# FADO
# ALEXANDRINO

# FADO ALEXANDRINO

## *António Lobo Antunes*

*Translated from the Portuguese by*
**Gregory Rabassa**

Grove Press
New York

The translator gives heartfelt thanks to
Maria João Antunes, who so expertly checked
every jot and tittle of the manuscript.

Grove Press
841 Broadway
New York, NY 10003

*Published simultaneously in Canada*
*Printed in the United States of America*

Grateful acknowledgment is made to Paul Simon Music for permission to reprint
lyrics from "The Boxer," copyright © 1968 by Paul Simon.

Library of Congress Cataloging-in-Publication Data

Antunes, António Lobo, 1942–
[Fado Alexandrino. English]
Fado Alexandrino/António Lobo Antunes; translated from the
Portuguese by Gregory Rabassa.—1st ed.
p.    cm.
Translation of: Fado Alexandrino.
I. Title.
PQ9263.N77F313    1990
869.3'42—dc20                                                    89-25981
ISBN 0-8021-3421-1 (pbk.)

Designed by Irving Perkins Associates

First Paperback Edition

*This book is dedicated to my friends*
*Helena Silva Araújo*
*José Almeida Costa*
*Luis Sobrinho*

# Contents

*Now the years are rolling by me*
*They are rocking evenly*
*I am older than I once was*
*Younger than I'll be*
*But that's not unusual*
*No it isn't strange*
*After changes upon changes*
*We are more or less the same*
*After changes we are more or less the same*

—Paul Simon, *"The Boxer"*

*Part One*

# BEFORE THE
# REVOLUTION

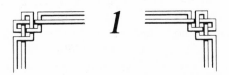

1

$A$ MID his colleagues, dragging his bag, he went out of the faded barracks building and immediately made out on the other side of the grating, on the sidewalk, a kind of sea monster of faces, bodies, and hands that was quivering, waiting for them in the ashen noontime of Encarnação where traffic lights floated randomly, hanging from the mist like fruits of light. An invisible airplane was whistling above the clouds. A platoon of cadets ran by, almost next to them, chewing up the gravel of the parade ground with the jaws of their huge boots, spurred on by a quartermaster whose empty eyes looked like those of china dogs on sideboards.

"What a shitty month of March"

the transport corporal muttered to his left, the knapsack on his back stuffed with African knickknacks that ragged one-armed blacks fob off on soldiers on leave in cafés in Lourenço Marques: tinfoil pipes, wire bracelets, horrible fetishes hastily carved with a jackknife in a miserable tin-roofed hut by some native. And he thought I'm in Lisbon and in Mozambique, I can see the houses in the lower middle class neighborhood section and the trees in the jungle at the same time, the gouty little gardens and the straw huts devastated by machine-gun fire, the octopus with happy anxious arms calling us and the enormous, gigantic silence that follows ambushes, peopled with soft

3

moans like the protests of the rain: he peeked under the Mercedes on the trail, and the guy sleeping in the cab a foot away from him was staring at him now with the distant distraction of corpses at wakes, their smiles softened into the amiable indifference of portraiture. He saw once more the commander taking leave of the battalion in the post gymnasium, the acid shine of his rimless glasses, the fingers held out, soft, to the soldiers at attention, almost propped up by gymnasium wall bars, and he thought I'm still in Mozambique, at the outpost, sitting at the bar watching night come on: the orderly handed out the malaria pills at dinner, a slight drizzle falls in the Encarnação afternoon, the Lisbon afternoon, making the soft smell of wet wood rise up from the coffins, the round smell of earth, and soon hundreds of insects will rise up from the tar and scatter, buzzing, on the streets of the city just as in the woods of Omar, until after a while they disappear out there in the darkness of the shelters. The transport corporal moved his duffle bag from one shoulder to the other, angrily breathed in the dampness of the air:

"Look at the fucking weather we found here."

Heads clinging to the grating, faces split into enormous laughs, confused, sharp, mingled voices called us. An aged sergeant in a white lab coat came out wearily to smoke by the door of a building with a red cross on the wall, went back in again, dragging his feet, and the soldier caught sight of the corner of a desk, glass cabinets, the rows of ever smaller letters for the anguish of nearsighted people. Lisbon, he thought, disillusioned, twenty-eight months of dreaming about the stinking city and finally Lisbon is this, while a beer truck, growling on the gravel, came through the main gate past the sentry's toy musket, bits of Sandeman wine and Binaca toothpaste emerged from the rooftops, the officers were playing cards in the mess hut, waiting for their dinner soup. But there wouldn't be any attacks today, there wouldn't be any attacks ever again: the trails, the bombardments, the hunger, the massacres had ended, here I am again in the Encarnação district and in the rotten little houses that were like abscessed teeth near the foul-smelling open gums of sewers that Cape Verdeans with picks were listlessly digging.

"The flu for sure," the transport corporal prophesied, "a week of hot-water bottles and lemon tea until the sneezing goes away."

He was sweating in the bunk, his weapon by his head and an infinite weariness in his limbs. I'm going to die. The doctor looked at him with his hands in his pockets, absentmindedly, a half hour later someone told him to roll over on his belly, and at the same moment they gave him an injection in one buttock for malaria, the pain spreading through his flesh as if a suddenly fiery molar was now white-hot in his tail. Completely motionless, his eyes closed, he felt his own blood pouring on the cushion, against his neck, just like a wounded animal running away, and around him the peaceful sound of the trees and the voices shouting at them from the other side of the grating in confused merriment: each leaf, he thought, is a trembling tongue, each eye a knot coming out of the wood, each body a branch bending down, startling and effusive. The General Services lieutenant trotted madly through the Mercedes' elongated shadow, whose mouth opened in a bottomless yawn, and on the walk embraced an old man writing in the air with the tip of his cane, undecipherable initials of emotion. He stumbled over the bag, carefully avoiding stepping on his neighbor in bed, who lay on the Lisbon pavement in a repugnant pool of intestines, turning his eyes aside so as not to find the bullet hole in his ear, and he noticed that the octopus of people waiting for them in happy anguish was twisting and stretching with colic beside the main gate, swallowing up the troops one by one with the carnivorous shriek of kisses: They're going to eat me too, he thought with terror, they're going to eat me with their tentacles of sleeves, shirts, neckties, topcoats, pants, sad worn widow's weeds, they're going to pulverize my joints with their vehement and imposing affection. The General Services lieutenant was carrying a screaming child around his neck, then a graduate disappeared into a whirlwind of pushing and pats on the back, and the soldier remembered him in the jungle, a mortar on his back, walking bent over through the underbrush in the quiet of the morning in the direction of the abandoned black quarters where some warm unglowing coals were dying out.

"If this weather keeps up," the transport corporal complained, "I swear that even my soul won't be of any use."

The airplane broke through the clouds with its landing gear aggressively down and approached the hidden landing strip like a great awkward and rigid dove, full of square pores of windows, a long red line down its metal back. Slowly, painfully, as if he were putting the pieces of a forgotten game in place, he put back together inside himself the city he had left two years before amid boat whistles and military marches, when the ship left the pier followed by the gull croaking of families, who flew around the hull like enormous afflicted and funereal birds, waving the open January umbrellas over the olive waters. It was the first time I saw my father fly (he thought, lying on the mattress while the engines of the packet ship shook his lungs and made the urine in his bladder slosh), and he kept on flying in my memory in the wake of the propellers as it went away, quarreling with the birds over a frothy dinner, until my sister's only letter reached Mozambique:

Abílio I hope very much that when you get this you will be in good health and happy myself and my son are well thanks be to God in spite of the fact that Vítor doesn't give a penny for the child and makes a scene here at the door every time with slaps and threats Abílio I've got some very bad news for you and it is: father kicked off they were doing folk songs on TV and I was only paying attention to that when to tell him to go to bed I touched him on the shoulder with my finger and he fell over onto the sofa like a rag doll and his elbow knocked our departed mother's lamp onto the floor that transparent one where you can see the wire and which was given to her by the lady where she worked days Dona Márcia at the haberdasher's promised me some good glue to fix it we had the wake day before yesterday and almost all the neighbors came Mr. Honório the boss Salgado cousin Esmeralda and the nieces who brought the poor crippled woman from number fourteen in a wheelchair you remember how we used to throw stones at her windows and she would holler hoodlums hoodlums at us Uncle Venâncio from the post office took care of the death certificate the undertaker's bill is being paid on time if you happen to have anything send it on because he was your father too and it isn't right for me to put up all the dough myself there were wreaths of flowers a small one with a purple ribbon from his friends at the café and another one of mine so pretty that Osório from the soccer team said to me hey missy Otília it makes me feel like dying myself and I answered right back rest easy with the cough you've got you won't have long to wait for your turn that's why the funeral had a hearse priest six taxis and three private cars a woman I work with at the factory lent me a skirt and a shawl everybody was sorry you weren't there and send you their condolences and best wishes I hope you come back soon and safe and sound you see so many cripples on the streets a hug from your sister Maria Otília Alves Nunes goodbye five hundred escudos would be fine for me.

Now (he thought when he finished the letter and put the envelope into his bag) the old man is still flying, his umbrella open, under the ground, his mouth full of mud and clay, with his little blurry pensioner's eyes carefully watching a ship that isn't there going off filled with soldiers in the direction of Africa, more and more insignificant on the stamped-paper blue of the river. The transport corporal was examining the low sky of Lisbon mistrustfully, in the same way that a tongue slowly feels an aching tooth: rolls of harsh dark rudderless clouds, and a strange feeling of hollowness, emptiness, as if the ceiling of the city were a slope of immense translucent steps that don't lead up to any door.

"A case of pneumonia at least," the guy predicted shaking his head sorrowfully as he would on patrol when after the mines had exploded, the men would come together, mute, not knowing what to do, around a lacerated, bleeding body.

The octopus behind the grating was slowly growing smaller, clumps of people, each group surrounding a soldier, were leaving the small square of Encarnação, where traffic circled patiently like a great, weary ox, turds of smoke fertilizing the skinny trees that imprinted delicate bronchi, branches, on waxen wall plaques. Only a small group remained, doggedly lined up by the main gate, so close now that he could make out the features and arms that hugged the shadows to their chests (anxious, like the blacks vainly glued to the barbed wire, cans in hand, in hope of some leftovers from the battalion's mess), women, men, old people with wrinkles, furrows of the resigned expectations of the poor, clumsy shoes, like shapeless stones, planted on the smooth sidewalk slabs. The recruits brushed against them again as they trotted by, goaded by the shouts of the officer candidate and the kids sergeant, who followed him like a shepherd's dog, insulting a fat man who was lumbering painfully at the tail end of the column, liquefied with despair and fatigue, the buildings of the post squatting insignificantly in the rear: the Army was all over, the shooting was all over, death was all over, night after night in the blind, peeking through a small hole at the quick orange light of weapons. One, two, three eager hands grabbed the transport corporal by the jacket, by the stripes, by the buttons on his tunic, as if they were dividing precious spoils among themselves, a tiny old woman in a shawl hung on his jacket weeping, leaning her face against his belly, timid, contented, emotional, my sister probably couldn't come because of the kid, and the bitterness of not having anyone to call him, push him, wet him with kisses, the corporal was smiling in confusion, not understanding, We're still in Africa, we're still following the remains of the trail, still crossing through the white muteness of the mornings of war, the smell of manioc on mats and the slow odor of black people, we're still standing in front of the high wheeler that blew up, the broken back of the driver splayed over the steering wheel. He came out of the main gate dragging his bag and searching with his eyes, unable to find the bus stop: even the bus stops have changed in this country, goddamn it. People passed in a mechanical hurry, faces, chests, limbs moving with increasing speed. A blindman with an aluminum cane was swiftly tapping on the corner, the loudspeaker for a sale turned its gabble loose from atop a pushy little truck: the guys with greasy briefcases and dirty collars who were exchanging African money for Portuguese money had evaporated, on the esplanade beside the sea, for the soldiers going on board, twelve percent, fifteen percent, twenty-one percent, thirty percent. There wasn't a single figure left clinging to the grating, and a redhaired boy covered with freckles, with a delivery basket on his shoulder, gave the information to Go down two blocks to the electrical store and take number forty-seven. The boy's pupils were green, their rims speckled with tiny yellow spots, the rain was like a kind of damp dust twinkling faintly in the air, the wooden Gypsy houses surrounded the district with the pestilential disorder of a native village: children, lame donkeys, stones and automobile tires on the galvanized roofs. Can the squat building in Buraca still be there behind the railroad tracks and the sad night-weeping of the whistles? (The bag drags along at his heels like a tail.) The picture of my nephew in the seashell frame on top of the sumptuous TV set? As he walks, he tries to remember the setup: the toilet, the room, the candy-box lids that served as pictures on the wall, the water tank, always out of order, showing the slats in the framework like bones. A line of people, almost all women, is waiting silently for the bus:

tomorrow, they'd sung in Angola when I passed through, I'm going to light a candle at the Muxima, I'm going to São Paulo fort, I'm going to see the bilious-colored water of the bay. Forty-seven finally stops with a sharp sigh of brakes, and after the metal door draws back with the sound of a folding screen the women begin to get on, heads down. The driver taps his fingers on the steering wheel and takes off with a leap amid a rattle of tin. The soldier grasps one of the chrome pipes or leather loops that sway from the ceiling, holds his bag between his knees, and watches a quivering parade of streets, avenues, unknown buildings, skeletal little dusty squares under a hazy sky. From time to time a buzzer sounds, the vehicle slows down with successive squeaks of springs, and ends up in a faint with a final shudder: the people getting on and off have the same bitter and confused tilt, the same faded clothing, the same infinitely distant aged features. (On taking leave of the chaplain at the post, he thought Never again will I see this guy, never again will I hear this guy's voice on the parade ground, never again will I hear his useless latinizing around the coffins.) The bus rolls on again, slowly and with difficulty, more façades, more buildings, more trees, once open spaces now covered with a pimpling of shacks, sidewalks deluged with garbage, little kids, and dogs. The way dogs and small boys look alike in this country, he thinks, is the way they look alike in Africa: the same begging expression, the same dull hair, the same slack-lily limbs. The bus moans over a run-down aqueduct, turns to the left near the railroad, whose rails can be glimpsed at intervals in a cane field, and begins, asthmatically, the ramp up to Buraca: there's something familiar here, something indefinable and intimate that I know behind those small tiled porches, those birdcages hanging out windows, those shirts bellying down the clothesline.

"I grew up when this section was nothing but small farms with cabbage fields and poultry (he would tell me later in the restaurant where we met so many years later, ten or eleven, after returning from the war). At that time, Captain, Damaia looked like a desert, a rotten riverbank scattered with stones, my father had a couple of goats tied to a stake, bleating all day with resentment."

(Fall out, the major commanded in the post gymnasium, and Mozambique was over, pounding the right foot hard onto the floor and putting into that force the loathing I have for all of you, the dead, the one-legged, the wounded, the lack of cigarettes, hot meals, mail, and women, except for an occasional skinny, indifferent, big-bellied, ragged black woman.) He suddenly sees the narrow three-storied building squeezed between the grocery store and a chipped, old structure, he quickly pulls the cord, I've arrived, and the tepid people traveling with him look up with surprise: a bald-headed guy appears, startled, from behind his newspaper, like a hippopotamus in a zoo tank, with thick glasses befogged by news items and letters. He elbows passengers who cough, indistinct muttering is joined to the sputtering of the motor, and he gets off, hugging the bag that trails its languid aversion on the ground, and he stands stupidly on the sidewalk, following the bus as it goes off with the indolent waddle of a fat person, with its inert, indifferent cargo.

"I didn't know what to do either (the second lieutenant would explain to me over the fish, sprouts, and poached eggs), how to answer so many questions, so many kisses, so much sudden and unexpected concern, so much interest in me. They touched me to make sure it was me, mixed their living breath with mine, loaded down with dead men, and then the thought came to me What now? Did you ever think What now?, Captain, when you got home? Did you ever think How the hell am I going to forget all that? Were you ever bothered, all alone, in Lisbon, by that empty space of the days to come, the hours that needed to be furnished in some way, did you ever think how hard it is to take off a uniform and be a civilian, that all I know how to do is pick up a piece and go hunt niggers in the woods?"

"When I got off the bus in Buraca, my sister wasn't there," the soldier said, "she'd gone shopping with the kid or something, I waited a hell of a long time at the door to the building."

"Don't stand there looking at me with a foolish face, come in," she said and the soldier made out a woman more or less his age, with a plastic bag in one hand and a kid in the other, staring at him with vaguely happy, vaguely annoyed arid eyes, who closes the door with her hip, goes ahead of him, shaking off the dust, along a dirty corridor (more boxes of trash, traces of doormats, the plaster on the ceiling dissolving from mildew), and she goes to put the bag down in the kitchen, where the polar-bear refrigerator's growl grows louder, while the son, standing in the middle of the living room, is examining him with eyes large with surprise, between a Mobil calendar showing a girl with dazzling naked breasts, and the fishbowl of a turned-off TV set. He sits down, half-frightened, on the edge of the sofa (It was here my father died), spots the picture of the old man on a sideboard, the ancient photograph of a man with a mustache and a watch chain, imposing as a pope on his holiday throne, he leaps up, from the kitchen comes the sound of lids clanging, the noise of drawers opening and closing, a stool falling, he goes over to the window and there are the bedraggled buildings of the district, the scrubby lot where they used to play soccer, with goals marked by stones or berets or bottle fragments, piles of rubbish, men moving trash with poles, and farther up the faded greens of Monsanto in the listless noon of March.

"She asked me if I intended staying there at home," the soldier told me. "Me still groggy like I'd just woken up, and she only asking me if I intended staying, like there wasn't anything else in the world, you see, Captain, that interested her, whether you stay or you don't stay here, maybe I can fix you up a place in the living room for a few days."

The plastic curtains were the same ones, only darker and sadder, the same ugly cheap furniture, the same china plate from the Algarve on the side-

9

board, the same smell of a clogged toilet and neglect everywhere, our father's pensioner's newspapers piled in a corner, yellow edges curled up like turkey feet, and the surprise of a man's loud jacket on a hanger, on a line that stretched across the room and which the clothespins grasped like plastic sparrows, their beaks holding socks, jockey shorts, a funny shirt printed with hula dancers raising their hands to a sky of palm trees. The sister came back from the kitchen, drying her bitten nails on her skirt:

"A month after our father died, she shacked up with the concierge's cousin," the soldier said, "a mulatto who worked at the airport restaurant, always in dark glasses, even at night, fingers full of rings, who wore her out with kids and beatings. Result: I had to rent a room elsewhere."

"You look green," his sister told him, pensive. "Didn't they feed you good in Mozambique?"

What a difference separates us now, he thought: You're talking to me now like I was a stranger, no kiss, no hug, not a shadow of affection: he closed his eyes and the octopus of faces, gestures, exclamations, anxious laughs, moved in his head again beside the main gate of the post, on the misty morning in Encarnação.

"Dark glasses, even at night, the kind with gold rims, completely dark, Captain," the soldier repeated slowly, contemplating the circle of foam on the glass of beer. "You could never tell where the guy was looking."

"Did you bring any funny diseases back, maybe?" the sister asked, mistrustfully, arranging some cloth roses in a vase. "Nits in the bladder, bugs in the stomach, or something, how should I know, something contagious."

The son, sitting on the floor, was amusing himself tearing up a magazine, there was a lack of furniture, of pictures, there was a lot more emptiness than before, the clay Don Quixote with a broken lance uselessly threatening the chandelier. And cracks, scratches, and lumps on the wall, too, a bitter neglect that was unfamiliar to him. The sister ran a quick cloth here and there, puffed up the pillows on the couch, got furious at a blowfly that came in through the window, tracing broad, exasperated circles in the room: The mail plane, he thought, buzzing on Thursday mornings, invisible in the jungle, that the sister was chasing with great spectacular gestures of anger, so as not to lay into me, not shout You lost your place here in this house, go away, while the mulatto put his key in the door (the quick, decisive turn of the master of the house) and stared at him, impenetrable from the threshold, behind the famous gold-rimmed dark glasses.

"I didn't even sleep there that night," the soldier explained to me, a thick lip of white foam over his mouth and his shoulders curved over the table as if he were running. "I stayed on the third floor of a rooming house in Calhariz, with the trains getting into my ears all night long and the lights of the coaches slipping along the ceiling, that white succession of little quivering squares like at the end of the movies in the mess hall. The bed moved for hours and I got the idea that there were wheels under the mattress and I was galloping through a funnel of houses, away from Buraca, toward Monsanto, the woods, the church steeples, the horrible neighborhoods of Amadora, the gardens in the park: so I woke up with the pain of a sword in my kidneys and train whistles in my ears like you can't imagine, Captain."

And Lisbon waiting for him in the street: closed shops, the wrinkles in the wrapping paper of mist, small trucks peeling off with the signals through the chill silence of the morning, cardboard cutouts of people at the bus stop, having to wait until nine o'clock to go into a drugstore and buy some aspirin.

"I was married and had a daughter this high," the second lieutenant said, smiling at the spoons the waiter was serving the meat with. "I was living on the Rua da Mãe d'Água, below the fountain, and after intimacies, even with the light off, I could see the round ball of the paper lamp, looking like an enormous moon, sowing Japanese ghosts in the darkness. (The breathing of his wife beside him and of his daughter in the other room flooded the floor with a murmur of sounds that rose and sank like the soft flutter of a dress. An appliance suddenly broke into a rumble in the darkness like a tractor climbing a hill, the hands of the alarm clock gesticulated motionlessly on the bookcase, and the round paper moon was floating, held by a green cord, close to the ceiling, blown by the soft breath of the stars outside, like pieces of an undecipherable checker game. Time, damn it, has swallowed me up, too, he thinks, this beer tastes like the bottom of the barrel.) When I go along the Rua da Mãe d'Água, most of the time I can't even remember the building, Inês in the kitchen, her back to me, moving noiselessly about in her tennis shoes, the bottoms of her frayed jeans touching her heels: see how easy it is for people to forget things, Captain."

"That afternoon," the soldier said, "I went to see my uncle to look for work. The old man had a small truck, did moving jobs, there was the idea of sharing in the business, and the next day I was already loading and unloading bureaus, tables, chairs, washing machines, pianos, helped by a couple of poor devils in coveralls, unlighted cigarettes in their mouths, who wore ILÍDIO in faded letters across their backs, from shoulder to shoulder."

"So you got back yesterday, eh?" Uncle Ilídio barked from the mess of his run-down desk. Without looking at him, he shuffled through dirty files in the tiny hole that served as an office, full of notebooks, vases with flowers, boxes of binoculars, cobwebs, papers, and shaky shelves lined with bundles.

He was a small, asthmatic man, almost completely bald, in whose features was concentrated a cosmic ferocity that had no object, fed by the hesitant bellows of his lungs: he would be silent from one minute to another, look at the dirty hanger from which his greasy topcoat swayed, and his ribcage could be seen swelling and deflating under his shirt in an afflicted way, like a frog's gullet.

"You're no sooner off the boat," the old man wheezed, "than you come to me looking for a job."

He contemplated his knuckles angrily and barked at him furiously:

"I hope you had the good sense to have lunch, at least."

"He was always like that," the soldier explained to me. "He would carry on when he liked people."

His hand moved by the glass, chasing ghosts away:

"He had a stroke in November, his left side all paralyzed, I'm the one who takes care of practically everything. We'll go *pfffft* some day too and it doesn't seem true, isn't that so, Captain?"

"I presented myself at the bank a few days later," the lieutenant said. "I sat down in the office, closed the door, and thought There wasn't any war, I didn't spend twenty-odd months in Mozambique with a carbine on my shoulder, I made up silly things last night: dysentery, stagnant water, the dead, the wounded, the sapper officer who lost an arm defusing a mine. I thought There wasn't any war there wasn't any war there wasn't any war there wasn't any war, and I slowly began to forget. When they brought me coffee at eleven o'clock in the morning, I'd never left Lisbon, and Africa was the names of the rivers we had to draw in school and you forgot right away, going on to mountains, grammar, or the branch line of Beira Baixa. I looked at people, Captain, secretaries, colleagues, clerks, attendants, I took care of applications, I looked through proposals, signed reports, and I thought It's true that I was here, what kind of shit could I have drunk to have sucked in so many dreams last night?"

The uncle went out of the warehouse, pushing him, breathing his heavy angry fish breath at him, and he went along, driving him out onto the sidewalk (carts of vegetables, baskets of flowers, first-floor windows with old gossips, eyes like holy images on the windowsills), over to a signboard that rocked on its staff, off its hinges: two steps, damp shadows smelling of cooking, tables draped with paper, a screaming radio, and in the back, behind the counter, a fellow with a vigilant neck pulling the chrome levers of the coffee machine up and down. The uncle raised his arm and a second fellow laid out napkins, forks, and twisted knives that looked as if a mule had trampled them a moment before, plates with chipped edges, a pitcher of wine, two glasses, bread, a triangular plastic toothpick holder: by the waiter's speed the soldier guessed that the old man and he knew each other.

"I'm not having anything," the uncle panted. "A leprous donkey steak for the lad here."

The other customers could hardly be seen in the darkness of the tavern (So they won't notice the swill they're swallowing, snorted Mr. Ilídio with a raucous laugh), shapes bent over, a scraping of silverware, hazy light scattered in successive reflections from the stove on the tiles. The old man kept switching a matchstick from one corner of his mouth to the other while he rapidly chewed the meat, the potatoes, the egg, the roll, but the lunch descended, almost intact, along the gutter of his esophagus.

"The check"

the uncle ordered, observing the surrounding shadows with distasteful sarcasm. Outside, on the street, the rainy March of the night before was running down the decrepit façades like the makeup of a weeping old woman.

"We went back to the little office," the soldier explained, "him in a broken-down chair that creaked and me standing in front of the desk, as motionless as possible, Captain, so as not to upset a single sheet of all that paper, all that junk."

(The uncle stopped looking at the soldier completely, drawing imaginary lines on the back of a dirty bill, and suddenly he looked at him with his dull eyes and declared, in a peremptory whisper

"What are you waiting for, idiot, you've started work as of right now.")

"What bothered me most was the house," the second lieutenant said. "I arrived home from the bank, and there, Captain, I really felt strange. Not at work, not at the restaurant, not downtown, in the car, maybe because I turned the music on the radio up loud and the commercials and the announcer's voice distracted me, and then, you know how it is, when a guy is driving all he concentrates on is not running into the guy in front or having the guy in back run into him, and there are people on the sidewalks, all those faces, each one different from the other, always running along and changing, but, then, I parked the car, went up the steps, put the key in the door, and there I was, things turning out badly for me, the strange feeling as usual: I looked at the tables, the shelves, the ashtrays, and I asked myself Where the hell are the trees, because I didn't see the trees, understand, the barbed wire, the shelters, the jungle, I put down my briefcase, lay down on the couch with the newspaper, my wife appeared, smiling, and I leaned forward in the hope that a familiar camouflaged shape would arise out of her shadow."

"That night he ordered me to eat with him," the soldier said. "He didn't invite me, he ordered me, Captain: he lived in a hole at the foot of the Campo de Santana, in a twisting alley inhabited by barbers and cats."

An ageless woman, her neck covered with vitiligo splotches, opened the door for him, shuffling her slippers, cast on him one healthy eye and another, blue and empty, that seemed more penetrating than the good one, and said:

"You can tell it's Ilídio's nephew a mile away, come in."

Walls covered with damp lumps, nail holes, insect droppings, there was unmatched furniture, an open magazine on a rocking chair, Benfica tiles, on the sideboard among cheap, orange-colored faceted glasses, my mother's picture, with the timid ashamed look that I knew so vaguely.

"Don't pay any attention to the disorder," the woman excused herself. "I went to the welfare doctor today and spent four hours in the waiting room."

His mother's photograph followed him tenaciously, tirelessly, throughout the room, like the Jesus with a visible heart and strumpet's mouth in a sacristy calendar, a window in back slammed violently, and the uncle, in his undershirt, insulted him, Hello, boy. He still bore his usual furious expression, and a kind of scowl tightened his tiny eyelids. Good evening, sir, I replied, thinking I didn't feel comfortable calling him anything else, damn it. They finally sat down at the table covered with a disgusting black-and-yellow-checkered tablecloth, the woman busied herself with the pots, the uncle, embarrassed, silently scratched the back of his neck with the huge fingernail on his pinky: It's wild how the old man looks like a toad, the soldier noted, the same round trunk, the same skinny arms and legs, the same big mouth. I was about to begin the vegetable soup when a girl in a lumber jacket came into the living room Hello Mother hello Godfather, and me with my spoon in the air, with a foolish face, my eyes playing Ping-Pong between the girl and the old man: So you ended up marrying a widow like the rumors I heard, you still got hung up with a wench more than ten years older than you, and that's why grandmother would protest and scream if they mentioned your name, and the celluloid ball bounced from uncle to girl, who held out a clump of fat sweaty fingers Pleased to meet you, sat down at the table, brushed away some crumbs and pieces of crust with the back of her hand, leaned over and began to swallow her soup, a thin girl, Captain, with a nose that was a touch broad and with a scar on her cheek, and lively, sudden movements, like a sparrow.

"Did you mount her?" I asked, looking for my handkerchief in a pocket.

A crab flew in front of us, an arm's length away, landing where the officers of the patrol were whispering on top of the mustard yellow drum.

"That was only a long time afterward," the soldier said, "months and months went by and she didn't even look at me." (And his mouth was smiling, fixed and hard, pasty, like the dummies in a store window.)

"Did the war make you quiet like a fish?" the uncle asked, furious. "Don't you know how to talk?"

The soup was over, he blew his nose in his napkin and covered up a monumental belch with the palm of his hand: he felt his stomach swollen with gas like the stairs and corridors of the subway at rush hour, the wind like people and more people trotting up the stairs of his insides, the squeal of brakes, unexpected jolts, gusts of froth: Am I nervous because I've come back or because I'm here, with the old people and her, in this mean, stinking house that I don't know, spitting bone after bone onto my fork? I'd never had so many in one bite, Captain, as during that damned dinner: the uncle browsing with his chin in the plate, his asthma straining and wheezing in his throat. I would have liked more oil, but I was ashamed to ask for it, the potatoes were sticking to my tongue, the sprouts were impossible to unravel, they were stuffing him. The second lieutenant, cigarette between his fingers, coughed slightly across from me:

"With the shit they fed us in the jungle, Captain, I'd forgotten domestic niceties completely, the coffeepot steaming like the dead mouth of Vesuvius, the etiquette I'd unlearned in the Army, the foolish little social graces that held me back."

He began to eat the soufflé, facing Inês's contented, smiling, anxious expression, and it didn't taste like anything. Not anything: only a soft mass of which he partook with the indifference of an ostrich, with a melancholy, urgent greed: to see the bottom of the plate quickly, to see the bottom of the plate as quickly as possible, and, perhaps, to have appear, painted on the ceramic or the plastic or the glass, the jovial childhood figures, good-natured Mickey Mouses, dancing Donald Ducks, a girl jumping rope by a playground, the pale recompense for tortured lunches and painful dinners inserted in his mouth (Open up) by the maid's swift spoon. In the kitchen courtyard, in summertime, the plants grew up out of their pots toward the sky, sheltered by a geometrical mesh of wire. The second lieutenant, glass of wine in his hand, smiled at his wife:

"It was great." (So many wooden objects spread about the living room, he thought, chairs, stools, panels, shelves, and a sudden suspicion gnawed at his insides: Where did you get the money for this, you bitch?) The uncle's stepdaughter, who was peeling a pear over the piled-up ruins of her fish, seemed to be mocking his anxious embarrassment:

"So what was it like there in Africa?" the old woman asked, picking up the plates and taking them away to the kitchen in a pile. She moved with difficulty, dragging one of her slippers exactly like the fat bitch at the post when she'd broken a paw and would lumber along, weaving like a ship. The girl raised her chin to hear him better. It really was great, the second lieutenant repeated to his wife's worried face at the exact instant when the daughter, in the neighboring bedroom, began to cry, the uncle, his hands flat on the tablecloth, impatiently demanded his coffee, the neighbors' flush toilet unloaded with a tremulous rusty retch: the soldier cast his humble eyes around, stopped on the ocular globe of the dusty light, hanging from the ceiling by a twisted cord without the trace of a shade protecting it. From the other apartments, muffled distant voices came through the walls, the helicopter carried the unrecognizable body off to Mueda, wrapped in a shredded blanket like a useless bundle. The girl, her knife motionless, was still waiting. He drew out of his throat, like a kind of sob, the most neutral voice he could muster:

"Pretty much like here, ma'am," he said.

## 2

T H E lieutenant colonel peeped out of the third-floor window of the command headquarters (an office with rococo desks, flags, bookcases, the eternal appearance of the tepid, gloomy, heavy idleness of military posts): down below, a soldier on fatigue duty was trimming the plants in their pots, cooks were plucking chickens, the radar at the airport was spiraling in the distance like a sunflower made of wire.

"They've all left already," he said without moving his lips, looking down at the deserted main gate. Another lieutenant colonel and three majors were in the room, each holding a glass of port wine with his fingertips. One of the majors refilled his glass from the bottle on a metal tray and raised the glass to eye level. He had the broad hips of a woman, sagging jowls, and a strip of decorations on his tunic.

"Arab oil," he approved. "It's been almost thirty months since we've had a drink of this."

The other lieutenant colonel passed around a wooden box with small Spanish cigars, but the one who'd come back from the war didn't even notice the tobacco: he stayed by the window, pushed the bridal-veil curtain back with his hand, his back to the rather sad birthday party being celebrated by five gloomy, worn-out men. The walls of the office, freshly painted, perspired with a nauseating smell that seemed to come from the soft body of the admiral framed over the bookcases, examining them with his blind shoat eyes. A few tall buildings stood out in the distance: the mist was breaking up into slow-moving dirty strips that retreated and regrouped in weary sloth. The majors lighted their cigars from one another's, joking unenthusiastically, and a thick, acid smell spread through the room: Africa, the lieutenant colonel thought, the soil of Mozambique after a rain, crickets loosening their wings in their night song, the communications officer standing at attention in the doorway, very serious, a piece of paper in his hand:

"May I?"

"How's your wife?" asked the post commander, who would pull up his pants in a clownish tic from time to time. He'd been the best student in his class and a rather good swordsman, but now, there, in front of him, he looked like a shy and simpleminded old man, anxious to please, as if he were begging for a job.

"I haven't had time to get to the hospital," he answered harshly, immediately repenting the roughness of his tone, and shrugged his shoulders: she got a little thinner with the radiation, but you know what family letters are like: they'd alarm us less if they told the truth. (And he thought I can't remember if you were pretty when I first met you, I'll have to open up the drawer with the photographs and startle myself with the garbage of the past.)

"I'll bet nobody knows you're back," the commander hiked up his pants with a stronger tug. "You've got my car at your disposal downstairs."

The communications officer took a step forward and held out the message:

"We leave for Lisbon on the twenty-sixth."

The friend put out his cigar in the middle of the glass ashtray: the lights on the highway could be seen, more trees, clusters of houses, as if the city were lighting up from inside itself like one of those moving stages in a nightclub: Manager, send every whore in Lourenço Marques to my table.

"You're not the only one who got himself fucked up in this," the fencer moaned. "Take a look at me: who'd take me to be forty-five? Shit. And now, in August, if you can imagine, Guinea."

He stood looking at the letters, not believing, searching for matches in his shirt pocket: the flame lighted up parts of his long face, two deep, vertical grooves at the base of his cheekbones, the reddish brown scar on his jaw, a map with colored marks in the rear. The communications officer cleaned his glasses with a handkerchief. The guard posts looked like little cubic mounds in the silence, facing the dark threat of the forest. The lieutenant colonel stroked his thin hair, raised his head, and the other one looked at his light, hollow, inexpressive eyes:

"Give it to Major Albuquerque, he takes care of everything. You can go."

He went down the headquarters stairs without returning the salutes and sat down beside his valise and duffle bag in the backseat of the commander's black Volkswagen, driven by a rough-looking corporal with a small blond mustache:

"The Cancer Institute," he ordered in a dull, quick voice, in which words devoured each other like angry dogs.

The tires squealed on the pavement and the car took off in the direction of the main gate, dragging the painful tin rattle of its mudguards along, and sank into the Encarnação district traffic in the shadow of a huge six-wheel truck.

"Lisbon swallowed us all up, Captain, everybody off in his own direction, the way a covey breaks up," the second lieutenant said. "And now here we are together after ten years, not the same ones: a lot happened in that time."

The communications officer rested his elbows on the tablecloth and leaned toward me, forgetting about the fish, his eyeglasses softly gleaming.

"When we arrived, in seventy-two, I'd belonged to the Organization for five years. They didn't want me to make myself scarce or go underground, or for me to get a government job: it was important for us, Captain, to have people in the Army, find out what was happening from inside, work within the machine: we knew that the only possibility for change had to come from there."

On the way to Sete Rios the lieutenant colonel didn't take his eyes off the back of the driver's neck, his short crew cut, the freckles or pimples or carbuncles along his collar. The Volkswagen smelled of the commander's cigarettes and aftershave, butts were piling up in the metal ashtray on the door, all twisted, like worms: Why in hell do they write to us in Africa, he thought, with the same caution they use with convalescents and children, why do they lie to us with the infinite concentric meandering of imbecilic half-words: The cobalt treatment has cheered me up a little, love, I don't feel any pain, I haven't lost any more weight, the doctor's very nice, he knows you, he was in your class in high school.

"And then I got the picture," the lieutenant colonel told me, a stunted little chick-pea, terrible in gym, always hanging around the priestling who taught Morals, full of pieties, alms collecting, masses, getting revenge for the beatings he got as a child by opening up people's bellies.

There were a lot of patients in the waiting room, silent and sheeplike, waiting for a door to open and for their names to be called, for them to be observed, poked, medicated, advised, sent off with a prescription in hand: Come back next month, or the one after, or the one after, or the one after, be patient, there might be an opening at that time. Close together on long benches, papers, cigarette butts, and tangerine peels on the floor, the ash gray of a granular light clouded their sloping faces, and a woman in a smock was sweeping up the trash from beneath a thousand legs into a wooden receptacle. An infant's pacifier fell onto the filthy tiles and the mother stuck it expeditiously back into the mouth that was opening wide for a tremendous howl. The yellowish man beside them, so thin you could say he was a frame, was reading the newspaper, carefully smoothing the pages with his thumb-nail: the last stop, the final getting off, the sad end of the line: guys from funeral parlors must pop by here every day to take a count, add them up, calculate the number of coffins.

"I went away, of course," the communications officer explained to me, delicately lifting the skin off his fish with the tip of his knife, "but, for obvious reasons, I didn't get any farther than Paris. You can't imagine, Captain, the number of informers the political police had spread around abroad."

He asked a middle-aged worker who was limping and carrying a bundle of clothing for the women's infirmary, and following carefully the complicated directions he was given, went up the stairs, stumbled on steps, got lost in hallways marked up with penciled phrases and he ended up coming to rest in a tiny laboratory where a bald-headed man in an apron, his hands in his pockets, was examining a row of test tubes in a wooden holder.

"Ten years is a long time, damn it," the second lieutenant said, shaking his head slowly. "Just look at how much I've changed."

"Three kids, Captain," the soldier confided to me. "I find myself cleaned out halfway through the month."

He tried to retrace his steps, but he felt lost in a labyrinth of walls, corners, steps, doors that didn't open, elevator buttons he didn't dare push. Every so often he would cross paths with a gurney piloted by two women orderlies (one of whom was invariably holding a bottle of serum in her raised hand like a standard), on it a fellow with closed eyes and a gutterlike mouth, like a deceased sparrow. Chipped walls, fragments of notices held up with pink adhesive tape, a circular stain, a giant splotch of mucus like the yolk of an egg: at times he imagined attics full of corpses who, like him, had wandered about lost in that maze, windows shutting off the uniform melancholy of the afternoon, smelling of ether, disinfectant, and toilet piss. At the echo of his steps and the sound of his afflicted wheezing, the humble and silent crea-tures at the entrance immediately made way (As when he would hear the appeals from companies under attack on the radio, he thought, lying prone on top of the corporal in the midst of the whistling, listening to the cries of pleading panic) until he pushed a screen aside and found himself suddenly in the middle of a room flooded with beds and night tables painted white, in the center of which a group of fat-bellied doctors was in solemn conference. "My wife died in seventy-two, the day before we got back from Mozambique," the lieutenant colonel said, meticulously splitting a toothpick into equal-sized little pieces that he then lined up parallel on the tablecloth. He coughed and his temples tightened like those of an exhausted dog.

"I didn't get there in time for the funeral."

And I thought, looking around at the bald heads, the gray hair, the worn-out faces that were smiling and chewing and talking: We got old for nothing or is it still possible, can anything still be possible? Because for me that was the worst part of it, the eventuality that we've screwed ourselves in vain, that we've worn ourselves out for no reason.

"Even the concierge in the building where I was living in Barcelona," the communications officer explained, "used to go periodically to the PIDE thug at the embassy and tell him what the Portuguese in the house were doing. Naturally, we made our contacts far away from there, in cafés, parks, churches, on the subway, but almost with the same care, the same precautions as in Lisbon."

"Ten years, Captain," the lieutenant repeated in disbelief. "Ten years without anybody catching on."

The lieutenant colonel attempted to walk timidly through the infirmary (maybe his dwarfish schoolmate, ever so important now, was hovering about there), he saw a spiderlike creature withdraw the bedpan from underneath his buttocks and put it on the floor, observed for a second the extremely thin hairy thighs that were moving, the pair of huge eyes that were looking at him without curiosity or shame, just floating, like vague swans on the surface of an absolute indifference, he saw torsos lying there, deprived of substance and weight, just like the black men that South African helicopters brought in from the jungle for the clandestine plantations, he pulled out his pistol by the command post, the guy was looking at him, weak on his legs, without alarm or hate, and I wasn't capable of firing, of seeing him double over, without any protest, and fall in a pile on the ground. One of the doctors, hooked about the neck by the ends of his stethoscope, looked at him questioningly: Can this be the boob from high school, he thought, but in reality he felt frightened and foolish, at a loss for words, so he began to retreat until his hand touched the metallic cold of a doorknob. The wards, enormous suddenly, were looking at him with what seemed to him to be immense reprobation: Seriously, I didn't kill him, the lieutenant colonel shouted silently, I didn't squeeze the trigger, I didn't even raise the barrel of the weapon up to the height of the rags on his chest. He opened the door, terrified, and once more the rather dirty corridors, the torn posters, the outhouse obscenities scrawled in pencil on the wall, the usual labyrinth with disinfectant and ether, orderlies with basins, or bundles, or boxes of dressings, or guiding little nickel-plated carts loaded with meals in tin plates. The sky had turned blue on the other side of the windows, above the tile-covered teeth of the roofs, beyond the balconies with pots and plants and the field of television antennae, whose fruit, quivering raindrops, hung from the wire branches. A tiny elevator, teeming with young nurses chatting and laughing, vomited him into the vestibule where once more he came upon the sad, ashen people who were waiting for their consultations in silence. He asked an old man with body odor and a Tyrolean hat and then a small man with a sad little beard Where is the receptionist, please? They gave him hurried and long-winded opinions, and the lieutenant colonel walked aimlessly among wooden benches and spittoons until he came upon a row of windows just like the openings in doghouses, too low for his height. He leaned over and faced the opaque and painted face of a woman: What can I do for you? The other workers were writing tediously, snarling on the telephone, going through file drawers. The woman listened to him, chewing on her pencil: she had a broken tooth right in the front of her mouth, but her cheeks, covered with makeup, looked round and solid, and a soft perfume came up from her hair. This is the business office, if you need information, go to the windows in back, and an arm rattling with bracelets arose solicitously from down there and pointed its extremely long fingernails to the left: a resigned line of people, the dull sound of rubber stamps, the lieutenant colonel obediently waited his turn behind an aged nun in the half-shadows of the end of the corridor, while someone behind him gasped for breath the whole time, he leaned over again Could you tell me where? Now it was a fellow with diabetic breath who attended to him while going through papers, agitated, very nervous, constantly wetting his fingers on a round sponge, who pulled a thick folder from a shelf, ran his forefinger down pages, shouted an insult at an invisible colleague, searched through notebooks, more folders, loose documents, finally ceased, lighting his cigarette with a recalcitrant lighter, while, moving his lips, he deciphered a dossier with a blue cardboard cover, It's my sad duty to inform you, my dear friend, that your wife passed away and her body has already left the Institute, the family took it away immediately after the autopsy according to what's written here. He thought There's got to be some mistake, no office ever functions properly in Portugal, they mix up names, they mix up dates, they mix up lives, they mix up children in maternity wards, what else can I say? What's the ward? he asked. There isn't any ward, the diabetic answered listlessly, a patient came in today and took the deceased's place. My wife was getting better, I got a letter from her a few days ago, the lieutenant colonel roared, clutching the grill of the window with such force that his fingers turned white: the line snaked around in the shadows, intrigued, halitosis turned his head and said, Oh, Mr. Mendes, you'd better come over to my window. Mr. Mendes had the look of someone from outer space and the suave manners of tyrannical office managers. The diabetic drifted away deferentially, ceding his place, and Mr. Mendes took stock of the lieutenant colonel's insignia and, with the intimate stateliness that obtains between commanders, offered, Is there some small complaint with which I can help? I lifted the revolver up to shoulder level, fired, and the black man fell into a sitting position, his hands on his stomach, staring at me without animosity or surprise: a trickle of blood was slowly running down toward his pants, the soles of his feet formed a complex geography of wrinkles and ruts and fissures. He stood with the pistol by his hip for a long time, fascinated and terrified simultaneously: the black man spat out a kind of vomit with difficulty, his hand weakly, casually grasped blades of grass. What did I do? Mr. Mendes was smiling expectantly, adjust-

ing the knot in his polka-dot necktie, the lieutenant colonel wrinkled his
nose, sniffled, leaned farther over: I got in from Mozambique today and all I
want is for someone to give me the number of my wife's room. Mr. Mendes
immediately cast an indignant sidelong glance at the diabetic, who hastened
to show him, confusedly, his papers, all in disarray. Another fierce sidelong
glance: Come now, give it to me in some kind of order. He was wearing a ring
with a black stone above his wedding ring, as a baby they'd fastened a gold
pin to his chest that said DON'T HOLD ME IN YOUR LAP, he would wake
up with a bed full of piss until he was sixteen years old. The boy from outer
space studied the documents with careful deliberation, writing sage phrases
ball-pointedly in the margin. The people behind the lieutenant colonel were
complaining,

("As if some shapeless animal," he explained to me, "some kind of saurian
were hovering around my neck and whispering")

he received a very grave look from Mr. Mendes, who twisted his solemn
mouth, opened it to make a speech, closed it, opened it, closed it, finally
ordered the diabetic to Open the door for the officer so we can talk more
easily. At that point, however, I'd already understood and I started walking
toward the exit without even looking at them, I could hear them calling me
from a distance Would you please would you please would you please like
bird croaks during the equinoctial tide, by some narrow little stairs at the far
end of the building I reached the garden where a peasant in coveralls was
lovingly watering the flowerpots, and I, empty (he told me, his elbows on the
table, lighting a cigarette, ignoring his dinner), with no anguish, no displeasure, no affliction, no anything, I, completely blank, trotting past the worn
walls toward the black Volkswagen from headquarters, I, avoiding a stumble
over the hose, I, leaping over the drooping plants and the geometric hedges
of the lawn, I, passing patients and visitors and nurses and doctors and
the devil take them as they came and went, I, twisting among the rumps of
the parked cars, I, opening the door and sitting down in the backseat, in the
rectangle of the mirror I saw the questioning eyes of the driver, instantly
awake after dozing at the wheel, Go on to the Anjos district and straighten
your beret, he ordered, are you a soldier or a pimp, during the whole trip he
chewed on the filter of a cigarette he didn't light, stared like a stuffed owl or a
wax doll at the houses, the streets, the alleys, the mews, the small squares,
empty (he described himself to me), still empty, he pointed out the building
to the blond driver, wouldn't let him help him inside with his suitcase and
duffle bag, went up to the third floor without looking into the elevator mirror
that was clouded with scratches, the black man's body relaxed finally, his jaw
drooped in a strange grimace, his hand, palm up, was pointing at the straggly
treetops, I killed him, I killed her, the smell of gunpowder pricked his nose, I
killed her with my almost complete lack of news, my lack of interest, my
coldness, nobody was waiting for him in the vestibule and the excessive

neatness of things alarmed him, he pulled the cord on the blinds and came
upon his own picture, in uniform, on a low table, ashtrays without any butts,
the television set, books, Who'd come by here to clean everything up? he
went into the bedroom, where the bed, covered by a crocheted spread, took
up almost the entire rug, he turned on the lamp on the night table on his
side, and the walls glimmered with concentric circles of light, It makes me
afraid to turn the knob on the closet and find your clothes, your shoes, the
belts hanging from a strip of cloth, he got undressed slowly, dropping his
field jacket, pants, shirt onto the floor around him, Bury him outside the
compound, he ordered the first sergeant who came running up, and while he
was taking off his socks the black man was beginning to fall in front of him
again with a slowness that had no end, curled up about himself like the coils
of a still, the noise of the shot kept echoing in his ears, he turned on the
shower faucet and the glassy stream of water deformed the image of the
stretcher that was moving off, rapidly, in the direction of the trenches,
preceded by the small obsequious shape of the sergeant, Dig the hole fast,
dump him in it, get this over with, for God's sake, he came out of the tub
dripping, groping for the towel, Why the hell didn't I have you come with
me, set you up in a peaceful place in the nearest village so I could visit you
when I was on leave, we could have been together, talked, made love, feeling
your tongue licking the hair on my chest during the whirlwind of orgasm,
your arched body lying there to receive the whiplashes of my blood, eating your eternally insipid meals, lounging around with you on the porch in
shorts, breathing in the night, the breath of Africa, loaded with mysterious
insects, sparks of strange lights, huge shadows, stars without a name, and
hoarse and happy voices, shivering, he got a towel from the pile in the hall
closet and took a peek at the kitchen, no plates in the dishwasher, no cups, no
frying pan, no forks, the stove without any gravy stains, the refrigerator
immaculate, a bottle of spring water all alone on the shelf in the door, My
son-in-law has probably been here and sopped up all my whiskey, there was a
little gin left in the bar in the living room, and he tipped the bottle up to his
lips in an automatic movement, without thinking, and at that exact moment
the telephone began to ring, By now they must know I'm back, they're
looking for me all over the city, sorrowful, grave, serious, full of gooey
understanding and resigned advice, Come to attention, the lieutenant colonel bellowed at the guerrilla, you're talking to a white man, I want to know
what the Frelimo movement is hatching up against us, in the background the
soldiers, perched on some crates, were sipping beer at the improvised bar,
the black man stared at him without answering, he opened the catch on his
holster with his finger, Everything you people are preparing to fuck our asses
with, you son of a bitch, he picked out a shirt and a pair of pants and got
dressed slowly, looking out the window at Lisbon's fatuous tranquility, the
soft afternoon colors, the slow, sick traffic, If you'd been with me you

wouldn't have died, you wouldn't have let yourself die in the insistent and courteous way animals give up, When's the next attack, you bastard? the black man's reddened eyes, devoid of sentiment and suspicion, dissolved into a kind of bloody tincture of iodine, How many mortars, how many bazookas, how many recoilless rifles, he looked in the drawer for the cardigan that he wore around the house, This filthy rag will be good for cleaning the tub someday, his wife would threaten jokingly with her forefinger in the air, he drank another swallow of gin, trying to remember her physically, her face, her expressions, her voice, and a dim figure came slowly back to him, a watery face, transparent nods, sounds that broke up, liquid, at a great distance, he squatted on the floor with the bottle between his legs and the telephone kept ringing loudly, he remained standing in the same spot, pistol in hand, when the sergeant touched his elbow We've finished that little job, sir, How is it they've finished that little job, he asked himself, since the black man keeps falling down in front of me, since he constantly crumples to the ground, his hands on his navel, facing my anguished affliction, You went to Angola and Guinea with me, the lieutenant colonel thought, but not to Mozambique, you'd gotten thin, you complained of pains in the breast, you'd sprawl out in a chair sometimes, your eyelids sweaty, letting an absent and hazy look pour over me, the doctor advised tests, X-rays, complicated examinations, you said goodbye on the dock in a coat that was suddenly enormous, your wedding ring kept slipping off, bracelets slipped off, your shoes danced on your feet, the gin was slowly making his heart beat faster, Old, I'm getting old, I can't take alcohol the way I used to, he inadvertently hit the ashtray and the butts scattered across the rug, The black man's eyes, you see, don't accuse me, don't condemn me (he told me, breaking up another toothpick onto the tablecloth), I was the one who was accusing and condemning myself, I was relentlessly destroying myself, he nodded yes to the sergeant and pushed open the door to the office lined with maps and charts, with a small window that opened onto the abandoned native village, straw roofs fallen in, beams, the abandonment devoured by grass, the extremely optimistic letters from Lisbon confused him, if the tests are normal, why aren't they clearer in what they write me, why haven't they given me any justification for the operation, the X-rays, the medicine, he leaned too heavily on a circular table with three legs, full of bric-a-brac and small boxes, and that precious junk glided along the length of the doily and fell on top of him, the lid of a porcelain heart breaking into a thousand pieces, the telephone, unceasing, continued its shrill and monotonous outpouring: If I'd been here you wouldn't have died, I'd have grabbed you by the wrist and wouldn't have let you die, I'd have explained to you that I need you, because the house is getting enormous, I can't breathe all by myself, I've got something in my ribs, a latch, a key that's tightening, discomfort, agony, a nameless upset, tomorrow I'm moving into the barracks without unpacking my bags, How many recoilless rifles, you piece of shit, how many mortars, how many men, he was wearing cheap rubber boots and his legs straightened, thin, chocolate-colored, to his khaki shorts, he tried to get onto his feet, carrying the bottle, and he keeled over on his weak limbs, in an unexpected mirror he caught sight of his open mouth, his messy hair, his unfocused eyes, he sat down in the office and took the whiskey out of the drawer while his index finger squeezed the trigger interminably, We caught this monkey, Colonel, on guard in a village of supporters, he didn't even see us, the first and the last one we got, fell into our hands, like a rabbit, he pictured his wife in the cancer hospital, just like the people he'd seen a few hours before, the same exhaustion, the same paleness, the same giving in to death, goddamn it, the gin is giving me heartburn, it makes me want to chuck my guts through my mouth, the telephone keeps on vibrating with its sobbing call, he bumped into an easy chair, into another, into the heavy bookcase, into the door

("In spite of what you suppose, Captain," the communications officer said, "after the Revolution the struggle became much more difficult in a certain way")

he reached the hallway, headed toward the bedroom, but the walls were wavering, the ceiling was wavering, the floor was rising and falling, trying to make him lose his balance with every step, unexpected steps made him tip over, lean, wave his arms like a beginning skater, Dying just before I got home is in poor taste at best, I hate you, How many bazookas, you shitty nigger, how many Russian instructors, what trails have been mined and make it snappy, What am I going to do now for a whole year behind a desk, giving orders to superannuated sergeants, and then Angola again, or Guinea, or Mozambique and twenty-odd months of war, weapons, coffins, faces weary of surviving their own fear every day, their own unrest, their own little stubborn despair that won't evaporate, like acid in the thousand little openings in their skin, and suddenly an enormous explosion blinding their ears, frightening the bats hanging from the trees like Spanish lace fans, the black man squeezing his belly with his fists, the trickle of blood, his afflicted ears vibrating to the rhythm of the sound, he went into the bedroom and there was the telephone, indignant, insistent, insufferable on the night table beside his picture, he finished the bottle of gin, which rolled along the rug, he held back the vomit with his sleeve No, I'm beyond the age where I can drink like that, he looked at the made-up bed You probably went shopping, you'll be back in just a little while, putting the plastic bags from the supermarket in the pantry, the canned goods, the vegetables, the eggs, the frozen fish, the meat, you'll come into the living room complaining about the prices, you disappear to make dinner, come back to clean out the ashtrays, at first, and until I got used to it, I was bothered by your exaggerated mania for order, everything symmetrical, everything gleaming, everything excessively polished, what am I going to do with this stinking nigger who won't stop falling inside me, his belly busted, what will I do about this nigger who won't ever stop falling inside me, every minute, with a busted belly, it's one or the other of you who's calling me on the phone, either you or him, I pick up the receiver and I hear Hello love from the other end, he bumped into the corner of the bed when he tried to reach the instrument, wildly grabbed the window curtains, the lights will go on down there in a little while now, he straightened up with difficulty, his stomach bursting

("No, all joking aside, tell me if it's easy, Captain," the soldier asked me, "for a guy to get by in these times with a wife and three kids?")

his head dull, his limbs entangled It's you, asking me to come get you in the Baixa because you can't find a taxi, or maybe It's just that I stayed at Maria João's apartment with the baby, I'll be home in fifteen minutes, The black man's that I've got to tell you about, I've got to tell you how much I miss you, he went along the edge of the rug, How much I love you, just imagine the rotten, tasteless trick they played on me at the Cancer Institute, you can't imagine what boobs they were, he reached out for the telephone, brought it up to mouth level, and when he was about to answer, he stopped, put it down beside him on the pillow, stretched out on the mattress, retching and vomiting, and he hugged the Bakelite with all his strength, as he would the living body of a woman.

3

"WHAT about you, Captain, has life been all that easy for you?" the soldier asked me.

The communications officer was living with his deaf godmother and a fat female dog with black and white spots, a mongrel, in a very old flat with enormous rooms on the street behind the Feira Popular amusement park: in summertime the bedroom window would be open directly onto the carousels, all lighted up, so that every so often a wooden elephant or horse would spin around the floor for a few seconds, cloaked in the sugary smell of fritters, before disappearing again in the direction of the Gypsy woman's tent, where she predicted thromboses, inheritances, and shipwrecks, or the soft drink and juice stands, piloted by girls in décolletage with the wise, appraising eyes of loan sharks. The godmother and the bitch resembled each other in that they limped on the same leg, suffered from the same ailments, shared their diet of kale and bream, and trotted around him like a windlass with whimpering and blear-eyed joy.

"I don't know," the soldier responded, "when you take a good look, you can see that our captain has aged as much as we have."

"Esmeralda," the godmother barked into the dressing room, turning her head on rusty bones with difficulty. "Esmeralda, come see who's here."

A third decrepit being, smelling of starch and hot clothes, appeared with the hyssop of a sprayer in her fist, and stood there adoring him in a silence of startled passion where loving ragged memories crept in: baptisms, a tricycle in the rain in the backyard, tincture of iodine, birthday parties. Hundreds of clocks went back and forth ceremoniously among porcelain buddhas, plates from China, pictures of naval lieutenants with great martial mustaches. The rotten stench of piss impregnated the rugs, and the old women fluttered about inside the smell like divers, spitting out of their mouths the little face-powder balls they breathed in:

"The young master," exclaimed Esmeralda, fascinated, looking for the handkerchief for emotions in the torn pocket of her apron.

"My godmother died in seventy-five," the communications officer said, "worn out by the PIDE's coming to the house before dawn looking for me for questioning, making threats, talking jail. Esmeralda went blind after that, in a poorhouse in Combro: I visit her at Christmas and she doesn't speak, doesn't hear, doesn't understand, doesn't know me. Those two old women hated Marcelo Caetano because of me, Captain, they thought the dirty bastard was personally out to screw me."

He walked out along the long hallway (the dampness thrived on the upper walls next to the ceiling) and he found the bedroom exactly as he remembered it, exactly as he had left it: the bed, the desk, the closet, the spines of the books casually arranged on the shelves, just like incisors stuck into superimposed gums: I'll wait a month or more for them to contact me, he thought, and until then what kind of excuse can I palm off on the old girls?

"The next day my daughter appeared," the lieutenant colonel explained to me, "and I woke up while she was cleaning up the vomit. I hadn't been drunk in years, friend, I threw up tons and tons of food. I made a damn lot of work for her."

There was some kind of very far-off sound, like that of a man walking or two things rubbing against each other, and the sound kept getting closer, closer, and closer, within reach. He tried to grab it with his fingers, but his arm, his shoulder, his whole body wouldn't obey him: he opened his eyes and made out a girl in the mist, the face of a guy behind her, the husky vibrations of voices that his heavy skull, just like a stone with aching angles, understood in a defective way:

"Father," the girl quacked like a duck in the haze, "do you feel all right, Father?"

He remembered waking up from the anesthesia when they took out his gallbladder, perceiving other people through a distorted filter, the surgeon's words reverberating, incomprehensible, in his brain, the gush of an open faucet hurting his eardrums like the endless stab of a knife. Two aspirins, the lieutenant colonel thought, a glass of milk, and I'll be fine, as the objects around him were becoming clearer and he was becoming aware that the back of his neck had been cut up into tiny little crumbs, held together by the film of his skin. The girl (She doesn't look like me, she never looked like me) leaned over threateningly, it seemed to him, like a huge building that was collapsing, smashing thick, fearsome blocks of saliva around it:

"I'm going to get you some water, Father."

A month of plunking his ass on café chairs, reading newspapers, buying semiclandestine books in that little tobacco shop on the Avenida, nodding from boredom at rerun matinées, inventing jobs to calm the old women down, until a harmless phone call set up a date on a park bench: underneath the fifth tree, he remembered, almost always underneath the fifth tree, counting from the top of the street. And in the course of those unoccupied and impatient days his comrades were probably spying on him, observing him, measuring him from a distance with prudent caution, getting together to discuss his case in smoke-filled garrets, in houses on the outskirts of Lisbon, in stores, in garages, waiting for reports that never came, that never would come, perhaps, from cells in Africa.

"The young master," moaned Esmeralda, foolish with happiness, moving her double chin to the digestive rhythm of the clocks.

From the window, the amusement park in the daylight had the appearance of a skeleton with iron vertebrae, decorated with extinguished bulbs and mascaraed giraffes, waiting for the ticket offices to open in order to break out in a trembling, twirling, exploding circle of disjointed beams that a motor would push with feeble farts. He unpacked with the dog rubbing about his ankles, the second lieutenant turned out the light and the bed became a dark ebb tide of sheets, where their breathing rose and fell like waves in the darkness. A tablet fizzed in the bottom of the glass, getting smaller and sticking to the sides of the glass, sending off a lively cloud of gas in the direction of the surface: the lieutenant colonel tried to lift his jaw from the pillow, but his brain, independent of his shoulders, had become a lunar rock that no force in the world could budge: anchored forever to the mattress, he would witness the slow passage of the years with the pathetic anguish of statues.

"We made you some codfish cakes," his godmother informed him from the door.

And she put on an air of comic confidentiality, which spouted from her nose under the not-so-clean gray locks of her hair:

"I just can't tell you what's for dessert, it's a surprise."

"Son of a bitch," the communications officer muttered, helping himself to the cake. "A week doesn't go by that I don't think of that old woman."

And, as a matter of fact, for two weeks he read newspapers, buried himself in movie theaters, hung around cafés, looking for nothing, abstract and funereal, leaning like a willow over an empty coffee cup, bored with the conversations, the waiters who moved about the tables, the billiard players in back, moving the markers with a disdainful cue. At night, lying down, he would disconsolately thumb through back issues of *Seleções do Reader's Digest* while the wooden elephants came and went through the open window, the necklaces of light on the ceiling and the motorcycles from the Pit of Death thundered through the neighborhood with catastrophic acceleration: The PIDE, he thought, could it have broken up the Organization? What about Olavo, Emílio, Baldy, and that stocky fellow, half-crazy, who wanted to go right out and plant two-pound bombs at the headquarters of the Ping-Pong Federation because he couldn't stand the sound of the balls' *toc toc toc toc toc toc toc* on the cement floor? Had they branched out into new groups during his absence, new cells, new guerrilla commandos, or, instead, been reduced to four or five strong-willed and stubborn students handing out leaflets, testing out classmates, writing hurriedly on the walls of buildings with red spray paint in quivering letters DOWN WITH DICTATORSHIP? Could there still be enough money to pay party workers their miserable salaries, order weapons from Algiers or Morocco, bring prisoners fruit, cigarettes, sponge cake, magazines? The lieutenant's limbs crept out slowly, conquering the soft resistance of the covers, his mouth found the perfumed angle of a shoulder and he climbed along the neck with successive kisses, en route to the ear.

"Put it in," the woman demanded in a quick, urgent voice.

"Let's see if you can drink it without spilling," the girl said, cupping her hand under the rim of the glass. "Ten minutes from now you'll feel great, word of honor."

Inês pulled up her nightgown, settled on her back, and the lieutenant's fingers touched a tuft of stiff hair and inside the hair an oblique little grotto that was becoming damp and sticky. An arm went around his neck, looking for the gap in the buttocks, rubbed his anus, and squeezed the tender, swollen root of his testicles. The paper moon of the lamp came and went, yellow against the trees, and when he reached the bus stop in front of the movie theater (a completely idiotic detective movie, mongoloid and disconnected, a typical American product), a fellow bumped into him in a casual way and kept on walking in the direction of Estefânia and its melancholy little pool, amazed, surprised, excited, incredulous, sinking into the houses: (Was it true? Was it true? Was it really true?) he recognized the thin back and short little steps of Olavo, whose huge frayed overcoat, as always too large for his tiny trunk, dragged on the ground with the ridiculous nobility of a priest's vestments.

"At last, they hadn't forgotten about me, Captain," the communications officer said, "at last, they were surviving, at last, they were working, at last, the report from Mozambique had arrived and I was still a steady guy."

He let him get twenty, thirty yards ahead and began to follow him, hands in his pockets, close to the buildings, stopping from time to time to look in a shop window, a crippled beggar showing the filthy scars of his stumps, a drunk, head down and stubborn, mumbling his cosmic fury to the footpath through the grass, shaking his furious little fists at the trolley tracks.

"You've got white hairs too, Captain," the soldier said triumphantly, examining me, "you've got wrinkles too, you've got a belly too, I bet you wear glasses to read."

Without looking back, Olavo went around the statue of Cesário Verde, which darkened a small rectangle of grass, and went up a short slope where cars were parked on top of the island, one after another like dead fish. The sun was revealing the tumbledown and leprous masonry of Lisbon more clearly, the scaffolding, the shopkeepers, the apathetic and neuter people. He sat up on the bed, his daughter put the glass on the night table, and his blood began to course, gradually, in no hurry, along his shoulders.

"My love," the woman breathed, wriggling, her legs wide apart so that his penis could hammer hard at the end of her vagina. (The string on the intrauterine device is uncomfortable, shit.) "My love my love my love my love."

"When the battalion gets together again here after ten years," the soldier asked me, bitter and sarcastic with wine, "how many of us, just tell me, will have bitten the dust by then? Seriously, Captain, level with me."

From a distance the communications officer was keeping his eyes not only on Olavo's trail but on everything he thought might be suspect around him (Just like the jungle, he thought, like the war, alert for sounds, colors, movements, the brightness of the landscape): the idlers, the shopkeepers in the doorways of their deserted establishments, a diligent policeman putting tickets under the windshield wipers of cars, lifting them delicately, like insects, with two dextrous fingers, until the tiny fellow evaporated into the shadow of a doorway and he waited ten minutes or a quarter of an hour, standing on the grass with the most idiotic and guilty look in the world.

"I was always like that, Captain," he explained with a timid smile, spoon suspended over the saucer of custard. "I could never get used to being underground."

The lieutenant colonel tried to get on his feet and the room rose before him, so different by day from the night before, without any shadows, threats, phantoms, that he thought to himself Yesterday afternoon is a lie, your death is a lie, the cancer hospital is a lie: in just a few minutes you'll come out in your robe with breakfast, coffee, toast, orange marmalade on the bamboo table, and to my relief, my life, will once more get back onto its usual track, the post, family dinner, the movies on Saturday with my in-laws, and I'll gradually reach retirement age without any surprises or upsets. But he faced himself in the bathroom with his face a mess, crusts of vomit on his collar and his chin, his daughter's dark dress, his son-in-law's black tie, the remorseful misty faces, hopelessly serious, and he dropped down to the edge of the bathtub, anxious, confused, running the palm of his downcast hand over his disordered hair.

"Go down," the second lieutenant asked with his head already stuck between the metal braces of the bed, and the girl, resting on his ankles, slithered down another foot like a snake. His eyes, liquid and blind like those of a newborn baby, throbbed in the vacuum, the Cape Verdean garbage men were noisily invading the street, tossing cans around, and the small truck, with two lights swaying under the canvas top, was gobbling up garbage, empty bottles, leftovers from meals, hefty bundles of paper, pieces of chicken, with great huge mechanical gulps. With his cheeks burning and his heart beating, he went over to the door where Olavo had entered, trying desperately to put on the casual look of a regular tenant and still conscious of my horribly artificial movements and my look of a conspirator, and he went into one of those antique hallways, with no lights, a tiled floor, mailboxes stuck into the scabrous wall, and in back the concierge's cubicle smelling of cats and rotten fish. The outside light had trouble getting into that dingy, dusty den, with the air as immemorially quiet as in a museum, and the communications officer, with difficulty, made out a bannister, a spiral staircase, the hexagon of a dirty windowpane above. He took two oblique, lost, hesitant steps forward, which his shoes emphasized with harsh squeaks: he felt like fleeing, running away fast, getting back into the daylight outside, the city's known geography, and at that moment Olavo calling him, leaning over from the second floor, a small microscopic shape, wearing a tie, just like a tiny efficient notary, and the familiar little voice Wait, don't be foolish, come here.

"Whichever way, Captain," the soldier insisted. "Ten years from now, if we've both still lasted that long, the loser buys the winner a bottle of Colares."

He stumbled up the stairs (his soles were squeaking fearfully in the silence), reached the landing, and Olavo pushed him into a small room cluttered with furniture, a still life of hares and partridges hanging on the left, and from there into a slightly larger room, but just as melancholy, with crocheted curtains that kept the sun out, an infinity of chairs, tables, small tables with pictures (Of whom?), cabinets loaded with chinaware and glasses, a worn sofa whose legs bit the corners of a floral rug. The little skeleton opened the cabinet with bottles and poured himself a glass of anisette: the sugary smell came wafting over, at a distance from his nose, as if a geranium were growing on the floor above.

"Want a drink?" Olavo asked in his clear intonation, showing the gold medals on the label. "Authentic Spanish stuff, man, to celebrate your return."

"You don't want to take a chance, Captain," the soldier challenged me. "You're more scared shitless of losing than I'd want to be."

I wonder what kind of guy lives in this dump, the communications officer asked himself, perplexed, examining the furniture, the photographs (a man in uniform, children, the attentive snout of a terrier), the clay figurines on the doilies, a second still life, with more hares, hanging opposite a window which the dim afternoon lighted like a lamp, Olavo so satisfied, his cheeks puffing up after every swallow. Certainly not his, it was impossible to imagine him in a setup like that, resigned, useless, ancient: he surrounded himself, he could swear, with fervent posters and revolutionary slogans tacked to the wall, books read and reread by Ho Chi Minh and Marx, and ashtrays overflowing with the crumpled butts from endless discussions, which made mouths bitter with the rancid taste of heroic plans. The Organization has improved during my absence, the communications officer thought, it's furnished itself with sophisticated hideouts, more perfect disguises, come up with new types of battle: in anonymous caves bearded types without any questions or doubts assembled bombs, prepared bullets, made coded telephone calls, their palms cupped over the mouthpiece to distant contacts, asking for machine guns and pistols from comrades in Paris, who, in turn (he calculated), were doing business with enigmatic and greedy Moroccans in run-down neighborhoods. The regime was going to fall by our hand, secret police would turn up assassinated on street corners in the morning, cabinet ministers, scared to death, their clothes in tatters, would cross the Spanish frontier on foot, red flags would cover the fronts of buildings, squares crammed with raised fists would chorus the "Internationale."

"Father," the girl asked, trying to embrace him around the waist, "do you feel all right, Father?"

Vertigo, dizziness, high or low blood pressure, the emotion of his return, nothing serious, it's already passed. The smell of vomit distressed him, his legs tried to steady themselves in vain, he limped aimlessly about the bedroom (he should stick his head under the faucet and the cold water running down the back of his neck, over his hair, down his back), the tiles rose and fell like waves at the beach, the reflection of the light over the washbasin thrust a thousand incandescent needles into his eyelids. The woman took the lieutenant's penis out of her vagina and began to caress it while her tongue excited his nipples, lingered on his chest, slipped down his stomach toward his pubes.

"Drink me," he grunted with all the strength of his nerves concentrated on the stiff swelling at the fork of his thighs, ready to explode in successive little waves of fluid.

The daughter and her husband turned on the shower and helped him lean his head under the spray, while the lieutenant colonel sneezed and coughed like a snorting walrus.

"How did it go in Africa?" Olavo asked, as if he'd seen him just five minutes before, with the same casual tone that he would have asked How's the traffic downtown? They're shitting on me after all, the communications officer thought: they're using me for their own services and if I'm no longer useful they'll give me a plane ticket to Brussels and send me off to catechize immigrant laborers, roaring Mao's phrases to construction workers.

"People die," he answered cautiously, fondling a cloth rose in a vase shaped like a woman's arm. (I wonder who is the fool who lives in this bazaar?) "There's so much dying," he added resentfully, "that I figured that they'd forgotten about yours truly: I got here almost three weeks ago, damn it."

Olavo poured himself another anisette and smiled at him: nothing about his expression betrayed worry or sarcasm:

"The usual precautions, you know the setup. The PIDE's had an attack of nerves, last month they broke up a whole cell of the Communist party: twelve men, radio equipment, lots of papers, documents that ruined at least five years of work. And if they could land on the party, it would be much easier for them to pounce on us."

The son-in-law, wafting the smell of American tobacco into his ear, wiped his face, and objects were becoming progressively clearer. The lieutenant colonel looked in the mirror, surprised, his features in disorder. I'm beyond the age of kiddy orgies, he thought, the time for drowning your sorrows with the first swig in sight.

The second lieutenant's body quivered three or four times in short, de-creasing spasms, and it landed on the sheets like a burned-out motor or a shipwrecked sailor on a beach: Inês, huddled over his belly in a fetal position, kept on sucking him, with concave cheeks, touching his perineum with the tips of her fingers, and desire began to be aroused again, slowly, inside him, turning his blood into a froth of excited bubbles. Olavo put down his glass and measured the communications officer with his small inquiring eyes:

"As you can see, we've gone on fighting in the same way. They haven't touched a single one of our units and we're quite sure there haven't been any infiltrators among our sympathizers. (Who can brag about a tune like that? the communications officer thought. Go sell your snake oil to somebody else, because I've been around just as long as you have.) We won't do great things, but we'll do them little by little, safely: the indoctrination of basic units, the formation of teams, solid implantation in the working class, a few daring little actions, the gathering of facts. It's this last point, incidentally, that they told me to talk to you about."

"Are you superstitious, Captain?" the soldier asked, leaning across the table, brushing his ever-so-ugly tie against an empty bottle. (He's drunk, I thought, the shitty part about these battalion dinners is that everybody ends up tight as a drum: how many poor bastards have I driven home, singing, shouting, pissing on the backseat, effusive, so bothersome, so unbearable?)

The soldier's expression had become intimate, brotherly, oily, like an accomplice, with the alcohol eliminating the mile-long distance of rank:

"Never mind," he conceded. "Ten years from now, with the speed people get old, none of us will give a damn."

"The Political Commission of the Permanent Council," Olavo informed him, sitting down now, his legs crossed, on a monstrous wicker couch, showing pride in his unshined shoes, "has decided that you will stay in the Army in the name of the supreme interests of the Proletariat, and it's arranged a place for you in the Secretariat of the Ministry of War. We have to steal operational comrades away from the war, we need trusted revolutionaries inside the machinery, with their ears open and a mouth that knows how to sing at just the right time."

Radiantly he studied the cheap shoes, meticulously tied a loose lace: This guy has really got the soul of a notary, seriously, the communications officer said to himself, he's talking to me with the haughty confidence of a lawyer postponing a hearing. He went over to the window, trembling with irritation, pushed back the crocheted curtains, and he saw a miserable dog, hunchbacked, nosing into the contents of a paper bag on the pedestal of the statue of Cesário Verde. A gentleman with a vest and a dignified look was solicitously passing a rag over the top of an ancient Austin, replete with a pair of huge extra headlights. Two guys in coveralls were unloading refrigerators from a truck. The afternoon sun was reddening the graceless gray or brown or blue buildings of the Estefânia district, the trees were trembling with the breath of a nonexistent breeze. The woman buried her head on the second lieutenant's shoulder, her round, full, well-turned legs doubled over him.

"Give me a cigarette," and I stretched out my hand until I reached the box of matches, the tobacco, the ashtray lifted from some nightclub many years ago, at a time when they had fun stealing plates, spoons, emblems, menus from restaurants and hotels in order to collect mementoes of the second-rate Edens where we'd been, esplanades along the sea, sleazy boardinghouses in Beato, inns, the mysterious song of the eucalyptus trees at night, tinkling their zinc leaves. Olavo brought out a long rectangle:

"Everything's in this envelope, comrade," he explained. "Money, military papers, passport, instructions to be burned after being read. You'll enter the Ministry at the beginning of the month, take advantage of the week of relaxation you've got. In the meantime we've already arranged to have another comrade there help you out: you'll give him the reports on levels one, two, and three, and he'll take care of distribution and contacts." (To help out or to keep an eye on me? the communications officer wondered, mistrustful. They're giving me a headache with all this sudden caution.)

Olavo rubbed the shoe on his left foot against his right pant leg, quickly finished the anisette, looked longingly at the glass and got up: standing, in relief his tiny silhouette gave the impression that it was part of the furniture.

"I know that this old song," he said with the benevolence of a store manager begging one's pardon, "the precautions, the controls, the secrets, what you think is undesirable foolishness annoys the devil out of you. But there aren't too many of us, old man, it's been a hell of a job getting the Organization set up, the police can buy informers on every street corner, and if we slip up once, boom."

He put out the cigarette in the cellophane from the pack he kept in the wrinkled pouch, put some ridiculous dark glasses on his nose, and twisted up into a kind of scowl or smile:

"You're aware of the dozens of arrests that have been made because of stupid carelessness, not watching out," he complained as he straightened out the lace doily on the sofa, "the tactical changes they forced us to make, the hints we've been giving to the PIDE: the Committee on Defense and Security has decided that it's time to put an end to luxuries of that sort."

He came over to shake his hand and the communications officer felt in the palm of his hand, as always, the unpleasant damp bones of the other man:

"Give me twenty minutes before you leave," Olavo requested.

The door closed and he was alone among the portraits, the flowers, and the pretentious, decaying chests, sniffing around him the special silence of old houses, woven out of tiny vibrations, of clock springs being released, of the subtle oscillations of drapes, of the moans of furniture and floorboards that no foot steps on: A little while from now I'll go down the stairs and will have forgotten this building, I don't know any guy named Olavo, I've decided to stay in the Army because of the unemployment crisis, I live with my god-mother and an old female dog behind the Feira Popular. What, Officer? Coming out of the Estefânia, you say, Officer, right next to the statue of Cesário Verde? Pardon me for contradicting you, Officer, but that's impossible, I haven't been in that district in years, there must be some mistake on your part. He leaned over the photograph of an extremely fat woman, her hair parted down the middle, stood up again: A misunderstanding, Officer, an unfortunate misunderstanding, I'm an officer in the Portuguese Army, I'm defending my country, petty politics make me sick, I've got enough amusements of my own. Me in a group of terrorists, Officer, in an armed group against the Government of the Nation, against my country? For the love of God, Officer, a jackass idea like that could only come from someone having fun or out of malice. He washed Olavo's glass in the kitchen and put it in the cupboard, alongside the others. Immediately thereafter he took a deep breath (I'm coming, Mama, I'm coming, Papa), buttoned up his coat, and headed for the landing: the city still maintained its usual inoffensive, neutral, peaceful look.

"I put in a year and some hard work before they locked me up, Captain," he told me. "I got out of stir with the Revolution."

He carefully licked both sides of the custard spoon:

"Olavo was checking out Marseilles at that time, buying hand grenades from the Libyans, and I only got to find out a long time afterward that I'd been in his mother's place, that the fat woman with the part down the middle of her hair was his old lady: what simpleminded idealists, Captain, the police must have laughed so much at us that they fell flat on their asses."

The woman began slowly to lick and kiss the lieutenant's chest again:

"More," she asked.

4

THE sprawling body of the machine gunner obliquely stretched out over his, the face so close that he could smell the fetid odor of death, he slowly made room for the woman's naked leg on his leg, for the smooth stomach against his sweating side (I've got to get out of here, he thought in anguish, I've got to find the fucking radio corporal and call Mueda, in the midst of shots and shouts), the weight of the sleeping head on his shoulder, burning his neck with thin, peaceful breathing. As he was waking up the trees were turning into walls and furniture, the grassy ground was becoming the ironed peace of sheets, the Lisbon afternoon was taking the place of the Mozambique morning, the automobile horns from the street were coming out of the moans of the wounded scattered at random on the carpet amidst the disorder of the apartment and the woman's slippers. The lieutenant got away from the knee that was crushing his side and went into the kitchen to wet the back of his neck under the sink faucet, whose stream wasn't coming from a curved metal pipe, but from the throat of a mortarman destroyed by a grenade fragment, giving off a dark substance in spurts. He looked at the pile of dirty dishes on the left and the row of square cloths hanging from a set of hooks and his heart grew calmer, beat more regularly, more slowly: I'm on the Rua da Mãe D'Água, I'm home, the woman with the cane, as always, is slowly coming up the steps from the fountain to Príncipe Real, leading two blind bitches on a leash. He rubbed his groin, standing, against the tiles, feeling the cold of the porcelain creeping up his veins. The nightmare can go fuck itself, I've been back more than a month, tomorrow I've got a very important meeting at the bank, it's strange how horrible things cling to us, to our memory. He lighted a cigarette from the big box of matches on the stove, grabbed the ashtray of beer-bottle caps bent by the bottle opener and lay down again next to the full body of the woman, who let out a disconnected phrase from her open mouth, moved forward, and drew her elbows back in a soft, toadlike spasm, resting her arm on his shoulder without waking, like an oar on a boat at anchor.

"Maybe I should have stayed in Africa that time," the lieutenant confessed to me. "Before the Revolution and Independence and the Russians taking over there, of course: it's just that it's taken me a little while to get used to Lisbon, Captain."

With the back of his head resting against the headboard and the smoke rising up from the space between his fingers, frightened, he was getting used to the familiar objects, in the same way that people recovering from a stroke learn all over again, syllable by syllable, the forgotten vocabulary that they already know: that picture, that knickknack, that painting, that door over there, as if the things lacked and at the same time possessed a past, painfully reconstructed in a kind of difficult archeology of the emotions. The city itself, in his absence, had become the same and different and was being displaced by an artificial setting identical to the reality he had lost and yet subtly different, where masked actors played, with more touches of white in their hair and more penciled wrinkles at the corners of their mouths, the friends of three years before, when the war was nothing but a vague threat in news items in the papers, wounded, dead, decorations, glorious victories. The woman moved slightly on the mattress like a turtle at the bottom of a fishbowl, her pubes rubbed against his navel, the clump of swirls had been cropped in the summer, and the lieutenant put out his butt and softly began to fondle that damp, resting hedgehog which was licking his fingers with the tender membranes of its mouth. The afternoon was growing dark on the window, the globe of the lamp was slowly swaying, rising like the moon from behind the geometric shadow of the table, the smiles on the pictures there spread throughout the room, returned beneath the glass in an afflicted flight of birds. He slid his hand along Inês's stomach up to the curve of her breasts, underlined with his tongue the shell of her ear (I can hear the sea so clearly in your ears), an empty bottle rolled along the floor, startling the gas marigold of the heater in its small enameled home, a rake of nails caught his kidneys, his testicles grew small in the lining of their skin pouch, he pushed the woman's legs away with his heels, the neighbor across the way was carrying on a shouting conversation with someone on the street, a Pekingese on his lap, and taking advantage of the cadence of his voice, like a surfer riding a favorable wave, he opened a path to the verge of an orgasm in a swirl of foam.

"A Pekingese in his lap, Lieutenant?" the soldier asked, restless, indifferent to the liquor. "A Pekingese on the Rua da Mãe D'Água?"

"I didn't know them at all, they'd moved in there a few months before," the lieutenant replied. "A fag painter and his black lover from Senegal who babbled French and stumbled over the words. The neighborhood had got full of faggotry all of a sudden."

When he ran aground on the sands of the pillow, just like the corpse of a seagull that the waters bring up and pull back with dreary slowness (no shots now, no moans, only the thick oily peace that followed an ambush), the paper moon hovered peacefully in the shadows over the blur of the furniture, and the hay-feverish telephone was sneezing in the corner of the room, calling them with an obstinate and implacable mechanical ferocity. He fumbled for the switch on the lamp (I'm going to knock over a book, a doll, some ceramic piece of shit, one of the two thousand precious potsherds you surround yourself with), the lights outside were quivering in circles on the ceiling, roses with successive shaded rings, clearer on the gray wall, he pulled the cord and my body, naked and defenseless, suddenly appeared on the bed as on an autopsy table, with a second body beside it, also inert, muttering protests into the pillow: She's been wounded, the second lieutenant thought, I'm going to call the Mueda hospital for a helicopter, and he walked along the carpet trail, his limp penis swinging back and forth, trying to figure out where the mines were in the irregular surface of the floor, over to the corner with the telephone, which was twisting and rocking in a colicky rage. He squatted down with the invisible weapon across his knees, lifted the receiver (twenty minutes, half an hour, *toc toc toc toc toc toc toc toc* over the tops of the bushes), and the disagreeable, masculine, authoritarian voice of his mother-in-law cut through his skull like an incandescent dagger:

"Who's there?"

"It was always like that, Captain," the lieutenant said, helping himself to my cigarettes without asking. "I would be making love or have just finished and at that very moment the sly old bitch, who seemed to sense it, would call me at home to interrupt my fun, get my mind all screwed up, file my horns down. She kicked the bucket last year from cancer of the pancreas and her husband married the housekeeper, a short little woman with a mustache who at that time at least didn't boss him around: I'll bet he took the servant to city hall like somebody going to Fátima, on his knees, thankful for a miracle."

Squatting down, without any clothes on, peering anxiously around the calm of the walls (A recoilless rifle hidden in the shelving of the cupboard? A mortar in the door frame?), the murmur of the code flowed into the showerhead of the mouthpiece:

"Spider Two calling Godmother, Spider Two calling Godmother, over."

"My second lieutenant," the soldier said, "was off his rocker for a long time: if the doctor hadn't got to him with his crazy pills, he would have had a fucking lot of beatings."

The monster hesitated for a moment, disconcerted, then returned to the charge with morose roughness:

"Who's there?"

Inês, leaving off sleep, lighted by the dentist-chair clarity of the bed lamp, whose glare erased shadows and shapes and illuminated the anemic tones of the dying on faces, was aiming the pistol sights of her erect nipples at the lieutenant. The sheets, at an angle, covered the fan of hair between her thighs, the apple of her behind stood out against a dark background of books. The voice repeated, irritated:

"Who's there?"

Here I am in Lisbon, shit, really in Lisbon, he thought, no mine is exploding under my feet. So he sat on the couch and answered

"It's me, Mother"

with a resigned small sigh of defeat.

"Our wives' fucking families on top of our own fucking families are too much to take," the communications officer decreed, picking his teeth, "you get smothered under such a mob. The only good thing about the war is that at least we're orphans for two years, with little letters now and then to play the part of sons and husbands."

"What's that spider business all about?" the mother-in-law asked suspiciously.

"I couldn't figure it out either," the lieutenant covered very quickly. "Crossed wires, coming at the same time."

"It's strange," the mother-in-law commented after a silence. "Would you please give me Inês?"

In the painter's apartment across the street, a silhouette against the light was going through a kind of oriental dance behind two red curtains. The concierge's bitch, a tiny, horrible creature, eternally pregnant and endowed with an incredible capacity for noise for such a diminutive animal, was barking angrily down below: Thirty or forty more years of this (and if not this, something like this), the lieutenant thought, discouraged, and then I'll die: a short or long illness, loaded with fear, indignation, suffering, and after that, and suddenly, nothing. Nothing: Inês's eyes were beginning to come alive, the sides of her face were folded up in the imitation of a smile, she curled up on the mattress and indicated the telephone with her chin, without words: Who is it?

"Your mother," the second lieutenant explained, and she shrugged her shoulders with indifference, annoyance:

"Tell her I went out," she suggested in a low voice. "Some excuse, I don't know, that I've got a lover, that I went to church, to the hairdresser, to the supermarket to shop: those are the only four things she respects."

The man covered the mouthpiece with his hand, as if telling them to be quiet, in the neighborhood of a village the patrol was spreading out into a semicircle in the brush:

"It won't work, she'll call up again ten minutes from now. Get rid of her with something foolish and quick."

"The fact is that little by little," the lieutenant colonel said, swatting at an invisible fly with his napkin, "I got used to her absence: I stopped seeing her everywhere in the apartment we shared, I stopped expecting her submissive face in the living room when I came in, I ended up putting her pictures in a desk drawer. I remarried a few years later and I noticed one day that the pictures had disappeared: my present wife isn't very enthusiastic about my past."

(And I imagined a furious, fat, disheveled creature in a terry-cloth robe trampling on the frames with the run-down heels of her shoes.)

"We worked like slaves," the soldier said, "and the business was doing fine. If my uncle hadn't stuck to old-fashioned methods so much, we'd be rich today."

"Are you still there, Jorge?" the mother-in-law asked, puzzled. "How come Inês hasn't come to the phone?"

The lieutenant pulled the cord over to the bed, sat down on the mattress and handed the receiver to the girl: Spider Two calling Godmother, Spider Two calling Godmother, whistling, squeaking, croaking, and a faint, muffled breath answering from the other side of the world: Godmother here, Godmother here, over.

"Yes?" Inês said, stretching, asking for a lighted cigarette with her middle and index fingers. "Mother?"

The second lieutenant kissed her knees, her thighs, her navel, laid his head on her breast, next to the bottom of her throat, closed his eyes: I just met you, we're holding hands and running along the beach, I'm going into the Army in April. He hears the waves breaking on the seawall, laughter, shouts, the brief, rapid, instantaneous squawks of the birds, the struggle to lift your skirt up in the pine grove, taking your panties off, the pine needles and the twigs hurt my legs, my elbows, my ribs, ants were crawling all over me under my shirt, the bra got torn (Just look at that just look at that just look at that and what now?), he was biting her ears, her hair, the quivering curve of her back (Stop it you beast you animal I don't want to let me go) and the little bloodstain on the ground, your tears, me with my hands in my pockets, all upset, leaning against a eucalyptus tree (I'm serious I love you I'll marry you don't cry) and you upside down on the ground, your legs still open, sobbing.

"No, Mother, I'm fine," Inês said, looking for the ashtray with her eyes, and she wrapped herself in the sheets, her back to the lieutenant, offering him the inflated, firm balloons of her behind. (The girl was still struggling in his memory and he thought Four years, God, the way time flies.)

"My uncle, Captain, never wanted to make any changes in the business," the soldier explained, leaning back in his chair, ordering another bottle. "And in the moving business, if you don't modernize, you go under."

"The usual chatter," the lieutenant explained. "The eternal, everlasting, idiotic usual chatter, hours and hours on the phone, exchanging bits of foolishness, setting up canasta games, backbiting."

"Dinner there tonight?" Inês asked, hugging the pillow in fetal inertia. (The brightness of the light erased ridges, edges, and angles on her, transforming her into a rose-colored substance fluctuating under the bedclothes, contracting and expanding like a digesting intestine.) "Of course we can, we don't have anything planned."

"And then eating there all the time," the lieutenant went on, "every night from Lisbon to Carcavelos and from Carcavelos to Lisbon and me bored stiff with that shit, Captain, there isn't an inch of the Marginal Highway that I don't know by heart."

The huge house in the middle of a neglected garden, the German shepherds leaping about the car, rubbing their big snouts against the windows, pulling their lips back to reveal their sharp teeth, resting their paws on the top, appearing and disappearing in the glow of the headlights in a grotesque ballet of backs, tails, and flashing reddish eyes (Down Roy, down Bazooka, down Bruce), the incredible succession of parlors, corridors, bedrooms, alcoves, stairs, busts of the grandfather at every turn, portraits of the grandfather everywhere, the excessive splendor of the furniture, the brothers- and sisters-in-law who moved about in the rarefied atmosphere of smoke with the waving motion of fish, the mother-in-law knitting in front of a turned-on television set, the husband, short, a subsidiary, leafing through magazines, putting his glasses in his pocket, wrapped in the conforming humility of a vassal.

"After field rations, to have lobster bisque, breaded shellfish, linen napkins, silver tableware," the second lieutenant described. "Do you know that kind of setup, Captain? I always had to remind myself that my father was a clerk, you see, so I wouldn't get in too deep in those waters."

Beyond the pine grove, in the distance a person could make out the scaly blue of the sea, a bodiless wind disturbed the treetops, green insects came out from the cracks and spaces between the roots, unfolding the silk-veined paper of their wings:

"For God's sake," the second lieutenant begged, "stop the tears, I promise on my life that I'll marry you."

"An hour from now at the most," Inês assured her, "we'll be there by then, Mother. Just the time it takes me to put on a blouse and a skirt."

She put the telephone aside and put out the cigarette. Just like your uncle, he thought, when he calls me into the manager's office at the bank to give me instructions, watched over by the ever-present bust of the grandfather on its cubic marble pedestal: the same wrinkle in the middle of the forehead, the same ironic mouth, the same profile that the years would be sure to fill out, conferring upon it the solemnity of a tribune. The girl looked at the night in the street through the semitransparency of the curtains and announced We're dining in Carcavelos, without asking me what I wanted to do, you understand, without asking for my opinion.

"I got home and told the old lady I was staying in the Army," the communications officer told me, picking up crumbs from the tablecloth with a thumb moistened by spit. "Since her father had died a lance sergeant (a fat fellow with a mustache at the head of the bed), it was obvious that she would easily accept it."

He helped her up, brushed the pine needles off her clothes (the bloodstain had completely disappeared, swallowed up by insects or by the earth's deep throat), he searched in his pants pockets for his handkerchief to dry her tears with, and they went up the front steps in the light of a blue-colored lantern that made the shadows of the garden even larger, while the dogs leaped and barked in disorder with restless jubilation. Inês rang the bell that was hidden by a loose vine branch: the maid opened the door (a big, mannish woman in her forties, sexless, who shooed the animals away with a wave of her arm, Good evening, miss, Hello, Hilária, and the dogs galloped into the hairy hedge toward the vague parallelopiped of a garage, crammed with crates of tiles, planks, old tires, unfinished boats, and the remains of furniture. Leading a ten-year-old girl by the hand, the black catechism teacher came toward the second lieutenant, who was waiting for him beside the wire fence:

"Four contos," he bargained in garbled Portuguese.

This fool woman doesn't see fit to say a word to me, I'm a real zero here, I'm beginning to get the feeling that I don't exist, he thought, handing his topcoat to the maidservant, who tossed it casually onto a huge spiked chest: and there they were spying on him from the hallway, the busts, the portraits, the hateful photographs.

"Four contos, Lieutenant sir," the black man repeated. "Bargain goods."

He trotted along various Arraiolos rugs that led him toward the living room (Inês had evaporated into thin air, maybe she'd gone into the kitchen to say hello to the loving muzhiks), hearing distant voices, the funnel sound of the television, the record player in one of the back bedrooms. He checked his necktie in the mirror with a carved frame, which returned an image that was wavy from imperfections in the glass, but the successive wall lamps only pulled him forward, flopping like a crazy butterfly (I'm going to marry you, don't worry about it, I'm going to talk to your parents tomorrow afternoon, the motionless blue tones of sea and sky came together in a perfect, orange-colored straight line), and he finally came out into a large, stiff, pompous chamber inhabited by people, porcelain figures, chairs, a silver samovar on a kind of throne, murmurs, décolletages, bodies, carnivorous, restrained, well-

bred laughter (When I was a little boy I always imagined that the world
ended at that little geometric junction of colors and beyond it there were only
ghosts out of dreams, angels and dead children calling me with penetrating
doll winks, everything floating along smoothly in some indistinct liquid). He
greeted elderly ladies who smelled like empty perfume bottles, gentlemen
clutching double whiskeys as if they were their last canes, false teeth clacking
together like the ice cubes in their glasses, ice cubes that clacked together
like teeth, he looked up and down at the barefoot little girl with the callused
feet of a stork and an incredibly dirty dress, he studied her round eyes,
expressionless, distant, and neutral, the stomach swollen from hunger, he
took the matches out of his shirt pocket (How many centuries has it been
since I made love to anybody?), he cleaned the soles of his boots on a rock and
bargained in return, observing the misty silence of the woods:

"One conto."

"Luckily they assigned me to a regiment," the lieutenant colonel said,
lining up the pieces of a third toothpick parallel to the others. "If they'd stuck
me behind a desk in the Ministry I would have flipped my lid in a month."

He saw the mother-in-law knitting on a velvet sofa, next to a creature with
purple hair and a necklace of yellow balls that hung down like a clamp from
her scrawny neck, and he started making his way toward the monster Ad-
amastor through a cane field of fans, large vases, chests with little drawers,
busts of the grandfather, trays of aperitifs, exclamations, glug-glugs, children's toys, cackles, conversations.

"One conto?" The catechism teacher struck his chest with his hand, most
offended. "One conto? One conto, Lieutenant sir? Did you take a good look
at the girl, white man?"

He made her spin around so rapidly on the dirt and trampled grass that her
limbs got all tangled up with each other like strings of spaghetti, he opened
her mouth to show him the short, stubby, infantile incisors, ran his proprietary hand over her nonexistent buttocks, and he gave the officer an askance,
afflicted stare:

"One conto for my virgin niece, Lieutenant sir?"

"I would like to ask for Inês's hand in marriage," he explained, choking
with extreme embarrassment, to the couple who were listening in a hostile,
impenetrable silence.

The mother-in-law offered her cheek distractedly, the skeleton with purple hair held out an exaggeration of rings to be kissed, the stones reflecting
the light intensely, like the spangled jackets worn by rich clowns. Some
Basset hounds scurried under the easy chairs, a freckle-faced little boy,
stretched out on the rug beside a pee stain, was demolishing a toy car with a
hammer.

"One conto five hundred and a bottle of liquor," the second lieutenant
offered, feeling his penis swelling uncomfortably in his pants: How many

centuries, really, had he gone without getting his ashes hauled, he tried to calculate mentally: Seven, eight, nine?

"I needed to see people, to breathe," the lieutenant colonel explained, adjusting with his pinky the position of one of the little pieces of wood. "I was never a man for paperwork: lock me up in an office for eight hours a day and I'll go nuts."

The father-in-law laid his magazine on a table with a double glass top filled with mollusks, pieces of coral, conchs, ebb-tide delights. The whale stopped her knitting, startled, and lifted her mouth, round with surprise, toward them:

"We were thinking about March, if it's all right with you, Mother," Inês said. "Jorge goes into the Army in April."

The catechism teacher lighted the cigarette the second lieutenant offered him and pondered the figure. He always wore a necktie, a greasy rag twisted together over a ragged shirt, and on Sundays, in a splurge of elegance, he furnished himself with a spectacular pair of glasses with scratched lenses and temples that had been repaired with pink adhesive tape, along with a plastic belt with the number 007 on the huge buckle. A toe stuck out through a hole in the age-old tennis shoes.

"Two contos," he concluded, like someone honorably agreeing to a peace treaty. "Two contos and the jug of booze to drink to your health with, Lieutenant sir. We keep our eyes on the girl, she doesn't lay ordinary soldiers, she hasn't caught any disease."

"Go into the dining room," the mother-in-law ordered, counting her stitches, "and ask Hilária to take care of you: there must be some codfish casserole left over."

Purple-head arranged her curls with outlandish flirtatiousness, fluttering the outlined wings of her lashes:

"What's become of Inês, I haven't seen her?"

"Two contos," the teacher said again, "and a family hut just for her and the lieutenant to talk in. Mother's for it, father's for it, brothers and sisters are for it, I'm for it, we'll give a goat as a dowry if she gets pregnant."

"Why such a rush to get married?" the mother-in-law asked, surprised, surrounded by her stern, innumerable marble busts. "When you come back from the Army there'll be time, won't there?"

The husband wriggled in his chair as if he were screwing his behind into the cane seat:

"Be still, Jaime," she cut him off with a sour snort.

The second lieutenant tripped over one of the Bassets, which, frightened, took refuge behind a drape, passed by the father-in-law, whom nobody was looking at, treating him like a stranger, in the vicinity of the ocean liner of a piano, as he patted his pockets in search of his pipe lighter, he kissed some more sumptuous rings smelling of nail polish and baked cod, counted out two contos and gave them to the teacher, who immediately sank them into the rags that were his pants. The little one, indifferent, was looking at the deserted billet and the recoilless cannon pointed at the woods and covered with an oilskin tarpaulin.

"I'll give you the jug of booze tomorrow," the second lieutenant decided, "after I check on the shipment. Anyway, you're lying like a dog, you shitty nigger: a girl that size can't be more than seven years old."

The catechism teacher, without getting angry, wrinkled his face up into a wise smile: Just like the smugglers in Lisbon, he thought, the slick bastards who fob off radios, fountain pens, watches, towels, tape recorders, all of it flashy and not worth a damn, on stairway landings in apartment houses:

"She comes from short stock, Lieutenant sir, she's ten," he guaranteed. "She bled for the first time last month."

One or two of Inês's cousins brushed by without seeing him, floating along the carpet puffed up in full sail with a heroin breeze behind them. Overly well-dressed types were discussing loans, debts, stock-market maneuvers, banking operations. He saw himself vaguely in the next parlor, with people leaning over gaming tables, somewhere he heard the nauseating business of your uncle's artificial anus, my boss's: Precisely, my dear boy, when you come into the family business I will demand more of you than of the others, don't think for a moment that I'm going to make things the least bit easier for you: and the shit tumbling into the rubber sack hanging by his navel. The dining room occupied by a huge, devastated table (What plague of locusts passed through here?), an old man dozing in the corner, a shrimp pâté in his hand. As he poured himself some red wine he heard Inês calling to one of her sisters in the hallway (I bet they got high on some grass in the bathroom, the collective roach going round from mouth to mouth), high-heeled shoes walked over his back, a baby was howling, and he flooded his plate with codfish observing the black girl (How many millennia without a decent fuck?), who barely came up to his waist, and whose submissive impenetrability fascinated him.

"I'm going to have them clean up the hut for our lieutenant today," the teacher promised with exaltation befitting a fancy-dress ball: large tobacco-colored rain clouds were gathering in the east, a sudden wind was whispering along at ground level, it would start thundering at any moment: the zipper lightning wiggled sporadically, piercing the belly of the jungle. He coughed, waited a moment, coughed again, the people waiting, impatient, the mother-in-law thrusting her needles into the skein, the father-in-law tamping his pipe with his fingers, the second lieutenant took them both in with the same awkward, panicked glance (I've got myself into a fine mess, there's no doubt about it) and he went ahead in a dying voice that faded with every word, shameful and exhausted:

"Inês is pregnant."

"Mariana was born seven months later, Captain, a little before we sailed off to war," he said, having another custard. "She looked like a shriveled little monkey yelping in the crib to me, my parents swore that she was beautiful. Now she's a grown woman, her breasts are forming, would you like to see a picture of her?"

The teacher greeted him with successive bows at the doorway to the hut, accompanied by a boy on crutches whom a spinal illness had left deformed:

"Your bride's brother, Lieutenant sir," the religious man introduced him, most courteously.

It had stopped raining and the grass was gleaming, the trees were gleaming, the afternoon was gleaming, the tiny hens, inspecting the ground with the worried look of supervisors, were gleaming, the clear peace that precedes African nights, broad and clean, like well-washed lungs, was gleaming, just like an endless concave piece of lace. The boy on crutches was hopping restlessly around me:

"Did you bring the jug of liquor, Lieutenant?"

"Inês pregnant?" the father-in-law asked, frozen.

"Be quiet, Jaime," the woman commanded, chasing off the Bassets with her heels. "When did you say you were going into the Army, child?"

The old man dozing in the corner took a distracted bite of pâté and fell back into a coma worthy of an executive, drooling crumbs onto his vest. The lieutenant pushed open the door to the hut (it smelled of dried manioc, the poor, uncomfortable, nauseous smell of manioc dried on mats, the corpselike aroma of the chalky roots, like twisted femurs, coming from the roof) and he found the little one in a huge decrepit double bed, with wedges and bits of brick for legs, hugging a straw doll, staring at him with her eternally enigmatic eyes, strangely adult, while behind Inês the pine branches swayed and on the horizontal scaly sea a white fringe of foam quivered:

"Take it easy, stop that, I don't want to," she pleaded with her eyes closed, pushing his arms away with the outstretched arms of a blind girl. I'll take off your panties, thought the lieutenant, whose very erection made his movements difficult, I'll take off your panties and I'll have you. He looked at Inês, lost, anxious for help that wasn't coming, he blew his nose, coughed again, and dissolved into an afflicted contemplation of his shoes:

"What did you say your name was?" the mother-in-law asked disdainfully.

In addition to the bed there were one or two broken-down chairs, a basin with water, a bar of soap wrapped in a sheet of newspaper. The girl undressed with childish haste, without putting down the doll, and she stretched out on the mattress full of lumps and hollows, studying the straw roof with the transparent marbles of her eyes. (A few flashes of lightning continued to flare, scattered, toward the river.) Six or seven years old, the second lieutenant thought, unbuttoning his shirt and his pants, unlacing his huge, stinking boots while desire (How many centuries, damn it?) was creeping up his thighs, slowly, like the column of mercury in a fever thermometer. He lay down, completely naked, alongside the little one's fragile salamander profile, and he began to probe, as in a pocket, the skeletal outline of her legs. The father-in-law was lighting his pipe, uncomfortable, sucking in the smoke with the broad buttocks of his cheeks. The lieutenant noted with great embarrassment that his shoes were in urgent need of half-soles, and he tried to hide his frayed cuffs, pushing the sleeves of his shirt in as much as possible. He penetrated the girl, who was clutching her doll, furiously conquering a mucous resistance, and he felt his body softening, almost at once, like that of an insect freeing the dampness of its wings from its whitened chrysalis. So he raised his chin and looked straight into the mother-in-law's acid bifocals:

"My name is Jorge," he said.

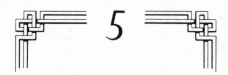

5

"Was it hard for me to get used to the work, Captain?" The soldier laughed, amused, spitting olive pits into the palm of his huge hand. "If you'd had to go through a life like mine, you'd know that the only hard thing is not eating."

He would get to the warehouse at eight in the morning, with the panes in the high windows, next to the tin roof, all cracked, sooty walls, the words NO SMOKING in red, pale like lipstick on an old shirt, furniture and crates and cabinets missing legs, which a stingy light struggling in from God-knows-where illuminated, revealing dusty surfaces, stuffing eaten by rats, bases for bidets, his uncle's birdcage office at the entrance with its ruin of a desk and indescribable disorder of file folders. It was there, Captain, on the outside, of course, that we would wait for the day's job (Moving the contents of number such and such on such and such a street to such and such an avenue, picking up a heavy old piece of junk in Caneças, going to some address in Caxias to pick up two pianos for Amadora), stamping your feet on the ground to keep warm, smoking cheap cigarettes, looking at the pale sky through the cracks in the roof tiles while the fat pharmacist across the way rolled up the shutters of his shop and the first old women huddled on their terraces, shrouded in their crocheted shawls. There was a kind of shaky porch on the second floor where

you left your lunch pail, changed clothes, and ate, a gate in the wall around
the madhouse next door where miserable little men in brown uniforms
gesticulated among angry trees. Mr. Ilídio would come in at eight-thirty
without saying good morning to anyone, breathing through his buffalo
asthma in a fright of snorts and wheezes, face stubbled and eyes inflamed
from the torture of insomnia, he would pat his jacket looking for his key and
shut himself up in the cluttered cubicle, jotting down figures, complaining
about the disorder of the papers he was sorting out himself, elbowing and
with his legs pushing aside bundles of old newspapers, barking his irate
conversations with creditors or friends into the telephone while he scribbled
on a greasy pad with the tiny stub of a pencil. They would wait like that,
doing nothing, for almost the whole morning, sizing up the women selling
fruits and vegetables on their crooked tricycles, listening to the gnawing of
the rats deep inside the warehouse as they scurried among the worm-eaten
legs of bureaus, leaning idly against the whitewashed walls in their coveralls,
and suddenly the office door flies open, the spongy toad face looking at them
with hate, the chubby hand angrily waving a piece of paper, Come here, all
of you.

"There were only three of us working there at that time, Captain," the
soldier recalled, in a soft voice, tenderly peering into the sweet mist of the
past. "An old man who was missing three fingers, who'd been in prison a long
time ago for beating up a cop, and he drove the truck that was falling apart,
bouncing a string of earthquakes over every pothole in the street, me, and a
skinny guy who never said anything, whose wife was in the hospital because
of seizures. Later on things got better, we bought two small vans and we had
eleven people working, including a lady with glasses who always had a cold
and would come at the end of the day to correct my uncle's boo-boos in
writing and put everything neatly into a book with a black cover, bound like
the kind notaries have or the ones in church, little by little the file folders
were getting to be fewer and fewer, the disorder decreased, new fountain
pens appeared on top of the desk, a blotter, flowers in a glass with water, and
the old man, frightened at the cleanliness, half-crazy, as if he didn't recognize
the place, snorted, all worried over that unlikely exaggeration of neatness,
Captain, sighing for his garbage bin."

"I almost never went home during the first few weeks," the lieutenant
colonel told me. "Everything so neat, unlived in, nothing out of place, made
me think, I don't know why, of death. As a child I never imagined it with
skulls and leg bones and ghosts and corpses laid out in the usual coffins: if I
thought about it, it was always an excessively orderly room, with objects
exaggeratedly in their places, that would appear to me. Or maybe my
grandmother's old sewing machine in a corner by the window, with a basket
of clothes waiting to be sewn alongside, the shadow of a lamp on the wall and
a complete absence of people. That's it, the complete absence of people,

understand, that's what frightens me: the silence of city squares at night, nobody there, galleries where our own steps are walking out to meet us, restless, and when we cough the bronchitis goes back into our throats, disagreeable and sour, like swallowing vomit."

Because of the old man's asthma, which was aggravated by tobacco smoke, they would put out their cigarettes, decapitating the glow with their little fingers, and they would put the butts into matchboxes, behind their ears, into their pockets, to smoke later, the three of them bumping along in the rattletrap little van through the disorderly city traffic, having a hard time seeing through the dirty, hazy windows, as if they were looking (buildings, avenues, squares, vacant lots, the strange mixture of disparate, random elements that make up Lisbon) from the other side of the mist of a dream. Dragging their tennis shoes or boots, they went up the worn-out steps of the uncle's cubicle, the old man missing three fingers uncovered himself respectfully, as at the entrance to a chapel, displaying the freckles and scabs on his bald head, and they crowded together before the boss, torturing their berets uneasily with their fingers, while Mr. Ilídio removed the flower from the glass with the infinitely disgusted look of someone touching a repulsive creature, and threw it (irritated? surprised? ashamed because of them?) into the wastebasket, where a confused and endless mound of paper was piling up, puffing and fermenting into a slew of invoices.

"I'll bet that after you people left," the communications officer suggested, reaching his unsteady arm out for a swig of red wine, "he fished the flower out of the basket again and stayed there all afternoon looking at it: your uncle had the makings of a poet."

"The furnishings on such and such a floor on such and such a street to such and such a number on such and such a square," the asthmatic croaked, handing them a page from his calendar where he had the addresses written down. "And the truck back here by seven, I don't want you making the stations of the cross at any bars."

"The warning was for the quiet fellow," the soldier explained. "He couldn't handle his wine and he'd stagger in after a job with the old man and me, scared shitless, holding him up. He'd whistle, dance the tango, roll on the ground, cackle like a hen, tell me about his daughter who'd died in infancy from an intestinal disease, the hospital, the tubes in her nose, her belly sewed up from the autopsy, he'd end up slobbering his snotty tears on our shoulders. Finally he wouldn't be able to stand on his own two feet, he'd hang onto us, beg us to take him to the cemetery to visit the girl's grave, and it was no use explaining to him that it was after seven, that there wasn't any grave, that it had been more than five years ago, that her bones were in the common grave mixed in with all the others: he wasn't listening, he kept on insisting, monotonous, confused, slow, stubborn as hell. We were in the habit of stopping by a dive in Chelas, the quiet fellow knew the owner, they'd played soccer together, they'd played as rookies on the Operário team, there were a lot of framed autographed pictures on all the walls, more flies than you could count, a pleasant breeze in summertime, the four of us drank a toast to Operário, a one-armed man who sold lottery tickets took out his wallet to show us a picture of the famous forward line of the all-star team (Manecas, González, Zuzarte, Pires II, and Zézinho) next to the numbskull smile of his granddaughter dressed up as a flamenco dancer, he bought a round at the expense of the Christmas lottery, in this dive there were even two rusty loving cups and a small showcase with medals in it, we were beginning to get high, Captain, from the strength of the Bucelas wine, bodies weaving flabbily, gestures waving stiffly, a hefty woman in an apron was roasting little birds on an earthen stove, The boss's lady, the owner proudly introduced her, I gave up soccer for this piece, we looked at her pockmarked face, her bulging belly, her varicose veins, the long hairs on her legs, and nodded yes. For a dish like yours, Mr. Paz, I'd go so far as to hang myself, the lottery man flattered him with conviction in hopes of a free drink, or just think, maybe, he really liked that sad sea lion, there are men who get excited over hags, the boss gave a mild, listless pat on the creature's behind and forgot about her the way we sometimes happen to pet a dog, there you are, now get along with you and keep watch, do you get what I'm trying to say? the workers at the foundry on the corner would put sparrows on their bread and the juice would run down their chins, their teeth crushing and slowly sucking the bones, the quiet fellow was embracing all the urchins with weak enthusiasm, our van was blocking the street and a line of cars, small vans, and tricycles was protesting behind it, we came out as it was getting dark, Captain, the building fronts tinted by night with a purplish plaster, the buildings changing color, the faces changing color, the trees changing color, the very sounds changing color, everything was becoming fragile, vulnerable, made of glass, if the voices, for example, were to have fallen onto the sidewalk, they would have broken into a thousand shreds of syllables, we were walking very stiffly, with great care, afraid that our hazy heads, delicately balanced and weightless, would fall off our shoulders, afraid that our eyeballs would slip out of their sockets onto the ground, just like marbles, and at the same time heavy dizziness, porches that wobbled, an upset in the stomach that was turning into vomit, the motor started up and our bodies, detached, slouched on the seat, the old man clutched the steering wheel and belched every other second with a breath that was enough to scare off beetles as it spread throughout the cab, we got to the warehouse and my uncle was at the door waiting for us, Captain, pulling on his suspenders, snorting with indignation, with rage":

"Where the hell have you been, you bums?"

The weak, sparse bulbs in the place, hanging from the ceiling, blinked their firefly antennae, revealing and hiding the immense area of shadows where the stacked furniture gave off a scattered crackling of wood. In the office cubicle the flower, now crumpled, had reassumed its place in the glass, and the soldier thought You've fallen in love with the bookkeeper with a cold (interminable and chaste kisses fluttering over infinite accounts to be added up), and if your boss lady even dreamt of it, you old devil, she'd make your life hell, broken dishes, threats, shouts, beatings, your grouper for dinner eaten in the tense silence of catastrophe. At first he'd slept in the warehouse, wrapped up in rotting ragged blankets, with the seat from the van, smelling of leather and sweat, for a pillow, with the india ink sky coming in through the broken windows, freezing his bones and his veins. He was terrified by the idea of rats running across his body, thinking he could feel tiny little feet, tiny little bellies, tiny little teeth devouring his testicles, thinking he could make out tiny little greedy sharp eyes spying on him in the dark. One dawn he awoke as he was being shaken hard, he sat up in a panic in the midst of the trash and the dust (they must be eating his penis, his stomach, his ribcage), at first he only felt cold and startled, but then he noticed a figure standing, almost touching the light bulbs and the cobweb stalactites on the ceiling with his head, and it was my uncle, Captain, his outraged asthma snuffling over me. Who gave you permission to sleep here, goddamn it. He got dressed quickly, drowsy, with Mr. Ilídio insulting and upsetting him. I don't want anybody in the storeroom, damn you, do you think this is a hotel or something? and at the same time he helped him button his shirt, fix the sleeves of his jacket, stopped him from slipping on the stairs, from time to time some automobile went off down the street, there was the pharmacy, closed up, the houses all alike, the damp silence of that March, the dirty-milk sky, the sparse grass between the small squares that dog urine was killing, the old man stopped to catch his breath, leaning against a park bench, he was pressing his open hand against his chest, one of his knees was shaking (He's going to give himself a spell, I thought), a pair of men, almost tied together, disappeared down the steps of the underground urinal, whose neon sign spread out its antiseptic moonlight like a kind of powder onto the flower beds around.

"I shacked up with her for a good long time," the second lieutenant explained, lighting one of the cigars that the second in command, shrouded in a thickish cloud of smoke, was passing out all along the table. "She got pregnant, she miscarried, she got pregnant again, so as far as I can figure, Captain, I've got a nine-year-old bastard in Mozambique."

"My nephew's going to come and live here at home," the uncle wheezed in the direction of the hazy figure that was moving vaguely, halfway down the hall, beyond a half-open door. The apartment at those hours looked even uglier to him, more uncouth, more worn, smelling even more from a lack of cleaning, of fried food and cat spray. Mr. Ilídio turned on the switch and the soldier drew back, huddling, under the harsh light: a sloping ceiling, a bed to be assembled, without sheets, an enameled washbasin, the portrait of a big old woman in a seashell frame: It's here.

"Isaura will get you some sheets tomorrow," the batrachian croaked, turning his back on him suddenly and he thought Who the hell is Isaura? The girl? The other one, the one who clears the table? He fell asleep with his clothes on, the light burning, without even taking off his shoes, his uncle was roaring somewhere, angry, I found him on a pile of rags, like a beggar, he's almost as big an idiot as I am, the gray dawn was turning the walls and floor the color of ashes, his legs felt beaten, his kidneys ached, good morning.

"She slept there too, Captain," the soldier said, pouring the pits into the plastic ashtray, "in a little room right off the entrance, on the left-hand side of the vestibule. Sometimes when I passed by I'd see a thread of light under the door, the dame worked during the day at an electrical appliance company and studied at night, when I got in from the movies or from shooting pool or from a cathouse with friends, I got the urge to knock on the door, but I didn't knock, I wished she'd let me in, talk to me, get interested, look at me in a serious way, her chin in her hands, in the middle of her open books and notebooks, I felt like having a woman take an interest in me but I didn't have the courage, I went into the bathroom in hopes of getting my nerve up but it was useless, I stared at myself in the mirror and decided I'm going over there, I'll knock, sit down on the bed and let myself talk, I insulted my own reflection Get a move on, you faggot, I pulled the chain of the toilet over the calm waters of the bowl, I heard my uncle's cough in the hallway, I hesitated, motionless in the dark, while my palms got greasy from panic and I finally gave up, mad at myself, shutting myself up in the cubbyhole in back, thumbing through cowboy magazines in a rage. At dinnertime, if she got back early from her classes and ate with us, I never dared talk to her: my uncle, in his ever-present undershirt, getting grayer and grayer, covering his barrel chest, was picking his teeth in silence, Dona Isaura was fighting with the silverware in the kitchen, and the girl (her name was Odete and her father had died at a grade crossing, he was one of those people who wave the green flag at trains and on one occasion, drunk, he tripped on the rails and the locomotive cut him in two, neat as a prayer, leaving one undamaged shoe, a piece of cloth, and the yellow bugle smelling of wine) was peeling the usual pear over the remains of the chicken. The soldier thought Today I'll pull it off and today never came, until he found out the name of the school from a cousin, the one she attended on the Rua Pascoal de Melo, he downed three glasses of *ginja* liquor in a row in a grocery store bar to take stock of things, and he was able to make it, in a new suit and wearing a tie, to the bus stop, his hands moister than ever, waiting, unsteady and oppressed, for men and women carrying books to come down the stairs of a corner building with a plaque on the veranda of the first floor, REPUBLICAN DAY AND NIGHT SCHOOL, SECONDARY COURSES.

"Move the furniture from an apartment in Cascais to a place in Pedrouços," the uncle shouted. "And if you drop anchor here later than five o'clock, you're fired."

"She never talked to me, Captain," the second lieutenant said, "I was never able to drag a word out of her. She'd hug her doll all the time, looking at the adobe walls, the little windows, the ceiling, with the same indifference, as if I were transparent, you see, as if I were dead, as if I didn't exist. At first I thought she was sick, mentally retarded, an idiot, something like that, then I remembered that blacks can't stand the smell of whites and that it must have been that, repugnance, nausea, agitation, and only after quite a few months had passed I got to understand."

"Don't tell me you were waiting for me?" Odete asked, intrigued. (What straight teeth, the soldier thought, what a pretty smile.) She was wearing a pleated skirt, a blouse, a silver ring on her finger, worn low-heeled shoes, and like the others who were leaving the REPUBLICAN DAY AND NIGHT SCHOOL building in groups, she was carrying a briefcase with books and notebooks under her arm. He thought, If I say yes she'll be sure to make fun of me, if I say no I'll look like a fool, what was I to say, Captain? He shrugged his shoulders, unable to look straight at her, scratched his chin with the long nail on his little finger, the display window of a nearby jewelry store looked like an enormous golden sparkling ice cube. The uncle gave them the piece of paper with the addresses and, wheezing, charged into his cubicle: a red rose, just like a painted vulva, was growing out of the glass, the bus appeared in the distance, coming around the small square. The soldier clenched his fists hard (the blood made his skin throb like gills) and he said very quickly, like someone diving off a board without knowing if there's any water below, I've been here since nine o'clock because I wanted very much to talk to you.

"I arranged to work until all hours in order to avoid going to bed," the lieutenant colonel said, taking another toothpick out of the box and starting to break it meticulously into pieces exactly the same size as the others. Or else I'd read the newspapers, without seeing the words, with the lines dancing and mingling in a devilish confusion, or I'd walk along the parade ground, kicking stones, listening to the officers' conversations in the lighted mess, distorted by the distance and the thousand echoes of the night. But if I went to bed and turned out the light, she would appear before me, dead, sallow and thin like a funeral candle, blaming me for abandoning her for no reason, leaving her to die in a cancer hospital, for not forcing my schoolmate, pistol in hand, to save her. So I spent weeks wandering around the deserted buildings of the post, passing through the dormitories like a ghost, the offices, reception rooms, until the windows grew pale, the trees slowly grew out of the ground, verandas and windows slowly materialized on the building façades. Then I would finally open the door of my room, get undressed, struggle with my pajamas, and stretch out on my back on the mattress, with the pillow propped up against the back of the bed, tense, stiff, eyes wide open, smoking. Odete moved the briefcase over to her empty armpit and measured him mistrustfully:

"What put that idea into your head?" she asked with a defensive tone. (She was the suspicious sort, Captain, the soldier explained, the kind that pushes people aside the first time without warning.)

The van staggered painfully along in the direction of the highway, caught up in the traffic like a woman's hairpin in tangled hair. The heater, out of order, was giving off an unbearable smell of burning rubber from under the seat, there was a large horn hanging from the rearview mirror, a row of colored postcards hung along the dashboard, the transmission produced a rusty sob of metal scraping against metal as soon as the old man, cursing, stepped on the starter, they got into the bus one after the other and the door closed with a tomblike sigh. Odete sat beside a window, staring at her own three-quarters reflection in the glass, and the soldier thought So what am I going to say to her now?

"The little bitch hated me, Captain," the lieutenant muttered. "During one of her pregnancies I caught her beating her belly with the straw doll, trying to abort. She refused to bear a child of mine, the child of a Portagee, the child of a white man: how could I be blamed for the war, tell me? And the catechism teacher, always so friendly, so pleasant, so subservient, bowing and scraping, he hated me too, only his mouth was smiling, his eyes, sir, they stayed sour and hostile. A guy can treat them nice, give them liquor, and, in exchange, they're capable of poisoning our lunch, everybody knows that blacks are a bunch of damned good-for-nothings."

"The trees on the highway passed slowly backward: there wasn't anybody who wasn't passing us," the soldier stated, "even a foolish yellow tricycle, flopping and shaking like a runaway goose, piloted by a little man in a beat-up helmet." The old man, with his elbow out the window, was complaining about this piece of shit they gave me to drive, where every part, no matter how small, was straining and vibrating with an awful racket, every so often the motor would explode into little afflicted farts, the smell of exhaust would get into the cab. The girl was stubbornly looking at her own image, shaking her head with the nod of a mare taking a drink in order to free the curls caught between the collar of her jacket and her neck: She wouldn't get involved with me because in a few years from now she'd have a degree and I'd still have a piece of furniture on my back like a Galician peasant, the fare collector was still relaxing up in front, dozing with his chin on his chest in an empty seat, lighted signs appeared and disappeared like a throbbing heart: the river in the background, the Marginal Highway driven away by waves, flocks of seagulls close by the sharp edge of the wall, the whitish light of March at three o'clock in the afternoon. He touched her arm and asked humbly:

"What are you studying?"

Odete's face aimed at me, Captain (Surprise? Annoyance? Indignation? Distaste?), her eyebrows raised, the scar on her forehead: close up like that she had an irregular face, with unpleasant and hard features, a sunken mouth, narrow shoulders, the flat chest of a boy. Thin threads of mist were rising from the water, the persistent rain was turning the houses yellow, the old man was cursing, struggling with the steering wheel. Any minute now, the soldier thought, this whole thing is going to explode like a goddamned firecracker, tossing everything up into the air like a trapshooting machine, nuts, bolts, handles, twisted sheets of aluminum, the quiet fellow's hands were shaking so much he couldn't get the flame of the match to his cigarette. They hate us, Captain, the second lieutenant stated, all those black bastards hate us, the one on crutches, for example, was certainly working on the little one to turn her against me, I gave them dried fish and without any gratitude at all, they cheated on me with her, they got to Estoril, made left and right turns, went ahead, backed up, got lost in rich people's back alleys behind acacia hedges, walls with grillwork gates and stone lions, ending up going down an unexpected little lane with small shops, suspicious-looking ground floors, broken-down boardinghouses, carts piled high with cabbages and lettuce, the soldier got out and showed the paper with the address on it to a café owner, who came to the door offering endless instructions with a toothpick in his teeth, the old man, irritated, shifted into first, spitting out curses in a low voice, and the van, choked up, started coughing in a succession of spasms, a park with empty swings, a church, buildings under construction reduced to geometric cement skeletons, and, immediately after, from where the ocean could be seen, a row of buildings in front of a slope strewn with sacks, tools, planks, blocks of fake marble next to the Electric Company substation that the café owner had mentioned. Stop this piece of shit, the brakes squealed like living creatures being hanged, and there it was: the set of buttons for the bells, a porcelain panel in the vestibule, the twin elevators painted green, the girl drew back hesitantly (Relax, I'm not going to eat you, little one), fleetingly showing the spines of her books, answered Science, and her voice, slightly disturbed, was swallowed up in the roar of the motor.

"I don't know which is more of a drag, Captain," the communications officer complained to me, scratching the bottle of cane liquor distractedly with his finger. "Shooting in the jungle or moldering on the second floor of the Ministry, surrounded by sergeants in civilian clothes, sallow and threadbare, with ruined livers, smelling of medicine. I would look at them from my desk and think So these are the poor devils the Organization wants me to indoctrinate, how in hell can you teach Marx to dead men? The walls were slowly crumbling into lumps of dust, fragments of plaster were detaching from the ceiling, the bulging floor groaned: everything faded, monotonous, lifeless, and the Tagus River through the window, also gray, groaning in the same way with its quiet protest as if the keel of a boat were treading on it. The Revolution seemed so unthinkable to me, so absurd in a country that was worm-eaten, resigned, and empty, and my existence seemed to me to be going along like a dream inside a dream, where ungraspable slogans and red flags fluttered randomly."

"I used to like studying too," the soldier said timidly, "but my father stuck me in a workshop when I was twelve, I got meningitis right after that and turned dumb right away. If I can stick with this job for the rest of my life it'll be a miracle."

The quiet fellow closed the elevator door, pushed the button, and almost instantaneously (a quiver on the rubber mat, a slight wavering of chrome plate, the thin, soft whistle of the mechanism) the metal cage stopped on the seventh floor (the little light bulb with the number seven on it swelled up and contracted with the cadence of a pulse), they went out into the hallway, lumbering and huge in their Ilídio Movers coveralls, which, because of the cloth, transformed them into great muscular creatures, rang the bell, oriental music was tinkling as if from the bottom of a well, a man in his fifties, with sandals, *missanga* beads, dyed-blond hair smiled at them from the vestibule. The soldier caught a glimpse of a lot of paintings of nude boys leaning against the wall or hanging from hooks, a table covered with sheets of newspaper, tin cans, bottles, brushes, the portrait of a black man in a velvet frame, book shelves, fat sofas, a Siamese cat rubbing against his legs, and in the room on the side, unmade, in disarray, with the breakfast tray forgotten on top of it and a spread like a fringed shawl, square, gigantic, giving off a strange perfume, the bed.

"We should have left a lot more casualties, Captain," the second lieutenant asserted, pouring another shot of cane liquor, "we behaved like idiots toward those bastards. Taking care of them, mess leftovers, insect repellent for the rheumatic, reading lessons, medicine, protection from terrorists. Two contos for a savage who didn't even know how to fuck is highway robbery."

Come in, the blond gentleman invited them pleasantly: a stick of incense was burning in a kind of thin candleholder, he was sloshing along up to his knees through thick-pile rugs of indefinite color. Large wooden crates and cardboard boxes had been prepared for them already, but it was a mess we hadn't dreamed of, dragging all that stuff downstairs from the seventh floor to the street, loading it into the van, covering it and tying it (a rain like soap bubbles was floating in the air), going back up to the apartment to tackle tables and cupboards, and I got the impression that the more junk we carried, Captain, the more was still left, chairs, assembly parts, consoles, chests, dressers, the old man was sweating, glassy-eyed, staggering under all that crap, this sack of dictionaries, that bunch of strips, that bundle of plates and tureens, He's going to pass out, the soldier thought, he's going to collapse right here pretty soon, the quiet fellow, with a cigarette behind his ear like a grocer, would materialize and disappear, tireless like the cuckoo in a clock.

"Why don't you enroll in a course?" the girl asked with distant polite interest.

They finished loading and went back up there, to the hairy carpet where they walked as if in a kind of swamp, their shoes sinking into the thick mud of the pile. The blond gentleman, who must have been closer to sixty than fifty, swelling a pair of tight, lilac satin slacks, said hesitantly The paints are left, I'll need one of you to help me pack them, he pointed voluptuously to the portrait of the black man and added Désiré is at the place waiting for you, the moving men looked at each other, indecisive, You there, for example, the blond man suggested, smiling at me (and his eyelashes fluttered softly like the little tufts on fish in an aquarium), wouldn't you like to give me a hand, tufts of grayish hair stuck out through the buttonholes in his shirt, the quiet fellow and the old man disappeared into the vestibule, the twin sounds of the door opening and closing, the distant whistle of the elevator, I began to put the tops on the cans, wrap them up in old magazines, pile them up in a corner, and the bastard was watching me, Captain, still smiling, he was wearing a funny thing on his wrist, something like a handcuff, and an enormous ring with some complicated engraving, the bus stopped like a ferryboat mooring, I held out my arm for Odete to steady herself as she got off and I felt the quick, alert tendril of her fingers through the cloth. They went along on foot, unable to find any words, scowling like two strangers, the soldier looked for some cord to tie up the brushes, There must be some string in my bedroom, the man in the purple slacks remembered, come get it with me, when they got to the uncle's place they both took out their keys at the same time, the green carpet was even thicker, softer, had more algae and sludge and tender light substances from the sea, and as soon as they went in the blond gentleman grabbed him by the shoulders Pretty boy, pretty boy he whispered, searching for the snap on his jeans, I've got the urge to lick you all over, here's five hundred escudos for your tenderness, the folded bill crinkled in his pocket, they pushed open the door and the darkness of the apartment was greater, thicker and closer than the darkness of the night, the uncle's scratchy breathing vibrated and echoed along the walls that were invisible in the shadows, the way water in wintertime runs down the ancient walls of Sintra. So much money, Captain, it was like a thunderbolt to me in those days, the blond gentleman smelled of turpentine, medicine, old age, and women's perfume, he unbuttoned his Ilídio Movers uniform, kissing him on the neck, under the arms, his chest, his stomach, I didn't feel anything, Captain, I swear I didn't feel anything, just tingling and fear and wanting to laugh. I'll bet she won't invite me into her room, the soldier thought, I'll bet she's going to shut herself in and study, he caught a glimpse of the light suddenly turning on, an encyclopedia on a shelf, a run-down desk and half of

Odete's face in the crack See you tomorrow, the other one untied his canvas shoes, took off his socks, and began to lick his ankles and calves while he reached out his enameled nails toward his testicles, twisted his hair, fondled his penis with a hand softened by creams and lotions. See you tomorrow, he replied heading for his niche, lacking the courage to invite her to go to the movies, the zoo, stroll along the Avenida, take a boat ride across the river, the blindman laid him down on the carpet like a castaway on a beach and sought out the space between his legs with his dilated mouth, With the five hundred escudos I'll be able to take her out to dinner, buy her some shellfish, fine wines, half a lobster, a spider crab, women are a matter of money, How sweet the sweat of your groin is, my treasure, the one with the bracelet snorted from down below, a distance, Captain, a long way away from myself, Your lovely tomatoes taste so nice, the sky through the window was slowly turning brown, like a dirty puddle, a bundle of wires without a bulb hung down from the ceiling, the fingers didn't stop, patiently tweaking his buttocks, Two contos, Captain, just imagine, all that just to screw a nigger kid. The soldier noticed that the man was undressed too, because he felt his naked flesh against the skin over his kidneys, Tomorrow I'll buy her a ring, a pin, a handkerchief, some present like that, tomorrow I'll have money to take a taxi home, enroll at the school, get me a striped suit that will make her fall on her ass in love. The down of the rug smelled like an African hut, he was living with Désiré, Captain, a great big black from Senegal with a ring in his ear who sculpted awful-looking African fetishes in the corners, the window was fading away little by little, the outline of objects was fading away little by little, the noises themselves were fading away little by little into a single buzz of sound, What muscles, pretty boy, and at the precise instant he came, in the hallway he distinctly heard her latch closing back there in the shadows like a last door.

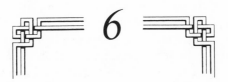

# 6

THE lieutenant colonel got to his table in the mess and the two majors and the chaplain, who were waiting for him chatting over the empty plates, stood, straightening their ties in a clumsy hurry. By the scattered dragging of chairs in the dining room he perceived that the other officers were also standing at attention, and he vaguely noticed, indifferently, familiar faces looking at him, two or three orderlies in white jackets, the horrible oil paintings on the wall showing African landscapes (forest fires, rivers, huts, jungle), the windows with plastic curtains in front of the infirmary and barracks, everything old, dusty, tarnished, soulless. He moved his chin around, sat down, heard the dull sound of the chairs on the tile floor once more, thought Screw all of you motherfuckers, and leaned back to be served his soup, That usual nauseating slop, remember? he asked me, little globs of oil and withered greens. The plaster cast of the unit's insignia with its faded warlike emblems over his head, the voices rose and fell with the hum of waves, diluted, onto the squared-off sands of the tablecloths. The men in white jackets took away the soup and approached with enormous platters of stew.

"For me, dying," I said to the parallel rows of little pieces of wood, "wasn't empty rooms with nobody there that you spoke about, Colonel: it was the mess at lunch and dinnertime, men with glass eyes chewing in defeat chunks of potatoes and meat in a big run-down room, waiting for the big fat ships that would carry them off to war."

"You would see them come in, distressed, all mixed up, pleading, passing through the inner section with folders full of tests, EKGs, medical reports, and testimonials under their arms," the communications officer explained, his crow's-feet still young and skeptical in the frame of his glasses. "They would hunch over under the sergeants' harshness, breaking out into excuses, hovering around in fawning circles. Take a look at my case, friend, have a peek at my urea, I've got cirrhosis, a chancre, spinal trouble, three overseas assignments under my belt, I can't ship out, fix me up with an assignment that'll get me out of this, some tactic, some trick, some way out, any kind of a maneuver, they'd sweat, loosen their collars, pull up their tunics showing the folds in their bellies, Just take a look at this damned thing, the stretched belly I got from being in Guinea. Those old men were so afraid of facing death that we felt more sorry than disgusted, Captain, more disdain than anger, and there they were back the next day with new complaints, new whining, new weeping, new tests: the sergeants would take their papers in a kingly sort of way, I'll append them to your file, Colonel, I'll send them to the Medical Corps right away today, and as soon as these characters had slipped away, disbelieving but hopeful, shuffling their hesitant shoes on the office floor, their anxious hopes were tossed into the wastebasket, torn up, and, unhurriedly, without enthusiasm, without drive, the typewriters went on monotonously batting out useless and endless memorandums."

"The captains are getting restless," one of the majors commented, taking a second serving of stew, "they can't accept the minister's ideas concerning the militia: what good is the Academy, Commander, if some guy from out of nowhere comes up almost as fast as we do?"

The lieutenant colonel was chewing in silence, his head lowered, having a hard time hearing the officers, as if his insomnia of the night before had interposed a blank between his ears and the others' words, an infinite void that a few disconnected and twisted syllables managed to cross only with difficulty. He finished his meat, thrust his weary spoon into the pudding, felt the recent lack of a molar with his tongue, and drank, with his eyes closed, two demitasses of coffee, one after the other, in order to shorten somewhat the immeasurable distance that separated him from the faraway, almost nonexistent presence of the others.

"They gather together at night, in one of their rooms, spend hours on end discussing things in low voices," the chaplain reported, searching his pockets for the little tin of tiny pills of diabetics' sugar which leave a powdery sweetness on the tongue. "A petition with hundreds of names has been making the rounds and I can only pray to God that it's not some bit of treason on the part of the communists."

The world, with the third cup, began to become real, palpable, clear, free of the phantoms, shadows, and thick clouds that sleepiness had accumulated and which hovered in his head mingled with rich memories, fragments of lovemaking, summer picnics, his wife, young then, smiling against the bluish tops of the pine trees. He swallowed a snifter and the taste of alcohol, lighting a trail of gunpowder down his throat, succeeded in planting him in the dull drudgery of the military post, in the uncomfortable dining room of the officers' mess with a fearsome vase of flowers on each table (Uglier than the ones here, don't you think? he asked me, wrinkling his eyes listlessly) where characters condemned to war chatted, argued, or remained silent, waiting for the recruits to gather on the parade ground for afternoon instruction with the lazy sound of weapons and boots.

"It's not a matter of communism, of course," the other major said, "but you can't deny that it does have a touch of insurrection about it, whether there are reasons for discontent or not. Did you notice, Commander, the mimeographed sheets, the pamphlets the captains are handing out in the bar, the complete disregard for the obligatory channels of the chain of command?"

I was a captain when you were born, the lieutenant colonel suddenly thought, I was stationed in Vendas Novas, barking at a company of cadets, they called me in, gave me my passport, informed me Three days, congratulations, I spent hours in uniform at the jitney stop, with a canvas bag in my hand, sweating with joy and from the heat of the August noon, until in the fishbowl of the maternity ward I saw a tiny, restless, yellow thing with a huge mouth opened uncommonly wide howling noiselessly, you. I'm going to start crying, he worried in the corridor where there was an increase in the whispering, the visitors, men smoking, cigarettes ashamedly cupped in the palms of their hands, nurses always in a hurry, a man wearing a lab coat and a competent look, I'm going to start crying in front of this whole bunch, the baby was sleeping now, with clenched fists, exactly like the other half-dozen infants in identical cribs, he knocked, embarrassed, timid, filled with emotion on the door of the room and without waiting for an answer, went in.

"I didn't have children at the right time, Captain," the communications officer told me, focusing on the peeling label, "and now it's too late to have any. There's got to be someone who when I kick the bucket can sweep all my garbage out into the street."

The lieutenant colonel stood up, the majors and the chaplain got up, the officers pushed back their chairs in a respectful hurry, he cast a slow random glance about the room, serious faces, short hair, grim military faces, he went quickly through the lounge, with the orderly, also in a white jacket, behind the bar, card tables in the back, fringed sofas, musty old prints of battles, lumpy, hanging crookedly on the wall. The hazy sun lighted up the trees in the courtyard, with a pool of rotten red fish amidst the slime, a fat-bellied lieutenant saluted from a distance. He went up the steps to the office two at a time, and the orderly, who was dozing on a bench by the entrance, leaped to attention, opening his mouth. From the outer office a tumultuous stomach growling could be heard: They're stamping, copying documents, typing, the lieutenant colonel thought, and it really bores the hell out of them, dreaming from time to time about the women on the ancient calendar hanging from a nail where month follows month in the same smooth unending dullness, the naked blond woman whose body looks like a smiling big-bosomed window on a vast sea of flesh. He turned the knob, the same desk, the same flags, the same cabinets full of cardboard folders that he would never read, that he refused to read, endless confidential reports about Guinea, or Angola, or Mozambique, extensive communiqués dealing with the logistical situation of the Army, authoritarian and contradictory orders from the Ministry to the commanders of Military Districts, Do this, do that, and nothing, understand, was really done, he told me, shrugging his shoulders, the Army was a kind of big shapeless machine that moved, slowly, through inertia, no blood pulsed inside of it, years and years of war had stuffed us with straw, dried us out, destroyed us, replaced our livers, stomachs, lungs, nerves with a kind of, you know, a kind of lifeless stuffing. And year in, year out, fuck it all, Africa.

"I used to go there from time to time, Captain," the soldier confessed, "if I wanted money to take her out with, to go to the movies, go for a walk, to the beach. Once we were in bed and right then and there the black man showed up, stripped, dancing, with marks and spirals in chalk drawn on his chest, and he crawled in between the sheets too, squealing: I earned a conto taking care of that queer pussycat couple who would scratch each other, tinkling bracelets, feeling their behinds, biting each other's neck, meowing in French. Naturally, I never mentioned that to Odete, I'd have sunk into the ground if I ever thought she might have guessed."

The lieutenant colonel went to the window, hands in his pockets: the platoons were forming on the parade ground, hurried along by the ferocious screeching of the officer candidates, here and there the wind was raising whirlwinds of dust that ran into the trees, the wall, and the buildings under construction beyond the barracks, windows marked by large white crosses. Someday, he thought, the master builders will manage to attack the river with their sinister blocks pregnant with exhausted sleeping families, who gather together in the morning in numb piles at the bus stop, where the steam clouds of their breath look like the balloons destined for the words of comic-strip characters. A huge cloak of idle hours unfolds anxiously in front of him, the coffee brown sky foretold rain: thick dark rolls slipped over the unequal rooftops, a cluster of quartermaster troops were playing soccer in the distance, in the cement rectangle streaked with a thousand cracks, surrounded by the silver-colored limbs of the plane trees. A corporal on crutches was hobbling along with difficulty, clinging to the wall, heading toward the infirmary. The office smelled of wax, mildew, rotting papers, old age: he picked up the phone, squeaks, a dull click, a male voice, Yes? My car at the main gate, he said dryly, I'll be right down.

"Sometimes she'd look at me," the soldier said, "she'd lean over and comment For someone who moves furniture, you're living high on the hog. And me The lottery came in, or We got a fantastic tip from a foreign customer, or I've been saving up for today," and he would buy her a soda during intermission at the movies, or buy her tickets for all the merry-go-rounds and all the Bluebeard's Castles at the amusement park, the two of us eating cotton candy among the plastic skeletons and hanged dummies. Désiré loved to dress up as a woman and spin around on the carpet, with long fingernails, high heels, and a wig, smoking American cigarettes in a tortoiseshell holder, and the man would shove me away to grab him, shrieking in an excited way Je t'aime je t'aime je t'aime. They'd met on the Métro in Paris, Captain, the black man was playing the flute on a platform flooded with bearded types sketching on the cement in order to pick up a few pennies, and the old man fell in love at first sight and brought him back to Lisbon, paid for by a rich brother who would have given his soul to cover up the scandal of a fairy in the family, a very important engineer, the owner of factories, enterprises, businesses, with a cancer in his gut, shitting through a metal tube buried next to his belly button. I never saw the engineer, Captain, I only found out about him because out of charity he was buying the foolishness the man was painting and must have burned it all right after or given them away to the poor as Christmas presents, the lieutenant colonel passed by the still closed office of the second in command (I bet he's on his fourth or fifth brandy down below there in the officers' mess, red faced now, confused now, getting his words and hands all entangled now), he went down the stairs and there was the black car with the driver behind the wheel and the radio shouting as usual, a small corporal, skinny, strutting, a taxi driver in civilian life, who'd replaced the previous commander's redhead who'd finished his enlistment the month before. He got into the car before they could open the door for him and leaned back, sick of the everlasting smell of tobacco, against the dirty seat. Maybe at last it wouldn't rain this afternoon: there was no wind blowing now among the broad leaves of the trees, the shadows were imprinting themselves on the gravel, growing near and moving away in neat waves. The driver's ears were pitched backward like those of a coach horse, waiting for an order that was long in coming, the tendons (or veins?) of his neck were trembling, the motor of the Volkswagen, turned on, was sobbing. The lieutenant colonel opened the window on his side, turning the piece of broken handle that was left, and, unenthusiastically, he inhaled the dry and dusty air of the courtyard: Take me home, he ordered.

"I used to do that a lot in those days," he told me, straightening the position of the little pieces of wood on the tablecloth. (So many white hairs, short and thin, I thought, and the receding hairline on the guy's forehead.)

"If I'd spent another rotten minute at the post I would have exploded, so I'd go off to the Belém Tower, or to the Jerónimos, or to Guincho beach, or to the Alcântara docks, and for the rest of the afternoon, without getting up from the bench, I'd smoke cigarettes and stare at the water, the ships moored there, the slime on the rocks, the kids. No, I never worried about what the corporal thought, fuck the corporal. Night was falling and there I was, quiet, watching the colors radiating out of the sunset, the factories of the Cova da Piedade that were being swallowed up in the dark, the lights and their inverted reflections, fragmented and yellow, floating on the black oil of the waves. And, later on, little by little I began to get the smells straight, the rotten odor of low tide, the high water's free, savage aroma of a young girl's braids or loose hair, the old woman's vaginal smell, unreal and harsh, of the earth that had had no rain, the perfume of hyacinth or a decomposing corpse from the trawlers riding at anchor. The glow of the cigarette moving about and growing smaller, the characters waiting for me in the mess, impatient, spoon in hand, watching the door in hopes of seeing me enter from one second to the next. That lazy son of a bitch and us here putting up with his nuttiness, the corporal, that one, not a peep, one or two times out of a whole year he asked my permission to piss, I saw his out of focus, threadlike silhouette, standing very straight, behind some bushes, but that afternoon, unexpectedly, without my wanting it to, it came right out of my mouth Take me home, and you can't imagine the confusion I brought on because of that."

"It wasn't the first time this had happened to me, I'd already had to deal with that stuff a long time ago," the soldier declared as he grabbed the medronho brandy and drank it with great avid and angry swallows, "but this was for money. Before the Army I'd worked in a body shop in Arroios, and some of the boys there would round out their wages on the Sodré docks, the Avenida 24 de Julho, the Praça da Ribeira: the guy would lean against a lamppost and pretty soon the fairies would start buzzing around him like flies in the summertime, two hundred escudos, three hundred escudos, six hundred escudos, well-dressed old men would slip him a conto in exchange for some sad, silent, sneaky, painful petting, afraid of police patrols or plainclothesmen, underneath the nearest stairway." His fellow workers had invited him to go along, Come on, let's have some fun with the old farts, but he stood back, watching them from a distance, relaxing on a bench, and afterward he'd help them change the money into beer and snails in the filthy dives in the lower part of town frequented by stevedores, worn-out whores, and drunken beggars while the gloomy morning rose up out of the river with a dull soapsuds light, coloring the pale, rusty houses on the shore with its hesitant mist. Only in Africa, that's life for you, Captain, did I get to lose my cherry and I was the one who paid.

The lieutenant colonel hadn't been home for a month and the building looked smaller and older to him than how he remembered, a four-storied cube right next door to the firehouse and its bright red equipment of hook-and-ladder trucks, smack against other identical cubes, modest looking, with a scattering of grocery stores, haberdashers, silk merchants. The noonday sun on the street did away with all shadows, a pack of weepy-eyed mongrels were following a bitch's proud behind with their soft snouts. At intervals beyond the tile roofs of the buildings there would be a glimmer of the quivering surface of the river, cemetery crosses, microscopic bushes, tiny far-off structures.

"I lived there for twenty years," the lieutenant colonel said, fastening his dark, sharp eyes on the space between mine, "and it seemed to me that I'd never noticed the tile work, the stucco decorations on the façades, the little garden with its bandstand and anemic roots burned by the clandestine pee of kids and cats, the empty apathetic faces of the people. So I got out of the car as if in some unknown, foreign country where I'd happened to land, asking myself What the hell is this anyway, where have I ended up?"

He dismissed the driver with a quick wave of his fingers in no particular direction (Come back for me at five) and stood motionless for a moment, trying to recognize the shape and the tonality of the sounds, attempting in vain to gather together the sparse memories that were ceaselessly fleeing him. The way goddamned time gets away from us, he thought, because even the image of his wife was becoming diluted and was slowly evaporating, replaced by the hard, authoritarian frown of his daughter, who would come to visit him from time to time at the post, There's a girl downstairs, Commander, keeping tabs on him, spying on him, criticizing him, railing at him for his lack of care, lack of neatness, negligence, telling him that the concierge, the one whose husband had been in France as a construction worker for years and who didn't seem at all upset by the fact, would take care of cleaning the apartment once a week until her father came to his senses (As if she were talking about some foolishness, some childish whim, he told me, accepting a cigar, as if I were really carousing or angry with the family) and decided to come back.

"My daughter was devilishly strong," the lieutenant colonel concluded, breaking up the three rows of toothpicks with the knife in his hand. "I imagine she must have already decided to break up with her husband at that time, because whenever he was mentioned she'd put on a grim face that had to be seen to be believed."

What did I come here for? he asked himself, perplexed, looking at the building fronts, the small shops, the brownish grass in the little park that a city worker was combing with a rake, what interest have I got in this place? He didn't know the neighbors except for the retired couple on the second floor right, melancholy and humble, who one night, in their slippers, tripped over each other in order to speak to him, asking him to protect their godson from traps in the Army, fix him up with a spot as clerk or supply man, look after him, Major sir (because he was a major at that time, the same as now, and he went off into a kind of bitter smile, he was expecting a promotion to general any day), don't let them give him too hard a job or treat him badly, or send him off to fight in Africa. The lieutenant colonel, astonished, remained silent during the whole speech, a copy of *Seleçöes do Reader's Digest* on his knees, listening to them, and it was his wife who saved the situation by offering the old woman a glass of water and an anisette for the man, who was wearing a shabby braided smoking jacket and too-long cream-colored trousers, which ended in successive folds over his checkered slippers, while she assured them, yes, everything possible would be done, Dona Inês, rest easy, Artur is quiet like that, but he's deeply concerned with people, if he helped the grandson of the woman who owns the haberdasher's, you can imagine what he will do for you people, another glass of water, some more anisette, death is the only thing that can't be fixed, Mr. Barbosa, no trouble at all, come now, Artur would even have been offended if you hadn't come to him. Now, yes, he thought, opening the door, calling the elevator, lighting a cigarette, the dead woman's features were coming back to him, her thin mouth, her short neck, her nose, her plucked eyebrows, moments, episodes, conversations, places were coming back into his memory, her Treasury official stepfather looking him over with animosity, her provincial mother, fat, approving, arranged meetings, moments alone, inventing pretexts to leave them by themselves in the parlor sitting stiffly on the cane settee, he in his cadet's uniform, she pulling down her skirt with both hands, uncertain, dazed, neither one daring to touch the other. He stepped onto the rubber mat in the elevator and found a man with deep wrinkles and graying sideburns in the mirror, in whose dim features there was a mysterious continuation of the pathetic innocence of the lost cadet, the man he shaved every day now and out of whose throat there emerged, by a strange quirk, his own voice. His father, cane in his lap, settled in his invalid's chair, brought his lips over to his ear in order to be able to say:

"The years pass, boy, the years pass," he mumbled with satanic satisfaction.

Are the years what pass? the lieutenant colonel asked the man with wrinkles and graying sideburns who was staring at him with an undecipherable and hostile frown, or do we simply get close to ourselves, independent of time, in some bed or other in some hospital or other, in the haze of pain that precedes the tranquil and complete emptiness of death? The way his father died, in his sleep, in his wing chair (we figured that from the sound the mikado wood of his cane made when it fell to the floor), the way his mother's chin collapsed into the plate of spaghetti at dinnertime and her eyes remained floating, astonished, over the grated cheese, the way you died among the dying and the greenish skulls of Jews, the way officers and men died in war when the dust and the explosions and the smell of gunpowder drifted off and you came upon bodies still in the cabs of trucks or scattered about on the grass, menacingly still, shouting without any sound or protesting without any words, the way we're dying here, Captain, in this neighborhood restaurant, sitting at an endless table full of bread crusts and glasses, getting drunk on the cheap booze of our own wake.

"The years pass, boy," the old man repeated carnivorously, with fragile, thin shoulders protected by the frayed strip of a shawl. "Oh, fuck it all, boy, the years pass."

The landing smelled of detergent and wax, and on the other side of the door there was a mixture of energetic cleaning noises, the electrical digestion of a washing machine, and a merry voice that was singing:

"It felt even stranger with all the noise," the lieutenant colonel said, looking for the ashtray among the pile of dirty dishes, and finally, with a dexterous maneuver that surprised me, he ended up using the edge of his demitasse cup: the cylinder of ash slowly broke away and the round pale yellow ember of the cigar looked, in miniature, like the struggling orange sun on a misty day. "I was expecting the usual silence," he explained to me, "the usual quiet of the tomb, the usual immobility of objects in their place (my daughter had even carried off my parakeet), I felt like roaming about there, nosing into drawers, running my finger over the porcelain objects, getting undressed, stretching out on the sheets, my eyes closed, letting myself, you know how it is, float on the mattress, hands behind my head, free of ideas, projects, remorse, and I find a regular revolution going on on the third floor at Graça, water running, suds, the radio on, someone beating the doormat on the balcony with great vigorous whacks of furious efficiency."

He hesitated, wanted to go back (the light in the elevator that had carried him up went out, he heard the whistle of the other one that was starting up with a jolt), he ended up fearfully pushing open the door to the vestibule like a sneak thief, sticking his nose in through the crack, seeing a still-young woman's hazy figure at the end of the hall going back and forth between his room and the one that had been his daughter's and was now transformed into a kind of repository in the middle of the apartment, full of suitcases, broken blinds, a wicker basket piled high with dolls and toys (The years pass, boy, the years pass, the sardonic voice of the old man went on imperturbably), a broken carving, horrible African fetishes. The apartment (he clarified for me later) had ceased to be the apartment he knew, the silence, the order, the absence of dust, of excitement, of movement, and his curiosity was aroused by imagining what his long married life might have been if instead of the dead woman a different creature had lived with him in the little apartment on Graça in a noisy uproar, it excited him to calculate the possible degree of difference in his life, whether he would have been happy or unhappy if the bed in the room had given off jubilant battle cries instead of the dull, habitual modesty, where bodies came together chastely, with the lights out, fearfully touching each other in the motionless coitus of butterflies.

"Good afternoon, Colonel sir, excuse the disorder."

The smile (he remembered) with the gold tooth in front, the big, erect bosom, the firm, ironic, challenging look: the body of the concierge had filled out, her haunches still quivered like those of a protective animal, she was wearing plastic slippers, her hair was tied back with a fishwife's kerchief: On Sundays I would see you go out to the movies and your mare's thighs and your firm muscular haunches would light up a kind of tremor of desire in me, the dizziness of someone who stands up quickly and feels his head light as a bubble, floating, free from its neck, in the density of the air. I wonder what happened to the son? the lieutenant colonel thought, recalling the pale, skinny, serious child crawling on the ground in front of the building, pushing a little wooden train. Dead? At boarding school? In France with his father? He began to wander through the rooms without knowing what to do (What's happening to me, where am I, really?), deafened by the tangos on the radio, looking through the windows at the firehouse, the park, the steep streets sloping toward the river, the clear sky buttering the rooftops, light clouds, just like the ones circulating in his blood, the shameful and pleasant tingle of feeling himself with somebody, of sharing that tomb that was decorated with ancient pictures and sofas whose backs and arms were covered with crocheted doilies, while the smiling concierge, resplendent and lithe, poured from a basin into the toilet and cleaned the bathtub, armed with an enormous jar of powder, resting the curve of her waist against the edge. At that moment the training platoons were forming on the parade ground, and the major, hands behind his back beside the bugler, was barking out orders to a forest of rifles.

"I'd been thirteen months without a woman," the soldier justified himself, pushing the hair back from his forehead with dry fingers. "Thirteen months, Captain, with the war, and the dead, and the lack of food, the lack of cigarettes, the malaria, and the rats in the barracks, just tell me if that isn't too long for someone who's twenty. (Another half hour and you'll have had it, I thought, you're all hopped up.) Today, for your information, I could go a hundred years: a guy gets toughened up, he gets calluses on his ass from the kicks he's taken. So if the urge got too bad, I'd go to the sentry post by the native village, call the first black who appeared, give him twenty escudos and tell him to drop his pants right there, behind the sheet metal and the woodpile. With a machine gun in the right hand and money in the other, there's nobody who won't obey you, nice as pie, not saying a word, and let's go, they've got no choice. Twenty escudos, Captain, twenty escudos for me to get into the fart-hole of a dumb nigger, the two of us shaking like leaves from anger and disgust. (And the silence of the jungle, I said to myself, the rotten armpit smell of the earth, the oilskin tarpaulins over the recoilless cannons, men in uniform wandering aimlessly among the straw huts, a very old black woman squatting, wrapped in a blanket, cooking lizards on dying embers.) Every time I remember (his skin grew tight at the temples, a purplish vein throbbed on his forehead) I almost puke, so help me."

## Before the Revolution

The lieutenant colonel circled around a little in the apartment, frightened, lost, trying to make the least noise possible (but the floorboards squeaked, his shoes squeaked, his joints squeaked if he moved them, and his breathing squeaked, suddenly boiling over, filling the entire space of the apartment), while the concierge, on her knees, naked under her dress, was scrubbing the tiles, the siren in the firehouse gave its call, fell silent, started up again, I wonder where the fire is, the woman asked aloud, lifting her head up toward him, her breasts were rising and falling, full under her clothes, Am I still capable, the lieutenant colonel asked himself, can I still do it? the eyes were measuring him, challenging him, the siren drowned out words and gestures with its spiraling howl, the chairs shook, the cupboards shook, the photographs shook in their frames, the night tables shook, the bed itself shook and both of us shook, he told me, awkward, confused, clumsy on the sheets, an abundance of legs, toes, stomach folds, kisses, I was losing my breath, my father was celebrating in his invalid's chair, the years pass, boy, the years pass, the cleaning woman's heels pressed on my kidneys, Come on come on come on, the arm pushing on my neck made me lick the pillow, I'm going to die, the lieutenant colonel thought in a panic, some spring or other is going to break inside of me, he closed his eyes and his wife and the concierge became one vacillating image, the siren curled around itself and stopped with a little sigh, like a light going out, and as he turned over on the mattress in order to get up, sitting with the blood still throbbing in his stomach, he made out, first in the wardrobe mirror and immediately after, turning his head, framed in the doorway, his daughter looking at them from the threshold, covering her open mouth with her hand with the infinite surprise of a child.

# 7

No one in the section worked in uniform, and if it hadn't been for the few soldiers who waited for their orders in the pestilential corridors, reading the newspaper, sitting in bishop's chairs opposite the majestic desks, one might have thought he was in any old dusty office near the river, with the Cacilhas ferryboats, enormous gulls brushing against the closed windows opening onto balconies, and a tongue of dirty water on the ground loaded with debris, the groans of loose boards rocking up and down. The statue of King José in the center of the square trotted motionless toward India in search of eight-armed concubines. Blind beggars sold useless items under the arcades, staring at people with the lily white stupefaction of their eyes, and the curtain of the sky was like a piano under the gloved fingers of the clouds.

"My job there, Captain?" the communications officer asked, rapping his wine glass with his custard spoon. "I set up trials and hearings, I filed, I was itchy, I was bored to death, I cautiously tried to indoctrinate mongoloid and superannuated lieutenants and sergeants, instilling in their pea brains homeopathic doses of Marxism. And I contributed to the classless society by knocking myself out at lunchtime explaining to the reserve major the advantages of people's democracies."

We ate in the narrow little alleys surrounding the square, similar to a clump of veins that cloak the swelling of a tumor, in tiny, smelly, poorly lighted restaurants with the bill of fare written in chalk on the wall and a constant buzz of voices swimming in the shadows. The day completely ceased to exist in those fogbanks of smoke where the smell of cooking clung to the roots of your hair like a tarantula with a thousand oily legs, the major listened to him, drowsily, picking his teeth, a cripple with theatrical mannerisms and a carnation in his lapel circulated among the tables vainly showing an accordion of lottery tickets, the waiter took the pencil from behind his ear to add up the bill on the tablecloth, drew from a kind of cloth pouch under his apron the crumpled and faded banknotes in change: and once again the arcades, the statue, the squat little tugs coming and going with their cigarette-holder stacks stuck deep in their mouths, a ragged fellow playing the accordion, a cap with no coins in it at his feet. The concept of democracy, Major, goes back to the Greeks, which is the same as saying a long time, they were even the guys who invented the word, just imagine, old women begging, filthy children, Gypsies, amputees silently exhibiting the misery of their stumps to people trotting by in a hurry to the boats, or, in other words, majority rule, you understand, our government, and a quarter of an hour later he was disconsolately looking over papers, taking notes, typing, maybe he could recruit the skinny quartermaster there in back, maybe the lieutenant, who would lean his head back from time to time and, as if he were performing a circus act, put three drops into each nostril to relieve his sinusitis, wasn't such a thoroughgoing fascist after all. Why did I keep on believing, Captain, because I did keep on believing, word of honor, for a few years more, and now that I don't believe in anything, what can a guy hang onto?

"Month after month," the communications officer whined, "eating in goddamned dives, which fucked up my stomach and my guts, in the company of poor devils hounded by the blood from their hemorrhoids and twenty or thirty years of beans and greens, who on Sundays, in pajamas and with a stubble of beard, would water the flowers on the balcony, dreaming about the absolute immobility of retirement." Sitting befuddled at his desk amid the sheeplike breathing of his colleagues and their repugnant, sticky, stinking sweat, the communications officer imagined vast fields of peasants with their clenched fists raised belligerently, rough, responsible, serious, capable of turning the universe into something undefined but obviously stupendous, somewhat in the same way that paralytics dream of a speed record. And all the while the inescapable sleepwalking of the river, the daily coming and going of the ferryboats, the swarm of beggars in the arcades would penetrate him every so often with the November of an acid doubt: What if it was impossible, what if we never got anywhere, and what if old Uncle Marx had been wrong, Captain? The pamphlets they gave him to distribute in those days in the empty offices after work seemed like clumsy, silly fairy tales to him, meant to hoodwink ingenuous people, the work of Olavo, Emílio, Baldy seemed meaningless to him, and he would walk home, hands in his pockets, bumping into lampposts and people, night slowly descending inside of him the same way that it did over the avenues of the city, first only a vague, hesitant trace of pink and dark blue above the tiled-roof gums, then an imperceptible alteration in the tonality of the air and the sounds, sharper, more strident, more solid, more lucid, followed by a vague penumbra that fell over things like a thin organza veil, which started to dissolve the trees and building corners, making the streets wider and the squares deeper, and, finally, the lights on the lampposts went on, the silhouettes were suddenly multiplied by two or four or five, or eight on the sidewalk, his aunt's flat, the place setting, Esmeralda in the kitchen, the dog smelling his shoes, the decaying melancholy of the rooms, the old woman's prie-dieu in the hallway and the incredible multitude of little plaster saints in pious poses spreading spun silk smiles around.

"The hardest thing in those days as far as political militancy was concerned, Captain," the communications officer said, putting his custard spoon on the tablecloth in order to attend to the residue on his chin, "was the lack of contacts, of friends who were in with us, of the orientation of comrades. Everybody took off in his own direction, understand, far away from the others, we never saw each other, never talked, we could be in jail or dead and only the invisible and unknown guy who coordinated us would know about it, we'd leave reports in an envelope on the counter of a pastry shop or a café, but we wouldn't get any answer, any letter, any telegram, any voice on the telephone, no confident and serious fellow with a tilted face would come looking for us, and all of that together, goddamn it, made you lonely as hell."

He would dine quickly on the porgy, without salt because of his aunt's diet, smiling vaguely, without speaking, at the questions from the old woman, on whose yellow cheeks tough masculine hairs were beginning to grow (the way things are going, one of these days you're either going to turn into a wild boar, or you'll die and I'll have to put away the whole fish all by myself), put his napkin into the plastic hexagonal ring, excuse himself, and shut himself up in his room, lying on the bed with his clothes on, without untying his shoes, looking at the lumps in the ceiling with the hard stare of a corpse or out the window at the lights of the amusement park, the little metal gondolas on the ferris wheel that gravely rocked back and forth high above the balconies of the buildings, the little cars on the roller coaster going along noisily over their loose tracks built on top of a kind of scaffolding, amidst the shrieks of delicious fear from the riders. Until suddenly, one morning, she appeared.

"She?" the lieutenant colonel asked, surprised.

"I still did some jobs at the amusement park," the soldier said, his hair disheveled, separated into grayish locks. "Hauling the furnishings of complete restaurants, tables, chairs, refrigerated cases, carting planks and braces from the Electronic Flying Saucers, filling the van with giraffes, elephants, and horses from the figure-eight-shaped carousel, picking up and carrying, all broken-down, the Pit of Death, where guys with little mustaches and high boots rode inside on motorcycles. The quiet fellow was crazy about those jobs, he would stand with his mouth open in front of Little Gypsy Dora's tent, she was a big fat woman in a turban sitting by the door, roasting sardines over the coals, or wandering around with us through the alleyways of the park where performers and workers, in shirt-sleeves, were adjusting fixtures and pipes with great energetic hammering, and they'd eat lunch in the shade of a piece of canvas with holes in it, fishing with their forks for pieces of chicken on battered tin plates. So that in the daytime, with the sun cruelly exposing the mends, the filth, the lack of paint, and the sores of poverty that the lights disguised, everything seemed smaller, uglier, very depressing, and desolately poor. Dogs and chickens trotted all about, girls were hanging out wash on the run-down rear of the World of Illusion, and if the wind was blowing, purplish dust rose from the ground in whirlwinds and got onto faces and arms, suffocating and sticky. You lost all desire to buy any tickets at night, Captain, when the windows opened, the music spread out from the loud-speakers tied to trees, in the Monaco Dance Hall, above the casino, you could see the soft, thin outlines of girls, creatures shut up in tiny little dens were selling cotton candy wigs spun around a stick, sweet hairs that dissolved in your mouth like a little mist of threads. The quiet fellow, who was really intrigued by those defunct miracles, stood petrified in motionless fascination in front of the little cages of the Whip or the papier-mâché witches in Bluebeard's Castle, who rolled their eyes and shook their haunches, driven by some unexplained machine, finally got to talk to Little Gypsy Dora, who invited us to eat inside her tent, rich with little silver paper stars, plastic skeletons, and black drapes. Little Gypsy Dora, whose real name was Alice da Purificação Fialho Cruz, picked the magic crystal ball from the center of the table, tossed it onto the ground like any old object, and the old man drew back to the door, frightened": She, the lieutenant colonel repeated, pointing his fork at the communications officer, who was she? Calm down, don't be afraid, Dona Alice said to him, it's just a piece of glass that isn't worth a cent. She gave each of us a plate with ragged edges, Captain, brought in a platter of sardines, and the four of them sat down to chew, with their elbows on the complicated signs of the zodiac. A satin dress embroidered with planets was hanging from a plastic coathook. The fortune-teller, regal and slow, with a double chin, immense breasts, and an archaic bun of hair, looked like the queen in a deck of cards, and the quiet fellow leaned over her gradually, the way little monkeys do over the felt bellies of big mother monkeys. The old man, itching to get going, was sucking on bones, frightened, agitated, rest-less, afflicted, the red wine was softening our veins, we were touching and handling Dona Alice's breasts with the pretext of saving her from the swarm of flies that buzzed around with steadfast insistence over the tails and bones,

the quiet fellow, loose limbed now, accompanied the astrologer inside behind a ringed curtain, looking for the pepper salad, we heard the cascade of
an earthenware bowl breaking, the sound of a stool falling, and right after,
Captain, we began to hear panting, sighs, the rustle of cloth, the guy's
anxious cough, whispering that rose and fell in the heavy air of the tent, the
old man tugged at the soldier's elbow Let's blow, let's get out of here while
there's still time, all that Gypsy woman has to do is put the evil eye on us and
we'll go blind or get paralyzed in the legs, the communications officer wiped
his forehead and his chin with his napkin, hid it away again on his knees,
smoothed the cuffs of his shirt, sat up in his chair, and opened his mouth wide
as if he were going to shout:

"She," he explained in a low voice. "The contact that Olavo had alerted me
to, remember?"

He hadn't expected it to be a woman, he hadn't expected it to be that way:
in the course of his barren underground years he'd become accustomed to
hunched, threadbare men who either talked in a roundabout way or too
precisely, telegraphically, hurriedly on some street corner, to the bundles of
paper they handed him quickly, without looking, in inoffensive suburban
cafés where widowed ladies sipped tea with lemon and nibbled shrimp pâtés,
he'd become accustomed to somber meetings, hazy with smoke, with the
participation from time to time of extremely ugly female students of Law,
Medicine, or Mathematics, sectarian and fierce, who implacably shot down
all arguments with endless quotations from Lenin. So when she came into
the office carrying a briefcase under one arm and under the other the
adventure novel (*The Return of Captain Blood's Great-Granddaughter*) that
served as a sign of recognition among members of the Organization, her hips
bursting out of her extremely tight jeans, with a pleasant, disarming sim-
plicity, greeting the sergeants, who already knew her and who melted away
with aged pleasure at their worm-eaten desks, the communications officer,
incredulous, his mouth open, thought Either the comrades have taken over
the Miss Portugal contest or the chicken soup I had for lunch has made me
weak in the head.

"And yet, Captain, outside there, through the window," he continued,
"still perplexed, still confused, still astonished, the river, the square, the
statue, the buildings went on the same as ever, the traffic lights on the avenue
to the railroad station went on and off indifferently, a giant tanker was
heading down in the direction of the river's mouth, and there she was, fooling
around with a hunchbacked lieutenant, patting another on the back, asking,
with a facetious air, about the wife of a third, going out without even looking
at him while her buttocks went alternately up and down like the buckets of a
waterwheel. Her long hair curled down over her shoulders, her long nails ran
over the cover of the book as I deciphered the message of her fingers with
difficulty Subway station, Six o'clock, Today," his dumbfounded heart
stopped suddenly, started up again, stopped, and the communications officer

asked himself with surprise What's this? What's this? What's this? They finally left Little Gypsy Dora's tent when the quiet man came out from behind the curtain proudly zipping up his fly, after an infinite silence in which a kind of echo of moans lingered, the soldier took leave of the futurologist who was fixing her bun, holding the hairpins between her tight lips, Thank you very much ma'am, he thanked the sardine smell where two dark eyes and a dirty stained apron floated, the old man gunned the motor of the van, very irritated, calling them, I don't even want to think about what's going to happen to me later on at night, he muttered on the way to the warehouse, he braked suddenly to avoid a dog, speeded up again, spirals of sand danced around them, the geegaws on the mirror swayed, the dashboard shook with ague, and the quiet fellow happy, eyes closed, was leaning back on the seat, fondling his sated balls.

"I never had a fortune-teller," the second lieutenant complained, drawing arabesques in the ashtray with a matchstick. "You sweating on top like the devil and the dame figuring out invisible star maps: Mercury in Sagittarius, Mars in Aries, and the full moon in Scorpio. Little Gypsy Dora, you say?"

The communications officer invariably felt a horrible claustrophobia in the subway, in that eternal subterranean neon dawn peopled by torn advertising posters where trains passed through in an almost unceasing succession of wheels, disappearing into great black tunnels punctuated with miners' lamps. He arrived ten minutes early according to the large round clock on the platform, whose enormous hands moved from mark to mark with the short little leaps of a rheumatic, and he leaned against the scale right beside the stairs, waiting, watching the people buying packs of cigarettes or chocolate bars from vending machines gaudy with chrome and mirrors. Waves of people flooded the platform, disappeared into the lighted cars, and were immediately replaced by a new batch of riders, gentlemen with briefcases, women in a hurry, girls dragging their schoolbags along the filthy floor, dignified old men with stickpins in their ties, serious, antiquated, uniform, solitary faces: What can their lives be like, what do they do, what do they think, where do they spend their vacations? He smoked two cigarettes, holding onto the scale, with growing anxiety: feet sweaty, jabs in his stomach, an urge to piss that made him twist his legs the same as on the night before an exam, very cold, very hot, very cold again. He saw the long shanks moving once more, the free and easy laugh, the Morse code of the fingers on the cover of the book, he saw the soldiers bent over their desks in ulcerous silence once more: Does she have a husband, a man beside whom she sleeps night after night, merry, therefore, jovial, happy, freeing her unstained laughter in the vault of her room? A worker in an oversized peaked cap was trying in vain, during the gaps between the torrents of passengers, to clean the platform with a broom and dustpan, cigarette butts, pieces of paper, rinds, fruit pits, spittle, the crowded trains came and went, the riders shoving each other ferociously to get in, every so often there would be insults, shouts, curses, faces wrinkled into a circle of threats, lips drawn back, baring sharpened, interminable teeth. The old man went out through the gate of the amusement park with a clatter of tin, She's already laid out the cards for us by now, she's put a curse on us, she's fucked up our lives, the little raffia doll hanging from the rearview mirror by a string was dancing in all directions. He thought he saw her, he took a step forward, an unknown face looked at him, startled, and the communications officer drew back in confusion Sorry sorry sorry: after twenty minutes he was getting her mixed up with every girl who appeared, She most likely isn't coming, I got the wrong station, time, day, I got the signal from her fingers all backward, he rested his arm disheartenedly on top of the scale, and right then a voice Excuse me, please, I want to weigh myself, he turned his head, a train came to a grumbling halt by the platform, the people were elbowing their way in through the automatic doors that opened with a kind of sigh, and, just as he'd seen her in the office, jovial, smiling, ironic, calm, she.

"You people, civilians, dared conspire inside the Army?" the lieutenant colonel asked slowly, his tone troubled, outraged. "You people tried to undermine what had cost us so much work to build?"

"Coming out of the Ministry I ran into a girl who went to school with me," the girl explained, "I couldn't get away from her any sooner. Every time I have a job set up things like that happen to me."

Her green eyes, or brown, or brown and green, her hands and feet too large for her body, her thighs that aroused a strange kind of hunger in him, the light, frothy smell of flesh, as if her blood, her muscles, and her tendons were rising up like little bubbles of pink champagne toward the surface of her skin, as if she were made from the same igneous and gaseous matter as dreams: I'm so damned ugly, the communications officer thought, she must find me rather unpleasant, pathetic, ridiculous, beat-up suit, ragged fingernails, glasses, a row of pens and pencils in my jacket pocket. He moved off the scale with a deliberately casual leap, feeling idiotic with every word, every gesture, and they began to walk slowly along the cement floor of the station, you with those heels a touch taller than me, and I was ashamed of that too, even if nobody noticed except for a blindman sitting on a bench with a violin case opened in front of him, playing tangos and boleros insistently out of tune, and the guy's dark glasses followed us implacably: Could he belong to the PIDE? They reached the warehouse with the old man still trembling with fear, and the uncle, hands on his hips, snorting his everlasting rage, howled at them from the door What were you celebrating with your boozing, you shitheads?

"I've been waiting for this contact for a long, long time," the communications officer said, "they guaranteed there'd be more comrades working with me at the Ministry."

"A complete net," the lieutenant colonel whined, stupefied. "A complete net of bomb throwers, trained abroad, aiming to destroy the morale of the military."

The communications officer stepped back a little to allow the man with the broom and dustpan to pass: the ad for some brand of detergent, framed in aluminum on the curved wall of the station, poured out a flow of mixed and bright colors before them, red, white, green, blue, and intense yellow like a breath of passion. The girl looked for the drops in her pocketbook amid an indescribable confusion of a handkerchief, purse, datebook, compact, gum paper.

"The usual precautions, you know how it is." (A well-scrubbed voice, clear, adolescent, and still sure, authoritarian, ready to go down singing the "Internationale" aboard the *Titanic* of Marxism-Leninism-Maoism. She had more balls than I did, she believed more than I did, Captain, and I'll bet she still believes, meeting in dens, corners, deviously defending the Chinese.) Olavo must have warned you that the Organization can't afford to play around with matters of security: Always the same line, he thought, always the same shitty line and with so many adjustments they ended up not doing anything really useful, nothing that could scratch, reduce, bring the fucking government to account. The PIDE was getting better at going after us and we, in return, all tied up in chicken shit, were doubling our precautions.

She put two pieces of gum into her mouth and the fetid air of sweat and filth and oil and garbage of the platform took on an unsuspected vegetable freshness when she spoke.

"You just got back from Africa, you don't know what's been going on here lately. (The voice adult now, professorial, a touch irritated, Captain, over my infinite ignorance of the realities in the country: it figures that she considered me an idealistic schoolboy, anxious for utopian demonstrations, for unthinkable mass movements, for the fall of fascism through the shouting of high-school students. It figures that in the committee she'd been against giving me party work, it figures that she would have preferred for me to stay on ice for years and years, under observation, waiting: and a bitter doubt in my head, an itching in my ears, an annoying enticement in my fingers.) Especially right now," the girl added, avoiding a round splotch of spittle, "when something important is finally being prepared."

"I'll be damned if this isn't going to be the last time you people do any loafing," the uncle threatened, outraged, pacing up and down in his glass cubicle, opening the desk drawer where he kept his asthma spray, squeezing the rubber ball in a frantic rage. "I'll be damned if I won't fuck up your life for you, you bastards."

"It isn't just petitions, Commander," the chaplain repeated, alarmed. "There are meetings, conversations, provocations, it's a real attack on regulations."

"You've got to keep your eyes and ears wide open," she advised him,

79

"you've got to step up your work: we want a report a week at the least, starting now, the fire's going to get hot as hell. The captains are restless, there's been widespread discontent, a wave of protest, and all this is beginning to come together, little by little, into a universal challenge to the government. Well-organized politically, properly oriented toward promoting the unyielding defense of the working class and its interests, the most enlightened officers can easily take control of the situation and blow fascism to kingdom come."

"What do you say we go for a little whoring after we leave here, Captain?" the second lieutenant suggested, his tiny eyes gleaming like little venomous metallic dots. The back end of his twisted necktie was sunk in the dish of custard, his shirt, open halfway down his chest, revealed tufts of hair, a small whitish, gelatinous patch of skin.

"What?" the communications officer exclaimed with great surprise. "What?"

A drunk, drooping over a bench near them, was vehemently and laboriously arguing with himself, slapping his knees, a group of schoolgirls was gathered together in a cluster of whispers, laughter, and proud little breasts, the hand on the round clock was making its little leaps forward over a high tide of heads: Everything's passed me by, the communications officer thought, why in hell don't they ever talk to me about these things, why do they keep the meat for themselves and leave me the charity of a few little bones, some skin, some fat, some useless leftovers? The girl (Call me Dália, use Dália with me, and he, resentful, The usual nom de guerre, the code name of the whore your mother was, you're probably Fátima or Ana or Isabel) managed to make a translucent pink bubble with her elastic gum, and she drew the bubble in with her tongue and brought it back inside her mouth. Her girl voice was still professorial and enervating, and she discoursed as if she were reciting material she knew backward and forward: You'll meet the guy, get the picture? tell him this, that, and the other thing, and don't deviate a quarter of an inch from what we've set up, don't give out the smallest detail, the most specific bit of information, a name, a plan, something excessively concrete that could put us in danger: tragic features, ashtrays piled high, stacks of pamphlets to stuff in Lisbon mailboxes during the predawn hours, the exalting, exultant, catechumenal clandestine atmosphere, where words burned with anxious enthusiasm. The girl took his arm and the communications officer could feel her light pulse pressing through the cloth of his jacket.

"It's best like this," she explained, "people will take us for lovers and they'll be less suspicious. There are informers everywhere, they might know our faces."

"You're going to work like stevedores," the uncle threatened, pounding his fat little fist on the desk, scattering invoices with disconnected waves of his arms, tossing the ever-present flower into the wicker basket in a surge that made him lose his balance and tip over the glass of water, forcing him to grab one of the metal shelves in order not to fall backward onto the floor. "I'm docking you for this time, damn you, no one will ever give you a job."

"I'll contact you whenever possible," Dália consoled him (the chewing gum no longer had a smell to it, reduced to a soft repulsive substance that hid her teeth). "Be prepared for some great news in the coming months."

The red flags, the revolutionary hymns, people running, tear gas, shots, paving stones, blood, chants, slogans, propaganda, the firm, unyielding, victorious fight against the revisionists in Moscow, the manipulators of peasants, the subtle, bureaucratized traitors of the working class, the Organization working legally along with slum dwellers, labor unions, factory workers, students, Olavo, Emílio, Baldy, me, with a card pinned to our lapels, up on a platform, orating in the midst of applause, shouts, confusion, the aggressiveness or contentment of the obedient faces listening to us: one more year, the girl guaranteed, and fascism will burst like a boil, the secret police will be dissolved, the Army will abandon the colonies and join up with the genuine communists, one more year of patience, one more year of struggle (her eyes shining with hope, her childlike smile, her hand squeezing the thin bones of his arm as if they were a bundle of matches) and we'll have, you'll see, soviets, agricultural cooperatives, worker management, we'll become happy.

"I felt that the Estado Novo was rotten but secure, Captain," the communications officer said, eyes lowered, cleaning his glasses with his breath. "We were sick of the war, sick of persecution, sick of the PIDE, sick of unfulfilled promises, but I couldn't understand very well how all that would end up, how it could end some way someday, since it seemed eternal to me, immovable, smoothly stonelike. Even you, who were in it, did you believe it?"

Across from his aunt's house, along the fence of the amusement park, the ticket offices were opening up, with hunched-over heads inside, the first lights were going on, the whitish neon halo reduced the trees to profiles of paper cutouts, without any volume, and it sketched out a kind of cupola over the halted seats of the ferris wheel, which swayed softly in the air, hanging from their iron bars. He went up the stairs that creaked and sank under his feet like old lifeless limbs and on the landing he flattened up against the acned wall (a cortege of ants was climbing upward across a nodule) to make room for the heavy widow with a cane who lived opposite and taught clarinet at the Conservatory: We're going to run off the bourgeoisie, my lady, we're going to be free at last, and the teacher's clenched fist rose up in sympathetic assent, her huge, unmatched haunches mounting in festive jubilation, the orthopedic shoe crushed the boards of the stairway in vengeance. He was to rouse up the building at the proper time, he would set up a Marxist cell of enlightened tenants, he would head the defense nucleus of the neighborhood, destined to reorient or prevent possible conservative deviations, against the obscurantism of a misinformed populace, against the siren song of panicking social democrats, against dazzling capitalist temptations. But the clarinet teacher limped out of sight below, alien to the cyclopic reforms of the nation (We have to go ahead in phases, Olavo would inevitably advise, cleaning his debatable fingers with a nail file, we must move with caution), the loudspeakers in the amusement park were pouring out a twisted paso doble that seemed to be filtered through successive layers of limestone, the smoke from sardines, fritters, roast chicken burned the eyes and rolled in wandering ellipses around the lampposts: Instead of plotting revolution, why don't you take a ride on the roller coaster with me, Dália, why don't we walk holding hands, licking ice-cream cones, in the craft pavilions (sheepskin coats, capes, gourds, leather purses), why don't you let me see you home, goddamn it? He rubbed his shoes on the muff of the doormat (WELCOME), went in, and the dog didn't bound in his direction to nip his heels, pull on his shoestrings, lie down languidly on her back for him to scratch her fat black and white belly covered by two rows of nipples.

"The talk in the subway took place on the day Lady died, Captain," the communications officer said, thumbing through his memory with the melancholy attention given to albums of childhood pictures. (You got old too, I thought, you lost your enthusiasm and your illusions too, you've got white hairs in your mustache too.) "It's always sad to see an animal that you've known ever since it was little die, practically the only living creature I felt close to there at home."

"The Organization told me to tell you that your activities are more important than ever," blushing, Dália tried to motivate him. (You don't know how to lie, dope, you're trying to help me and you're screwing up.) "You're doing a most useful job at the section level of the Ministry, and it's absolutely necessary for you not to deviate from the directives you were given."

And very low, in a kind of accomplice's whisper:

"It'll be any day now, word of honor."

Stretched out on the kitchen floor, not moving, vomiting, sighing as she stared at him with the damp jelly of her eyes, purple drool hanging from her mouth, Lady's breathing slowly grew fainter, her eyes were nighting over, her hindquarters shaking, her hair standing on end from time to time, her tail dragged afflictedly across the floor. Esmeralda was twisting her apron with her thumbs, his aunt, leaning against the stove, suddenly became a hundred years older:

"I had her call the vet already, I didn't talk to him because I can't hear." He made excuses, said he couldn't come, that he didn't have anyone he could send: the bleat of a goat trembling with insecurity, anguish, and the communications officer was startled to discover an indecisive little girl underneath the wrinkled rind of that stiff septuagenarian, who addressed all the angels and saints of her prayers with haughty superiority. She came down with some kind of sickness this morning, an embolism, colic, a heart attack, poor thing, she's been wilting all this time. Isn't there some infirmary near here at least, can't they relieve her suffering at least?

"Some whoring after all the speeches, Captain?" the second lieutenant tempted, rolling his eyes comically and running the tip of his tongue over his lips. "In order to remember the cabarets we went to on leave, to take the rust off our hammers the way we used to when we got back from the jungle and covered the table with bottles of champagne, remember?"

Mulatto women in gaudy dresses leaning against the wall in the darkest corners of the club, middle-aged women done in by nights on end with no sleep, the pathetic striptease of a clumsy creature, with no rhythm or grace, introduced by a fairy emcee in a bow tie, with a roll of drums, our hands judging, feeling, pinching, touching knees under the table, going up along legs with the avidity of a centipede, and so many of the dead protesting silently in my blood: we'd close our eyes and they'd reappear, stubborn, insistent, inert, sleeping with their eyes open on the edge of the grassland, sneaking into the whores' perfume, into the deodorizing taste of the whiskey, into the anxious fury of desire: he went out into the street, covered two blocks, turned left, and in the distance made out the luminous, rectangular, opaline sign in the midst of other letters, designs, arabesques, all pulsating: São Roque Medical-Surgical Center, 24-Hour Service. It's good for something, the communications officer thought, my knowing every inch of this stinking neighborhood from having done so much walking. He rang a bell, waited a second, rang again, and the sound seemed to buzz, far off, without any answer, in a zinc cavern, until finally a character in a lab coat, half-hunchbacked, opened the door for him grudgingly, yawning because of the nuisance or from sleepiness.

"If I don't catch this train I've had it," Dália whispered before running to the car where people were pushing each other, listlessly, complaining. "Don't do anything on your own, I'll look you up."

"Yes?" the hunchback asked, looking him over with irritation, almost without moving his mouth, with one of those faces that are swollen from an abscess. "You're nervous, pal, tell us all about it here in the waiting room."

Formica chairs, seats upholstered in checkered cloth, magazines on a small table missing a leg, pictures on the walls in lacquered frames showing children and landscapes and swans, heavy glass ashtrays, a cheap mat, the kind they sell at Guincho beach on Sundays, serving as a rug, a gaudy brass chandelier hanging from the ceiling. It smelled of halibut liver grease, disinfectant, and sweat, a record player was bellowing in the next room, the hunchback roared, drowning out the music, Turn that shit down, Emília, and almost immediately there was a terrifying silence.

"Whores, Captain," the second lieutenant urged, spilling some white wine, without noticing, on the tablecloth, where it spread out rapidly like pus vomit. "We'll barge into some joint, take all the women for ourselves, have a bash like in the old days."

"So what ails you?" the man in the lab coat asked in a professional tone, cleaning a spot on his sleeve with his forefinger, wet with his spit. (And he managed to catch sight of her for a second more, struggling in the welter of shapes, before the doors closed, a whistle sounded, and the train started off in the direction of a dark, irrevocable, endless tunnel.)

"Are you the doctor on duty?" the communications officer replied, drying the back of his neck with his handkerchief. (For a second, just for a moment, but it was as if her hand, you see, was still holding my jacket, as if her voice was still going on, imperturbable, putting forth her infantile orders: Where do you live, Dália, give me your phone number, let me call you up in the middle of the night if I can't sleep, let me hear your laugh, concave like a womb, in my long insomnia dawns, before the first vacillating, tenuous light over the rooftops of this city that I detest to the point of nausea, these cataleptic, unbearable morning streets.)

The hunchback, distant, turned his tiny yellow eyes on him, came forward on the rug with the twisted little step of a scorpion:

"There's no doctor after six at night, friend, I'm the only one here, for shots, bandages, blood pressure, a pill or two for the nerves." The record player started up again, this time a touch softer, the hunchback opened his mouth, I drew back a couple of feet fearing another frightening bark, the smell of a stew came floating through the door, and the lieutenant colonel said, picking at the space between his teeth with a fingernail:

"When a guy gets involved with a housemaid it's next to impossible to get her off your back."

The last car evaporated into the tunnel in the shape of a round light bulb going away, the walls, the advertising posters, and the cement of the platform stopped vibrating, the trooping steps of a new load of passengers were coming down the stairs all in disorder, and the communications officer imagined, as in movie documentaries, hundreds of branching horns, reindeer horns, clashing as they galloped along a wide snowy plain inhabited by strange red pines that were weighing scales. The long neon tubes on the ceiling gave way progressively to the dim chandeliers of the waiting room, whose light might have been said to be filtered through the ecclesiastical modesty of cloth eyelashes, and he heard his own voice, timid, awkward, stumbling over the syllables like a chorus boy in a surplice:

"Could you please take a look at a dying dog?"

The record player fell silent as the needle squealed in the grooves, the hunchback stared at him with astonishment (A dog? A dog? Are you kidding?), someone shouted from behind a curtain Hurry up Amílcar, soup's on the table, disconnected noises of plates and silverware could be heard, chairs dragging, children crying, scolding, and the hunchback, huddled in his lab coat, continued looking him over with infinite surprise, as if he were face-to-face with a two-headed calf or a crocodile with acne:

"A goddamned dog? Was it a dog you were talking about?"

"Amílcar," the shouts insisted, "hurry up or everything will be cold."

The hunchback finally shoved a vial of bluish liquid into his pocket (One teaspoonful with each meal and get going

AMÍLCAR!

or I'll be the one dying),

pulled him out into the vestibule (some broken-down cupboards, a foggy mirror with a carved-look frame, knickknacks, more magazines) and from there to the landing, where the smell of disinfectants and pharmaceuticals was almost completely diluted by the musty air, Don't forget, the technician advised, one teaspoonful

AMÍLCAR!

with every meal, the shouts com-<br>plained

The beans have lost their taste, the communications officer went confusedly down the steps feeling the weight of the syrup in his jacket, and outside it was completely night, very dark, opaque, rain-sad: you couldn't make out people's faces twenty or thirty yards away, haloes of lights came closer and disappeared, spreading thin shadows over building façades, people reduced to insignificant little shapes waved from the top of the Great Ferris Wheel to their frightened families, and when I got home, Captain, Lady had died and I threw the blue liquid into the garbage. I went to get a hatbox in the storeroom, dumped the pins, lace, pieces of felt, fake jewels that were inside into a drawer, my aunt was still leaning against the stove, not moving, her jaw drooping, Esmeralda, taking refuge in the enclosed balcony, was wiping her eyes with her apron, he grabbed the dog by the neck, her small body, covered with slaver, soft and still, made him nauseous, and laid her in the box, and the crackle of the tissue paper made the old women shudder, he covered her with newspapers, went back out to the street, hesitated beside the garbage bin right next to the entrance door, on the sidewalk opposite they were constructing a row of buildings on a vacant lot beyond a student boardinghouse and a Protestant church, he borrowed a shovel from the watchman, who was warming his hands over a fire of boards, and when he sank the blade into the sand, the grass, the roots, the fruit pits, the pebbles on the slope, I raised my head, saw both their figures watching me from the balcony, not moving, and beyond the figures the carousels and little iron trains of the roller coaster whirling in the midst of the smoke and the colored lights, heard the music, the exaggerated hawking for the Pit of Death, the baleful laughter and fake shrieks of terror from Bluebeard's Castle, and, I don't know if you understand, Captain, but I got like an idea in my head, or bladder, or liver, or guts, or the prick that can fuck me over, a goddamned rage for all of us.

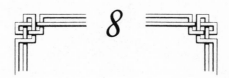

8

"As soon as I landed," the second lieutenant said (scarlet faced from the wine, the cane liquor, the plan for whoring, the more and more sickening and rarefied air of the restaurant, while a fan on the ceiling was spinning around in slow whirls), "things with Inês began to go bad, I don't know why. We'd probably got unused to each other over the months, we acted like two strangers, we'd lost the habit of life together, we'd ceased knowing each other completely." (The blades of the fan were slowly spinning, like spoons, in the thick cream of the smoke, a kind of radiator with blue cylinders hanging on the wall was chasing off fat summer mosquitoes. Through the open door the Lisbon night and the Lourenço Marques night drew close and merged like naked bodies touching, the buildings across the street looked like the Indian Ocean from a distance, with porthole lights rocking, standing out in the dark. The second lieutenant, tight, tense, attentive, hunched over in his chair, stared at the squares on the tablecloth like someone following a guerrilla trail in the jungle: In Africa, he thought, you forget about being with people, you become a kind of irascible and afflicted beast, cruel, frightened, alienated carnivorous animals, desperately clinging to the crutch of a machine gun.)

Two, three, sometimes four times a week, on arriving home worn out from his work, up to here with the bank, sick of meetings, speculations, market analyses, figures, wanting some silence and rest, he would sit down on the couch, exhausted, legs stretched out, would open the newspaper eyeshade without seeing the letters, and right then, just when he was beginning to doze off (It's two hours to dinnertime, I can get some perfect rest for a little while), the telephone would break loose and each lament would give him a little jab of pain, like a knife, in his ears, chest, head. He would lift his arms up, groggy, to cover his ears with his hands, and suddenly a small silence, his wife's ceremonious voice Hello? and immediately after, sweetly, agreeably, warm, Yes, Mother. (And he, putting the newspaper on his knees, feeling his muscles all swollen and painful, his skull still off center from the noise, his eyes painfully covered by their lids, just like curtains of sulfur going up and down: Why is it that you never talk to me that way, why this coolness, this distance, this bitterness?)

"Is it my fault that you don't like my parents?" Inês asked, furious. "When you married me you already knew what they were like."

No, Mother, dining there would really be just fine, it would save me an awful lot of work, I don't have to ask him, Jorge will be delighted I'm sure: the figure hunched over the low telephone table, hair loose, myopic fingers feeling for the nearest ashtray, the child finally asleep on the backseat, carrying her with her arms around his neck, weeping for sleep, home: I hate you, Inês.

"The chick was promising me all that, Captain," the communications officer said, carefully putting his glasses back on his nose, "revolution, the fall of fascism, the people up in arms, freedom, the devil's own, and I was everywhere at once, with notes, memorandums, letters, trying hard, you can imagine, to seduce sergeants who couldn't care less, but what was for sure is that everything at the Ministry stayed just the same: the same hopeless dragging of feet, the same dusty uselessness, the same pleading colonels, the same noiseless immobility, the ferryboats coming and going against the mustiness of the windowpanes. In those days Marxism appeared just as utopian as it does today, and yet, imperturbable, steadfast, idealistic, I went on believing."

"I'll only be a minute getting ready so we can dine in Carcavelos," Inês advised, running past on her way to the bedroom. "Would you be so kind as to put the little one's things in the basket?"

Diapers that would come back in a plastic bag cruelly smelling of shit, the pacifier, a string of rattles, a rubber bunny without a face, chewed after months of teething. The baby protested, squirming, and the second lieutenant muttered You must be crazy hungry, I bet your mother didn't give you any lunch, spent the whole afternoon on the phone, drinking whiskey and cackling a lot of bullshit with her girl friends. When he leaned over to pick the baby up from the crib all his bones creaked and cracked, his joints pulsated with pain, a vise twisted him, tighter and tighter, inside his thorax, the bell went on ceaselessly, massacring his ears. By the bathroom door he caught sight of his wife on tiptoes at the mirror, enlarging her eyelids with vials and brushes, transforming her mouth into a disdainful wound, hiding a pimple on her chin with a dab of cream. What have we got in common, he thought, where the hell did we ever get the idea to get married? We used to go to the movies in a group, to parties in a group, we ate out in a group, we played tennis in a group, we water-skied in a group, I cut classes regularly during the first year of Economics, you never set foot in the Hungarian teacher's ballet classes or the French lessons at the Alliance, I liked your simpleminded ways, the silly way you laughed, shrugged your shoulders, danced, your rather foolish enthusiasm, without any put-on, the way you chirped out clichés, I was pleased with the luxury of your parents' home, the furniture, the paintings, the silverware, the impeccable profusion of maids trotting back and forth with the obstinacy of an anthill. One Saturday we happened to be side by side in the Condes movie house (The Condes? the soldier ex-claimed in surprise, I thought upper-class kids went to the Tivoli), an abso-lutely awful film that took place in the Middle Ages, with bearded characters talking endlessly, we couldn't get tickets for the São Luís and the orchestra seats stank of cheap perfume, nylon stockings, and sweat, a field of round, dark stones that were heads spread out in front of them all the way down to the huge colored rectangle of the screen. Inês was restless in her seat, ever so bored, her dress rustled with every movement, and it was as if I could feel in the depth of my testicles, Captain, every pore of her body, every inch of her skin, the soft contact of her clothes, our thighs one against the other: I'm hungry to get close to you, I'm hungry to hold your hand, and suddenly, without my expecting it, when a wild battle of tin swords was starting up on the screen, your knee pressed strongly against my pant leg and I remained absolutely motionless, incredulous, amazed, thinking It was just by chance, it can't be on purpose, it's a lie, hoping, you know how it is, that it would last forever.

"I'm ready," Inês shouted, quickly putting away on an unseen shelf jars, containers, tubes of mascara, brushes, the little magnifying mirror that deformed your face and turned it into a twisted and threatening mask. "You can go down to the car with Mariana."

The next week he summoned up the little courage he was capable of and after scratching lines out innumerable times, he finally wrote her a clumsy sonnet, asking for her love: he waited almost a month for an answer, the girls in the group stared hard at him, they whispered funny little things to Inês (Everybody's read it by now, they're going to make up a slew of shit about me), he didn't dare get close, kept to himself, sullen, bashful, Inês Hello, and the second lieutenant, inaudible, Hello, until one night at a dance, when he was leaving, he found a piece of graph paper from a notebook folded in the pocket of his topcoat. He only came across it in the dim light of the streetcar on the way home, the conductor standing waiting, clicking his punch, my name on the outside in large block letters, he opened it trembling and there inside, Yes. I'm going to faint, he thought, this is so good I won't be able to take it standing up.

"I still must have it someplace or other at home, Captain," the second lieutenant confessed, reaching for the strawberry brandy among the many empty and full bottles on the table. A page torn out of her school notebook, a childish hand: and for years after I considered that note the greatest thing in the world.

He settled his daughter in the child's seat hanging on the back of the rear seat by two chrome hooks, and the spotlights that illuminated the fountain on the Rua da Mãe d'Água lighted up the nearby walls and trees against a mysterious background where trunks swayed and shadows swirled. He put the basket in the trunk, and down below on the Praça da Alegria the usual and disjointed concert of angry horns could be heard. From time to time an entranceway would light up, people would come out chatting, and shortly thereafter a car would appear, backing up along the row of parked automobiles. He pulled a knob, put the key in the slot in the steering wheel (You're never coming down, the second lieutenant thought, furious, you're probably answering another phone call), and the motor started up softly, making the rather dirty windows of the car buzz. Chewing on a cigarette, hands clutching the steering wheel, arousing the Fiat from time to time with a spasmodic gunning of the engine, angry at Inês's indifference and his own mushy subservience, he waited.

"Have you any idea," the lieutenant colonel nudged me, his voice stretching out the syllables with the uncertain drawl of a drunk, "what it's like to be caught by your own daughter stark naked humping the cleaning woman?"

What am I going to answer now, the second lieutenant pondered, terrified, what am I going to say when I see her, what's it like to be in love? At the end of the following week, instead of joining the group as usual at the entrance to the movies, expectant and timid, he remained shut up at home in horrible indecision, smoking, walking through the rooms, refusing any lunch, snacks, dinner, his nose wrinkled, constantly washing his oily hands, answering with vague expressions what his parents and sister, all intrigued, asked him, his eyes fierce, as if he were seeing them for the first time, at the pictures, the knickknacks, the piece of square that could be seen from the balcony, the rear of buildings, eaves, the asymmetry of sooty chimneys. At nine o'clock in the evening the telephone rang, his mother, who was knitting beside it, answered, Just a moment, she looked about the room for him, called him with her chin, Jorge, his father laid his open book down on his chair and went out, he heard the metal latch on the bathroom door turn with its customary squeak and immediately an abundant flow from the faucet, A girl, his mother announced, my legs began to shake, hesitate, bend, my guts were rolling in my belly (You turned out to be a great big coward, Lieutenant, the soldier said), I'm going to make a fool of myself, he thought, I'm going to look like an idiot, his mother (What's wrong?) passed him the phone without understanding, he put it to his ear, staring in confusion at the old picture of a baby on the wall, his breathing was making the curtain rise and fall, he coughed into the mouthpiece, and her voice, small, clear, hesitant, asked from the other end Is that you.

"No, seriously," the lieutenant colonel repeated in a sticky voice, "an old man humping a cleaning woman in the presence of his daughter, just picture the scene. For weeks and weeks I was all upset, running away from the kid."

The light in our entrance went on, revealing the sad moribund plants by the doorway, the elevator, Inês's tall body prancing down the steps. She greeted the concierge, who was leaning against the mailboxes, chatting with the lady in third-floor left, with an evasive nod, I signaled her with the headlights, and the woman, still putting on her jacket, sat down heavily onto the seat and immediately pushed in the car's cigarette lighter. The enchantment of days gone by had disappeared completely, Captain, the enthusiasm of days gone by, the fever of days gone by, the inextinguishable urge to hug her, kiss her, fondle her breasts of days gone by: a slight boredom, a nuisance, a ritual that each time lost more of its sense and meaning. He unbuttoned his collar, loosened his tie (Is it my spine or my muscles or the three hundred joints that are aching all at the same time?): What are you waiting for, Inês asked dryly. He lifted his foot too quickly from the clutch, the Fiat leaped, sobbed, fell silent (I never saw anyone so clumsy, she observed without affection), they finally went up Príncipe Real with some difficulty, aiming to get on the freeway, they went past the French Lycée, picking up speed, with the little one crying in the back (Teeth?), and beyond the Viaduct the motionless blotch of Monsanto mingled with the also still spots in a sky speckled by the flint of stars. Wrinkles of clouds lay in folds over the river like the creases in a crumpled sheet.

"What impresses me most, Captain," the second lieutenant said, pushing his hair back, "is the fact that everything in my life has changed without my being aware of it, it's not at all like it was before, the people, the places, my own age, exactly what I needed never to change. As if north was south now and I was drifting without a compass, looking for something to guide me. This sure feeling, you understand, that it's too late and I've lost my way home, or, if I find it, I'm touching a wall, a corner, a blind alley with my feelers."

They ran into each other two or three days later in the vicinity of the Alliance (an imposing, venerable building, with a flagpole in front, high stucco ceilings, dark paintings, old-fashioned desks) and Inês's smile, childlike, happy, loving, lighted him up like those badgers in animated cartoons when they fall in love with long-lashed lady badgers and little red hearts appear all over their bodies and they squeak like bedsprings. They would walk a few blocks at random, not speaking, until I got the courage to reach for her arm, give her my hand, feeling her soft palm in mine, the fingers interlaced tightly with mine, and I, then, How many hundreds of times have you done this before, how many sons of bitches have you loved before me? I didn't say anything because if I spoke I might just ruin everything, Inês isn't going to find the nonsense I talk the least bit amusing: and I felt giddiness, hot and cold flashes, indescribable cramps, my ears turned into little fleshy fires, singeing the hair of my temples. The people who passed us seemed vague and shapeless, lighted up by the streetlamps or the shop windows, a very erect gentleman, with hungry eyes, stiff and hesitant at the same time, was waiting patiently for the little dog he had on a leash to finish offering its millimetric trickle to a tree trunk, traffic was flowing along the avenue with a twinkling of lights and shapes.

"No, I wasn't in class," Inês explained, "I go to class as little as possible. I thought it was a good idea to meet you here because it's far away from my parents' Lisbon place, there's no danger of anyone seeing us."

A voice just like the one on the telephone, still withdrawn, innocent, finding its way through the words like a thread of water, but stronger, clearer, more fleshed-out, and the second lieutenant felt a weakness in his legs again, his insides contracting with pleasure, a buzzing in his ears, and for a second he remembered his mother's face as she handed him the phone. It's for you.

"What I wanted to be was a real ballet dancer," Inês revealed in a tone of pompous confidentiality, "but my father is very funny about things like that: if he had his way none of us girls would be allowed out in the street."

He began to go up onto the freeway, right behind a small truck spewing thick smoke from its exhaust pipe, the shrubs along the roadside were protesting to the wind, and, he thought, shifting into second, You said that, and I pictured a kind of one-eyed monster, all hairy and scaly, giving off terrible scowls, locking the family up in closets in their rooms, and I was afraid at that moment that he would tear my letter into a thousand pieces, slashing furiously, opening and closing his gigantic sharp talons, limping after me like an ape, all bloody, through the alarmed city streets.

"And in the end, Captain," the second lieutenant said, bumming a cigarette from the quartermaster next to him, who was smoking some pestilential unfiltered foreign butts, "what I met up with was a pleasant quiet little man, ordinary, inoffensive, tyrannized by his wife's disdain, his wife's money, his wife's curt military commands, completely silent in a corner of that enormous parlor, hidden by the piano that was just like an abandoned threshing machine, chin in his hands in front of the chapel glow of the television set."

It was a year later, more or less, that the lieutenant met him, that he entered the Carcavelos house for the first time, with no place for his body or his hands, frightened from the first by the number of cars in the yard, by the size of the garden, by the water in the swimming pool where swarms of reflections went off and on, by the tiled façade overgrown with braids of wisteria, by the sickening and remotely agreeable smell of money: brokerage houses, buildings, land in the Alentejo, two commercial centers, several companies, interests in a bank. And there inside a crowd of people circulating, plates in hand, who came together, separated, chatted, laughed, kissed Inês and ignored him completely or conceded him a distant and distracted interest, if that, leaning like curious hens over the silver trays placed around the large oval table with a showy porcelain object in the center. (There were other tables on the grounds, a tennis court, golf flags, and, farther off, blond children playing at bowls.)

"This is Jorge," Inês introduced him to her mother, who stopped listening to a lady on in years, to examine him with sudden sharp attention. Her pale eyes measured him, appraised him, estimated, guessed his weight, and tossed him away:

"If you haven't had lunch yet, help yourself," she offered in a way completely lacking in friendliness. "Inês, child, see what your friend wants."

"It seems to me," the communications officer cackled triumphantly with a perverse laugh, "that you succumbed to the temptation of capital."

While he was chewing his food, leaning against a sideboard, he was taking in the oil paintings, the draperies, the small tables, the rugs, the heavy, imposing luxury of the house, the servants going about with trays, three or four Bassett hounds, continually being stepped on, whimpering under cabinets. I've got nothing in common with these people, he thought, I dropped in here like Alice on the other side of the looking glass, and he smiled at Inês who was coming over with two glasses of sangria in her hands: The beginning of the end, Captain, he muttered desolately, twenty-one years old, one-hundred-percent boob, the post at Mafra waiting for me.

At the end of the freeway, after the gasoline pumps, the Marginal suddenly appeared with the river opposite, pitch black beyond the wall, sown with a constellation of anchored boats.

"Can't you go a little faster?" Inês commanded harshly. "Mother's probably been waiting centuries for dinner."

She handed him the glass, pinched his cheek, and the second lieutenant thought How come you like me, I don't dress as well as these guys, my manners aren't quite as polished, are cruder, my face is less delicate than theirs, I don't know the people who come visiting or the hotels they stay in or the cities they talk about, my father works as assistant to the manager of a second-rate printing company, sooty and dirty, I'm not a count or a millionaire or an artist or a celebrity, I flunked miserably the first year of Economics and live in an apartment in Marvila where not a single piece of furniture is worth a damn. As if there'd been some great big mistake in all that, Captain, a mistake that they were bound to end up discovering, a deception that they would catch in the midst of expressions of horror, giggling, snide remarks, derision. He swallowed a forkful of codfish with difficulty, answered Inês's smile with an embarrassed scowl, noticing that a bald-headed priest and a languid lady loaded down with jewels were observing him, Any minute now they're going to order me out through the kitchen door, pointing their fingers, but the figures mingled and disappeared, casual, obsequious, or vaguely friendly, large painted eyelids, elastic mouths that had no end, moribund breasts, imposing bald heads, he finished the codfish and stood with the empty plate in his hand, extremely timid, not knowing where to put it down, Inês had gone off to greet a couple who waved to her from a distance, and the second lieutenant, unprotected, leaning against the wallpaper like a condemned prisoner against the execution wall, was thinking in terror It's now, they're going to kneel down on the carpet, squeeze the trigger, shoot. And yet, Captain, I went back the following Sunday, and the one after that and the one after that, I learned to kiss women's hands and to talk urbanely to the men as one equal to another, I got along with a cousin of hers, a wild guy with bags under his eyes, bloated, on the borderline of drunkenness like teetering on the edge of a swimming pool. The cousin worked (Does he still?) at the family bank and from time to time he would phone him for a fling with some dancers from the Casino, or Belgian models, or freckled creatures (tennis players?) passing through Lisbon, picked up before dinner at bars in the hotels where foreigners stayed, where the staff received him with respectful slavish bows.

"Capital, my son, inevitably leads to sin," croaked the communications officer, imitating the tone of a priest in the confessional. "As penance you will say five Hail Marys for the benefit of the classless society."

The high-tide waves were exploding against the wall and climbing up through the shadows with a burst of foam, the automobiles were driving slowly along the wet surface, houses in the darkness followed one after the other in no particular order along the railroad tracks. In the backseat Mariana was whimpering with impatience, fatigue, hunger: Eat dinner, return home as quickly as possible, take a pill, fall asleep. His eyes were burning, he had practically no feeling in his legs, a painful palpitation was devouring the right side of his head, treading on his brain, dragging along on his neck, his arm, with disagreeable and sudden jabs of pain as Inês's voice penetrated with monotonous rancor:

"I'll bet they're on their dessert already."

"The child is living or was living with her mother, Captain," the second lieutenant declared in a blank voice from which all feeling was bitterly excluded. "I would have her on Saturdays, every two weeks, and later on she'd visit me to ask for money. A week or so ago, you know how it is, she came by my place with a mustached character who greeted me with a grunt, dropped onto the living-room sofa, and lighted up a cigarette, Helder here's got me pregnant, I need ten contos for an abortion, and me looking at her, not answering. That at the age of fourteen, mind you."

He searched forlornly for the picture of his daughter in his wallet, inspecting the tiny compartments filled with calling cards, calendars, phone numbers, assorted papers, and he finally showed the very old photograph, full of yellow spots, of a little girl in pigtails and a white dress pretending to hug a dog.

"Helder," the second lieutenant said in a dead tone, "plays drums with the Demons of Rhythm, boxes at the Andorinhas, and he witnessed the scene with all the tranquility of a zebu, stroking his mustache with his square fingers. (As if he were there to protect you from me, he thought, as if he'd come to tell me that This is how things stand, so fork up the dough, because feelings don't interest me one damned bit.) It seems that they're living in a building on Martim Moniz with twenty or thirty other idiots like themselves, shooting up heroin, listening to screeching music, scratching their bellies, and thinking themselves the chosen people. I haven't laid eyes on them since, I get news about Mariana here and there. They didn't even tell me, Captain, if the baby ever was born, whether it was a boy or a girl, its weight, its health, the color of its hair, foolish little things like that. Maybe if I hadn't got divorced everything would have been different for her, she would have stayed in school, brushed her teeth, would still be a virgin, what the hell."

About two months before going into the Army, he invited his parents to meet Inês (by then the old woman would hand him the phone without a word, clutching the knitting needles with her weak, recriminatory free hand) and took them out for pizza at an Italian restaurant by the park, full of the smell of roasting coffee beans and smoke, where people moved about as if they were swimming with difficulty in a fishbowl full of fog. Six Chinese, looking all alike, occupied the next table, smiling at each other over their polka-dot neckties, modest and very well mannered, the waiter's sweat dripped into the salad. He didn't want to stay home out of shame, afraid that Inês would compare the luxury of Carcavelos with the modest, irregular, dusty flat in Marvila, over whose scratched furniture his mother would listlessly, year in, year out, pass a rosary, a third of it wrapped around her wrist, and where the beat-up springs of the couches pinched buttocks like the tips of fishhooks. His father, his shirt collar dirty with dandruff, was chewing obstinately, silently, buried in his plate, answering with grunts from his full mouth his son's desperate questions. His mother fixed the timid spangles of her eyes on Inês, twisting, rigid with bashfulness, the hem of her skirt (an exaggerated and cheap flowered dress that would have provoked hilarity on the part of everyone in Carcavelos), and you were looking at the three of us from the unmeasurable distance of a microscope, with a horror impossible to define, not speaking, putting little pieces of bread into your painted mouth with the precise movements of a metronome. But you didn't break off our love affair (Why?), you didn't leave me (Why?), the telephone continued to ring faithfully at night in the worm-eaten silence of the living room (Why?), the group still got together for the movies, for a night club, for parties, the love affair was becoming official, sluggishly, slowly, I continued taking the train, second class, to Carcavelos, if I couldn't manage to wheedle from the old man the ancient Ford, in ruins, covered with a striped cloth, and parked permanently by the door, its radiator, full of holes, obliging them to stack a tinkling bunch of jugs on the rear seat.

"A coup d'etat, she announced," the communications officer muttered, shaking his incredulous head. "With that goddamned calm in the streets, in factories, in conversations on the bus, only a lunatic like me, Captain, believed it. And yet, all of a sudden, *bam*, the people rallying in Carmo, tanks in the lower city, soldiers with machine guns on the corners, the PIDE in jail, the government in ruins, great big headlines in the newspapers."

Inês let him stroke her body, her breasts, the bare part of her legs, pull down her panties to feel her hair, sniff the smell of her neck with his boar's snout, she would touch him too, lean her head back, moan, and in her outline, clear against the thick blue of the sofa, breathing rapidly like a tired animal, she would acquire the pink attraction of movie actresses on posters. The second lieutenant heard the voices of the servant girls in the cellar, the lawn mower trimming the grass, the throat of the swimming pool swelling up, the carpeted silence of the veranda. His underwear was damp with desire: he didn't imagine, didn't reason, he was only touching her, his hands went up and down, rumpling her dress, he tried to unbutton his fly with his eager fingers, caught up in the buttons: Wait, let me help you, Inês whispered, and I, of course, Captain, inside, Oh what experience, oh what a wise whore, because I'd fallen in love like a calf, you see, everything I could imagine, the most passionate and imbecilic, and in the end, what can you say, it was the first time, her casualness, her poise, her worldly airs had disappeared completely, and in the pine grove a frightened little girl rose up in her face, Be careful, be careful, don't hurt me, but I did and she cried out with one or two moans or short wails, biting me with all her strength on the shoulder, the muscles of her vagina had softly expelled my penis, and there it was, on the tip, the little drop of bright crimson varnish, a brushstroke of blood.

"Well, now that I'm old, Captain," the soldier said, sucking on and picking his teeth with his tongue, "the moving business doesn't interest me: if I'd really made a serious effort at it I'd have been a millionaire today, driving around in a Mercedes, nice and fat, talking big, presiding over athletic clubs, with a mistress set up in Restelo. The way it is, you see, I work as little as possible, I have my few beers on Sunday, play dominoes with some friend or other who shows up: the same old thing, habit, the crap of age forty, hunched over, giving up, you know how it is, Captain. A few months ago I had a phlebitis attack in one leg, and since then I haven't felt like doing anything."

"Is it my fault that you don't like my parents?" Inês complained, moving in her seat. "We haven't even got to Santo Amaro and you're already getting sullen: do they want to pull out your nails without anesthesia or something?"

Trees, the wrathful spite of the sea, trains playing hide-and-seek in the night, above the houses the patch of sky heavy with rain on the hillside: It wasn't that I didn't like her folks, Captain, the father, especially, made him feel sorry, so useless, so pathetic, so worthless, so extinct, condemned to stroll like a shadow through the enormous rooms or draining melancholy whiskeys in front of the defunct television set. It wasn't a matter of liking or not liking, it was just that he felt, felt foolishly, without knowing why, that he was betraying some imprecise, indefinite, vague but certainly important things, the guys at the printing presses, the dirty lead dust on the windowsills, my mother serving soup in the run-down living room, whose unbelievable furniture had belonged to my grandparents and uncles, betraying successive generations of anonymous merchants in their tile frames, or, maybe still, something I could never find words to describe, or simply nothing, nothing, nothing, only a nameless uneasiness without any consistency or cause. Lying side by side, embracing, they listened to the domestic sounds coming from the house, the vacuum cleaner, the telephone, voices, and beyond the windowpanes, far, far away, the sea.

"I got married five or six months later, after my basic training," the second lieutenant said, rubbing the scar on his forehead with his wrist. "Music in the church, tons of flowers, four hundred guests, a damned confusion. Inês hiding her three-month pregnancy under her white dress, and I never saw her look so beautiful as on that day."

Weeks before they'd invited the second lieutenant's family to Carcavelos, and the old man, in spite of the efforts by Inês's father, remained stubbornly silent, staring at the corner of a picture frame, huddled in his grain-colored suit: We want your son to work with us: and the humble, servile, grateful smile of his mother, the expression of a seamstress who'd discovered in a cupboard drawer the most complicated and obviously false brooch that exploded like an aneurism on the low-cut neckline of her dress. Your mother, your mother's brothers, your mother's friends were looking at us, at the little frightened island we formed, as at a strange species of extinct animal, and I saw that the old folks, if they could have, would have beat it into the kitchen to eat with the servants, I could catch stagnating in the old lady's eyes the begging pardon for having been born in Amadora, for going around in slippers all day at home, for not playing cards, for adoring cheap magazines, for not knowing the people everybody knew. But Inês's parents pretended they didn't notice, one dish followed another without any cataclysmic phrase (Please, God, have them bear up under it a little more, I prayed in silence, have them get by with no grammatical mistakes, no toothpicks, no mangled verbs, no looking at the servant who was serving them from the side with a feeling of equal to equal) and when it was all over your family came to say goodbye at the door, we took a taxi home, and you can't imagine how relieved I was, Captain, able to breathe calmly again.

"Off to the whores like before," the lieutenant colonel snorted pensively into his glass, "off to the whores to remember the war. Since we're living such idiotic lives, why shouldn't we do that, goddamn it?"

"And you didn't even know that the Revolution was coming," the communications officer asked, surprised, "not even that the country's drawers were bursting at the seams?"

Well, he certainly didn't notice, but there were still a few years to go, right? It had been the war, he'd come back from the war and zilch: there wasn't any talk of that in Africa, there wasn't any talk of that in Lisbon, Inês, in her letters to Mozambique, almost always limited herself completely to Mariana, to Mariana's little tricks, to Mariana's first words, to Mariana's ear infections and stuffy noses and vomiting and lack of appetite, his mother complained about her back trouble and guaranteed that his father didn't write because You know him only too well, but he thought about him all the time, You're the only son we have, no feeling at all about the Revolution, only when it was very close at hand and his wife's family began a hurried transfer of funds to Germany and Switzerland, getting rid of companies right and left, wanting to make a deal for the bank, when he noticed a touch of affliction in their faces and he stared at them perplexed, questioning, without understanding, until his father-in-law called him aside into his study, turned off the television, turned his back to the mahogany cabinet by the bar and the ice cubes in his glass were like castanets in his hand, pointing to one of the easy chairs in the library full of encyclopedias and hunting prints, leaned his fat and inoffensive little trunk over him, and whispered in the usual strangled, loony voice, We've had it now with the Communists in.

"I say yes, the whores, when Major Ribeiro finishes his speech," the lieutenant colonel whispered into his glass of strawberry brandy. "A night on the town like the ones in Mozambique with a pistol pointed at the doorman's balls. If anyone from outside comes in here you know what you'll get."

Leaning on his elbow, beside the curved and naked body of Inês, the second lieutenant heard the ton-heavy steps of the caretaker on the gravel underneath the window, the swishing spin of the sprinklers on the lawn, the whispers and conversation of the maids in the pantry, the breathing, calm now, peaceful, of the girl (Relax, love, nobody's coming until seven o'clock), the immeasurably distant roar of the sea, which he could imagine dying with successive sobs on the beach that would be cleansed, still without its April umbrellas, watched over by the cardboard buzzards that were gulls. Just like in Sesimbra, Captain, with Ilda, the bank secretary who worked with me, a skinny single girl, quiet and pimply, who lived in Algueirão with her uncle and aunt, on Saturdays she'd go to Caparica with a swarm of girl friends, also single and quiet, in a single and quiet Citroën, she would buy cheap movie magazines and platonically fall in love with the successive single and quiet economists who never noticed her, her protruding ribs, her pectoral lollipops, her sucked-in cheeks, her strict widow's weeds. Just like in Sesimbra, in the hotel, Captain, where from time to time we'd spend a couple of days hiding out under the pretext of business trips, contacts with foreigners, complicated and urgent deals. Ilda would get undressed in the bathroom and make me close my eyes until she pulled the sheet up to the level of her long nose of a toucan with a cold, hiding her nonexistent breasts and the acne blooming on her neck. Her sharp knees and elbows ruined my legs, her lunar worm body stuck disagreeably to mine, she swallowed pills for her thyroid and her little bird's heart was beating rapidly against my chest. We would stroll on the sand, chat with our hands in our pockets, I would talk to her about what was bothering me, the bad scenes with Inês, the damned job, the shitty little episodes of everyday life, I thought If I'd married you you'd have me stuck in three floors in Cacém, without any telephone, decorated with cheap knickknacks and bargain furniture, you'd read the paper in bed, use powdered deodorants, my parents would feel themselves on the same wave length as their daughter-in-law and I would go around, pleased as punch as they say, with it all. My wife never asked me anything when I got home, Captain, she would glide a fleeting kiss over my forehead and run off to fix her makeup while I slouched in the living-room chair, Why not go whoring? why not celebrate the ten years of war? the funny-looking painter in the building opposite appeared on the balcony with a palette in his hand, a lawn mower was buzzing persistently in the depths of his memory, the voices of kitchen maids, echoes, the caretaker's boots on the gravel in the garden, there's the Carcavelos house, going up to the rusty gate, the enormous red eyes of the dogs leaping in the dark, there's the usual dull chatter, the usual dull lethargy, Down Tiger, down Miss, down Bruce, the big heads with tongues hanging out coming through the open car door, Inês going up the steps of the porch, ringing the bell, disappearing into the lighted vestibule with her daughter hanging around her neck, if whores can help us forget, hell, let's go whoring, and me quiet by the car, Captain, fists sunk in my pockets, understanding for the first time the dark, impenetrable, almost solid hopeless silence of my father.

"My uncle's wife was hit by a stroke the year we got back from the war," the soldier explained, weaving from the wine, lighting the communications officer's cigarette with a precarious match. "We were all settled at the table and just then, boom, we heard a hell of a noise in the kitchen."

The uncle, in a sleeveless undershirt, his face engulfed in the glass chandelier that tinkled like microscopic chimes if someone opened the window, shook and snorted at the head of the table in his usual three-hundred-sixty-degree rage, directed at the obvious and collective swinishness of the world, Odete was gathering the skin and bones of the fish onto the edge of her plate with her knife in order to leave a half moon of space for the fruit rinds, the unmatching furniture was breathing softly in the shadows, blown on by the lace lungs of the curtains, on the sideboard the mother's picture lighted up and went dark, Aunt Isaura was scrubbing pots in the kitchen, where the light spread out, crawling along the uneven floorboards in a kind of milky phosphorescence, and all of a sudden, Captain, all that could be heard was the sound of the water from the faucet, there would have been a hollow, rhythmical silence, except for the old man and the wheezing of his asthma and the hoarseness of his limitless fury, and then a pan fell onto the stone floor, a coffeepot rolled irregularly along, limping on one wing, almost to my feet, and just like in movie avalanches, Captain, first the threat of a clump of earth bouncing onto the stones, then another clump, threads of sand, and finally a huge and onrushing curtain of earth tumbling downhill in a storm of dust, out came the sound of cans, tin, aluminum crashing against the tiles, a pile of chinaware breaking on the floor, my uncle got loose from his chair with a kick, threw his napkin ring onto the oilcloth table cover, a glass of wine tipped over and the liquid was dripping onto the wooden floor, Odete followed him without letting go of her knife, and they came upon Dona Isaura stretched out in the kitchen, her eyes open, her nose on the stone floor, coated with bile, or mucus, or spittle, or a touch of vomit, surrounded by pots and pans.

"I never saw so much junk around one person, Captain," the soldier said, cleaning the wax out of his ear with the extinguished match. "She'd lost her slippers, her fat knees were shaking, peeping through the door to the backyard where pale cabbages could be seen, the chestnut sky, one or two indistinct trees, hens scratching the matted ground with their claws."

"What are you waiting for, go get a taxi," his uncle roared at him in anguish, looking for his jacket among the dish towels hanging from a strip of wood studded with rusty nails bent into hooks of a sort: You don't even know what you're doing, the soldier thought, all you need to do next is look for your shoes in the silverware drawer.

He ran to the corner of Gomes Freire, where an uninterrupted flow of traffic was going up and down the avenue lowing like reindeer, and he stationed himself beside the hunchbacked newsman, who looked at him with surprise, making desperate signals with his arms at the passing cars. He imagined the concentration of neighbor women called by a strange tropism of funereal sunflowers, his uncle and Odete dragging the limp body over the raffia mat at the entranceway, the urgency of waiting to see him arrive in a tumult of diesel gut-grumbling, Aunt Isaura drooling, her eyes closed, wallowing on a seat, but no car obeyed his waving, vans and trolley cars streamed past him clanging, rolling and shaking, clusters of people in a hurry, as indifferent as mannequins, tried in vain to cross the street, a policeman with his hands behind his back stood puffed up under the majestic plumes of his cap in front of the brushes and bottles of a drugstore. Farther on a character in a beret who was watching him with hate surreptitiously grabbed a cab and smiled at him, satisfied there inside, a vengeful, triumphal little laugh: He fucked me up, he stationed himself on the other corner and he screwed me. He threw him an inoffensive gesture with his arm when the car was already far enough away so the man in the beret wouldn't see him, and a fat fellow with a briefcase, in an attendant's uniform, pounding his foot on the edge of the curb, gave off a sympathetic curse as he got into a bus whose automatic door opened with a long metallic groan. If they tore down the buildings that wound down toward Martim Moniz you'd be able to see the Tagus, the soldier thought, the tugs, the cranes, the rusty freighters alongside the dark stones of the piers, and suddenly he got the dizzy feeling of the alienation of the world with respect to him, Just let me catch something, kick the bucket, tomorrow dawns and I'm dead, the gang, keeping out of it, go right on walking to work, the hours roll around on clocks, maternity wards fill up with screaming pregnant women, and me dead, it's not fair, dead like the war dead in their quartermaster coffins in the depot, sealed with lead by the carpenter's welding torch, waiting in a stack in a corner, transported to Lourenço Marques and there, from warehouses crammed with uniforms, seeds, bundles of tobacco, dust, loaded onto the old ship that sailed off in the direction of Lisbon on foggy mornings, whistling a lament.

"Have you ever looked at dead people's eyes, Captain?" the communications officer asked, knocking over a toothpick holder with his sleeve. "They don't reflect anything, friend, they're burned-out bulbs, glass globes incapable of light: just imagine what it's like to be that way all of a sudden, stretched out flat on your back, hands on your belly, with a cloth over your face like furniture in summertime. I don't know about other people, but if I start thinking about that I'll go nuts."

"At my wife's funeral," the lieutenant colonel announced, stifling a yawn with his hand, "twenty people at most came. At most. At the very most. The priest galloped through his Latin the whole time, and at the end he came over to ask my forgiveness for speeding up the ceremony because he had eight baptisms right after and the doctor had advised him to keep his tension down. In any case, you can rest assured, he guaranteed me, patting me on the back, with the prayers I gave her she went straight to Heaven, like on a spool: she might have got a quick look at Purgatory from a distance, but no flame singed her, I can swear to you."

If they keep on drinking, and they're *going* to keep on drinking, I thought, observing their unkempt hair, their faces oily with sweat, their lax limbs weak, moving over the tablecloth like inert elephant trunks, in just a little while they'll be crawling under the table on all fours, vomiting the remains of the meat over each other, stumbling, belching, shoving each other in a blind butting of billy goats, rolling on the filthy carpet on the floor amidst grunting, meowing, scratching, and snoring. A taxi finally stopped, the soldier fought for it determinedly against two persistent schoolgirls, one of them cross-eyed, who flitted about like pullets, he finally got the front door open (the sign NO SMOKING leaped up at his eyes like a hot coal in a grill), sitting down on the green plastic seat beside the meter that was vibrating and ticking, telling him to go to the Rua da Alameda in a dull, exhausted voice.

"It's to take a sick woman to the hospital," he explained to the driver, a mistrustful insect who was wearily twisting in his seat, guarding the cigar box with his money in it under his thin little legs. "My uncle's wife had a stroke just now."

"Is she still alive, at least?" the man asked, putting the cab into gear, hugging the steering wheel, a different low gear that produced the sound of zinc against zinc, a spoon having a hard time scraping the lumps in a pot. "If you're trying to get out of an autopsy, let me tell you right now that I'm not driving a hearse."

"That was the way it always was, of course, Captain, it was always that way," the second lieutenant said, shrugging his shoulders resignedly. "The kid whining on and on and me driving without saying anything, with a hell of an urge to smash the two of them, hit them over the head with the crank, see the blood pour out of the holes in their ears. So mad I wasn't even looking at the road in front of me."

At the entrance to the alley there was already a flurry of neighbor women in aprons, street vendors, customers from a nearby bar, cigarettes in their mouths, dispensing warnings and advice. Guys in yellow jackets were unloading crates from a soft-drink truck and offering detailed explanations to a man in a hat who was mopping his brow with a handkerchief. The widows in the windows, heads leaning out, were chirping like parakeets. And all along the alley, in tiny little open spaces where one could see flowers, narrow gates, clotheslines, very old men in slippers were slowly rocking in wicker chairs.

The taxi stopped with its motor running while the driver unwrapped a cough drop from a mess of paper, the people silently moved apart, opening up a kind of passageway to the door of the house, the widows fell silent for a moment, staring at him with the sharp bird-varnish of their little eyes, the sweating man respectfully took off his hat, a strand of hair over his baldness, and the uncle appeared in the vestibule, in a jacket with the collar turned up over his undershirt, buttoning up his fly, teetering on his summer shoes.

"We had a hell of a time getting her into the cab," the soldier said, opening and closing the matchbox with a half-gassy smile: "You can't imagine, Captain, how much that old woman weighed. And then there was always an arm, a leg, her head sticking out, it was a hell of a mess getting her onto the seat: if the guys from the soft-drink truck hadn't helped we'd still be there."

But the whole family did in fact fit, he and Odete in back with the patient, moistening the back of her neck with a damp cloth, and the owner of the Ilídio Movers in front, suspenders hanging down along his baggy pants, beside the driver, who started up with a jerk, almost running over the boy from the bar, who was relating the misfortune to two startled soldiers in minute detail. He turned around and through the window he could make out the alley that was disappearing into the darkness, while the boy, stationed in the middle of the street, outraged, gave them the finger with each hand.

"Is she alive?" the driver asked the uncle uneasily, touching the *figa* charm on his mirror as a precaution. "Because if she isn't, I'm going to lose the devil's own time at the hospital giving my name, showing the papers for the taxi, waving the permit in their faces, putting up with the cop at the entrance."

Dona Isaura, lying on top of us, was whistling like a cow in a coma, and she would sprawl out from time to time, piercing my belly with the sharp point of her elbow. Odete, squeezed in between her mother and the door, kicked against one gigantic buttock in order to breathe, and the sick woman's gray head wobbled back and forth like a porcelain Chinese figurine parallel to the taxi floor.

"Alive?" the uncle exclaimed with a whack of protest on his chest that brought on an immediate coughing attack. "We're just taking her to the hospital to get her pee analyzed, understand? It's a mania we've got here in the neighborhood."

Gomes Freire again, the Campo de Santana, surrounded by a wall of asymmetrical, disjointed buildings, the statue, the Grecian pomp of the Faculty of Medicine with its unbeautiful columns, a stretch of ramp, a tunnel, a man in uniform who ordered us to stop and came over to the car with the measured step of a cardinal or an ostrich. The uncle tried to roll down the window, but the loose handle came off in his hand, and he finally leaned over the skinny driver, who looked like a martyr in a religious painting, ready to accept any misfortune, like someone preparing to dive.

"We've got the dying wife of the commander of the Guard here," the asthmatic whispered as he would a state secret. "We came in civilian clothes because it's a secret: the family doesn't want any news to get out."

Astonished and respectful, the ostrich took a step back, Odete managed to get loose from the buttock with a stronger pull, and the body slid down like a partially filled wineskin until it got stuck between the two seats with a weak grunt of protest. The one in uniform let them pass with the nod of an accomplice, the taxi leaped again as if the driver's heels had sprouted spurs, the uncle, irate, threw the handle out the window (What kind of a shitty wagon did you get for us, damn it?) without the driver, who was no doubt waiting for one of us to stab him in the back, daring the slightest complaint and on the left and on the right the small unpainted buildings of laboratories and infirmaries appeared, maids in checkered robes, small ramps with sclerotic flowers trying in vain to survive in pots without water. A pile of debris rose up against an unfinished wall, yellow dogs were nosing carefully in the bouquet of the gutters.

"Is it much farther?" the soldier asked the narrow and motionless shoulders of the driver. "The patient is squashing our feet."

Ambulances with blue lights on their roofs, more taxis, firemen carrying canvas stretchers, and there: a wide door, a somber haze where shadows moved about, a cluster of funereal people at the entrance: You get to wait five or six hours, Captain, it's enough time for a man to be able to die nice and slow.

"Five or six hours, up yours," the uncle roared, snorting furiously with the muddy intonation of a lungless person with only two dubious porgy gills. "You just watch me take care of this in a flash, friend: if she's to be signed in, sign her in, if she's to go home, give us the prescription and let's go. I don't take much stock in doctors' talk, though, damn their hides. And if a cab isn't here when I get back my boy will shave your beard with a few good socks, we've already got your license number memorized."

They parked behind a police Volkswagen with three solemn-looking fish-faced types leaning back on the false leather seats, and we began a useless attempt to deliver Dona Isaura: her body, stuck between the seats, resisted, her gray bun fell apart in a rain of hairpins and dirty hanks of hair that hung down in front of her face like stiff barbed wire. Night was falling all around them, scattered bulbs were lighting up in windows with broken and loose blinds, the blotchy outlines of the buildings took on an unknown thickness, the faces of the people blended into an inseparable amalgam of features. Odete got one of her mother's arms loose (fingers like sausages, purple nails, a thin wedding ring squeezing her flesh), an adolescent fireman pushed solicitously on the other side, one of the policemen was piping oaths of eternal love to the corporal of the squad into the microphone, creatures with limbs in casts were stumbling toward the exit steps, escorted by the sorrow of their families.

"How about a little help, guys," the uncle ordered a pair of individuals in white (white jackets, white pants, white shoes) who crossed paths with him on their way to the trash bin. "Or do you want to read in the paper tomorrow, damn it, that patients are dying right by the door of São José Hospital?"

The ambulance people lent their stretcher (a complicated affair, quite heavy, with wheels and straps), and they finally managed to extract the old woman's stubborn body from the taxi by pounding it, one foot with a shoe on, the other one without, the varicose veins in her thighs showing, her twisted mouth sighing unrhythmical croaks, an ammoniac stench emanating from her clothes. Odete, squatting, fixed her mother's blouse (you sexy devil, the soldier thought immediately), the miser covered the old woman with a blanket that had lumps of vomit and blood on it, and Dona Isaura immediately took on the worthy look of a real dying woman, lying on the canvas like a downed elephant, her right eye open and her left one closed in a skeet-shooting squint.

"Just the taxicab part was like a bullfight, you can't imagine," the soldier said, pushing away the drunken barracks corporal, who was trying hard to sit on his lap. "More people gathered to watch than at a sideshow, each one pulling on a piece of flesh or clothing where he happened to be, it's a miracle they didn't tear the poor woman into shreds right there. And my uncle directing the operation, hollering, encouraging some, bawling out others, insulting the rest, as if he were taking charge of, you can imagine, the removal of a grand piano from a very small room, come on, come on, a hair to the left, hold it, turn her completely over, that's it. If the old woman hadn't had an attack before, she certainly would have had a stroke right there with all those maneuvers, all that hollering, all that pandemonium, the crutches and legs in casts grew in number, taking in the scene from close by."

The uncle immediately conscripted the taxi driver to carry the stretcher along with someone who happened to be there, taken by surprise, by chance

(Me? me? me?), from the group of most interested onlookers (Instead of standing there like a boob, come help the poor woman at least) and he burst martially through the emergency entrance of the hospital followed by the fireman, Odete, and my stupefied surprise. Night had fallen outside, the small buildings of the wards had disappeared completely into the darkness, the outline of the trees was no longer visible against the starless sky, imprecise shapes floated behind the blinds from time to time (and the soldier imagined sleepwalking cirrhotics floating along in striped pajamas through extremely long and terrifying empty corridors), the motor of an electrical generator was shaking somewhere, like in Africa, Captain, in case the lights went out, remember? and we'd bump along, feeling our way from bunk to bunk, looking for our beds or the barracks door, in our shorts, to pee in the damp night air, sniffed over by the miserable dogs on the post.

"Hospitals remind me of the PIDE infirmary in 1973," the communications officer said, "with guys locked up and howling with pain the whole night through."

A kind of frozen cloister, unreal with neon, patients everywhere, covered with bandages, sitting on the floor, staring at us from the distant haughtiness of suffering, litters, covers, and beds crowded together in an indescribable confusion, urinals, catheters, cotton, squatting Gypsy tribes eating in silence, clerks carrying papers, drunks snoring on long wooden benches, moans, whimpers, sighs, vomiting attacks, two stone archways bearing the signs MEN and WOMEN, leading to the dankness of the toilets where the accumulated feces looked like reefs at low tide, and inside, bustling around empty cane couches, doctors with stethoscopes hanging from their necks like wine stewards, examining, with learned frowns, X-rays of bones held up against dull, lighted surfaces. They laid the old woman down, her mouth more twisted than ever, next to the washbasin where the Hippocrats were gathered in cabalistic consultations, and they, decked out in long papal albs, looked at us as if we were completely transparent standing there in front of them, as if we really didn't exist, putting their enormous serious heads together to study the round swelling of a knee or the antediluvian angle of a maxillary, discussing fractures and tumors in calm voices. (And the soft, dull light, he thought, impregnated the room with the atmosphere of a main altar after a massacre of Christians, supplied with incense by a basin full of dressings yellowed by pus.)

"Of course, they didn't pay the least bit of attention to us, Captain," the soldier said, finally putting the box of matches away in his pants pocket. "They shit on us, of course. My uncle was roaring with rage, touching, gentle all of a sudden, this one and the other one's back, the driver and the fireman ended up sneaking out, Odete sat down on a corner of the bench, chin in her hands, next to a girl who was whining and pointing to her ankle which was out of joint. Finally a sullen character broke away quietly from the council, ordered Take the blanket off her, to the wall behind him he muttered The mania for blankets these people have, he gave some weary hammer taps on the old woman's arms and legs, stuck a pin into the schistoid soles of her feet, looked into her eyes with a tiny light, wrote quickly on a prescription pad, tore a sheet off with a rapid motion, stood up, brushing invisible crumbs from his coat, gave the piece of paper to my uncle, said Stroke, there aren't any empty beds here, take her home, one of these pills with each meal. The uncle opened his mouth (to protest? to plead? to invoke some hypothetical protector, a recommendation, an important warning, an express order, Take her in, from the commander of the Guard?), but the doctor, already far off, having forgotten, unattainable, was touching the belly of a wailing little girl stretched out like a codfish, and he ended up halfway there, stupefied and mute, having a hard time getting his asthmatic breathing through his tight snook throat." The soldier went out alone in search of transportation, passing cautiously over a melancholy hell of people lying and whimpering, and the almost solid texture of the night that had completely devoured buildings, trees, the city, in which he sensed a bitter threat of rain, riddled by the colored lights of the ambulance and the headlights of the patients' cars, made him feel like a mole digging his subterranean path through the muddy labyrinth of darkness. The hint of an advertising sign floated lightly in the distance, and there was no lighted window anywhere.

"I painted a picture like that," the painter said, naked, on his back in bed, surrounded by shelves of African sculptures, stroking the soldier's forearm. "It's called *Black on Black* and I sold it to the Bulgarian embassy."

How old is this guy? the soldier thought with distaste, looking at the other's fat and unappealing body, his parrot feet with twisted toes down below, the roots of his ankles that broadened upward, little by little, into his plump thighs lying on the sheet and into the grayish clump of dying hair of his pubes, smothering a prick in its blond-dyed tangle, and then the protruding stomach, the woman's breasts, the round absence of muscles. The black man was asleep, rolled up on a mat on the floor, among canvases, easels, bottles of turpentine, stains, and cans of paint, exhaling in his sleep through the toothless-octopus opening of his thick lips incomprehensible phrases in French. The soldier could barely distinguish his own clothing mingled in the half-shadows with the clothes of the other two, the moving-company coveralls, the socks, the stained, dirty shoes, the painter's bracelets tinkled when he touched him, he had several necklaces around his throat, and the melting mascara ran down along the wrinkles of his cheeks. The three usual bills were waiting, folded, on the night table, held down by the photograph of an apocalyptic weight lifter (To my darling pussycat from his Kid Gomes, who always remembers him) framed in a metal square. I pick up my money, the soldier thought, sneaking a look at the time on the artist's wristwatch, and I beat it away from the Rua da Mãe d'Água as fast as I can: maybe there's still time to pick her up at school, maybe we can gab a little bit on the bus home.

The communications officer shook his head in amazement, disappointed, disheartened, moving the lighted end of his cigarette around the rim of his saucer:

"Me fighting for the Revolution like a numbskull and all of you worried about getting yourselves out the best you could."

He finally managed to get a taxi, out of which a man all doubled over had climbed, clutching his stomach, escorted by two friends or acolytes or colleagues or brothers-in-law, holding him up under the armpits. The driver was counting his change, leaning over the hazy pale light of the dashboard: a strong fellow, ill tempered, with pockmarks and boil scars on his neck. They brought the old woman out on the firemen's stretcher, bumping into legs, trunks, heads, soft bellies along the way, which protested just like the belly-button horns in talking dolls, the doctors went on studying X-rays and smoking with dreary exasperation, balloons of serum floated in the air, patients with tubes in their noses slid from one side to the other in big beds on wheels, and at the door they had to lift Odete's mother up to put her into the cab, her chin bouncing from shoulder to shoulder, while the pockmarked man, blind to their efforts, and whose violent, nasty disposition was several points above the uncle's, was gunning the motor with acid impatience. The electrical generator shut down and you could make out the chirp of crickets and the croaking of frogs, stopping and starting up again in an untranslatable and endless Morse code.

"She got sick at the worst time, Captain," the soldier said, scratching his head with his long, mistreated fingers. "The business was growing, we'd rented a second warehouse with even more rats, cockroaches, and cobwebs and crates than the first one, we'd taken on people, were making payments on a new van. We were working twelve and thirteen hours a day, the old man was turning the office accounts over to me, little by little, and right then and there, just imagine, she had to decide to have a stroke."

The painter turned over in bed to kiss his neck (Three bills is almost the price of that dress you always gobble up with your eyes in the shop window by the school), the springs in the bed, equally decrepit, creaked wildly on their frame, the chandelier on the ceiling lighted up his red hair (I'll let him do his thing, I'll let him have a little fun and then I'll leave), the driver settled in his seat, pointed with his gigantic thumb (he was missing two fingers on that hand) at the door of the hospital, and announced in a voice like a boulder rolling down a cliff:

"There's no doctor who isn't an absolute son of a bitch."

"Living out her infancy on the back seat of the Fiat," the second lieutenant said bitterly, "how else would you expect the kid to turn out, Captain?"

They piled into the cab, holding the old woman who was weaving, without any strength, spraying watery vomit on them, and my shoulders rubbed yours from time to time, my knees were up against yours on the curves, your skirt, your hip rubbed against mine, and the streets of the Lisbon night unfolded one after the other like the tubes of a spyglass, cardboard façades, spooky entranceways, deserted squares, a halo of blood around the uneven outline of tile roofs. The cold that came before the dawn was shaving their backs, puncturing the thickness of their clothing with hundreds of icy stilettoes.

"I don't want to have anything to do with those bastards," the driver was explaining to the uncle, giving great slaps to the steering wheel. "If anyone gets sick at home, my friend, we take care of him with tea from the herbalist."

It'll be daylight soon, the soldier thought, the shadows are evaporating, making the buildings emerge from the darkness just like reefs at low tide, tin alarm clocks gush out like arteries brutally cut by a sudden knife, the light of the lamp slowly goes out and an imprecise gray, a fog of fatigue, a sudden and colorless clarity, enlarges the branches, uncovers forgotten details under the eaves, transforms signboards into words that shout and burn if we listen to them. Odete's wrinkled face, up against the glass, was observing the fading of the streetlights without any curiosity, the shine of the trolley tracks, the men with yellow rubber vests who were washing the street with the help of long hoses which doubled over and rolled interminably along the pavement, run over by tires in disjointed little goose waddles. It'll be daylight in a minute, the soldier thought, lighting a cigarette, the trees in the jungle are moving softly, the radio corporal, squatting down, rolls up the canvas of the tent, the leaves give off a transparent sweat of dampness, the black man is going to wake up on his mat and make coffee for the three of us, the painter, awake, runs over my body again with the soft, slow hands of a woman.

"And might we know where the gentleman's been sleeping?" the uncle asked, already dressed, razor in hand, half of his chin shaved, half waiting to be shaved, confronting him in the vestibule with an ominous smile under the lather.

"Herbalist's tea and that's all there is to it," the driver repeated, peremptory and convinced. "Sunflower seeds, peanut butter, medicinal food, damn it, pure food."

And with a roar, as if he were turning a tremendous secret loose to the four winds:

"I'm not afraid to say it, my friend, I'm a nature freak, I don't go along with pills."

"You don't have to believe it, Captain," the communications officer admitted in a confidential tone, because the chairs were being moved about and speeches were being prepared in back, "but during all that time, until I was arrested, she was just about my only contact, so that I began to wonder if the Organization, Olavo, Baldy, the whole crew, still existed. I worked, I went to the movies on Mondays and Thursdays, I was bored to death, I shut myself up in my room on Sundays to read poorly printed pamphlets in small type by Engels and Marx."

"Better off than we'd ever been or ever would be," the soldier said. "The catch is that the golden age of Ilídio Movers was a sun that didn't shine too long, with the old woman's attack my uncle's drive disappeared, he hollered a lot less, he'd be lost in his thoughts, he stopped nagging the workers, using the spray for his asthma, shouting. The trash in the office disappeared, the flower vases multiplied on the shelves while the paperwork got less, the bookkeeper began to come in during the morning to help him run the business, to correct invoices, to bark orders at the drivers, to set up loads, to answer the telephone, an ageless woman with glasses who looked at them all with the air of a princess on her property and shut herself up with the old man in the glass cubicle, all smiles, all pleasantries, all caresses, giving little tugs, ridiculously daring, to my uncle's cheeks. And the business he'd handed over to me, Captain, from that moment on, nowhere to be seen: meaning that I'd lost out with her illness, too, don't you think?"

"With doctors," the driver explained in the voiceless voice of four in the morning plagued by bronchitis and tobacco, "you come in and go out just like that, on a stretcher. Look, they killed a goddaughter of mine with meningitis in Estefânia, and, to top it off, they cut her up for an autopsy like a chicken in a restaurant kitchen, they weighed her liver on their butcher's scale, sawed open her head to take out her brain: they like to do bad things to people, chum, if they can't destroy a guy they get no rest. Take linden tea now, hah, did you ever see anyone bleed out of the ass from drinking it?"

They stopped at the door of the house (the sides of the taxi brushed against the empty dawn garbage cans and the narrow berm along the sidewalk), the uncle took a roll of bills out of his pants pocket and leafed through them in a miserly way, his forefinger wet from his lower lip, Odete's mother gave off a machine-gun burst of farts from the cabbage-leaf layers of her skirts (She can't even hold her shit anymore, poor thing, the driver commented, distressed: he opened the glove compartment, from inside, amid the rags and detritus, he exhumed a plastic bag of little black grains, Have her swallow a spoonful and tell me about the results later), the uncle tucked the bag into his pocket, grumbling indistinct thanks, they dragged the old woman along the outside corridor up to her bed, tripping over rugs and bumping into furniture, the pockmarked man followed behind, going on at length with enthusiastic herbalist propaganda, Dona Isaura's twisted mouth, which the absence of her false teeth pleated into concentric soft flaps, was spitting out vague and disconnected phrases at them, the wounded brightness of the morning was enlarging the size of the misfortune and that of the cupboards, what an incredibly big body on the sheets, Captain, what legs, what eyelashes, what an enormous nose, I looked at Odete and I thought Today I'm going to get you, today I'm going to pop you with my prick, fine manners were over along with politeness and from here on this is all going to be stud-horse stuff, Uncle Ilídio was shaving in the little round mirror in his bedroom, which magnified on one side and didn't on the other, and where the dawn was reflected in a

thin, sad circle, and he said, after the driver had left, Hang in here, I'm going
to the drugstore to fill the doctor's prescription, he went out with shaving
cream sticking to his ear and one suspender down, beside the bed there was a
fringed rug with a design of deer, the kind that are sold from door to door by
supple and equivocal Gypsies, a kind of Jehovah's Witnesses of smuggling,
the soldier thought, Odete, leaning against the window, her profile lighted as
in bridal photographs, was looking out at the absence of voices on the street,
the complete lack of breathing of steps in the dying night and me, to myself,
Hurry up before the old man gets back loaded with packages, smelling of
cotton, disinfectant, ether, lift up her skirt, pull down her panties, go in, a
half dozen little sighs, that's that, she hurriedly straightening her hair and
clothes with her distressed arms, the sick woman was moving her legs under
the crocheted spread, the zipper of his fly up, the satisfied, victorious smile,
discreetly triumphant, It's raining, Odete said from the window and I
thought, scratching my balls through my pocket, I can't do it, I can't do it, I
can't do it, I raise my head from the deer on the rug and I come upon Uncle
Ilídio's angry disapproving shoes hard by my nose, the eternally greasy laces
undone, the rain's tiny teeth were biting the roofs carnivorously, dripping
onto the floorboards through a hole in the roof, I'm going to get a plastic
container, a coffeepot, a pan, the neighborhood dog barked as if he were in
the room behind the chest, present there with frightened blue eyes, between them, I've got the urge to kiss you, damn it all, and I can't manage it,
I've got the urge to touch you and I can't manage it, I've got the urge to
gobble you and I can't manage it, a picture of Dona Isaura and the uncle, arm
in arm, was looking at him with disapproval from the oval doily on the night
table next to a glass of water covered with a cardboard circle, the place
smelled musty, of closeness, sweat, a lack of soap, Look how it's raining,
Odete said to him, and the soldier went over to the window and to your
straight body leaning against the curtains, explain arithmetic to me, teach me
French, make me feel less weary in this dawn that's bleeding like a wound on
the head. What about the Revolution? the communications officer asked,
irritated, did you all shit on the Revolution? Maybe she likes women, the
soldier thought, maybe I've made a bad impression on her, the girl's wet hair
hung down over her forehead like dull algae, he leaned out, lifted his elbow
to touch her shoulder, the buildings sunken in mist were slowly rising from
the pavement, and that color of the sky, Captain, the anxious cold of morning, and when I was about to hug her, imagine my luck, Uncle Ilídio putting
his key in the door, going down the hall like a rhinoceros on the attack and
appearing in front of us, eyes lost, silent, and defeated, the packages of
medicine piled up against his chest like Christmas presents.

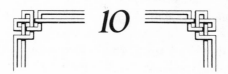

## 10

THE orderly knocked on the door with the two usual soft raps (Why not one, or three, or a volley of kicks, curses, punches?), he raised his eyebrows from the papers, said Come in, and the china figurine of the corporal stood out against the light of the threshold, effeminate and thin, in the same irritating equivocal posture as always. A sergeant went by along the gallery, carrying the enormous double chin of his belly in front of him: How long, the lieutenant colonel thought, will I have to put up with these types?

"Captain Mendes, Commander," the orderly announced in a thin oboe voice, the complicity of which displeased him.

"I received them once, I received them twice, I received them three times," he told me in his disillusioned and aged tone, with weary words and phrases full of wrinkles and fatigue, "and there was no way I could decide. I was afraid of losing the shit I'd earned over all those years, you see, the command post, the promotions, the certainty of not dying of hunger, the nice little life I'd become accustomed to, without any complications, crap, or annoyances."

Captain Mendes took a few steps forward on the carpet and stood there waiting: Me, fifteen, twenty years ago, the lieutenant colonel thought, me, an idealist and an imbecile with some hopes still: don't worry, you're going to lose your illusions any day now, my dear simpleton, don't worry, pretty soon you'll turn into a dead turd like me. He got up and before going over to the window showed the other man a bundle of photocopied papers written in a cramped conspiratorial hand, sprinkled with corrections:

"What's the meaning of this chatter, Captain?"

The wind was raising yellow earth from the parade ground, flowerbeds, the cement barracks buildings, shaped like the base of a pyramid or a parallelepiped, toy jeeps rolling along beside the trees: Twenty years ago I would have been involved in this for sure, I believed in people, in comrades, in the possibility of change: not now, son, there's no adventure that can convince me anymore. Captain Mendes, ugly, tall, ungainly, looked the papers over quickly:

"A study of our situation as compared to that of the militia, Commander," he explained in an apparently opaque, superficial tone. "And, also, a half-dozen critical comments on the situation in the country and overseas in general: as you can see, almost all the officers have signed it."

The trees, the wall, and beyond the wall the city: crummy little houses, the Vila Franca traffic, factories, the incipient beginnings of the province.

"Two hundred odd names already, Commander," Captain Mendes announced, standing in the middle of the room, looking around with his little bloodshot octopus eyes. "We expect that the ones who haven't signed will do so soon."

"In short, it's a question of a rebellion, pure and simple," the lieutenant colonel answered, stroking the breasts, thighs, buttocks, legs of the cleaning woman, whose face exploded with a mute, carnivorous smile, while the major in the gallery broke the obedient silence of a soldier on fatigue duty with roars: Your hands call me, your knees grab me, your mouth asks for me. "I suppose," he added, thinking I'm not going to be able to penetrate her, "that this has been circulating freely around here."

I was against my daughter getting me another maid, I stood up to her carping, her warnings, her threats, I demanded that the concierge continue working for me, every week at the infirmary they give me a vitamin injection, a spiral of my blood climbs up, dark, in the syringe. Twenty years ago, goddamn it, I was shaking with malaria in India, the force of the rain was knocking the flimsy boards off the porch roof, geckoes skated lazily along the ceiling. Captain Mendes placed the pile of papers on the desk with a gesture whose delicacy surprised him, like that of certain mechanical arms manipulating insignificant metal fragments:

"Active solidarity in every unit in the country, Commander. Majors and captains, but a lot of lieutenant colonels, too, and junior officers."

Ash gray sky, ash gray buildings, ash gray streets, ash gray mist: a shitty winter, a dull spring, raindrops bouncing in the air: even the green of the branches looked gray to him that morning, the pale, listless faces, heavy and dispirited movements. He tore the manifesto up and tossed it into the wicker basket underneath the flags:

"I only hope you've got a clear idea of what you're getting into," he stated without conviction while he lay down on top of the cleaning woman, thinking I hope to God I make it this time, I hope to God I'll be able to. The luminous hands on the alarm clock were outstretched, his wife's picture, near him, gave him encouragement, she was quite serious under her faultless hairdo. After the rain the suffocating humidity, so he settled down on what was left of the porch, fanning himself with a piece of newspaper. The white uniform hanging from a wire hook, dripping and stiff, on the wall.

"May I say something, Commander?" Captain Mendes asked, advancing one rough lobster step on the carpet. Doors were slamming, the washing machine was sobbing away at its work, the remaining rooms in the house were advancing and retreating to the rhythm of the irregular beats of his heart, the cleaning woman's smile was gradually changing into a continuous guttural moan, her heels, scaly and hard, were squeezing his buttocks. He stood stock-still in the middle of the office, waiting: Twenty years ago would I have had the courage if they tempted me, would I have gone along with the others in a crazy thing like that? Mendes coughed to clear his throat, and he thrust out his crooked chest, his ribs little bumps under his shirt, in his direction. An artery in his neck was softly throbbing between two tendons:

"We would like to know if we can count on your express support, Commander": We've still got that at least, a respectful look, a sense of rank, by God. "As you can see, a lot of high-ranking officers have already signed, your joining us could never be considered an isolated position." And the lilacs at dusk, distant thunder, movement in the underbrush, the girl who would come through the back door, slipping in silently, just like an enormous caterpillar, anointed with creams and oils, into the bed. The lieutenant colonel turned his back on the captain to look distractedly at the showcase with the unit's standards and trophies. Up above the photograph of the admiral in white was flabbergasted, with an expression of absolute stupidity.

"The puzzle hasn't been put together completely, as I see it some pieces are still missing," the lieutenant colonel replied prudently, hugging the woman's energetic body like a fetus. "And later on, confess to me, where is all this going to lead?"

"A fluff revolution, Captain," the communications officer lamented, his eyeglasses, foggy, were taking on the changes of a sea mist without the fish of his eyes inside, "a real fluff revolution. A petit-bourgeois coup controlled by the revisionists in Moscow, who'd infiltrated the Army with the siren song of social democracy. What we were after was a real popular uprising led by the peasants, by the working class, by oppressed people in general, the path toward absolute socialism."

A large, slippery caterpillar who never spoke, eternally wrapped in a long green cloth, almost inert dark limbs, an absence of breasts, a face without cheeks, the flint or bulging wooden knots or convex metal of her eyes sparkling on the pillowcase. And not a cry, not a sigh, not a caress, an enigmatic and passive indifference. She must be an old woman today, the lieutenant colonel thought, an old woman stationed at the door of her mud hut in the village, with a part down the middle of her hair, a spot on her forehead, and gray hair falling down loose, watching the rain furiously dissolving sheds and palm trees.

"Everything is written there, Commander," Captain Mendes argued, jiggling his long legs, "I frankly don't know what additional facts you need to lend us your support. We're sick of being scapegoats for the politicians, we'd like to contribute to a peaceful and constructive solution to the problem. As one military man to another, Commander, you certainly must agree that there's no way out of the overseas war. General Spínola, for example, advocates a federative solution."

She didn't even speak in the morning when I left her in the tumbledown house beneath a huge thunderclap, where invisible hands were torturing the clouds as if they were bread dough. The trees were agitated with tics, the brimstone light was shedding quick copper-colored flashes over the few unmatched pieces of furniture. Not a word, not a sound, her damp fingers extended, an absolute lack of expression on her face, the jeep heaving hesitantly in the windstorm, battered by loose leaves, trash, gusts of water, splashes of mud brought up by the wheels, just like spit. Through the body, the words, the face, the tunic of Captain Mendes, he saw the house growing smaller in the distance, the restless river, the anguish of the woods, his own heart, microscopic, vibrating. Now you're watching the rain fall in some village or other, cookstoves fashioned out of three piles of stones over a small cone of hot coals and twisted logs, you died of fever during the last monsoon, and you're fattening up the earth with the transparent cartilage of your bones. The lieutenant colonel ran his afflicted hand over his hair:

"I'll let you know my decision at the opportune moment," he said, and opened the office door, and the cleaning woman encircled his neck with her avid arms: Such jelly eyes you've got, such a curve you've got in your ear. As you might imagine, a matter like this can't be resolved in a minute (Feeling myself ridiculous, you see, insulting myself inside, finding myself to be a fool of fools), there are all kinds of factors to take into consideration. (For example: should I marry the cleaning woman or shouldn't I, should I take her to a boutique so she could dress better.)

Captain Mendes moved a tin ashtray an inch or so, put it back in place, ran his distracted finger over a flat surface as if he were looking for dust, straightened the insignia on his shirt, touched the ribbons over his left pocket.

"We thought we could count on you, Commander," he confessed with a suddenly firm intonation, unexpected in that man whom one could call incomplete, anemic, put together from wire and stearin. "Tomorrow I'll tell my comrades we were mistaken."

And to the movies, the lieutenant colonel thought, on nights when nobody goes? He pictured himself on the concierge's arm, examining shop windows along the way, leisurely and attentive, discussing colors and prices, the posters for the coming movie, I know that actor, that actress, maybe there'll be time next week. A company appeared, marching along the parade ground, microscopic people, rifles on their shoulders and in camouflage dress, swinging their arms in rhythm.

"No, you weren't mistaken," the lieutenant colonel said very quickly, lifting the maid's skirt in order to touch her on the tight skin of her stomach. (That's it, he thought, that's exactly it, no definitive yes or no, vague diplomatic paths that lead through the different hypotheses.) "The question is, you understand, that it's a matter of a problem too important to be faced with a light heart, to let ourselves be dragged along by emotional decisions that have cost us so much in the past. I especially don't want you people to think I'm closing the door on you. (Touching your breasts, hefting them in my hand, moving it down along the smooth beach of your stomach to the strange damp and final hedgehog between your legs, the living, salty creature of your pubes.) The evaluation you gentlemen have made of the military situation is mine exactly (And why not get married, really, seat her at your table in the officers' mess, in lace bra and panties, in the midst of the stupefied officers, order her to roll her enormous, provocative, amber-colored mammaries from one side to the other, singing a strange bird trill through her overly painted lips, with her legs crossed?), we can, at best, disagree on the solutions arrived at: self-determination, federation, independence, have you thought, perhaps, about how far that can go? General Spínola can say whatever he likes because he's up there on top, there's no one who dares meddle with him, if he were to turn cartwheels on the Rossio the General Staff would all clap: we're dancing to a different tune, no one is knocking himself out to make life easy for us, we won't miss any competition for promotion. (Now circulating among the tables, exaggeratedly swinging her hips, throwing him kisses, shaking her long hair dyed carrot red, smoking through an interminable silver-plated holder.) A punishment assignment in Guinea is the least one would get, and therefore the necessity of studying the matter deeply, weighing the pros and cons, the advantages and disadvantages, the possible consequences for us: I'm an old fox, my friend, I've learned that you pay dearly for playing around."

Captain Mendes tapping lightly on the backs of the easy chairs (or on the spherical buttocks of the cleaning woman?), impatiently moving his trunk back and forth (You're mounting her, you devil, you're enjoying yourself on her body), snuffled, wiping the sides of his nose with his forefinger and thumb. But no lump under his shorts, the absence of any projection of his penis by his fly, no little damp spot of sperm: impotent too? inhibited? the shame of fornicating in public, of seeing himself getting off, lowing like an ox, in front of me?

"If the commander will excuse me," he interrupted in a perfectly normal voice (Can it be that sex doesn't interest him? the lieutenant colonel wondered, intrigued. A eunuch without any hormones, an invert the best hypothesis?), "your objections are groundless because it's people like us who hold operational power, who really command the battalions. A general's stars, you know quite well, aren't worth a damn, we can do whatever we want in the country. Guinea, Angola, and Mozambique agree with us, a reluctant regiment or two will join in at the last minute as a matter of self-defense. We've got the Army, the Air Force, the Special Forces, and a good part of the Navy. (He masturbates all by himself in the bathroom, huddled over the toilet, the lieutenant colonel decided, he's scared to hell of women.) I can guarantee, Commander, that if you don't accept, the battalion will go ahead if it becomes necessary to go ahead, under the orders of the highest ranking officer, this one or that one, and your career, promotions, and reserve status, whatever, will slip through your fingers, farther and farther away."

The companies were forming laboriously on the parade ground now, the men clutching their rifles by the barrel, the bugler, beside the major, was softly blowing his instrument, while the cleaning woman, on all fours on the mattress in the filtered afternoon light, was vainly trying to excite him with her mouth, looking backward at the uselessness of her efforts: a soft, sad little thing, an insignificant little trunk, a piece of cylindrical skin, worthless. Why sometimes yes and sometimes no, tricky, why that anguished, inexplicable, intermittent functioning? Age, he thought, it's got to be age, forty-eight years are unforgiving. Captain Mendes withdrew toward the door with his strange lobster steps.

"I'll pass on your words to my comrades, Commander," he guaranteed with an absurd solemnity, as if they were both wearing swords at their waists, Aramis mustaches, plumed hats and huge-buckled belts, touching now a terribly ugly bronze figure of a black man squatting with a bowl on his unequal knees: These filthy bastards do like their heroic moments, the lieutenant colonel thought, vaguely watching the breakup of the battalion, just like a large body exploding, their glorious tirades, theatrical answers, useless phrases. Captain Mendes, feeling the abundance of the cleaning woman, who had sat down on his lap and was rubbing her unbelievable carrot-colored cups against his chin, raised his mouth to the ceiling as if he were going to howl and exclaimed in a pathetic monotone In a matter of hours I shall inform the conspirators of Your Highness's idea; oh, royal Arthur, will it be too late for thee to change thine intentions?

The ship began to leave Goa behind on an ocher-colored morning (ocher sky, ocher earth, ocher trees, ocher lightning, ocher people), the rain-wet face was dissolving into chestnut-colored pieces of features, the rocking of the deck pushed us against each other like broken clay fragments, the Indian girl wrapped in her cloth whirled from palm tree to palm tree, my house in India was slowly dying, with its uneven dressers that the water drove against and was destroying.

"This is how it stands," the lieutenant colonel said, his hands behind his back, looking at the deserted parade grounds, the miserable end of the March afternoon: "Give them the message that within two or three days at most I'll give them my final answer."

"You were playing two horses at the same time, Colonel," the soldier laughed, poking him in the kidneys with a jolly elbow. "The colonel was going to come out on top no matter which way it went."

A fellow was going on at the head of the table, constantly interrupted by applause, shouts, laughter, and over the telephone I ordered my car, to take me home. The orderly at attention, quartermasters, sergeants flitting about, the sharp sound of typewriters in the main office, the flat smell of sweat in the corridors, the long, graceless steps with the rigid majesty of a church, the main gate, the well-known route, the usual neighborhood, the firehouse, home. Captain Mendes kept appearing to him at every moment, crossing over the carpet with his crustacean movements, addressing him with pent-up vehemence: The government is rotten, Commander, we've got all the conditions for seizing power: and then a swift, meteoric promotion to general, chief of the General Staff or the National Guard or the Police, four stars on his shoulders with no effort, no risk, no deceit, without knocking himself out for the manifesto, decorations, women, banquets, an embassy, foreign missions, the hypocritical and obsequious adulation of politicians, a guy in uniform by his door, the respect of his neighbors.

"But the government might not have fallen, right?" the soldier said. The maneuver could lose its synchronization, units not advised at the proper time, the government resisting through the PIDE and loyal garrisons, the undecided falling to the other side and there he'd be in with compulsory reserve status, retirement, a hollow ending with no benefits or advantages, his daughter abusing him for his incurable simplemindedness, his hopeless stupidity. A hell of a decision, Colonel, what a shitty choice.

A mechanic with a screwdriver was working on the elevators in the vestibule (only an ad from the *Reader's Digest* in the mailbox), shouting instructions to some buddy above, entangled no doubt in a complex mechanism of pulleys, and he walked up, across the landings in the dark, to the apartment (Tell your comrades, please, about my fatigue, tell them I'm suffering from the endless fear of losing the little I've won), opened the door, rolled up the blinds in the living room, dropped onto the sofa and the dead woman didn't come and the cleaning woman didn't come, no glass of water on a tray, no tranquilizer, no hand on his shoulder, only the heavy hostility of familiar objects (Nothing here ever liked me) and the immense silence of the rooms in shadows. He grabbed the little Bakelite animal of a telephone and in order not to feel alone he dialed the tireless number that gave the time, a female voice excitedly swallowing time, and then another one at random, which kept ringing in the emptiness of an unknown apartment, with no voice answering him. Whom did it belong to? the lieutenant colonel thought, having forgotten the series of numbers in the meantime. He imagined an old crippled woman, her hair in disorder, in an armchair with a polka-dot cover, a piece of oilcloth over her knees. He put the receiver onto its metal cradle, turned on the faucet in the bathroom, took off his tie, removed his tunic, and massaged the Play-Doh of his cheeks, chin, forehead, neck in the warm flow of water: do things with his hands, move his arms, don't stop, keep busy. And, after all, I haven't got any political ideas, fuck it, I haven't got the slightest interest in spending months in the Fort, having my picture in the papers, giving my daughter grounds to pester me, drive me crazy, come see me with her dope of a husband at visiting hours, solemn, regretful, obediently recriminative.

"When the Caldas coup failed," the communications officer said, starting on another drink of brandy, "damned if I wouldn't have sworn then and there that it was all over; the PIDE on its toes, the government redoubling its vigilance, widespread shifts of units, it was finished. Besides that, Dália disappeared and after a few days, one morning they came for me at home."

"Father, I swear, you haven't got the least bit of shame," his daughter shouted at him, hands on her hips, at the door of the cell, examining with disgust the bed, the porcelain toilet bowl, the washbasin, the chair, the detective story open on the table. "No sooner do I turn my back than you come out with some jackass thing for sure."

"If you'd joined up with us," Captain Mendes murmured sorrowfully, comforting the little man sitting on the edge of the mattress, "you wouldn't be in the sad position you find yourself in today, Commander."

"When I got divorced he was five years old, you people don't know what it cost me to raise him," an old woman with astute eyes and a mole on her nose bleated, sitting most naturally right there on her own coffin. "I took in sewing for almost twenty years so I could send him to school, a cousin of mine, a brigadier general, advised me Put him in the Army and you can relax, I'll fix things up to help the boy, he was in India, he was in Africa, but he never got too far, you see, he married a stenographer from the neighborhood here, a nice girl, but not too well-off, I tried to bring him to his senses, but no use, I threatened him, but no use, and the results (the threadbare sleeve of her dress swept the dusty atmosphere of the room) can be seen here."

"Mother," the lieutenant colonel pleaded, drying himself with the towel, "don't go away, Mother."

"I read about it in the Caldas paper," the soldier said, applauding the speech by the guy in back, "and I didn't believe even half of it. Garbage thrown into the people's eyes so they could raise prices, I thought. Do you remember, Captain, what a pound of sugar cost in those days?"

"Two or three more speeches," the second lieutenant snorted, having some more Cartaxo wine, "and we'll sneak out unseen, crawling if we have to. I'll bet none of them will notice."

The lieutenant colonel looked unsuccessfully at the bathtub, the tiles, the terry-cloth robe behind the door: his mother had disappeared in a disenchanted flash, and yet he got the strange impression, putting down the plastic lid of the toilet, that he was sealing up an irrevocable tomb with a simple gesture of his hand: I killed you, I drowned you in the yellow, foamy water of the toilet bowl, now you're heading down to the river through a complicated geometry of pipes. Sometimes, as a boy, he'd find a gentleman of some years in the sitting room, smelling of hair tonic and shaving lotion, holding a bouquet of flowers wrapped in cellophane against his chest as if he were exhibiting a trophy. His mother, all smiles, would chat with the both of them, handing out soft, equal pats, flirting with phrases that infuriated him (I really can't decide yet which of the two of you I like better), she would lay him down and when she leaned over to kiss him, the lieutenant colonel would feel himself submerged in an unknown and strong perfume, which brought on a vague and shapeless feeling of desire in him. And a few minutes afterward, he would hear from the bedroom next to his laughing, creaking, tender protests, the old gentleman's afflicted cough, pecking kisses, a whispering of grave, sharp words, panting, long gulps, and finally an enormous convex silence filled with the fatigue of two bodies.

He went back to the living room and from the balcony, hands in his pockets, was studying the demolition of the building across the way when Captain Mendes's voice rang out with unexpected energy at the back of his neck, coming from a corner table loaded with encyclopedias and portraits:

"Do you refuse to contribute to bringing down the dictatorship then, Commander?"

The gentlemen succeeded each other, less well dressed and pleasant each time, the darkened wallpaper was peeling, the flush toilet went for weeks with the pull chain out of order, the water running tumultuously in his sleep until something began to happen almost daily, a man quite a bit younger than his mother, with a small mustache and a light-colored suit, all duded up, named Gonçalves, would shamelessly feel her in front of me, lick her throat, hold her around the waist looking for her breasts, and, starting with the following week, the chinaware, the silver, the pictures inexplicably began to disappear gradually, followed by the best sofa, the bedroom dresser, the large mirror, and the sewing machine. His mother began to work by hand until Mr. Gonçalves disintegrated in turn, giving way to a very old gentleman to whom his mother would complain, weeping, and he would console her by giving her chaste little pats on the shoulder with a hand full of old-age liver spots, and after that two silent men with cigarette butts behind their ears brought the machine back, a few more modest but gaudier pieces of furniture, shining with varnish, took the place of the former pieces, pictures made from candy box lids, with Styrofoam frames hung from the walls, the man, who was a retired supply sergeant, piled the table high with egg cakes for dessert, his fingers caught up in the strings of the packages, gave him lead soldiers and wooden warplanes, and touted the Army to him. In no time you'll be a general, boy, but what he got in the end was jungle and malaria and rain, the misery of isolated mess halls, daily death, insomnia, anxiety. The man, for the benefit of the neighbor women, was a cousin and a brigadier general, but nobody believed the fib, he told me, splitting toothpicks on the tablecloth, everybody in the neighborhood knew perfectly well, you understand, that it was a question of her lover, his mother frequently dyed her hair blond in an attempt to hide her age, she wore dresses that were more and more flashy and cheap, gaudy necklaces around her low-cut neckline, rings with large glass stones, she imitated movie actresses and darkened her eyelashes, and, one Sunday afternoon, the brigadier general cousin was reading the newspaper on the couch and suddenly he looked at them without saying anything, opened his mouth, some thin froth came down over his chin, and he was still, halted on the accident news page, with the shapeless bored expression with which they buried him two days later after a wake turned upside down by the appearance of his legitimate family, children, grandchildren, nieces and nephews, a girl who insulted the two of us in front of the flowers and the corpse as we clung to each other there, wrapped in discreet grief.

The hands flapped like birds as they applauded the speech, a red-faced officer was roaring with enthusiasm, the speaker, confused, was drinking a glass of white wine to overcome his emotion, a kind of assault tank, prickly with teeth, was tenaciously biting the walls of the building under demolition, giving it zebra stripes of scratches and cracks, the lieutenant colonel stretched out on the sofa and put out his arms, pushing ghosts away.

"A typical petit-bourgeois attitude," the communications officer whispered to me. "The fear of losing privileges that stops them from acting."

"Fifteen minutes more," the lieutenant colonel promised the second lieutenant, "and we'll get out of here. The movies, church, whores, whatever you want."

The elevator workers must have finished their job because he heard a slight hiss of cables on the landing, voices, the sound of the metal screens of the doors that contracted and expanded like gills in the silence. Why aren't you coming today, why aren't you coming in here, apron and feather duster in your hand, lifting your fishhook of a hand up quickly for the money on top of the refrigerator in the kitchen?

"You should have joined the revolt, of course," the old gentleman opened, the newspaper on his knees and the hardened snail drool crystallized on the wall of his chin. "The main qualities of a military man worth his salt are the proper use of the means at his disposal and a quick decision."

His mother, whistling with plumes and bracelets, half her face hidden behind an immense fan, boldly touched Captain Mendes on the chest with the tip of her glove.

"We'd be enchanted, take my word for it, if you could visit us tonight," she invited in a soft whisper, showing the beginning of her knees. "You were such a great help to my boy, poor thing, in the dilemma he's found himself in."

"Dilemma, Captain," the soldier scoffed, leaping like a kangaroo for the brandy bottles. "The problem our lieutenant colonel had, if you'll excuse my boldness, was he was so scared he couldn't stand on his pins."

"I lost out on a spot as director general because of him," his son-in-law accused. "The secretary of state knows I married his daughter, I'm lucky to have stayed on at the Ministry marking time."

"He says he didn't understand too well what was fluttering around in the air," the second lieutenant explained, making a face. "Do you believe he didn't know anything, Captain?"

"I felt hemmed in," the lieutenant colonel protested, pouring himself some gin at the small living-room bar all agleam with glass, "Mendes's intimations left me positively in a bind. Deep down I didn't care who was in power as long as they promoted me at the proper time, gave me assignments I liked, guaranteed my retirement."

"And the month after Caldas," the communications officer said beaming, "the real coup, the hymns, the applause, all those people setting us free. Even if the PIDE had tried, there wasn't any time to screw things up: some interrogations, a few whacks, that was all."

Another combat veteran began to talk after having extracted a thick bundle of folded papers from his pocket, opposite his mother's apartment the assault tank had already completely destroyed one wall and its tracks skidded down onto the dusty rubble of the ruins, while the motor gave off thick, dark smoke from underneath the driver's seat. A group of onlookers was curiously following the operation, square chunks of sky could be seen through the exploded windows, the lieutenant colonel rested his glass on the arm of the sofa and at that instant the telephone rang: My daughter, my brother-in-law, you? Some beggars were scavenging in the ruins, a man in a cap was signaling to the tractor, farther off a siren rose and fell at the firehouse.

"Yes?" he asked into the mouthpiece with a tired sigh, with the disagreeable taste of alcohol at the top of his throat. It had stopped raining and the ship was moving faster now in the muddy waters, not rolling, leaving India behind, the ruins of India, the palm trees of India, your dead silence, on the road to nothing. Sitting on her coffin, in the middle of the living room, his mother was looking him over disdainfully.

"Commander?" a small uninflected voice said to him in the earpiece. "This is Captain Rodrigues, the officer of the day. I'm sorry to bother you at home (Why don't you get it up?), but just now a column of the Caldas da Rainha

Regiment has left headed toward Lisbon, and they're calling for the support of all units to help them bring down the government. On the other hand (get it up, just a mouthful, normally I'm competent with one or two gins), instructions to the contrary also came in from the Ministry of Defense. The majority of the personnel are at the post, the officers' opinions are divided, and in view of what's going on, I'd like you, Commander sir, to give me orders as to what I should do."

His mother, very old now, was carefully combing her long white hair with the pathetic, trembling theatrical gestures she had used in the past, she was decorating herself with pins, bracelets, necklaces, pantagruelian fake rings, lace, she lifted her skirt to show her skinny legs clad in spectacular black and blue stockings decorated with transparent rosettes that hung down loose over her bones, and the lieutenant colonel thought for a moment he could make out the gray threads of her pubes, whose lips were closed, protruding like those of a pouting mouth. A second wall fell noisily in a cloud of tiles and the old gentlemen came out behind her, smiling, chatting, offering each other cigarettes, patting their knees, looking at him with compassion, wafting their censers of toilet water over his head with deep reprobation. The lieutenant colonel slowly sipped another swallow of gin, gaining time:

"Isn't Major Ferreira there?"

"I went down the steps of the prison in the midst of applause and cheers," the communications officer said, "and I couldn't believe what was happening, Captain. The fall of fascism, you see, had become a kind of dream for me, an illusory goal."

"And that's another reason I'm calling you, Commander," the little voice went on in its determined flat intonation. "Major Ferreira is asleep in his office after such a dose of brandy, you'll excuse my saying so, that he's in no way capable of making any decision. And we couldn't wake him up even with a dozen buckets of water over his head: right now you can't count on him for anything. And Major Osório isn't here. Both the Ministry of Defense and the Caldas regiment want an immediate answer. What shall we tell them, Commander?"

The old gentlemen were delicately shaking the powder from their shoulders, his mother, installed on the coffin, was pinning a gigantic, almost obscene cloth rose by her low-cut neckline, whose petals were just like superimposed tongues. The man with the little mustache, standing behind her, was massaging her shoulders and smiling. The end of the March afternoon was tearing the houses apart. The concierge put the key in the door, sneezed in the vestibule, and appeared on the threshold in her slippers.

"Hello, sweetheart."

"Tell them," the lieutenant colonel answered, leaning over to the second lieutenant with a wink, "that we'll go on to the whores in just a little while."

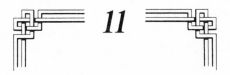

## 11

"IN the morning?" the second lieutenant, his mind on the cabaret, asked the communications officer, who was putting talcum powder on his outstretched arm to absorb a stain on his sleeve. "You were arrested in the morning? How did that happen?"

"And I was going to stay in Africa, Captain, get a job, set myself up in business, marry a mulatto girl," the soldier told me, opening his eyes yellowed from wine wide. "Just look at the mess I got myself out of."

I'm not sure how it all happened, the communications officer thought, it's not clear in my memory, there are gaps in what I can remember, like a group photograph without faces, or an unfinished drawing, or those games with numbered dots that you have to connect in order to make a figure, a profile, a landscape. He was sleeping and the doorbell suddenly invaded his dreams, it spread out in a monotonous stain, tireless, strident, his head rose up to the ceiling, he heard Esmeralda cough in the next room, the dog in the apartment upstairs barking continually, he opened his eyes and a blue mist filled the curtains, the houses seemed to be sketched out in rough charcoal crayon, the bulbs in the streetlights flickered like the flame of a kerosene lamp, Esmeralda stumbled down the hall protesting and all the while that fishhook of sound torturing him, preventing him from touching his cheek to his pillow for a bit of silence, making him seek a new position between the sheets which would protect him from the raging persecution of the bell that was chasing him all over the mattress to stop him from falling asleep. He became aware that his aunt was also getting up (the slats on the bedsprings were moaning), he heard distant male voices, as if diffracted by a wave of water, the servant's sharp complaints, the little cars on the ferris wheel hanging down and swaying on their iron hooks in an emptiness of clouds, clear down to the smallest detail, like the branches of a tree at dusk. I've got to get into my bathrobe, the communications officer thought, I've got to see what it's all about, but his weak legs wouldn't obey him, his muscles wouldn't obey him, his trunk, boneless, wouldn't obey him, like during attacks in Mozambique, remember? when mortar shells would begin to fall inside the stockade, opening up just like great big flowers of light in the surprise of the night, and we wrapped up in blankets in our bunks, without the strength to crawl from the barracks to the shelter, thinking Fuck the shrapnel, fuck the war, a little while before I'd taken two tranquilizers, leave me alone, goddamn it, I need my sleep.

"The regiment didn't join in the Caldas coup," the lieutenant colonel explained, "and Captain Mendes thanked me a few days later for my tacit support of the ideals of the Movement. Except that on the 25th of April, just to change things, I got completely swamped in foolishness."

"See what fear can do, Captain?" the soldier whispered, indicating the old man with his mouth. "At least our lieutenant colonel was a hero for a week."

The voices came closer, treading quickly and harshly along the hallway (It's my chest they're crushing, the communications officer thought, twisting in his bed, they're walking over my back), his aunt and Esmeralda were whimpering timid, ill-defined complaints in the rear, the door burst open, striking the bookcase violently, quick fingers sought the light switch on the wall, the moon, like the narrow tip of a fingernail painted ash gray, evaporated, the same as the spiral filaments of the streetlights in the immobile numbness of the morning, the communications officer sat up, feeling for his slippers with his feet, and at that moment the chandelier on the ceiling blinded him, the furniture rose brutally out of the shadows, two men came over to him (I've had it), Esmeralda in her nightgown, her rosary around her wrist, was chirping vainly by the door of the room, his aunt, her hair down, leaning on her cane, was looking at them with eyes huge from sleeplessness or surprise, Put on some pants and a jacket, boy, a bald-headed guy ordered, older, rising as if by miracle over the shoulders of the other two, Don't be frightened, ladies, this is a joke, a prank, we're buddies of his, a tranquilizing calm, a friendly, respectful smile, and his face suddenly tense, suddenly authoritarian, Are we or aren't we your friends, old pal? the old women were fluttering about the room like hens, bumping into the desk, knocking over the wastebasket, flattening up against the closet door handles, the two guys were going through the shelves, throwing books onto the floor, rummaging through drawers, pulling posters off the walls, Starting revolutions, mister hero, the leader commented, getting his smile back, plotting like a Guevara, you son of a gun, a paternal pat on the back, a pamphlet shoved into a bag, Your nephew, my good lady, is a busy young fellow and I like busy young fellows, the wooden animals on the carousel were emerging out of the morning mist with their painted eyelashes, the giraffe was quietly staring at him from the windowsill, the photographs of the performers of the Pit of Death were waving on the canvas, the communications officer picked up his pants and the jacket he had worn the night before from the chair, got into them without taking his pajamas off, trying to get his confused head working, Who turned me in, how long will I be able to take it, what will I end up confessing to, the two guys were sorting through handbills, examining his letters, looking for false bottoms in the furniture, the bald-headed guy, persuasive, kept on calming his aunt and Esmeralda, For the love of God, take it easy, a few silly questions and you'll have him back by the middle of the afternoon, and meanwhile more Marx, more Engels, more Lenin into the bag, handbills, cheap little books, magazines, communiqués, photocopies, How would Olavo act in a mess like this? the communications officer thought, still dizzy with sleep, looking at the disorder in the room, one bag, two bags, three plastic bags of revolution, tied up with a string in the claws of the police, the streetlights had gone out, dying slowly, the buildings, day-time ones now, had the same incredulous pale tone as the old women, a kiss for one, a hug for the other, See how well-mannered the kid is, the head man said to his colleagues as if he were dressing them down, as if he were calling their attention to him so they could take him as an example, and there was the long hallway strewn with religious traffic signals, the sacred varnish of the eyes of saints, the sinking down the stairs with the old women up above, terribly afflicted, flapping their wings on their railing roost, the cold of the street, the car by the door, up against the alley wall, We even brought along a chauffeur for you, my fine fellow, the shove that propelled him pell-mell onto the seat, a slamming of doors, a smell of tobacco, the dull dawn traffic lights, deserted streets, a glimpse of branches, shop windows that quickly fell behind, the steady, balanced engine roar, and then a wide entranceway, the bald-headed man telling him, Get out there, Robespierre, tongs that grabbed him, clutched him, squeezed his armpits, an office worker nodding at a desk with a telephone, three or four quiet guys leaning against the wall in the corners of the hall, stairs, a kind of glass birdcage with chairs, a cubicle without any furniture, Get in there, a key turning, a window that was too high up, the uniformly snot-colored sky, I've had it.

"Do you remember the PIDE in Africa, Captain, their little brown barracks that looked like a bunker smack up against the old slave quarters, their agents who would come to mess with us sometimes, weapons on their belts, drinking coffee with us?" the communications officer asked me, scraping a splotch off the lens of his glasses. Without his usual glass mask he lost his normal look of a math teacher, his features took on an unsuspected innocence, a childlike smile hovered over them like the air bubble in a carpenter's level, between the lipless mouth and the round, unformed nose of a baby. (And you into politics, I thought in disbelief, you conspiring, running risks, hiding papers, writing on walls, moved by a wearisome ideal that became crystallized in a spray of words making up an imperative order.) I was in the habit of taking a walk in the village in the afternoon, followed by the watchful silence of the dogs, imitating the movements of my own shadow, which stretched out before my feet like a rug, I would go up to those fellows' quarters and inevitably one or the other would be leaning against the wall, or playing with puppies, or chatting with truck drivers, and he would invite me in, offering me some whiskey, brandy, or some drink or other, in a room lined with large maps marked with little plastic flags, with a crucifix or a portrait of the admiral president on the wall. I was getting to know the dungeons, the huge radio sets, picking up information, learning details about the agents, finding out a little about how that strange machinery functioned, and on one occasion, just imagine, the subinspector, the sweatiest guy I've ever known, constantly mopping his brow with the tattooed arm of a carnival wrestler, showed me the interrogation room, where a black man, his knees on a very thin iron bar that he was gripping with his fingers, was receiving a rain of blows from the jailer, who was kicking him and whipping him with a lash made of small metal rings, grunting like a shot-putter with every blow. The prisoner's swollen lips were bleeding, his nostrils had been reduced to a kind of fleshy pomegranate, deep, slanting welts covered his sides, and I suddenly thought, terrified, Maybe they fucking well know who I am, maybe they know all about the Organization, the pamphlets, Olavo, the bomb plans, what if when the black man drops, in a pile of disjointed muscles, they put me there and start up again, but hell, Captain, there came the customary lemonade or whiskey, the friendly handshakes that the agents exchanged with us, the usual daily complaints about the isolation, the malaria, the rashes, the heat, the meager pay, the war, playing checkers until suppertime, I lost all the games because in my head a guy was endlessly beating and kicking me, because the dungeon doors were closing behind me, because questions were coming from all the little flags on the maps, Who are your contacts? What's your system for messages? What's the address of the printer who's turning out all this shit against the minister? and me on my knees, with an iron rod under my fingers, thinking, terrified, With the first blow they'll break all my teeth, crack my jaw, what will the pain of a crushed humerus be like?

He remained in the cell for hours on end, first standing, then squatting, leaning against the door, and finally sitting on the filthy cobblestone floor, gathering his thoughts, preparing answers, inventing excuses, while he calculated the approximate time by the color of the sky in the rectangle of the opening by the ceiling, the thick butcher paper of morning, the small drifting clouds of midday, the shadow of doves of afternoon, When are they going to call me? When are they going to feed me? he felt like urinating and there was no place to do it, not a single crack, small hole, grating, he used all his strength to hold back the piss in his bladder, a suspicion of doves gave way to the tenuous dark colors of dusk, less than fifty or a hundred yards away people were coming home from work and here I am, streetcar, newspaper, dinner, whole families hating one another at the table, the old women whispering their tenth rosary at least, staggering along the hallway, kneeling down at their prie-dieus, afflicted, ever so concerned, tireless, the aunt was attempting to converse in shouts on the telephone with a relative who was a director general, who, according to her fantasy had powerful friends with the police, the ferris wheel was slowly beginning to turn, the animals on the figure-eight carousel were appearing and disappearing in a din of music and laughter, the smell of chicken and fried sardines was fluttering along in a compact mass down the block now, pitch black in the opening, one tiny star, and all of a sudden a neon lump, very faint, lighted up behind a dark plate in an inaccessible corner, I'm hungry and not a single sound of steps, of people, of breathing beside him, to eat, to chew on fish, chew on meat, chew on fruit, swallow a tureen of vegetable soup, under the guidance of the working class and its most lucid and courageous democratically elected elements we will build an egalitarian and socialist nation in Portugal, I don't know any Organization, don't know Olavo, don't know Dália, don't know Baldy, I have no idea what you're talking about, I'm an officer in the Army and I demand full recognition of my prerogatives, I know nothing about bombs, nothing about weapons, nothing about clandestine pamphlets, they're holding up dinner for me and it's so late, he turned his jacket collar up, squeezed his legs against his swollen belly, a true Communist must be strong in adversity, It's only a matter of time, she said, great things are being prepared for something soon, she said, Some green soup, for example, just a spoonful of green soup, and outside there, on the other side of the door, the sound of shoes, keys rattling, conversations in different voices, a peeping shout into the distance, his aunt, desperate in her deafness, was howling her laments into the telephone, the bolt was pulled back, a broad figure appeared against the light on the threshold, the bald man's heavy humor Shall we go have a little chat, Fidel? his bladder emptied like a punctured tire, getting out of control, torrential, furious, cataclysmic, comical, a hot jet of urine let go, uncontainable, running down his leg.

"Were you ever called in for an interrogation, Captain?" the communications officer asked me, carefully replacing the glasses on his nose with the slow movements of a jeweler, the alcohol making him even more pompous and slow. (And, I thought, How much has this guy swilled down, how drunk is he? A drunken ex-revolutionary talking about the Revolution is worse than a former priest saying bad things about the Vatican.) "I swear to you that

hellish things happened in that building in the Chiado. I went there on duty
after April 25th and everything looked small, harmless, crude to me, a kind of
house of horrors in daylight, wide open and ridiculous. Maybe that's what it
had already been before the coup, maybe it was only good to strike fear into
little innocent angels like me, but I can guarantee you that people went
through some pretty rough times there. I handled a whole lot of briefs for the
trials of agents, inspectors, informers, and guards, and I wondered, with the
fellows sitting all upset on the other side of my desk, How could I have been
scared of these guys, how was it possible that half a dozen idiots had terrified
me? You, Captain, for example, weren't you scared of them?"

The piss was running down his pant legs and hindered his movements,
making him run along with the short little steps required by a tight skirt
beside the bald-headed chief (A true Communist must be strong in adversity,
a true Communist must be strong in adversity, a true Communist must be
strong in adversity), first through a much longer corridor than the one at his
aunt's, except without any runner, prie-dieus, or burnt smell from the oil
lamps by the saints, with a sad little wick floating in a teacup, and then (The
stain on his pants was perfectly visible, what a drag) through offices full of
bustling types in shirt-sleeves, just like the ones of the night before, working
beneath round wall clocks that accompanied the admiral's picture. Ten
o'clock, the communications officer could see, I haven't eaten for almost a
whole day, they went up some half-hidden steps in the corner of a little room,
a current of air made it more laborious and difficult for him to make his way,
his sock, wet, was drooping down over his shoe, another cubicle, but this one
furnished with a table, a typewriter, paper, file folders, two or three unmatching chairs, a fan on the ceiling, a lighted bulb giving a yellow gleam to
the objects around, and the obtuse circus strongmen who had emptied his
bookcases and stolen his books, conversing with their primitive grunts. The
bald man settled down with a sigh before the keyboard, invited him to sit
down with an urbane and friendly gesture, opened his face into a huge, fierce
smile, placed a sheet of paper in the machine, and the soldier's curiosity
What was he like, Lieutenant, did they give you a heavy beating, Lieutenant? slowly rocking back and forth on an ebb tide of bottles. A common
individual, the communications officer thought, the look of a civil servant, a
bookkeeper, a department-store cashier, a grammar-school teacher, fifty,
sixty years old at most, freckles on his bald head and little lizard limbs, he
probably was taking medicine for an ulcer or prostate trouble or asthma,
hemorrhoids most likely, an anal fistula, migraines, angina, at home his wife
making life a frenzy for him. The Hottentots stationed themselves, hands in
their pockets, on both sides of my chair, the bald man consulted a file, jotting
down occasional notes on a pad in a laborious hand, clasped his hands in a
priestly blessing, smiled again with disquieting pleasantness, staring at him
with his tiny, sarcastic little eyes, and inquired in his usual mocking voice,
dragging out his words, So how is this revolution business going, comrade?

"My head was kidney-level with the other two, Captain," the communications officer said, crumbling a cork, "and I could smell their strong breath, sense the slightest ripple of their skin, the play of their muscles, and I was sweating in panic, I thought In just a little while they're going to start beating me, a closed fist came toward my chest, a rubber blackjack worked over my stomach, a true Communist is strong in adversity, but what would Lenin do in my place? the piss was evaporating on his legs, the bald man cracked his knuckles (a flat wedding ring and another ring with initials showing), bowed obsequiously, and reminded him, with ironic good manners, Let's get down to business, son.

"I don't know what you're talking about," the communications officer stammered with an insecure cough, hesitating out of mistrust, fear. (Hello? Hello? Hello? the aunt was chirping into the telephone, signaling Esmeralda for her to translate the silence, certainly full of saving explanations from her important relative.) "I'm an officer in the Army, I'm not interested in politics. You have no right to hold me here. I haven't eaten anything at all for twenty-four hours, this whole thing is absolutely illegal."

"Did you let him have it like that, Lieutenant?" the soldier asked with admiration, "did you throw those words into his face?"

The bald man stroked his cheek while his smile went all the way around his head to the back of his neck like the equator on a schoolroom globe: He looked like a proud father, Captain, ever so happy over his son's abilities:

"Very good," he approved enthusiastically, "your lesson right on the tip of your tongue the way I like it. Let's see if you can get a hundred on the test with the second question: what's your role in the Organization?"

The one on the left just patted his cheek with a sign of praise, then a blow: the chair fell in one direction, the communications officer in another. A sharp pain in his behind, I must have broken my coccyx with the fall, the bald-headed man turned his bored face to the policeman who had hit him.

"Good heavens, Edgar, what kind of behavior is that? Help Che Guevara up and remember that bad manners are a nasty thing."

They set the chair back up (Good boys, good boys, the bald man encouraged them), they picked me up under the armpits and dumped me onto the seat like a dead clown. His spine was throbbing, his neck had hit the baseboard of the room, his shoulders and his thighs were trembling (From lack of food? From the beating? From the fear?), Guevara is a little listless, give him some pats to liven him up, and those guys, Captain, worked over my body like you've never seen before, with the boss looking on, leaning on the desk, jolly as ever.

"We'll cut out in ten minutes," the second lieutenant whispered, looking at his watch. "Whose car are we taking?"

The bald man raised his fat arm, they stopped beating him, the new speech, monotonous, soft, not vehement, never-ending, the pages seemed to be piling up higher and higher, the lieutenant colonel was strategically measuring the distance between his seat and the door, Will we have to crawl out of here, and I thought, annoyed, Over leftovers, rinds, twisted beer-bottle caps, crumbs? a true Communist is strong in adversity, no one is touching me, no one is hurting me, the smile spread out, confidential, for him What's your role in the Organization, dear boy? and the black man's red eyes staring at us through the slits of his swollen lids, the broken lumps of his lips dilating and contracting like marine corollas, the boot of an agent, covered with hobnails, rose alongside his carotids with an anxious slowness, a dull sound and the man was rolling on the cement, his limbs in confusion, in a bundle of rags that slowly quieted down like the feathers of a slaughtered turkey.

"The Organization?" the communications officer asked, he'd lost his glasses in the fall and the surroundings had given way for him to a funnel of colored blotches where shapeless forms were spinning about, as if seen from behind a curtain of anemones. They transferred me to Caxias two days later, Captain, with a bunch of prisoners just as beaten up as I was, in just as bad shape as I was, bouncing and bumping with the rough ride, I didn't get to know anybody in jail, the people formed cliques and shit on me, nobody had any contact with me, no one came over to talk to me, and every so often, you can imagine, they would call me into the office for the usual questions, for the usual round of kicks and beatings.

"What about your comrades, Lieutenant," the soldier asked with indignation, suppressing a belch, "didn't they do anything for you during those weeks?"

"Now, a little wider awake, let's go back to the beginning, my treasure," the bald man ordered patiently. "What's your role in the Organization, how do those bunglers operate?"

No, the communications officer thought, nobody did anything, nobody helped him, they explained to me later that they were extremely careful about their actions, that the PIDE had planted stoolies everywhere, that they couldn't, shouldn't sacrifice the supreme interests of the working class by risking themselves in a bourgeois way for a single militant in danger, and maybe my lack of belief, my doubts began right there. Because for me, Captain, communism was just that, a complete solidarity, you see, a sharing that offered me what I didn't have at home, an ideal of complicity that would help me endure the loneliness of my life, which was visited only by the giraffes on the carousel spinning in a phosphorescent glow on the ceiling.

"We can make it crawling," the lieutenant colonel calculated, sluggish with wine, sketching a very complicated design on the paper tablecloth, "if none of us rises more than a foot from the floor and if we stay casual looking so as not to attract attention. Just in case, it would be best to keep watches, rings, chains, bracelets, any shiny objects in our pockets. You, Captain, let me have the keys to your car: I'll lead the way, I'll get in on the driver's side and unlock the doors. In eight minutes I want everybody in the vehicle, in uniform and with proper weapons, ready for the final attack. Is there anyone who wants any doubts cleared up?"

The communications officer suddenly became aware of something like grains of rice on his tongue: he spat them out into the palm of his hand and they were fragments of teeth, his saliva thick with blood, his nose completely anesthetized by the ether of the blows. The bald man, exceedingly polite, hastened to scold his colleagues (I don't know what kind of an education you people got in school that you don't know how to behave like normal individuals), offered to get him a glass of water, was quick to furnish the name of a dentist friend of his, A skillful young chap who can fix all that up for you, very cheap, in a matter of seconds. I was pressing my gums with my handkerchief, I'd lost one of my slippers and the naked foot, very white, was curled up like a strange worm on the stone floor: If I don't speak, these bastards here will still kill me, tear my arms off, crack open my head, leave my belly twisted like a figure eight, a true Communist is strong in adversity, he accepted the water, the bald man hurried out, came back immediately with an aluminum cup, and instead of giving it to him to drink, pretended to trip, unexpectedly, throwing the liquid into his face, and for the first time the policeman's affable smile twisted into an unforeseen and horrible expression of hate, his jaws grinding in fury, his eyes boring into him pitilessly, the muscles of his cheeks hardening, a sandpaper voice rasping in his ear Are you going to sing or not, you son of a bitch, If they start off in a very friendly way, Olavo had warned him, relax, because after a while they'll take off the sugarcoating and that's when their tune starts to get serious, they kept Emílio standing for six days and when his pins gave out on him they'd beat his back until he stood up again, people call it the statue treatment, but they've got other specialties on their bill of fare, the lieutenant colonel traced out a sketch of the path from that point at the table to the restaurant door and from the restaurant door to the car door, in a warrior's confidential whisper he gave the password: *cabaret*, countersign: *whores*, shook his subordinates' hands, wishing them good luck and, knocking over glasses, requested Don't forget to cover my retreat, shoot straight, and don't waste bullets, the water cooled his swollen face, he licked the circle of his lips in order to get more of that agreeable wetness into him, but they shut his mouth with the blow of an elbow, pulled his hair and he was soon on the floor again. You're going to sing every song there is, my lovely, the bald man prophesied in a faint voice now, going slowly off, they're going to call you the canary of Caxias pretty soon, he staggered back to his cell, shoved by a guard, spent hour after hour stretched out on the mattress, unable to move, sailing through a kind of sleep inhabited by painful tacks, waking and sleeping the way a ship appears and disappears in the lively September tides, he didn't touch his food, he received a supplementary beating for having soiled his drawers, he spent some days in the prison infirmary dreaming of the seats on the ferris wheel, a fat man in a lab coat gave him injections, the doctor listened to his heart without a word, examined him with a radioscope in a dark room illuminated by the bluish atmosphere of a miracle, and me thinking about giraffes on the carousel, Captain, me seeing them dance at an angle on the wall, ridden by people who were pointing at me and laughing, Olavo, Dália, Esmeralda, my mother with me as a child around her neck, in Odivelas, so many years later I felt her arms again, her breast, the smell of her neck, Three broken ribs, the doctor mumbled, but there must have been some kind of infection because I was pissing blood, so they gave me some pills to take every six hours when they remembered and they didn't remember very often, there were two other beds in the infirmary, in one a bearded guy, skin and bones, connected to an oxygen tank, unable to talk, one morning the man in the coat covered him with the sheet He died, in the other a boy whose legs and pelvis were fractured, he must have taken a heavy beating on the head because all the time, his eyes wide as a madman's, he kept singing the anthem of the Volunteer Firemen of Bombarral, the fat man in the coat told him to shut up and he, even louder, We fight earthquakes and fires, you could see the ocean through the windows, insignificant little ships, fringes of foam, What's this bastard doing here still? the doctor said, indignant, putting out his cigarette on the sole of his shoe, and they sent me back downstairs, I had a fever because I was shaking so much I could barely stand on my legs and right afterward that afternoon the bald man called for him, sat him down for the millionth time in the same chair, the same room, Confess right here and now your secret love to the inspector who adores you and who's been opening up to you, talk to me about that Organization, They think there are a lot of us, the communications officer thought, they really think we're a danger to the government, and (something that had never happened to him before) he felt like laughing, breaking up into belly laughs in front of those three cruel rhinoceroses who were insulting and beating him, felt like laughing, pissing blood, at the pompous phrases that solemnly placed him at clandestine meetings, a true Communist is strong in adversity, what really matters is that they've got some of my teeth, fucked up my health, made a fearful scarecrow out of me, I got into this game of cat and mouse without their asking me anything, automatically, as if by definition they were the torturers and I the guilty slave. In coming months things are going to happen that you never dreamed of, Dália had advised him in the subway station, this country is going to take a wild turn, pal. As a diversionary maneuver, the lieutenant colonel planned, one of you will go to the bathroom, attracting the attention of that corner of the table toward you, Fortunately you find this is a joke, fortunately you have a good opinion of me, the bald-headed man congratulated himself, I've always liked faggots with a sense of humor, he got up, came around the desk, took the brass knuckles out of his pocket, he said Hold him up, he's just back from the infirmary, he raised his arm and began to hit, his little round mouth grew and shrank, in search of air, like the scarlet fish in spherical childhood fishbowls, And nothing from your comrades, Lieutenant, the soldier was amazed, your comrades as silent and quiet as mice, but not just my comrades, he thought, the old women too, not a single letter, not a single book, not a single visit, everybody's lost interest in me, Marxism-Leninism-Maoism is a piece of shit, with the help of cups and glasses and ashtrays the lieutenant colonel explained the operation again, a dish of olives fell to the floor and the shiny little spheres, black and green, rolled off in different directions in oily silence, They're drunk, I thought, they're drunk beyond recall and now until the night's over I'm going to be the orderly for these sad, aging warriors, the two policemen grabbed him forcefully, he saw their white bony fingers on his shirt, the bald man put away the brass knuckles and started kicking, Watch out for the man's balls, Inspector, you'll kill him, but the other one, like one possessed, You think it's a joke, you whore bastard, you think it's a joke, you're going to find it a lot funnier when I really fuck you up, when I turn your bones into baby food, the communications officer felt, without any concern, that a piece of his stomach had broken off and was floating around on the liquid in his belly, Blood tastes sweet, he thought, amazed, his jaw in pieces, swallowing himself with a kind of pleasure, blood is sweet and thick like jelly, the second lieutenant, a cigarette in his mouth, immediately volunteered for the diversionary maneuver to the bathroom, You'll be decorated posthumously by the chief of the General Staff in person with the Order of Saint James of the Sword, the lieutenant colonel promised, the Motherland gives fitting reward to those sons who sacrifice themselves for her, the lights in the carnival all went on, the motorcycles in the Pit of Death accelerated with a hellish noise, the little cars in Bluebeard's Castle left, sidling off on a shadowy course between skulls and coffins, the giraffes on the carousel galloped on their turf of loosely placed planks, pushed by an enormous rack wheel, on the back streets with restaurants the smell of food, like an octopus, clung to one's hair, the Great Ferris Wheel began to turn, the metal seats swaying slightly, the second lieutenant got out of his chair and assumed a squatting position, ready for the signal from the lieutenant colonel, who had raised his arm with his eye on the clock, the bald man stepped back to give himself more drive, Watch out for his nuts, Inspector, the man can't take even another tickle now, Wait'll you see the big joke on you now, you son of a bitch, the other one said, lowering his bald head and burying it furiously in his stomach amidst shouts, laughter, talk, lights, music, and the swollen, soft body of the communications officer fell from up there, from one of the top seats, from where one could see the buildings, and the rooftops, and the advertising signs of the city, and it piled into a confused mixture of rags alongside Little Gypsy Dora's tent.

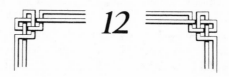

# 12

A SMALL sloping street in Intendente, parked cars, the lighted sign blinking Bar Club Madrid, Bar Club Madrid, Bar Club Madrid, next door to a shuttered closed grocery store, the doorman, the ever-present policemen, and the poster with photographs of women illuminated by a red bulb that spilled its misty blood over the sidewalk. The doorman took a little ticket book out of his pocket and said Two hundred escudos per head, while a policeman watched us silently under the visor of his cap. I parked the car between a small truck that smelled of chickens and an empty taxi, in front of a tiled building where old women on crutches received bank-clerk boarders and letters from nephews in Venezuela covered with stamps and postmarks, the sky, the color of the inside of a shoebox, pressed down on the roofs, the windows stared at me with the disquieting attention of torn-out eyes, and if I had put my ear to the scaly façades I most certainly would have heard dozens of faithful watchmen snoring in unison, in a chorus of T-shirts from the belly up. An out-of-tune bolero was seeping out of the fissures of the cabaret like smoke from a pot. The lieutenant colonel flashed his ID to the policeman who came to attention with a limp salute, and the doorman, surprised, discreetly buried the ticket book in his pocket: Most likely, I thought, he thinks we're from the vice squad, most likely he thinks we're wasting our time inspecting this dump. At ease, the lieutenant colonel told the sleepy and, for us, martial guard, Battalion forward. We marched along bumping into each other, still dirty from the sawdust and peels on the restaurant floor, the bolero grew louder and there was an orchestra in back, with a fellow in a white jacket and circumflex eyebrows whispering dramatic confidences in Spanish into the microphone, huge empty tables, the ladies on the poster, almost all blond and fat, installed on long-legged stools by the bar with the shivery stances of sick storks, and a gray-haired gentleman in fancy pants was moving about the miserable cave with proprietary airs, while a smell of perfume, thick as rat poison, made us hesitate in the polar atmosphere, stabbed by a vagabond focus of light, like the sharp eye of a dentist seeking out cavities in an open mouth. The gray-haired gentleman sidled over, displaying the professional smile of a benevolent diplomat, the lieutenant colonel leaned forward in an attack position, and we immediately formed around him as if for the assault on a native village. The enemy, scared to death, backed off smiling, a kind of hyacinth in a vase outlined on his cheeks, a waiter appeared out of the shadows and whispered something in the ear of the ambassador, who straightened his pearl-colored necktie with his unsteady fingers, This way, Colonel, please, the waiter asked pointing to a circle of infinitely distant chairs, the lieutenant colonel, staggering like a walking doll, turned his head over his shoulder and ordered us Follow the native guide, a twisted beer-bottle cap was still stuck to his dusty elbow, the manager and the waiter advanced backward, signaling like the attendants who direct maneuvers in garages, the communications officer was stepping on my feet, the soldier was pushing me from behind with his invisible weapon, the second lieutenant, on his knees, was protecting us from a distance behind a curtain, making the sound *Pum pum pum pum pum pum pum pum* with his mouth, we reached the table after a stormy trip, which the danger of antipersonnel mines hidden under the floor prolonged considerably, the lieutenant colonel clicked his heels at the gray-haired gentleman and declared modestly Mission accomplished, General sir, the second lieutenant appeared on all fours, settled down next to me with difficulty and shouted to the waiter Champagne for the men quick, the circumflex-browed man of the boleros was embracing the microphone poignantly, making unnatural love to the amplifiers, What a damned bunch, I thought, what kind of a stinking mess have I got myself into, a group of natives, with slicked-down hair and sideburns, was sucking beer in a corner, watching us with the absolute impassiveness of Lisbon blacks, a second waiter placed a candle in the center of the table and our faces emerged from the darkness like the bony, pale masks of a horror movie, the wandering beam of light drew other bodies, other shoulders, other motionless creatures out of the darkness, a small door marked Ladies, a glass case full of antediluvian boxes of chocolates, the musician with dark glasses who was martyring the piano with his cruel, spiderlike finger bones. All of this, I thought, is sad and poor and pretentious, like a hearse without a coffin, these drapes, these curtains, these silver-paper stars, these false twinkles, and these lying gleams, I think I am correctly interpreting the feelings of the commander-in-chief, the lieutenant colonel declared, in promising you at this point in time a collective citation and a military cross to each one of you, in addition to five days' leave in Lourenço Marques, in the company of beautiful women excited by our military dash, ladies of the best society of this beloved overseas province that we are so gallantly defending, and in fact, slipping off the high-legged barstool with the unhurried avidity of insects, they were coming close to us, twisting like crabs, on the precarious balance of stilts, obese creatures with extremely impressive platinum hairdos, gold teeth carnivorous in the shadows, deep décolletés like Hertzian waves, immense breasts and hips looping over their girdles in bulges of flesh, earrings that quivered like the lights of a train. They placed several bowls of popcorn on the table and two sweating chrome buckets, the necks of champagne bottles were pointing their cork bullets at the ceiling, the manager, hands behind his back, was shoving the girls in our direction with imperative invitations from his animal trainer's chin, the bolero man was now gnawing on the bone of a tango with the bark of a watchdog, the first women attacked the table with a tinkle of tin bracelets like frogs on the edge of a pond, down their gullets they poured whole cups of fried potatoes, peanuts, pumpkin seeds that they chewed with impassive placidity, the lieutenant colonel got up to urinate and suddenly, bent over and hesitant like that, he looked to me like a fragile, defenseless, melancholy gentleman on in years, without any hope at all, leaning on the backs of chairs on his way to the toilet. My name is Abílio, what's yours, kid? the soldier asked a huge mulatto woman who was eating popcorn eucharists with soft indifference, the manager, calmer now, kept watch over the level of alcohol with the metal measuring stick of his eyes, the gentleman on in years finally disappeared, on difficult legs, around a bend in the bar. Could we have been like this already ten years ago? I asked myself, could we have been as dead as now already, so finally dead without appeal as now?: the light licked the spectacles of the communications officer who kept whispering sweet nothings into the ear of a menopausal frog who was clutching her glass with her enormous fingernails in a vegetable sort of way. In just ten minutes, a graveyard voice promised, we will present our fabulous international show and our first striptease act will be by the famous Italian dancer Melissa, runner-up throughout Europe for her most difficult specialty, coming expressly from Milan for an exclusive act in the Bar Club Madrid. The tangos had given way to paso dobles, the saxophone music twisted about on the platform like a centipede on its back, there was a knock on the office door, the second lieutenant said Come in without interrupting his reading, equipped with a red pencil, of the pile of papers in front of him, quick little steps closer and closer, the singer brandishing a pair of castanets in a funereal sort of way,

I work in the moving business, the soldier explained, I should have got rid of them here and taken off for home because I start at the branch tomorrow, already angry with myself, mixing the bleachy bubbly with my finger, the second lieutenant raised his hand and came upon the eternal primary-school-teacher's dress and the Sunday-school-teacher hairdo of Ilda, a hog-hunchbacked redhead was diligently caressing the back of my neck, Who's going to send for a bottle just for the two of us, who? and the curved nose nibbled at me with the sharp, horny kisses of a godmother, a wet hand was undoing my fly, opening and closing like an oyster, over my panicking testicles, the man at the piano was furiously beating out the notes as if he were squashing them, like cockroaches with a slipper in his bedroom at night, the lieutenant colonel, in back, was returning to the table, rowing against the currents of his wine, If Olavo saw me, the communications officer said, he would have ordered me to memorize three hundred pages of Lenin a day for a year, the second lieutenant put down his pencil, pushed the papers aside with his elbow, We hadn't been together for a few weeks, Captain, I would speak to her distantly in the bank dining-room and that was all, Ilda hesitated, put her belly up against the table, seeming to be getting her balance or getting her courage up or whatever it was she had inside, checked the clasp on her purse, wiped rice-cake crumbs from her sleeve and suddenly leaned over him I'm pregnant, the second lieutenant What? and she more assured, less trembly, louder, You heard me, I'm pregnant.

"If you're the kind who washes his hands," the lieutenant colonel whispered to me, fumbling his way back to his place, after doggedly bumping into the wall countless times, just like a toy car winding down, "don't miss the little one in a bikini who hands people soap and a towel: twelve, thirteen, fourteen years old at the most, but each breast, each thigh, each leg capable of making a whole cemetery get a hard on. When the chick smiled at me my bones went soft."

"Switzerland, Luxembourg, it's all the same to me," Inês's mother said, "what I want is the money out of here as fast as possible, we'll worry about interest later."

The music stopped, In just a few minutes our first strip number, and it started up again with the jerk of a train pulled by the saxophone's struggling engine, painfully climbing up a rise of flats. The champagne was making us levitate in our seats, made us capable of biblically walking on a lake of mineral waters, floating through the lights and smoke, like strange drunken birds, bumping into each other with the feathery fluttering of jackets. What? the second lieutenant repeated with great surprise, what? bodies clinging to each other on the small circular dance floor, insignificant men ready to be devoured by all those blond tresses, all those man-eating behinds, all those naked breasts: It was a rough moment, Captain, everybody in the financial world sensed that something serious was about to happen, that the Army was worked up, that the political police couldn't control the situation, that busi-

ness groups were breaking up, that the government was impotently witnessing all that, my mother-in-law's family was selling companies and stocks for a
song, the mulatto girl was devouring the soldier to the rhythm of castanet
teeth that were chewing, slicing, breaking, and her torso was gradually
dissolving in the scintillating dress, there might be a few pieces of bone here
and there on the floor that the cleaning woman would sweep up the next day,
mixed in with the trash and cigarette butts, toward the door, at the time that
the grocer was unlocking the door of his narrow realm of detergents and
potatoes, Ilda observed, down below there, the owner of the notions store,
with legs that were Manueline with varicose veins, washing the showcase,
perched up on a stepladder, in the midst of beggars, lottery-ticket sellers,
street peddlers, and the fierce hurrying people with pale assassin's eyes from
the Baixa. At the far end of the avenue, after a row of geometric trees, one
after another, successively smaller and smaller, of traffic lights, a thin lozenge
of river could be made out that buses and streetcars, limping along in the
distance, hid and revealed with magician's hand passes that had no mystery
about them. Fourteen years old and not a single wrinkle on her, the lieutenant colonel whispered, everything tight, everything firm, everything lean,
just the muscles of a young mare on her back, just soft fuzz on her belly: I can
imagine spit without tobacco smell, eyes without gum, the excited little
hamster moans. The second lieutenant, quite nervous, lighted a cigarette on
the filter end, a horrible burned taste filled his mouth and nose, he put it out
quickly in the square marble ashtray, left his desk waving the nauseous fan of
his hand to drive off the smoke, the telephone rang. No, no, I didn't forget,
thank you, tell them to come into the meeting room and Dr. Costa Nunes
should take care of things until I get there: the chubby fag bastard, wearing a
polyester shirt with wild cuff links ugly enough to scare you, lecturing with
his mannered warble and his oily mannerisms of a priest to a platform of
submissive executives.

"Ilda, eh?" Inês chortled, "if she looks like her name, my God."

She wasn't to blame, she didn't want it, she always used the usual precautions except the pill that the lady doctor wouldn't let her take because of a
risk to her delicate veins, hemorrhages, thromboses, varicose veins, there'd
never been anything as draggy as this, right? who in hell knew why it had
happened now, and the second lieutenant, behind her, was looking at the
beggars and drunks on the street too, the notions store woman who was
closing her stepladder and disappearing into the shadows of old magazines
and ancient carnival noses with elastic for the neck, into the store, the
painted, motionless plaster Tagus, and the nearly white sky clinging to the
tense, exasperated, fearful heads of people: The city's caught us like rats,
he thought, early in the morning, the Sanitation trucks will pick up our
swollen, repulsive, putrid little gray bodies.

"Sónia, do you swear?" the communications officer was astounded, offering a light all around with his hasty lighter. "Should I confess to you, young lady, that my dream has always been to marry a Sónia? Can you believe it?"

Dr. Costa Nunes was taking slow notes on a pad after inviting his subordinates to express themselves, one after the other, their bankers' imaginations, their financiers' deliriums of titles and money, while the second lieutenant hated him minutely and the soldier, apparently intact, returned to the table proudly escorting the huge mulatto woman who was touching up her lipstick, funneling kisses into a round mirror, while the successive pleats of fat gathered together, double chin piled onto double chin, to the tiny watchful eyes of the undaunted chameleon, ready to roll up its fly in the glass loop of saliva. The hunchback was pinching the lieutenant colonel's belly button, putting her hand into an opening in his shirt, the girl with the towels was moving about on the side, like a tarantula, in her web of bowl brushes and urinals, Inês nodded on the seat of the car, beaten by the waves of the Marginal that were leaping over the wall as if someone were furiously flinging buckets of water from the darkness onto the pavement in a dust storm of drops:

"A sweetheart at work just like any other imbecile," she laughed, wrinkling her nose, slicing him up mercilessly with the razors of her eyes. "What surprises me is where you got the imagination to go that far."

When her menstruation stopped she wasn't too upset, it was normal with her, sometimes it was ahead of time, sometimes behind, but after a few days she got spells of nausea, giddiness, vomiting, morning sickness, they would set a cup of tea in front of her, something would come over her and zap, before eleven o'clock she hadn't swallowed a thing and there was no way for the blood to come, as soon as she woke up she would examine her panties and there they were, clean, she slowly began not to understand, to become concerned, to worry, with the greatest embarrassment she bought an analysis kit at the drugstore, one that was advertised on television and that her cousin, a practical nurse, the mother of three children, used, but she didn't dare try it out of fear, a fake doctor's report, she wouldn't go out because of her nerves, she had insomnia attacks, frights, strange dreams at night, she thought she heard a baby crying in the deserted hallway, the crying, calling, sobbing of a baby, the second month vomiting and indisposition lessened and yet no pain in her head or in her ovaries no pink drivel on her sanitary napkin, she finally dribbled a thread of urine into the test tube, waited for a few terrible hours, with three useless tranquilizers in her gullet, leafing back and forth through a suddenly unreadable novel, she peeked, saw the brown circle at the base of the liquid, deciphered the instruction pamphlet once more, examined the tube again, shook it in hopes that the circle would dissolve and nothing happened, looked at the paper again without any illusions now, the little paper, Pregnancy.

No bus now, no streetcar held back the river, a bright yellow freighter was slipping toward the mouth, the sky was moving on and breaking up in successive banks of clouds, a promise of blue was watercoloring the rooftops: the mulatto woman put the neck of the bottle between her teeth and poured a pint of champagne down her guts, the drums beat the way they did at Punch and Judy shows announcing the spectacle, the spotlight halted over the empty dance floor, the grayish ambassador in a tuxedo arose out of the shadows dragging a microphone, he gave a few experimental taps with his finger which echoed monstrously in the room like the clearing of the throat at the Last Judgment, and he acknowledged the applause that nobody was giving him: Ladies and gentlemen good evening to all and our sincerest best wishes for an enjoyable soirée, accept the best wishes of the Bar Club Madrid which is honored to present to you good people the first part of its extraordinary international show, filled entirely with performers of known fame and established merits, especially brought from the casinos of London, New York, Paris, Monte Carlo, Rome, and Singapore, in a completely exclusive act that under no circumstance, I regret to tell you, can be televised. And to open our fabulous parade we have the pleasure of seeing in the flesh (a background of piano and accordion way out of tune) the incomparable Swedish acrobat Charles and his most beautiful partner Janete, just arrived this morning from Las Vegas to prove to us through their unequalled skill that the law of gravity, ladies and gentlemen, has become passé.

"I don't believe one little bit in those television devices," the second lieutenant answered contemplating the distant form of the ship, squeezed by the Pombaline vertebrae of the houses. Right under the window the usual invalid was settling down in the passageway on a piece of blanket, placing his dirty beret between his legs, touching the pants of people with the repulsive sores on his stumps. Bebex, the Chemical Angel Gabriel of the Twentieth Century: How can you still swallow those idiotic lies?

"Switzerland, Luxembourg, Germany, wherever you want," the mother-in-law spurred with an urgent whine, "but get moving, I can already catch the smell of communism around here."

No, it wasn't idiotic, there he was insisting with his usual stubbornness, after the analysis she opened up to her practical-nurse cousin, incidentally, you can rest easy, I didn't mention your name, she ended up that afternoon consulting an unknown doctor on the other side of Lisbon, paid the nurse in advance, the doctor told her to lie down on the sofa, tied her legs to a kind of hook arrangement, a glove came toward me moving the yellow sausages of its fingers, the lampshade on the ceiling had fringes and spots, the sausages slipped inside her body with smooth skill, my practical-nurse cousin gripped my hand, some feeling of the stomach, a metric tape to measure the bones, Please get up, the ball-point that filled out a card, friendly pats on the shoulder, Let's set December twenty-second as the due date, three or four big-bellied girls were sitting in the tiny waiting room, just like the Spanish dolls in a maid's room, the door closed behind us, *poom*, and there was a notary's office on the first floor, civil servants behind their windows and a long line of people down along the steps, each one with his piece of stamped paper and patient dull eyes, and there outside the afternoon sun on the tiles of the building façades and the roofs of the city stumbling over each other down to the docks, with fat pigeons, skinny gulls, the frozen arms of derricks and the pyorrheal warehouses along the bank, abandoned and empty like dwellings of the dead.

The incomparable Swedish acrobat took a few small leaps out of the darkness, tight in yellow Dr. Denton's, sparkling with bangles and glass beads. He was short, dark, with sideburns, a typical Nordic from Marvila, and when once he made a slip, out of the dark foliage of his mustache the impetuous Fuck it all of a Viking escaped. The beautiful Janete, tiny and assy, with long hair streaked with straw curling down in disorder over her shoulders, twirled about the artist who was repeating lamentable leaps backed by an orchestration with the tragic rhythm of catastrophe.

"It's none of your business what I found out, how I found it out, who told me," Inês shouted furiously, "all I care about is that you've got a lover at the bank."

Ilda leaned her head onto the windowsill and began to cry, and the second lieutenant thought, unaffected, You're ugly, unkempt, not too feminine, with dandruff on your shoulders, how did I ever get to sleep with you, damn it, how was I ever capable of that? I didn't know her too well, Captain, I never knew her too well, the mess she could have got me into frightened me, the inevitable whispering in the section frightened me, if Inês ever dreamed of it, if Inês's family ever dreamed of it, and the busts of her grandfather grew tremendously on their ebony pedestals, twisting in grimaces of anger, in convulsive threats. The day changed color, his insides gurgled, the air was solid and unbreathable, heavy, the one called Charles disappeared with somersaults, came back for a moment, his arms outstretched as a way of thanks for the nonexistent applause of the audience, the beautiful Janete followed him, wiggling her imposing hen-turkey rear, the words came out of my mouth without my wanting them to, like an uncontrollable fart, And who's so sure the child is mine, and no sooner had I finished the sentence, you see, I realized I'd screwed it all up. The orchestra fell silent, the ambassador dragged the microphone out onto the center of the stage again, carefully adjusted the height, with the shadow of his lashes falling over his chubby cheeks, And following Charles and Janete, who have just given us such an unforgettable performance, the Bar Club Madrid brings you the lightness, the enchantment, the gracefulness of the well-known French performer Madame Simone, the craze of the Moulin Rouge of Paris, who will show us her moving, skillful little birds for some moments of dream, poetry, and careful precision. Now only the piano was playing, softly, fountains of hemisemidemiquavers rising and falling like the sighs of a child, the silhouette of the musician hunched over the keys as if he were eating them, the hunchback asked the waiter for some more popcorn, Ilda turned around with such an angry twist that the second lieutenant, startled, retreated a step, I never thought you were so common, I never thought you could be so cheap. Madame Simone, a fat old woman with a dangerously low-cut gown that dragged sumptuously on the floor with a soft murmur, was accompanied by several cages of pigeons or turtledoves or some kind of big ugly bird, that moved about, flapping their wings, stirring up the smoky atmosphere, and they lighted on her head and shoulders, dropping between their pink feet the quick, soft spittle of their feces in an uncomfortable intimacy. A fellow with a bow tie and scarlet jacket laid tin toy cars on the floor which the creatures, with serious and stupid eyes pushed with their beaks, obstacles which they leaped over with joyless ease, an electric train where, with jerks and starts, very stiff, they rode over turns of rail, scattering loose feathers about, transparent grain husks, and the smell of shit, and, finally, they all perched motionless on the metal tree that Madame Simone gripped in her mouth, while the fellow in the bow tie, legs curved and eyebrows fierce, was mentally preparing a barbecue for any of them who disobeyed. The orchestra celebrated such prowess with a jumbled frenzy of rhythm, and the lucky spectators at the Bar Club Madrid, the first and only Portuguese to have the good fortune to witness the indisputable skill and poetry of the impressive little birds, inspected, blowing on the white feathers that fluttered every-where and in their noses and throats, the fantastic thighs of the blond woman, clutched by garter meridians, like someone looking for sad house-hold treasures between the cushions of a sofa.

The shadows had also been changed into a kind of big smelly cage run through sporadically by the flutter of wings, cooing, sighing, peeping, by fluctuating outlines and from time to time thick drops of shit would fall onto the tablecloths, sent down from the drapes and molding of the ceiling where a few perverse doves had found a niche, pecking at the blue, yellow, green, brown, white kernels of the spotlights, laying eggs in the folds of the curtains, confusedly fornicating in the piano, slipping outdoors into the night in hopes of some equestrian statue where they could drop anchor between the bronze testicles of the horse or the eyes of regicides, sheltered from the cold by rusty moss. Madame Simone, hand-in-hand with the fellow in a red jacket, came back on stage rolling her ancient body with all the grace of a locomotive, and bending over in an awkward bow that made the vast withered mass of her mammaries pop out like the cartilagenous heads of twins peeping out and hanging down in the course of a birth. Straightening up with another creak-ing of joints (Something, I thought, a gear, a spring, a rod, the motor is going to go out of commission inside the craze of the Moulin Rouge), she threw kisses, holding her fingers together, to the mute audience, the gray-haired manager presented her with the same bouquet of false gladioli, smelling of plastic and cabbage, that moments before he had offered the beautiful Jan-ete, and Madame Simone disappeared, shaking her abundant silvery mane like a restless horse, followed by her aide in the bow tie who was, I suddenly discovered, the tomb-voiced singer of tangos and boleros. Ilda rummaged in her plastic purse, drew out a wrinkled, endless man's handkerchief from deep inside, wiped her goat face in whose granite wrinkles puddles of stagnant tears were festering, checked the thousands of hairpins in her bun, pushed away the second lieutenant who was trying to hug her with artificial affection, I just came to tell you, I don't need your help in anything, and he, swallowing the urge to wring her neck, But what's wrong with our talking, what's wrong with our having a little talk, don't be foolish, sit down for a few minutes, forgive me for what I said, I didn't mean it, it just came out.

"Jorge?" the mother-in-law asked, authoritarian, and he was struck with the feeling that one of the nasty plaster busts was asking for him, lowering the corners of its protruding mouth. "Finally, damn it, you're harder to get hold of than a cabinet minister. I want you to arrange a way for me to change thirty thousand contos into dollars by tomorrow, I've got a carrier I can trust going to London."

That was at the end of March, Captain, less than a month before the coup, the bank in a quiet uproar, the main shareholders pulling their chestnuts out of the fire fast, the value of the stock more and more fictitious, the prime minister reading speeches with his ass on fire to a gang of generals who couldn't even support the weight of the stars on their shoulders, Inês making a scene with me night after night, not because of love, you understand, out of pride, out of the pain of being bypassed, shouts, insults, nastiness, jeering, and if that wasn't enough I was suddenly saddled with a child, and from Ilda, in the midst of this damned mess. No, seriously, listen, how would you have got out of it in my place, Captain?

"Thirteen years," the lieutenant colonel snorted, all alone, into his champagne glass. "Could an old guy put up with a high yellow like that?"

"I won't have an abortion," Ilda stated. "But you can rest easy, I won't cause any scandal, I won't make it hard for you, I won't get you in trouble, I won't ask for any money."

Madame Simone was followed by the astounding Bulgarian magician Mikael Mikaelov, who turned milk bottles into newspaper cones that were transformed into the Portuguese flag and he asked for the help of the audience in the Oporto accent typical of Slavs, the Smith sisters from California, with the gracious consent of their casino in New York, in a double show of strength, a pair of muscular mares (one of them, besides, was the most beautiful Janete, the partner of the Swedish acrobat a while back) knocking themselves out in somersaults and leaps, Marina Madragoa, the most recent discovery in the fado, accompanied by her own group (the twister at the piano and the caterpillar on the saxophone, who had changed jackets for the number) and after a few minutes of nil expectations and absolute indifference (Prepare yourselves, ladies and gentlemen, for the matchless number awaiting you), the striptease champion Melissa, envy of the most celebrated stars of Italian cinema, and singularly resembling the goddess of the fado with the difference that she kept silent while the singer, undone by lyric inspiration, had howled as if in pain into the microphone like a fire-engine siren with an earthquake in its rear end. The soldier, his head nestled on the flat of the mulatto's arm, was fervently kissing the sensuous scar of her vaccination. The communications officer, after having put his glasses into a pocket of his jacket, was suffocating his cough in a blond thickness that quickly devoured him like quicksand in an adventure movie, the final hyperbole a wave in the air.

But she wouldn't sit down, Captain, she wouldn't talk to me about my suggestion of an abortion, my suggestion that she think it over, think better about it, she looked at me like I was a stranger, turned her face away if I got near her, smiled with scorn or indifference or pity, standing there in the middle of the office, holding that plastic aunty purse that she always used in front of her belly, and in the middle of what I was saying she opened the door and left without even a goodbye, not out of rage, understand, not out of hate, but because I had really ceased to exist for her, she'd left me behind for good in her distant past, in the old things, disagreeable and sad, that gradually lost color until the feeling that suffering gave them evaporated, the only thing they had possessed after all: I would still run into her two or three times at the bank, she didn't say hello to me, I didn't say hello to her, I would call her and she'd hang up on me in a snit, and then the Revolution, my quick flight to Brazil in the rush of Inês's family, and when he came back, five years later, he tried to look her up in the personnel section they informed him that Miss So-and-So had stopped working at the bank, her apartment had been bought by an agricultural engineer who was very helpful and full of goodwill but who was completely unaware of the whereabouts of the former tenant, he didn't dare go to the section of the bank and find some friend of Ilda's, if one or two were left maybe, who could help him, so not only did he not get to see her again but he knew nothing about the son or daughter that she was carrying in her womb, if it had been born, if it hadn't been born, if it looked like me, and a week hasn't gone by without my dreaming about a baby, pacifier in its mouth, accusing me. I never thought you could be so common, that you could be so cheap, Captain, you can't imagine what it's like for somebody to have a child whose face he doesn't even know.

"Thirteen years, goddamn it," the lieutenant colonel muttered to himself, alone, fondling his glass, "who wouldn't like to drive his nail into a chippy like that?"

The champion of Europe finally got out of her panties, tossed them to our table with a broad sweep, the skin of her breasts glowed, her chubby thighs quivered, her behind shook. The second lieutenant lowered his eyes, cut off a belch, and smiled all around, ashamed, excusing himself:

"It's hard to take so much shit, don't you all think?"

*Part Two*

# THE
# REVOLUTION

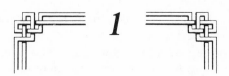

# 1

ODETE'S cries and his uncle's asthmatic belching awakened the soldier with the same instantaneous anguish, suddenly on the alert, just as he had awakened before in the jungle at the first unusual sound, the first whispered order, the first shot. He quickly slid onto the floor, sweating, caught up in the sheets, feeling in the space around him for his weapon, the streetlamp lighted up the building across the way and a portion of the room (the clothes closet, the washbasin and its mirror, Dona Isaura's Saint Philomena on the wall), the sticky egg-white of dawn was growing like algae on the rooftops. Military marches were coming out of the living room, guitar music, male voices singing, an announcer was reading a short speech from time to time, and after that, after a brief endless silence during which blood was held back, kept in suspense in the veins, waiting, more marches, more anthems, more choral groups, more music. He sat down on the floor, turned the room lamp on and his toes rose up out of his pajama legs, stiff and pale, like those of the dead. The lumps from last winter's dampness stood out on the ceiling, the box full of cowboy magazines that served as a night table touted a brand of wine to the soldier: there were no trees, no bushes, no grass, no blacks gripping Czechoslovakian rifles, staring at him suddenly with the strawberry pudding of their eyes: only Odete and his uncle, who were chatting, or getting excited, or arguing in the parlor, the unusual outpouring from the radio, the immense heaving of the old woman in the double bed, her existence half-racked in the divergent spasms of a crab. He wet his hands, the back of his neck, his face, (a guy passed by the window running in the direction of Gomes Freire, followed by the echo of his own shoes on the pavement), dried himself mumbling to the blanket, put on one of his slippers, held his other ankle in the air, indecisive, I'm going back to bed, I'm not going back to bed, I'm going out there to peek in on what's going on, the radio of the neighbor above was transmitting the same discourse, the same songs, the same anthems, people calling to each other from balcony to balcony, he looked at the clock, Six in the morning and all this excitement what's going on, he ended up leaving his cubicle with just one slipper on, limping, quickly buttoning up his fly, through the open door of her bedroom he saw Dona Isaura gasping on her mattress underneath the huge rosary hanging on a hook, vials of medicine, a second Saint Philomena, hands clasped, surrounded by a crowd of angels and the light in the hallway on, and the light in the bathroom on, and the light in the pantry on, They're going to pay a fat electric bill at the end of the month, he thought, they've hit the jackpot in the lottery or they're crazy, he stopped at the parlor door scratching his belly, perplexed, his uncle, in his drawers and undershirt, was coughing on the sofa, Odete, her hair down, in her bathrobe, was fiddling with the dials on the big ancient set, two slices of vulgarian sandwiching a song, the needle slipped along the dial but only one spot was working, the lashes on the lampshades cast chaste yellow ovals onto the floor, touching and treading on it like the converging eyes of a cross-eyed person, showing off the dull designs of the rug, schematic deer repeated one after the other in faded monotony, and at that point Odete raised her head and saw him, Hurry up, come here, they're overthrowing the government.

It must be some kind of joke on the part of the radio station, the soldier thought, there's no end to the crap the advertisements put us through, the stinking music they make us swallow, maybe some wild old nut burst into the station with a handful of papers, I've got a crazy idea, let's shake people up with this.

"We can't go out? We can't go out?" the old man croaked indignantly to the Last Supper in the background, won in a small-prize lottery. "That's all I needed, kid, I've got a whole stack of moving jobs today."

The soldier sat down in one of the uncomfortable seats, a straight-backed chair, at the dinner table, leaned his face on the cool surface of the oilcloth, closed his eyes and Odete and the uncle went away, the fall of the government went away, the old man's cough sounded dull, without any echo, far off, growing smaller in the immeasurable grotto of the parlor, the bulbs of the lamps wrinkled up and lost their brightness on his eyelids, To sleep, and suddenly the imposing tone of the announcer pulling him brutally out of his sleep and the outraged barking of his uncle This is crazy nonsense, damn it, if those bastards think they're going to stop me from going to work they're wrong, go get dressed, dummy, so we can get started earlier.

"And that was the first time," the soldier told me, "that we went to the warehouse together," battered along alleyways by shouted radio conversations. Unshaven men leaning out of windows like worms in an apple, dogs overturning forgotten garbage cans, the doorman at the crazy house standing by the entrance, holding his transistor to his ear as if he were listening to the ocean waves in a seashell, a bitter chill froze their legs, the uncle was snorting If they threw the government out on its ass they won't rest till they set up one that's even worse and they'll turn us out on our heels begging, Command Post of the Armed Forces Movement, and Mr. Ilídio bitter, Look at those guys, just look how happy they are, damn it, it even looks like they're going to save the world, it was seven-thirty in the morning and the workers hadn't come in yet, no one was waiting for them by the chains on the door, the old man searched for the key in the enormous handful in his pants pocket that stood out like a hernia and he kept on getting them mixed up nervous as he was, Shit, the sound of rusty metal protesting and the iron accordion shrinking with a kick, I bet the cocksuckers have taken advantage of the hullabaloo to get out of working as though the fall of governments and troop movements on the radio let anybody off, get the loaded van there out for me and just the two of us will try to do the job and you can rest easy that when we get back I'm going to screw your fellow workers' asses. The soldier went carefully down the cement incline slipping on patches of oil and puddles of water, climbed into the cab, started the motor, there were two more vans and a Mercedes rotting and rusting away in the shadows, not to mention the usual furniture, the skylight up above and dust and cobwebs all about, the tires danced on the wet pavement, he knocked something down that shattered noisily, finally he found the ramp, the uncle, all choked up with anger, was hanging a piece of paper Be Right Back on the office door, Let's go to the Baixa, the old man roared, and don't come to me with that shit that your insurance ran out last month, after a while they began to find infantry troops on corners, tanks, soldiers in helmets with bazookas on their shoulders, almost no cars were on the streets, a young lieutenant made them stop, Traffic is cut off, friends, I've got some urgent business in the Chiado, the uncle replied, our little van won't make any difference, but the other one had already turned his back on them and was deciphering the piece of paper that a weary corporal, beret askew, had just run up with, they backed off, took half a turn and headed into Entreposto, Rato, Escola Politécnica, the soldier turned on the radio and the marches and guitar songs thundered in the cab where everything was trembling and vibrating, all by itself, waiting for a cataclysmic explosion, the music was cut off, the voice of the announcer began talking again, Shut your mouth, you bastard, the uncle roared, like a man possessed, feeling around for his asthma squeeze-bottle in his jacket pocket, noble buildings, antiquarian, the Príncipe Real garden shimmering with light and almost right then a tank lying across the road, men in uniform, mortars, troop carriers, and now a sergeant approaching, all excited, pistol in hand, Get the hell out of here before I take a shot at you, We were amazed, Captain, we'd never dreamed of war equipment on the streets of Lisbon, Mr. Ilídio, stupefied, didn't even open his mouth, some people in camouflage dress, standing on a bench, were listening, their heads together, to the martial anthems coming out of the radio, the sergeant, his jaw up to door level like a carnival dummy, was looking at us, his little eyes staring like a bird's, I spun the wheel while the stuff hanging from the rearview mirror fluttered like something with malarial fever, I went into first, into reverse, first again, my feet couldn't get onto the pedals, the wheels wouldn't obey, the sergeant was staring at us with firm mistrust, Come on, come on, come on, get out of here, Mr. Ilídio terrified, hissed, and ten minutes later we were jerking into the warehouse, boarding the ramp that led to the door, with the van's rear full of pieces of furniture knocking against each other and getting mixed up. A flock of pigeons sitting on the wall across the way took flight at that moment, cut diagonally across the trees set out in a kind of park, disappeared over the rooftops of the laboratory, the bookkeeper, her place arranged with the proprietary air of an office, filing folders, waved to the uncle in a friendly way over a vase of gladioli (There's no way for you to hide now, you old devil, the soldier thought, outraged), the old man, the quiet man, Isidoro the Mulatto, and another man they called Peeker because he was cross-eyed were dancing around like clumsy bats among bidets and pianos, Isidoro the Mulatto was brandishing a microscopic radio, shouting to those left They've got everything under control, they've surrounded the president and his ministers at Carmo, but Mr. Ilídio, scowling, crushed his elation instantly, I don't want to hear about that shit, the lazy bums who took today off are through working here.

At eleven o'clock Carmindo, a mustachioed fellow who'd started work in March and was living with the bookkeeper's goddaughter, appeared on a motorcycle, he took off his helmet and his hair stood up on end, It was a real hassle before they let me through, Mr. Ilídio, they've even got warships going back and forth across the Tagus, they don't want anybody to sneak out of their houses, and a whole wave of people pouring down toward the Chiado heading for the PIDE, for the Carmo, if it hadn't been for a major they would have clubbed an agent of the secret police to death, he kept saying he wasn't, a middle-aged guy, his face like a muffin, crying, and the uncle from his glass-cage office, Even with a cops-and-robbers story like that I'm docking you two hours at the end of the month and you're lucky I don't fire you, he ordered them to load the small vans and his cough was sobbing, muffled by the crates, he took the spray out of his pants pocket and squeezed the rubber ball into his afflicted gullet, it was easy to see that the bookkeeper was scolding him, smiling and tender, the old man and the quiet fellow left in the new Peugeot, we stood there scratching our backs against the scabby wall, the rats were galloping about in the corners of the warehouse, and right then the noise of the truck again, the broad white hood appearing up there, They won't let us through, Mr. Ilídio, you can't imagine the mess we ran into, my uncle opened his desk drawer, pushed aside balls of twine, stained sheets of paper, hinges, a pencil sharpener, boxes of screws and nails, a paper punch, hinges, a pencil sharpener, several keys, a pair of broken glasses, an empty picture frame, he finally found a bottle of pills, put a round one on his tongue, threw the flowers into the wastebasket and drank the water in the vase, swallowing the tablet, fell listlessly, his eyes vacant, into a wooden chair, muttering indecipherable conclusions, the announcer was becoming, communiqué by communiqué, more optimistic, more victorious, more triumphant, promising at every instant the fall of the Government, Democracy, Freedom, the worn-out batteries in the old man's radio made it difficult to understand the verbiage: clustered on a beat-up velvet couch we listened, intrigued, without catching it too well, the bookkeeper rapped her knuckles on the glass calling me, she was making up her eyes and mouth now, wearing tight dresses, with hair spray, and a smell of lavender sachet which reminded me of winter, rain, idle Sunday afternoons at home, with the rain coming down, monotonous, the breaks in the tile roofs, I dashed up the scratched cement steps, the bookkeeper had lovingly put the flowers back on the desk, and my uncle, convulsed, his fists to his temples, raised a panic-stricken trembling jaw to me, Hurry up on out there and find out what's going on and come back here and tell me, because he didn't understand a damned thing, because everything had taken the shape of a strange nightmare for him, a great big lie, the world against him all of a sudden, a flood, a shipwreck, a disaster, a tremendous threat, life turned upside down, impossible to be lived, all the while digging the spray tube out of its case, putting the little glass thing to his gums and *pfffft pffffft pffffft*, as if he imagined the medicine would put everything back in place the way it was before, that his anxiety would disappear, that his anguish would cease, that compass faces would freeze into position, They're going to arrest the ministers, mulatto Isidoro announced, his hair kept smooth with tons of desperate grease, they're going to put them in with the monkeys and the bears at the Zoo, in the neighborhood, not even the bar had opened, no women were to be seen on the streets, what a drag, the soldier took the small van out of the warehouse, he tried to follow a complicated route toward the Baixa, but at a certain point in the distance he spotted an Army Berliet loaded with guys in camouflage dress, so he parked with two wheels on the sidewalk along a very narrow street and proceeded on foot, hugging the walls, in the direction of Camões, where the soldiers were thicker, people were applauding the troops, offering them food, cigarettes, milk (What's this all about? he thought, amazed, what's this all about?), shots rang out near São Carlos, Everybody to the PIDE, a very tall boy roared, hair wild, wearing the checkered shirt of an amateur actor, valiant men trotted back and forth holding cobblestones in their hands, officers were arguing beside the statue, there wasn't a single pigeon in the square, a platoon of marines was marching toward secret police headquarters, commanded by a lieutenant with decisive movements, clutching his pistol holster, Kill the cocksuckers, the boy proposed, kill the bastards, a confused wave of bodies dragged him to the front of a large building (and the river and the sky, ash gray, there in the background), surrounded by a crowd that was shouting, insulting, throwing bottles and stones at the windows, the marines approached the door cautiously, and right then a middle-aged guy ran out from inside, arms raised, and right away a crowd of people fell on him, beating him with fists, shoes, sticks of wood, tearing his clothes, knocking him to the pavement, the man's nose, jaw, mouth, eyebrows were bleeding, until the lieutenant grabbed him by the torn sleeve (another kick, two more kicks, another punch in the ribs), turned him over to a sergeant Put him in the jeep with the others, somebody was shooting from inside the building, a body slid down along the wall opposite until it fell into a sitting position with a look of surprise, the marines entered the building with rifles ready, a weapons carrier made its way along, blowing its horn, up to the front of the movie theater across the way, shots, just like insignificant bubbles bursting, moans, protests, curses, Let's set fire to all that shit, let's burn those sons of bitches like rats, a naval man with shoulder boards (A commodore or something like that, I always get Navy ranks mixed up) appeared in a window on the second floor asking for calm, waving his arms up and down like a bird that's forgotten how to fly, and a short time later, escorted by marines, a few dozen guys that people called names, spat at, tried to attack, were led to the vehicle, which took off, still blowing its horn, turned right at the end of the street, disappeared, we scrambled into the building paying no attention to the indignation and protests of the quartermasters, and we came upon what looked to me like just any old government office, just like all the others, desks, chairs, files against the walls, the ever-present photograph of the pig-faced admiral in a white uniform with a blue sash and great big medals on his belly, typewriters, straw wastebaskets, papers scattered all over, empty jackets swinging on the coatracks.

"That's all?" Espreita asked, throwing a carved candlestick at a great big rat. "You want me to believe that the PIDE was only that?"

No, of course not, the soldier thought, but not much more in the end: files, radio sets, cameras, rooms with no furniture, with big thick doors, with bulbs behind glass covers next to the ceiling (That's where they did their torturing, the quiet man explained, and that's where they squeezed your balls into mush with a kind of pliers), and not a single gaunt prisoner, no bones in the corners, no torture-chamber cellars like in the movies at the Odeon, white-hot irons, manacles, lead balls, terrible instruments. The people took the pictures of the admiral off the walls, leaving bright rectangles on the plaster, they fought fiercely over ridiculous souvenirs (fountain pens, erasers, rubber stamps, printed pads), overturned tables, dumped things off shelves, plugged up toilets with rolls of blotting paper and trash, every so often a strident carnivorous howl could be heard in some room He belongs to the PIDE he belongs to the PIDE, and blows rained down on curved backs that protested, shrieked, tried to flee, that ended up falling to the floor, weeping, until more marines began to arrive, rifles at high port, with a trooping of boots, and they drove us all out onto the street, the energetic lieutenant explaining in a thick voice Leave the cleaning up of this to us, let us do the work the way it should be done, the people dispersed grudgingly, carrying their useless little treasures, two guys were fighting over a piece of chair, a gentleman with a mustache and his tie loosened in his collar was roaring DOWN WITH THE ESTADO NOVO LONG LIVE FREEDOM, but a hulk with suspicious eyes asked Aren't you with the PIDE, maybe? and he shut up at once like a flower closing, disappeared in terror into the midst of the people who were trotting toward the Largo do Carmo, summoned now by an invisible loudspeaker, ALL TOGETHER LET'S BRING DOWN THE GOV-ERNMENT, military vehicles, a crowd, soldiers, a great confusion, urchins hanging from the trees in front of the headquarters of the Republican Guard, the sentry boxes empty, officers up on the roofs of cars, megaphones at their mouths, holding back the people from forcing the gates, knocking down the doors, milling around and bumping into each other at the trolley stop like blind cockroaches. What would my uncle say if he saw this, what the devil would the old man think of it, a captain was suggesting surrender to the rows of empty windows, tanks came and went, slowly, amidst a vociferous tangle of tongues, disparate, disordered, incomprehensible slogans were chanted, which amateur actors in checkered shirts like the boy at the PIDE were trying to bring together, waving their arms like choirmasters, FREE-DOM FREE-DOM FREE-DOM, Just a matter of hours, an enthusiast in a goatee informed him, tomorrow you'll see them swinging from the lampposts on the avenue, but there weren't any executions, Captain, there wasn't any blood, there wasn't even a serious revolt, the ones who were in charge before are in the driver's seat again, after a few years in exile, after a few months in jail, so we go on just the same in this shitty country, so much joy, so much work, so much racket for what, finally a general with a monocle arrived in a car and the crowd cheered, the soldiers pushed the people back with their rifles, more orders, more anthems, more shouts, his uncle's hand inviting him into the glassed-in office, his melancholy, dispirited face, agonizing, the bookkeeper sitting at the desk, ball-point ready, waiting.

"So," Mr. Ilídio snorted in a murmur, "have they started sacking yet, have they started robbing honest people?"

He'd sent the workers away, sick of their restless, inquiring expressions, perplexed, of their whispered conspiracies, their furtive glances, they were to return tomorrow for the afternoon loads, the bulbs were swaying lightly from the rotten roof beams, dusk was creeping in on a slant through the incisions of the small windows, the sangria-colored sky was devouring the chimneys, and there was no sacking, no robbing, and we have continued until today with our little moving business, and that was almost ten years ago and here we are again in the stagnant, serene, corpselike, unchanging tranquility of times gone by. The general with the monocle got out of his car, his decorations and insignia sparkling in the sunlight, disappeared into the big building on Carmo accompanied by two or three dignified civilians, very thoughtful, wearing neckties, a few seconds of expectation, a few elastic minutes that lasted an eternity, more characters climbing up trees, the roofs of the surrounding buildings full of people, the choirmasters began to wave their arms again, more energetically now, FREE-DOM FREE-DOM FREE-DOM, he thought he saw Odete leaning against a young fellow in glasses with a flag but no, it wasn't she, it was a shorter and uglier girl, with a guitar case by her feet, the captain with the megaphone would confer from time to time with second lieutenants and sergeants who would stand on tiptoe to talk to him, an ocean of heads would come together and spread out, bubbling in a froth of eyes, gums, noses, chins, his uncle got up out of his chair, came outside, hands in his pockets, peeping at the night, the lights that were going on in the mournful little garden, the stray dogs, an ambulance leaving the Capuchin Hospital down below, he came back inside, swallowed another pill and guaranteed, in a funereal way, his eyes on the stained Mobil calendar on the wall, There's going to be one hell of a revolution in this country, we're fucked for sure.

"He saw his business turned to rubbish, sinking, sinking, going under with no way out," the soldier explained, furniture falling apart in the warehouse with no one to claim it, Ilídio Movers without any orders, ruined, and not just Ilídio Movers, Captain, endless lines for meat, vegetables, milk, people getting skinny, poorly dressed, with hungry faces, packs of thugs with beards robbing honest people on street corners, military jeeps shooting out after the firehouse siren of the mandatory curfew, wavering imperatively through the lightless streets, over furtive shapes falling back, along the sidewalks sniffed by enormous gray and shaggy dogs. Gasoline had disappeared, militiamen in khaki took away cars with ferocious hooks, traffic consisted of excavated trembling buses filled with worried and serious passengers, one came across foul-smelling corpses on cellar steps, in vestibules, in the embassy neighborhood, in the few shops still open, with empty windows and clerks half-hidden behind empty counters. And the hospitals overflowing with wounded, covered with dirty dressings and bandages, thousands of people held prisoner in stadiums and bullrings, firing squads shoving guys with hands tied behind their backs up against the bases of statues, the machine guns, the protests, the weeping, the pleas, red flags on public buildings, Russians and Chinese everywhere, giving orders, occupying the government palace, strolling about with the air of masters of the city, and Odete But what kind of a mania is that, what kind of fixed notion, the Estado Novo is finished along with the political police, that's all, and Mr. Ilídio, desperate, When you have to eat your own shit, when they make you shack up with a Czechoslovakian, come talk to me, this business of parties is the trick they're using to get a better grip on our tails.

The general with the monocle finally came out of the Guard headquarters, without showing any emotion over the enthusiasm, without acknowledging the applause, settled down with the solemn gentlemen in the car that immediately began rolling out of the square, breaking off branches, with gestures, signals, victorious smiles, the crowd rapped on the doors with their knuckles, greeted him, shouted, more tanks were arriving, their cannons pointed at the deserted building, more officers, more troops, a fellow carrying a flat basket was handing out carnations, and suddenly the soldier remembered My grandmother's house was near there, on that terrace where you can see the Tagus, and coming into his mind, intact, was the old woman's run-down, almost miserable first floor, the imposing picture of the Sacred Heart of Jesus in the vestibule, the lumpy uneven floor, the eternal profusion of cockroaches in corners, strange hairy raffia sofas, fat women in aprons stirring pots in the enormous kitchen, the long table in the dining room, with an oilcloth cover, and a dozen or two girls excessively made-up, excessively extravagant, excessively sleepy, some in slips and bedroom slippers, others with false eyelashes drooping down, waiting for the soup tureen, painting their nails or their lips, arguing, chatting, brushing their hair, showing the huge pale spheres of their breasts through their neck openings. I used to have lunch in the midst of them, Captain, dazzled by their clothes, by their perfume, by their long hairy and smooth thighs, by the prickly little hedgehogs I imagined down underneath their belly buttons, by the round dampness of bodies close together, by the sea sound of their conversations, by my grandmother who would pull my ear every so often, who would cast a glance in a circle around the women, benevolently authoritarian, wearing an ivory rosary around her fat neck, who forbade me to play in the hallway of the place with numbered doors on both sides and prints showing monks in sandals and with naked girls in their laps: Your mother, uncle, my mother's mother, who got upset over your marriages, didn't want to hear your name mentioned, insulted Dona Isaura (the afternoon sun was creeping across the floor like a yellow worm, uncovering new imperfections, new defects, new holes in the wood), the one with fierce deep eyes, who immobilized the girls into a respectful panic.

"If they took the prime minister away in an armored car, we're lost," Mr.

Ilídio lamented with his head in his hands. "It won't be long before they'll come looking for us, with pistols, here at the warehouse."

Tables confiscated, bidets confiscated, pianos confiscated, all those useless rotting old things, the dust itself and the rats and the cobwebs confiscated, the shop sealed up by cross-eyed militiamen, the bookkeeper flinging her arms about in despair, waving her purse, behind bars. You would approve of this one, this Dona Emília, Grandmother, she belonged to your race of falsely quiet, falsely generous tarantulas, when I fired her she threatened me with the police, wanted to hit me, drag me through the courts, she sent her son, a great big printer, to threaten me with a beating.

"Don't be crazy," Dona Emília said dryly. (If you were in charge of a whorehouse there'd be good screwing at least in Portugal.) "What have you done for them to arrest you?"

The number of people on the square kept growing, a lot of them carrying flags and radios as at a soccer game, the trees were a tangle of arms and legs and attentive, expectant, voracious eyes, a tank came out of the crowd, headed toward the Guard headquarters, open mouths, hundreds of teeth gleaming in the sun in the green froth strained through the leaves, elbows pushing me, arms getting entangled with mine, acid breath blowing on the back of my neck, and enthusiastic sweat in my nostrils, and all of a sudden, Captain, I felt four, five, six, seven years old again, submerged by the fantastic, heavy, terrifying proportions of adults, the square had been transformed into my grandmother's endless dining room, filled with rectangular images of little saints and dubious nymphs, occupied by hundreds and hundreds of awakened, tawdry, languid, half-naked whores, who were darkening their eyelids with brushes, filing down the calluses on their feet, shouting mechanically and rhythmically, FREE-DOM FREE-DOM FREE-DOM, strolling in front of the headquarters on Carmo in transparent underwear or in bath towels, their shoulders glistening with droplets, waving to me from a distance, funny, comical waves, ironic leers, gay, graceful gestures, as if I didn't notice, Captain, as if I were a ridiculous, half-idiot dolt of a child, as if I hadn't secretly spied on the bedrooms along the hall and hadn't seen them stretched out on the bed, thighs apart, after having got undressed with surprising swiftness, pushing down the bedspread, folding their clothes, accompanied by soldiers, older guys, young kids all hot and bothered and bashful in Sunday ties and jackets, as if I hadn't spied on the bodies awash on the mattresses, the squirming of hips and behinds, the dark almond of the pubes that they would wash while straddling the bidet with the liquid from a straw-covered jug, the uncle opened the desk drawer again, shuffled through the junk inside, took out the bottle of pills, put a tablet in his mouth and from the depths of his chair lifted up his eyes wild with fear to them:

"Everybody in the can as quick as a flash, you'll see, they'll requisition my trucks for their services, make me put up Bulgarian engineers and Polish spies, order me to sleep on the living-room floor wrapped up in an old blanket, shivering."

And Dona Emília to me, indignant, Look, look, he's gone crazy, he's off his nut, he's got a screw loose somewhere in his head, drinking the water out of my vases, stuffing himself with pills, accidentally swallowing the geranium leaves, you're a member of the family, get him to a doctor right away, a cousin of mine went on like that for months on end until they got his blood pressure down with a salt-free diet and he was fine, the shouts grew in intensity, the crowd undulated like the wake of a ship, the armored car, looking like a tin can, went through the headquarters gate, nothing could be made out through the peepholes, maybe some shapes, some shadows, some imprecise silhouettes, At least those bastards won't be giving anyone a hard time anymore, an old man wearing a beret and a carnation in his lapel said, right next to the soldier, They'd never given me a hard time at all, Captain, it was all the same to me, I didn't care whether it was these or those just as long as there was work and a little money at the end of the month for me to invite Odete to go to the movies or to the beach or to the dances at the Estefânia Club, the first floor, an orchestra, fierce mothers riding herd on their daughters, sitting around the room on stern watch, a few boys threatened the armored car with their fists, spat at the little windows, insulted the shapes inside there, Fascists, bastards, sons of bitches, the people again began to shout FREE-DOM FREE-DOM FREE-DOM obeying the tinny voice of an invisible microphone, the syllables pouring together in an enormous roar, the soldiers were protecting the Guard headquarters now, the guys perched up on the trees were sliding down the trunks and we began to break up little by little, from time to time a shout He's from the PIDE, he's from the PIDE, and running, shoving, blows, swats, a man, bleeding from his head and mouth, struggling in vain in the center of an angry whirlwind, I seemed to be getting a glimpse of Odete everywhere, even in the mannequins in shop windows, and I was always wrong, What if I've fallen in love, I thought, what if she disappeared and I went around butting my head against walls, all upset, we finally convinced my uncle to go home and there were a lot of people talking on the sidewalks or from one balcony to another, we left the bookkeeper at a bus stop, under a small green canopy, and in his uncle's eyes the soldier caught the difficulty, the despair, the anguish of separating from her, The same thing happened to me, he calculated, frightened, it's strange what happens to old people, they've got wrinkles and illnesses and kidney stones and they can't hold their piss and still and through all they persist, machine-gun squads here and there, on street corners with carnations stuck in their uniforms, multilipped flowers that were withering, night had fallen completely and the usual dogs were nuzzling in garbage cans with slow voluptuousness, cars were rooting sadly alongside parks, men already drunk were talking and arguing about the Revolution in crowded dairy stores with bottles of anise and chocolate in their dirty display windows, the bookkeeper remained behind there, all alone, staring at them with melancholy and apprehensive eyes, suddenly so unsheltered that the soldier felt a kind of pity for her loneliness, he pictured a rented room at the end of an alley, an ancient bed that creaked, dresses concealed behind a sketchy cloth drape, but his uncle, wheezing, plowed into a corner bar right next door to a barbershop, shoved people out of his way with his frog elbows, laid his hand flat on the stone bar marked by purple circles from glasses, the proprietor, sleeves rolled up, brought over an oblique, inquiring smile, and Mr. Ilídio, ogling the hourglass shape of the naked girl on a calendar, Two shots of clear stuff to raise our morale. I wonder what Dona Emília looks like without any clothes on? the soldier thought, coughing, blind with the tears brought on by the bagaceira, the raw grape liquor, while his bones, rubbery now, were filling up with alcohol: still desirable, without any wrinkles, her breasts sagging a little, her belly smooth, or, maybe, repulsive, covered with hair, enormous moles, big soft behind, cellulite on her thighs? His uncle was swallowing shot after shot, and since he kept ordering them by twos the soldier was also tossing down that transparent thick liquid that lighted up a painful stearin wick in every corner of his insides, while the uncle was slowly getting involved in the conversation between a hospital orderly and a mail-man with a speech defect, furnishing points of view, asides, warnings, the hospital orderly was in favor of freedom, to the mailman it didn't matter, they were taking advantage of the Revolution to have a few drinks besides the usual Sunday ones, at a certain moment the bar owner covered the girl on the calendar with the national flag and wrote on the not-too-clean plaster LONG LIVE DEMOCRACY, What the hell is democracy? the soldier thought, his shoes beginning to rise weightlessly from the floor, his arms fluttering like seaweed, his head freeing itself from worries and annoyances and climbing up through the smoky air of the bar like a gas balloon, Mr. Ilídio was explaining at great length to the mailman the functioning of an asthma spray atomizer and several curious bystanders squeezed the rubber atomizer, the way tires are pumped up, into the inside of their mouths, Open your lungs, my friends, the uncle was announcing, stumbling over chairs, spraying the customers with the apparatus, open your lungs to springtime, someone pushed him, annoyed, and the uncle fell facedown onto a domino table where four old men, skinny sucked-in cheeks, jealously hiding their pieces from the myopic curiosity of the others, broke out into croaks of indignation through their toothless gums, the soldier, his legs wobbly, helped him up, rowing in the vacuum, and they went back to their drinks, Long Live Democracy, Long Live Freedom, Mr. Ilídio howled in a senile little yelp, the old men were trying in vain to set their game up again, cursing in an incomprehensible spittle of obscenities, Mr. Ilídio called the bartender over with the hook of his forefinger Red wine for everybody in the name of the

Revolution, and almost instantaneously, you know what it's like, even when he was picked up, even uncomfortable, even shaken constantly by the shoulders, on the sides, by voices, by people's knees, he broke into a snore.

The armored car finally disappeared, Captain, followed by a swarm of people, and after a few moments the crowd left the square, singing anthems and songs he'd never heard before on the radio (I prefer romantic music, he confessed to Odete later during a break at the movies, looking at a showcase with pink baby clothes, Spanish songs that send a tingle up your spine because they talk about love), the soldiers also withdrew from the square with the exception of seven or eight guys in camouflage dress who protected the headquarters against the chill of dusk, the soldier sat down on a bench, hands in his pockets, watching night come on, you couldn't see the river now and the opposite bank was a bunch of trembling little lights twinkling in nothingness, the buildings rolled up and twisted first before stretching out, gigantic, among the trees, I'm five, six years old and this is the time my grandmother's establishment begins to operate, the first people ring the bell, the girls, painted, in very short dresses and high heels, wait, all composed, in that little parlor with a ceiling ready to fall, full of torn velvets and mirrors, sipping fake martinis through pursed lips, the old woman, in an apron and slippers, hair loose, checks the rooms one by one, the bedclothes, the bidets, the jugs of disinfectant behind the doors, a strong smell of cologne and cooking makes me dizzy, the women's long shinbones make me dizzy, the large breasts almost showing make me dizzy, the dark nipples, the throats, the backs of necks, the round elbows make me dizzy, the mirrors that throw images against each other make me dizzy, That bastard Ilídio has no regard for, I don't want him here, the grandmother muttered in the direction of the curtains, the bastards my children are, they don't know how to do anything but show no regard, anyone who saw them would think I'd brought them up that way, the huge Sacred Heart of Jesus received waves of bald gentlemen in the vestibule with the obsequious smell of a majordomo, they finally dragged themselves home, his uncle and he, embraced, greeting everybody, pissing at every lamppost, stammering marches, muttering in unison FREE-DOM FREE-DOM FREE-DOM, Odete stood looking at us, mouth open, on the straw mat, not answering the Hello that neither of us gave her, Be calm, kid, my uncle advised her patriotically, down with fascism and oppression, Dona Isaura was snoring in bed, a triumphant announcer on the radio was giving news of the complete victory of the Armed Forces Movement, they collapsed, flies open and shirttails hanging out, onto the sofa beside the oilcloth table cover, and when I closed my red and painful eyes, Captain, a swirl of whores and soldiers came spinning inside my head, calling me, accusing me, insulting me, until after three or four farts or sobs or belches, if you'll excuse me, I fell asleep.

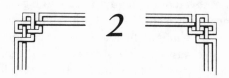

2

The telephone rang and moments later the lieutenant colonel's hand moved in the darkness, feeling around, touching the granulated skin of the carpet, looking for the receiver: his fingers ran into a slipper, a coil of wire, a fallen book, open in the darkness like a wound, bleeding letters: the noise went on indifferently, with mechanical tenacity, stripes that were paler now were turning the spaces between the slats of the blinds blue, the squat forms of furniture could be made out as they took on shape and dissolved like waves in the sea, the metal heart of the clock was beating softly, anxiously during the brief, rhythmical moments of silence between rings, his hand finally found the smooth plastic surface, he lifted it to his mouth, and listened to himself mumble through successive curtains of saliva and bronchitis, Hello.

"Artur?"

The shadows smelled of the cleaning woman's dark body, of the thick, strong mixture of sweat and cheap cologne that she was made of, weak sighs still crept across the pillow, she straightened her hair as she sat on the edge of the bed laughing: the small voice repeated, weak and hesitant, like the struggles of a little dog, in the numb funnel of his ear:

"Artur?"

A truck passed on the street and the lieutenant colonel wriggled under the covers, uncomfortable with so many sounds pushing and pulling him, drawing and quartering him, cutting up his insides. Still confused, he rested his other cheek on the pillow, the bones of his face sank deliciously into the froth of the stuffing, and the breathing in his ear once more, the anguish of the small voice that was pursuing him like a ferret with its afflicted haste:

"Artur? It's Ricardo, I'm calling from the Ministry of Defense. (He imagined sounds, coughing, orders, hurried steps, discussions.) A few blockheads are going around playing at revolution and you've got to get to your unit as fast as possible, bring them to their senses, instill order: we can't let ourselves tolerate adventurism of this sort."

The lieutenant colonel inhaled the concierge's thick smell that was slowly coming off the bedclothes and hovering over him in solid swirls of flesh, he moved again, rested the back of his neck against the bedstead and said goodbye to the maid, who was waving to him from the door, buttoning up her knitted jacket, with a funny little farewell.

"So long, pussycat."

"What's that?" Colonel Ricardo asked, perplexed.

"Nothing, don't pay any attention to it, I was talking to myself," he murmured very quickly. "What time is it?"

"Going on four o'clock. The secretary of state says we haven't got any time to lose, we've got to straighten that bunch of kids out one way or another before anything foolish happens, any mess that can't be remedied discreetly. Your headquarters controls the entrance to Lisbon against anyone coming from the north, a half-dozen half-tracks placed here and there, a few dozen men you can trust, decisive, able. You've got to use your prestige with the younger officers, and it goes without saying that we're all counting on that, we're asking you to help avoid a childish piece of asininity no matter what it costs."

"Shit," the lieutenant colonel complained, waving at the empty door with a smile, "you people won't even let me sleep."

He remained sitting in the dark with the instrument hanging in his hand like a dead bird, until he reluctantly squeezed the switch on the night-table lamp (the light made him curl up over himself like a worm) and looked at the square clock whose springs were throbbing rapidly like the neck of a dove: three-thirty. Either that piece of shit is slow, he thought, or Ricardo is lying to hurry me up. There they were, your choice, the same old junk, clothes on the chair, the picture of the dead woman in the silver frame, examining him with that eternally alarmed and apprehensive smile. Maybe he should have advised the Ministry of Captain Mendes's intentions, maybe he should have done something before now, maybe with a little tact he could have got rid of that annoyance: how many columns from the provinces, how many armored vehicles, how many companies, how many Indians on the warpath? He went to the bathroom to urinate and run some water over his hair, dazzled by the light that was too bright, he put on his uniform and kept getting the buttons mixed up (How strange it was living alone, where these rooms had become great compartments), he felt around on all fours for one of his shoes under the bed, his head congested with blood and a sharp buzzing in his temples, limply knotted his tie in front of the mirror on the dresser, fighting against the languid and inert desire to get back into bed, close his exhausted eyes against the pillow, cover himself with the blanket, and fall asleep: the telephone rang again (More orders? More information? More alarms?) without the lieutenant colonel's answering, thinking This is the route you follow every night after you say goodbye to me, your slippers trot along the carpet, your energetic straight trunk, the decreasing merriment of your laugh, the elevator was a long time in coming, creaking and swaying on its rotting cables, he pushed the button without daring to look at himself in the rectangular mirror in the rear, full of defects and scratches (the face of someone dug up from the grave, the creased face of an old man), the garbage guys were running for their green trucks with diagonal red and white stripes on the rear end, the coldness of the night was freezing me inside my uniform, my testicles were two numb little kernels buried in my belly, my beard, which was growing, rustled in the darkness like bushes by the sea defending themselves against the waves in chinks in the rocks. Weary advertising signs blinked here and there, the dying halo of streetlights slipped its weightless hand over the backs of parked cars whose flanks were wrapped in a gelatinous mist of dampness. The crooked buildings slowly sank into the asphalt.

"Artur?" the anguished little voice of a while ago spoke out in his head. "It's Ricardo, I'm calling from the Ministry of Defense, a few boys out there are going around playing at revolution." And while he was searching in his pockets with stiff fingers, still thick with sleep, for the keys, he remembered the small, redheaded, always nervous shape of the other man, the sparse wine-colored tufts on his forehead, punctuated with freckles that would light up alternately out of fear, indignation, surprise. The garbage truck was gobbling up crate after crate with fearsome gurgles, the workers, almost all Cape Verdeans, were noisily tossing the empty containers back on the sidewalk, they hung on the running board, advanced ten, fifteen, twenty yards, jumped off again running, putting crates onto the moving platforms that went up and down like muscular iron biceps, lifting up great dark plastic cups to their mouths, the car's battery refused to work, a faint little light was quivering on the dashboard, You've got to use your prestige with the younger officers, it's absolutely imperative that you help avoid a childish bit of asininity, and the worry, the doubt, the panic in his voice, the freckles on his indecisive, frightened forehead on fire, sergeants going back and forth with messages in their hands, radio operators encoding orders, the secretary of state bringing grave generals together in his office, he pushed the Volkswagen with the help of the night watchman, dead drunk, who always gave

him complicated salutes and whose useless rusty enormous sword held him
back, entangling in his legs, toward a steep slope by the firehouse (Why don't
they have their coups d'etat at three in the afternoon, why in hell aren't there
civil servants to handle revolutions?), and listening to the stubborn sobbing of
the engine, the cylinders skipping, and finally running, harshly, continuously, the beam of the headlights stronger, façades, windows, doors, the
Formica look of the buildings (I'll bet that behind those walls there's nothing
but a carpentry mock-up of boards, paint cans, shavings, smudges, uncombed hair and fleeting faces, the usual backstage confusion), he caught the
smell of the concierge on the seat next to him and he looked at the empty
place with astonishment, a smell that was rustic and pretentious at the same
time, sardonic and tender (How quickly you became accustomed, not complaining, to my silences, my rare grunts, my tight face, the stiff absence of
affection in my body), green, amber, red lights that made him stop, start,
stop, start again, he ran his hand over the seat, That's not where the smell is,
it's on me, the biting odor of armpits, groin, the long biological-science-book
mammoth hairs of the vulva, the little radio on the dashboard wasn't working, whistling, shrieking, belching an incomprehensible stew of words, her
diligent fingers on my penis, up and down in quickening cadence, What an
empty city at night, so uninhabited, so dead, and going around the Encarnação circle, the berm sown with a hedge like a cake of shadows, the long
wall at the post, painted white, with two or three rows of barbed wire on top,
the concrete tower with its extinguished searchlight, just like dentists' round
lamps, and the main gate at the end, the inside obscured by a tangle of
shadows: Ricardo is sick in the head, who wants to get mixed up in any
troubles now. He stopped the car, blew the horn, one or two dim figures in
camouflage dress (Camouflage?) appeared, staring at him, and finally from
the sergeant of the guard's cubicle a figure emerged at a trot, at attention with
a pistol in his hand (Second Lieutenant Baptista?), leaning over the window,
cupping his hand over his eyes, opening the door, and saying in a rapid,
uncertain tone, You're under arrest, Commander sir, please get out. Armed
soldiers had surrounded the Volkswagen, someone was working the difficult
hinges of the gate, shouting could be heard, the sound of armored vehicles on
the lawns by the barracks, a jeep, weaving, squashed the grass and the
marigolds in the flower beds with the great round boots of its tires.

"What the fuck is going on?" the lieutenant colonel asked, annoyed,
observing dark shadows, accusing and timid, that surrounded him. "And put
those rifles away, you might get wounded by mistake," while he thought Go
back home, get into bed, fall asleep, shit on all this, and then, as the sound of
the armored vehicles increased and the buildings of the regiment filled with
busy movement in the darkness, Ricardo is right, these guys are crazy, you
don't make a serious revolution this way.

The soldiers hesitated, confused, one or two of them withdrew the butts of their rifles to unload the round (To sleep), but Lieutenant Baptista, still pointing his pistol, determined, small and squat, his eyes enlarged immensely by the lenses of his glasses, snorted around him What did I tell you to do, you bastards? and to the lieutenant colonel, blinking his enormous eyelashes that moved up and down like a fringe of stiff wire (Even my mouth smells like your mouth, how strange), Be so kind as to accompany me upstairs.

"Baptista, just imagine," he smiled, with an enterprising woman on each side, shaking his sad, long ears over the glass of champagne. "Chubby, ridiculous, timid, always alone reading in some corner, I never thought he was worth a red cent."

A corporal disappeared over the gravel of the parade ground with the Volkswagen (the rubber groaned and sang like a pair of new shoes), the figures in the duty sergeant's office calmed down gradually like hens on a roost, the cloth wings of their uniforms settled down, the howls from the radio were coming through the half-open door, Lieutenant Baptista touched him lightly on the flank with the pistol (Even his uniform smells of her, even the air around him smells of her), and they began to walk in the darkness, next to each other, tripping over the mismatched sound of their own steps, in the direction of the mournful building of the administrative offices, through whose windows a deathlike, nightmarish glow was sifting, just like those indecisive dawns of disaster that insomnia invents: Like when I wake up in the middle of the night, the lieutenant colonel thought, with your muscular and energetic mare's body softly entwined with mine, a leg over my legs, a sharp elbow digging into my neck, and nothing turning the shades pale, the room is a pitch black cube that retracts and expands to the rhythm of the cleaning woman's lungs and her imperative bad breath, the terrible, fierce odor of her armpits, sown with tiny tufts of algae, as if two other mouths had grown underneath her arms, reduced to the sponginess of gums. I would wake up, get the thick granite weight of your thighs off me, prop the pillow against the headboard, sit up in bed, and my eyes would grow large, feeling about the furniture and the silence of the apartment, the distant drip of the kitchen faucet, the floorboards that creaked, alive, as if some gauzelike ghost were treading on them. I take a pill, I don't take a pill, I slide down a chemical slope in the direction of a coma, and right there the alarm clock starts sobbing (Five o'clock in the morning shit), the concierge moves beside me, uncomfortable, still chatting with the same fantastic animals of her dreams, protesting, arguing, the bad breath grows stronger, the acrid perfume of her armpits fills the whole room, like a pair of twin badgers stinking up the breath of a tomb in unison, and then groping for, turning on the lamp on the night table, a sudden light that splinters objects and explodes your brain, and after that the place slowly, painfully taking shape again, clothes on the carpet, window frames, a piece of stucco chipped off near the ceiling, the woman's kinky hair emerging, studded with hairpins, from the sheets, the myopic eyes sleepy, the usual annoyed expression, I've got to leave, love, and I couldn't figure out if I detested her or liked her, if I really had any regard for her or only needed some kind of company, it didn't matter what kind, a woman, a Siamese cat, a puppy, a parakeet, something alive and warm and moving that made you feel alive too, hating her and desiring her while I kissed her goodbye, wrapped up in the covers like an animal (I've got to send you to the dentist this week without fail, I've got to ask him to clean your teeth), and staring at her, upset with myself, while she slipper-shuffled out of the room to the landing, buttoning up her blouse, slipping on her cardigan, feeling the hairpins, carrying that repugnant sum of smells with her, the street door slammed and the dull echo resounded through the deserted rooms for a long time, the lieutenant colonel put the sleeping pill on his tongue, swallowed it without water and felt the tablet going hesitantly down his throat, he put out the lamp and lay still for a long time, his eyes open, like a cornered dog, pondering the soft and enervating texture of the silence.

While the second lieutenant and he were approaching the administration building, whose shadow turned shrubs and dry flower stalks blue, the sluggishness of sleep was slowly drifting out of his brain in the same way that mist dissolves, a remnant of confused clouds was swimming away from him into the distance, inside his eyes a column of armored vehicles was forming on the parade grounds and the lieutenant colonel thought, dispirited, Ricardo's right, the characters at the Ministry are right, it really is a revolt, seeing the armed soldiers, unexpectedly warlike, swarming into the vehicles, commands, countermands, shouts, confusion, an agitated, sulfuric fever in the air.

"Get in there," Lieutenant Baptista ordered him with no respect whatsoever, shoving his pistol into his ribs. It must have been going on six o'clock, a dirty, whitish halo, slimy with cold, was beginning to watercolor the trees, the outline of the buildings, the broad emptiness of the airport in the distance, walls, shacks, no pigeons, chimneys. Almost six o'clock, he thought, the city rising up out of the dark, confused and bland, like a soufflé taking its shape from a glass mold, wide-open windows exploding outward, a strange bustle in the mess: Am I really here or just dreaming it, Ricardo's phone call, his anxious haste, the idiot threat of a military coup that he invented, he climbed the long stone steps in front of Lieutenant Baptista, who was breathing heavily behind him at kidney level, and in the office of the vice-commander, guarded by a corporal with a machine gun, he came upon some officers with lost eyes, smoking in silence with great worried wrinkles on their creased foreheads. The priest, leaning on the windowsill, clutching his beads, was observing the maneuvers of the gray vehicles down below, the platoons in helmets, armed with mortars and bazookas, climbing like insects into the Mercedes trucks, a guy on his knees on the gravel working a walkie-talkie while the morning fermented in the midst of superimposed clusters of clouds, the trees became trees in fact and silhouettes turned into people, the sounds were taking on their usual everyday hoarse tones, Lieutenant Baptista turned the key in the lock from outside and there we were, prisoners, counterrevolutionaries, fascists, bourgeois, Nazis, I, two majors, the chaplain with his rosary in his soft seamstress fingers, a half-dozen terrified captains and junior officers, some in uniform, others in civilian clothes, others still in a strange mixture of peaceful and warlike garb, as if we were awaiting a summary judgment in the courtyard behind the barracks buildings, led by a vociferous and bearded leftist raising his accusing clenched fist all the while. The Mercedeses left in a column, fanning out the gravel, preceded by two or three weary jeeps, rust colored, whose engines were missing a beat, like an old man's heart, and an early timid sun, diffuse, out of nowhere, spread out its open fingers like a fan over the flower beds, just like the acid and stellar luminosity of an aquarium. The lieutenant colonel sat down in the vice-commander's chair, with the majors and captains looking at him hopefully, as if they were awaiting something from him, an order, a smile, a call, a definitive explanation, he rested his elbows on the desk, pushing folders aside, and he was already starting to fall asleep, wrapping himself in a cobweb with a sticky weave where everything was stretching out and losing color, sinking into a soft and concave coat of mail that fended off spikes and thorns with his gestures, when the key turned painfully in the lock (Or inside my skull?), hurried steps resounded on the carpet, from a great distance he heard the voice of Captain Mendes, he opened his eyes with the stubborn difficulty of an oyster, and he made out three or four men in camouflage dress with rifles, motionless boots on the fringe of the rug, while the captives approached in silence, obliquely, slow and sleepwalking like men condemned to death: It can't be, he thought through a wavy curtain of mist, a thick, invincible gauze of surrender and fatigue, I don't understand anything, there's something wrong in all this, there must be some mistake.

"As you probably know," Captain Mendes advised, suddenly imperative, authoritative, lodging the barrel of his weapon in his armpit like a thermometer, "some hours ago the Armed Forces Movement initiated a series of patriotic military operations that have as their aim the fall of the present government and its quick replacement by a regime that will respond to the legitimate aspirations of the Portuguese people (Still the same old speech, the lieutenant colonel said to himself, startled, still the same shit phrases, now even soldiers have taken to talking like politicians.) I give you my word of honor that before nightfall the Marcelista dictatorship will come to an end."

"And what dictatorship is going to follow it? Confess," the chaplain squeaked, swinging his rosary back and forth. "Atheistic communism?"

Sunk in his chair in a kind of algaelike languid torpor, which reduced his bones to an uninterrupted flow of bubbles, the lieutenant colonel was gazing out the window at the now energetic morning sun against the battered and now unmysterious buildings of the post, the weary daytime trees, bereft of shadows, waving their arms pathetically in the excess light, the small, deserted infirmary, open wide and showing its tonsils of beds: Are even the patients running around attacking ministries, arresting deputies, shooting district governors? His mother, dressed in a black low-cut gown, casting a dark, fatal, evaluating look about the stupefied officers, touched one of the majors on the back and pointed him out bitterly with her fan:

"The minute he was born I had a feeling he'd never amount to much."

Captain Mendes wavered on his endless, thin tarantula legs, withdrew the rifle thermometer from his armpit: How many degrees did it go up, the lieutenant colonel thought in his dreamy fog, how much warlike fever has this guy got? He didn't seem entirely at ease, his pained eyes were searching for some object which he could grab, to touch a pitiful crutch for his own timidity, his own surprise at suddenly finding himself a revolutionary, a plotter, a conspirator. A broad-shouldered character, without insignia, unshaven, wearing an Air Force uniform, placed himself next to Captain Mendes with fierce hands behind his back and unleashed a quick, hurried glance over those present, haggard from lack of sleep:

"All units and practically all officers have joined the Movement," he announced with an ill-humored scowl that turned the tight skin under his eyes purple, "you gentlemen make up some of the few exceptions we've had news of. Only as a precaution, I repeat, only as a precaution (he pronounced the syllables as if all the teeth in his mouth were aching), we're obliged to hold you here until the operations under way are completed. Once those are done, we'll let you know what your fate will be, and each case will be carefully weighed. For now, and provisionally, the command of the regiment is in the hands of Captain Mendes."

"Tell me one thing," the chaplain asked, holding up his rosary and striking the pose of a martyr, "are you a bolshevik?"

"And all that, you understand," the lieutenant colonel explained to me, pushing away one of the fat women in the club who persisted in hanging about his neck, whining insistent, incomprehensible words of affection through the thick tubing of her mouth, "looked to me, combatants and noncombatants, jailers and prisoners, and especially the idiotic atmosphere we were caught up in, like a ridiculous piece of fiction, a puppet show, a complete farce, idiocy squared, cubed, raised to the tenth power, which a little discipline and common sense on the part of the Ministry would have resolved in a minute."

"Bolshevik?" the Air Force man muttered, wrinkling his brow, intrigued. "Bolshevik, what's that?"

And he imagined dirty, skinny workers, the unmistakable victims of the Estado Novo, with hollow faces and dirty fingernails, intoning the "Internationale" in tiny, modest living rooms, burning with cigarette smoke and emotion, worms in rags, gnawed by illnesses, who were limping out of their shantytowns to attack, mewling with jubilation, the poor boxes in churches, the silver crowns of the saints, the vestments in the blackwood cupboard in the sacristy, You've got to use your prestige with the younger officers, the chaplain kneeled down, surrounded by shelves of files, maps, and wire-enclosed cabinets, and burst into prayer, eyes closed, aloud, like a pilgrim at Fátima, he thought he was going to die, you see, he thought he was going to be shot by Lenin in person, Come on, Father Nunes, cut out the sissy stuff, the drill major advised, quite shocked, a mustache of sweat clinging to his lip, the veil of fatigue and sleepiness that separated him from the world wasn't going away, it was going up and down, the lieutenant colonel noted with a slight, almost delighted surprise, They must be waiting for me to say something, approve the operation, encourage them to carry on, they must want me to offer them my name with a kiss on the hand in order to convince reluctant officers, the paratroopers, for example, the marines, a few friends of the Army, and me there, stretched out in a chair, indifferent to the Ministry, indifferent to the Movement, indifferent to the confused agitation all around me, distracted, weightless, vaguely smiling, floating inside myself like a tasteless perfume, while the people were looking at me in silence, amazed, with convex, twisted faces deformed by the fishbowl glass of my torpor.

"There's still time, Commander sir, for you to join us," Captain Mendes said in a casual, hollow tone, with his head down, adjusting his belt buckle, trying to reach a neutral tone, a dry bare bone of words.

Just like Colonel Ricardo, he thought, like the secretary of state, like the guys who right now are shitting with fear at the Terreiro do Paço, clinging to the telephone, to the radio, to the supporters who've suddenly broken away from us, as evasive as leaves falling from a tree: and it gave him the idea that they'd all suddenly discovered themselves at the same time, that I'm a steady fellow, a two-fisted guy, and he imagined the freckle-faced thin-haired man explaining to a worried group of generals You gentlemen will see, we're secure as far as Artur's concerned, there's no problem, and the maid's smell still clinging to my skin, her bad breath making her harsh, withered flower grow in my mouth, her hand saying goodbye between the bedroom and the hall, Bye-bye.

"I'm in, what the fuck," proclaimed an older lieutenant from General Services, giving a little leap as if the floor were burning him. His fingers, restless, went in and out of the pockets of his shirt: Do I have to sign something? Has anybody got a sheet of paper with a seal to lend me?

"They haven't stopped calling you," Captain Mendes told me, not listening to the other one, who was anxiously rummaging through the files, knocking things over, in search of a fifty-escudo stamp, a perforated little rectangle that would save him. "I had them switch the calls up here, we'd like you to straighten things out with the Ministry, Commander."

The General Services lieutenant had placed a sheet of paper against the wall and was writing laboriously, chewing on his tongue: more trucks were roaring on the parade ground, more shouts, the sound of soft objects falling: Corpses? he thought, confused, could some be dead? The Air Force man whispered something into the ear of one of the centurions in camouflage dress, he galloped off swallowing up his own shadow with his huge boots, and the echo of his footsteps rolled around and bounced off each other along the endless corridor on the way to the stone steps. One of the majors lighted two cigarettes at the same time and stood looking at them with a stupid, indescribable scowl, the second major was fluttering around aimlessly, bumping into the furniture like a wounded bird, no one was talking, a thick, sweaty tension spread out through the office, and at that moment the telephone began to sob with repeated moans, insistent and stubborn, like a hungry pup. Colonel Ricardo's voice seemed to be coming from Saturn, refracted and diluted by thick, innumerable, colored towels of water. There must have been taps everywhere, interference, whistling, effervescence, mechanical coughing swallowed up and sank the words, which would suddenly return to the surface, all agitated in a disorder of insects.

"Artur?" the redhead asked. "Artur? Damn it, I finally got you, you're harder to reach than the pope, they keep telling me you're not there, that you've just left, that you haven't got in yet, that you'll call me later, the usual excuses, the usual lies, Jesus. Here they're telling me that you've joined the coup for sure, that your unit is furnishing logistical support to those nitwits, those lunatics, and I've been defending you like a Doberman, swearing to them that you're loyal to the government, that you've got your men under your control, that sooner or later you'll blow the whistle and calm them down, that your armor will head downtown, that you'll take care of your part in the whole affair in a wink of the eye."

The voice went under, came back to the surface, sank again, listing like a dying transatlantic ocean liner, he called desperately:

"Artur? Artur? You didn't hang up, did you, Artur? I'm going to turn you over to our General Mendonça (What? he thought, that idiot?) who'd like to give you the directives of the General Staff personally."

Silence and then squealing again, a kind of cooing, the mechanical coughing of a while back, the wires crackling, nuts and bolts dissolving in a prolix mush of sounds.

"Colonel Esteves, General Mendonça here," he announced, unexpectedly close by, in the middle of a pause in the interference, the lugubrious voice of a hoarse parrot. "The instructions are the following, would you please jot them down. It doesn't matter if they hear us because if you're quick enough you'll take them from behind no matter what they do."

It was followed by a furious storm of noises on which individual phrases still floated, just like drifting boats, and not just individual phrases, friend, as if they were talking in code, calls, songs, so loud that he held the receiver a few inches away from his ear, breathing in your smell in the officers' uniforms, in the wire-mesh cupboard, the flags leaning against the wall, in the ocher stains, tobacco colored, on the paint of the ceiling: I haven't gotten up, it's early, the alarm clock hasn't gone off, I pop another half a pill into my mouth and keep on sleeping, in a restlessness of agonizing nightmares, until I wake up painfully, like jelly, at eight o'clock and then the inevitable daily, stabbing thought, What now? that keeps on resounding like a threat of pain through the deserted apartment, even if I urinate, even if I shave, even while I'm putting on my shorts, undershirt, shirt, trying to comb my graying hair, I brush my teeth and my mouth fills up with the light minty foam, I go out into the street, not having eaten, with your body and my age on my mind, to have a cup of coffee in the nearest pastry shop, dirty with nighttime sawdust and yesterday's cigarette butts, which the rachitic little handyman hasn't swept away for the sad, aloe-colored, dim and mournful morning in the city: Still winter, goddamn it, when is the sun going to come out in this country? And the customers with eyes puffy from sleep, the customers with the slow movements of sleep, the customers with rumpled clothing, ugly, dispirited faces, numb exasperation. The storm lets up a little, the words on the telephone, solid once more, were taking on new consistency and strength, talking to him now about the Navy, the strategic importance of the Navy, guns aimed from the river at key points in Lisbon. The lieutenant colonel stretched in his chair, pulled an invisible sheet up to his neck: take communion with a couple of pills, turn off the switch to the sun, doze off.

"General sir," he said softly, taking advantage of the brief clear space of a pause. (The way my words are evaporating, he thought, the way everything around me is evaporating.) "It isn't worth wasting your Latin lesson on me, I'm not going to obey any of the orders you've given me."

The General Services lieutenant, fanning the sheet with his revolutionary support to dry the ink, stared at him with stupefaction: his little mustache, along with his eyebrows, quivered with terror, just like an imprisoned member, his throat was going up and down, most upset: I wish they'd leave me alone, the lieutenant colonel thought, I wish they'd let me sleep.

"Have you gone crazy, Esteves?" the general asked, outraged, in a volley of belches, a wave of electrical hail that was buzzing. (Captain Mendes took a step forward on the carpet.)

"No, I haven't gone crazy and you heard me perfectly, General sir," the lieutenant colonel explained with the didactic sweetness of someone in love. "I have no intention of lifting a finger in favor of the government."

He put the phone in its cradle (General Mendonça's voice was shouting Just a minute just a minute just a minute, in the midst of explosions, alternating current firecrackers, Bakelite yawns, and the gurgling of a sprinkler), stared at the window opposite with blind eyes, and slowly stretched: just a tiny effort, reaching out to the left with his hand, grabbing the bottle, opening it, dropping one of those bitter yellow circles into his mouth, and waiting for his blood to thicken and slowly become motionless inside him until his body slipped, inert, into a deep swamp of sheets and oblivion, where his fingers at times touched the rotting and repugnant faces of the dead, coming closer and going away, drifting, with their enormous accusing and swollen eyelids. The telephone wept one or two oblique protests and fell silent, the sound of assault cars was constant on the parade ground, soldiers shouting, the heroic military marches on the radio, laughter, the chaplain had withdrawn into a corner between two flags, murmuring inaudible discourses with the valiant scowl of a person in the confessional, the day seemed ready to explode with light, lancing the clouds like soft boils, the doorknob turned and the Air Force man entered the office smiling, We've got practically everything in our hands, the lieutenant colonel opened up an imaginary bottle, poured the contents into his hand, got more comfortable in the chair bed, put his tongue out, Captain Mendes spoke solemnly, turned toward me, "In the name of the Movement, Commander sir, I thank you for the collaboration you have offered us," but the lieutenant colonel instantly dismissed the speech with a shrug of his octopus shoulders: What a dark night, he said to himself, what devilish silence in this apartment, no reflection, no glimmer of life in these shadows. His own voice, independent of him, wavered, rose and sank again, suddenly grew, suddenly diminished, evaporated sometimes, on the edge of silence, with slimy rhymes, was taking on an unexpected sureness, weakened later, became ossified again, authoritarian and sharp immediately after, while he looked at the cleaning woman, half-dressed, half-naked, unrolling a stocking from her perch upon a pile of dossiers, right behind a monarchist second lieutenant with a signet ring, most concerned:

"Please stop raising the flag, Mendes, I'm not supporting the revolt for exactly the same reasons that I'm not supporting the Ministry, if you people had been the ones to telephone, you would have got exactly the same answer in your faces: it's too late, I've got two or three strong sleeping pills in my gullet, the only thing I'm seriously interested in is getting rid of all this light and getting some rest."

And the strangest part, he explained to me as he let his idle arm wander over the round thighs of the cabaret women, was that I was being sincere, no, seriously, listen, completely sincere, because in a certain way I still think along the same lines, I don't give a shit for military coups and maybe that's the reason they're going to take their time in making me a general, because what's important for me is not waking up in the middle of the night, not finding myself sweating, completely lucid, terrified, sitting in the midst of scattered bedclothes, pursued by the terrible faces of the dead and now, too, since I've been drinking more, by swarms of fierce little carnivorous animals, snakes, insects, ferrets, globular toads, eating each other up in a cruel vegetable silence. Because since Africa, understand, and especially beginning with the death of my first wife in the cancer hospital, going there, just back from the war, coming into the deserted apartment, I started emptying bottle after bottle, coming home from work, nailed to the sofa in front of the television set, in hopes of pacifying a painful, nameless anguish in my insides, without any definite place or origin, a moving flame, avid, iron jaws gnawing, the slow stubborn acid that was consuming him. Captain Mendes left behind a radio set, where communiqués and songs alternated, on top of the desk blotter, and for a long time he listened to the decreasing sound of boots in the hallway, imprecise voices that drifted off like clouds, the virile hoarseness of the stocky pilot on the stairs (a reserve colonel, he found out later, a fellow who died a few years back with his whole family in an automobile accident), the General Services lieutenant remained in the same spot, stupefied and standing at attention, his stamped sheet in his hand, a sergeant brought lunch, brought tea in the afternoon, brought dinner, soup, meat, wine, bread, and I didn't touch anything, sleep came over me and disappeared like the shadow of a castaway on the tide of a beach, the outline of two officers blended, grew, separated one from the other in an infinite lethargy, someone turned on the switch to the ceiling light and a thousand sparkling acid slivers buried themselves in his eyes, his neck grew smaller on his shoulders, like a polyp in an aquarium, dozing, the door opened, he saw Second Lieutenant Baptista in the doorframe, walking noiselessly toward them as in the elastic and insubstantial center of a fog, The military operations are over, you can leave, shouts, sighs, coughing, whispered commentaries, profiles that disappear one by one, he wants to ask them to turn out the light and no phrase takes shape in his throat, from far away he hears Captain Mendes who might be calling him and he doesn't see him, the hand full of invented pills pushes him slowly toward a hollow, uninhabited depth where words and pale flashes revolve laboriously, they touch him, shake him violently by the shoulder, Commander sir Commander sir Commander sir, and gasps of unknown breath by his ear. The dirty old man fell asleep, the cleaning woman's leg stretches out lazily over his, the usual stale smell of armpits explodes in his face, shouts and singing from the soldiers on the parade ground, great happy boots, rifle butts hitting each other, metallic vibrations, trucks, and me, up there, sunk in the quicksand of my sleep, opening and stretching out the cartilaginous pincers of my arms, rolling around in my mouth with difficulty an onomatopoeia, a call, a children's song that no one answers.

$A$FTER a month or two they stopped summoning him for interrogations, ceased beating him, and the communications officer thought spitefully, They must have got some fresher information elsewhere, they've infiltrated the Organization, a PIDE in a beard who seems a fervent Maoist. Someone talked and with a flip of the finger they completely broke up our comical network of precarious little cells joined together by the tenuous threads of spittle from dubious organizers. From his cubicle he could glimpse a stretch of shore just beyond the wall, the guard with a machine gun on a kind of cement throne, distant houses, tiny automobiles on the highway under construction, trees, clearings, conical piles of rubble, and the long hours, Captain, much longer than in the Army, days without end, stretching out like endless Basset hounds, nights that smelled of urine and sweat and where, mingling in the dark, were the frames of bunks, shapes lying down, wakeful-ness, coughing, breathing, the sound of tentacles sucking, of bare feet stumbling in the direction of the stinking tile shell of a toilet. No one visited him, he got no letters, most likely the old women hadn't found out anything and were going around bewildered, searching for him in hospitals, in clinics, in emergency rooms, he's not here, ma'am, we haven't taken in anyone at all with that name, and his aunt, quite deaf, sticking her neck forward Eh? or maybe they wouldn't let them talk to the communications officer, which made him imagine his godmother and Esmeralda, defenseless, insignificant, afflicted, leaning against each other by the prison gate with cakes they couldn't give him, with cigarettes they couldn't give him, with clothing they couldn't give him, and finally, with the string of useless presents hanging from their fingers, trotting away toward the little railroad station, where, from time to time, a shrieking, quivering effervescence of windows would stop moving. The prisoners, withdrawn, kept to themselves, didn't talk to each other, didn't smile at each other, didn't ask questions, ate in silence, extremely mistrustful, tense, spying on each other out of the corners of their eyes, and some of them at least, he'd swear to it, beyond any doubt, had plotted together in the same offices, the same universities, the same companies, had argued in warehouses, in the rear of garages, in crowded restaurants, in cancerous rooms about self-developed socialism or the viability of half-term Marxism in Portugal, in favor of armed struggle, against armed struggle, beer, furious discussions, angry differences, Shall we plant a bomb in the Assembly, attack a police station, or what has Fidel got that we haven't got? and more beers, more arguments, more anger. But the Organization, understand, gave the impression that it didn't exist in fact, that it was a clever and simple invention of Olavo, Emílio, Baldy, meant to trick boobs like me, pick up a little money from dues, income from the sale of the poorly printed magazine, whose grimy letters stuck to your fingers, and then the three of them, their pockets full of bank notes, would go to eat at our expense a great variety of crabs at the Portugália, or the Monte Carlo, or the Império, or the Trindade, slapping each other on the back with great satisfaction, the perfect hustle, the story of the ideal con man, each with an apartment in Linda-a-Pastora, with parquet floors, finishing touches in aluminum, heat, and a marquee above the entrance, and if we complained to the police we would be the ones who screwed ourselves by acting against the Nation, against our Sacred Overseas Empire, the inalienable Christian values of Western society. Or maybe, who knows, none of that, and that pinched little guy who always has bronchitis at the corner of the table is one of us, the great big mulatto who's in the same row of bunks as I is one of us, the older man who came back last week from the infirmary in elbow crutches is one of us, it's just that there certainly must be police spies among them and that's why they don't approach me, pretend not to know me, look at me with transparent, distant eyes, one of these days I'll wake up with a message in code, Good morning comrade, in my pocket, and the old women, confused and rigid, sitting next to each other like a pair of cockatoos on a single perch, staring at the swift parade of walls and houses, one after the other, riding along toward Lisbon: the amusement park will open any day now, music, shouts, calls, the ailing motors on the carousels, the smoke from the food stands, the hot dogs, the hamburgers, the shadows of the giraffes spinning around on the figure-eight ride and Olavo who waves at him, rumpled, hair uncombed, deformed, laughing, from a wooden elephant. Slowly, indirectly, without noticing, he had begun to hate them, no, seriously, hate them, What am I doing here? What am I going to do when I get out of here? Emílio and Baldy filled his dreams, masquerading as clowns, pointing at him with their great white gloves and jeering at him, squirting spurts of artificial tears through their painted eyes, a pitiless spotlight exhibited him to the dark, circular mass that was the audience, he ended up fleeing in his underpants, running along the alleyway, pursued by the out-of-tune music of the orchestra, by the persistence of the spotlights, by the catcalls of the audience, he would awake tossing on his mattress and would hear in the silence, right next to him, the furtive chords of endless pissing, great open mouths sounding off, the rustle of bedclothes, bodies awash in sheets, the sharp and distant whistle of a locomotive in the darkness, opening her belly, full of sleeping night people, with the sharp knife of its cry, and still farther off, dull, lapping, sad, the miserable moaning of the sea.

"So, Captain," he said, quickly lighting the cork-tipped cigarette of a skeletal blonde and pouring into her glass with the gestures of a wine steward the sulfuric champagne they had been drinking for an hour, their stomachs, guts, livers reduced to calcinated cracklings, I'd gotten used to the idea of growing old in prison, waiting forever for the trial that never came, that never would come, drinking watery soup, eating raw potatoes and spongy bread from the night before, until they'd find me dead on the mattress in the bunkhouse with the crystallized sugar of a rim of saliva around the rotten fruit of my mouth. And finally, you see, when I no longer hoped for anything from anything, when I'd become used, like an old mongrel, to the deserted prison courtyard and its three or four stunted little trees, to the highway under perpetual construction down below, traveled by microscopic bicycles, hangdog carts, and rare dark automobiles, to the musty days and the tumultuous nights when the waves, leaping over open fields and chimneys, would break at his ankles with a dying scum of foam, when I had even become accustomed to the indifference and silence of the others, on the day after Emílio's arrival at the prison, there came that complete confusion, soldiers, cheers, reporters, the hubbub, freedom, people going out the main gate dazzled by all the hugs, all the smiles, all the joy, all the flashbulbs, all the interviews and me thinking, pushed, pulled, cheered, hugged, photographed, I want to go back to my bunk, cover myself with the stinking pillow, wrap myself up in the dirty sheets, eat the rotten Sunday fish, stay on there: misery is only hard at first, Captain, a few weeks later, like in the war, if they had come to take away our rags, bedbugs, lice, dingleberries, we would have felt a strong nostalgia for all that. And I didn't give a particular shit for going back to the phoniness of political militancy, to reading Lenin and Mao Zedong, to heated arguments when I was sick of the class struggle and cigarettes, to my job on the Terreiro do Paço, with the tugboats slipping, sobbing, past the windowpanes like big fat fatigued goats, filing away cases, taking notes on cases, unfiling cases, an occasional movie, rarely, a guilty drink at a bar, and then walking home, hands in my pockets, through streets with windows and display cases and electric signs turned off, dreaming vaguely about contradictory, impassioned, and stupid plans, having a woman with rollers in her hair, ugly or pretty, what the fuck, Dália, for example, in her housecoat, waiting for me, reading detective stories in bed, belly up, tenderly touching with my foot an ankle that isn't mine. Maybe all I was at that juncture, Captain, was a failed social democrat, a dangerous individualist obsessively preoccupied with his tiny little useless happiness, a privileged person with a bad conscience, gnawed by a sense of guilt for not having gone hungry, not having nine brothers and sisters, a shack in Galinheiras, a drunken father vomiting up pieces of chicken in alleyways, a grandmother in the Mitra poorhouse among hundreds of petrified and motionless octogenarians, moving the broken tongs of their gums backward and forward with alligator swallowing.

He saw Emílio in the courtyard before lunch, his head shaved, leaning against the wall, and he recognized him in spite of the swollen state of his features, the destroyed left eye, drooping like a withered lily, the wounded tangerine pulp of his mouth. He thought about speaking to him, hesitated, advanced a step, hesitated again, gave it up (I bet there's a bunch of bastards watching me from the cement towers, from the balconies, from the windows, from the kitchen entrance, from right down here even), he took a long aimless walk under the pale, dull morning sun caught up in the lumpy fatness of the clouds, he passed by near him as though casually, blowing his nose and sneezing loudly with the idea of catching his attention, of waking him up out of that kind of drowsiness of a defeated boxer held up by the curving support of the ropes, but not a blink, Emílio didn't move a finger: enormous, cubic, with eyes that were neutral, disinterested, extinguished, dead, he was filling himself like a sunflower with the heat that didn't exist, and he'd become thinner, was missing some front teeth, and they'd broken one of his wrists during the interrogations and his legs were wobbling slightly, weakened, reduced to the curved masts of his bones. He wouldn't even have recognized his mother if she'd been brought there, the communications officer said indignantly, with a swarm of frantic red flags breaking out, reborn, inside him, clenched fists raised wrathfully, ardent soviets, metal workers advancing, stones in their hands, against the water cannons, and the shields, and the visors, and the clubs, and the rubber bullets of the police. He approached again, diagonally, lighting a cigarette that trembled (from nervousness? excitement? enthusiasm? rage?), the Organization wasn't finished, the Organization, goddamn it, continued on, unknown comrades meeting in unknown but predictable places, with a touching and idiotic innocence, continuing courageously, childishly, armed with books, pamphlets, posters, defying the dictatorship, printing communiqués and newspapers, making deals for pistols, hoarding explosives, planning scientific attacks that could never be carried out against banks and police stations, the cells are growing, friend, membership is increasing, Olavo, dizzy with fatigue, goes hurriedly from meeting to meeting, advising, ordering, suggesting, Emílio, the communications officer called in a low voice, standing in front of the huge bulk of his friend, almost liquid and igneous in the growing light, Emílio, and at that moment the siren broke out with the call to mess in a twisting flame of sounds, the prisoners began to move, dragging their slippers, toward the mess hut, I bet they're going to stick us with the same soup, the same sprouting potatoes, the same ribs without any meat, Emílio, the drooping eyeball moved and sank down like an extinguished bulb, Does it hurt, Emílio, the pulp or petals of his mouth slowly formed an inaudible word, he got closer with a listening ear, stretched out his arm to the other's chest, When did they catch you, Emílio, have you been here long? and his fingers, Captain, nails purple from being kicked, stepped on, hit, tried to grasp, without succeeding, one of the loose rocks sticking out from the wall, his knees bent a little, he had crust and marks of filth around his ears, and all that on the eve of the coup, just imagine, the bastards were working conscientiously right down to the end, he smelled, like old people, of dry shit and medicines, those packaged disinfectants that are dissolved in a basin of water, a white powder on the bottom that you have to stir and move around with your hand, and not just an incrustation and marks but also scars from recent wounds, lumps of dirt, cobwebs, trash, In which cubicle, the communications officer wondered, in which stinking dungeon had they put him? the bald-headed inspector, mace in hand, drawing back and thwacking as he grunted his zeal of an able functionary, In the balls, damn it, let me hit him at least once in the balls, the siren suddenly stopped, we were the only ones in the courtyard and the guard on the cement tower barked from up there What are you waiting for, you bums?, The sun's going to break away from the clouds, I thought, it's going to catch us with the instantaneous speed of a punch, a kick of light, a terrible, solid whack of heat, right beside Emílio's big body a busy caravan of ants was disappearing and reappearing through the cracks in the plaster (They're the ants from Omar, the communications officer thought in fright, the red, carnivorous ants of Mozambique who are coming back), Emílio's cheeks had become flabby, his legs were more bowed, a bubble of saliva spread out and burst under his nose, the communications officer steadied him with a strong grip on the torn waistband of his jacket, What's become of the others, what's become of Olavo, what's become of Dália, the cop on the cement tower began to come down carefully along the spiral staircase, insulting them, pointing with his machine gun, I was shouting louder and louder without realizing it, without caring, indifferent to the

PIDE man, to the PIDE man's weapon, to the reprisals of the PIDE, Does the Organization still exist? Does the fight against the regime still exist? How are we working now? the red ants from Omar were crawling up Emílio's back, sides, shoulders, muscles, the same as they went over the open, infected wounds of the sick black men on the steps of the post, along the lips of the wound, over the iridescent crystals of blood that incessantly form and dissolve, What the hell kind of shit is this? the guard asked, Didn't you hear the lunch call? but the communications officer was shaking his friend's shoulders, not listening, Olavo? Dália? Baldy? how come they never got in touch with me? how come they're leaving me to rot in here? how come none of them give a goddamn about me? the inspector was looking for his stomach with the cudgel and hit him, the bulb on the ceiling, at the end of a twisted wire, was blinding him, the floor was wavering, the two policemen were holding him up by the armpits, Emílio's jaw drooped, the deformed artichoke of his nose fell to his chest, his fingers fell down alongside the seams in his trousers, What are you doing to the guy, damn you? the guard asked, pushing me away with the butt of his gun, Let me get him in the nuts, the inspector asked, wild, out of his head, let me clean up this swine once and for all, the guard took a step back, I took a step back, Emílio's huge body seemed to be trying to advance toward us, speak to us, embrace us, his big hands rose up slowly like two great useless wings, his knees were wobbling, the shadow of a fleeting clarity lighted up his eyes again, and the guy flopped, big as he was, facedown onto the ground, right at our feet, without a moan, just like a plaster statue falling over. And, as always, from behind the houses, the trees, the open spaces, the railroad tracks, and the scabrous little station, beyond the beach full of detritus and seagulls and the slimy mouths of sewer pipes, reaching us unexpectedly, dull, whining, and sad, coming from all directions at the same time, encircling us with the gelatinous, contractible threat of the shapeless octopus of dreams, was the miserable lowing of the sea. The communications officer was trying in vain to pull off the blonde's gold earring with his teeth as she twisted from his amusing tickling:

The PIDE man took a whistle out of his pocket, blew it, and right away three or four guards came who said He's dead and dragged Emílio out of the courtyard, pulling him by the ankles and wrists like a slaughtered bull, and they took me to the encounters again, to the interrogation room after leaving me alone for a long time. They considered me important again, Captain, and while I was climbing up the stairs I was thinking Olavo is next, Baldy is next, Dália is next, maybe two hundred years from now, when the regime is over, in the city that won't be a city anymore but some other kind of thing, I can't even imagine what, they'll erect a monument of aluminum and plastic to the quite dead heroes of the resistance, to the quite dead and anonymous forerunners of socialism, maybe two hundred years from now someone will remember us in the annals of History and in the ruins of Peniche and Caxias they'll find a Pompeii of shinbones, pieces of bunks, the remains of cells, and, on the ocean side, with a rusty trawler beneath, the fluted and unoccupied surface of the waves, almost on the horizon line, buried in a kind of eternally morning dust.

But, instead of the ferocious bald man of previous times, the inspector was a skinny, middle-aged man, continuously straightening the knot in his tie with his restless fingers and taking out heartburn pills, who limited himself to a few hurried questions, scribbling on a schoolboy's lined pad, full of doodling and designs, which he pulled out of his jacket pocket. And he didn't see the two hefty policemen from before, replaced now by a guy who looked completely bored, lacking any sort of zeal, with a matchstick in the corner of his mouth and smelling mercilessly of martinis, who didn't even give him a patriotic and Christian whack, limiting himself to attempting to contain a rain of belches with the palm of his hand and leading him back to the bunkhouse without any insults, kicks, or threats, scratching the hair on his belly through an opening in his shirt.

"They must have already been suspicious about the Revolution," the second lieutenant suggested, his diving arm disappearing into the vast interior of a low-cut neckline as through the opening in a fishbowl. "They must have known what was being plotted and were all going around quaking with fear, pulling their chestnuts out of the fire, getting ready to take off. You wanted Central Committee treatment, old boy, torture, a good solid beating, solitary, you wanted to feel important, prove to yourself that you existed, but you no longer held any interest for them, you weren't worth anything to those guys anymore. In a certain sense the Revolution screwed you: it made you understand that when the chips are down, nobody cares a plugged nickel about anyone else."

"Maybe you're not aware of it, Captain, or you'll laugh at it, or find it idiotic," the communications officer explained, triumphally spitting the silver-plated ball from the earring into a glass of champagne, arousing the dozing liquid, which hastened to fizz along the glass walls like hundreds of tiny panic-stricken creatures, "but between the PIDE men and us, by dint of living together, in a manner of speaking, a heavy love affair came out of it, a strange closeness, a kind of marital relationship with its inevitable foolishness, its jealousies, its whims, its reconciliations, its crises and envies, its appalling stupidities. They gave the orders and we obeyed, they hit and we took it, they treated us badly and we didn't even protest, they insulted us and we didn't react, but that was just it, understand, the way we got to like one another, the equivalent of tender little domestic acts of married couples, the exuberant expression of our wedded bliss."

"Excuse me, Lieutenant," the soldier said, slipping down in his chair in hopes of escaping the monstrous mulatto woman who had him by the neck and was tickling him under the arms, "but you're drunk as a lord. If I was you

I'd order a cup of strong coffee, an Alka-Seltzer, some Pedras water, or I'd go outside and get some air."

The communications officer put his hands on the edge of the tablecloth, leaned over me, and breathed the thick vinegar of his breath into my face.

"No, listen, if somebody took a beating instead of me I'd feel relief and envy at the same time, if somebody went for interrogation instead of me I'd feel relief and envy at the same time, if somebody was punished and put on a starvation diet instead of me I'd feel relief and envy at the same time: I didn't really notice it at the time, of course, I needed to stand back, I needed distance, but in all the years since then I've had more than enough time to think about it."

"Completely soused," the soldier went on, muffled, pushing away the mulatto woman's two insistent hands. "Soused to the ears."

"And do you know how I ended up, Captain, do you know what became obvious after weeks and weeks of deep, obsessive, uninterrupted thought?" the communications officer asked with his nose almost against mine, his eyes growing and shrinking like gills behind the afflicted circular convex lenses of his glasses, while the blonde absentmindedly drank down the earring with an affected gesture. "I ended up thinking it was the best marriage I ever had, I ended up thinking that without my realizing it I'd spent the golden years of my stinking existence in Caxias, and that all of a sudden without warning, brutally, bang! I was widowed."

"Seriously, don't you want to go outside with me, Lieutenant?" the soldier offered. "Get a little fresh air, get some color, relax, get away from this shit for a while? The fact is, Lieutenant, word of honor, if you could see your puss in the mirror you'd be scared."

"Listen, if it wasn't like that, with people rolling over with joy when they're mistreated, when they're stepped on, when they suffer," the communications officer argued, poking me in the ribs with his finger, "why do you think the dictatorship was tolerated, Captain?"

There were rats and spiders and centipedes in the bunkhouse, the boards creaked painfully all night, threatening to break, a perpetual, nauseating bad odor floated among the bunks, similar to the corpse smell of October low tides and their pus foam, pieces of plaster were slowly breaking off from the ceiling, just like psoriasis scabs, Emílio was lying facedown on the dark earth of the courtyard, the guard, the barrel of his weapon aimed at me, lifted the whistle to his mouth in a very slow, interminable movement. The communications officer didn't eat lunch, didn't eat dinner, showed up late, unruly, empty, for the usual formations, answering to his own name in a faraway voice, one of those echoes of childhood that drag along, lost, in houses where no one lives, syllables roosting on the old furniture of the throat like lame doves, he lay down on the straw stuffing of his mattress before the others did, without taking his clothes off, and he passed the whole night with his eyes open and spherical, floating in the shadows, surrounded by sighs, unsteady, irregular breathing, dry bronchitis, shapes that expanded and retracted like fetuses under bedclothes stained with vomit and urine, from the Guincho area the despairing, almost inaudible snoring of the palpitating beacon on the sharp edge of an escarpment. From time to time a prisoner, paralyzed from sleep, stumbled his way to the clogged urinal, slipping on the ammonia of the eternally muddy tiles, brushing by him, coughing, he would lie down, spiritless, on the sheets: I wonder, the communications officer thought, if they killed Olavo too, I also wonder if they put an end to Baldy, I wonder if they locked Dália up in Peniche or deported her to Cape Verde: in spite of all, they must be easier on women, I wonder if tomorrow or afterward they'll lock me up in some room and put a bullet in the back of my neck, boom, and right then he suddenly became aware of the cloudy, little, skittish clarity of dawn, of a lusterless moonlight on the window frame, of that fragile glasslike silence that the slightest sound will break, he went outside with the soldier, leaned against the wall, near the garbage bins and a large metal container, the sign of the Bar Club Madrid was going on and off with the rhythm of a varix of a vein, coloring my shoes with its blue polish, Feel better now, Lieutenant? feel more relaxed? a willing redhead and a guy with his hair plastered down closed the door of a crumpled Peugeot on them and it took off with a jerk, moaning, as in a gym exercise, the gearbox squealing, just like the jeeps in Africa, Much better, buddy, don't worry, he answered, cleaning his glasses with his handkerchief, we'll strut our stuff again in a little while, at seven o'clock the siren didn't sound, no guard came to holler at them, the prisoners looked at each other startled, there weren't any PIDE men around, how strange, on the cement towers or rounding them up, all bunched together by the barbed wire, with machine guns, what's going on? they went out, intrigued, in a group, helping each other stand the shock, to the deserted mess hut, stone-topped tables, benches, the crippled half-idiot worker busy at the ancient cataclysmic stove, the smell of coffee and, on a shelf above the bread bag, next to the tin cups, a portable radio barking out military marches and (the world suddenly turned upside down) subversive, forbidden songs. The cone of light from the headlights of the Peugeot (I'm going to vomit my dinner right here) was striped by the slanting marks of the rain, the night watchman, sheltered by a hat the size of a canopy, was checking locks, taxis were coming and going, slowly, their motors gargling.

"Fine, fucking fine, no dizziness, no nausea," the communications officer said to the soldier who was watching him worriedly, his chin shining, smoothing his wet hair back. "There's nothing like a breath of fresh air in the snout to hose down your thoughts."

They took their usual places in silence, in front of the carcasses and mugs of watered coffee, they chewed in silence, bent over, mouths close to their plates, while the marches and anthems followed one another in the pantry, an announcer gave an indistinct communiqué, which the worn-out batteries turned into an incomprehensible mishmash of sounds, a hash of sounds, no, if you want to know whether I didn't find it strange that there was an absence of policemen, orders, shouts, I was still imagining what might have happened to Dália, Olavo, Baldy, I kept on thinking about guys making bombs in secret, illuminated by an indestructible Faith, thinking about fervent student rallies, thinking about the Organization, watching Emílio die, seeing them dead, bullet holes in their temples, flowers of blood like the crystals in a kaleidoscope, I continued listening to the slow and deep breathing of the sea and a piss flute falling into the stagnant urine in the latrine, Not that I don't want to keep you company, Lieutenant, the soldier stated, wiping the stalactite from his nose with his sleeve, leaning against the precarious support of a display case, but would you rather be alone, Lieutenant sir? the idiot limped over to the table and whispered They're all together in the warden's office, All of them? a prisoner with a mustache asked, All the ones who didn't run like rabbits when the Revolution started, and us, completely surprised, What revolution, damn it? we paid closer attention to the transistor, but only marches, only anthems, only disconnected speeches, when we finished the incubating mud coffee we saw that, contrary to custom, the inner doors of the jail were almost all open, that they hadn't even taken the typewriters out of their cases in the empty office, that there weren't any coats hanging on the hooks, that a strange orderliness predominated in the silence, you could come and go as you pleased with no one stopping you through the rooms, along the corridors, in the offices, in the guards' own quarters we took warm showers in their bathroom, lathered ourselves with their soap, dried ourselves with their towels, the one with the mustache was carrying the cripple's battery radio under his arm and whenever the music was interrupted for a communiqué or a speech, we clustered around like wasps by their nest, trying in vain to understand the irrational bubbling of the words, what's he saying, what did he say, what's going on, the communications officer, the collar of his jacket turned up and hands in his pockets, closed his eyes and the paso dobles came to him, made faint by the rain and the walls of the club, in a swirl of saxophones, accordions, and castanets, a rightist coup? a leftist coup? the prisoners, indecisive, ended up walking aimlessly along by the wall with the stumbling blindness of scarab beetles, and in the middle of the afternoon the diesel sound of the crowd arrived, calls, chanting, slogans, the soldier trotted off, shoulders hunched over, on the way to Andalusia and champagne, the doorman was desperately stamping his feet on the ground to keep warm (Someday he'll tread on the paving stones with the soles of his shoes, someday he'll sink them into the earth), a megaphone from a lottery for the blind was howling encouragement, the PIDE people had disappeared somewhere in an endless confabulation, If you people could only see the wild crowd out there, the idiot said, you'd jump for joy, but we didn't know,

Captain, whether they wanted to free us or hang us, string us up right there from the dying trees across from the waves, the man with the mustache suggested that whichever it was, we should behave like choirboys, novice nuns, model prisoners, when night fell we went back to the mess hall and the gimp, that old son of a bitch, had taken off and there wasn't a crust to eat, damn it to hell, and the uproar increasing on the other side of the wall, and slogans, and anthems, and megaphones caterwauling, we were getting up from the tables when two majors and a civilian appeared at the door, It's from the right, we're fucked, the man with the mustache snorted, but no, just imagine, The oppressive dictatorship is over at last, the civilian announced in a saintly way, his necktie askew and his shirttail trying to pull out of his pants, today we've seen the long-awaited dawn of freedom and democracy, your undeserved and terrible imprisonment (what I had right then was fierce hunger and pain, an aching back), gentlemen, is over.

"I'd never heard talk like that, Captain," the communications officer said, removing a piece of dirt, a black mark, from his glasses with his fingernail, "since the time I used to attend mass when I was little, with my aunt always telling me to kneel, stand up, sit down, and hitting me in the ribs with her missal that had a mother-of-pearl cover, again, Kneel, stand up, sit down, clean the crud out of your eyes, you've got wax in your ears, show some respect, stand up, and the priest would come to the wooden communion rails, chat about Paradise with hundreds of old women in veils, in the florid and exaggerated language of the elect." The majors stood on either side of the civilian giving the homily like two acolytes, wearing capes, they listened to him with lowered heads, motionless, taking in his counsel and pious advice like catechumens, Stand up, kneel, sit down, stand up, kneel, sit down, wipe your eyes, show more respect, stand up, the sign of the Bar Club Madrid was growing and swelling in the rain, the wine seemed to be dissolving inside me, taking refuge, insignificant, in some angle, some hole, some hidden recess in my body, leaving in its place a restless vacuum, a white anguish, a shapeless solitude, your great dreamy indifference when I return home later, your displeasure, your weary disdain, We will build a new Nation, a Nation without dungeons or shackles, the civilian was orating, on the tragic ruins of our fascist heritage, the majors lighted cigarettes and were casting incense over the dormitory chapel, the bunk altars, the stunned prisoners, mouths open, We will erect the true shrine of Equality in this beautiful, unequaled garden spot situated by the seashore, This guy's crazy, the man with the mustache whispered, this guy is definitely crazycrazy, the rain was softening the buildings and the metallic texture of parallel nighttime lead plates, the windows were becoming round and slowly dripping, as if there were drops of window frame falling all along the building façades, the chimneys were wilting, the panels of tile fading away, the flowerpots on balconies were a confused repugnant mush of flowers, Pretty soon now, the communications officer thought, the worms in the oil lamps will drag their sick light down to the tar, maybe if I sit down a spell on the step of this doorway, if I just sit down a spell on the step of this doorway, Consider yourselves from this moment forward the anonymous but useful carpenters who are energetically building a better Portugal, Completely crazy, the one with the mustache insisted, Stand up, kneel, sit down, sergeants appeared, quartermasters, a lot of photographers, pushy types with long hair, tennis shoes, gripping microphones, interrogating everybody indiscriminately, the idiot, startled, was witnessing the sudden intrusion clinging to the radio as to a last life buoy, strangers not in uniform were embracing us along with great, sturdy pats on the back, Who are these guys greeting me? the communications officer thought, who are these happy characters that I don't know? if Olavo at least, if Baldy at least, Come ye, my friends, the priest roared with a broad gesture, to the cyclopean tasks that await without, a pimply, hairy thing hung a microphone upside down by my mouth, Specify for our listeners the subhuman conditions under which you lived in here, a photographer ordered him Hold it and blinded him cruelly with a sudden bright light, we began to walk in a column toward the exit gate, and beyond the wall were shapeless mouths that you could sense boiling in the darkness, howling, I wanted to turn back inside, run to the bunkhouse, flee, pull the sheet up over my head and forget myself, waking up tomorrow to the harsh, familiar, imperative routine of always, drinking the watered coffee, eating, wandering about the courtyard, listening to the sea and the wails of the misguided gulls, remembering the streets of the city from time to time, the hidden little restaurants, the Organization, What can you tell them about the fall of the oppressive regime? What tortures were inflicted upon you people here? Did they make you practice unnatural acts with each other? the imperious command Look sad, and another sudden, horrible quicklime tearing in his eyes, a new slap of light on the startled, defenseless face, the people in the courtyard, lighted up by floodlights for movies, television, newspapers, around which there were hundreds of moths, mosquitoes, gnats, the soft and sticky insects of April, they were chanting confused religious hymns, the priest came down the altar steps heading outside, it was already night and I had a headache, fright, a wish to take a taxi home, there was shouting, applause, they grabbed me, stuck more microphones by my mouth, the streetlights were going on along the great black pit of the sea, a sticky dampness clung to movements and clothing, he felt his hair all tangled, his palms wet, the weave of his pants prickling his legs uncomfortably, no stars were to be seen, only ash gray splotches that broke up and rolled along, and in the courtyard, following the stairs to the vestibule by the sentry's hut, to the gate, to the civilian who was still orating, still speechifying, slowly, measuredly, episcopally, dozens of floodlights, bulbs, flashes from cameras, roaring megaphones, the nave filled with the faithful, the priest stretching out the sleeves of his cassock in a kind of soberly triumphant blessing, and the communications officer made out, first from the smell of syrup and rotting plants, then from the dry-leaf sound of false teeth, hundreds and hundreds of old women clutching missals with mother-of-pearl covers, standing up, kneeling, sitting down in a kind of carnivorous Christian drive that frightened him, Clean your eyes, the indignant voice of his aunt hung over the rest, how long since you've had a bath?, They won't let me go back inside, he thought, they won't let me hide in my bunk, What do you feel like, unexpected for you, I imagine, at finding yourself free? and he savored the idea of answering him Like shit, some prisoners were lifted up onto shoulders, others had family waiting for them and were lost in endless emotional displays, and the memory came back to me, Captain, that I didn't have any money when it came time for the collection, not a single coin to put into the tray, I ended up splitting a taxi with a character carrying a guitar case, The Feira Popular amusement park, he told the driver, the tide must have been coming in because no smell of stagnant water on the rocks, of rotten slime, of dead crabs filled his nostrils, the taxi took off with jerks through closed rows of church biddies, he continued to turn around to look at the prison, but the bodies of the old women blocked the wall, the iron spikes, the cement towers, he dropped off the man with the guitar, silent and wondering, at the Marquês de Pombal circle (What was that dope doing in Caxias?), the statue, the lion, the park, all that jazz, and then the driver stopped by the door of his building and declared solemnly You don't owe me anything, I've always been with the Opposition, the rain stopped, he headed for the cabaret again, reached the worn doormat at the entrance, rang the bell, he heard the voice of the soldier beside him Back in shape, Lieutenant sir? and there they were, gentlemen, in the dim red light of the landing, dyed-blond hair, painted cheeks, and great gaudy plastic necklaces, each with her glass of champagne in hand, asking the lieutenant colonel and the second lieutenant for cigarettes as they hugged the old ruminant bones of their waists, his aunt and Esmeralda waving at him from far off, out of focus, through the years, slow and avid (Do you have any bank notes, deary?) smiles with no affection.

# 4

H E was shaving in the little concave mirror, pushing up the hairs on his neck with his finger and discovering unexpected, gigantic hairs the size of stalks, upset because it was late already, he was going to hit a lot of traffic on the Praça da Alegria and he made a fatal cut on one of his sideburns (I'm going to have to shave them off and be left with a horrible Easter-egg face), when the telephone rang three or four times, he heard Inês's haughty voice asking Hello? a long silence, she hung up the receiver, he grabbed the green bottle of aftershave that one of his sisters-in-law had given him on his birthday, and as he twisted open the metal cap he saw his wife's unkempt face behind his shoulder, mouth open, eyes suddenly awake amid vague streaks of makeup, the hand that had held her up on her way to the bathroom anxiously scratching her armpit, touching him on the arm.

"At first I thought I'd given my mother-in-law a heart attack, Captain," the second lieutenant said, applying friendly little pats to the soaked side of the communications officer who was huddling in his chair like a dying sparrow. "A heart attack, a stroke, an aneurism, some kind of spell that would have straightened her out for good, can you imagine the relief? An end to the phone calls, an end to the dinners, an end to the awful boring soirées, sitting

186

on the edge of a sofa, cigarette between my fingers, listening to talk about viscountesses and Fátima."

"It was Mother," Inês murmured in a subdued tone, in an unusual, tragic tone. (And my hopes went down the drain, my joy flickered out like a candle: the monster's still alive and kicking.) "There's been a communist revolution overnight, there's shooting all over the downtown section, the rabble is out to hang decent people from lampposts. Mother has ordered us to get to Carcavelos as soon as possible, just imagine a gang of toughs breaking into the apartment and carrying Mariana off."

Men with bloodshot eyes, drunken bricklayers, mechanics eager for rape and silver shops, bootblacks with huge brooms beating up on poor defenseless businessmen: the open bottle of aftershave was exuding the sharp masculine odor of the Herculean cowboy on horseback on the label, the little one was starting to cry in her room, the second lieutenant, in his shorts, was staring stupidly at the metal cap in the palm of his hand, incapable of making a decision, with drifting, stagnant ideas: What now? He perceived from the turmoil that Inês was getting dressed in a hurry, without washing, pulling so strongly on the dresser drawers that everything was spilling out helter-skelter onto the floor. He ran the comb through his hair several times, each time parting it in the wrong place, he pulled on pants, a shirt, a jacket, a pair of unmatched socks, the first shoes he could find under the bed with the tips of his toes (They're probably coming up the Avenida shouting, they're probably stoning cars and shop windows, setting fire to banks), they put the can of baby food, two or three plastic toys, and some still damp diapers pulled off the drying rack on the balcony into the wicker basket, Move it, move it, move it, Inês was shrieking desperately, searching for her cigarettes under the sofa pillows, on the table next to the record player, by the dishwasher, by the bidet, grim-faced types in gray uniforms with a hammer and sickle on their lapels commanded by Cubans or Czechoslovakians or Hungarians or Russians were battering down the door with rifle butts, locking us up in the shower stall, throwing furniture out the window, treading on books and paintings with their boots, lighting rags soaked in alcohol, and the three of them, terrified, listening through the tiny lighted crack in the tiles where the toilet was dripping into the foul-smelling pond of the bowl with the slowness of a clock, the explosion of burning wood, the crackling of headboard and sheets, twisting with pain, eaten by fire, the explosion of light bulbs, the bookcase crashing noisily onto the floor with its confused load of books, papers, photographs, porcelain doves, a tin bank in imitation of a prayer chest, vases of flowers whose stems rose up like afflicted flames pointing toward the damaged panels of the ceiling.

They finally found the cigarettes and the lighter on the windowsill (and the second lieutenant got a feeling of ominous tranquility on the street, the deserted square in the background, with guys holding machine guns most certainly hiding behind trees, ready to fire on us, a final silence in the cloudless morning), they didn't run into anyone on the landing or in the vestibule, Inês was brushing her tangled hair in the elevator, I was carrying Mariana around my neck with the basket in my free hand, the concierge, on her knees, was vigorously scrubbing the steps (Good morning, ma'am, good morning, doctor) and her grimaces and movements were the everyday movements and grimaces of always (The Russians are going to cut her throat for sure, it wouldn't be long before they'd slice her neck), he put the girl in the backseat of the car, got behind the wheel, unlocked the door on Inês's side, felt something hard, cylindrical, and metallic in his palm, he opened his hand and a virile cowboy came galloping up from his skin, a slight, small masculine smell spread through the Fiat and he saw that without realizing it he'd brought along the silver-colored stopper of the bottle of lotion (I'm really a lot more nervous than I thought, damn it), which he ended up tossing out the car window with an irritated flip.

"So Czechoslovakians, eh, so Hungarians, eh, so hooting everywhere, eh?" the communications officer commented, laying his glasses on the tablecloth and wiping his wet cheeks with his handkerchief. (How naked his face is, I thought, how terrifyingly nude, obscene, without his glasses.) "Millionaire exploiters of the unprotected working classes are cowardly abandoning the country, carrying a fortune in bottles of aftershave."

But no, the top stayed there, between two stones in the driveway, until it was crushed or swept away or flattened or picked up by some kid, sparkling slightly like the panes in the windows, and once more, this time on a morning with practically no traffic, broken by a few lazy and hunchbacked trucks, the hedges and trees of the freeway, factories dizzily escaping to the rear, the Estoril exit, the entrance to the Stadium, and there in the background, its intense blue bordered by the hazy line of Barreiro, the sea, the cursing of the waves against the wall, the sudden, strange smell of Sunday in the middle of the week, of idleness, holiday, not going to work, lacking only the usual fishermen at Caxias, at Paço de Arcos, stubbornly, courageously swallowing the cars' exhaust, motionless, heroic, and covered with rubber like soft statues of solitaire players.

"You can mock it all you want, Lieutenant," the soldier said to the communications officer, "but no matter how much you make fun of it, it's easy to see that you haven't completely lost your mania for communism."

There was the Santo Amaro beach, covered by a cloak of seagulls, with little eyes just like cracker crumbs, mistrustful and sharp, opening their wings, closing their wings, pecking at seaweed, pieces of straw, reeds, taking flight all at the same time to follow the curved wake of a trawler, the Oeiras motel on the left where the clerk behind the desk, who in past times had worked at the same printing plant as his father, with the wink of an accomplice, didn't ask them for identity cards and facilitated for him secret, clandestine little nighttime morsels, he with Ilda, in rooms facing the Tagus (we'd lie on the bed with the window open, with the water at our feet, and the ticktock of your wristwatch embracing me from behind, and the uncomfortable, excessive boniness of your body, and always the nauseating disappointment in the end, the sweaty bodies ungluing, the quick shower, dropping you off at home at two, three, or four in the morning, returning to the Rua da Mãe d'Água without any words, any tenderness, any kisses, without the slightest urge to touch you, stroke you, at best my mouth on your head, See you at the bank, then, so long, and finding the paper moon on the chandelier floating slowly over the table, blown by Inês's sleep and the sharp chill from the balcony, by the enormous illuminated fountain that invaded the apartment with its masonry, its stone steps and its lack of water, and Príncipe Real up there, rustling in the darkness), and then continuing on to Carcavelos, lurching into the village, crossing tiny squares, narrow little streets, corners that the river or the sea (The river or the sea?) was eroding, climbing, going past the train station, continuing to climb, going around the first sign, the second sign, continuing straight ahead, opening the large white gate that creaked, and the German shepherds leaping along in front of the car, yelping, barking, their paws and snouts up against the windows, frightening Mariana who was screaming, Down Tiny, down Roy, down Bruce, finally disappearing at a gallop, in disorder, biting each other, into the shrubbery by the garage, the arbors, and the trellises in the garden, several cars were parked in front of the house, figures slipped along noiselessly on the other side of the windows (leaving Ilda, eyes closed, between the sheets, and running to wash myself, turning on the faucet on the bidet, straddling the porcelain and energetically soaping my penis and testicles), he flung open the back door, untied his daughter from her seat (Ilda lighting a cigarette, smoking, thinking about God knows what), Inês picked up the wicker basket and without waiting for him headed toward the bell on the porch (smoking and detesting me, Captain, hating me slowly, meticulously, examining my naked body with her pitiless opaque little eyes, devoid of tenderness, affection), the sound echoed enormously in a desert of portraits and furniture (great lighted ships crossing through my stomach, crossing through the night), the unpleasant maid, with apron and starched collar, who never paid the slightest attention to me and for whom I never even began to exist, her face wrinkled in a kind of mask, Hello Hilária, Hello missy, why in hell, Captain, do you think the dame never said hello to me, talked to me, because, damn it, you see, she'd look right through me, as though she were looking at a beggar or a phantom who had no interest for her (I would button up my shirt, put on my socks, pull on my pants, and a ship by my elbow now, and a trawler by your serious face now, there's no doubt about it, you hate me), Persian rug after Persian rug all along the hallway, marble slabs, paintings, eighteenth-century sideboards, porcelain pieces, complicated dishes in glass cases, a radio roaring out military marches, mingled voices in the distance (You certainly know that I'll abandon you someday, that one of these mornings I'll wake up sick of your skinniness, your pimples, your absence of breasts, your bitter resignation of a very ugly woman, that I'll inevitably trade you in for a busty stenographer or a redheaded secretary with long, well-turned legs, delightfully simpleminded), the second lieutenant's father-in-law, chin in hands, in his usual easy chair in front of the usual turned-off television set, in-laws and cousins, wearing neckties already, blazers already, prepared already for board meetings at banks and brokerage houses and real estate chains and factories, whispering solemnly in the corners, whiskey in hand, acting as they would at a wake, the usual male and female friends were coming into the parlor in small anguished and serious groups, the mother-in-law, in the center of the couch, stiff and tense in her dressing gown, surrounded by decrepit ladies-in-waiting in fur coats, older and more wrinkled suddenly, with loose strands of hair hanging down like the branches of a willow tree, she was running the huge rings on her fingers over her withered cheeks, she received his kiss distantly, looking at him with the same haughty indifference as Hilária (And I would lean against the small wall of the terrace, Ilda, waiting for you to put your shoes on, your coat, your gloves, your scarf, I leaned over the iron railing and the bougainvillea smelled of the sea and the sea of dusty purple sticky flowers, dull leaves, of the broad and deafening silence of the darkness, peopled by the motors of fishing boats up channel. The beach was a vague, imprecise, illuminated lump in the shadows, an ocher splotch, a white little fringe that advanced and retreated, and you getting dressed behind me, fastening your bra, trying to cover the acne with a cream that made it glow all the more, turned it raw red, on fire, repugnant, your skirt, the masculine shoes without heels, the metal clasp on your purse closing, click, her steps drawing near, I'm all ready), the mother-in-law gripping Inês by the African bracelets on her arm:

"Did you hear about those horrors on the radio, child? Do you have a good idea of what's happening, child?"

"Are you people sure that this champagne is any good?" the lieutenant colonel asked, pointing to the necks of the bottles in the silver-plated buckets. "The fact is, it makes me want to piss every two minutes and I've got a weight on my head you'd have to feel to believe."

"They've arrested the government and the president of the Republic, poor man, so courteous, a joy, what harm did he ever do to anyone, they've arrested hundreds of people, there are hordes of atheists out there, the kind who give women the pill, killing everybody, destroying churches, shooting Catholics. I'm not staying here, I've already told your father to get airplane tickets for all of us, I'm not ready for a band of savages to invade my house just like that and rape me and the whole family."

And to her husband, secondary, small, useless, huddled in his easy chair with a glass of cognac forgotten beside him, tuning the volume of the anthems on the radio:

"Come, Jaime, get a move on, take care of things, don't sit there like a frightened rag doll, like an ape, it's beginning to look as if you want them to put us in jail. I still wonder, word of honor, why I ever married a lump like you."

The second lieutenant went off obliquely toward the balcony where the sea was visible (But later on, fifteen or twenty days later, without noticing it, he would pick up the interoffice phone, dial Ilda's number, Do you want to have dinner with me tomorrow? and they would go back to the discreet restaurant in Paço de Arcos, always the same one, frequented by office workers and traveling salesmen, to the same red wine that made him light-headed, daring, pleasantly disposed, to the car where he would seek out the skeletal roots of her legs with the roving haste of his fingers, lowing softly like an aphthous calf Let me lick your throat, let me nibble your ears, and from the car, quickly, to the motel room, the washbasin, the bed, clothing falling to the floor as in a faint, the bodies dancing their disconnected routine under the covers, too many members, too much mucous membrane, too much skin, and me Grab it and drink me in, grab it and put me inside you), the sea of Carcavelos, the sea of Parede, the sea of Estoril, scintillating and quivering in the distance beyond the treetops, beyond the extension of the garden lawn where a sprinkler was spinning, the caretaker pruning the shrubbery with an enormous pair of shears, the roofs of houses, more lawn, more trees, the occasional white square of a swimming pool whose submerged tiles gave the impression that they were trying to leap out of the water like mad, scaly china fish.

"I telephoned the bank," the uncle said, "I told them who I was, I told them to call Bastos, they answered We're already looking after your welfare, or Take your time, or some threat of that nature, and they hung up on me. I don't even know who answered."

"A revolution carried out by the Army, just imagine," squeaked a micro-scopic, peremptory aunt with hairs on her chin, divorced from a fairy French count who would walk around the Algarve in August wearing a Roman centurion's sandals hugging huge Germans. (The count would visit the second lieutenant's mother-in-law when he was in Lisbon, a gray-haired man, on in years, well-groomed, quite mannerly, who would discuss interior decoration, family trees, fashion, and had an intense woman's smell about him.) "As if they didn't owe everything they are to Salazar, as if their obligation wasn't to fight blacks."

"It hasn't made me want to piss, Colonel sir," the soldier said, "but with whores' champagne you never know for sure."

"If you don't like making love to me," Ilda asked, "why do you bring me here?"

"Tucha was arrested two hours ago by some brutish sailors," a character pale with fear informed them, wearing a hastily buttoned vest over a pajama top. "Nico called me at home just now, she was crying. You people should leave Carcavelos as soon as possible before those sailors get here, hide at the farm, for example. I brought as much silver as I could get into the trunk of the car, I sneaked out through the service entrance without the chauffeur noticing."

"Are you listening to Ricardo, Jaime, are you listening to Ricardo?" the second lieutenant's mother-in-law sobbed, searching for the bottle of tranquilizers in the pocket of her dressing gown. "Will you wake up only when they're sticking a bayonet in your belly?"

"An aftershave top, eh?" the communications officer repeated to himself, dressing his face with the frame of his glasses. "Jesus, you must have been shitting in your pants."

"Of course I like making love to you, what a thing to say," the second lieutenant said. "There are times when you have nothing but goofy ideas in your head."

The sea of Carcavelos, Captain, the same sea as the one that was an accomplice with the darkness at the motel, except that it was luminous and broad and wide and bright, polished and young in the fleshy freshness of morning. Gulls could be seen far into the distance, tiny white traces appearing and disappearing, insignificant, in the distance, the German shepherds were chasing each other in confusion in the garden, terrified ladies in mink and contrite gentlemen were getting out of enormous cars in the yard, fixing their running makeup in vain with trembling little brushes: Tucha was arrested, Nuno was arrested, Duda was arrested in his office at the Company, On the other hand, the lieutenant colonel observed, the dames are drinking and nothing's happening to them except that they keep on asking for more bottles, more gin, more vodka, more martinis, more American cigarettes, more toasted canapés, more ham sandwiches, the alcohol hits their weak spot, that's what it is, women are so different from us, it's funny, Ilda, leaning on her elbow, was kissing my testicles, anus, the soft folds of my thighs, and her enormous shadow covered the ceiling, crept down the walls, she explored my navel with her tongue, they arrested Álvaro, they arrested Né, they arrested Duarte, I'd like making love to you if I liked you, if only you used a better quality of perfume, if you were only less ugly, damn it, if your discharge didn't smell like rotting canned cuttlefish, Inês's uncles and aunts, brothers and sisters, deep vertical wrinkles on their foreheads, were hanging around the telephone, asking, listening, answering, shouting gloomy bits of news into the parlor, the workers at the bank wouldn't allow the managers to come in, the Army had occupied the branches, grim-looking guys were rummaging through drawers, combing through papers, trying to catch, ears on the alert, the combination of the safes, With me it's just a little buzz on, Colonel sir, the communications officer said, buying smokes from a chubby girl in a bathing suit with a pink bow in her hair, but it might be that I've got a clogged bladder, Poor Né, the microscopic aunt lamented, they'll make him sleep in a filthy dungeon, But they didn't arrest anybody, Lieutenant sir, the soldier protested, they only did that a lot later, where did your wife's family get off inventing so much bullshit?, It's just that I'm not always in the mood, he explained to Ilda, if you only knew what's hit me lately, Mariana was crying from hunger, other children were crying, getting underfoot, the seamstress's daughter, her arm in a sling, was spying on the hubbub in the parlor from behind a curtain, the servants were serving tea from easy chair to easy chair, Inês's mother was offering her bottle of tranquilizers to her lady friends, How repulsive and aged they all are in the morning, I thought, surprised, this house is just like a panic-stricken henhouse, they started shooting fifteen or twenty feet away from us, behind some dry logs, some underbrush, so close that their camouflage uniforms and faces could be seen, the quick, red flashes from their gun barrels, we pushed each other, leaped, fell out of the trucks onto the sand of the clearing, we tried to crawl under the vehicles, one or two guys not moving, on their backs with their mouths open, Starting now I'm going to have more free time, I promise, they looked at us with fright, the machine gun on top of the minesweeper was stitching across the disorder, that goddamned mess, that goddamned confusion, the radio operator trying to get the battalion, They lost their heads, the second lieutenant explained to the soldier, deep down they felt guilty as hell for being rich, deep down they weren't at peace with themselves, deep down I wasn't at peace with myself either.

"I wonder if it's because I'm getting old," the lieutenant colonel said, "that I'm past the age for champagne now."

The skin of the sea looked like the taut rubber of balloons while he waited in the yard with Inês's father for the chauffeur to bring the big car around from the other side of the house. It smelled of the wet soil of the flower beds and the flask of brandy or cognac in the jacket pocket of the old man, torn away by his wife's nagging from his peace by the television set, his eyes puffy from weariness and lack of sleep. Above the second lieutenant on the second floor, people's alarmed conversations were buzzing, they'd arrested, they hadn't arrested, I'm going to sell the boat as fast as possible, the land in the Algarve, the apartments, the jewelry, the minks, and the gardener's pruning shears were chopping off their necks and the shrubs, *tack, tack, tack*, around the border, and the heads, separated from their bodies, kept on talking all by themselves until they slowly fell silent in the middle of a sentence like exhausted motors, If they don't put us in jail today they will tomorrow or the day after, do you still harbor any illusions that things are going to stay this way? the father-in-law was rubbing his hands, far removed from the agitation, the bellowing, the anguish, the noise of the automobiles coming and going without cease, contemplating the whitened edge of the sea with empty eyes, coughing lightly, cautiously, as if his bronchitis were made of glass, they helped the chauffeur load the luggage into trunk, Seriously, we're going to see each other some more, Ilda, seriously, I miss you, Ilda, seriously, we're going to spend some weekends out of town, and her small, incredulous eyes, her small, mistrusting eyes, her small eyes that gave in, consented, became enthusiastic, laying my body out on yours, hurting myself on the unexpected corners, the unexpected knobs of your bones, entering you with the blind haste of a member in an endless sleeve, Inês's father said Thank you, Augusto, we won't be needing anything more, and he kept on rubbing his hands like an absentminded schoolteacher, his nose pointed toward the lighthouse, An inert little squashed vegetable, Captain, an insignificant amoeba, a worthless homunculus, half a dozen faded hairs on the speckled top of his head, his horn-rimmed glasses, the eternal circumflex expression, dim and humble, the sun was beginning to warm and dry the ground, the sea was getting closer, a train scurried along below toward Lisbon, and me there with him, just imagine, as if nothing had happened, as if it were a day like any other, as if the fever, the fear, and the anxiety of the relatives didn't warrant any respect from us, looking at the trees, the streets, and the roofs of Carcavelos emerging from the light April mist, looking at the gardener, in jeans, who was opening the faucet now to water the flower beds, looking at the chauffeur who was going off to open the recalcitrant white gate at the end of the gravel drive, watching the dogs panting, barking, shaking themselves, quivering with impatience by the kitchen door, waiting for bowls of meat, dog food, water, I swear that only if you separate from her will I come back here with you, Ilda gasped, only if you get rid of her for good, her ankles wrapped around me suddenly on my buttocks, She's going to come, the second lieutenant thought, she's going to moan and shout and twist and bite the pillowcase in her spasms, she's going to squeeze me with all her strength against her thorax, her nonexistent breasts, the concave trough of her vagina, he tried to imagine in vain some image that would excite him (a movie actress, a girl met by chance on the street that afternoon, a lingerie ad, the woman on the second floor right in my uncle's and aunt's building, in a fur jacket, kissing and rubbing her nose against her dog's snout going down in the elevator), any memory that would make his orgasm coincide with the desperate, monotonous shoving, like a puppet on a string, of the woman, a delicate little wave, a surge of nothingness grew inside him, rolled up, broke in a brief, pale, sad, insipid faint, coming out from inside you and lighting a cigarette, hurriedly lighting a cigarette, and remaining motionless in the dark, with the light out, listening with eyes open, beyond the sound of your blood and the occasional activities of other guests (doors, running water, conversations, footsteps) to the undulating silence of the shadows.

"In my case, I don't know why, what makes me piss most is dark beer," the soldier announced. "Right after the first glass I'm like a regular fountain."

"It's like the cherry brandy my godmother used to make," the communications officer said. "If you like cherry brandy, Captain, it's my pleasure to invite you to come home with me, there still must be two or three jugs left in the pantry. On the condition that you don't notice the mess, of course."

"They guarantee that they're not going to arrest anybody, Father," one of Inês's brothers announced. "They guarantee that they're going to open up the jails and let everybody out."

"You're being naive, child, just imagine the attacks there'll be now, the danger in walking in the streets at night," the lady with purple hair moaned, hiding her rings, fingering the gigantic pearls around her neck. "All those thieves on the loose make me nervous."

"Let them explain the difference between thieves and communists to me," the uncle from the bank demanded.

"They might even order the churches closed," a fat sister-in-law conjectured, "and make us all go live in disgusting little hovels."

"The car's ready, dear," the father-in-law announced in the doorway to the parlor, rubbing his hands incessantly, caught between the piano and an Empire commode. "When do you want to leave?"

"Who'd like some cherry brandy at my place?" the communications officer invited all around, his glasses askew, slipping down his nose, enlarging the parallel wrinkles on his cheeks enormously, like magnifying glasses. "My godmother had a magic touch with things like that."

"Mother," Inês said, looking at the purple pigtails, "since they're not going to arrest people maybe it won't be necessary for us to hide out on the farm, don't you think?"

"What if they attack us, what if they rob us, what if they rape us?" shouted the fat sister-in-law, quite alarmed. "As far as I'm concerned, with that rabble out there I don't dare come out of my burrow, I swear, I'm even afraid to send the children to school."

"Help the chauffeur unload the car, Jaime," the mother-in-law ordered. "We'll stay for the time being, I still want to see how this is going to turn out."

A gang of bricklayers, cigarette butts in the corners of their mouths, were ferociously fornicating with the maidservants, a newsboy was pulling the necklaces off the old women and the little milk-colored spheres were rolling, scattering around the parlor, filthy women in slippers were taking the pictures off the walls, hoboes and drifters were unceremoniously shitting on the rugs, he put out the cigarette, lighted another, and at that moment, softened by the veil of the blinds, the distant sigh of the sea reached him. At the point where their flanks touched a little puddle of sweat was forming, from time to time my toes rubbed against yours and withdrew with revulsion (Could you have noticed that?) and I thought, intrigued, about what was going on in your head, in the dark, what ideas were in you, whether you liked me, whether you hated me, whether you would have preferred being alone in your single woman's room with a novel with a bright cover beside the alarm clock, in your bed, which I imagined to be narrow, uncomfortable, old, squeaky, sailing through the Olivais district out toward the river.

"What would have happened to me, Captain," the second lieutenant asked the drink-filled glass where vague little yellow dots persisted in bubbling, "if I'd separated from Inês at that time and married Ilda, if we'd rented a two-story apartment in Damaia, with a rear-balcony shower stall, not much furniture, beat-up sofas, prints in bad taste on the walls, what would have become of me, understand, if I'd gone back to being what I really was, what I really continued being in secret? But I never would have been sure that she loved me for myself, see? that if I were a poor devil like my father she wouldn't turn me in for the first economist that came along."

"For now," the uncle agreed, "it's the best decision. You won't gain anything by running away from Lisbon now, and, besides, the farm can always serve as a kind of last resort, something in reserve."

"Happier, less happy, just the same?" the second lieutenant asked. "When you come right down to it, Captain, it would have been hard to get any less happy."

He went silently down the steps behind the slight figure of Inês's father, whose mouth looked like a retractable and shrunken wrinkle, and he stood blowing the horn through the open window until the chauffeur appeared on the run, buttoning the gray jacket with silver buttons of his uniform, coming from the area of the kitchen where a hoarse radio was desperately playing the national anthem. The gardener was watering the large ocher pots against the wall, the sea, convex, looked ready to explode in a violent, reverberating froth of pus, Gypsies in rags were voraciously pillaging glass cabinets, commodes, dressing tables, pier tables, desks, screens, settees, coming in scabrous wagons whose creaking aroused the German shepherds, who were barking at them from a distance, protected by the branches of the shrubbery. The chauffeur, who had a strong smell of underarm deodorant, put the luggage back onto the ground, my father-in-law was watching him without seeing him, hands in his pockets, the two, three, or four hairs on the top of his head moving in the wind, I helped them stow the bags in the vestibule on the ground floor, dragging a trunk with metal studs and corners along the gravel on the ground, he felt Ilda's body swell up, the hand that was feeling around for his face, the dark clarity of the sea was undulating and vibrating through the venetian blinds, near and distant at the same time, he thought, uncomfortable, withdrawn, I don't feel like having you touch me, I don't feel like having you caress me, I don't feel like having you rub me, he tried making himself small, tiny between the sheets, evaporate, disappear, but the woman's fingers were running over his neck, his shoulders, his chest, descending, damp, across his stomach, dropping anchor finally at the tender, shriveled base of his testicles, they slipped his foreskin down the length of his penis (An unpleasant and hard little claw, Captain, a stubborn, tireless tendril), with the back of my neck resting in my hands, I was witnessing the insidious, oblique, distasteful, slow dilation of my desire, I feel like it and I don't feel like it, I want to and I don't want to, I'll give in and I refuse to give in, the acidity of your breath was drilling into my throat, a skinny thigh lay on mine, shrinking and expanding to the rhythm of her hand, Thanks a lot Augusto, Inês's father said to the chauffeur, disinterestedly contemplating, with dead eyes, the pile of sacks and suitcases, you can take the rest of the day off if you want, a small breast, slightly illuminated, was squashed against his flank, the other thigh nestled in the space between the second lieutenant's motionless legs, the nub went into a kind of greased tunnel, the moans, the protests, the pushing, the licking started up again more strongly, Glad to accept, sir, thank you very much, and thereafter, little by little, almost without noticing, he began to become excited in turn, Ilda rolled underneath me with the asthmatic sigh of a bellows, Swear that you love me, swear that you love me, swear that you'll never forget me, In that case, if it's all right with you, sir, I'll take advantage of it and visit my folks, Jaime, the mother-in-law's authoritarian voice called, where'd you go off to, Jaime? the husband, as an answer, stared at me with his thick eyes of vegetable submission and for the first time, Captain, I thought I understood him, by God, I thought I understood his obedience and his fear, Come now, Ilda commanded, bent into an arch, like someone sick with tetanus, on the folds in the mattress, the arteries pounding in my brain, my heart, suddenly huge, was working with the drive of a train, In another second I'm going to explode, the second lieutenant thought, in another second I'm going to turn into one of those bodies blown up by mines, with eyes so wide open with fright, peaceful acceptance, the chauffeur went off in his shiny leather boots, stepping lightly on the gravel like an acrobat walking barefoot over the broken shards of bottles, the carts creaked on their way to the gate, loaded down with silver and crystal, Jaime, didn't you hear me calling you, Jaime? the communications officer settled himself better in his seat, smiled, and stuck his skinny neck out at us:

"Agreed," he said, "when we scram out of here we're all going to my place to have a taste of the cherry brandy I've got in the pantry."

"Piss and dizziness, piss and dizziness, piss and dizziness," the lieutenant colonel repeated, looking at the transparency of the contents of his glass, rapping with his fingernail on the edge, aiming to stir up a surge of bubbles. "Are you people sure that this crap isn't screwing up my guts, isn't grinding up my prostate?"

"It's always best for you to have a little refuge at hand," the bank uncle stated, "and under the present circumstances I'd save the farm for a better occasion."

"Less unhappy, Captain," the second lieutenant looked ahead, "that's for sure. The Rua da Mãe d'Água, for example, I wouldn't even want to get within smelling distance of it."

"You two go back home with the little one," my mother-in-law decided, burying her tranquilizers in the pocket of her dressing gown. "If this takes a turn for the worse at any time I'll phone you."

A group in fur jackets, tranquilized, was playing cards in a corner, the cousins were drowning themselves in whiskey, Ilda finished before me and I felt her body collapse and soften under me, my blood suddenly in suspense, the world suddenly motionless, that's it, How quick this all is, he thought, how horribly unsatisfying and quick this all is, he found Mariana's basket squashed by the distracted buttocks of the fat sister-in-law, all the furniture, all these engravings, all these nineteenth-century landscapes marching off in Gypsy wagons, the brothers-in-law began talking horses again, bank operations, women, the aunts put shadow on their eyelids, the world, serene, was getting back on its usual tracks, the sea was penetrating the sky in a single, uniform, thick blue where boats floated like clouds, he looked for Inês in the kitchen bristling with cupboards and machines, went up to the second floor, opened doors, closed doors, peeped inside bedrooms with nobody in them, with bedclothes brutally tossed aside, a record player deafened him for a moment, he went on ahead, rug after rug, looking through the windows at the peaceful quiet of the trees, he pushed open a shutter and there were the two of them, Inês and her mother's friend with the purple hair stretched out on a divan, kissing each other, hugging each other, running their fingers up each other's legs, indifferent to him, in a languid, endless thirst. He felt dizzy, leaned against the wall, sucked in air with difficulty, stopped hearing the sounds of the motel, leaped up from the mattress. Drops of light were lazily floating in the distance:

"It's very late, after four o'clock," he explained to Ilda, stammering. (And his own voice, desperate and tense, stood out, foreign to him in the darkness.) "If we don't get ourselves ready fast it'll be morning when we get to Lisbon."

5

"Even after the coup, Captain," the soldier said, "Ilídio Movers continued to do all right. But something was missing, you see, maybe it was my
uncle's drive, his enthusiasm, stuck in his glass cage now, not caring about
anything, examining his bookkeeper's flower, maybe the thrashing of his
asthma all the time, maybe our panic about his racking attacks. He was doing
well without doing anything, not through work, the way it happens when you
shut off the water, what's left in the pipes keeps on dripping halfheartedly out
of the tap, you know that at any minute, after two or three drips, *pffft*. It
wasn't the Revolution or the complications that came after that made our life
difficult, it was Dona Isaura's stroke that ground us down."

At first a nurse would come at the end of the day, a little woman on in years
and not too clean, who lived down the street and, it was said, performed
abortions behind the scene, to give the sick woman a shot, and every month
or so a skeptical doctor would look down at the bed from a distance, fanning
his melancholy equine head, take a pad from the pocket of his gabardine
jacket and prescribe illegible and confused scribblings translated by the clerk
at the pharmacy into syrups and pills that Dona Isaura refused to swallow,
turning her twisted mouth in a vehement denial while her more open eye
would fill up with a hatred of terrifying lucidity. But she got weaker, thinner,

slept all the time in a restless sleep of sniffling and muttering, she would constantly urinate on the sheets, a foul-smelling mist of ammonia would spread throughout the apartment, dust was accumulating on the rotting furniture propped up by cardboard and wooden wedges, fatty leftovers from dinner, just like the slime of entrails, were left to dry repugnantly in the stone sink. Uncle Ilídio chatted with the nurse and she put down the syringe to dedicate herself to summary, nominal operations of cleaning up, vaguely washing a sheet from time to time, giving a distracted brushing to the crusted plates, opening the tight rear windows that opened onto a tiny garden suffocated by two hens and three cabbage plants, and whose only visible characteristic was that of flooding the rooms with voracious, thick swarms of flies that feasted on the old woman's mattress with its recent residue of piss. The pessimistic doctor disappeared, leaving behind an immense avalanche of packages of medications, accumulating slowly everywhere like tidal flotsam, and hidden in his jacket the uncle brought home the flower vase, setting it in the center of the dinner table, and he would spend the whole evening wheezing alongside the dying petals, which he slowly munched with his globular ox eyes.

"And later on the bookkeeper began to come by the apartment," the soldier said, "she proposed and disposed, giving orders to Odete, the boss, and me, changing the location of things with a commanding way at lunch, taking the place of Dona Isaura, who was bubbling out her diarrhea and hawking up spittle onto her blanket. Odete and I, Captain, would shut ourselves up in our rooms after coffee, she with the pretext of studying, me reading a comic book on the couch, and through the crack in the door you could hear the sounds of the neighborhood, the short, strangled sobbing of the hens, Mr. Ilídio's wife fighting with her pillow, and, above all, the voice of the bookkeeper, who seemed to be getting angry, or lecturing, or threatening, disagreeably and pointedly, throwing out darts of words at the inert, defeated hulk of the asthmatic, his eyes hanging on his lifeless flower like the grip of a clamp."

"No, no, that's not it, hell, the fact is I've had a lot to drink," the lieutenant colonel stated to the fat mulatto woman with the popcorn who was now swallowing a gigantic sandwich of cold-cuts in one bite, not listening to him. "Whiskey, martinis, vodka, gin, even medicinal alcohol for wounds in Mozambique, just think, and nothing attacked my guts like this shitty champagne."

The soldier kept on getting to the warehouse at the same hour, but the other workers were arriving later and later, nine o'clock, nine-thirty, ten, without having the uncle, at his desk, chin in his hands, far removed from the ringing telephone, bark curses and stimulating outbursts at them from the glass cage of his office. The big van, now broken-down, was rotting amid a mess of old furniture, looking just like a gigantic art nouveau ark with windshield wipers, the springs bursting forth through the torn lining of the seats, someone had broken the glass over the dashboard with a hammer, the rats were devouring the plastic covers and the rubber floor mats, running their tight teeth over the squashed edges of the windows, at eleven o'clock the bookkeeper would quickly come up the concrete steps, give the old man's motionless forehead a wifely kiss, change the flower in the vase, answer telephone calls, jot down orders, nose over the pages of the datebook she kept in her purse, spray Mr. Ilídio's open mouth with the asthma aerosol, appear noisily in the doorway, clapping her hands, and we would slowly come over, close by the sooty and cracked walls full of holes and stains, scratches, rubbed-out dirty words or insults or sketches in pencil, we would listen to the orders shouted out in a tense, exasperated tone, we got a piece of newspaper with the address on it, piled up a half-dozen chairs, tables, crates into the small van, laboriously went up the oil-covered ramp as the tires slipped from side to side like cakes of ice on a metal surface, and the fierce summer sun was waiting for us outside there, squashing trees and houses with its huge boots of light, the traffic lights in the city, the buildings with their tile designs, the statues, the awnings of confectionary shops, the old man was driving with his usual angular rage, the silent man sunk down on the seat was stroking his beard between us, and my uncle, I couldn't get him out of my head, leaning on his elbows on the broken-down desk, piercing us, without seeing us, with his stare, blowing an anemic little chill of winds out of his open mouth.

"Did you read this shameful newspaper?" Inês's mother asked indignantly. "They're going to give rich people's money away to everybody. Catholics are going to be able to get divorces, they're going to breed dozens of political parties. Jaime, please spare me, don't bring any more filth like this into the house, topped off with photographs of horrible communists on the front page."

"He was a different person then, Captain," the soldier said, "he'd always be a different person, and, underneath it all, it was that, I think, that was hardest for me to accept: I missed his rage, his fury, those strange hatreds for no reason. He'd grown soft, I'd grown soft along with him, the business was going to pot, neither one of us was getting anywhere. And any day now I'll have my own stroke, I'll start pissing in my bed and mumbling nutty things, and they'll put me in the hospital where I'll get thin, suffer, get covered with bedsores and vomit, die. Could I trouble you to pass me the champagne?"

And in the meantime he would still visit the Rua da Mãe d'Água when the old painter would telephone him, whispering like a poplar, at the job, all timidity, all niceties, all sweetness, all the suppressed volcano of tenderness, insulted by his silence, by his not wanting to know, by his absence. The bookkeeper stuck her tart head out of the cage, roaring at the guys There's a gentleman on the line for you, I was pushing the blackjack cards out of reach, cards with naked women painted on the reverse, with long blond hair and high heels, the ceiling bulb, hanging by a precarious cord beside the skylight with scratched glass and twisted iron molding, was dancing like a pendulum, revealing and dissolving faces, hands, piles of boards, mattresses, silvery cobwebs of a fragile, inconceivably delicate crochet, I knocked my hand softly on the side of the open office door, Dona Emília was adding up figures on a machine, Mr. Ilídio, his eyes closed and hands resting on his belly, was twiddling his thumbs like a baby, I'd never seen him like that, the soldier said, never seen him so far out of it, so fed up with everything, the way he was then, the woman pointed to the phone, You ought to know by now that phone calls are not allowed during working hours, and me, Captain, Hello? and the voice in my ear Hello?, I'd like for you to come by right after dark, I'm dying to see you, pussycat.

"So we were almost neighbors in those days," the second lieutenant said, "so you were making your living in the apartment across the way, at the fruit's place. You must have seen my car a dozen times, my clothes hanging out to dry a dozen times, I don't see how we never ran into each other there."

"If you people could only take a good look at their faces, if you could hear the wild things they promise, you'd faint with fear," the mother-in-law insisted, annoyed, cooling herself by fanning with a fashion magazine. "All I can say is that Salazar, who was no dummy and went to church, must have had good reason to put them in jail. Or do you children want me to believe that the members of the government were all Nazis, that there were concentration camps in Portugal? Oh, Jaime, if another newspaper comes into this parlor, I'm leaving. Take your choice."

"I didn't run into you or anybody else because I took precautions, Lieutenant," the soldier explained with a smile of apology. "I wouldn't turn on the light at the outside door, I carried a pair of dark glasses in my jacket, and as soon as I hit the open spaces I would high tail it to the Praça da Alegria. I had to be particularly careful, right? if Odete ever suspected I'd be done for."

"Father Manuel," the purple-haired lady was scandalized, "told me, and from a trustworthy source, that the socialists want to force all women to use the pill just so they'll fall into mortal sin, just so they'll be on the bad side of the pope. That's only one step away from outlawing seminaries and the Saint Vincent de Paul Conference."

The tinkling of the bell spread liquidly, languidly through the apartment, the ever-present smell of turpentine, tubes of oil paints, atomizers of perfume, sticks of incense stuck into apples burning on commodes, mats on the floor, African sculptures, unfinished paintings everywhere, reduced to colored splotches, the painter, in sandals, bare chested, brushing his blond hair away from his temple with fingers covered with cheap rings, You're riding high, Odete observed, where did you get the money for dinner, for the movies? the painter pulling him into the vestibule by the waist, barring the door, hanging onto his neck with his arm covered with old-age spots, Relax, I didn't steal it, the soldier was annoyed, the smell, the words, the bracelets, the actions of the guy were making him sick to his stomach, A sight for sore eyes, you scamp, It's too bad, the communications officer offered, that they don't have pills for a sour soul.

"A sour soul, Lieutenant sir," the soldier asked, "is that wanting to hang yourself?"

Odete didn't like the vampire films at the Condes or the Argentine melodramas at the Odeon and she would drag him, against his will, to the theaters on the Avenidas Novas where they showed complicated, incomprehensible stories, Italian or Polish or French, that always lulled him into a tremendous wish to sleep: but I'd be aroused by the motionless presence of your body beside me, the elbow that from time to time, on purpose or by chance, would rub against my sleeve, the girl's attentive silhouette, lighted by the cone of light coming from a tiny window on the second balcony, What would happen if I put my hand on your knees, What would happen if I pushed my leg against your leg, but he lacked the drive, he lacked the courage, he would drag himself out at intermission, his eyelids drooping, leaning beside her against display windows of children's clothes, automobile accessories, watches, disconsolately licking a Popsicle, throwing the stick into the metal ashtray with a little water in it, and as soon as his fingers would reach into his pocket for his cigarettes, already the people would be lining up funereally to go to their seats, standing up, sitting down, standing up, excusing themselves, begging their pardon, coughing, whispering in the dark, and on the screen the incomprehensible, complicated story began again with its gloomy situations, the actors gabbing on without a break, the subtitles appearing and disappearing before he had a chance to read them, he wriggled about in his seat, snuffling and holding back farts, trying to get into a comfortable position for an endless nap, Odete would lean over to him and whisper Great, isn't it?, Yes, of course, he thought, yes, of course, he answered, I've never seen anything that could be compared to this, Désiré isn't here, the painter explained, he fell in love with an Italian accordion player, he left his clothes behind, his sculptures, and he took off, and his fingers were unbuttoning my shirt, his teeth were biting my chest, How can people like campy crap like that, the soldier wondered, endless gabbing, no guns, no fighting, no great chicks, not an Indian to be seen anywhere, That black guy will be back, don't worry, the soldier consoled him, the one the cannibal's in love with is you, and the old man herding him into the bedroom, drawing the curtains, lighting a reddish little lamp, more sticks of incense, colored candles, I'm not interested in Désiré, my chubby little dove, I'm interested in you, your skin, your smooth hair, your big tool, he would always open his mouth coming out of the movies, stretch, and Odete, indignant, What a dolt, what a boor, you only get worked up over brutish things that aren't worth a cent, I've never known anyone with so little sensibility, good Lord, we walked down to the subway station and all of a sudden, still daylight, just a little nothing of a shadow falling on the buildings, all the streetlights at the same time, pow, all the neon signs at the same time, pow, we'd have a steak and egg with French fries at the beer garden, spitting out the lupine shells into the startled palms of our hands as if they were our front teeth after a fight, your movements were light and soft, the curls on your head fell down by your throat and it gave me the urge to touch you, hug you, squeeze you against me, and instead of doing what I really wanted to, I asked Do you want any salt?, Do you want any pepper?, The meat's good, isn't it? nonsense like that, you know how it is, to get me away from my wanting you, to get you away from my wanting you, the conversation of a fool, a dope, and you looking at me almost with pity, almost in pain, smiling, mocking me above your flat breasts held in by your knit blouse, Don't take off your shoes or socks, the painter asked, shoes excite me, and his body stuck onto mine, Captain, his sad little behind rubbing against my belly, I lay down on my back on the white rug, gritted my teeth, did my duty, but then I had to stand for his caresses and complaints for half an hour, an hour, sometimes longer, lying on top of me and tickling my testicles, talking about his life, getting me aroused, Why don't you ever read worthwhile books?, Odete asked, why only cowboy novels? why only comic books?, So, big again you're taking advantage, the painter said, nibbling at my ear, So big and so pink just for me, all the way home I was so ashamed of being a swine, I was so ashamed of not studying, swearing to myself Tomorrow I'm registering for night school, and I wouldn't register, Tomorrow I'm going to a bookstore and buying some books, and I wouldn't go, even now, for example, being treasurer of the Águias do Paço da Rainha club, and we've got a little library in a wire-mesh bookcase, I prefer checkers, or dominoes, or billiards, The lighted windows, Odete, gave me a crazy urge to marry you, to have dinner with you, in pajamas, and watch the news on television, go to bed, a toothpick in my mouth, imagining the slow curve of your kidneys, You flirt, you scoundrel, the painter was whispering, digging his flanks with his fingernails, such bad manners, getting like that in front of me, the old man's head sank, moaning, between his thighs, the thin blond hair frantically rubbing against his navel, and always, as usual, when we got to the door, Odete Good night and she would shut herself up in her room, me Good night trotting down the hall disappointed on the way to my cubicle, the soft fat-person sound of Dona Isaura rolling in bed, my uncle's passive asthma, I would get undressed by feeling without turning the light on, bumping my knee against a chest, stumbling into unexpected furniture, limping over to my bed, and sitting for what was like a hundred years with tense muscles and curved, alert body, like a beast, trying to catch the sound of your cough or your footsteps there in the distance, at the other end of the apartment, smelling your distant presence in the silence of the darkness, imagining that you were coming along barefoot, that you were coming along noiselessly, almost not touching the floor with your feet, that you were lying down beside me and the two of us were lying that way, watching, without sleeping, the same as in the movies, the tiny rectangle of the window, pale in the phosphorescent mist of morning. .

"Months and months dreaming about a woman, Captain," the soldier said, tapping on the tablecloth to the rhythm of the music, "wanting things, inventing things, suspecting things, despairing: she's got a boyfriend, she hasn't got a boyfriend, she loves me, she doesn't love me, how many people at work have asked her to have an affair, how many boyfriends has she had already, is she a virgin or sleeping on the sly with a married man, a character in a lettuce green Mercedes waiting for her to come out of night school, thoughts like that, can't you see? poison my head, make my lungs ache, give me gas, stop me from thinking, from being in a good mood, from concentrating on my work. I was unloading a piano and her smile appeared before me, I would hear the old man's muttering while he drove the truck and it was Odete's voice I was hearing, I would go to the café and her laughter would ring out behind me, making fun of me, I'd turn around quickly, scared, nobody. I lost quite a few pounds, dark circles were forming under my eyes, the face of a corpse, wrinkles, I couldn't get to sleep, Dona Isaura's doctor prescribed some ampules to take before lunch and dinner and not even then, Captain, I've got the idea that people who fall in love with a woman start to rot inside."

"Exactly what happened to me with Dália," the wet-bird voice of the communications officer peeped as he balanced on the perch of his chair. "And to top it off, the fuck of it is that if a guy gets there it's always flatter, always worse, things never happen the way you think, life starts to fall apart, and when we come to, shit, crash, the plate's broken into pieces and you stand there looking at it, there's nothing left to do."

Starting at one in the morning, the painter invariably began to drink: barefoot and nude, his soft behind dragging along, he would head to the closet full of brushes, canvases, bottles, tubes, pots, old newspapers, easels, and cans of paint, coming back with a bottle of vodka or turpentine in his hand, he would lie down on the bed again, kiss him, wallow on his back hugging the neck of the bottle, and in a minute, after some hawking, start up with an uninterrupted outpouring of lamentations, Désiré was a pimp who only wanted American cigarettes and printed T-shirts, a low-class nigger without talent whom he'd taken in out of simple Christian charity and he was all the time swapping him for the worst lowlife ass-fuckers in Lisbon, for the commonest sons of bitches in the whole city, a man-eater looking at my Pekingese with criminal intent to barbecue, in the matter of venereal diseases alone he'd caught seven doses from him, and the soldier Why don't you drop him?, Why don't you live by yourself? and the painter, weeping, makeup running down his cheeks, I don't know how to get along without him anymore, Abílio, I've become accustomed to him, what do you want me to do, I swear I can't get along without him, Even fairies can fall in love, the lieutenant colonel observed, outraged, even fags suffer from that, Désiré would stay away for two weeks before he heard from him, not even a phone call, or a letter, nary a word, he would come back as if nothing had happened, put his key in the door, Bonjour, and I'd forgive him, I'd take him in, hugging his waist, having forgotten everything already, crazy over his attention, the pleasure, the joy, and the cocksucker didn't give a damn, Abílio, the cocksucker laughing as if it were a big joke, the cocksucker sucking the marrow out of my bones, asking me for money, Get my watch out of hock, get my ring out of the pawnbroker's, I owe Eustáquio five contos, hurry up and get me in the clear, the soldier was moving away to the opposite side of the bed, driven by the breath of wine that was wrapping up the words, as he felt around the rug on the floor for his shirt, his shorts, the painter would fall silent from time to time to sob into the sheets, He'll end up vomiting on me, I thought, he'll cover my back with the rotten remains of his lunch, he'll forget the usual five hundred escudos, but no, Captain, there was the bank note on the dresser asking me to put it in my pocket and beat it, the guy's sentences were riding one on top of the other more and more, it was hard to make out the syllables, the meaning, the liquid was running out of his mouth down his chin, down his throat, while I got dressed in a hurry, without a sound, putting on my pants, jacket, necktie, An ingrate, the painter was mumbling, an ingrate with no excuse, my beloved ingrate, the little sticks of incense were burning in the scorched skin of the apples now, If I don't get out of here I'll suffocate, the soldier thought, this smells like a bar and a church at the same time, I grabbed the bank note, stuck it in my pocket, the painter tried to sit up on the mattress, the bottle got away from him, rolling on the floor, Where are you going, sweetie pie, he asked me, Where are you off to now, but his eyes closed, his arms fell, in just a minute he'll be snoring like a hog, I closed the entrance door slowly, pushed the elevator button adjusting my collar, tightening my belt, struggling with my shirttail, the Pekingese gave him a farewell lick on the ankles with his flattened snout, and there outside the fountain, the green shadows of the trees, the run-down cabarets on the Praça da Alegria, he went up Conde de Redondo, surrounded by the calls of whores on corners, the vestibules of fucking houses displaying in the dim light their spiral staircases with eroding steps like the teeth of corpses, the houses leaned and twisted in the darkness, the sky was a horizontal pane of glass mournfully echoing the sounds, his heart beating fast, his weary breathing, the front of a building expanding and contracting like gills in death throes, receiving and spitting out the cold breath of the night, in the Capuchin Hospital, on the right, hundreds of patients were coughing up their cancerous lungs in unison, this has been a strange summer, all the urgent and contradictory news items in the papers, finally the Rua da Alameda, his neighborhood finally, finally the alley, the garbage cans on the sidewalk, the everlasting profusion of downcast, flea-bitten stray dogs sniffing along the gutters, the last drunk royally installed on a step, next door to a bar, hat on the back of his head, laughing silently with his mouth open, an endless laugh, it was two, three, four o'clock in the morning, With the painter I was never sure when I could get away, when he was loaded enough to break out snoring, muttering a lot of complaints, wrapped up in the sheets and the dense thickness of his breath, forgetting about me, the light was on underneath Odete's door, a frame of thin light between the plaster and the wood, I wiped the soles of my shoes on the doormat and without noticing, Captain, word of honor, I turned the porcelain knob, went in, turned it again, and I stood there, arms hanging down, at the entrance to the room, surprised at myself, all embarrassed, nervous, in the middle of the books, notebooks, folders, paper, prints of paintings tacked to the wall, trying desperately not to see you, not to look at you, afraid of the repugnance, the indignation, the disgust, the fury, the infinite disdain on your face.

"And that's how you started rotting inside, old buddy," the second lieutenant said, "and that's how you began to get into an agony that had no way out. They should have taught us in school never to open a closed door, especially if there's a woman on the other side."

"Was that at the time they nationalized the banks," the lieutenant colonel asked. "The time of the confusion about the Revolution?"

No, the soldier thought, before that, some time before that, during the period of the bed of roses of democratic idealism, with us all softened up, as the communications officer would have said, by antifascist blessedness, like fat little bitches, romantic, generous, getting along, while political parties were getting ready, behind our backs, step by step, to slaughter each other, snarling behind their artificial cardboard smiles, carnivorous, pitiless, ferocious during the calm that still obtained during the sweet peace of May, June, July, during the sweet peace of August, on the beach Sundays with fellow workers, the nephew of the bookkeeper leaning out of the truck on the highway at girls, Would the young lady allow me to keep her company?, Would the young lady allow me to introduce myself? they played ball on the sand, pulled each other into the water, hid each other's clothes, on one occasion, at Fonte da Telha, they made dates with a group of girls who worked at a woolen factory, took them to the Volunteer Firemen's ball in a second-floor hall over the ambulances and fire trucks, but they refused to go with us to the Ilídio Movers warehouse to make love on the decrepit couches amid rats and dust, and they went off angry after an interminable argument on the corner of Intendente, two or three of them, full of lace, frills, and flirtation, were ready to accept, but a short mulatto girl, pockmarked, refused at the last minute, attacked by inexplicable scruples, and they ended up in a house of decrepit sluts on the Rua do Mundo, banging, one after the other, the only creature available, a redheaded mastodon who didn't even take the trouble to unbutton her bra and remained the whole time gelatinous and immobile without a single effort at tenderness, it was almost morning when they left, the eaves of buildings were taking on a suspicion of blue, municipal workers in orange vests were hosing down the pavement, it had been a few months earlier, Colonel sir, my body hurt from sunburn, my kidneys ached from the sun, political parties were on the attack in the newspapers, crucifying each other in diabolical tones, pricking each other with communiqués, demonstrations, and notes, flirting with the Army, preparing subversive activities for September, the president of the Republic, in monocle and gloves, was vociferating for the benefit of the usual apathetic crowds, groupings on the extreme left, eternally restless, were agitating, the mulatto woman ordered a second sandwich and her cheeks, enormous and elastic, filled up and withdrew, oily, like those of a frog in a pond. It must have been toward the end of August, now that I think about it, a few weeks before the painter turned up dead in Cruz Quebrada, near the sewer outlet, floating, disfigured, in the midst of excrement and waste, the newspapers printed the story, forgot about it the next day, picked it up again when Désiré was arrested, accused of killing him I don't remember how, a knife, a rope, his fingers around his neck, I was upset for a time, afraid that I'd see guys in uniform or plain clothes appear at the warehouse or at home or in a café, grim faced and stony, and they'd drag me off to the station house, take my picture front and side with a number on my chest, shine a light into my eyes, force me to confess by beating me to dozens of assaults, rapes, robberies, frightful things that Odete would read with horror in the newspaper, that my uncle and sister would listen to, greatly impressed, on the radio, but they sentenced the black man to twelve years in prison (Blacks were made to be found guilty, the judge in Lourenço Marques roared, or do you people want us to find whites guilty?), and he was growing calmer, rediscovering a kind of joy in the complicated, sad miracle of being alive.

"Underneath it all you felt guilty about the faggot," the communications officer declared, "guilty for having taken him months on end, for having squeezed something out of him, for having looked down on him. Underneath it all you didn't feel so good about yourself."

"What about Odete?" the second lieutenant asked, "didn't she notice that your dough had suddenly run out?" (That's one of the few things, you see, the lieutenant colonel stated, that women never fail to notice, one of the few things that dames have eyes like spotlights for.)

She didn't notice because he would often accompany his fellow workers to the Sodré docks, she didn't notice because he would always run into some old man ready to get rid of a few bills in exchange for a drive through Monsanto, a quick visit to a solitary homosexual's apartment, decorated with baroque and pathetic good taste, for a short stop at the Montes Claros parking lot, with huge trees branching out over some timid and voracious bald head. She didn't notice because the wages at Ilídio Movers were shit-pot cheap and the bookkeeper refused to stretch them out, and what he earned at night in urinals and public parks, besides being amusing, was enough for some fine frolics at lunchrooms on the waterfront, poking each other in a friendly way and making fun of the transvestites who took off their artificial hairdos in order to down man-sized drinks. Some of those women with beards, tattoos, and cream makeup would stay with us into the early morning hours, more beer, more wine, more squid salad, more giblets, and their makeup breaking up like rotten plaster as the hours passed, opening ruts and breaks on their cheeks and foreheads, the colors crystallized on their necks, their eyes grew baggy from insomnia under their numb-owl lids, their voices grew thicker, their gestures became masculine and decisive, the lunchroom worker would turn off the neon sign by the ceiling, and in the bright light of morning we would leave, escorted by those strange and sexless amphibian animals, high up on the inconceivable stems of their heels, who take refuge in furnished rooms in Santa Marta or Alcântara, waiting in the nests of their iron beds for the favorable return of dusk.

"Guilty as hell as far as the fairy is concerned," the communications officer insisted, "thinking it was because of you that he killed himself or was killed."

Well, be that as it may, you end up in time being friends with people, Captain, having a little regard, and then the queers didn't make him especially sick (I'll bet you even liked them, the second lieutenant laughed, I'll bet you even got your kicks that way), he'd known dozens of them, old and young, and in all of them he noticed the same fragile eyes of cornered animals, the same desperate, afflicted loneliness, if you want to know the truth, they awakened more pity in him than anything else: transvestites, for example, he had dealings with quite a few, a restaurant worker, a stevedore, one from a good family, son of an engineer, who wanted to be a dancer and called himself Tó Zé, and the cubicles where they slept aroused confusion and pain in him, those tight little damp compartments, with small windows on an entranceway, so narrow you could barely put your arm between the frames, and a fearsome pile of men's and women's clothing everywhere, dresses, shoes, pants, neckties, a kind of truss to flatten and hide testicles and penis, mirrors with light bulbs all around like theater dressing rooms, and lots of bottles and flasks and atomizers and hooks and razors and photographs cut from magazines, he would play checkers and cards with them, listen to their confidential stories, their upsets, their misery, he watched them shave and get themselves ready, with anxious care, for their long and sinuous nocturnal explorations from corner to corner and from bar to bar, haughty, suspicious, standoffish, and unsteady, he helped them put on the wax to get rid of their leg hair with sighs and squeals, straightening out the helmets of their wigs, he didn't hold back from going down into the street with them, helping them down the stairs, eating with them in the filthy dives on Intendente, Just as big a faggot as those characters themselves, the second lieutenant muttered, just as broken-down shabby as the guys themselves, I'll bet that every so often you'd go to bed with the stevedore for nothing, he'd go up your fart-hole and you liked it, It did happen to me, but it was with the engineer's son, Lieutenant sir, the soldier replied without being offended, and it wasn't important, you see, an accident, foolishness, it just happened, we were playing cards, it was almost dark, there wasn't much light in the attic and a lot of clothes hanging on a line, dresses with spangles, miniskirts, embroidered blouses, garters, stockings, he caught my hand, crossed fingers with mine, a few joints extended by false nails, some without, he stared at me with the most abandoned and pale eyes in this world, he smiled a smile of entreaty and abandonment at me, me waiting with the trump card in the air ready to win the pot, the engineer's son laid his cards upside down on the table, passed his silky nun's hand over my cheek, stepped on my ingrown toenail, silenced my complaint with a kiss, he'd had paraffin injected into his breasts to give them shape, he had almost no balls, almost no dick, a little bulge, a few stringy hairs and nothing else, maybe you won't believe me, but it was practically like being with a woman, believe me, the same smell of the flesh as with women, the same moans, the same movements, if you can't use sugar use those little pills that diabetics use, isn't that it?, You faggy bastard, the second lieutenant insulted him, you son of a stinking bitch, and the soldier imperturbable, And ten minutes after that, after buttoning up my fly, I played my trump and won the game, a dress with shoulder straps, with bangles, rubbing its fringes against my face while the outside was getting rid of its usual roof full of doves and taking on the terrible hollow depth of a well where sounds fall backward like castaways, without a single sound, Captain, he was making me feel pity, understand, half-man, half-woman like that, like the statues in stone water tanks on squares, bearded with slime and seaweed, his eyes made me feel pity, his smile made me feel pity, it wasn't always for money, it wasn't always looking after my own interests, it was out of friend-ship too, out of companionship in loneliness, I left him up on a stool, powdering his nose at the bar on the Rua das Pretas when night was begin-ning, spreading out in successive waves over the bottles of rosé, spreading out like a fan in the darkness of the alleyways, engulfing buildings, chimneys, windows, display cases, with its thick granular rolls, three or four gentlemen on in years, with avid cheeks, were already taking up positions around the first amphibians, who were flirting with gestures and little laughs, Ciao sweetie, Tó Zé shouted at him in a wifely way, holding his compact, the old men drew back, indecisive, and the soldier withdrew in shame, That's all I needed, the lieutenant colonel lamented, having had a fag in my command, Shame, Captain, like the time he closed the door to Odete's room behind him, his heart stopped beating and he came upon her in her nightgown and glasses reading a book in bed, in the middle of the poetry and the prints on the wall there was a tiny radio, a battery set, filtering out classical music, the kind with violins, a drag, on the night table, any number of notebooks, a porcelain jar full of pencils and pens, pads, no smell, no perfume, an atmosphere of chaste seriousness in the starched sheets, in the clothing folded on the chair, in the hair held back with rubber bands, And now, the soldier thought, what am I going to say now, Odete took off her glasses, put them into the book to mark the page, and seemed to be waiting on me, you know how it is, for some kind of justification and me without words, me empty, me sweating, and me with my heart now slow now at full speed, trembling with nervousness, Ciao sweetie, Tó Zé's red nails were waving, my grandmother was giving orders, pitiless and benevolent, to her army of whores, and the soldier had an intense wish to see himself in the corridor, far away from all those papers, all that learning, all that ecclesiastical indifference, She's going to break out in a howl, he thought, she's going to scream at me in fury, she's going to kick me out of here, he thought about the cowboy magazines on top of his chest, about how the idea of the broken springs on his bed was delightfully pleasant to him at that moment, slipping under the covers and escaping in that way from those tiny little opaque eyes that were observing him, examining him, dissecting him, quartering him, Odete put the book on the floor beside her slippers, still looking at him, Uncle Ilídio was coughing through the wall and his fierce fish asthma, tumultuous, invaded the room, agitating curtains and papers, he tried to say Don't be upset with me, don't scold me, but his voice wouldn't come out of his lungs, see, the sounds got all stuck in his throat, he turned around all confused, he happened to come upon the doorknob, felt himself run through with curiosity, or with fury, or with surprise from Odete, Get myself out as fast as possible, the soldier thought, run out, evaporate in the air, and I already had one foot in the hall, I was almost safe, almost at peace, almost free, the sweat was drying on my sides, my muscles were taking on their obedient normal texture, my arms, legs, head, what luck, submitted to me again, he whispered Excuse me, whispered Good night, made a kind of wave with his hand when she, just imagine, Captain, without my expecting it, without my asking for it, without my wanting it, called me over.

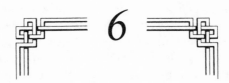

6

T H E Y held him at the post for a few days, dazed and with nothing to do in the midst of all the confusion that followed the coup, that debasement, that unbelievable disorder of the early days (he grunted, hair in disarray, the tip of his necktie dipping into the glass of champagne), the military vehicles coming and going ceaselessly, angrily coughing their way across the gravel, the breakdown of discipline, the lack of respect for rank, the groups of unshaven soldiers making fun of the priest's actions, until an order came from the General Staff, just imagine such nonsense, promoting spider-legged Mendes to colonel and telling me to report to the Ministry: room after room, rugs, clerks, disorder, Wait a little while, they'll see you soon. He sat down on an uncomfortable chair watching a concerned bustle of sergeants, a half hour later a lieutenant signaled him from a distance Please, pointed to a long wooden bench in an antechamber with a high ceiling that had stucco flowers at each corner, Colonel Ricardo requests that you wait five minutes, Colonel sir, and he, quite surprised, Colonel Ricardo? but the man disappeared now, brandishing a handful of papers through a doorway hidden behind a mouse-colored screen. And more sergeants, more second lieutenants, more corporals trotting back and forth with painful haste (The rabbit in *Alice in Wonderland*, I thought, multiplied ten, fifty, a hundred, a thousand times,

212

running, tail up, looking at his watch), a general like the Mad Hatter came from behind a green curtain, a brigadier disappeared around the curve of an archway (a playing-card jack from the end of the story), voices rose and fell, telephones rang, virile boots trod the stone floor, the mouse-colored screen moved aside, the hand and face of the lieutenant again and, immediately following, Colonel Ricardo's freckled bald head, split in two by an enormous smile, They didn't tell me you were here, old man, come on over here, come in.

"Say," Dália told the communications officer, "Caxias was good for you, you put on weight, it's just a filthy rumor that the PIDE doesn't treat people well." (And he closed his eyes and remembered, as in a dream, Caxias, Peniche, the sea's sound of clothes being washed in the darkness of the night below, gnawing at the sand with its persistent teeth, blotches of foam, the lights of boats far off in the distance, light and dark reflections on the water. He didn't recall the cells or the corridors or the guards or his prison mates or the tough guys at the interrogations, the murderous, expressionless, tiny little dust-colored eyes, leaning over and whacking: he remembered the sound of the waves, the moaning of the waves, the odor, more imagined than smelled, of the waves, the white birds in the morning and the brown birds in the afternoon poised on the cliffs, the way in which the clouds stretched out, orange-colored, with the indolence of a sleeping woman, he remembered the sea at Caxias, the sea at Peniche, waking up early in the morning with a damp taste in his mouth, the flavor of wet canvas, rusty planks, items from a shipwreck that rolled around, salty, in his mouth. Yes, he answered Dália, while the white birds, the brown birds all took off silently at the same time inside his skull, rising straight up to the sun, I put on weight, I had a good time, I had a fine vacation, this business about a revolution is a bore, don't you think?)

Colonel Ricardo, still smiling, gave him a few friendly, paternal pats on the back, sat down behind a majestic, endless desk (A minister's desk, the lieutenant colonel thought, an emperor's desk, with polished legs and top, two telephones, a rearing horse in bronze, a desk blotter edged in leather, a lamp with a parchment shade at one end) and he put the tips of his fingers together with clerical slowness. Stucco cornucopias hung baroquely from the ceiling, a thin, squalid sky filled the enormous windows:

"I hope you didn't take the conversation we had the day of the downfall of fascism seriously," he declared, concentrating his look on the round glow of his wedding ring. "As you can imagine, I was obviously testing your democratic feelings."

(So many birds, the communications officer was amazed, I go up the steps at home and find them croaking, flapping their wings on the rocks, cleaning their feathers with their beaks, moving from stone to stone with little leaps on the autumn twigs of their legs, hungrily spotting the crabs at ebb tide. I open the clothes closet and a flock of seagulls bursts out of the coat pockets, hitting the walls, disappearing in confusion down the hall on their way to the street, I go to the bathroom where the equinoctial wind roars in the faucets, the tile of the washbasin, the toilet, the bidet sparkles with scales of water in front of me, and the square of the mirror, filled with blue tiles and my enormous eyes, suddenly takes on the vast nearness of the horizon. I lie down and the springs rock softly like a boat at anchor, with the lamp on the night table floating over the motionless waves of the sheets. It was really a good thing that they caught me, he confessed to Dália, showing her the scar of his broken jaw, you can't imagine the pleasant memories I've brought back from Caxias.)

"Obviously, since I was with the minister and the generals," Colonel Ricardo went on easily, displaying the swarm of red spots on his hands, "it was better to be in on the movements of government supporters in order to pass them on to our troops, to quash them at birth, if possible, through opportune contrary orders. And, just between the two of us, something was done along those lines: you, for example, who've known me for twenty years, I'll bet you caught on to my idea right away, and you went along admirably."

"So," the second lieutenant said, "they repaid your insight by kicking your ass out of the regiment."

"After five days," the lieutenant colonel clarified, serving himself, uneasy, some champagne. "They must have spent all that time deciding What the hell are we going to do with this guy?"

It wasn't just the sky that could be seen through the large windows of the office and their patriarchal cretonne, but the river too, just as dull, just as dirty, just as gray, the color of the stucco on the ceiling and its exuberant baskets of fruit, clusters of grapes, apples, pears, bananas, streaked by a thin thread of fissures and cracks, the river, the back-and-forth of boats from bank to bank, the statue in the center of the square, a round railroad-station clock on the front of a building, the steps went slowly down to the water with the lingering of a caress. A major knocked on the door, came in with a fat briefcase, Colonel Ricardo raised his eyebrows in comic resignation, signed half a dozen documents that the other handed him, waited, unwrapping a cough drop, for the door to close again and the hangings to stop moving, and he leaned over with a confidential, secretive tone, broadening his smile:

"In spite of what I've said and repeated to the members of the Military Junta, that you're more than to be trusted, that you're on our side, that you've always hated the Dictatorship, those guys, what can I say, without my understanding why, tighten up, look at me suspiciously, hesitate, end up promoting, just imagine, that dunce of a Mendes, on the demand of those damned captains it seems, and they put him in charge of the unit, contrary to my opinion, contrary to my suggestion, contrary to my request. That your attitude was doubtful, that you hadn't really fallen in with the coup, that even if it's true that you told off General Mendonça, it's also true that you didn't help the boys, that, when contacted, you kept putting off your answer, idiotic arguments like that, how should I know, stupid reasons, completely inconsistent things. They even hinted, just imagine how paranoid those idiots are, that after you hung up on the secretary of state, you fell asleep in your office surrounded by subordinates and the chaplain, that you watched everything with the eyes of a sleepwalking ox, disinterested, indifferent. The Navy flunkies wanted to retire you to the reserves without any more discussion, I stepped in there, said Halt, if you retire Esteves to the reserves retire me too, and I demanded (Colonel Ricardo, inoffensive, chubby, short, scarlet with indignation, his furious fists on the table before a circle of defeated warriors) that they appoint you my adjutant here in the bureau of officers: You promote me to brigadier general and I promise that I'll lead the man along the proper path. This, obviously, for just a short, temporary period, until you can get a regiment or a promotion. With the cleanup that's taking place, you know, there'll be ranks of general to be passed out or sold. And those guys, scared shitless, had no other way out, they had to go along with me."

One of the telephones on the desk began to bleat, Colonel Ricardo picked up the receiver, said Yes? and remained listening, grunting occasional monosyllables, with a concentrated frown that brought his features together in a swirl of bumps, marks, hairs, and folds up at the thin focal point of his nose: everything in that room was too big for him, the dark paintings in carved frames, the impressive hangings, the worn plush chairs, the solemn atmosphere of a papal audience. Everything's too big for you, you poor devil, for your wordy explanations, for your mean little cheating, for your shitty little ambition.

"What's on your mind?" Colonel Ricardo asked, hanging up the telephone. "These revolutionaries are killing me with work, you'll be quite useful to me here. If they had their way, you know how it is, all senior-level officers would be thrown out, we've got to give in in a few cases to give the ones left some space to maneuver in. Cleaning out, promotions, transfers, that's the kind of boredom that's waiting for you. You'll look over service records, draw up a memorandum, reach your little conclusion, we'll discuss the decision to be made together, I'll take what we've decided on upstairs and the jerks can do whatever they think best, we've got nothing to do with that. I put my balls in the fire for you, I'm not going to do it again for anyone else."

"My, what a fine little damned friend you fixed yourself up with, Colonel," the communications officer said with an acid little smile. "I sure wish I could have got someone to make a sacrifice for me: if it hadn't been for the Revolution, I'd be looking out my window at the sea right now."

"Not just more weight," Dália insisted, "you're more grown-up. And you remind me of Trotsky, with that glowing little beard of a leader of the masses."

Colonel Ricardo answered another call, hung up, lighted a cigarette (With one of those silver lighters, I imagined, that you get after twenty-five years of conjugal martyrdom, mutual dilaceration, cruel, resigned hate), leaned back, examining his smoke with satisfaction, sought him out again with his gelatinous lilac mole-eyes:

"You'll start tomorrow at nine-thirty, there are dozens of items pending. And then, the more generals and brigadiers who fall, the more your chances of climbing up grow. With a little bit of skill and luck, a touch here, a touch there, a few old dodderers out in the street, not bad, you'll have your stars before the end of the year. You're three slots behind me for promotion, aren't you? Look, starting next week they'll give them to me: easy, right?"

Too big for you and too big for me, the lieutenant colonel thought, I don't feel right with these luxuries, Mama: the three rooms in Graça, a mess for lunch and dinner and movies on Saturday are enough and more than enough for me, imagine me commanding a Military District, chatting with ambassadors, with fine ladies, with important people, giving cocktail parties and dinners? Colonel Ricardo got up, he got up too, fingers lax, waiting: the redhead came around the mahogany spread of the desk and jovially poked his freckled forefinger in his belly:

"Major Fontes and Lieutenant Cardoso have instructions from me to help you in any way necessary." The voice dry now, sharp, authoritarian, devoid of the gentle, fraternal inflections of a moment ago. "We've fixed up an office for you next to this one, you'll come to go over things with me at noon. Of course, I'm not even considering the possibility of your not accepting the position."

He unwrapped another cough drop noisily, grabbed him forcibly by the arm: the fat little hand looked like a toad, a speckled lizard, a repulsive and slimy creature poised on the thick, shit-colored fabric of his shirt, and the lieutenant colonel had an intense urge to shake that strange little vermin off his elbow, it must have been provided with suckers that would go through his clothing, bite into his flesh and tendons, and slowly, implacably and tenaciously suck out the thick liquid of my blood. Colonel Ricardo's bald head, with red and white little hairs standing on end, was glistening, his smile grew again and a row of false teeth, horribly perfect, rose from inside his mouth like an obscene plastic flowering.

"From here on you won't come in without knocking, you'll ask my permission to smoke, and try to get in the habit of addressing me as brigadier. These might seem like silly little formalities, but we've got to start somewhere to get a little discipline back into this game."

Major Fontes stepped back to let him pass, closed the door delicately behind him, and pointed with his chin to a cramped cubicle: two tables, an antiquated typewriter covered with a funereal cloth. Shelved cabinets stuffed with books and papers, the nail from which the photograph of the pig-faced admiral had hung was rusty, waiting for the photograph of the future president. A dying light crept sadly through the curtains, and at the Naval Arsenal next door a sergeant in white leggings had taken the place of the sentries:

"Colonel Ricardo picked this room for you personally, Colonel. I explained to him that there are other bigger ones that are empty, but he insisted that you like to work in a relaxed place, a peaceful place, that if you were taken out of a hole in the wall like this, no one could get along with you, you'd be grouchy as a dog."

The Naval Arsenal and after the Naval Arsenal, instead of the river, houses, small shops, a parking lot, spindly trees, a piece of square, traffic lights thinned out by distance: He still hasn't finished getting even with me, the lieutenant colonel thought, he still hasn't humiliated me enough, he won't get any rest until he fucks me up completely.

"Colonel Ricardo," the second lieutenant asked suddenly, "wasn't he that general that turned up dead a few years back half-rotted away in a car in Sesimbra?"

No, he was a cousin of that one, the one who committed suicide, but the way things turned out, all in all, it didn't make much difference, he ended up in the hospital, all full of tubes and bags of serum, tied to a whole mess of machines: he had a heart attack during a military parade, the troops parading and him twisting around on the platform, pulling off the medals and buttons on his chest, roaring, crazy with pain, his colleagues holding his arms and legs, opening his collar, giving him worried pats on the cheek.

"It's really nothing great," Major Fontes excused himself, looking at the chipped walls, the chipped ceiling, the chipped window frames, the melancholy and poor Lisbon that stretched gracelessly along toward the waterfront in a stumbling row of uneven tiled roofs. "I said the same thing to Colonel Ricardo, that there were other offices, other solutions, that we could, I don't know, swap with the adjutant sergeants, and he, no, no, no, it's just what you wanted, Colonel sir, that he knew your habits backward and forward, that a modest place like this would even bring back memories of your mother's place in Chelas, that you'd feel out of place in a different room. Well, if you'll excuse me, I'll have them bring you some cases."

"Can you see him?" a lady in a medical smock asked, entrenched behind the half-moon of a counter. (It smelled of medicine, silence, whispers, illness, oblique shapes scurried along the waxed floor.) "Visiting hours are from three to four, you'll have to wait in there a while."

Chelas, right or wrong, was just like that, but isn't it true that all modest neighborhoods are alike, Marvila, Chelas, Buraca, Paiã, Olivais, Moscavide, Benfica, the same buildings, the same little moribund gardens, the same filth, the same stray dogs, the same strips of posters falling off the walls? There was no elevator, of course, there wasn't much room, of course, he had to walk diagonally through a confused tangle of tables, chairs, pier tables, wicker objects, pictures, dolls made out of seashells or clay that trembled with ague when the toilet was flushed hard, shelves lined with paper doilies, of course. The neighbors were soldiers in the Republican Guard, store cashiers, retired bookkeepers, a café worker who wrote poetry and had won second prize in the sonnet at the Jogos Florais of the Academia Estudiantil e Recreativa Os Oito Unidos de Lisboa, of course, men put on striped pajamas when they got home from work, of course, radios tried to bellow louder than the weeping and complaining and whining of the children, unsimilar smells of cooking mingled and dissolved in sticky dampness. And yet, you see, don't think that in spite of a lack of comfort, a lack of money, and the singing of drunks on Sunday nights in the bar next to the coffin store, my life in those days wasn't good. It was good: as my mother used to say, heaven will protect little people like us.

He spent the morning shut up in his cubicle beside the prehistoric type-writer, taking notes on dossiers, thumbing through notebooks, using a red pencil to underline words, phrases, whole paragraphs, with his tongue in the corner of his mouth as if he were smoking a soft piece of squid, editing page after page of Ministry of War paper with a seal, which a quartermaster with long nails would come to pick up at eleven o'clock and bring them back typed shortly before noon. While he was heading for Colonel Ricardo's office, with the sound of his shoes echoing on the marble floor (they must have been marble, those whitish worn lozenges run through with small blue veins), he took a casual look at what he'd written and he was attacked by the uncomfortable evidence of having put together a bunch of idiotic, unconnected statements with pompous and useless expressions, which the other man would disdainfully throw away into the wicker basket kept for the mental crap his underlings had shat. The woman in the smock, holding the telephone like a violin between her neck and shoulder, called to him through the glass, and the lieutenant colonel dropped the Brazilian magazine full of near-naked bathing beauties, politicians in dark glasses, and soccer players, and went over to the Formica-topped counter:

"It's five after three (a coquettish smile, a gold tooth, a pretentious, ironic voice), just in case you like your friend better than you do the newspapers."

And with a suddenly professional intonation, fixing her hair with the flapping palm of her hand:

"General Armando Ricardo, microcardiac infarction, room twelve: at the top of the stairs, to the right."

"Not bad for the first day," Colonel Ricardo conceded, examining the pages with quick glances. "But what's missing is less benevolence and more aggressiveness, in order to defend democracy in an effective way, to keep the objectives of the Revolution intact: out of nine doubtful officers you only propose the retirement of one, and even then he's a harmless little lieutenant who won't stand in the way of anybody's promotion. We'll never get there that way, Artur: give me at least ninety percent of the higher-ranking officers retired into reserve status, they were the bastards who supported the regime. Give me the details and I'll fix them up here and there and convince our little captains in diapers with their Guevara manias: they're a slippery little bunch, you see, but if you give them a pat on the butt you can do whatever you want with them."

The lieutenant colonel went up the hospital steps feeling the receptionist in a smock observing his movements and the cut of his jacket, critically guessing the price of his clothes. On the landing he passed a woman who was weeping, supported by a young fellow, much younger than she (son? son-in-law? relative?), the wall lamps, turned on, gave the sad atmosphere of a church to everything around, the faces of the nurses and the aides looked dispirited and rainy to him. Long corridors, numbered doors, the smell of alcohol, oxygen tanks with a valve and gauge on top leaning in a corner. Room five, room six, room seven, room eight, room nine, metal ashtrays screwed onto the walls, and behind some doors muffled murmurs, conversations, indistinct sounds, running water.

"Did Brigadier Ricardo give you a hard time, Colonel?" Major Fontes asked, smiling without malice. "If it were left up to him alone, all the officers in the world would be retired by decree."

Room twelve: he turned the chrome knob, went in, and there was the chubby body in a metal bed, the red head, the thin hair in disorder, sunken into the pillow like a filling in a tooth, a bottle of serum, hanging from a hook, dripped into his arm, his pajama top open and his chest covered with clamps and wires, which disappeared into a kind of television set with a metal case on the blue screen of which surges of little flashing waves quivered intermittently: Boy, look how yellow you've got, the lieutenant colonel thought, look how old you've got, you bastard. And he pictured him laid out on an autopsy table, rigid, pale, stark naked, with a block of wood under the back of his neck, while a doctor in a rubber apron approached, scalpel in fist, raised his hand, and scratched the general's stomach with the painful slowness of a plow. The lieutenant colonel closed his eyes as quickly as he could so as not to see the gelatin of the intestines pour out onto the stone tabletop, the clots of blood, the translucent little froth that bubbled up from under the purple anemone of the liver. There were other corpses on other tables, that of Major Fontes, that of Lieutenant Cardoso, mine, a window with frosted glass panes, a dentist smell that pecked at his eyelids, orderlies in coveralls washing the floor with the long, hairy strokes of a mop. He wondered how old the woman in the smock could be. Forty, forty-five, forty-seven, was she single, married, a widow, what could her name be? Plucked eyebrows, polished nails, dyed hair: just the opposite, shit, the cleaning woman's fingers were square, wrinkled, masculine, her trunk was too thick, lacking any grace, great peasant feet moving about the Antarctic of the sheets. General Ricardo looked at him with difficulty, his mouth open, breathing with difficulty on the pillow, a shadow of a smile broke out for him, for a few seconds, on his gums, his free hand walked like a crab a way along the edge of the mattress, stopped with the pincer of his forefinger in the air, the streaks on the television screen continued on, impassively, with their strange luminous march. I'll bet forty-seven, I'll bet from a good family, I'll bet a widow, all that sarcasm had carried off a husband in a wink: now the doctor was cutting the ribs with an instrument that looked like a pair of pruning shears, and the twin gray casings of the lungs could be seen, the decomposed fruit of the heart wrapped in a case of pink cellophane, membranes ferociously slashed by a scalpel.

"Good afternoon, Ricardo," he said to the dying eyes, dulled by weariness or terror, and the fellow's index finger trembled just a tiny bit, his Adam's apple leaped on his throat, a small marigold of spittle bloomed at the corner of his lips.

"The sea?" Dália was puzzled. "What's this business about the sea?"

"From colonel on up," Colonel Ricardo ordered energetically. "Invent solid reasons so I can ask for a complete cleanup, leaving a half a dozen quiet fellows, of course, to protect appearances. So that beyond our doing an inestimable service for the Revolution, just between you and me, it'll be our great opportunity, Artur."

"I must have gone over more than five or six hundred cases in a short time," the lieutenant colonel grumbled, cautiously feeling his bladder: This shitty champagne is going to put an end to my kidneys, I swear. "There's no single soldier in existence about whose life I'm unfamiliar, about whom I haven't filed memoranda, advisories, reports that Ricardo would change afterward whenever he could into recommendations for retirement to the reserves, slowly opening the way, with the patience of a scarab, to a four-star position for himself. Because that, you understand, was the only thing he was really interested in: being a general, commanding a district, attending commemorations, parades, oath taking to the flag, from the top of a decorated platform. And with my help, fuck him, he got it, in less than a year."

"How many did you shoot down today, Colonel?" Major Fontes asked with a nervous laugh. "Have they swept me out yet?"

"Do you mean, Colonel sir, that that was what the Revolution was all about?" the soldier was surprised. "Do you mean that the Revolution was the big fish swallowing each other, like in a brawl, seeing who woke up on top in the morning?"

Not really the Revolution, he thought, but behind the scenes, in the dressing room on the coup, the colonels, the brigadiers, and the generals whose help the captains had over a certain period of time to legitimize the bastard origins of democracy, to ease the restlessness of capitalists, businessmen, emigrés, and to calm the United States and Europe, assuring them that there wouldn't be any Cubas in the peninsula, any cataclysmic bearded guys in fatigues, smoking cigars, and planting sugarcane and busts of Lenin everywhere. Not the Revolution or the ones who made the Revolution, but the voracious, cancerous microbes that fed on it and hovered around it, political parties, influence ploys, personal hatreds, the insatiable little ambitions of frustrated people: I want to be a marshal, I want to be rich, I want to be a minister, I want a boat, a house with a swimming pool, a color television set, an expensive mistress, I want twenty thousand creatures applauding me, waving flags and banners enthusiastically, I want to grind down the others, I want to crush the others, I want to cream the others, I want to be left all alone, heroic and in bronze, on the highest pedestal. And in the end, Jesus, miserable in a bed, full of tubes and wires, laid out in some little hospital, panting with the silent panic of a dog about to faint, his freckled hand limping like a crippled lobster along the edge of the mattress, evaporating in urine, diarrhea, pestilential breath, and foul-smelling sweat in the disarray of his sheets.

"Let me warn you, I don't like this at all, Artur," Colonel Ricardo threatened, furiously scratching out my recommendations, my memoranda, my reports, making corrections in the margin, cutting out whole sentences, underlining passages. "In this way not only won't we get anywhere, but we'll leave a bunch of fascist generals having a good laugh at our expense. (A tugboat came in through the curtains of the window with the sun, shaking the stucco flowers on the ceiling.) Do it any way you want, uncover, scrutinize, sink yourself into the garbage and, once and for all, get rid of these guys for me because if the Revolution runs aground these sons of bitches will land on us like hyenas."

He moved about, stammered, got all indignant, suddenly stood up waving the typed pages, withering me with his pink little anxious eyes, storming back and forth in the papal office with his hands in his pockets, roaring, muttering, snorting, barking, shouting, patriotic all of a sudden, socialist all of a sudden, antibourgeois all of a sudden, busy with the high destiny of the Nation all of a sudden, ready, all of a sudden, to carry alone on his shoulders all of its thirty-five thousand square miles of belfries, silence, and forgetfulness.

"Not just the sea," the communications officer explained to Dália, leaning against a huge poster full of aggressive peasants brandishing sickles, mutely chanting the "Internationale": "The birds, too, the cliffs, the transparent shades of the afternoon, the shrubs and small trees on the rocks, whose branches the wind was reducing to a calcinated texture, the boats coughing out their little exhaust smoke on their way to the river's mouth. Since I didn't have much to do, I spent my time counting them: I got up to twenty-seven one afternoon."

The patient seemed to recognize him from an infinite distance through the successive waves of mist, the little waves on the television screen speeded up, the tip of his tongue came out trembling along lips that were as dry as the earth of the Sudan. He's going to tell me something, the lieutenant colonel thought, leaning over him, he's going to talk to me: he put his nose almost next to the redhead's nose, shook him on the shoulder and felt an inert round mush of flesh that quivered and grew soft in the palm of his hand: Brigadier General Ricardo sat up, twisted with rage, in front of him, while the tugboat went off in the rarefied atmosphere of its smoke until it blended into the ash gray outline of Barreiro and the stout, starched folds of the curtains.

"Democracy is the most serious matter I know of, Artur, I can see now that I made a mistake in defending you, foolishly getting myself involved so they wouldn't screw up your career: with these shitty briefs of yours, you're prejudicing yourself, me, and all of Portugal. (Now it was a smaller, hesitant vessel, a fishing boat, with one or two tiny figures on deck, that was battering blindly against the windowpanes with stubborn insistence, trying in vain to find a gap in the wood through which it could enter, ending up disappearing over the automobiles and trucks on the square with a slow, asthmatic listless-ness.) Only a few of these guys need to get out of the way, for me to get my stars next month."

"Ricardo," the lieutenant colonel called, putting the cone of his mouth at the redhead's hairy ear that was just like a wrinkled, deaf conch with no sea sound inside. "Ricardo, you old bastard, it's me, Artur, it's my turn to fuck you in the ass."

"You can soften the story all you want, Colonel sir," the communications officer said, fishing the lieutenant colonel's necktie out of the glass of cham-pagne, "but a whole flock of guys was put into the reserves all at once. I was there, I saw, they'd come in to pressure us, and the sergeants were confused, perplexed, worried, just like us."

They'd appear in the afternoon, in civilian clothes, looking older, with hunched shoulders, pockets full of boxes with decorations, and commenda-tion diplomas rolled up under their arms, insisting on being received by the minister, the general, the brigadier, the colonel, the major, one of the invisible captains of the coup, I have a name to defend, a career, just two months ago I was awarded this medal, look, and they'd open the boxes with a snap of the springs and display pieces of metal that gleamed on the blue, or green, or brown, or red velvet, I'm just a soldier, I never supported the regime, please put this petition through, these pages stamped with seals, this letter, give it to the minister today, to the general, to the brigadier, to the colonel, to the major, there must be some mistake somewhere, just look at the injustice in all this, no, seriously, I'm the one who's asking you, read the first page at least and you'll see, twenty-three years of strictly military service, with no demerits, as for the tours in Africa, damn it, we were obliged to accept them, I never killed any blacks, I only wanted to bring my men back in one piece, but the mines, the ambushes, the mortars, sometimes one of my men would be left without a leg there, sometimes a vehicle would be blown up into the air, but collaboration with the regime, the answer is no, but fascist organizations, the answer is no, but the Legion, the Youth, the Militia, the answer is no, long live the liberating coup d'etat of April 25th, they invited me several times and I always replied Holy patience I'm a democrat, knock on some other damned door, and now, my friend, without any warning, without any motive, without any reason, they pay me back like this, they publish my name in the newspapers, they drag me indecently through the mud, here's a kick in the ass and start walking, beat it, disappear, we don't need you, as if I were some mangy dog, understand, a soul in damnation, as if I had leprosy, or nits, or something contagious, they'd rest their hands flat on the sergeants' desks, rocking with indignation and fear, they'd drop into chairs, mopping their brows with a handkerchief, straightening their ties in order to give their fingers something to do, almost sobbing in panic, I'm a general, damn it, they can't treat me like a pile of shit, damn it to hell, the sergeants would take their petitions, letters, protests indifferently, Relax, it will be turned in tomorrow, General sir, yes, I'll have it sent to somebody who can resolve it, General, The sea at Peniche, the communications officer was explaining to Dália, the sea at Peniche, dozing off and waking up in the night, my dozing off and waking up in the midst of a monotonous, fleeting cocoon of murmurs, the acid taste of foam in the tasteless taste of my saliva, my mouth full of sea like that of a castaway on the beach, I always had respect for the rank of sergeant, you know, I have fine friendships with the people under me, we've always got along famously, never any problems, if you don't believe me ask your comrade Cosme, your comrade Rocha, your comrade Marques, do me a small favor, what do you say, if they reinstate me, you can count on me, hand in these photocopies personally, this bill of particulars, these papers, Ricardo, the lieutenant colonel whispered, Ricardo, you old son of a bitch. What a great pleasure to see you exploding, the chubby redhead's mouth bubbled on the pillow, the haze over his eyes went away, So much the better that you can hear me, Ricardo, so much the better that you know it's me, the waves on the television screen speeded up, sparkling spasms sobbed all along the convex glass of the screen, the drops of serum dripped slowly into his arm, disappearing into his vein through a plastic tube fastened to his skin with pink adhesive tape, You must have the feet of a sea bird, Dália, the communications officer thought, long and bony, with long thick nails, feet for walking on the rocks, for leaping on crags, the feet of a white bird, of a brown bird with its breast feathers disarrayed by the wind, feet scratching my feet on the dunes of the bed, moving slightly, standing at an angle on the bathroom tiles, coming and going in the stunted room, going away and coming back, cartilaginous, with an awkward swiftness, avoiding pebbles of shoes, pebbles of slippers, sleeping beside me, not moving, on the mattress, straight and scaly and hard, rubbing the fleshy part of my leg with your heel, running along me from the end of my shinbone to my knees in a simultaneously absent and fierce carnivorous caress, feet in shoes, in rubbers, in stockings that hide the bulging tendons, the dark skin, the lumps of the joints in the toes, the muscles of the ankles, of the little pebble of the fibula, feet for taking flight at the end of the day after a short, painful trot on the sand toward a hollow on the coast from where you can spy on the night with round, fixed, luminous eyes, feet for my kisses, Dália, for my tongue to fill the space between your toes, to rub my nose along the thick surface of your flesh, to bite, lick you, caress the under part of your knees, searching with my chin for the delta of your hair, the vigorous vibration of your thighs, the harsh, wet, swollen wound of your vagina, feet to climb up my belly, up my chest, up my throat to the sudden stagnant musty green silence of my mouth, feet on my side, on my kidneys, on my behind, linked together on my anxious back, the generals would leave, discouraged, hopeful, wounded, reticent, they would linger at the door (They're going to try to give us money, they want to, but they're reluctant to offer us money), their pockets swollen with decorations, carrying briefcases of commendations tight under their arms, they would finally go out into the hallway with a pathetic decreasing sound of shoes, the sergeants would start typing again in their usual sluggish sloth, General Ricardo, completely awake now, was staring, terrified and disbelieving, at the lieutenant colonel, who was slowly pulling the adhesives off his arm, The sea at Caxias, the communications officer told Dália, is half-sea, half-river, it smells like a toilet, drainage, vomit, rotting corpses, the dung of seagulls in a flock on the wall with dirty feathers, it smells like poor homes, armpits, cold meals, unwashed dishes, he pulled the tube of serum out of his arm and the yellow liquid went on dripping onto the rug, standing beside the bed, imperturbable, motionless, quite straight, saluting, the lieutenant colonel was smiling in an almost friendly way at the patient who was searching, his desperate mouth open, in vain with his soft fingers for the button for the bell, the phosphorescent streaks on the screen had changed to discharges of irregular spasms, to sudden incandescent vibrations, a bulb began to blink on the upper left-hand corner of the apparatus, a metal buzzer was sounding, General Ricardo's hand flattened out weakly onto the sheet, his eyes retreated, without disbelief or fear now, into the shell of their sockets, the leaps and slashes on the television screen had disappeared, the light of the bulb was continuous and stronger now, a peaceful horizontal line was crossing the screen, You're not afraid of me anymore, the lieutenant colonel thought, you're not afraid of what I can do anymore: on leaving the room he heard the buzzer bleating again in the hallway. What a wild idea, Colonel, the second lieutenant murmured, what a crazy notion you had, he passed a young doctor gripping a stethoscope who was trotting hurriedly toward number twelve followed by two nurses with caps askew and syringes in their hands, he went downstairs peacefully, whistling softly, stairs that a charwoman on her knees was waxing, he stopped for an instant at the empty entranceway to examine a painting in a pine frame that by means of fearsome pictures of carbonized lungs and people coughing explained the drawbacks of tobacco, and he heard the scoffing voice of the lady in a smock, protected by the wall of her counter, surrounded by telephones and registers (Close to fifty, certainly, she must be close to fifty years old at least), who asked him in the friendly ironical tone of a while back, Is your friend better now?

"Much better," he answered, pushing aside the shutter (a few steps down, a neglected flower bed, shrubbery, the impatient traffic on the Avenida right below, traffic lights that changed color with lax facility). "So much so that we even managed to make peace, how about that?"

*7*

"L ET the sea rest in peace," Dália suggested, pushing away waves and
birds with the back of her hand. "Let's be serious now, my dear vest-pocket
Trotsky, did you bear up under it all in the end?"

"I know from my own experience how fucked up you can be if you can't tell
a woman that you're head over heels in love with her," the soldier said.

The seat of the Organization was operating out of a decrepit second floor
in the Bairro Alto, near the Largo do Camões, with a faded façade covered
with paintings on stone of sickles, hammers, grim-faced workers in front of
cranes and smokestacks, arm in arm with harvest maids and barefoot fishermen in caps and checkered shirts, which the coming winter would dissolve
into a disjointed paste of colors. Next to the door, posted in a display case, in
capital letters a slew of insults to the bourgeoisie in power and to the siren
song of Soviet revisionism that lulled the masses, and there inside, in old,
uncomfortable, and icy rooms, with chairs and tables falling apart, posters,
quotations from Marx, Lenin, and Ho Chi Minh, red flags, a plaster bust of
Engels (looking like my grandmother, right down to the beard) on a small
pedestal of wooden slats, with cigarette butts, ashes, scraps of paper, indefinite filth on the floor, a tiny counter where coffee, orangeade, and cheese
sandwiches were served to asexual and ugly creatures, who picked their

teeth with their fingernails and stuck out their pinkies as they held the plastic cups.

"Are you prepared to see that deep down you're just as bourgeois as I am?" the second lieutenant asked. "That the same little insignificant details horrify you? The only thing that separates us is the fact that my class status doesn't make me feel guilty in the least, and I don't feel any obligation to be a scapegoat because of it."

I, on the other hand, the communications officer thought with bitterness, went on for a long time split between the dark, painful sadness of not having been born a carpenter, or a mechanic, or a sewer worker, and the impossible desire to reconcile that remorse with my atavistic aversion to bad table manners, wrong verb tenses, hair with dandruff, and the dogmatic assumption of leadership by self-proclaimed leaders of the proletariat repeating with conviction, tirelessly and passionately, truths from a hundred years ago with the same sinuous and ardent inflection to cells of the Organization, at university meetings, in the Rossio on May Day, with a couple banners, a couple posters, a couple of dozen unconditional enemies of soap and comb. Weeks, months, years believing, wanting to believe, pretending that I believed, fobbing off flyers at the Ministry, prospectuses and confused doctrines, fighting against the stony deafness of old sergeants, and at night, in the musty floor on Camões, looking down on pastry shops, pimps, snot-nosed whores and drug peddlers, the endless stormy sessions with the comrades of the Central Committee presided over by Olavo's skinny figure at the other end of the table, deciding on a proposal for a strike by the metal workers, which would never take place, an attack on the president of the Republic, which no one seconded, a popular uprising that would leave the whole country indifferent and sunk in its usual dull drowsiness, anesthetized by the false deviationist promises of the social democrats. Weeks, months, years waiting in vain for the Long March, still shaking when a character in a topcoat (a policeman? an inspector? the secret police?) approached me, waiting for weapons from Algeria and Tunisia, manufacturing time bombs with broken-down alarm clocks, ending up talking about birds and having coffee in the Bairro Alto beside the clear, interrogative, impatient round eyes of Dália.

"Me a bourgeois?" the communications officer was indignant, he straightened the frame of his glasses with his ring finger. "At least I put my body to the test, at least I took a royal beating in Caxias."

"Ricardo had a first-class funeral: camellias, rifles, the head chaplain saying masses for him," the lieutenant colonel stated, drying the tip of his necktie on the tablecloth. "There wasn't a single military man who didn't show up at least to make sure it hadn't been one of the guy's tricks, to make certain at least that he'd finally kicked the bucket."

And the communications officer pictured the open casket in the church, a pair of freckled hands, pricked by the doctors' needles, folded over his uniformed belly, the family pale from lack of sleep, downcast like doves at dawn, and hundreds of old military men in black ties, exultantly sorrowful, hovering over the corpse in the basalt light of morning, just like fat, hesitant fish around a strange coral reef of ribbons and flowers: Olavo came over to him with his quick little insect walk, and touched his arm with two pointed fingers:

"The comrades are waiting for you to start the meeting," he announced in his monotonous grave little voice, eternally confidential: "It looks like great things are in the works."

"And in the end another bourgeois," the second lieutenant lamented ironically, "in the end just as big an elitist and as decadent as I am. Explain to me, please, what program for change the communists are putting forth, explain to me what there is that people can still believe in."

A large table, people sitting around, more flags, more banners, more posters, on a lame cabinet a wrinkled and heroic Lenin serving as a paperweight for a pile of projects: they, the ugly ones, the ones with long nails, the ones with a finger held out, the ones with exuberant and imposing bad taste, believed during that period, still believe perhaps: Was that what made me feel less than the others when I sat down beside them, could it be envy, jealousy, shame about my reticence, my hesitation, my doubt that made me uncover ridiculous weak points, grammatical mistakes, onion breath, dirt spots, salivating as they spoke? Avenging my hidden inferiority, avenging my idiotic taboos?

"What fault is it of yours," the second lieutenant asked, "that you weren't starving as a baby, what fault is it of yours that you were brought up among clay figures of saints? Open your mouth and close your eyes, my boy: with a few glasses of champagne this will all pass, the illness that wine can't cure has yet to be discovered."

Lopes's gray hair stood up as he put out an unfiltered cigarette in the aluminum saucer he was using as an ashtray, and he picked little pieces of tobacco off his tongue with his thumb and forefinger:

"Comrades (the buzz of conversation lessened and ceased, heads turned in the direction of the voice, someone coughed in the silence, muffling his mouth with a handkerchief). Comrades, trustworthy information has reached us that a reactionary blow against the glorious conquests of the working class is being hatched and will strike soon (What conquests? the communications officer wondered, surprised, playing with an extinguished match). We know that the right has been conspiring at military posts, we know that landowners and capitalists are collecting money for the coup, we even know the names of some shady characters from the old regime implicated in the plot. The Portuguese Marxist-Leninist-Maoist Organization is obliged, as the only legitimate vanguard of the oppressed, to prevent by any means we shall decide here today the cancer of fascism injected by criminals, malcontents, and opportunists from undermining the now healthy but young and vulnerable organism of Portuguese democracy."

Pompous statements like that, he thought, brought on frenzied arguments that lasted well into the night, snuffling with coffee and cigarettes, until the pigeons returned to the Largo do Camões in stumbling, sleepy flocks at dawn. Dália was dozing in her chair, an old man who always had a toothpick in his mouth clutched by a broken denture plate, who'd been a glass worker, was snoring in a worn-out easy chair with uneven springs, slashing wire corkscrews, that pinched the backsides of unsuspecting people, the outlines of buildings were frozen in the cold. Lopes, all worked up, hair all over the place, circles under his eyes, was advising all the militants, without distinction as to position or duty, to redouble their energies for revolutionary vigilance and the preventive use of truncheons. And then, you know how it was, he said to me, opening and closing the plastic imitation tortoise frames of his glasses, things began moving with incredible speed, the general resigned following a whole day of demonstrations and barricades, they named a new president, the indecisive Army was split, quartermasters in the department talked politics over their forgotten typewriters, Esmeralda complained about the rise in the price of fish, the price of meat, the price of fruit, the price of bread, his aunt, greatly alarmed, was all over the place, crossing herself and holding her beads at the innumerable little shrines along the hall, when comrades tried to put up posters on corners in the Baixa, they were beaten up, they didn't know by whom, This is only going somewhere if we hit back, Olavo muttered, this can only lead to a few little bombs, my children, they even began to make some, they even tried to buy machine guns in Morocco, but the Chinese and the Libyans didn't send any dollars, the guys in charge of accounts were constantly complaining, the mimeographed newspaper ceased publication because of a lack of funds, and one afternoon Olavo pushed him over to the bay of a window, We've got half a dozen military rifles buried in the Alentejo, if we don't rob a bank, we're finished.

"Oh, my God!" the soldier was alarmed. "Rob a bank just like that, Lieutenant?"

Not a big bank, we haven't got the wherewithal, Olavo clarified, a small branch in Algés, near the market, boxed in by a grocery store and a furniture shop, three or four tellers at most, no police in the area, Dália gave excuses at the Ministry, she would get up early in the morning, spend the day spying through the windows on the movements of the tellers and the customers, at the beginning of the month a silent, patient line of retired people blandly waiting for their pension checks, stretching out through the lobby almost to the corner of the Avenida dos Bombeiros with its red and shiny fire engines. At the site where they had torn down the bullring, there was a circular and dusty empty lot now, which traveling circuses occupied in August with their impoverished tents, all around squat houses and modern buildings, the bus stop, and, farther on, the shelter and the long platform of the station, a strip of beach, bearded with weeds, crossed by packs of downcast dogs, and the river's parallel friezes of yellow froth, depositing its poor and eroded trash that held no mystery onto the sands. In order to lay out the details of the operation, Olavo got together every week with Dália, the communications officer, an extremely thin cello player who wore a muffler, with spidery fingers and an infinitely inoffensive and gentle look, and whistled strange pieces of music all the time, and the former glass worker who would snore, crammed into the easy chair after five minutes of talk. Maps with variously colored arrows, crosses, and dots were unfolded, This little square here is the bank, these circles are the places with the greatest activity, the supermarket, the butcher shop, the school, the arrows are possible escape routes, the crosses are the positions each one of us will take, What about the car? the cellist asked, cracking his knuckles, we're going to need a car to get out of there, It wasn't rich people's money that you people were going to steal, the lieutenant colonel said in an accusatory tone, it was the savings of retired people, what kind of shitty communism is that?, Rip off an automobile in Pedrouços, cars are one thing there's no shortage of in this country, Olavo explained, by the way, do any of you know how to drive?, Let the rich pay for the crisis, Colonel, the communications officer answered disdainfully, let the rich come up with the dough for people who haven't got any, the important thing at the time was to raise the morale of the working class, lift their spirits with plans, leaflets, newspapers, let them know that there were people fighting for them and show them the way, organizing demonstrations, explanatory sessions, lectures, peace marches, throw capitalism and its bloodsuckers in their faces, Dália, the communications officer, the cellist, and the old man looked at each other in embarrassment, none of them had ever sat behind the wheel, What kind of shitty militants are you, Olavo was indignant, pounding on the table, who are unaware of everything, no matter what? Lopes, when he was consulted, put out his unfiltered cigarette in the small tinfoil plate piled high with butts, fell silent in an endless strategic meditation, ended up pushing back his gray forelocks with the impetuous inspired gesture of a maestro, and ordered Give Comrade Pires here some money, have him enroll in driving school and take half a dozen lessons, the old man protesting all the while Me? Me? jabbing his chest with his thick, disbelieving forefinger, he didn't want to accept, he couldn't, he refused, he was sure he wouldn't understand the whole mess of gearshifts, blinkers, pedals, his dentures were moving around in panic, loose in his mouth, but Lopes scolded him firmly and severely, What's become of our revolutionary discipline, comrade, what's become of that unconditional devotion to the sacred cause of the peasantry, and the glass worker ended up chewing his toothpick in silence and staring at us with the most terrified eyes in the world, What if I run over somebody, damn it, what if I ram into a wall? The next day we saw him go by at five miles an hour beside an instructor with a little mustache, desperately clutching the steering wheel of a blue Volkswagen like a castaway on a cork life preserver: he just missed a fruit cart by inches, he went up and down the street three or four times, disappeared blowing the horn and turning on all the lights down the Rua do Loreto, weaving out of control on the trolley tracks. As the lessons progressed, however, Comrade Pires was growing enthusiastic, pulling people by their annoyed sleeves at headquarters, I can shift like a dream now, I can back the crate up now, I passed a truck by the Jerónimos today. He would leave earlier in order to study the traffic laws, inflicted endless lessons about traffic signs on the others, This one with just a cow is to let you know there are animals about, This red and blue one means no parking, Do you people know what right of way means? at a Central Committee meeting he came to suggest that they buy five blue Volkswagens in order to improve the Organization's image, to show those hicks of Portuguese that Maoists are not as dirt poor as they think (You people may not believe it, you can go fuck yourselves, but it's the surest way of winning bourgeois elections, I don't care if we haven't got the money to buy even a pair of roller skates), Dália, deeply involved, requested an indefinite leave in order to continue her scouting of the bank, accompanied by Olavo now, the maps with crosses and dots and arrows grew in number, the plan was taking shape little by little, You stand here, you there, we two will go in, with that numbskull face of yours who would ever think to mistrust you, the other comrades, Captain, talked to us with deference, respect, Lopes announced at the Permanent Secretariat, energetically putting out his cigarette, the shock brigade will go into action quite soon, I only want to let you know in the meantime that capitalism is going to suffer a hard blow in the Lisbon area, but they all knew the details, they'd all seen the maps, they'd all put forth alternatives, suggestions, ideas, Why not a drugstore, drugstores are easier, why not follow the methods of the Basques and arrange the assassination of a primary-school teacher, or a nun, or a tax collector, killing night watchmen, for example, is duck soup, they're almost all hunchbacks and the ones who aren't hunchbacked have bladder trouble, a baker's good, damn it, early in the morning there's no one on the street, you sneak up behind him with a knife and the man's buried in croissants right there. They were opening the amusement park, finishing the final touches on the restaurants and carousels, refreshment stands, ghost castles, the roller coaster, amusing devices that jolted and shook people up until it made them, pale as plaster, shriek with fear, vomiting up their insides onto the ground under the tender care of their families, and the communications officer woke up to the exhaust of the motorcycles in the Pit of Death spinning him around on his pillow like insistent wasps, freeing him from unbearable nightmares of shots and shouting retirees. His aunt's cane was pecking down the hall, Esmeralda was in the kitchen complaining about her aching back (Don't get off the track, you son of a bitch, the second lieutenant snorted, tell us how it went), and he was thinking, in the dining room, over coffee and toast, How many colonels put into the reserves am I going to have to endure today, how many brigadiers, how many generals, how many fat, bald-headed bastards, a cold shower, the nauseating taste of the toothpaste in his mouth, the subway to the Rossio and then going down to the Baixa on foot, to the Column docks, hands in his pockets and jacket collar turned up (I've got to buy a topcoat and some gloves), while sleepy guys were opening the coverings of shop windows and lowering their awnings, tailors, watchmakers, goldsmiths, travel agencies filled with exotic posters and pictures of tropical sunsets, Leave the sunsets in peace, the second lieutenant insisted, nibbling on the blonde's throat, what happened later? and along the river the tugboats, the nauseating and sticky mist that smelled of gasoline, rotten shellfish, and seagull corpses rising up from the water, tiny fishing boats, a rippled sky, the bronze king in his motionless trot, the long, endless, geometric buildings with archways and their vendors of lottery tickets, alarming blindmen with vague and terrible eyes, Forget about everyday things, the lieutenant colonel ordered, and get on with the imbecilic story I can't bear listening to anymore. Until Olavo, Captain, with great airs of mystery, called the shock brigade together, shutting himself up with them in a tiny room without any Lenin, either in bronze or plaster, only a benign Mao Zedong, infinitely fat, smiling on top of a cabinet, a school blackboard fastened to the wall and lots of colored lines drawn in all directions on the black background. The cellist, who was allergic to chalk, began to sneeze and blow his nose, with red eyes, all choked up, What a shit bunch of antifascists these birds turned out to be, Olavo complained immediately, you should get out of politics, carry a picture of the pope in your wallet, and belong to the Christian Democrats at best, It'll go away, it'll go away, it's nothing, the musician promised, suffocating, the sound of a Ping-Pong ball could be heard back and forth from the floor upstairs or falling *toc toc toc toctoctoctoctoctoctoctoc* onto the floor, sharp shouts on the street, radio music, arguments, Tomorrow everybody here at ten o'clock without fail, we're going to lay our lives on the line for the working class, comrades, Olavo pointed theatrically to the laughter of the obese chinaman and added pompously Let us courageously follow the incomparable example of the Great Helmsman, But why that kind of language, the soldier was surprised, why so many hard words in just one sentence, I couldn't sleep all night long, the communications officer complained, I spent the whole time, without moving, listening to Esmeralda snoring, my aunt's wheezing, and the creaking of furniture, the garlands of lights from the park came and went, driven by the wind, into the gelatinous interior of my fatigue, the loudspeakers were throwing blasts of metallic syllables into the shells of my ears, the bed was an uncomfortable seat on the roller coaster that was tumbling down dizzily, without stopping, in the direction of the dawn, he got up very early, turned on the shower, thought that someone was calling him, but it was his aunt's voice conversing indignantly with the phantoms of her dreams, You would do well to shave off that mustache, Eduardo, she whispered, the skin on my face is a mess because of you, the water that fanned out from the ceiling hurt his fingernails and bones, made his stomach contract, he soaped himself quickly, dried himself off shivering, the tube of light that the tiles broke up made his features thinner and plowed new wrinkles into his cheeks, What a puss I've got, the communications officer thought, I look like a corpse with five years in the family vault behind him, he cut his chin shaving, stanched the flow of blood with a piece of toilet paper, and only after he was combing his hair, already dressed, did he notice the dried shaving cream clinging to his sideburns, he swallowed a cup of barley coffee and ate a couple of biscuits from the cookie tin with ladies in ringlets on the lid, slices of codfish were swimming in a plastic bowl on a wooden stool, Maybe a little later they'll be preparing the food for my wake here, surrounded by the desolate sisterhood of neighbor women, port wine, liqueurs, chicken croquettes on a spit, Lopes would write a moving editorial in the *Red Flag*, KILLED BY POLICE WITHOUT MERCY FIGHTING FOR HIS UNPROTECTED BROTHERS, and in the capitalist press, DANGEROUS THIEF SHOT BY FORCES OF LAW AND ORDER, or BEWARE, POR-TUGUESE: TERRORISTS IN LISBON, or maybe SIGNIFICANT NUM-BER OF SOVIET-MADE WEAPONS FOUND IN ROBBERS' VEHICLE: POLITICAL CRIMES PLANNED, MOSCOW FORMALLY DENIES INVOLVEMENT IN SHOOTOUT THAT RESULTED IN SERIOUS WOUNDS FOR TWO COURAGEOUS POLICEMEN AND AN EXEM-PLARY HOUSEWIFE, he went down the stairs at half past seven in the morning and was walking along the almost deserted streets of the city, looking at the buildings, the trees, the lifeless shop windows, the parked cars, tarnished sides dampened by the night, everything black, gray, white, and misty, without any color, without any reflections, without any shine, until around Saldanha the pale green tangerine of the sun became stuck in a space between roofs, magazine vendors were spreading photographs and mastheads on the sidewalk, watercolor animated façades and faces, at that hour Dália's alarm clock, the cellist's alarm clock, the old man's alarm clock began to ring, fatty bodies, fatty movements, gummy eyes and slippers, I want to wake up with you, Dália, in the morning I want to breathe you in, I want to drink in your sleepiness and the spongy flesh of your shoulders, I want to graze on the calm-herb sweat of your breasts, I want to die a sweet soft death in you, peopled with great sad eyes of animals that can't talk, I want to blow on the equinoctial birds of your throat, he took the subway at the Marquês de Pombal, sinking into the boiling and noisy catacombs of cement in a rush of office workers, stenographers, attendants, hotel workers, nurses, and panhandlers, he came to the surface at Restauradores like a seal out of breath, huge movie posters, cafés with chairs still on the tables, where they were sweeping sawdust and spit and rinds and matchboxes and cigarette butts into the street, he took the elevator to the Bairro Alto and his legs were trembling, and his arms were trembling, and his mouth was trembling, But look how nervous I am, damn it, after the tenth bank this will all be duck soup for me, the cashiers will hand over the money now as soon as they see me, the blood was dancing in his chest in unequal bursts, he went along hugging the wall, I'm not going to faint now, toward the irregular, shapeless incline, the Largo do Camões, his retirees who were flying off and his pigeons, with canes, bent over on the stone benches, he had a strange feeling, a kind of pain in his left side, he flattened his hand against his jacket and immediately got angry with himself, What kind of a shitty coward am I, fuck it all, it's nothing, he had a fleeting memory of Africa, the mines waiting for us on patrol, the coffins waiting for us in the warehouse, and yet what he remembered most were the disgusting stray dogs, skinny, resigned, stretched hungry by the flagpole, ears fallen, eyes jellylike, the wounds and scars on their flanks that swarms of flies crossed with folded wings, he remembered the frighteningly and surprisingly human side glances of the dogs, their heads, their hairy penises, and their human paws, their human trunks with backbone and ribs showing, he remembered the fear, the acceptance, the sugary human humility in their eyes, he didn't remember bombardments or ambushes or wounded bodies or his head splitting with malaria, he only remembered the solitary, hopeless melancholy of the dogs, because all I have left from the war, Captain, is a pack of stray dogs in the tormented depths of my memory. The communications officer turned left and right on the varicose streets of the Bairro Alto, the aneurisms of the alleys, the tumors of its steps, while from above the retirees floated down in hats and neckties over the eaves and cornices of the roofs: Which ones are pensioners, he asked himself, and which ones are pigeons, since they all feed on the crumbs of the wind? and he calmed down gradually, but when he saw in the distance the decrepit building of the Organization his knees went soft, his stomach gave a turn in his belly and he closed his mouth tightly so as not to vomit up the biscuits and the barley coffee. He waited, leaning against the door, smoking cigarette after cigarette (Like fathers in maternity wards, the second lieutenant laughed, just like fathers in maternity wards), for Olavo to arrive, find the key among the change in his pocket, and go ahead of him up the stairs to the devastated and dirty room of the Central Committee meetings, where, in spite of the open windows, the ever-present, unbearable smell of Lopes's cigarettes floated in the air, tinfoil plates overflowing on every side. Dália appeared with a different hairdo, dark glasses, and the shadowy and discreet smile of a Mata Hari, Just who do you think you are, Olavo asked her, annoyed, we're not here to play Al Capone, but no sooner did he turn around than he saw the cellist disguised as a Jew in a synagogue, with a hairy cotton beard, a tin crucifix on his belly, a priest's cassock, and sheepskin boots, and he stood looking at him openmouthed, green with rage, unable to speak, Are communists always nutty, Lieutenant, the soldier wanted to know, always soft in the head?, Are you people making fun of me?, Olavo roared, standing on tiptoe, hitting the wall with his fist and knocking over ashtrays, piles of paper, glue bottles with the brush inside, leaflets, rolls of posters, are you having fun with me, damn you?, This is so we won't be recognized, the musician explained softly, to draw police attention to Soviet lackeys, luckily Pires wore the usual rumpled suit, the usual toothpick in his plastic teeth, and the enormous joy of being able to drive a car with only one steering wheel, Stop this clownishness, damn it, Olavo was shouting, it isn't Carnival time yet, they must have been able to hear him hollering out on the street, Captain, because the greengrocers stopped hawking their goods, If you're going to go on insulting me, comrade, the cellist warned, I'll pull out of the robbery entirely and report what happened to the Conflict Commission, they finally withdrew sullenly, each to his corner of the room, staring with moody eyes at the erased slogans and defects in the plaster, Dália, the old man, and the communications officer trotted back and forth between the other two, pleading, arguing, railing, begging, after half an hour of painful diplomatic missions they grudgingly consented to shake hands, after the cellist took off the crucifix and cassock and appeared in the rubber shirt and pants of a frogman, The most practical thing, he explained, beaming, for a little operation of this nature, Olavo disappeared into the hallway and re- turned later with a hodgepodge of children's toys, cap pistols, water pistols, and machine guns that shot beans, Here are your weapons, he excused himself with an embarrassed expression, there were some real rifles buried in the Alentejo, we even had a map of the spot, but dig as we could, we couldn't find them, I spent the night shoveling here and there with no results, Comrade Nunes and Comrade Pinto are still there with picks, all covered with dirt, under the cork trees, the one who gets the machine guns will load them with birdseed from the pantry, the ones with the pistols, just in case, will fill them with water in the bathroom, it's still better than nothing and, besides, at first sight the bank clerks and the police couldn't even tell the difference from the real thing, the same size, the same color, the same shape, only the weight is different, mine, which was broken, the communi- cations officer said, was dripping through my pant pocket and a cold liquid ran down over my knee to my sock, the cellist had to put the cassock back on in order to hide the machine gun decently, as its flint gave off yellow sparks from its barrel, *tack tack tack tack tack tack tack tack*, it was after eleven o'clock when they filed out, sad and conspiratorially, from the headquarters of the Organization, Any day now, the communications officer thought, the rotting desks, the mountains of pamphlets, the slimy toilet, and the busts of Lenin will collapse in confusion onto the neighbor below, a grim-faced and solitary gentleman, middle-aged, who was accustomed to walking a tiny, terribly nasty dog called Sport in the Carmo neighborhood, any day now we're going to land there, the Central Committee, Security, the guys who come here to drink cheap coffee, in a cloud of plaster and dust, of rotten beams and lettered banners, right into the guy's dining room full of sideboards and ceramic partridges, It's already after eleven, Olavo snorted anxiously, his Bakelite weapon hindering his movements, get a taxi quick, before the bank closes. A triangular piece of river could be seen, a rusty tanker, the sky was cloudless now, the methylene blue of springtime, and the pigeons were circulating from church to church. The cellist's cotton beard was waving biblically before the windows of drugstores and bars of taverns, dark like wounds, where mingled shapes moved about as if swimming, Olavo paid the driver who was peeping, mistrustfully, in the mirror at that strange mixture of diver and cathedral canon, whistling through the false hair of the mustache that kept getting caught in his mouth, and the five of them stood all alone on a street with trolley cars in front of a building under construction protected by a network of platforms, and on both sides were the walls of gardens or factories, iron gates, stone pineapples, small buildings, sunken little shops, a goldsmith's, a haberdasher's, a corner funeral parlor crammed with little angels and coffins.

"The dogs, the bastards, the filthy swine, the sons of bitching dogs," the lieutenant colonel said, contemplating the miserable Mozambique post in the bottom of his champagne glass (and the trees in the jungle trembled in his eyes, and the nearness of death turned his teeth black). "We should have shot all the dogs when we left there, we should have cut the throats of every one, knocked them all off. They would come slowly up to us, lick our legs, the camouflage pants, the canvas shoes, follow us, limping, a few feet back, submissive and servile, going off again without barking, without complaining, dragging their weak thighs and rear ends, they would curl around the flagpole staring at us pitifully with their great big brown eyes without any lashes, during attacks they'd flatten their bony bellies against the belly of the earth, and during pauses in the explosions we could hear them whining softly like wounded soldiers and birds of night, we could hear them pissing with fear like us, they obeyed out of fear like us, they continued living out of fear like us." The colonel's right, the second lieutenant backed him up, we should have shot them all when we left, shot them and the people on the ship loaded down with old, exhausted soldiers, drunk on rosé, red wine, martinis, beer, dancing on the fading water on its way to Lisbon.

From time to time, through a crack in the wall, the urinelike chlorine breath of the river hit them in the nose, and they walked a stretch of the almost deserted street aimlessly in search of the ideal car for a bank robbery, trying doors that wouldn't open, triangular glass windows that were impossible to force, hermetically sealed tops, despairing now, cursing now, muttering now, kicking mudguards and tires spitefully now, the cellist, from the tunnel of his evangelical beard, insulted a pair of ladies of advanced age who were examining them with fright, dumbfounded by Dália's dirty words, a trolley car disappeared, ringing its bell, occupied by a motorman with hollow eyes and a few quick, indistinct shapes, Fuck it all fuck it all, Olavo was getting impatient, adjusting the plastic machine gun under his jacket, they tried one or two oblique cross streets unsuccessfully, a small square with a fountain without water, an alley that ended suddenly in a set of stairs that led to a second, twisted alley, Slow down, the old man protested, panting, you people will be the death of me, I'm taking heart pills, endless, painful minutes punctuated by Dália's frenzy, and there it came, finally, the enormous, majestic yellow Jaguar, bristling with bumpers and lights, coming to a halt near a wooden-slat bench, the bald-headed fellow blowing his horn inside there at some building, Olavo's quick whistled exclamation, Get that one for me, damn it, the cellist fighting with his cassock, ripping off buttons, pointing the plastic pistol at the stupefied cheeks of the driver, Get out, bourgeois, long live the Portuguese Marxist-Leninist-Maoist Organization, the old man got nimbly behind the wheel, clutching his chest, nervously trying the gear shift, the lights, the pedals, gunning the engine in neutral, the comrades stumbled, pushing each other, bouncing into the backseat in a hodgepodge of legs, arms, unlaced shoes, machine guns with birdseed and toys dripping water, the bald-headed man, hands in the air, begged in a panic Don't kill me don't kill me don't kill me, a fat woman with flashy dyed-platinum hair and an acrylic fur coat who came regally out of a nearby building, dropped her purse and began to scream (the guy's mistress? the guy's wife? the guy's sister-in-law?), the cellist, with the pistol still in his fist as in gangster movies, drew back toward the Jaguar, but missed his footing and fell, with the sound of tin cans, right on top of a motor scooter that fell over with him onto the sparse grass of a plot, Hurry up, Olavo moaned, pulling on his cassock, hurry up, that madam's going to rouse the whole neighborhood in a minute, but the cellist had got his ankle caught on a wheel and was dragging the scooter along behind him, Get rid of that shit, the old man commanded, indignant, that stinking priest is crazy, what in hell does he want a motor scooter for at a time like this? the bald man, on his knees now with his hands up, was looking at them one by one with infinite wonder, the creature with the exuberant platinum hair was pushing all the doorbells she could, hugging the wall of a building whose ground floor announced in great green letters GONÇALO IS A BUM, and the communications officer envisioned, emerging with their hair hanging down from the catacombs of their cubicles full of doilies, pottery bunnies, and Our Ladies with the malevolent smile of a cancan dancer, a fierce band of concierges on the warpath, armed with fearsome bowl brushes and plumber's helpers from toilets with a fatal flatus, who would hurl themselves upon them with a hail of curses. Help me get loose from this, the cellist appealed with shouts, and Dália detached the fallen scooter with kicks, crushing the brakes, bursting the gas tank, destroying the gleaming exhaust pipe, the bald man ended up flopping down onto the bench, loosening his tie and collar, breathing through his open mouth like a suffocating fish, the musician, his beard askew, finally got loose from the metal snare like a butterfly from a chrysalis, and dove headfirst, confusedly, into the Jaguar, Let's get out of here, let's get out of here, Olavo screamed, the old man pulled on the gearshift, let out the clutch, and the car lurched and climbed the sidewalk, bounced off the tricycle of a television repair company, off the bench with the bald man, who fled on all fours through the flower bed, crushing the dying, sad municipal plants (Hyacinths? Camellias? Dahlias? the second lieutenant asked), a lamppost bent over from the blow like a stalk in the wind, we went down a steep slope at supersonic speed, missed by inches a truck that was crossing in front with a fearful squealing of brakes, Did you people see the speed that this old boat has? the old man asked, amazed, looking back and forgetting about the steering wheel, the Volkswagen I learned on never went over fifteen, the green-tinted glass of the windows went up and down with the push of a button, the multiple speakers of the stereophonic radio flooded the car with dance music, sambas, boleros, mambos, foxtrots, The stinking bourgeois treat themselves well, the cellist observed, clutching the ribbon of the fake whiskers and taking an assortment of nuts and bolts from the motor scooter out of his shoe, I'm sure they eat elephant croquettes and ostrich stuffed with truffles for breakfast, The dogs, the lieutenant colonel thought in a rage, us sitting in the mess, eating what wasn't on our plates, drinking what wasn't in our glasses, playing very seriously in Africa at little dollhouse dinners, and the wretched dogs sniffing us biliously on the knees, jumping up to the oilcloth table cover, showing their sharp teeth, rubbing their hungry wet snouts against our fingers, the vapor lamp in the center of the table projected giant shadows that barked onto the walls, backs, tails, bellies, flat skulls, the night gave a blue light to the rickety wooden barracks, the little cement cube of a command post, the geometric and dark outlines of the weapons carriers, the shelters with poles and tin roofs, and out there, phosphorescent and imprecise, trotting, floating, swimming in the clear September shadows, with staring lilac eyes and the tight lower jaws of children, the dogs looked deeply at me with the mysterious or aggressive or penetrating or inexplicable opaque perplexity of dreams. The communications officer, who had abandoned his glass, his mouth extended, was drinking straight out of the tipped-up bottle of champagne, a bony lump was bouncing like a restless ball under the skin of his throat, and two threads of shining liquid, like drool, two silvery wrinkles underlined the angles of his mouth, slowly dying into his collar. The mulatto woman, leaning over, crushing the kegs of her breasts, was measuring him indifferently, devouring tons of peanuts, french fries, cheese tidbits, popcorn.

"Did you belong to that bunch robbing banks that the papers talked about, Lieutenant?" the soldier asked with a cadaveric censuring feeling. "Did you belong to that sect that killed two tellers and wounded an invalid waiting in a wheelchair for his pension, Lieutenant?"

Pictures of men with the fearsome faces of outlaws, touching interviews with victims' families, coffins covered with wreaths, the proper and unanimous national indignation, the strong communiqué from the minister, the transcription of the telegram of condolence from the president of the Republic, the photograph of the policeman who all by himself had overpowered three scoundrels, the testimony of the manager, the assistant manager, the second assistant manager, the cleaning woman, an emotional housewife who was carrying her husband's wages at that moment, a lucid psychologist, a stern politician, an indulgent psychiatrist, and a kindly priest, specialist of social violence at Swiss universities where the dark anarchistic impulses in white rabbits were electrically stimulated: Not exactly, the communications officer thought, placing the bottle on the sweaty ice in the bucket and riding the mulatto woman's huge pubes with both hands. Not exactly full-time revolutionaries, not exactly South American guerrillas in khaki uniforms from Nicaragua, Cuba, Venezuela, destroying armed units with bazookas and torturing ambassadors, sure of themselves, determined, efficient, but five excited and nervous characters waving ridiculous kids' pistols around, thrown together in a big luxury car, knocking down lampposts, flattening bicycles, making traffic cops flee in panic with their helmets, tipping over crates of fruit and vegetables in marketplaces, which spread out squashed on the sidewalk, regally ignoring traffic signals, roaring, blowing the horn, going forward, backing up, with the windshield wipers going at a furious pace, the blinkers going off and on like the throbbing of a carotid artery, Why don't we forget about the bank, the old man proposed, his eyes gleaming, and take a drive to Guincho to look at the dunes, the beaches, have a sherbet in Cascais? The streets in Algés are all alike, Captain, ugly three-story buildings, work being done on the berms, stacks of pipes, the surface of the road bumpy and full of holes, There it is, Dália would announce, and it never was, more houses, more little shops, more trees without any green, more of the dark brown presence of the river coughing behind us, You did a shitty piece of reconnaissance of the terrain here, Olavo was indignant, spitting involuntary birdseeds out the window, don't you even know where the hell it is? The cursed dogs, the lieutenant colonel thought, feeling an inexplicable fury growing inside him like a whirlwind, one afternoon after the thunderstorm, Major Gonçalves came out of the command post drunk, sinking up to his heels in the mud of the parade ground, he drew his Walther out of his holster and began shooting at the dogs at random where they were rolled up like scarves around the flagpole, cries and quick shots echoed in the saturated, sulfuric atmosphere of dusk, the lower branches of the bushes were waving, a pregnant bitch fell to one side, kicking, her throat torn by a dozen bullets, the major reloaded his pistol in silence, the muscles of his face tight with hate, and the dogs disappeared howling, bellies to the ground, into the hollow of the shelters, Are you people sure you really don't want to go to the beach? the old man insisted, merrily tooling down the road, did you really want to do the bank job?, Major Gonçalves held out his arm again, closed one of his eyes, squeezed the trigger (great clouds of rain were piling up to the north) and the bitch stopped twitching, serene suddenly. I wasn't mistaken at all, there it is, Dália shouted, pointing to a plate glass window, the outline of a counter, no policeman, capital letters in relief over the door, Stop this piece of shit, the cellist searching through the birdseed in his pockets, the communications officer nervously patting (Just like Zorro, the soldier commented) the plastic pistol in his pant pocket, Olavo was loading the bean machine gun, the old man turned the wheel, pushed down the pedal, but instead of the brake, he pushed the accelerator down to the floor, the Jaguar gave a short mechanical whinny, shook the mane of its headlights, the tires sang exultantly on the pavement, What's going on? What's going on? Dália protested, very frightened, the window, the counter, a round clock grew in size instantaneously in a tunnel that came out to meet us, Oh, mother of mine, the old man murmured in a dying tone, pulling levers and pushing buttons, and immediately the crash, the window in pieces, indistinct chunks of metal breaking off and flying in all directions, the car's body folding up like a telescope, pieces of plaster breaking off the ceiling, no typewriter, no clerk, no safe, nobody, just a liquid voice announcing (beside me? in front of me? behind me?), very far off, without anger or alarm, We've arrived, more pieces of plaster, more pieces of tin falling, I love you, Dália, I love your hair, your breasts, your smile, but they'd closed the bank the day before because there'd been a fascist revolution, comrades, because the people, Lopes explained to them didactically when he went to visit them at the hospital, led by the enlightened vanguard of the glorious Portuguese Marxist-Leninist-Maoist Organization, not only had the criminal reactionary plans aborted as they had demanded, but obtained, in addition to a broad amnesty, the nationalization of the banking system, securities, and several metallurgical and mechanical enterprises, so that, comrades, get rid of your splints and casts quickly so you can contribute your irreplaceable efforts to the building up of socialism that we've dreamed of, the major went over to the dead bitch and emptied his weapon into the leprous, muddy, inert body, my aunt and Esmeralda brought me orange cakes and a pile of magazines that smelled of the attic to the hospital, the doctors' coats floated ethereally among the beds, I closed my eyes and at that moment of dozing off (or almost asleep already?) the major turned the barrel of his Walther on me, Captain, I tried to drag myself to the shelter of the pillow in spite of the pain and the plaster cast, resting my hands and ankles on the ground of the sheets, a shapeless bark came out of me like a belch, I lifted my dirty rear to him asking Wait, and he (or the nurse holding up the syringe?) hesitated a second, took a step forward, and fired.

## 8

"I T was at that time, when you were going around crashing into bank windows, that my people, pissing with fear, rushed to get on board the plane to Brazil," the second lieutenant said. "The people, that is, the ones in Inês's family who still hadn't been arrested, Mariana crying and me bringing up the rear as a supernumerary, hair uncombed, unbathed, quite sleepy, with my pajama pants under those of my suit and the knotted waist string showing through a gap between buttons."

Life at the bank was becoming complicated, Captain, the managers trying hard to keep afloat in a bog of ill will, the employees didn't greet him with the usual hurried deferential bow as before, some would pass him without even saying good morning, just imagine, inflammatory pamphlets against the management circulated from section to section, conspiratorial meetings followed one after the other during working hours, the busts of the grandfather were slowly disappearing (Inês's uncle was discreetly taking them home at night in the trunk of his car with the help of his chauffeur), secretaries neglected things, indifferent to phone calls and orders, stenographers thumbed through picture-story magazines or idly polished their nails in front of abandoned typewriters, cashiers were out of sorts, without neckties, arguing with customers in loud voices, we were losing account after account with the slow, inexorable sinking of a ship.

"Exactly like us at Ilídio Movers after the old woman's stroke, Lieutenant," the soldier supported him, saying a slow rosary with his fingers as they went up and down the vertebrae of a skeletal blonde named Frances. "We could have been a first-class business today, with lots of loaders and vans, and because of her sickness and the dumb things we did afterward, we saw ourselves without any money by midmonth."

"Only when he died did those of us at the Ministry find out that Ricardo didn't have just one wife, he had three," the lieutenant colonel laughed into his glass. "All young, mulatto-looking and tall, good as gold, all dressed in the same way, with the same silvered nails and the same gaudy, aggressive grief, dragging by the hand little Ricardos in patent leather shoes and bowties around their necks, their eyes frightened little spheres that rolled around the funeral chapel on the verge of a panic of tears, I'll bet that's what killed him instead of the dirty trick, having to run from house to house, invent excuses, complicated lies, whole stories, justifications, put up with their hollering, cursing, jealous scenes with plates flying through the air, demands, the amused curiosity of neighbors. You can imagine what it must have been like being awakened at seven o'clock in the morning by three alarm clocks at the same time, eating three identical breakfasts, saying goodbye to three sleepy cheeks, going down in three simultaneous elevators, riding in three different Mercedes to the Column docks?"

"That's not what I can't stand," Inês's uncle protested without answering a panting telephone that had been bleating for centuries between a chrome-ringed ledger and a framed picture of his wife. "In spite of everything, the lack of respect is the least of it, what throws me completely is seeing bankruptcy on the horizon. For one reason or another I've had to double the dose of pills I take when I go to bed and God knows how many Sundays I haven't played any golf."

"What he needed maybe," the second lieutenant said, "were some hard-on pills, his fear of communists had made his tool go completely limp."

"Taking care of three women is hard work too," the communications officer put in admiringly. "I swear, I couldn't even dream about prowess like that."

"Throw some things into a suitcase and come to Carcavelos right away," the mother-in-law's voice ordered in an imperious little trickle. "I can't say anything more, the phone certainly must be tapped."

"Three great big women, you know how it is," the lieutenant colonel went into details, "the kind that have everything big, big tits, big asses, big legs, big shoulders, the kind who leave behind them a trail of perfumed snail spittle like a trail of desire, the kind who when they walk their behinds move like the oiled biceps of Mister Muscles in those contests, making great big flesh potatoes stand out under their skin. I couldn't believe it even when I saw it."

"What about their insolence?" the dense brother-in-law, the one with the insignia ring, was indignant, he was in charge of the Personnel Department, "Have you noticed their insolence, Uncle? They come into my office without asking permission, smoking, they address me in a familiar way, making themselves comfortable in a chair, all that's lacking is their wiping the mud off their shoes on my curtains. And the workers' commission, so ill mannered, protesting everything, constantly demanding privileges from me, time off, meeting places, that they should run the canteen because the pastry's no good, the soup's no good, because the custard is shit, not to mention free medicine, free consultations, free X-rays, aerodynamic toilets, air condition-ing, asses washed with rose water, Queen Maria beds for siestas."

"All that's lacking is for them to take a good shit on the top of my head," the second lieutenant lamented during dinner while the shadow of the paper ball around the lamp wavered slightly on the wall and the trees on the Rua da Mãe d'Água were printed in china ink, right down to the last branch, on the paper façades of the buildings. "All that's lacking is for them to fart on the busts of your grandfather that are still there."

The fraternal togetherness and euphoria of the first days were succeeded by a period of stormy confusion, heated arguments, curses, insults, with dignified types with the emblems of different parties on their lapels threat-ening each other with a beating and insulting each other in the halls, all choked up, furious, baring their wrathful gums like guard dogs on country estates. Work was piling up and nobody touched it, files and papers were accumulating, gathering dust everywhere, Paris, London, New York, Zurich, Amsterdam were giving friendly evasive answers and suggestions to post-pone any business propositions, the firms that had loans from us were going under without paying, the anemic satellite companies needed constant injec-tions of capital, Inês's uncle was in his office twisting his fat fingers, slipping his wedding ring on and off anxiously, he was aging a hundred years every day, your brothers and cousins were curing their anxiety in nightclubs, troublesome and quarrelsome, clutching their glasses of gin the way a sailor does a rudder that's out of order.

"Get in your car immediately," the mother-in-law was panting, "before the troops come there to grab you at home."

I almost never went out, Captain, I never went with them to discotheques or bars, but it was easy to imagine their rowdy arrogance, their well-cut blazers, the sweat on their sideburns, their stupid little eyes squinting, looking for a target amid bodies standing or leaping to the intermittent colored lights and sharp surges of music, it was easy to imagine the slaps, the kicks, the punches, the stupefied little cries of their girl friends, a tray of bottles tumbling down noisily and falling into a million shards on the marble surface of the dance floor, metal lamps rolling on the floor, a character staggering and holding his face, the devastating gorillas of the establishment clashing with the customers, the music cut off, all the lights turned brutally

on revealing indignant faces, or those in panic, or those holding handkerchiefs to their lips, the arrival of the police, squashing fragments and
splinters of glass underfoot, the manager parleying with the police, all calm,
all tranquil, all urbane, all very much in control of himself, spiraling diplomatic gestures with his lighted cigarette in a holder, and finally your brother
Pedro, or your brother Nuno, or your brother Tó pulling a little book out of
his pocket, signing a check on the hatcheck counter to pay for the damages,
their leaving, hair mussed and triumphant, leaning on girls in very tight jeans
and genuine fur coats, stumbling from trash can to trash can like defeated
boxers in the first light of morning. Because that was what impressed me
most, Captain: not the fear, not the decadence, not the animal desperation,
but the prideless madness of their defeat, an oxlike resignation, you see,
resigned to their lot with the humble acceptance of animals, drooling and
vomiting in the bathroom, grabbing their neckties with a hand that had no
strength, cheap bar liquor. It was in times like that, in those thick, bilious,
bitter early mornings without color, that the universe of rotting pieces of
junk, horrible still lifes, and Formica furniture of my parents took on, in
contrast to the profusion of Persian rugs, crystal, silver, and eighteenth-
century console tables, the piercing reality of something precious that had
idiotically been lost. I might still have been living in my bachelor's room,
witnessing at mealtimes my father's tight, bitter silence, been introduced to a
succession of invariably near-sighted suitors of my sister, timid German
teachers, engineers from modest State bureaus, skinny municipal veter-
inarians, creators of a new and transcendental method of artificial insemina-
tion in female hippopotami, I might have been studying Economics at night,
seducing the neighbor woman on the ground floor right, who worked as a
nurse in a hospital for mongoloids, in short, reasonably happy, anchored in an
everyday, familiar life without surprises, and, after the old folks had died, you
see, occupying in my turn the pretentious black bed of theirs under the brass
crucifix, the springs squeaking with every sleepy movement of my body.

"What's Brazil like, Lieutenant?" the soldier asked. "The farthest I've ever
traveled up till now was carrying some bedroom furniture in the van to
Badajoz."

"This is really it," the mother-in-law whispered in an unprotected and
fragile little glass voice, "now they're going to shoot us all: they've bombarded a military post and jeeps full of horrible soldiers are going around
arresting people in their homes."

Very early in the morning, as in novels, the second lieutenant thought,
hurriedly filling a suitcase with clothes, seeing Inês's frenzy out of the corner
of his eye as she opened closets, spilled out drawers, scattered jewelry in
disorder among blouses, skirts, plastic shoe bags, Mariana's knitted jackets.
This is really it: the door knocked down by rifle butts, a circle of dark and
ferocious faces, the dark eyes of machine-gun and rifle muzzles aimed at us, a

sergeant pushing us downstairs with his pistol into an Army truck parked on the sidewalk, the coolness of five or six o'clock on goose-pimpled skin on the back of the neck and the throat. Strangers arrested, too, also waiting for the next firing squad, moving their numbed behinds over to make room for us, the streets of the city fleeing behind through a slit in the canvas, fewer and fewer buildings, trees now, the brick-colored river, boats pulled up onto the mud along the bank, run-down wooden structures, the truck suddenly stopping, the sergeant's angry voice, Get out, hurry up, I jumped down onto the wet pavement of the roadway with Mariana hanging around my neck. A small old woman was hugging the sleeve of a very pale man, the skeleton of the bridge at Vila Franca de Xira was emerging from the mist from time to time in the shape of great sharp iron elbows encrusted in the greenish oil of the sky, they went down a slippery slope, sliding on the weeds, the dampness making it difficult to move and the sickening smell of stagnant water rising up in rolling waves of mist in the faded air, This really is it, he thought again when they lined them up shoulder to shoulder facing the neutral, absent faces of the soldiers without eyelashes, without noses, without chins, Mariana was playing with his chain, Inês was wobbling on her unsteady legs, on the opposite shore two men were bent over a small motorboat that coughed and fell silent, shortened by the distance and the fog, the sergeant placed himself between the soldiers and them, counted them, examined them closely, counted them again, They're going to shoot all of us, the second lieutenant thought, and he remembered his mother's intrigued expressions as she held the phone out to him, It's for you, the sergeant stepped back two paces, said Fire, the people fell on their faces or to the side, unprotected, in the mud, some tiny little poop-colored birds took flight from the reeds, I didn't feel any pain, any bullets, Captain, just a kind of wind going through my body, my belly being soaked in I don't know what, and a strange almost agreeable absence of strength, limbs that gave up, muscles that gave up, my soft bones piling up on top of one another like spaghetti in a pot, Mariana slid out of my hands and broke into a thousand pieces like an exploding doll, I tried to keep standing, holding my chest with my arms, a corporal came over still firing, This is really it, my mother-in-law moaned fluidly from a long way off, waving at me in a caricature of a goodbye, now you're really in a jam, Don't you want to answer? my mother asked me, holding the phone out, would you rather I said you've gone out?, I could still make out Inês's face, dirty with mud and what, through the growing imprecision of his eyes, looked like broad stains of blood, staring at him from the ground with transparent glass eyes, the little old woman was whining, dragging along behind him, This is really it, the second lieutenant agreed, and he flopped down onto a rock, looking left and right with unlimited surprise, looking at the poop-colored little birds, terrified, hiding in the reeds, This is really it, he believed, and the motorboat began to cast off gradually, blue stripes were spreading between the clouds,

It's not just my belly, he thought, it's my sides, my kidneys, my forehead too, it's this sudden, unfamiliar breath of air in my throat too, the sergeant put a cold tube to my ear, squeezed the trigger, and while everything was exploding, fanning out and falling apart with an interminable slowness, while an enormous silence came over the vibrations of sound, scattering it across the indistinct and horizontal ash gray plain, he perceived, unable to move, his mother shrugging her shoulders, putting the telephone back on its cradle, picking up her needle and starting to knit again, nestling like a dove in her usual easy chair.

They tumbled down the stairs, dragging Mariana behind them after the second lieutenant had checked from the balcony that no gray, threatening, terrible military vehicle was waiting for them down below, bristling with revolvers and mortars, and that was the last time, Captain, that I entered the house in Carcavelos, the last time I went through the iron gate that was always open and continued along the little gravel drive surrounded by boxwood trees and shrubbery, the way to the huge house up there, beside the tiled rectangle of the swimming pool, which wavered like a set of banners under the water, and where the statue of a child on a pedestal was reflected in a series of ripples. The last time the dogs leaped around me, tumultuously fraternal, yellow eyes glistening with friendly hate, the usual whirlwind of tails, snouts, paws, nails, barks, disappearing and reappearing with the carnivorous energy of springs, the last time that enormous building, made of dissimilar additions, diverse pavilions, contradictory terraces, windows that always looked at each other without feeling, would swallow him up into the whale stomach of its innumerable parlors peopled with large oil paintings, majestic porcelain, expensive furniture, his father-in-law's unfinished boats lying on the Persian rugs surrounded by forgotten tools, islands of sawdust and wood shavings. They hadn't run into any police roadblocks on the Marginal, the serene skin of the sea was covered with little spangles of light, there weren't any armed civilians with armbands checking cars, revolutionaries with fierce pointed mustaches inspecting the trunks of cars with a microscope, the seagulls swirled about the drains by the river in voracious ellipses, they turned right, next to the parking lot with a restaurant at the other end, where we used to stop at night sometimes, lights out, to feel each other's sex organs, anxiously facing the pale phosphorescence of the waves, the sun-drenched streets of the village unrolled like soft yards of bright-colored fabric, and for the last time the porch by the entrance, smothered in vines, the cracked cement steps, the outside light, the Saint Sebastian in antique tile, for the last time the doorbell echoing like a fire siren through the deserted caverns of the rooms, for the last time Hilária's haughty antipathy, looking at him with disdain from the top of her starched collar, for the last time her irritating good evenings, her absolute indifference, her frowning brow repeating You don't belong here, go away, none of us here likes you.

And, in a certain way, isn't it true, Captain? on that same day her huge, acid desire to watch my back going off was satisfied.

"Did you forgive your wife after you caught her fooling around with the other woman, Lieutenant?" the soldier asked while the skeletal blonde, hanging over him, was eagerly going through his pockets in search of cigarettes. "Did you swallow the pill without even blowing up, giving her a beating?"

Their bodies tight together, the old woman's purple locks mingled with Inês's light brown hair, fingers with long nails interlaced and letting go, cooing, whispering, giggling, trouble with skirts and stockings, the two nuzzled and afflicted faces that looked at him with surprise: we weren't in the war anymore, friend, my job depended on her family, if I left her, wouldn't they quickly fire me afterward? the old woman sputtered some kind of excuse, Inês sputtered some kind of excuse, and I accepted them as if I believed them, see? as if nothing abnormal had happened, and you might find it strange, but by the following week I'd almost completely forgotten the matter and we even made love from time to time on weekends in silent and mediocre pleasure. They probably went to the movies together, probably visited each other, probably undressed each other, sighing, in my bedroom, probably kissed and bit each other and rolled around on my sheets, probably panted like fish on my pillow, probably invited more lesbians and drank and danced and swapped partners, Inês probably made fun of me, telling ridiculous stories about me, inventing, enlarging, twisting, so what? I'd tried to fly too high for my wings, old boy, and it was only right for me to pay my dues, it was only right for me to screw myself up a little, it was only right for me to learn, at my own expense, what I really was: a lump, the son of an old typesetter, an innocent boob just drifting along. And it took a while for me to understand that, but I swear I know it today: you, for example, you can do your own thing, isn't there a job at the moving company that you can get for a dope like me?

"The things people will put up with, Jesus," the lieutenant colonel complained out of the corner of his mouth, "the number of fucking things we have to put up with."

Stretched out on his back in the mud among dozens of corpses and indistinct tall moving shapes, listening to the viscous lapping of the water, the whistling in the bushes, and the new-shoe squeaking of the frogs, the second lieutenant saw himself safe and sound, putting the bags down in the vestibule beside the life-sized ebony black man by the stairway to the second floor, he saw Inês's quick reflection in the engraved mirror, a pyramid of overcoats and topcoats piled up on the chest, the faint design on the rug, the brother-in-law, bald now, baggy eyed and extremely worried, arms in the air, They've arrested Gonçalo, they've arrested Mané, they've arrested Uncle Inho, they looked for them at home, at the bank, at the securities company,

Pedro was trying to call Caxias just now, but nobody answers, he's been trying to get General Ricardo at the Ministry for a long time now and no luck, he isn't there, he's not coming in today, he just left, try later, the usual nonsense, you know how it is, and nobody can get the idea out of my head that these bastardly soldiers aren't all tied in with the Russians.

"If Colonel Ricardo only could have heard him," the communications officer laughed, "he would have had another heart attack right there: so it's the Russians, eh? Your wife's family's something else, wow, always delusions of grandeur, Moscow, no less."

Lying on his back in the weeds and mud, his body slowly sinking into the water, he witnessed his own arrival, behind Mariana and Inês, in the family parlor with the stove (a structure of tiles and glass plates under a black metal chimney, built by the father-in-law to justify his complete idleness) and there they were, Captain, wafting about like terrified phantoms between the easy chairs and the bar, whispering solemnly in the sudden atmosphere of a church, cousins of both sexes, aunts and uncles, and the usual vague relatives who were almost strangers, there was my mother-in-law, conferring with the oldest brother, graying, responsible, wearing a pearl gray necktie, installed on the usual sofa, there was the lady with purple hair, sparkling with brace-lets and rings, who distractedly gave him her bony stork's hand to kiss (and the insignificant poop-colored birds were leaving the reeds one by one, and a second motorboat was coming laboriously down the river), I leaned out a window and the sea was throbbing its intense blue in the distance and the clouds were neatly reflected on its polished plate, an anxious voice was asking on the telephone Has General Ricardo come in yet? can you connect me with General Ricardo? the father-in-law was surprised, staring like a small owl at the oil painting, faded by the years, of a gentleman with a mustache and a watch chain, two or three busts of the grandfather presided disdainfully over things, assemblies of photographs on the tops of commodes, the monstrous stove looked like an altar for sacrificing lambs out of the Old Testament, Aren't you going to answer? his mother was surprised, don't you want to talk to your lady friend? and I had the urge to answer her (standing, hands in my pockets, facing her, my sides smeared with mud and a strange dampness crumbling my bones) Can't you see that I've died? can't you see that I no longer exist? because I was never alive in that house, Captain, because they always looked through me, you understand, as if I were myste-riously transparent to them, because my only and almost nil density came from the accessory fact of my being the husband of Inês, whom the lady with purple hair was consoling, stroking her shoulders and neck, pulling her forcefully toward her, putting her knee against hers, Say, Jaime, give the airline tickets to the children, my mother-in-law ordered, the soldiers climbed back into the gray truck that vanished, bouncing and shaking, into the shadow of an isolated little building, the cabin of one of those fiercely

solitary fishermen with great rubber boots that smelled of rotting fish and low
tide, Inês's father woke with a start from his sheep's meditation to give each of
us a slender little booklet with the humble air of someone distributing leaflets
on a street corner, At the airport at eleven at night, at the airport at eleven at
night, at the airport at eleven at night, he repeated with the soft murmur of a
prayer, we'll meet by the departure gate, the uncle clarified, the important
thing now is to leave here, get moving, get moving, find a friend's house,
anyone you can trust, someone the police and the Army wouldn't dream of,
and once more the sound of boots on the staircase, hinges flying off, hoarse
indistinct roars, square jaws giving orders, the marble busts of the grandfather were spying on us with the alarmed expression statues have, the in-
laws, the cousins, the relatives were serving themselves more whiskey, more
gin, more ice, while the wrinkles of defeat grew larger in the corners of their
mouths, Jaime, Inês's mother commanded almost in a shout, give the help
the day off and take the station wagon out of the garage for me, Belts, ties,
shoelaces, and money on this table, a quartermaster with a red stripe on his
sleeve and a big pistol on his belt ordered. Hold up your pants with your
hands and start walking single file to your cells, long corridors with iron bars,
people crowded like chickens in tiny cubicles, paratroopers with boxer eyes,
hours on end without eating and dreaming of chicken, steaks, sardines,
disemboweled straw mattresses full of lumps, stains from fruit rinds and
dried blood, Do you want to come to my house? the lady with purple hair
asked, helping Inês on with her coat and surreptitiously fondling the tendons
of her throat, and I, to myself, That's an idea, and I, to myself, Why not? and
I, to myself, Who cares, another bust, sardonic now, another portrait of the
old man making fun of my passivity, my consent, my inertia, You really
overdid it, Lieutenant, the soldier sympathized, you really let your wife do
what she wanted to, some nephews were floating around weightlessly on the
rugs or, airborne, were bumping into furniture, blown by the hot south wind
of heroin, one of the younger brothers-in-law, very tall, very thin, very ugly,
put a cassette of cartoons into the VCR and dropped, indifferent to everything, with long, languid arms, into a wicker chair, a monstrously human cat
and rat started a chase on the screen, Some of you to the farm, the bank uncle
advised, others to the apartment in Lisbon, others to Aunt Vera's attic, poor
thing, because since she's loony and spends all her time in bed repeating
nonsense, there's no danger of her being on to anything, and the second
lieutenant saw dozens of majestic contradictory clocks swaying in the
shadows, bound books, very old encyclopedias, a tea service on a cart, a
grand piano and a bookcase of operatic arias in an enormous living room, If
you people think you're going to inherit anything, the old woman would roar,
pointing to the worm-eaten cupboards, her cane trembling, furious, you
savages, get that idea right out of your heads because everything is going
straight to the Sisters of Charity, everything is going straight to the Museum

of Ancient Art, Say, Jaime, the mother-in-law ordered, put all the jewelry you can in the false bottom of the suitcase, the telephone rang again, my mother stuck her needle into the ball of yarn, grabbed the receiver Hello?, Two in each cell and be quick about it, the quartermaster barked, I'm not going to spend the whole afternoon here waiting for your excellencies to decide, It's your girl friend, his mother informed him in a whisper, covering the mouthpiece with her hand, saying that she's been waiting more than half an hour for you at the entrance to the movies, she's asking if you left very long ago, what do you want me to tell her?, I left two centuries ago, Mother, I'm on my way to Brazil, Mother, it's been ages, my God, when that took place, it's been ages since I was madly in love with her, it's been ages since I'd tremble and hesitate and stutter and my blood would thicken in my body all of a sudden just from seeing her, your face so different from the others in the middle of dozens of faces, your raincoat standing out, unique in the midst of dozens of raincoats, and soon my fly swelling uncontrollably under my coat, interminable winters of passion and wonder, afflictions, doubts, hope, I put the tickets in the inside pocket of my jacket, the cars parked in the yard were going down the gravel slope, crushing the loose stones with their tires, the dogs were barking, biting each other, rolling on the lawn, coming and going with leaps and bounds, tempestuously destroying the boxwoods, and there came to mind the first time we'd entered, all excited, blushing, holding hands, escorted by the mistrust of the concierge, the unfurnished apartment on the Rua da Mãe d'Água, there came to mind the first time we'd gone through the narrow little rooms, trying the faucets, checking the stove, seeing two little flowers of gas whistling beside the porcelain, imagining, inventing, discussing, adding my salary to the monthly allowance from your parents, It's enough, it's not enough, it has to be enough, I'm going to ask them to advance us the money for the rent, dear, I'm going to ask them to help with expenses, love, and your happiness, and your contented eyes, and your smile, Inês, the yellow paper lampshade carried from the shop in triumph, the plastic rods, the paper sphere, the wire circles that had to be hooked, separated, attached, Are you sure it's all right, Jorge? are you sure you haven't broken anything, Jorge? the enthusiastic excitement at the beginning that vanished quickly, so quickly, the fever of discovering, investigating closely, seeking out shops, antique dealers, mattress stores, china shops, furniture, utensils, the old fairy with a toupee and powdered cheeks, smelling of Spanish perfume, surrealistically named Espiridião, who took measurements of the windows discoursing, moving his rings, about hangings and curtains, his sudden accomplicelike, unexpected intimacy with Inês, her blind faith in the wordy opinions of the old man, Ask Mr. Espiridião first, dear, I've got so much confidence in his experience, dear, What do you think Mr. Espiridião would do in this case, dear? and Mr. Espiridião would decide, approve, disapprove, frown, forbid, greet her with two little fraternal kisses on the cheeks, grant me a bundle of limp fingers softened by creams and lotions, and then, love, little by little, love, habit, routine, boredom, the difficulty of parking the car among so many other cars, the first night that I thought I don't feel one fucking bit like going home, I don't feel one fucking bit like this monotonous existence of a jellyfish, the first drink at a bar, staying late at work, feeling unhappy, feeling guilty, feeling alone, feeling a fool for feeling unhappy and guilty and alone thumbing through some magazine or other surrounded by porcelain objects and postcards from the twenties, my quiet, vehement desire to live without you, to fry fish on a gasoline stove, to win, Captain, the adolescence I never had, Haven't you left yet? the mother-in-law asked, running about picking up silver objects, Still here waiting for them to come and grab you? the automobiles were disappearing down the slope followed by the effusive, irritating, uncontrolled gallop of the dogs, and for the last time the vestibule, for the last time the enormous ebony black man, for the last time the outside light and the tiles and the steps to the garden, for the last time the fantastic horned screamers moaning under the tranquil surface of the sea, for the last time the smell of earth and wet lawn and red and yellow plants in the flower beds, for the last time Carcavelos, for the last time in Lisbon the agreeable and smooth smell of rich people, Inês getting into the white Alfa Romeo with the air of an owner, the lady with purple hair touching her on the elbow in a seemingly casual way, snuggling in her fur coat, getting behind the wheel, and my wife rolling down the window, turning her mouth in my direction, looking at me as if I were an underling, or just a piece of shit, or a servant, telling me The best thing is for you to follow us in case you get lost on the way, rolling up the window, smiling at her whore of a friend, twitching her shoulders in a coquettish caper, their exhaust in front of me, the crushed gravel, my rage, the brake lights going on and off, Mariana's hand waving quick, childish goodbyes to me, I hate you, Inês, I so much want you to die, streets and streets, houses, yards, the sun high up over the March trees, and always, in the distance, now on the left, now on the right, obsessive, intense, sparkling, almost golden, the omnipresent presence of the sea.

"I'm sorry, Lieutenant, but it was all your fault," the soldier said. "A couple of whacks in time and any problem of a third party is settled."

"Three wives, how about that," the lieutenant colonel insisted with vague eyes, lost in a labyrinth of memories. "It seems that they got to be friends, it seems that they got to be like sisters, I don't know, they went to the movies together, had tea together, took their children to the doctor together, even lived in the same building until the next general came along. One of them was taken over by Brigadier Horta, they're going to be married, I've lost track of what the other two are doing today."

"Everybody knows that sharing a lover," the communications officer observed, sucking on a piece of ice as if it were a piece of hard candy, "has always been something that brought people close together."

The tide won't be long in rising, the second lieutenant thought, that smell of rotting mushrooms, that agitation in the weeds, that restless spinning of the water can't fool me: the tide's coming in and it will submerge my body, my mouth, my nose, my eyes, for a moment I'll be able to make out the dirty factory sky over the waves, the pestilential afternoon clouds, the worn buildings of Vila Franca quivering in the distance, the Alfa Romeo in front of me and the shape of the two heads buried inside there, going along, turning, going through a complicated series of small squares, avenues, streets, alleys (They want to avoid the soldiers, he deduced, they want to avoid running into any military trucks), neighborhoods I didn't know near the rushes along the railroad tracks and the miserable little building, zebra striped with lines and cracks, that was the station, trash accumulated on the berms, guys in gray repairing a telephone pole, they sped along a small, irregular, narrow lane and came to a house with a pointed roof, stone benches with crumbling lions' paws around an oval swimming pool, rose bushes, the metal cube of a stove with mingled smells, large glassed-in balconies facing the mountains, I pulled up beside the Alfa Romeo on a rectangle of tiles alongside the pretentious arabesques of the door, a gray-haired butler greeted him from the shadows full of chests and large mirrors with a ceremonious kind of bow, Hello Fernando, Inês said to him familiarly and the second lieutenant, to himself, You know him, you bitch, you must have come here any number of times while I was putting up with the shitty drag of work at the bank, lesbian teas, you pervert, long siestas in July in an enormous bed, whole afternoons oiling yourself on top of a towel printed with Snoopy by the pool, Not one single slap, Lieutenant? the soldier was surprised, no whack in the chops to bring things under control? a broad parlor, pillows, low benches, a complicated piece of sculpture on one corner, a small poodle dozing indifferently on the rug, the portrait of a kindly foreign-looking gentleman who looked like Maurice Chevalier (the same protruding lip, the same hat, the same wrinkled eyes), smiling at everyone with infinite paternal indulgence. The second lieutenant belched and felt around for the neck of a bottle with the rudderless sparrow of his hand fluttering hesitantly over the tablecloth:

"Not a slap, not a whack, friend," (the voice of a lampwick going out and lighting up, blown on by a breath of gases), I stood there stock-still in the living room, next to the drink cart, with Mariana hanging around my neck, stupidly looking at a gigantic black and green tapestry which represented a kind of hibiscus whose flowers were resting on a kind of palm tree, at the same time that almost noiselessly there danced around me a somnambulist rubbing of fabrics, talking, smoking, falling silent, getting drinks, getting up and sitting down on fat plastic sofas which creaked and groaned, me there, completely motionless, lighting a cigarette, looking for an ashtray with my eyes, taking a timid crooked turkey step on the carpet, hearing the mangy wheezing of the dog, hearing the cough of the butler in the pantry, hearing (or imagining? or imagining that I was hearing?) the effervescent protests of the sea, bubbling closer by now, almost inside him, following a row of little translucent dwellings and the wall of the Marginal bearded with mussels, snails, trash, algae, sitting on the floor Mariana was playing with conch shells, other speckled shells that tinkled, I should call my parents, I should tell them at least that I am going away, Right after dark I'm catching the plane for Brazil, Aunt Ilka, Inês asked the lady with purple hair (and the latter, smiling, Yes, treasure?), I'm worn out with all this excitement, can I rest a little bit upstairs? the picture of Maurice Chevalier nodded yes in its frame, Relax, Mother, don't worry, as soon as I get there I promise I'll write you immediately, the lady of the house coming over to him with the slither of a snake and the second lieutenant thought You're some old woman, you are, God, rotten underneath the makeup and the cream and the girdle, but he accepted a cognac, but he accepted a dish of saltines, but he settled into an antique rocking chair that went back and forth with the light unsteadiness of the deck of a ship, but I chatted about the Revolution with her, but I chatted about the communists with her, but I was sad with her over Mané's imprisonment, such a nasty thing, poor fellow, such a good person, he didn't deserve it, a bunch of long-haired soldiers, just like that, inside the door, just imagine the injustice, imagine the horror, imagine the shock, unbelievable that the Americans should let such a shameful thing happen, unbelievable that the Spaniards didn't intervene, the lady with purple hair was indignant, restless, he was nibbling on peanuts, Luckily Greg is working in Paris, luckily Greg doesn't know anything about this, and the second lieutenant closed his eyes and there were the insignificant little buildings of Vila Franca in the mist, there was the river, there were the broken bodies on the slope and the little motorboats bumping into each other, hoarse, between the banks, there was the Army truck going away, the mud and the bronchitis of the frogs that penetrated my body through the dark openings left by the bullets, not a slap, not a whack, friend, all that time at Carcavelos had polished me, perfected me, civilized me, varnished me, so I agreed, nodded my head, drank more cognac, chewed more crackers, Really, what luck for Greg, gosh, at his age (eighty-three already?, I can't believe it) this kind of misfortune, even for an Englishman, it's terribly confusing, how fortunate that when news gets abroad it's low-keyed, toned down, the voracious crabs of high tide were walking over Mariana's riddled paste-doll face, They're going to eat her eyes, the second lieutenant thought in panic, trying to protect her with his motionless arms, I'll bet they're going to eat her eyes, May I phone my father and let him know that I'm going away? he asked, pointing to the instrument with his chin, crabs grasping gelatinous pieces of intestine with their pincers, carrying us off slowly, laboriously, avariciously to the mud at the bottom, crabs and translucent fish and aquatic salamanders and a strange race of eels or snakes, They're going to suck out her bones, her nails, a half-dozen tendons, the thin threads of her hair, You're still a gloomy Gus, the communications officer was annoyed, unless you can torment yourself with sinister episodes you won't have any rest, he heard the noise of the swimming pool filling up in the garden, the siren of a distant ambulance, the little dog stretched, idly sniffed his ankles, fell back, indifferent, into his coma, he dialed the number of the print shop and saw men leaning over the machines, the monotonous noise, the milky bulbs on the ceiling, the dirt, the dust, the windows eternally dimmed by a dark film, the old man's filthy office, the lady with purple hair got up, put out her cigarette, and the filter tip, twisted in the ashtray, was tinged with red from her lipstick, I'd best go up to the bedroom and see if Inês needs anything, don't you think? the phone rang two or three times and right away the flat, undefined voice of his father, Hello.

"If I'd been you I'd have gone to see them in person," the soldier censured him, "if I'd been you I wouldn't have gone off without thinking about visiting the family."

"Were you afraid the soldiers would guess and be waiting for you?" the communications officer asked. "Were you afraid of a reception committee, carrying machine guns, at the Rua da Mãe d'Água?"

"What?" his father was surprised, muffled by the storm of the presses. "To Brazil? Right after dark?"

"If you'd like some scrambled eggs, Fernando's available," the lady with purple hair offered, with a sudden friendly smile that opened up here and there on her face the cracks of a building falling down: shriveled legs, shriveled breasts, the shriveled neck of a chicken: What attracts you to that character, Inês, what kind of shit draws you to her?

"To Brazil," the second lieutenant confirmed, shouting, in hopes that the old man would understand what he was saying. "I can't get over there right now, but tomorrow or the day after I'll write and explain everything."

Maybe his fear of the Army, yes, maybe his shame at running away, maybe the growing difficulty of facing his family, his father's threadbare suit, the ever-present match in his mouth, the rolled-up rag of his tie, his forefinger wet with spit to turn the pages of the newspaper, the exaggerated, tinkling, tremendous cheap jewelry his mother had: Their poor taste pained me, Captain, their broken-down furniture, their homemade liquor, their thick, endless, recriminatory silence at the table pained me, their excessive humility before my in-laws pained me, their mute begging your pardon, the way they chatted, said goodbye, the way they shook hands. It pained me to have gone suddenly from the oval crocheted doilies to the Persian rugs without dropping anchor at either place, not being a clay clown or an eighteenth-century cabinet, I was especially pained (I'll bet you're going to find all this idiotic, I'll bet you're going to laugh, I'll bet you're going to think I'm a numbskull) by the imposing kitchen clock over the door to the back balcony, whose face was a pot and whose hands were a knife and fork in aluminum, slowly eating up time.

"I can't hear very well because of the machines," the old man complained, shouting. "What's all this about Brazil?"

"Just last month I bought a clock like that at an auction," the soldier said. "They're nice."

"Wait till I close the door to see if I can hear you," his father roared desperately, and the second lieutenant pictured him crossing the office with a heavy step, cigarette in his mouth, treading on the floorboards and the scattered pieces of paper with his shabby shoes, pictured him pulling the grating that separated him from the shop, pictured him laying his glasses on the desk, stroking his poorly shaved chin, looking perplexed at the telephone, picking up the instrument again reluctantly: Son? Hello, Son?

"But Inês needed something, poor thing," the lieutenant colonel gibed, making his voice whine, "she needed Asiatic splendor, poor thing, she was weeping for my tenderness, poor thing: and you, you bear, watching the trains go by, right?"

"They work real fine," the soldier explained. "The motor never breaks down, instead of a bell they make the sound of a pot on the half hour and a frying pan on the hour, I don't understand what you've got against them, Lieutenant."

"Start all over again," his father ordered, "maybe I can get it straight this time. A flight to Brazil?"

"Which is the same as saying Take it easy, you boob," the lieutenant colonel was furious, "while I go give the customer what she wants. Drink if you want, smoke if you want, take care of your daughter if you want, feel free to call the butler, but don't get in our way: the chick upstairs is laughing at you, the chick up there making fun of you and you let them lord it over you, get you over a barrel, what a show."

"Soldiers picking up people for any old reason?" his father was surprised. "I haven't heard of anyone being picked up around here."

The Army truck disappeared on the wet road up there behind a little famished grove, the tide was dragging the body of the older woman away now toward the channel, mixed with chunks of mud, crusted slime, tufts of weeds, trash, other bodies with broken necks sunk in the water, the whistle of a locomotive dynamited the silence, shattered into a thousand pieces his white convex china surface, The people there in the neighborhood, of course not, old man, but they bombarded a military post in Encarnação, the parachutists from Tancos landed for a coup which failed, the commies had decided that Inês's family, capitalist types, businessmen, rich people, the church, were machinating some kind of revolution to knock them off their roost, so they were taking their revenge all over the place, filling the jails with poor devils, companies and banks are under guard by Czechoslovakian gorillas, just imagine, disguised as municipal construction workers, they'd love to get their hands on me, and his father ruminating, not frightened, in the midst of the noise of the machines, Is that so?, Is that how it is there? he finished his cognac, put the glass on the pane of a tabletop beside the approving and smiling Maurice Chevalier, Thank God you're in Paris, you bastard, thank God so he may fuck you in all his glory, he got up, Mariana, on all fours, waving her behind which was all puffed up by diapers, was surrounding herself with seashells, conchs, silver cups, oriental dolls of blue stone (characters with mustaches, birds, fantastic animals), the sounds of Fernando's catarrh came and went, casual as the wind, from the other side of the wall, His cough goes about spying on me, the second lieutenant thought, walking on tiptoe along the hallway decorated with ancient muskets, armor that reminded him of human lobsters, hunting prints swarming with hounds and horses, a dining room in the shadows with high-backed, stiff chairs, the library with its fat cowhide-bound volumes with gilt clasps, its photographs framed in fine leather, its large porcelain vases the color of burgundy, the stairs to the second floor, They've just given me the airline tickets, Father, of course Inês and the little one are going with me, the crabs were slicing up Mariana's nose, her gums, her tongue, around her cheekbones, If I stay here they'd have me locked up within an hour more or less, Father, the best thing is to take off for a few months, and the silence coagulating at the other end of the line, full of suspended recriminations, Why did you hitch up with, why did you get mixed up in, what was your idea in, but you didn't say anything, old man, you'd never say anything, you always passed through my life with an absolute muteness, total indifference, obstinately clutching the open pages of the newspaper, with glasses opaque from paragraphs and headlines, he went upstairs running his hand lightly over the varnished bannister, plants in pots, rubber trees, hairy ferns, a cubicle with an ancient desk with marqueterie, a wicker couch, lampshades, In that case, his father shouted, overcoming the noise of the monotonous tumbling of the machines with difficulty, the best thing is to hang up right now, boy, you can't tell, your phone might be tapped, and no emotion in his voice, no interest, no affection, no apparent displeasure, you sent me off in a hurry, you got rid of me in a hurry, Go to the airport, disappear, go, I know of cases, the soldier asserted, where parents don't like their children, Lieutenant, they hate their guts, I know of cases where they'd give everything to see them out of the way as quickly as possible, he went down the hallway, his head empty, finding an open door, he heard the purple-haired woman's unexpectedly masculine laugh, Inês's submissive laugh, combining, interweaving, mingling, a corner of a rug was visible, drawn blinds, a blouse on the floor, he hung up the phone and the sound of the printing shop kept weakly shaking in his ears for a long time, he turned back, made a signal with his arm to the sergeant who was following him, the uniforms ran past him, a rubber shoe bit Inês's blouse, he felt the penetrating sweaty smell of the men, he noticed the brown and green splotches of the camouflage suits and the dull gray barrels of the rifles, he went down to the first floor again with the slow caution of a moment before, and was going to pick Mariana up with her arms around his neck, and was going to answer the soldier That's not it, when the first cutting screech instantaneously tightened his guts in infinite anguish.

9

O<small>DETE</small> began her nursing studies and we got married right after that, the soldier explained. There's no need for me to say that the sun didn't shine for very long.

"You never read any books, you never read the newspapers, you've got no interest in anything, you're a full-fledged idiot." She was furious with him, wearing orange rubber gloves as she washed the dishes, full of hate. (Through the open window the hens were scratching around the kale in the garden.) "What crazy idea ever got into my head to make me throw myself away on you?"

"Marry Odete?" the uncle panted, looking at him with his dead snook eyes from behind the flower on his desk. "Isn't there some better notion you could get into your head, boy?"

"She began to humiliate me almost immediately, Captain," the soldier complained. "Humiliate me, put me down, show me to be the piece of shit I was. But no matter how low people may be, we've still got our pride, don't you think?"

Beyond the entrenched garden fence of boards and stones were other gardens, equally downcast and sad, tiled roofs, pieces of fence, a whole crop of television antennae, the vertical, tall trees of the Campo de Santana, completely motionless in the night, the hazy outlines of the buildings around: I would close the window of the cubicle, lie down, and I could hear the restlessness in the chicken coop, the soft gauze paws of a cat on the tin roof, and I would see the kale glowing, not quite black, not quite blue, in the darkness, the grooved, overlapping metal sheets, electric signs throbbing in the distance: One of these days I'm going to move into Odete's room, which faces the street's absence of mystery, I'll sleep in the midst of pencils, notebooks, poems, and paste dolls, and I come here in my pajamas, secretly, to take a peek at the vegetables growing out of the earth like the hairs of a beard, to catch a look at the enormous, violent, dim heart of the city raising and lowering the floor, regulating the intensity of smells and sounds, the distance of objects and the oppressed, afflicted beam in my chest creaking. I come here secretly and the kale swells up in the shadows, grows, spreads out, flourishes, covers the house, splits the pavement with the tumultuous strength of its roots, knocks down lampposts, the carts and tricycles of street peddlers with its stalks, devours the imprecise trees and buildings of the Campo de Santana, dries up the river, invades the factories on the other side with its gigantic snails and its gelatinous mile-long parasites, imprisons the seagulls and transforms the sea into an immense basalt plain full of defunct ships, in the craters of which dusty and congested lunar eruptions bubble up from time to time.

"If you already knew her temperament, why in hell did you get married?" the second lieutenant asked. "When you come right down to it, you're the one who's a masochist."

"Marriage is a big pear-shaped bore," Mr. Ilídio revealed, hoping that the bookkeeper didn't hear him, arranging the flower in the vase with his dirty nails. (God, you're afraid of her, the soldier thought, boy, that chick has got you on a short rein, you devil.) Do you want to rot away while you're still alive," the old man huffed at him, "do you want to die by degrees, do you want to wither away piece by piece? In your place, I'd cut out the poetry and stay just the way I am."

"Your mother and your uncle," his grandmother growled bitterly to him in the kitchen when he was a child, keeping a severe watchful eye on the preparation of lunch, "hanged themselves like the dummies they were."

"Just take a look at what's happened," his sister said in the small living room of her place in Buraca, pointing to hundreds of mulatto children. The trains trotted along their noisy way behind her, her husband, in dark glasses and a Hawaiian shirt, was in a broken-down easy chair deciphering the sports pages. There wasn't a single unbroken knickknack, the mirror on the cabinet, broken, exposed the worm-eaten wood of the door, the smell of a tomb came out of the water tap, dinner plates were piling up on the oilcloth table cover. His sister, her hair stiff and filthy released from the hairpins of her bun, took a step forward on her limp hips, pushing the flabby wineskin of her belly before her: she had a strong smell of lye, sweat, cooking, manioc, and infant's green diarrhea: Almost the same as in Mozambique, I thought, almost the same garbage, the same poverty, the same resigned abandonment, the same famished dogs nosing around: Is this what you're looking for, she asked, is this the height of your ambition?

"I don't see any need to rush our getting married," Odete said, licking a Popsicle during intermission at the movies, one of those complicated, sleepwalking films without any shooting or fighting that she always picked, God knows why. "Let me finish my studies first."

"Are you serious? Are you really serious? You're not pulling our legs, are you?" The quiet man, all enthusiastic, was cracking his ribs with great fraternal thumps. "Shit, old buddy, we'll have to lift a couple of extra ones tonight and clean the clams out of our guts as a way of celebrating."

And there were the elusive, smoky shapes in Alcântara, on the edge of the drive or among the trees, the cars with their parking lights on, brushing against them, coming and going in an oblique insistence, hesitating, stopping, timidly lowering the window. We'd go over to them, lean inside, discuss the price (Four hundred, four hundred fifty, five hundred) with worried, dim figures who repeated Get in, get in, we'd open the door, the weak plastic bulb on the ceiling going on, the figure would change into a worn-out, well-dressed gentleman with the retractile gestures of an anemone, and then to Monsanto, to the fence by the Gun Club, underneath the Bridge, or, with a bit of luck, an anonymous apartment in Restelo or Oeiras, sitting haughtily above the river, haughtily above the sea, the small vestibule, the stereotypical living room, the bedroom, the man smiling bashfully in the elevator, undoing his tie, untying his shoes, speaking to him formally, showing an interest in him as a way of masking his embarrassment, What's his name, where does he work, how old is he.

"In church?" Odete was indignant. "Are you out of your mind? I want nothing to do with priests."

The grandmother, her mouth twisted in disgust, leaned over the child's frightened ear as he pulled his spoon out of his soup and faced the tremulous, carnivorous, voluminous breasts that were getting bigger:

"I gave birth to a couple of jackasses, damn it, a pair of simple donkeys with a mania for double beds. But with the fool of a father they drew what would have surprised me would be just the opposite."

"Lots of lupines, lots of shrimp, lots of conchs, lots of crabs, lots of votive beer," the soldier said, a sign announced DRINKS SOLD ONLY BY THE GLASS. This bit today is on us, boss, morning being born on Ribeira, the table full of empty bottles and glasses, the now useless neon sign on the roof, faces tight from drink and fatigue, the urge to urinate in the pestilential toilet with broken tile, gulls out of control squawking over truckloads of fruit at the market, revolutionary slogans written in charcoal on the walls of buildings: a melancholy and dreary orgy, punctuated with monumental belches and copious vomiting on the sawdust on the floor, pale guys sliding out of their chairs like spaghetti, sleepy whores and acrimonious transvestites arguing over the bookkeeper's nephew in a pandemonium of threats, followed by a dawn of nebulous double-decker buses mingling with freighters on the Tagus, which drifted along in the rosé waves or fluidly went through the great gray building of the station, and in whose windows the inexpressive and hollow mannequin faces of the passengers appeared from time to time.

"I didn't see my sister for a while, Captain," the soldier said, "until one day she appeared before me at the warehouse, aged and filthy, with a baby around her neck and a crowd of kids of different ages hanging on her skirt. She asked me for the loan of some money because the mulatto had been fired from the airport restaurant for stealing or something like that."

He was helping the old man put a couch into the van when one of his colleagues called him from the bottom of the cement ramp leading to the street: Hey, Abílio, a woman with ten pickaninnies who haven't seen a bar of soap in six months is waiting for you up there.

"Would you please tell me what you've got against nursing?" Odete was annoyed. "Would you please tell me what you've got against my studying?"

Ilídio Movers was in business at the end of Luciano Cordeiro, at the end of Intendente, I knew the hookers around there like an old hand, and once in a while I'd get a free one, climbing steep, risky stairs in the dark after skinny girls, their eyes painted with coal dust and their nail polish cracked, for quick, clumsy lays in tumbledown iron beds, I'd strike up a conversation with them in their cramped little owl's nest attics, sitting on the porcelain bidet in my drawers and undershirt and scratching my armpits. I'd give them a ride in the cab of the truck, crowded in among the piles of swaying furniture, if they were going off to work, wiggling their behinds on dusty roadsides in Cova da Piedade, Seixal, Amora, the flea-bitten factory area of Barreiro or the marine barracks, we'd have lunch together, it happened sometimes, in smoky pall-bearer dives around the Morgue, so I thought It's Dolores or Berta or Celeste wanting to talk to me, Adelaide, who usually has me pawn her earrings or beads, Mafalda, poor thing, to complain about her pimp, something like that, Captain, I calmly finished with the couch, tied it to the rusty hooks with rope, climbed up the incline toward the sun (branches, chimneys, the broken outlines of buildings), went by the glass cage of the office where Mr. Ilídio, his asthma spray forgotten in his hand, was contemplating the flower with his fierce little defeated eyes, a skirt, a knit jacket, a vaguely familiar body, vaguely intimate, Was it Arlete?, I thought, but this one was taller and stronger than Arlete, more poorly dressed, too, Not Arlete, no, features of a face that the excessive light was dissolving, shoulders ground down by light, a clutch of tiny shapes moved about her, It's Clotilde, I bet, with her ever-present mangy dogs, the dozens of limping strays that always follow her, licking her varicose veins in loving submission, and five yards from where he was, slippers, fingers full of pustules, a face, you see, like my sister's looking at me without smiling, Clotilde, my eye, the soldier said to himself, Clotilde's dogs, my eye, a pile of dark kids, with skinny limbs, clutching the ruined legs, It can't be, I thought, It isn't possible, I thought, How many years has it been? four? five?, I thought, the green teeth, the wrinkled clothes, the initialed ring on the middle finger, not Arlete, not Clotilde, not Berta, not Mafalda, my sister, and she, without affection, wrapping more tightly the child she was holding in a filthy shawl, Hi.

"OK, study whatever you feel like and forget about the church," the soldier conceded. "I'll take care of the paperwork, I'll turn everything in at the registry next week."

"Two jackasses, goddamn it," the grandmother's gigantic breasts repeated, as she used a twisted spit to stir the charcoal in the stove, "two jackasses of the first order. With that little moron face of yours, boy, you certainly won't get much farther."

Not just miserable, the soldier thought, used up too, and not just used up, bitter on top of it all, and worse than bitter, hopeless: Dolores, Adelaide, Mafalda were probably still hoping, who can tell, for something in the future, an inheritance back in the country, an educated gentleman, an accountant or a bank clerk or somebody established, an emigrant on in years with a house set up in the country and a metal-colored car by the door, a fairy-tale prince who would pay for their lunch the next day and a nanny for their children, but her? She must have gone through the past months hocking the refrigerator, the furniture, the TV, the lamps, the gold chain, the exhausted sofa from their father's time, the little portable radio, the heater, while the mulatto, impenetrable behind his dark glasses, thumbed through the sports pages with absolute indifference:

"Zeca lost his job, Abílio," the sister said, wiping her nose on the sleeve of her jacket. "I came here to ask you for some help. To beg a little money from you."

Like that, just like that, and without any pride even, I thought, without any courage even, without any memory of Buraca even, when you turned me out into the street after I'd got back from Mozambique still dizzy from the war, go to hell: he saw the narrow building once more, shirts hanging from a line in the living room, photographs of the dead parents on the shelves, smiling slightly with that strange absent sweetness dead people have, the sound of the key in the door, Zeca coming in, lighting a cigarette, leaning against the wall, looking at him with a calm, empty expression, and the soldier, to himself suddenly, If I'd stayed in the Army and we were in Africa, I would have raised my rifle and killed you, and the soldier, to himself suddenly, Since when does a nigger run things in my house?

"I still can't understand what the rush is all about." Odete was surprised. "The world isn't going to blow up tomorrow, is it?"

"We need people here," I offered, "the ones we've got aren't half enough for the jobs. I'll talk to Uncle Ilídio and they'll take him on."

How many kids in all? Five? Six? He counted them: eight, kinky haired, yellowish, with hungry faces, one of them with clips on the eyebrows and his elbow in a plaster cylinder that was brown now, falling apart (He fell downstairs the day before yesterday, Otília explained icily), another so cross-eyed that his pupil disappeared under the corner of his eyelid, So that if the swine plague hit your brood, the soldier imagined, maybe you'd get back to being what you were before, maybe your life would be a little bit better at least.

"Zeca most likely won't be interested in working," his sister said. "Besides, he went off last week with all the money in the house and I haven't laid eyes on him since."

"I don't know of any nigger who isn't a complete bastard," the second lieutenant stated. "I'll bet my balls that he took up with some snot-covered slut in one of those shantytowns on the edge of Lisbon."

Shacks of wood and tin with rocks and used tires on the roof, mud, a heavy stench of filth, rancid food, and excrement, old black women with pipes between their gums, stirring up the small clay fireplaces, plastic curtains, lanterns amid crates and pots: For almost a whole week I went around with the quiet man and the bookkeeper's nephew looking for the guy in Alcântara, Benfica, Amadora, Casal Ventoso, Algés, squashing shit under my shoes, tripping on rocks, getting ourselves deeper and deeper in a concentric maze of garbage and jerry-built buildings filled with hollering, barking, crying, a silence that has no name, a whole week asking questions of indecipherable bands of Gypsies squatting in endless conspiracies, who looked us up and down before answering, with their long, overhanging eyelids, guided by the vague, directionless halo of taverns, where the wine came down out of the kegs with the slowness of blood from headless necks, one week, Captain, coming across opaque faces with dark glasses, and Hawaiian shirts staring at us, mute, in a dense and absolute indifference, very old and serious children, with mouths as stony as the rivers of winter, stinking and sweating and a whiff of fish and smells as hard as a punch, cripples moving about like dying spiders, dragging dozens of twisted and soft members along the irregular ground, and nothing, Otília, what you can call nothing, absolutely nothing, nothing at all, maybe in Jamor valley, maybe in Cabo Ruivo, maybe out in the country, maybe in the rotting boats that cast off from Alhandra heading nowhere, like rudderless balloons or uncontrolled blood clots in a vein, maybe under the Aqueduct, maybe in Marvila, maybe in Montijo, and blacks and Gypsies and donkeys in decomposing poverty, and we'd invariably end up swallowing the gloomy rotgut of defeat, elbows on the bar in a little corner establishment with a crew of barefoot drunks whose callused feet didn't even touch the ground, or by gaudy formerly redheaded women strung up by successive strands of glass beads, living with aged and historic wrestling champions, the Bear of the Caucasus, Chief Geronimo, the Masked Eskimo, who were growing fat, their eyes floating in alcohol, surreptitiously draining little glasses of white wine.

"Twenty guests at most," Odete imposed, "ten apiece and even then it's a bother. With mother ill I don't feel one damned bit like filling the house up as if it were a village festival with a full orchestra."

After a week (or four, or five days, or almost instantaneously, Otília?) he discovered that his sister, tired of waiting for Zeca, who was too invisible or volatile for her needs and tastes, had replaced him with a retired railroad worker and a solid pension check at the end of the month, his rheumatism doing away with any ideas of flight in him, a bald-headed gentleman, always lifting one cheek of his behind off the chair in order to put in some pain-killing suppositories, clutching a jug, with a blanket over his knees and with the face of a hopeless dog that grew animated between groans when he recalled the Beira Baixa line. A few varnished pieces of furniture with Formica tops appeared in the Buraca home, a rubber pillow for the hemor-rhoids and a huge picture of a horrible woman with white hair, her face twisted all the way to the left in an unpleasant smile, My departed Cecilia, the old man would point nostalgically with the quivering fingernail of his pinky, the multitude of mulattoes grew a little fatter, the sister began to sweep empty bottles and trash under the table and comb her hair on Sun-days, until the retiree's spine began to act up, he whined constantly, unable to hold his feces or piss in, waving his handkerchief every minute or so at nonexistent trains, which made the legs of the bed tremble with a disorderly galloping of shadows, and Otília exiled him and his dreams of freight cars and longing for his wife to the straw mattress in the little back bedroom, soon full of the unbearable smell of ammonia, empty suppository boxes, and the piercing shrieks of a dying parrot, which were joined by the photograph of the departed Cecilia, thrown by the sister with all her might through the door in the direction of heavy agitation under the sheets. One Sunday, on entering his father's house, he came upon a tall black man in dark glasses, a gleaming wristwatch, several rings, and a printed shirt, calmly reading the sports pages with proprietary airs in the wicker easy chair, rubbing his polished shoes against each other: Damião, his sister proudly introduced him, caressing the grease on his kinky hair, and after Damião came Agostinho and following Agostinho, Aristides and following Aristides, Minervino, the number of children grew visibly, his sister stopped sweeping the dust and combing her hair once more, and the old man, forgotten, moaned ceaselessly on his mattress there in the distance, clutching his cold jug like a castaway while the railroad cars slipped swiftly by, one after the other, on the walls, shaking the unmatched glasses and the crocheted doilies on the shelves.

"Not at São Jorge castle, no," Odete refused. "I detest those sickening peacocks hopping around the walls. The best idea so far is to have lunch in some pastry shop or other."

He spoke to the quiet man and the bookkeeper's nephew about stopping their wild goose chase through the shantytowns, pursued by the frightened rage of the dogs, but his colleagues had already grown used to the hazy little moonlight of the taverns and the heartburn atmosphere where grape liquor submerges guts and head, the quiet man had even fallen in love with a broken-down, exuberant dark woman, lame in the left knee, who ran a ruinous bawdy house set up in a former school in the Bairro da Boavista, frequented by a select clientele of newsboys, workers, furtive adolescents, and wandering unemployed thieves who would attempt to sell record players and battery radios to the customers, so they would wake up in the morning from time to time, with a little luck, alongside girls as skinny as sick mules, in compartments separated by cloth dividers with maps of Portugal hanging over their heads and blackboards screwed into crumbling plaster instead of the usual mirrors, where our sleepy faces would be transformed into chalked price-checking addition exercises stuck to the precarious pile of numbers of the sums, dimmed by the sponge of months. The black woman in the vestibule, a bottle of red wine within reach and fat lips fiercely painted down to her jaw and up to her nose, was collecting admissions and zealously watching over her mangy flock, while the quiet man, leaning in a corner, swung admiring round glances of passion in the direction of that vigilant empress of syphilis.

"The way she's going," the grandmother prophesied bitterly, fishing an infinite hair out of her bowl of soup, "I'll bet my life that any day now my granddaughter is going to turn into a first-class hooker."

I'd get up from the bed, Captain, it was a jerry-built pallet on top of some planks on the floor, listening to mixed sounds out there beyond the calico hangings, whispering, insults, farts, conversations, laughs, the authoritarian and ageless voice of the black woman invariably upsetting the quiet man, and I guessed it must be morning because little crystals of frost and tulips of steam were flowering in my bones. I stumbled over to the blackboard to comb my hair, a dull, thick night of slate framed in wood reflected my silence and my baggy eyes, ignored my body as if I had ceased to exist, you see, my surprise was offered the sibylline solution of a complicated mathematical exercise, where the figures leap-frogged over one another, mysterious as ants on a cake. The yawning whore murmured an emblematic, evasive phrase from a disconnected dream, the dogs in the shantytown were barking in the numbed alleys of six in the morning, muddied by the dew of the drains, roosters sharp as thorns wounded him from the broken fences of the gardens, the quiet man, daubed with lipstick like a carnival redskin, came out tucking his shirt into his pants, the bookkeeper's nephew, in a yellow helmet, was kicking the starter on his motorcycle in vain, All right, Odete, not at São Jorge castle, we'll find some pastry place near here, on the Rua da Escola do Exército I saw one with huge, three-tiered cakes, a bridal couple in sugar on

top, and egg-sugar icing all around the sticky paper plate, What time is it? the
famished whore asked, untangling her hair with her fingers, Only midnight,
go back to sleep, the soldier answered, buttoning his shirt, I never made love
at the Castle, Captain, I didn't have the nerve to invite her, for example, to
spend a Sunday up there, in the middle of the old stones and the ivy that
turned the sunlight into a kind of green curtain of gassy sludge, and when you
say Castle you're talking about the Cathedral or Alfama or the Miradoiro de
Santa Luzia, the motorcycle finally started, they clung together on the seat,
dead with fatigue, behind the yellow helmet, they took off toward the Baixa,
weaving unsteadily, leaping on the stones, I never went holding hands to
watch the pigeons and turtledoves and swans and ducks, I never went
holding hands to look at the river, Odete's kisses were distracted and quick,
her hugs had no strength or conviction, he stopped by the apartment to wash
his face and Dona Isaura's snoring thundered in the vestibule, with the tenth
black man in dark glasses and a Hawaiian shirt I lost interest in the narrow
little building in Buraca, I never visited my sister and her uncountable
collection of mulattoes again, I haven't been in the neighborhood for over
five years and they tell me everything's changed, and they tell me nothing
has changed, and they tell me everything's just the same, the ugly buildings,
the structures surrounded by scaffolding, abandoned construction material,
piles of rubbish on the ash gray vacant lots, the steeple of the Amadora
church far off, I didn't invite her to my wedding, naturally, I didn't invite her
to my son's baptism, I didn't tell her anything when he died of meningitis a
year and a half later, the social security doctor listened to the child with his
stethoscope, his name was Ezequiel, scribbled the name of some syrups on a
pad, snorted in a flat voice It's the beginning of pneumonia, no open windows
in his room, no drafts, no cold, and when they discovered the mistake,
Captain, the little bugger had got his brains all screwed up, and just what in
the devil is a beginning of pneumonia, explain that to me, three days in a
coma in the hospital, injections, bottles of serum, pills, nurses in a hurry who
never answered his and Odete's questions, the doctors evasive, the stretcher
bearers, and finally, one Saturday afternoon during visiting hours, a bald man
in a white smock opened his arms in fatalistic resignation, You're both young
and you've got your whole lives before you, what you need is courage, what
the hell, they performed an autopsy on Monday and on Tuesday the workers
at Ilídio Movers began appearing to offer their condolences, smothered in
flowers, my uncle had an asthma attack at the funeral because of the chrysan-
themums, during the priest's prayers, the bookkeeper was wiping her senti-
mental glasses with her handkerchief, a few old friends appeared, reeking
with wine, I visited the grave a few times, but right after I got divorced I
forgot, some time back I got a letter from the City informing me that five
years had passed and they were going to remove the bones, that if I didn't pay
for a plot in the cemetery they'd put them into the common grave along with

hundreds of mud-covered skeletons full of teeth sarcastically laughing at the gravediggers' shovels, so, Captain, right now he must be dissolving, with thin wisps of hair on his skull, amid hundreds and hundreds of leg bones, ribs, backbones, disconnected jawbones. Ezequiel? the second lieutenant asked, and he, Ezequiel, yes, not because I liked the name especially since I would have preferred Amândio or Teotónio, but because it was the name of Odete's godfather, who was a notary in Lamego and would send a money order and cardboard boxes of smoked pork sausages at Easter time.

"Three-tiered cakes, not on your life," Odete declared. "For the love of God, stop coming up with those bits of bourgeois foolishness with me."

The soldier had never noticed too much, Captain, how his wife would go out Wednesdays and Saturdays for night meetings at her job and he didn't dare ask her anything, she'd get back quite late, get undressed by touch without turning the light on, and if I sought out her body in the sheets, if I stroked her behind or breast, she would move away to the edge of the bed and breathe heavier and grow limp, pretending to be asleep: work or another man, it was all the same now that they'd been separated for a fucking bunch of months, it could have been a case of real meetings, it could have been lovers' meetings, what's certain is that almost immediately after the wedding, as soon as she got pregnant with Ezequiel, it was as if I didn't exist, you know how it is, as if I were a bothersome guest in the house. Maybe she secretly wanted me to die too, maybe she secretly hoped a cabinet or a piano would fall on me during some move, or she just didn't give a shit about me, everything she did was like she meant to say Since you're there, stay there, as long as you don't bother me, I don't give a shit. The funny thing, though, was that she had books with hammers and sickles on the cover and a cloth calendar with the picture of a Chinaman, along with papers and leaflets and brochures locked up in a dresser drawer. At that time all of a sudden, without any reason that I could see, she'd already stopped her nursing studies (all those arguments between us, all that talk of vocation, all that studying for nothing), she was working as a clerk at the Ministry of War, she improved her appearance, painted her nails and dyed her hair, lost weight, she wore high heels, dressed differently, her waist took on unexpected rhythms and men followed her on the street, eyes all lighted up, studying the ocean waves of her hips. The way things are it's possible that the Russians were paying her, Captain, the soldier was never strong on politics, but so much hammer and sickle stuff should wake a guy up, I kept on dragging furniture from here to there, transporting buffets, lugging cabinets across endless landings, getting home too tired to notice this or that, as soon as I sat my ass down in a chair I'd doze off, and Odete, disdainfully, You're a beast, you've got no culture, all you worry about is eating and snoring and I'm an even bigger beast because I put up with you, and the hate in her eyes, the rage in her movements, the impatience in her shoulders, until one night when he got home from work, they were living in Olivais at the time, on a drafty fourth floor with three tiny rooms, he put the key in the door, everything in darkness, an afflicted feeling of emptiness, no cooking smell, he turned on the light, books were missing from the shelves, Dona Isaura's picture was missing from on top of the tape recorder, the dinner pot was missing from the stove, a stocking fluttered on a chair like the leg of a hanged man, a piece of paper on top of the bed, Let's have a look at what it says, I thought, let's just take a look at the message, Odete's slanted, hurried hand, he opened it, I'm leaving you.

"Didn't you ever see her again?" the second lieutenant asked. "Didn't you ever hear anything more about the whore?"

"Go ahead and get married," the uncle gargled sharply with the little chuckle of a parakeet, the asthma spray pointed at his rotting teeth. "But if you think I'm giving you the week off, you've got another think coming, my boy."

I even went to the Ministry to talk to her, Lieutenant, waiting for her under the arcade when the workers came out, when a gray, shapeless, uninterrupted almost mechanical flow of people invaded the ferries to the other side, the thousand tongues of the Tagus lapping softly against the steps, the lights went on all along the parallel streets, giving an unimaginable depth to the façades. Not furious, you understand, not spiteful, not out of my head, not to beat her up, just sad, confused, perplexed, just to talk to her, just with the embittered, melancholy need to understand, but I always saw her all perked up, lively, happy, making forceful gestures, in the company of the lieutenant or a skinny, restless guy whose overcoat dragged on the sidewalk, so I didn't dare approach her, stop her, ask her to talk to me, so I always ended up, fuck it all, holding back, going with my bachelor fellow workers to a low-down dive (Hot Dogs, Beef Strips, Squid Salad, Assorted Sandwiches) by the Sodré docks or in the Bairro Alto, where they'd have dinner, drinking five or six glasses of red wine all by myself, going with them, unsure and vague, to the black woman's primary school and its drapes or little curtains stained with flies, and, in the meantime, the dust was gathering in Olivais, I forgot to pay the water bill and after a certain time, boom, they cut me off, he opened a tap and out came two stingy drops and that was the end of it, the neighbors greeted him as if they were sitting up with his corpse, the concierge's husband paid the overdue bills, the lady on the ground floor, the widow of a marine sergeant, tried to force a mangy bitch on him as a gift, the bedclothes smelled of your body for months, some shoes, left behind in the closet blinded me, I never went back to the Terreiro do Paço at six in the evening, never spied on her from behind a column, next to the stiff, stony restlessness of blind beggars, the ferries docking and leaving with an intestinal cadence, If you really want to grind yourself down, that's your problem, the uncle growled, but don't look to me, I won't help anyone commit suicide, they got married one Saturday afternoon in Arroios, at a decrepit registry where half a dozen women pianoed ageless typewriters, protected by a worm-eaten counter, and, right next door, a photography shop's display case exhibited a framed swarm of vapid smiling brides with long eyelashes, pensive and sweet, his fellow workers, in neckties, fearfully squeaking in their new shoes, made a methodical exploration of the neighborhood bars, and when Odete and he sat down opposite a serious lady shuffling papers, a dozen fierce brandy breaths floated through the solemn room on the second floor that was falling apart from worms and dampness, Mr. Ilídio's asthma spray was whistling in a corner, the bookkeeper, with an enormous brooch of blue stones in the shape of a millstone around her throat, was coughing emotionally into her hand, I looked at you fearfully, out of the corner of my eye, and you'd gone to the hairdresser's, and you'd fixed your nails, and you'd made up your eyes and face, and you were wearing high heels and a burgundy dress that I'd never seen before, Let's take off and bring some chicks along, the second lieutenant suggested, Let's get out of here and go to my place, and you had your lips tightly pressed together, Odete, in an expression of regret or doubt, So pretty, the soldier thought, so chic, your hands so beautiful, clasped on your knees, the serious lady put on the glasses hanging around her neck from a plastic cord, read some rapid phrases in a bound book, asked one or two harsh questions of those gathered which went unanswered, the sun was slowly eating across the floorboards, spreading out across the worn walls, driving the bloody shadow of the trees far away from the room, the creature drew a cross in pencil by the place where we were to sign and turned the register majestically around, the way someone passes the sugar bowl, toward my chest, Odete opened her mouth and I, immediately, She's got second thoughts, she's going to say to hell with it all, she's going to say she doesn't want to, but no, it was a belch, she wrote her name, right away, with the ball-point I loaned her, with the infinite slowness of blacks tattooing themselves in Africa, Captain, the asthma spray whistled again and the soldier thought Any minute now the sun's going to come through the roof, explode the stucco, brutally pull off the molding, dry up the century-old mustiness, and its little flowers just like fat polyps, reminding him of the brambles and the houses in Arroios, inside the bedroom, in turn the lady in glasses wrote out some regal arabesques, closed the book, got up, greeted us disdainfully, and disappeared, her episcopal vestments fanning out, behind a curtain, Four chicks aren't enough, the communications officer opposed, the champagne had enlarged his appetite, at least two apiece and that's the minimum, Since the motion has been made, I second it, the lieutenant colonel gave his support, two per guy is the minimum of minimums, and then a few insipid embraces, a few soft kisses, a midget in a striped suit who bore a camera shouted Hold it, and a magnesium bulb went off, What about the rings? a concerned voice asked, what happened to the rings? but there weren't any wedding rings, Odete didn't want any rings, I'm not a pigeon in a pigeon coop with little hoops with a name and a date, what for? you kept the little silver ring you already had on your finger, Now the family, the midget commanded, leaping around us, pushing Uncle Ilídio, very annoyed, between the two of us, Now the close friends, Now all the guests together, and more flashes of light, and more instantaneous blind eternities, and more bodies and faces suddenly motionless, smiling, staring on the paper, pale and anfractuous like pieces of limestone, Now me alone, fearfully stiff, Now you alone leaning against the palm tree in the square and your bored look, Odete, your hanging, withdrawn wrists, the impatient wrinkles on your forehead, the furious tension of your shoulders, She never loved me, Captain, she must have gotten married out of apathy, to avoid explanations, to escape boredom, she must have said to herself This one or some other one, it's all the same and I'll stop having to put up with my godfather and family worries, You're twenty-five years old and why hasn't it happened yet, listen here, girl, when are you going to make up your mind, What's the lucky man's name, The thing she's got under her skirt could turn into a wormy piece of fruit, or maybe, you see, she got married for convenience, because it was necessary, how should I know, for the good of the proletarian revolution, the unprotected and hardworking classes of our so martyred and yet so heroic country, because the party ordered her Pick some sucker you can use as a cover, an idiot, comrade, a boob, one thing there's no lack of around here is morons, and she sleeping leninly with our lieutenant and me wearing myself out lugging furniture all day long, screwing up my spine with bureaus on my back, getting slipped disks picking up sofas, and then, at night, you'd turn your ass to me and go to sleep, I could make out your side, a shoulder blade, a piece of neck in the tallow-colored light of night through the window, what can I do, damn it, with my hard on, Odete, what do I do with my wet pajamas, what do I do with my crazy hunger for you, if I touch you with my knee, your behind retracts, if I try to caress you, your muscles harden, if I look for your mouth, you run away like a skittish little drop of quicksilver, I've got a headache, I'm tired, I've got a funny feeling in my ovaries, Not now, the Arroios palm tree rubbing the Bakelite combs of its leaves against each other, the boys at work were sailing along without a keel over small lakes of grape liquor, mouth breathing, elbowing each other, laughing, they finally went off to their pickups, downhill to the bus stop, the bookkeeper presented me with a plastic imitation crocodile wallet with transparent pockets for the pictures of children and I don't even have Ezequiel's in it, we went home, Mr. Ilídio and I, in the moving van, we parked on the sidewalk, wiped our feet on the doormat, and no bubbling of intestines or throat from the sick woman's room, no sound of lungs, no slurp of saliva, just the sun coming in at a slant through the blinds and sketching parallel strips on the rug, I stick my diddly up my own ass, Odete, but what do you want to do with the hairy space between your thighs where I can't get

lost, can't sink in?, Uncle Ilídio ran down the hallway to blow out his
emphysema, his anguish, pulling on the knot of his necktie, feeling for the
spray in his pocket, he opened the window blinds and the kale and the
chickens rolled together, all mixed up, on top of the bedspread, on the scarlet
branches of which Dona Isaura suddenly smaller, her eyes and gums open,
motionless, was swallowing the edible hours of five o'clock on the church
steeple.

"I never did know she was married," the communications officer protested, "she never mentioned any husband to me, never any ties. I knew her
by her nom de guerre, Dália, we'd meet and go our separate ways at the
Organization, at the Ministry, or in the subway at most, she didn't wear a
wedding ring, she didn't talk about you, if I asked her questions she'd change
the subject, fool around, talk about the weather."

"So you two were going around tricking each other," the second lieutenant
said, "so you were cheating on each other."

"Isaura," Uncle Ilídio called, shaking the dead woman's knees, "what's the
matter, Isaura?"

"Seriously, listen here," the communications officer asked, "if I'd dreamed
she belonged to you do you think I'd offer you a share in one of these, eh?"

"Neither one of us believed it at first, Captain," the soldier said. "It
seemed so impossible to be dead like that surrounded by vegetables and
chickens."

"Put her in the van," Uncle Ilídio panted imperatively, "they must have
serums and shots and oxygen and a doctor and a nurse and every other
goddamned thing in the clinic down there."

You didn't cry that time, Odete, the way you didn't cry in church or at the
wake, or at the cemetery the next morning, four or five taxis following the
coffin under a black and gold cloth that looked like a bullfighter's costume
without sleeves, nauseating wreaths of flowers, the compunction of the
neighbor women, solemn old men, one of whom was horribly hunchbacked,
hat in hand, efficient and expeditious undertakers, the casket laboriously
lowered by ropes into a dark, rectangular hole of infinite depth, the sound of
earth falling, falling onto the wooden lid, the annoyance, the discomfort, and
the afflicted suffocation of the dead, the smell of mothballs from jackets and
you wearing green glasses, Odete, witnessing all that, impassively serene,
accepting the condolences of people almost with a smile, thanking them
without once lifting your handkerchief to your eyes, could you have been a
revolutionary already at that time? could you have been called Dália already
at that time? could our lieutenant have already put it in her if he ever got to
put it in? men brag, Captain, about so many things they haven't done as long
as they can tell stories about their tool, we went down the alley as fast as the
van would go, leaping sidewalks and knocking over crates, the clinic was a
small one-story building with several plaques with doctors' names between a

run-down restaurant and a shop selling china and unbelievable pink and
snot-colored glassware, I got Dona Isaura, who didn't weigh any more than
the white sponge of bones, just like a handful of hollow pieces of wood or a
bird's tibias, out of the backseat, Uncle Ilídio was anxiously ringing the bell,
cream-colored rooms, undecipherable smells of medicines, cabinets containing the pliers and long little mirrors dentists use, metal tables, basins with
dressings, rusty oxygen tanks, gurneys, Where can we lay her down where
can we lay her down where can we lay her down, the old man was whining in
panic to the empty walls, where charts with sardonic skeletons and pictures
of intestines and livers hung, and, finally, after hours of shouting, lamentations, and demands, a creature in a smock appeared, of indefinite age and
more or less of the female sex in spite of the deep voice and masculine shoes,
with a stethoscope around her neck and a syringe in her hand, who examined
Dona Isaura's eyes with a small flashlight, applied some scientific taps to her
elbows and bunions with the help of a long rubber instrument, ordered
her to breathe deeply, cough, say thirty-three, unbuttoned the neck of her
blouse, straightened her up, contemplated her for moments like a rare steak
and informed us She's dead, if you don't take her out of here right now I'll
have to send her to the Morgue for an autopsy (and the soldier imagined
bodies horribly quartered on marble slabs, stomachs and kidneys weighed on
a butcher's scale, craniums opened with a saw), Uncle Ilídio, in disbelief,
persisted Give her mouth to mouth resuscitation at least, a little electric
shock on the chest at least, those massages they give drowned people on
television at least, Your wife kicked the bucket more than an hour ago, the
androgynous woman doctor made herself didactically clear, I'll prescribe
some cough syrup for you under the pretense that it's bronchitis, and you
people get out of this establishment as quickly as possible, because a corpse
in here gives the clinic a bad name, patients needing a quick bandaging job or
with ingrown toenails will run away in fright if they catch the smell of a dead
person, Just tell me what trouble a little bit of serum is, just tell me what
trouble an injection of penicillin in the vein is, Uncle Ilídio pleaded, penicillin always perks a person up, the creature shrugged her shoulders,
annoyed, constantly looking at the door in case a whitlow appeared, or an
unexpected laceration, or an eyebrow needing care, Dona Isaura's huge
open, insatiable mouth was swallowing the bulb on the ceiling now, a can of
compresses and a flounced screen were silently evaporating in her gullet, I
guarantee that if I had known it was you, the communications officer swore, I
guarantee that if the slightest suspicion had entered my head, and at that
moment a big, fat orderly entered the room and all together we managed to
convince Uncle Ilídio, who was resorting to his asthma spray from moment to
moment as if to fill the room with the air of his displeasure, to take the
deceased woman back home, the orderly accompanied us to a dairy store
halfway home with the insight to bolster the widower with some energetic

and invigorating drinks of grape liquor, furnishing him with strange bits of advice and opinions of a dazzling optimism, while the deceased waited for us in the van, wrapped in a checkered blanket, we reached the alley with Uncle Ilídio explaining to us in a wordy way, between singing and belching, that he was damned, by God, if at the age of sixty-three he wasn't going to start living, he got our names mixed up, kissed us, wanted to dictate his will, overthrow the government, invent a dishwashing machine, enjoy Carnival, he finally fell asleep facedown on the living-room couch snoring like a rhinoceros, Odete and I (or should I say Dália and I, Lieutenant?) dressed her mother, struggling against the stiffness of her legs and trunk (and a little tuft of grayish, foul-smelling hair down there, and the skin of her belly repugnantly flaccid and ashen, and the swelling of her knees, even in back), we put on a pair of patent-leather buckled shoes that suddenly looked enormous to me and reflected and deformed our images like convex aluminum surfaces, pointing to the ceiling with the tenacity of traffic signals, we stretched her out on the bed, lighted candles by her head, received the first neighbor women, whom Uncle Ilídio insulted, Go to hell, in the confused vapor of his dreams, we served port wine and chocolate cookies from the grocery store and at nightfall the kale began to glimmer in the garden, puffed out like girls wearing a lot of petticoats doing handstands, the buildings in the area piled up around us enormous, colorless, heavy, threatening geometric shadows, whispering, huffing, cackling, brief swallowing in the restless chicken house, I've got such a craving for you to touch me, I've got such a craving for you to kiss me, I've got such a craving for your fingers to go up and down my fleshy piston, eagerly, slowly, deliciously. When you come right down to it, eight is too many, the second lieutenant decided, we'll take four along and I've got whiskey and music at my place, Just explain to me, Lieutenant sir, the soldier asked the communications officer, why in the devil didn't your lover like me? the neighbor women nibbled on the chocolate cookies, sucked on the port wine accompanied by Uncle Ilídio's monumental farts and they escaped outdoors with little unnoticed cat steps, the almost bald deaf-mute woman from the building next door was left behind, sitting on the kitchen stool clacking her false teeth and saying her rosary in an enormous state of shock, I got undressed, Captain, in the midst of books, notebooks, pencils, posters, and poems, all that wisdom that had been patiently stored up, you turned out the light and your nude thin body that wavered vaguely in the blue haze of the darkness came close to me, lifted up the sheet, lay down noiselessly and without a word beside me, the way a tongue slips into a mouth, I love you, Odete (or Dália now?), I love your nose, your eyebrows, the harsh stubble of your armpits, I lifted my hand to grip your shoulders, to lie on top of you, to bury myself in your indifferent legs, and at that moment I felt I was being stared at, I don't know how to explain it, but I felt that I was being stared at, I looked out the window at the kale, silk colored, gleaming in the garden, and right at my feet, on the dresser, almost perching on the bust of an evil-looking bald man with a beard, Lenin, the communications officer said in a low voice, That son of a bitch of a Lenin, the soldier corrected, that bastard of a Lenin, that biggest bastard of them all of a Lenin, was a chicken with great big crimson feet and a neck without feathers, watching me, you see, with the hard, solid, round, glass eyes, with the careful and devastating cruelty of an executioner.

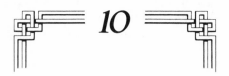

# 10

"Four of these lady friends plus the four of us makes eight hot whores," the lieutenant colonel told the second lieutenant, still suspicious of the champagne, massaging his stomach. "What will your neighbors say when they see us?"

Me, for example, I'm my mother, he thought, a ridiculous old woman who wore gauze, rings, perfumes, makeup, and creams, her artificial nylon eyelashes fluttering like insect wings, clumsily attempting to seduce the grocer in hopes of a little discount on a jug of wine, because I started drinking toward the end of my life, Son, because I sit down in front of the television for the soap opera with a tray of full glasses by my side and I go along sucking them up with a straw like kids' soda pop until the images on the screen get all mixed up with my present life, with my past life, with my friend on the floor upstairs, curled like a lizard around her cane, who brings me a package of wormy cookies from time to time along with questions bellowed out of her deafness, with my engineer lover, with my architect lover, with my industrialist lover, with my doctor lover, with my well-dressed, well-combed, solemn lovers, so mannerly, who would wind up the gramophone, give me diamond bracelets, cut my steak for me at dinner, fondle my buttocks and undress me in the darkness of the bedroom, gasping in bed, pulling me with great heaves of anguished haste, men pedaling, exhausted, on the bicycle seat of my pubis along the road to the stagnant unpleasant silence of the orgasm, men staining my sheets with their sad little tasteless juice, and Yes, love, and OK, love, and Any way you want, love, I'm my mother, the lieutenant colonel thought, I tell myself to comb my hair and brush my teeth before coming into the living room, tiny, wearing a necktie and patent-leather shoes, to greet Uncle Borges, or Uncle Rodrigues, or Uncle Mendes, before smelling their repugnant odor of hair cream, their odor of talcum powder, their odor of money, before tolerating their sickening soft fingers on my throat, I'm my mother in her Almirante Reis refuge on the miserable fourth floor above the sweet shop and the notary, hair loose, mute, in chemise and slippers, waiting for death beside the broken radio, a striped blanket over her knees.

"Eight whores," he muttered, his head full of motionless octogenarian women stabbing the dividing wall with their mineral eyes, "it's worse than a battalion of night watchmen with bad breath."

Colonel Ricardo had promised him You'll only have to put up with it in the Ministry for a few months until the little captains' revolutionary hard ons soften up a bit (and in addition to that it's even better if they've finally forgotten about you and in addition to that if they've finally forgotten you exist), so for the moment what I want is for us to go along with these bastards all nice and easy, But, he complained, I ended up rotting behind my desk in that cubbyhole until the November 25th coup, sifting through cases, taking notes, drawing up memoranda, clearing out generals and brigadiers and majors, no sooner did I hand in a report than I would receive a pile of cards, file after file piled up on my desk, and Colonel Ricardo, impatient with democratic fervor, You're terribly slow, You're terribly soft, What's happened to your energy, man, What's happened to your capacity for solving problems, man, the rain on the tiles seemed to be beating down directly onto the tin roof of his head, summer was dissolving his muscles into flabby fat, the sergeants who came and went with papers looked at him with sarcasm, disdain, pity, I'm not my mother, goddamn it, I'm not even capable of fighting for a decent office, the artificial lashes are falling off my eyelids, my bony haunches don't attract anyone, what chauffered automobile is waiting at the door for me, what grocer will trust me for a day for a jug of red wine?

"I've come to let you know," his daughter informed him, taking off her topcoat in the vestibule, "that I'm divorcing my husband. Since you never could stand him, Father, I imagine you're happy at the news."

"We're not clearing out just anyone, we're skating back and forth across the shit of their résumés, the General Staff is getting upset and the fault is yours, Artur," Colonel Ricardo accused him, pushing away a bundle of typed pages with the freckly back of his hand. "If we don't do a proper cleanup job, the ones who will be the victims of our benevolence will be us."

"Each one of us can handle two of them, hell," the second lieutenant protested. "Our commander is underestimating the combat capacity of his battalion."

"Bang," the soldier shouted, shooting with his index finger at the manager, who fell in a sitting position in the middle of the dance floor, holding his bleeding intestines with his shaking hands.

"I've never known a more disgusting guy," the daughter said, looking for cigarettes in her purse. "Disgusting like all disgusting things: I stood him as long as I could, but I couldn't stand him anymore, see, even his smell, even his breathing unnerves me."

"That whole year and a half at the Ministry, fucking up guys I didn't even know," the lieutenant colonel explained to me, "drove me crazy. I got to taking three pills at night and even then, I had an awful time falling asleep."

Jumbled dreams in black and white, legs pedaling idly in the sheets, a murky, infinite, painful, deadly fatigue on waking up, the concierge disappearing out the door waving, without coming back, a vague goodbye with her arm, faded days that were turning into gray weeks, weeks that were being prolonged into a marmalade of months, the firehouse siren and the motor of the water wagons plowing sharp furrows in my sleep, in my mother's old whore sleep in my place in bed, in my place in the bathroom mirror, in my place in the bathtub, in my place in the car, in my place in my body, so that every morning I would wrap myself in my complicated dresses, in my tulles, in my velvets, in my gauzes, I would create eyebrows between two soft wrinkles, water the scaly hundred-year-old crocodile pleats of my armpits with Spanish perfume from the drugstore (large blue flasks that smelled of faded violets and rotting fish), paint a huge red mouth between my sunken cheeks, adorn myself with the absurd pomp of tremendous cut-glass rings and gaudy necklaces worthy of a notions shop, which imitated garishly complex Russian jewelry, I would enter the Terreiro do Paço with an arrogant, imperial majesty, not returning the salutes of sentries and subalterns, go up the stairs of that huge, melancholy building inhabited by the ghosts of ancient artillerymen with mustaches, pale Cavalry officers eaten by the malaria of Gungunhana, and second lieutenants of shock troops proclaiming the Republic by the statue of the Marquês de Pombal in yellowing photographs replete with an enthusiastic and petrified crowd of stiff collars and hats, settle myself in the cubbyhole in the rear, cooling my double chin with my fan and daintily underlining paragraphs and phrases with thick, trembling lines of lipstick, I'm the mangy old whore my mother was, her cardboard vanity, I go into Colonel Ricardo's office at noon as usual (and there's the worried little bald head in the rear behind the vast varnished desk top) for the usual report (How many rotten apples thrown out today, Dona Elisa?), and there are the speckled little hands, suddenly lost, fluttering aimlessly, afflicted, not touching anything, over the stapler, the mute telephone, the green rectangle of the blotter, the rearing bronze horse with fierce flared nostrils, the fringed lamp, Colonel Ricardo's fat hands rose, hesitated, reached out childishly toward me. There's been a revolt, Artur, a devil of a mess, the paratroopers have taken over the television station.

"Him all mixed up and me figuring the guy was an important communist," the soldier commented, "me figuring the guy was taking orders from Moscow."

"Carlos is determined to come and talk to you," the daughter said, "he wants to come and cry on your shoulder, wants to complain to you. Get rid of the guy, any way you want, as far as I'm concerned it's all over."

"A revolt?" the mother frivolously asked Colonel Ricardo, vaguely annoyed or inconvenienced or intrigued, opening her fan that sparkled with spangles in an evasive, spoiled, spiraling gesture. "Is it someone I know at least?"

Like some kind of entertainment, see, he told me, fun and games, a rather unfortunate move by a friend with no imagination that day, but always good at choosing bonbons. As if it really were something of no importance that was only worth a casual glance, a superficial, slight, weightless interest, the usual ironic, merry look: Nobody you know, Mother, a few paratroop guys, some soldiers, some officers, and some anonymous civilians without enough money for even an hour in your sheets, without enough money to ring the bell, sit on the plastic covers in your parlor, drink your peach brandy, give me a paternal and smiling pinch on the cheek, Come here and say good evening to Uncle Ferreira, Artur.

"What the hell are you smiling at?" Colonel Ricardo was indignant, furious. (And Major Fontes green, Lieutenant Cardoso green, and a sergeant he didn't know with a wine-colored birthmark on his cheek, deathly green.) "Don't you realize the gravity of all this, don't you see it could be the end of us? The country devastated, our positions threatened, our promotions in doubt, in just a little while shooting all over Lisbon, and you, you bastard, grinning at me here, right in my face, extremely amused."

"I'm sure she lost her head, you know, that she went completely crazy," the son-in-law whined, terribly confused, the left side of his face lighted by the afternoon sun, cracking his knuckles: Do you think he's going to cry, Mother, do you think that he's going to pull his handkerchief out of his pocket at any moment now and blow his nose good and hard? "I want to leave you, I want a separation, I want to divorce you: Everything so fine between us and all of a sudden, she, without further ado, just imagine, comes home with that crazy foolishness in her head."

"One whore apiece?" the second lieutenant laughed. "Do you need hormones maybe, Colonel sir?"

"A little hard going," the concierge answered (and he suddenly missed his wife and had a bitter urge to cry): "but every so often, poor dear, he'd make it after an hour or so."

"An hour, that's awful," the communications officer said. "Wow, so you went soft all of a sudden too, Colonel."

"If he could run into a woman like me," his mother defended him (Thanks, old girl), "relax, my son would fulfill his duty with three strokes of his pen."

"A devilish confusion, Dona Elisa," Colonel Ricardo was desperate (and Major Fontes and Lieutenant Cardoso and the sergeant with the wine-colored birthmark nodded agreement): "the Army divided, contradictory information, garrisons against other garrisons, complete anarchy. And no orders from above, no message, no phone call, no instructions as to what we have to do."

"For the first time they ground him down without warning," the soldier exulted. "For the first time they caught him without a trump card to play. The guy must have been wiped out from the legs down."

"One whore apiece always turns out cheaper," the second lieutenant conceded. "When the bill comes for this cat-piss French champagne, it's going to make your hair stand on end."

"The paratroopers have taken over the television station," Major Fontes said, "they put the flag on the screen, interrupted the program and read a very radical communiqué, from the most extreme left wing, you can imagine. And now only military marches and incitements to a popular uprising. Is it your opinion we should join in, Brigadier?"

"She shouted at me that she's sick of me, that she's got a lover, that she wants to go work in Brazil," his knuckles were squeaking. "A whole string of nonsense, I even asked her at first if she was on drugs, there are so many lowlifes around smoking funny things."

"You're my drug, and, besides, you've given me a duodenal ulcer. Go to hell."

"He was a hell of a lot of work for me, a hand here, a hand there, a mouth there, with me at my wits' end to give him some pleasure," the concierge snorted indignantly, "and the son of a bitch, one fine day, Beat it, on your way, I want to marry someone else. He probably drank a whole bottle of monkey glands and didn't need me anymore to get his tool up."

"Bring me a set for the office right away," Colonel Ricardo ordered the sergeant with the wine-colored birthmark. "I can't decide whether or not our section should join in until I find out what's going on."

"The radio's going on as if nothing happened, Brigadier," Major Fontes alerted him. "Even if it's a real revolt, I don't think it will get very far."

"Come give the major a handshake, Artur, come say hello to the people, say it like this: Good evening," his mother whispered melodiously, shaking her bracelets, while the phonograph squealed out a paso doble that was way out of tune with the Castilian squeaks and belches of an accordion.

"For the love of God, Dona Elisa," Major Fontes protested, "I'm not a man to stand on ceremony, let the child do what he wants."

"Me, in any case, I lean toward taking along two," the communications officer insisted, his glasses buried in the blonde's hair, "but if you people don't want to, I'll give in."

"And could a person know now what it is you're going to do in Brazil?" the lieutenant colonel asked, leg outstretched, cleaning something off his shoe with his finger.

"If you could only get those idiotic ideas out of her head," the son-in-law suggested, "if you could only send her to a psychiatrist."

"A coup d'etat," Lieutenant Cardoso lamented, "right today on my wife's birthday and I've got my in-laws coming to dinner."

"A handshake for the lieutenant, Artur," his mother commanded, "what kind of obsession is that, not talking to people?"

"To work," his daughter replied, "the company's opened a branch and there's an opening for me as a secretary. And, beside that, as an extra bonus I'll see myself free of his crying spells."

"No, sir," his mother said. "If we don't teach them when they're little, trust me, once they're big we can't do a thing with them. Let's take a look at your ears, Artur, to see if you've washed them the way you should."

"Fuck it, Artur," Colonel Ricardo scolded him, walking back and forth on the rug with comical little leaps, "you sit there large as life on the couch, not saying a word, smiling. What shitty reason have you got to be so amused by this? Do you want to be cleared out? Do you want to be put in the reserves? Do you want them to screw up your life?"

"And not just my in-laws," Lieutenant Cardoso explained, "some cousins of hers who live in Oporto too. Twelve people. I've ordered lobster Newburg from a restaurant, I'm supposed to pick it up at seven o'clock. Leave the kid alone, Dona Elisa, he's old enough, time will take care of teaching him manners."

"All of a sudden," the concierge muttered, pulling on the zipper of her skirt, "he took up with a floozy, a chick with a cigarette holder, getting old, with a lapdog always around her neck, owner of a boutique on Sapadores. Me all trusting, covering him with caresses, and the guy sticking a knife in my back, sneaky. One of these days I'm going to that slut's shop and right there in the middle of all that cow's rags I'll raise a ruckus the likes of which you've never seen: I can't get the idea out of my head that she gave him some kind of tea to drink."

"Show her where she's wrong," the son-in-law asked, "that all this is foolishness that hasn't got a name. Just last February we bought the apartment, the man who's going to glass in the balcony is supposed to come next week, we haven't paid off the car loan. Please, sir."

Nothing, the lieutenant colonel thought, I'm thinking about absolutely nothing unless it's the fact that I'm the old whore of my mother in her ruffled girdles and fantastic, unbelievable satins, that I'm crossing my legs to your

280

surprise, your shock, your desire, in order to exhibit for you the hairy skin above my stockings, in order to rouse you with my pink garters and bows, in order to turn your head with my lace panties, in order to drive you crazy with my sharp knee bones, the sergeant came staggering into the office, purple faced from the effort, hugging the cube of an enormous television set whose cord was dragging along behind him like a tail, sliding along the waxed floor, Major Fontes and Lieutenant Cardoso helped him set it on the desk, plug it in, play with the dial, Careful with the finish on the desk, they pushed away the fringed lamp and the bronze horse, the mother searched for her glasses in her purse in order to see better, Colonel Ricardo, twirling his wedding ring on his finger, confused, in panic, installed himself in a small low sofa like a toad that had lost its strength, You didn't clean your ears, Artur, his mother scolded him, and your nails are filthy, how shameful, you're going to bed without any dinner for a week, and just then the screen suddenly lighted up, little grains of light twinkling like an October sky, an out-of-focus voice that came closer and closer and became clear, a shape, a captain discoursing with his eyes on them, Forgive him, Dona Elisa, you know better than we what children are like, If the two of you talk it could happen that she'll listen to you, the son-in-law was hopeful, it still could happen that she'll come to her senses, don't you think? You're lucky, you rascal, the good major has interceded on your behalf, my mother told me, you're lucky that I never refuse my friends anything, The bill for the champagne? the soldier was startled, don't talk fortunes to me because I've only got one conto in my wallet, Lieutenant. Shall we join in, Dona Elisa?, Colonel Ricardo asked hesitantly, shall we send a telegram right off stating our enthusiastic support for the lads in the coup?, Twelve settings, lobster Newburg, vol-au-vent, pineapple, and hazelnut mousse, the lieutenant recited, everything paid for yesterday afternoon, what am I going to do with the dinner?, I've got a great desire to know Rio de Janeiro, his daughter explained, and then, with all that sea between us, the guy certainly won't be bothering me, someone off camera must have been signaling the captain to speed up his speech or get off or shut up, because the eyes of the man in uniform kept turning away from us and his forehead became wrinkled, and the words were swallowing each other up, shapeless, like carnivorous insects, the man turned his head to the side, gesticulated, protested, and the signal was abruptly cut off, once again the little grains of light, once again the mobile, unstable scintillating dots, the national flag for a few seconds, a female announcer speaking with an artificial smile, introducing some movie or other, They've switched the transmission to Oporto, Major Fontes said, the best thing would be to hold off on the telegram, Brigadier sir, because the armed forces are giving tit for tat, cartoon perils began to follow one upon the other on the screen, What a poorly handled coup d'etat, boys, my mother commented disdainfully, aren't you people in the Army even capable of making a revolution in manners?,

The chiefs aren't answering, Brigadier sir, the sergeant announced, holding the phone like a hand-held showerhead, there's probably nobody at the palace, They've sneaked out, the lieutenant colonel thought, smiling, all that's needed is a little intrigue, threats, troops in the streets, armored vehicles, and they evaporate beautifully with a box of foreign decorations under their arms and their pockets bulging with military commendations and newspaper clippings where they're shamelessly called the Saviors of the Nation, Pillars of Democracy, Strenuous Defenders of the Poor, Lucid and Energetic Guides of All True Portuguese, weeklies mellifluously flatter their intelligence and courage and the guys with fire in their asses, dark glasses, and fake Carnival mustaches, fleeing to Spain, fleeing to France, crossing the border stumbling over stones, slipping on the weeds, falling into ditches, muddied and upset, scared by the Guard patrolling the area with fixed bayonet, scared by the barking of dogs in the silent darkness of farms, scared by the wind in the trees and the silhouettes of bushes, scared by the river and its unexpected, fleeting glimmers in the dark, the water murmuring like blood in the vein of a schist, the tiny shape of a rabbit scurrying among roots, and our decorations lost amid pine needles, our commendations cast aside in the panic of retreat, forgetting our composure, our slow dignity, our indisputable historic importance, Make your son behave, Dona Elisa, Colonel Ricardo requested, because even with the Nation in danger, he still hasn't stopped smiling.

"He must have met her at some boardinghouse on Intendente," the concierge said, her eyes white with hate, panting. "One of those boardinghouses for bitches in heat where fine ladies open their legs, groaning with hunger, for automobile mechanics and house painters."

Not at a boardinghouse, friend, the lieutenant colonel thought, scratching his groin in front of the television set while Lieutenant Cardoso was trying in vain (Goddamn it, they've cut the lines) to telephone home to cancel the dinner, the lobster, and the in-laws: not on Intendente, friend, not on Santa Marta, not in Monsanto, not on the Avenida, not on the street or in taverns with exuberant transvestites and discreet pimps huddling in the shadows by the bar with the outline of their switchblades showing on their pants pockets and long, vigilantly pensive hair, but on one of those absurd chance occasions that has presented itself to me, but only because one afternoon, coming out of the Ministry, hands in my pockets and nose to the stones of the pavement, sick and tired of cleanups, of trials, of papers, of notes, under the arcade I bumped into an aging blindman who was playing the trumpet on a canvas stool, and the blindman, in turn, opening and closing his arms like a great unbalanced bird, fell, giving off a pitiful C sharp, against the knees of a lady with well-groomed hair and a fur coat, loaded down with packages, which buried the musician with their many ribbons, their countless bows, their silky silvered paper, with the tremendous flat sound of a wall collapsing, and up in my face, indignant and complaining, there arose a thick fog of perfume in which the pearls on a necklace were vaguely shining, in the distance like a ship's lights, a jaw coated with cream quivering with anger, two imprecise eyes in a mist of cologne, furious first and appraising afterward, a wrist replete with permanent bracelets hesitating halfway between me and her precious items, and there below, on the ground, far away from us, the blind-man feeling around, ass in the air, for his trumpet and stool, with his scaly hands deformed by gout, advancing and retreating, just like dying corollas, in the spittle, trash, cigarette butts, dog droppings, and bits of paper on the sidewalk.

"Love at first sight, Father?" his daughter jested, putting her glass of vermouth down beside the picture of the dead woman and her pale, sad smile, which, little by little, was fading in its frame. "Fine, Father, congrat-ulations, when are you going to introduce me to my stepmother?"

"You really used yourself up in a hurry, Colonel," the second lieutenant commented. "Only four whores, seriously? In Mozambique you could take on two black women each time and still have enough of a hard on left for another shot."

"There's no way I can get through," Lieutenant Cardoso was afflicted, dialing the telephone number with the tip of a pencil for the thousandth time. "Everybody sitting at the table waiting, my mother- and father-in-law, my cousins, the couple from upstairs, an engineer and his wife that I don't even know, and no vol-au-vent, no hazelnut mousse, no Newburg, no pine-apple, no me: my missus will be sure to have a fit, thinking I ran the car into a wall."

"It seems that an armored column from the Commando Regiment is on its way to Belém," the sergeant informed in a whisper, covering the mouthpiece of the instrument with his hand. "It seems they're trying to screw up the Cavalry units there into an about face."

"Dona Elisa," Colonel Ricardo threatened, "you must know that if your son doesn't have the slightest respect for me and doesn't stop laughing, I'll give him a good whack."

"She reads too many books, sir, she's had bad advice, she wants to start revolutions in Cambodia, just imagine, she considers herself a feminist," the son-in-law bleated in a little voice that was slowly threading its way through the words like water from a broken pipe on the lumpy surface of the floor. "Nonsense like that, you see, her fellow workers feed her and she swallows it without chewing, like an ostrich swallowing a monkey wrench. What am I going to do now, please tell me, with the balcony people?"

"I'll make it rough for her," the concierge guaranteed, making her son blow his nose furiously. "I might make it rough for myself, but by the health of this little bastard, I'll make it rough for her first."

"Artur, Artur," his mother nagged as she followed the cartoon with benevo-

lent distraction, waving her gloved forefinger from her easy chair. "Do you
want to go a whole month without candy?"

I helped her pick up the packages, in some of which bits and pieces of
chinaware were rattling around, hailing a soldier on duty I called for one of
the Ministry's huge, imposing black Mercedes cars, with seat covers torn and
burned by the lighted tips of cigarettes, I shoved all that broken pottery, the
ribbons sagging now and the paper torn, onto the front seat, the cloud of
perfume got in behind the driver, murmuring thanks that I didn't understand
too well, I beg your pardon again, ma'am, my mind was completely somewhere else, and he remained in the shade of the arcade, touching a birthmark, watching the car with little fringed curtains on the rear window
disappear slowly, regally into the traffic on the square, Might I know what
you've got against Brazil? my daughter asked acidly, a ferry went off, mooing
from its bridge, the blindman finally found his trumpet, set himself up with
difficulty on his canvas seat, tried a tango, still wobbly from fright, pushing
with his dirty fingernails on the instrument's bruised keys, the gulls flew over
the boat shouting the protesting sobs of a child, and all of a sudden there
came to mind the far-off years when I made love to you in your parents' place
in Seixal in a faded building beside the river that always reminded me,
leaning like that, old like that, cracked and falling apart like that of the
remains of a shipwreck, full of furniture eaten by fish, by algae, and by the
teeth of the water, inhabited by people with wrinkled faces, porous and hard
like pumice, floating in the posture of the drowned in the thick pestilential
vapor that came up from the bank and entered in cloudy rolls through the
disjointed windows that hung on their hinges like molars with pyorrhea from
the thin sponge of their gums. The Tagus was a repugnant narrow band of
mud, squeezed in by decrepit walls and factory chimneys, in which small fat-
bellied boats languished, the remains of ancient docks reduced to caries-
ridden wooden beams, and sickly birds shivered in the recesses of building
façades, the sun struggled painfully against the reddish, almost solid mist of
afternoon, your grandmother, just like a folded piece of coral, was putting
down roots in the living room right in front of us, keeping watch with her
fierce little octopus eyes over my desire for you, an underwater parrot moved
to one side on its perch like the figures on Egyptian frescoes, emitting the
cooing of a dolphin from time to time, and there was some indefinable thing
of an anemone, some absurd thing of a ray fish about your gestures, you must
have had mussels or limpets or marine insects or tiny crabs under your arms,
in your groin, the little parlor was like a greenish fishbowl full of pebbles with
its knickknacks and vases of flowers that the ebb tide tilted in the direction of
the channel, you spoke to me and no sound reached my ears except that of
the tongues of water breaking listlessly against the hulls, the keels, and the
sides of the boats, your mouth tasted like dry seagull shit, the river could be
heard in the conch shells of your ears, your father's one-day beard repro-

duced itself like moss on the rocks, the bicycles they pedaled on the road went up and down like quivering shadows, like the strange streaks that run rippling along the sandy bottoms of lakes, night was falling and the village was decorated like the deck of a ship, the houses dissolved, the factories withdrew, the albatrosses fell asleep on the hanging rain branch of a cloud, hundreds of lines of glass drops hovering lightly over the roofs like faces over a cradle, the lights of Lisbon throbbed in a scattered, elongated, horizontal, endless swarm, running at sea level to Cascais, you said goodbye at the door and your skirt billowed out like gills, the lieutenant colonel, an officer candidate at the time, would take the last bus, the last ship to the city, and there behind, in back of me, Seixal sank with a sigh, with its skeletons of ships and shipwrecked houses, into the mud of the Tagus, until nothing was left but a flock of stupefied doves with no cornices to drop anchor on, and a great black hole in place of the buildings from which there arose, resting on nothing, the huge ash gray willows of absolute oblivion.

"The Commandos knocked down the gates at the Lancers Regiment with tanks and invaded the post, Brigadier sir," the sergeant, who was whispering questions into the telephone alerted him. "It seems there are wounded, it seems there are dead, it seems that there's hellish pandemonium in Belém."

"I can't come to dinner," Lieutenant Cardoso roared, "I'm on urgent duty here, the best thing is for you to send for the lobster Newburg at the restaurant, it's already paid for. No, I'm not lying and I don't know how long I'll be held up, I'll explain it all later. Yes, something at a very high level, a serious matter."

"What's she like, how old is she, what's her name, what does she do?" the daughter asked in one breath. "Seriously, Father, when are you going to introduce me?"

"Do you think I've got nothing better to do than chase after women?" Lieutenant Cardoso shouted into the telephone, indignant. "Do you think I've got any spare time for fooling around?"

"Why don't they let us know what's going on the way they should, Dona Elisa?" Colonel Ricardo protested, turning around in his chair, "Why haven't they summoned me up there to the High Command, with some general wailing in my face The situation is the following and the following and the following, this, that, and the other thing are happening, we're going to do, or we're doing, or we've done A and B and C? In spite of everything we're the Officer Personnel Section of the Ministry, goddamn it, not a pile of garbage they can shit on from up there. If a comrade stops by for news, the commander of a Military District, for example, what are we going to tell him, answer me that? And now what's that idiot son of yours still smiling at?"

Two or three days later (two days, hour by hour, he remembered perfectly, two days of notes and reports and file cards and crosses and pencil marks in the margins of the cases) the telephone rang in a different way (Or is it me just imagining that it was a different way?) in the cubicle, the thick Beira accent of the switchboard corporal announced A lady for you, Colonel, do you want to take it, Colonel? explosions, a kind of sandpapering that hurt his ears and head and reverberated down his spine, a double click, Please, and almost immediately a female voice, relaxed, polished, sure of itself, I wanted to thank you for the automobile ride on Thursday, Colonel, I wanted to thank you for your kindness.

"And it's not just the balcony man," the son-in-law insisted, desperate, "it's the car insurance, it's the deed to the apartment, it's the thousand and one bothersome little things that are pending and have to be resolved, orders at the grocery store, bank account, my clothes that she sent to the cleaners which I can't pick up because I haven't got the stubs, the address book she took off with, the bathroom faucet that needs fixing, the bottle opener I can't find even in God's right hand, the maid who's even stealing the detergent and bathroom disinfectant from me. For God's sake tell her I love her and try something, sir, see if you can make her come back."

"That fashion designer wants to eat his meat but she'll have to gnaw on the bones too," the concierge predicted in a threatening cackle. "She'll spend whole nights like me, playing the mandolin on his dick until she gets it excited."

"It's always the same old tune, Jesus," Lieutenant Cardoso sighed, lifting his eyes to the ceiling. "Where are you going? Who are you with? Do you think I don't know anything about your life? And crying, and complaining, and threatening, and hollering, as if I were a movie actor, as if I were the best lay in the world. I swear, I've had it up to here with her jealousy."

"There's nothing to thank me for, ma'am, I'm the one who should ask you to forgive me, ma'am, of course I'm more than ready to pay you for the damage I caused, ma'am": and a vaguely pleasant lift in spirits, the words were difficult, sticking in his throat, the blue pencil drawing arabesques on a petition, and also the fear that she would suddenly hang up and leave him all alone again, sustained by mountains of paper in the cubbyhole of an office, organizing methodically, in detail, conscientiously Colonel Ricardo's promotion to general. And the difficult sentences, the absence of any agility with his tongue, the plaque on his teeth that threatened to come pouring down with every syllable from the roof of his panic-stricken mouth: "If I damaged anything, if I broke anything, if I crushed anything, I'll make it up to you, ma'am."

"One dead, two wounded, the Lancers Regiment in their pocket in less time than you can strike a match, no support from units in the provinces," the sergeant said. "With this action the communists have lost the game, Brigadier."

Don't leave yet, talk to me about yourself, chat with me, the perils of the film continued uninterrupted on the television, the radio programs continued indifferently, as on normal days. Are you really certain there's been a coup d'etat, Quaresma?, Colonel Ricardo asked the sergeant on the telephone, are you really certain that the fellows haven't been having some fun?, You don't break up a home just like that, the son-in-law argued, you don't just leave a man all alone to take care of things, if only I knew a little something about cooking, it wouldn't be so bad, sir, No need for that, answered the nimble voice that gradually melted his bones with its wise tone that grew soft (And I caught her smell, he whispered to me, and I could see her eyes, and I rubbed my face on the silvery hairs of her fur coat), I'm the one who doesn't know how to repay your kindness, Colonel, people are so rude today that frankly I wasn't prepared for a gesture like yours, Try Pontinha, Quaresma, Major Fontes suggested, it might be that they've got some concrete information there, There was an opening in London, his daughter said, but it rains all year round there, no thank you, and I never did like blond men, the lieutenant colonel fished through his pockets, took out a bill, put it in the blindman's cap, and went back inside with his hands in his pockets, If you'll allow me, the best way to repay me will be for you to let me invite you to dinner, and then, to myself, I fucked up, I moved too fast, I'm going to get a great big no thrown in my face, Pontinha is a good idea, Colonel Ricardo backed him up, Quaresma, invent some pretext, a message, an urgent dispatch, and let me know if you come up with something from there, and, crossing the Tagus, Seixal didn't exist anymore, no bulb, no light, no vague glimmer of beacons, everything submerged, you see, he told me, everything, an old Spanish galleon under hundreds of feet of water that a tenuous, dusty glow haloed, the deck, the staterooms with their worn velvet, the broken forecastle of the bow, and there below, in the hold, your parents' living room with large chairs devoured by the scarlet hunger of lobsters, the curtains floating weightlessly in a boreal transparency of algae, the skeleton of your grandmother with a crocheted diaper dangling, like an apron, from the bones of the pelvis, and your fleshless arm still waving to me from the door the gelatinous and insubstantial goodbyes of an octopus.

"Don't sell our commander short, Lieutenant," the soldier scolded, "two lays a night are duck soup for him."

In any case, since you already got the idea, allow me to take the initiative of the invitation, the voice now tenderly nauseating like the dark sugar dregs at the bottom of a demitasse of coffee proposed, and the cubbyhole immediately grew larger, the row of leprous buildings all the way to the Sodré docks suddenly took on an inexplicable charm, the future became tinged with unexpected diffuse and strong hopes, and I pictured vast, smooth extensions of carpet (Oh, no, ma'am, absolutely not, it wasn't my intention to take advantage of you), tufted pillows on the floor (Of course I like fish soufflé, it's my favorite dish), niches in the wall full of Chinese pottery (No, I won't get lost, I know the street quite well), the bell echoed four or five musical notes in the extension of the apartment, the beginning of a song, like some automobile horns, a dog barked with anxious hate, sniffing the door, a brief electrical silence of timidity, expectation, fingers tightening his necktie, checking his shirt, smoothing his suit, They hung up on me, Brigadier, the sergeant complained, they hollered at me that they weren't giving any explanations to any communists, and there was the cloud of perfume smiling at him in the vestibule, long earrings and an evening gown, and my own face, pale, surprised, afflicted, in the imposing mirror in a carved frame, there was the solitary body and the hands without any belt to drop anchor onto, Me a communist?, Colonel Ricardo said, outraged, me a communist? tell me Quaresma, who was the son of a bitch who answered the phone? the lapdog was leaping hysterically around the woman, running, standing up, going off, coming back, and beyond the archway the lieutenant colonel could make out a long tablecloth on a table that was completely set, cut-glass tumblers, two lighted candles whose flames leaned in my direction, If my parents only dreamed of it, they'd cut me off, sir, the son-in-law whimpered, they'd lose interest in me, sir, you know how northern families are, sir, Dona Elisa, honestly, Colonel Ricardo asked the old woman, no, seriously, answer me as honestly as you can, do you think I look like a communist? he wiped his shoes on the mat, took a step forward, coughed, stiffly offered her the cellophane and the tulips and the ribbon like a marshal serving an attachment, I swear I've never seen such a pretty bouquet, the woman thanked him with the undulating murmur of a dove, why did you bother just because of me?, Communists, Dona Elisa, how unfair can they get, Colonel Ricardo was furious, accusing us of being communists and here we are courageously engaged, day after day, in a battle to the death against Marxism-Leninism, she put the bouquet in a porcelain vase, leaned back to catch the effect, lightly arranged the petals with her hands like a hairdresser perfecting a permanent, Whoever says two lays is saying seven or eight, Lieutenant, the soldier generously multiplied, his necktie over his shoulder, drinking the others' champagne with voracious speed, in matters of dicks our commander is king, What's wrong with Brazil? the daughter was surprised, the set-up is great, the pay is great, they're giving me a place rent-free in Leblon, Call me Edite, the cloud of perfume suggested, as her buttocks floated, hanging over the carpet, inflating and deflating to the rhythm of her steps in her ball gown (the skin of her naked back glimmered softly under the straps like the pink water of a bay of flesh), and now, Mr. Lieutenant Colonel, don't you want to disclose your name to me?, Her mania for jealousy, her mania about lovers, her mania that I've got nothing better to do than get involved with someone, Lieutenant Cardoso was angry, rolling along with rage, one of these days I swear I'm going to ask for a divorce and cut off this sickness at the root, Artur is great, it fits you to a tee, the woman cooed, wasn't there a prince, or a general, or some emperor called Artur?, Fontes, Colonel Ricardo bellowed, send a telegram off for me right away to Pontinha affirming in the strongest terms our repudiation of Moscow ideology, a white sofa with a low table, glass topped and covered with shells and fashion magazines, between two easy chairs, also white, at right angles to the sofa, a record player boxed into a bookcase, and frames with pictures, syrupy violin music as in restaurants, small aperitif glasses on a Chinese tray, A drink, Artur, while dinner is warming? and the aggressive smell of her crossed legs, the strong smell of her neck, the almost solid smell of her round shoulders, Who's the dame who's made a pimp out of you, confess, the concierge asked, who's the chick, so I can beat her to death?, A firm telegram, see, a kind like democracy yes dictatorship no, The perfume, my God, drinking in her perfume right down to the open space dug between her breasts, The revolution completely defeated, Brigadier, the sergeant on the telephone reported, the leaders under arrest, the paratroopers defeated and on their way back to Tancos, the country reentering its previous normal condition, they interrupted the cartoon, returned the broadcast to Lisbon again, a woman announcer with a calmer smile said that there would be a special newscast shortly, and while they waited, masculine military music flooded the screen, the lieutenant colonel rolled the glass back and forth in his fingers, installed in a corner of the sofa, extremely embarrassed, obstinately staring at a picture that showed a half-naked girl hugging an oversized colt, in the lighted apartments of the building across the way people could be seen bent over dinner, children, the irate gestures of a man ranting, the daughter took off her shoes, dropped them onto the floor, sat down on his legs, Maybe I'll come back from there with a mulatto, Father, a samba dancer, a soccer player, maybe I'll come back from there married to a berimbau player, confess, you'd just adore having little black grandchildren, Commit her, the son-in-law requested, commit her urgently because she can't talk straight, a psychiatrist friend of mine assured me that the only remedy for her is a sleep cure, A sleep cure, Dona Elisa commented, the idiot's gone completely out of his mind, don't you find it the most natural thing in the world for a person to be sick and tired of a man, Brigadier?, You're practically not drinking anything, Artur, the woman laughed, would you rather have some vodka or can it be that my presence is making you nervous?, I'm going to get rid of her jealousy once and for all, Lieutenant Cardoso swore, I'm damned if I won't get rid of her jealousy once and for all, begging the major's pardon but at this moment I really want the Revolution to go fuck itself, I really want the communists to go fuck themselves, I really want the anticommunists to go fuck themselves, the only thing I'm really interested in is for that dame to stop bothering me, driving me crazy, The president of the Republic is going to read a statement to the country, the sergeant announced, it seems that some advisers are going to be interviewed on the radio, That telegram, goddamn it, Colonel Ricardo was getting desperate, that little telegram announcing our unswerving solidarity with the winners, our deep satisfaction with the reestablishment of public order and the existing democratic regime, don't forget to stress Order and Democracy, Quaresma, and even now, is it intentional, Dona Elisa? that idiot son of yours can only smile, And all of us, you see, the lieutenant colonel told me in a low voice, Ricardo, Fontes, Cardoso, the sergeant with the birthmark, the concierge, my old lady, my daughter, my son-in-law, me, weren't in the fancy office at the Ministry, in the midst of its church hangings and its enormous windows, facing the military marches on television, but in Seixal, beside the river, huddled in a circle in the mud of low tide, in the midst of fat-bellied little boats and ancient docks reduced to caries-laden wooden beams, with the eternal birds shivering with grippe in the nauseating recesses of building façades, hazy Lisbon in the distance and a great marine and horizontal silence all around us, while Edite took off her black lace and purple bows in the reddish orange light of dusk, her white, fat body surging up out of her bra, her girdle, her garters, her panties, lying down on her back, moving her legs like a crab on a plank lapped by the last wave, and, above her, the gulls broke away like leaves from the rain branches of the clouds, carelessly shouting the stubborn, cruel, colossal, sharp, infinitely sad, ferocious calls of a castaway.

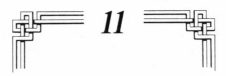

# 11

A F E W days before he'd had lunch with Dália at the Parque restaurant, a small, glassed-in, dirty establishment with iron tables, riding up above the city, clouds of insistent flies always landing on the steak and potatoes, looking out over the rice balls and bowls of lupines at the Avenida descending toward the river and the rooftops that the sky was turning iridescent with a delicate, veined blue transparency, the white, almond-cake splotch of the castle, edible boats within reach of one's fingers poised on the water like milk buns in the cases on the counter. Have you noticed how Lisbon's brightness dissolves, abolishes, subverts distances, Captain, the communications officer asked me, adjusting the frame of his glasses with his forefinger, have you noticed how the person next to us is suddenly miles away physically, with clouds crossing over his ears and temples and factory smoke fogging his eyes, and, on the other hand, the statue of the Marquês de Pombal in a chair next to ours, his rusty imposing presence sipping lemon tea with broad, bronze historic gestures. We ate on the terrace of the Parque, surrounded by shrubbery, drifters, swans, and stray cats, the gravy on the meat and the manager's sweat were similar and mingled, and if the head touched his forehead it would have tasted butterfat and mustard, a fellow in coveralls was lazily watering the grass with a plastic hose and the constant, monotonous, phosphorescent sound of an endless nighttime piss, as when a man gets up in the dark, dopey with phantoms, and the dreams run off without interruption through the opening in his pajamas onto the porcelain of the toilet, and his head weaves weightlessly in the mirrors, and his puffy fingers get entangled in the buttons, bald-headed guys chewed their own noses, their own cheeks, their own lips, skewered on their forks, between potatoes and beef, Dália made a discreet signal with her fork for me to lean over, I want to tell you something very important, pal, my chin hit the saltshaker, What is it? the waiter, who was carrying pieces of chicken just like the toasted thighs of a baby, turned to look at me with the little wrinkles of his eyes, weary from tons of custard puddings and friendly computerized Japanese fairies, and she, in a low voice, covering her mouth with her sleeve, in the pompous tones of the Archangel Gabriel announcing the arrival of the Messiah, We're taking the revolutionary step on November 25th, the days of the bourgeoisie are numbered, comrade.

"And you were so simpleminded you believed it," the second lieutenant said, disgusted. "And you were jackass enough to jump at the chick's words."

"Do you like baked fish, Artur?" the cloud of perfume asked, her carnivorous legs were growing huge in the black mesh stockings through the slit in her dress, completely filling, imposing and soft, the cushions on the sofa. The music from the record player went away from them from time to time, the same way in which the wind sometimes goes to the highest branches of the pines: I bet you're going to fall in love with my recipe for *robalo*.

"I already know that line by heart," the soldier said, "I've heard it whispered by over a thousand girls. It's part of their method to catch us, Commander, it's part of the tricks women use. From that standpoint they haven't got any imagination at all: I learned to cook from my mother, darling, ever since I was a little girl what I've wanted to do most was keep house, sew, iron, dust, wash dishes, it was the necessities of life, you see, that made me take a job, be a secretary, a stenographer, a hairdresser. Wily whore shit, Colonel, lies meant to trick boobs like us. I'd almost swear you let yourself follow the line like a dope, I'd almost swear you married the madam afterward."

I jumped at the chick's words, yes, and I believed in the Revolution, in the fall of the bourgeoisie, in the approaching, imminent final victory of the working class, the communications officer thought, and if after all these years she promised me again any day now the ineffable, sweet, obvious, utopian joys of socialism, I'd believe it again with the same ironclad, unshakable, adolescent conviction, I was ready to go out into the streets, machine gun in hand, singing the "Internationale," ready to shoot every reformist who got close to me, every bearded pro-Soviet type pasting posters on the façades of buildings where nobody lives, with broken windowpanes, green and hollow like rotting teeth. I believed, Captain, Olavo, the cellist, the old man, Baldy, Lopes, the lucid wordy comrades in the Bairro Alto believed, and I spent my time ardently imagining through the windows of the dirty restaurant at the top of the park, beyond the trees, the flocks of geese and the shrubbery without lushness, the deathless working class coming up the Avenida in a frenzy of anthems and flags, pitilessly hanging social democrats, bosses, police, and the lackeys of Capital from lampposts, and proclaiming Marxism-Leninism-Maoism at the Rotunda in the out-of-tune strident sounds of loud-speakers and marches. The castle was slipping down toward the river until it touched the clear luminous back of the water with the transparent fingernails of its crenels.

"So, at seven o'clock, a meeting of the Central Committee at headquarters for the final instructions from the Secretariat," Dália whispered, afraid that the cakes and the Bakelite toothpick plates were listening. "One or two weeks more at most and bourgeois democracy will be all over and revisionist deviators will be finished once and for all."

"How's the fish?" the cloud of perfume leaning over him above the glasses and silverware challenged, her large ever-so-white breasts swinging like censers in her low-cut gown. (It won't be long before she opens her mouth and swallows me, the lieutenant colonel feared, it won't be long before she'll be unceremoniously chewing me as if I were a forkful of *robalo*.) "If you find a dish like that in a restaurant I'll give you a piece of candy."

"I married her, naturally," the lieutenant colonel confessed, "I fell for her like a dope, naturally."

You were talking to me, all excited, all passionate, like an idealist, unrealistically, optimistically, generously, ingenuously, restlessly, stumbling enthusiastically over your words, about vigilance committees in factories, serene union leaderships fighting and going beyond the zigzagging inertia of the undecided and the desperate useless death throes of the right, the unctuous and funereal priests, who would abandon the Nation in a big black boat loaded down with missals, chasubles, and monsignors, a Nazi flag waving at the stern, automobiles replaced by exalted proletarian bicycles, all of us pedaling jovially to offices, stores, docks, workshops, reciting Chinese slogans against hated American imperialism and against the even more hated Soviet imperialism, and what I really liked, Captain, was confessing to her in an antirevolutionary way over the now cold steak and the froth of the beer as it crystallized into a veil of white rings inside the empty glasses, Forget about Marxism-Leninism-Maoism and give me a kiss, forget about Comrade Ho Chi Minh for a minute and come with me for a little something behind the restaurant where the cook throws away his garbage and the dinner leftovers in big metal pails, so I can touch your breasts, so I can touch your stomach, so I can suck on your neck, followed, spied on, peeked at by clusters of tramps and dogs who curl up for the night shivering on dry branches, liquor bottles, filthy rags, and rolled-up newspapers, send the meal away, shit on socialism, lift up your skirts, lie down on the grass, hold what I can feel growing in my shorts and stick it in you with a short, hoarse, isolated animal grunt, into your hold. And instead of that, Captain, instead of paying the check and dragging her outside by the arm, I kept quiet, I didn't say anything, nodded yes, made an effort to be interested too, factory committees of course, union leaders obviously, priests expelled, but what a relief, we're setting up the paradise of authentic popular democracy in rotten Europe, sordid and unlivable, polluted by Coca-Cola, disposable cigarette lighters and bubble gum, undermined by the cancer of multinationals and by the infamous exploitation of liberal economics, let the land be fertilized immediately with the fat intestines, full of the egg sweets, of the rich. I got interested, I approved, I stirred the coffee endlessly with the little tin spoon, and to myself, in secret, I want all this to flop, I want all this to fuck up, what do I care about this, there are some very convenient bushes up there ahead of us, Dália.

"I detest frozen fish," the cloud of perfume said, repeating the dosage with the precious gestures of a goldsmith. "You won't believe a word of it, but I swear to you that I'd rather starve than eat those horrible filets. More lemon, Artur? It's great for the nerves, it's got a lot of vitamin C in it, my father, who was in the merchant marine, would make us suck a whole one every day, without any sugar."

After dinner, the lieutenant colonel thought in panic, a liqueur, a brandy, a cordial, a whiskey, tiny glasses tinkling with ice, the two of us sitting side by side on the sofa, all alone with a pale and intimate light on in the distance there, slowly going away in the oily silence of ships, her body getting up, buttocks swaying, to turn on the radio, to change the record (tangos, sambas, boleros, rhythmical, aphrodisiac maracas), getting closer to me, lightly touching her leg to mine, squeezing her thigh against my pant leg, her large liquid eyes clouding over and staring at me, her mouth opening into a corolla with a piece of peanut husk sticking to her front teeth, her hand casually stroking my fingers on the edge of the ashtray, her breath more and more intense, closer and closer, her oyster-colored eyelids slowly closing (Our commander's a whirlpool, the soldier explained energetically, any pussy that gets too close gets sucked in), and what if I can't make it, I was concerned, what if I can't get it up, what if I'm unable, and what if I cut the usual sad figure I do with the concierge, the check finally came on a scratched plastic saucer, a small pink paper rectangle marred by a sum, the communications officer was going to confess I love you Dália, maybe the bushes right out there opposite, but his voice, without his knowing why, betrayed him, became serious, responsible, alien, asking maoistically What time is the Central Committee meeting, comrade, what time are we going to get instructions from the Secretariat.

"So you never put it in her," the second lieutenant was disgusted, "so you spent God knows how many years watching the trains go by."

"Four," the communications officer was precise. "Or maybe it's still going on, who the hell knows."

## The Revolution

Because sometimes, Dália, I feel very relaxed at the Ministry, working, they tell me There's someone to see you in the hall, and suddenly, how stupid, not wanting it, not thinking about anything, I get the idea in my head It's you, and suddenly I imagine that I'm pushing open the frosted glass of the door and finding you sitting in the vestibule waiting for me, and that you're smiling at me, and that you're talking to me, and that you're going down the stairs with me, Dália, on the way to the street, just like the last time, the last times I saw you, the same forefinger poking me constantly in the chest while you indoctrinated me, the same Marxist ardor, the same leninlike drive, and the same hochiminhesque fever, the same unshakable, utopian faith in an oriental socialism, in a uniform made of ticking, sexes that are differentiated by the bars on their bicycles, and the Great Wall of China crossing the Tagus and snaking through Beiras toward Spain, I suppose, you understand, that I'm quite relaxed at work, the telephone rings, It's for you, I casually reach out my arm Yes, and you Hello, and that day we have lunch again at the Parque restaurant, and that day the flies again, the garbage, the filth, the heat, the haste of the waiters, the case of cakes that stops me from seeing the river, the dust that mingles with the flour, the flour that mingles with the salt, the salt that mingles with the dust, the dogs, the tramps, the beggars, the Gypsies, who always walk like a cat along a wall, the shrubbery that used to be behind the crumbling building, the slanting sun lighting up the branches, the metal trash cans, the bones, the leftovers from meals, you opening my pants and pulling down your panties, putting me

(not that way, wait)

inside you,

your breath on my neck, your fingernails gripping my shoulders with all their strength, it still goes on, Captain, I still carry her around in my head now that I'm living alone on the street by the amusement park amid worm-eaten prie-dieus, withered flowers and large chipped chairs, now that I need someone to clean the rooms and chat with me, warm up my hot-water bottle, serve me tea with lemon if I get a cold, curl her stomach around my stomach in the darkness, defend me against the wooden giraffes on the carousel that roll in and out through the window frames, I'd like you to take a look at a very pretty mother-of-pearl object, Artur, the cloud of perfume sighed, come in here and let me show it to you, and her behind fluctuated and the music lowered its volume, a corridor with prints of birds, the door to the bathroom half-open, imposing gold faucets in the shape of fish, innumerable bottles on glass shelves, and, just as the lieutenant colonel feared, the rectangular, gigantic, huge bed, raised up on a kind of altar or platform with two carpeted steps, the lace bedspread, puffy-cheeked twin pillows leaning against one another like loving heads, a dresser with an oval mirror and more bottles, more perfumes, more tubes, more sprays, more creams, more boxes, more tweezers, the celebrated mother-of-pearl object that was a horrible peacock, almost life sized, perched on a wooden roost, I've had it, the lieutenant colonel realized, all frightened, if I don't quick invent some kidney stones I'm going to undergo an awful humiliation here.

"Comrades (Olavo's voice, tremulous, cavernous, almost funereal, the plaster busts, tremulous, cavernous, almost funereal the characters around the table, tremulous, cavernous, almost funereal) in the name of the Secretariat of the Political Commission, I have the honor to announce to you that as a consequence of our efforts, of our militancy, of our persevering and uncompromising revolutionary work, the death rattle of bourgeois democracy is finally in sight."

"In that case, one whore for each of us," the soldier negotiated, intimate now, fraternally patting the backs closest to him, "and two, of course, for the exclusive use of our commander: respect for rank, bowing to authority, you gentlemen know how it is."

"I've got a lash in my eye, Artur," the cloud of perfume suddenly winked, opening and closing her eyelid, frowning, leaning backward, sticking her fingers desperately into her eyes. "See if you can get it, damn, see if you can get it out."

"The Secretariat of the Political Commission of the Central Committee is expecting us," Olavo added with a baleful intonation, "now that Marxism-Leninism-Maoism is ready to free Portugal from the infamous yoke of the bourgeoisie, the land barons, the estate owners, the capitalists, and the exploiters, to close ranks more than ever, comrades, and complete without cowardice or faintheartedness, unthinkable in a word, the vital tasks on the 25th of November, a date that will be engraved in gold in the annals of Lusitanian History as the bright, shining irreversible glow of the socialist dawn, which we are still committed to, as the legitimate and only vanguard of the working class, peasants, proletariat, and, to sum up, I don't have to stress it, comrades, the immense human mass of the exploited and the oppressed that imperialism has pitilessly produced for decades if not centuries."

"Don't say no, Commander, don't be modest," the soldier was encouraging him tirelessly. "Am I right in saying that two are too few for you?"

"Not that eye, the other one, Artur," the cloud of perfume complained, twisting around like a lizard, stamping her foot on the floor. "And be so kind as not to gouge my breast with your elbow."

"Did you talk to the defenseless," the second lieutenant asked the communications officer, "with all that bullshit chatter?"

The tinfoil ashtrays overflowing with butts (And people understood you? the second lieutenant went on, are you sure people understood you?), the thick smoke burned his eyes, weighed down his head, and made silhouettes and faces hazy, turning them imprecise and neutral, devoid of features (Don't move, ma'am, stay calm, I've almost got it, the lieutenant colonel asked, holding depilatory tweezers at the ready, leaning over the round afflicted pond of an eye), the cellist, with the flippers and rubber suit of a diver under his open shirt, the old man motionless, Dália motionless, the Central Committee motionless with disciplined attention, listening deeply to Olavo's lengthy speech, the dogmatic commonplaces, the pompous phrases bereft of meaning, the usual nauseating inanities, the arm that went up and down rhythmically as if he were directing an invisible chorus, and yet, Captain, the communications officer stammered, suppressing a belch, we'd been arrested, beaten by the police, we'd languished in Caxias, in Peniche, in Lisbon, with fever, with aching bodies, vomiting, urinating blood, inventing a sky different from the one we saw from the window, we went on hunger strikes, held rallies, meetings in factories for half a dozen workers in hard hats, indifferent and apathetic, explanatory sessions to denounce the political situation to guys who weren't listening to us, stretching, yawning, leaving the room before the break, taking more shit, whether from the Soviet revisionists or the other Maoist parties that also claimed for themselves the unlikely title of the legitimate and only vanguard of the oppressed, and on whom, as they did with us, the aforesaid oppressed shat (Of course they understood us, come on, the communications officer answered with conviction, all we needed was for them not to understand us), How can I be quiet if you move away from me, you dog, the cloud of perfume howled, furious, get away and give me the tweezers before you fuck up my eye.

"OK, OK," the soldier conceded, "one apiece and let's drop the subject."

Even the busts, even the banners, even the standards seemed to be fluttering idly in the midst of tobacco smoke, the irregular buildings of the Bairro Alto softened and twisted all around us, darkened, faded, lacking in consistency, made of plastic or wax, diffuse forms moved about outside like fish, and they could have been seagulls, they could have been pigeons, the devout pigeons of churchyards, the senseless pigeons of the Chiado, the hashish-high pigeons on Camões, the gulls that soar, restless, from the river, over roof after roof, searching in vain in eaves, tile statues, cornices, for a ship's mast to perch on, with the help of a blackboard Olavo was explaining the details of the coup, The paratroopers will come from Tancos during the night, they'll take over the Television and the Airport, it's a cinch, the Cavalry Regiment will occupy the radio station, the Lancers will surround Parliament, the troops from Queluz and Encarnação will cover the entrances to the city, the Navy is traditionally on the left and there won't be any problems there, the population of Amadora, comrades, will neutralize the Commandos' headquarters by means of a stiff barricade of trucks and pickups, and our shock units will be responsible, along with the indispensable task of inciting and giving moral support to our bases, of encouraging those who are hesitant, sensitizing the undecided (and the smoke was so thick now that they couldn't make each other out, they seemed to be just vague, gassy shapes without any form) for the following specific missions, comrades, for the proper fulfillment of which you will receive the usual water pistols and bean machine guns, gulls crossed paths with the blue-tailed peacocks on the battlements of the Castle and turned their heads this way and that, beaks open, and hard white tongues out, surprised by the absence of water, How can I grab the lash, you lump, the lady in the evening gown was impatient, if you can't even hold a shitty mirror the right way.

"I hope that in spite of the flop of the bank robbery they won't insist on splitting us up," Dália's voice whispered to him hopefully, coming from nowhere like that of *arvéloas* in boulders, diminished by the dark brown thickness of tobacco. "After so much training they can't deny us a second chance, hell, they can't deny us showing them what we're worth."

"Say, child," his godmother asked him from the corridor, lovingly dusting some fifty bald Saint Anthonys made of plaster, stone, small shells, plastic, aluminum, cloth. "You haven't got mixed up in politics, have you?"

On Saturdays and Sundays the Nineteenth Combat Brigade Mao Zedong, or in other words, the old man, the cellist, Dália, Olavo, and I, driven by a fervent, unwavering guerrilla enthusiasm (Maybe there wasn't any other brigade, the second lieutenant suggested perfidiously, maybe you and your buddies were the only Chinamen in Lisbon), would get together at ten o'clock in the morning, in tennis shoes and red gym suits, with the initials of the Organization on the back, in the fourth-floor apartment of the musician on Santa Iria da Azóia, two tiny, dusty little rooms full of lined paper and instrument cases, with an extremely ugly Beethoven, looking like Karl Marx without a beard, angry on the wall, the sounds of automobile horns and the rustling of trees from the small square down below, and the domestic noises of the neighbors, toilets flushing, children, cutlery, anger, and coughing coming through the walls, we tacked up a target on the door frame, we twisted our faces up into snipers' masks, we shot off frantic chicken feed with the tin-plate shotguns in the direction of the silhouettes of heads drawn on paper, we would apply judo grips to each other from the manual *How to Tear Your Boss to Pieces in Ten Easy Lessons*, we invented a secret vocabulary for the use of the group, from which we were constantly forgetting the words, we went downstairs in twos, under the orders of exhausted, wheezing sighs from Olavo, on whose cheeks an anemic trace of a beard was trying to grow now, and we jogged one or two blocks outside (closed shops, glimmering dim barber poles, garage entrances, a Jehovah's Witnesses temple in a cellar where illuminated and severe creatures dropped down morosely), watched indifferently or attentively by policemen, pursued by the barking of dogs, jeered at by youths, their upper lips dirty with mustaches, who were shining shoes on café terraces, we would return staggering, salivating anthems, to the musician's apartment, losing our footing on the chicken feed or slipping on the puddles from the water pistols, and we would settle down into ancient, precarious chairs with broken straw seats, arguing about tactics and inventing attacks over maps of tissue paper, colored with arrows, lines, and crosses, vehement, energetic, happy (Happy, the lieutenant colonel was surprised, happy about what?), gorging vitamins for the muscles, effervescent tablets against fatigue, which dissolved in the glasses into geysers of bubbles, going madly up and down, getting smaller and smaller until they disappeared in one last whispered little cusp: and Dália's little-bird voice, coming from nowhere, diminished by the thickness of the smoke, God willing, they won't break us up now, after all this hard work.

"When are you going to cast out the sin of communism and become a proper person?" his aunt asked, crossing herself before a huge Saint Expeditus, masquerading as a Roman centurion, who was making love to an ivory Archangel Michael with the honeyed silk of its eyes. "You won't rest until you've got all of us in the poorhouse."

"The Chinese worship gods with eight legs," Esmeralda explained, "they bathe in a very filthy river and fill the streets with white calves. I can't understand your inclination toward them, you never liked cows that much, child."

"Hey, man, step back there for a second, goddamn it, just don't move for a second," the evening gown commanded in desperation. "If I don't get this bitching lash out, we're going to spend the night at the São José Hospital."

The lieutenant colonel drew back three paces, he knocked over a vase with his elbow and it shattered on the floor (Damn it, Artur, shit on you, you only came here to play the jackass), he ended up dropping down, sitting on the edge of the bed, but he leaped up instantaneously for fear that he would step on something fragile and precious, while the woman in the mirror, tongue out, pulling and pushing back her eyelids covered with blue dust, extracted a thick bristle from herself and by herself with the nickel-plated tweezers that suddenly gave off sharp, surgical flashes, which she displayed triumphantly all around, to the indifference of the portraits and the melancholy fringes of the lampshades, like a bullfighter showing off the award of an ear to the thousands of handkerchiefs, coats, applauses, and hats in an excited bullring.

"Brigades Four, Five, Six, and Seven," Olavo's voice recited, drawn out in the haze, having difficulty cutting through successive opaque waves of smoke, "will back up the encirclement of Commando headquarters, leading sympathizers and consolidating bases, and preventing the inevitable and most dangerous infiltration by counterrevolutionaries and fascists."

"Evidently they haven't changed the combat groups," Dália was happy, also dim and distant. "Evidently we're going to work together again."

"I got it, I got it, I got it," the cloud of perfume shouted to the lieutenant colonel, fastened to the thick pile of the rug as if screwed in, "Gosh, Artur, what a relief, don't be grumpy, come give me a big old kiss to celebrate."

"Brigades Twelve and Thirteen," Olavo said in the neutral tone of a press release, "will take an active part in the attack on radio stations, furnishing our revolutionary military comrades all the logistical help needed, and maintaining constant contact with our headquarters for that purpose."

"What a complicated business, Lieutenant," the soldier was impressed. "Was it really the way you're telling it, seriously?"

Seriously? the communications officer thought with a toothpick halfway between the plate and his teeth, seriously the smoke, seriously the books, dirty and creased by fingers, read and reread and discussed and underlined, seriously the aggressive posters with fists in the air, the pamphlets, militant words scratched on walls, the little mimeographed newspaper, the discouraging sessions at factory entrances for indifferent workers, the eternally failed attempts to fight illiteracy in shantytowns with the idea of converting them later, the way missionaries in Africa did with little black children who were doomed to hell, to Marxism-Leninism-Maoism, saving them from the gloomy capitalist purgatory with its demoniacal agents and its diabolic leaders, we would take along notebooks, pencils, erasers, greasy multiplication tables, a scratched blackboard, we would set things up in the midst of the dust, the tin roofs, the Gypsies' lame donkeys, the garbage, the rat shit, the barking of the dogs, and the mineral mistrust of the old people, we would begin by teaching the vowels and nobody listened to us, A Apple, E Elephant, I Ink, O Oats, U Uncle, women with slack haunches were dumping out enameled bowls from the doorways of the houses, a drunk was leaning against a tree snoring, ash gray sheep were grazing on the pieces of paper that the wind was blowing to and fro, Dália was writing fervent capital letters on the blackboard, children with restless adult eyes paused, examining her thighs, Dália repeated the letters didactically, looking at them, guys in undershirts were sitting near us on kitchen stools, chatting, spitting, playing cards, taking swigs from a wicker-cased jug, a turkey was dragging its emphysema around us, the drunk was thrashing about in his sleep, upset by horrible nightmares of cities without bars, A Apple, E Elephant, I Ink, O Oats, U Uncle, the cellist bellowed, furious, trying to get away from a dog that was growling at his shins, we ended up in defeat, gathering up our notebooks, pencils, erasers, greasy multiplication tables, and the scratched blackboard, we went down the steep, dug-out walkways, stepping on calf dung and long widow skirts, toward the bus stop beside the wire fence around the campground where Swedes in shorts communicated in a soda-water language under huge eucalyptus trees that smelled of empty throat lozenge boxes, number 42 arrived with a whinny of brakes, the automatic door opened with the whistle of an asthmatic blowing out the candles on a birthday cake, we got in, clutching the rail, wiping our shoes on the metal steps, and we disappeared, puzzling over our cultural defeat with every painful, piercing break or bump in the pavement on the way to the tumbledown headquarters building, eternally wrapped in a haze of tobacco smoke from the members of the Central Committee, where the red flag hung, defeated, on its staff, without the shouts of the street vendors and the arguments of neighbor women to awaken it to its erect and heroic future as leader of the oppressed masses.

"Was it serious?" the communications officer asked, offended. "Was it serious? Of course it was serious, idiot, in the Organization there was no playing around: us, for example, they ordered us to kidnap the president of the Republic, see?"

"Oh, Artur, this doesn't seem like you," the cloud of perfume meowed, trying to drive the bewildered lieutenant colonel in the direction of the bed. "Don't be afraid of me, I won't eat you."

"And while we're at it, why not the pope?" the second lieutenant suggested, a bottle of champagne in each hand, the back of his neck leaning on the mulatto woman's broad shoulder. "And while we're at it, why not the Dalai Lama? Or the prior of Beato? Or the big boss of the CIA? Or my mother-in-law for a little variety? You can't imagine the lift you people would give me if you kidnapped my mother-in-law."

"I bet you're kidding us, Lieutenant," the soldier said. "As far as I know the president of the Republic was never kidnapped, as far as I know nobody was daring enough to try that."

"And how have you people arranged for us to get into the palace?" the old man was interested. "They must have a whole army of sentries at the gate."

"That's not it," the lieutenant colonel sighed, catching his breath, kicking about on the bedspread, pushing away lace, bracelets, and locks of hair. "It's your necklaces that are hurting my neck."

"Wearing the uniforms of Venezuelan brigadier generals," Olavo elucidated, opening a trunk full of military uniforms from 1914 and tin Yugoslavian decorations, prizes from packages of baby cereal. "We'll go along there to the guy's office, calmly, at a stately procession pace, with pistols in our pockets, salutes to the left, salutes to the right, what dummy is going to be suspicious of us?"

"The president of the Republic, imagine that," the second lieutenant complained. "That's the way friends are: instead of getting rid of my mother-in-law for me, which, besides being much simpler (getting to her house, a few little shots and that's that), would be doing me a personal favor, you decided to lay hands on the relative of a stranger."

"I'm going to be the ambassador from Denmark," the cellist decreed, anxiously rummaging, as at a sale, through the contents of the trunk. "Isn't there a diplomatic outfit here, a jacket, a sword, a peasant's cap at least?"

"Open the clasps and take them off," the cloud of perfume ordered urgently, slinking along the bedspread, twirling the pathetic, exaggerated billiard balls of her eyes, surrounded by the hanging wire threads of her huge lashes: Now I really am caught, damn it, the lieutenant colonel thought, all upset, now I really am screwed up. Her hands were furiously opening the neck of her dress, lifting the skirt, urgently tearing at the black frills of her panties: "Open all the clasps of my body, Artur, put your tongue in my ear, squeeze my thighs, kiss my breasts, hurry up and take off your shirt and tie, so I can feel your muscles, lick your chest, feel myself branded (Did you ever

hear such nonsense? he was resigned, did you ever hear such foolishness?)
by your hot iron."

"Why not like a lady from Seville with a bun and a comb in your hair?"
Olavo was angry, generously distributing epaulettes around while remnants
of ribbons fell softly to the floor. "Do you think this is a masked ball or
something?"

"I can't believe it," the soldier was appalled. "The lieutenant mixed up in a
mess like that?"

"My mother-in-law should have been the one," the second lieutenant
insisted, enthusiastic, "if my mother-in-law was set up and then, with the
whole family cooperating with you, it would have been all the easier if you
took on the little job. Me, for example, I'd take charge of poisoning the dogs
with a couple of little chops laced with cyanide. I can just picture the
monsters puking up their guts in the garage, wow, rolling around in convul-
sions in the midst of old tires and unfinished ships."

"The boy goes around not saying anything, he won't take any phone calls,"
Esmeralda said, apprehensive, preparing the dietary roasts in the kitchen.
"There's nothing serious going on, is there?"

"The Danish ambassador or nothing," the cellist griped, trying some rusty
gentleman bullfighter's spurs on his tennis shoes. "With a riding crop, a
dictionary, a unicorn, and a Swedish accent, nobody will be able to tell that I
haven't just arrived from Copenhagen."

"What a delightfully loving little thing, such a tiny little thing, so loving,"
the cloud of perfume whimpered, poking with the tips of her fingernails
through the lieutenant colonel's terrified fly. "Come here, my jewel, my
pretty, Mama's going to make you big in a minute."

"When are we going to take the dames to your place?" the lieutenant
colonel asked the second lieutenant. "As for me, I've got tangos and waltzes
and stripteases coming out of my ears."

"We should arrange for a black car, with curtains and smoked glass, the
kind cabinet ministers use," Dália proposed. "Everybody respects a cabinet
minister's car."

Of course it was serious, Captain, the communications officer affirmed
energetically, inviting the magician's assistant over to the table with gestures
to smoke, drink, and eat (and no life in the apartment by the amusement park
anymore, where silence coagulates over the surface of things like curdled
milk, except for me, and no one enjoys the shadow of the wooden horses that
rolls around the walls, and no one chats anymore with the portraits of the
dead so that their smiles will grow, like sweet pale plants, in the sad vases of
their picture frames, no one gets the Bakelite float of the toilet fixed when it's
out of order, no one except me lights the angry blue marigolds of gas on the
stove with a timid match), of course we got dressed up in a serious way, the
old man, Olavo, and I as Venezuelan brigadiers, covered with tinfoil medals,

gilt cords and Christmas tree decorations, colored sashes and rubber daggers (only me listening to the silence on the surface of things, only me sniffing the immobility of the dog asleep behind the closed doors), the cellist with his plumed hat, crushed and shaped characteristically for ambassadors from Denmark, dragging along the floor over his diver's suit the cloak of a typically Nordic chamberlain, the wooden rings of which kept hitting each other and clicking, and Dália, furnished with such thick glasses that they blinded her and made her constantly bump into the corners of furniture, stationed beside the musician with a pencil in one hand and a pad in the other, taking without pause the quick, continuous stenographic notes of a perfect secretary. Of course it was serious, Captain (but the smell of the rooms changed as the flowers went on dying, the buds spread out over the pieces of dry mortar, the old dresses hung, unused, on the racks in the closet like snakeskins on the branches of trees, and not just the smell, the light as well, that dim clarity alighting, yellowed, as if in the now transparent thick innards of objects, and not just the light but the taste of food, the smell of dinner's beef boiling in the pot, the taste of the water, the watch taste of the morning toothpaste), of course it was serious, Captain, we went down the groaning wooden stairs that twisted and protested, alive, like great worn-out lizards, under our shoes, we took a taxi at the Largo do Camões in order to avoid at least a repetition of the sad catastrophe of the bank robbery, the driver looked us over with wonder, people stood stock-still on the street examining us, astounded, the magnificent mixture of outfits, Dália, standing stiffly behind her glasses, was stumbling all over the place like a blind cockroach, clutching her pad, two ladies in leopard jackets were following us openmouthed (Say, Artur, the cloud of perfume asked, intrigued, twisting her fingers obstinately on the definitively dead tool of the lieutenant colonel, does this happen to you all the time or did the dinner hit your weak spot?), The Belém Palace, Olavo ordered with a heavy South American accent, the Danish ambassador, in front of us, was holding his snorkel like a scepter, a little Ping-Pong ball at the tip imprisoned in a kind of rubber birdcage, we went along the 24 de Julho down a slope of antique stores and lawyers' plaques dispensing art nouveau advice to their clients on the second floor, a square, traffic lights, the stifling nearness of the river, broad dark buildings gnawed by greenish caries, sciatic trolley cars limping along on their rails, Orglup flipknoque zbntz? the cellist asked, pointing to the Bridge with a curious forefinger, Schulptmn trzbz glop glop, Dália explained, ceaselessly writing, the driver, most startled, turned off the car radio in order to listen better, Damn it, the old man whispered, I forgot my heart pills back there, Don't even think about going back, Olavo hissed, unswerving, when the final victory of socialism is at stake, Klpt brozni glapniox, the ambassador solemnly approved, the taxi driver, a bald middle-aged man, was trying to locate us in the rearview mirror with his startled little eyes and kept getting his gears mixed up (But this little cock of yours is stubborn, Artur, the cloud of perfume commented, redoubling her zeal, the little devil, the more kisses I give it, the smaller it gets), we turned left with a jerk, right, left again, one-story houses now, deserted little bars, a soccer field gobbled up by underbrush, low garden walls, the old man took off his cap with a straw visor and felt his sides, unsuspected wrinkles were growing on his cheeks, This is beginning to hurt like the devil, word of honor, stop at a drugstore so I can buy some pills, Long live undying Marxism-Leninism-Maoism, Olavo snapped back at him, unmoved, Tlac tlac problium psblt? the Danish diplomat was nervous, rocking back and forth on his worried behind on the seat, Drgt zzzzzzzz flop gugu, Dália advised, taking pity, The whole country is waiting on us for this just and absolutely necessary act of liberation, Olavo whispered, in the name of the working class I demand that you cease this business of reactionary personal feelings and bourgeois sentimentalism at once (The guy managed to be a drag right to the very end, the second lieutenant commented to the communications officer, why in hell did you put up with him for such a long time?), the taxi guy, frightened and confused, was desperately sticking out his ear toward us, anxious to know what we were talking about, Slop mnq brum? the cellist joined in pleasantly, offering his pack of Três Vintes, and the bald-headed man, very nervous, hastened to explain to him in sign language that he hated tobacco, that right there on the dashboard was a sign pompously stating NO SMOKING, the lieutenant colonel, lying on his back on the bed, had his shorts pulled down to his knees and his undershirt, the tip of his tie, and the wrinkled tail of his shirt pushed upward, and he felt ashamed, foolish, ridiculous, with a crazy desire to disappear, flee, evaporate into the air, wishing he'd never accepted the woman's invitation, never rung the bell, never come in, never had dinner, never, shit, fallen into the childish trap of the mother-of-pearl peacock in the bedroom, A drugstore, the old man begged, tearing off his medals, if you don't find me a drugstore quick I won't be present at the triumph of the proletariat over dying capitalism, Gjmnm urms toflse, the ambassador muttered, out of sorts, and the alarmed, inquiring eyes looking for us in the mirror, Hang on, we're almost there, Olavo advised in a low voice, hang on, the palace is in sight over there (nor did I hide the prie-dieus in the attic, nor did I take the dog's box off the balcony, there are still underpants and undershirts belonging to the old women hanging on the drying rack, there are still bottles of perfume and drops for high blood pressure in the dresser drawers), the tarred terrace in front of the gate, the trees, the stock-still sentries beside their confessional boxes, no traffic around, no police jeeps patrolling the area, Have you tried vitamins at all, Artur? the cloud of perfume inquired, stroking her chin with her rings, softness like that isn't normal at your age, it seems to me they've got capsules you can take that can give life to a dead man, the car went up to a plane tree and stopped, Olavo dug some Venezuelan money out of his pockets to pay the fare, Clmt jarnytz obaia, the Danish ambassador complained, indignant,

offering the driver a handful of menthol hard candy and tops from soda and
beer bottles, mixed in with cigarette butts and pieces of matches, the bald
man sat staring at those Nordic coins, his chin sharp with surprise like a
crocodile's, A capsule at lunch, a capsule at dinner, Artur, she consoled him,
and at the end of the month you'll be a Tarzan you never dreamed of being, I
can't stand on my feet, the old man murmured, with decorations flowing
down his uniform jacket, pretty soon I'll start howling with the pain, Rnhopl,
rnhopl, Dália said softly behind the lenses that transformed her eyes into
confused, imprecise, wandering little microscopic drifting dots, the shadows
of the branches were slipping down to the ground with the lightness of water,
going off and blending, the long sword Olavo had was leaping behind him
like the tail end of a broom, the cellist advanced decisively toward the palace
like a burglar toward a jewelry store with no alarm system, and we didn't
even get twenty yards from the place where the taxi had dropped us (the
length of the corridor, God, Captain, you've got no idea how long the
corridor is now, trotting and trotting for hours on end along the dusty carpet
and the door to the room farther and farther away, and the doorknob of the
bathroom shining, mockingly, from the antipodes, and the saints in their
niches looking like milestones on an endless highway), Dália, dizzy from her
glasses, was zigzagging like a mole among obstacles in the sunlight, Eternal
glory to Marxism-Leninism-Maoism, Olavo roared at the indifferent treetops, gripping the armpit of the old man, whose ungoverned legs were
staggering and trembling, Hhlorph marxiskt lenivan maoara bum bum, the
diplomat vigorously approved, a flock of dogs was trotting heads down at the
opposite end of the square, I shouted Watch out, the guy's going to fall, watch
out the guy's falling down, seven or eight medals rolled onto the pavement,
Dália, blind, was getting lost, gripping her plastic pistol, bumping into
bench after bench by the river, Flap orgoin tzaun? the cellist asked as he tried
to free the toy machine gun from the wooden rings of his cloak, the lieutenant
colonel, standing, was dispiritedly buttoning his fly amid sardonic mirrors
and suddenly ironic porcelain boxes, comforted by maternal pats from the
cloud of perfume, It's nothing, Artur, it's not important at all, Artur, after a
few boxes of capsules you'll see how the two of us will die laughing at all this,
Artur, Give me a hand here, comrade, Olavo called him, holding up the
other general by the waist, give me a hand, I can't hold onto this colleague,
Chtok chtok, Dália was peeping, dashing down some steps that led to the
docks, I ran toward them tripping over the spurs and at that same instant (the
furniture was also enormous, gigantic, infinite) the old man slipped through
our fingers (the bulbs in the ceiling, pale and dirty, more distant than stars),
humid, slippery, gelatinous, and he began twisting with horrible grimaces in
a patch of sunlight (Even the breeze on the curtains is different, the communications officer explained to us, even the sound of my lungs on the pillow),
muttering through the ring of his lips one final, definitive Venezuelan curse.

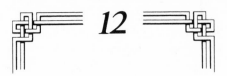

**12**

"I WANTED to leave the club before dawn, Captain, because there's nothing in the world worse than the face of a whore in the light of day. They turn off the spotlights and the ball-shaped little mirror that rotates on the ceiling, the musicians put away their instruments on the bandstand, unhook the microphones, put on their topcoats (ordinary topcoats, just imagine, just like yours and mine) over their red ties and tuxedoes, turn up their collars, open the door, a sad toilet brightness slants in, lighting up the tables and chairs, the garbage cans and buildings outside are visible with the painful clarity of an abscess, the threat of the clock suddenly unleashes very far away somewhere a throbbing inside us, a shiver of affliction rises up my spine to my shoulders and I, understand, without realizing it, without paying any attention to it, begin to shake. It's the time when whores, dressed like rich clowns, leave cabarets, stumbling on their exaggerated heels on their way to trolley stops, with the last cigarette burning, forgotten, in their fingers, like the rear lights of a train swaying all alone on the last car on the way to nothing. It's the time, Captain, when Lisbon is a desert of building façades pierced with a cold that an icy wind keeps shaving and shaving, in which the trees slowly emerge from the morning mist and the squares and streets fill up

306

with whores with hazy bat eyes wrapped in their garish fake-fur coats and their artificial rabbit stoles, the time when hundreds, thousands of rich clowns with long red or blond hair, or hair black as shoe polish, return, clumsily, to their fourth-floor rooms without elevators, waving their glass-bead purses with the sharp ends of their fingers at the rare, furtive, slippery, fearful taxis that don't respond. At six in the morning, see, when the garbage, the sheets of paper, and pieces of newspaper roll along the sidewalk blown by an invisible, nonexistent mysterious mouth, when the fountains in squares are in suspension in the air and the bronze statues in the pools lift their rusty members in motionless goodbyes without any direction, Lisbon is a city of worn-out whores, corroded by false champagne and whiskey made of drug-store alcohol, a gloomy circus that a mute trumpet mournfully backs up, observed by an opaque windowed loge. When I was little I would wake up early in the morning sometimes in the middle of tumultuous and unusual dreams, summoned by a smell of sweat and cheap perfume, by the tinkling of innumerable bracelets, by a swish of clothing, by a strange collision of necklaces that blended in with the groaning of dresser drawers, the creaking of the floor, and the marine breathing of my parents in the bedroom next to mine, grumbling like walruses between their sheets, I would go over to the balcony, mistrustfully push aside the curtain, and there they were, on the sidewalk, tightening their neckerchiefs in front of the extinguished sign of the Flamingo, dozens of spidery women in black stockings and very short skirts, looking like acrobats, contortionists, trapeze artists, the ladies with trained dogs from the Coliseum, waiting with the quiet affliction of little owls for the arrival of a savior bus, coming confusedly from down there, out of the mist of boats on the river, dancing on the fat haunches of its wheels. I would fog up the windowpanes with the avidity of my nose and would wipe them clean with the anxious sleeve of my pajamas as the whores multiplied in the street in the tragic, menacing, terrible postures of clowns, with a saxophone or an accordion in front of the bangles of their breasts, reaching out to me with their white gloves, their raised eyebrows, and great scarlet smiles between their painted cheeks, while an out-of-tune orchestra began to play behind me with an enormous thunder of plates, a focal point that constantly kept changing color followed me, drifting along in a zigzag through the room, the gloves, the arms, the eyebrows, the smiles, almost reached the win-dowsill, heavy, swollen hips were smothering me, black patent-leather shoes crushed my bladder, the piss of affliction ran down the legs of my striped pajama bottoms, the volume of the orchestra grew, echoing through the rooms, until it mixed with my mother's voice, which deafened me com-pletely, lifted me off the floor, took me away from the curtains, carried me around her neck to the bed that had been hers when she was single, and her mother's before her, and her mother's mother before that, and she left me alone on the mattress, spying with fright at the balcony where the faces with the long red or yellow or black hair of Lisbon whores were attached, twisting in gloomy, strange grimaces of invitation or rejection.

So I wanted to leave the club before dawn, Captain, the five of us, the fat mulatto woman, the magician's helper, the two faded skinny girls, stationed like candlesticks on either side of the lieutenant colonel, insatiable for peanuts and vermouth, and the striptease goddess Melissa, whose name is Adosinda, has pimples on her shoulders and was a servant in Oporto in the house of a kidney specialist, coming out while night mercifully covers the circles under our eyes, the crow's-feet, and the white hairs, hides our paleness, the wrinkles in our suits, the twisted ties and the lumpy shirts, before the numerous, uncountable army of whores invades the city with its gloomy circus of excessively deformed creatures with gums bursting the plaster of their jaws into pieces, like grenade fragments, remember? the army of people coming back from the war on leave to Lourenço Marques, and the moaning of the sick wouldn't leave us for a second all through the night, we buried our mouths, our noses, our ears between the teats of a black woman and kept on, shit on it all, hearing them thrashing and moaning in the post infirmary, getting up before dawn, Captain, going up with you people to the third floor on the Rua da Mãe d'Água, lighting the lamp with a yellow paper shade, serving whiskey to everybody (there must be enough glasses in the cupboard) and disappearing with the magician's assistant into Mariana's room, facing the lighted fountain, legging it naked on top of the insignificant body of the woman, surrounded by paste dolls, rubber ducks, and teddy bears sitting on the shelves, examining us with their inexpensive little stupid porcelain eyes.

"And how long were you in Brazil, Lieutenant?" the soldier asked, as his face appeared alternately in the rotating lights of the club: an asymmetrically twisting face, huge green teeth, hollow eyes, irregular pumice skin, damp from soap and sweat. "How long did you work down there?"

"The old man died two or three days later from an aneurism, in spite of the serum, in spite of the apparatus, in spite of the catheters," the communications officer said. "We held the wake at Organization headquarters, and we carried him off to be buried in a coffin engraved with a hammer and sickle, covered by the red flag of authentic Marxism-Leninism-Maoism, with dozens of militants with remorseful raised fists bringing up the rear. Olavo and Lopes gave speeches at the cemetery in the middle of the crosses, tombs, and plaster angels, in the name of the mourning proletariat, Dália tossed a carnation on the grave, an older lady, dressed all in black, was weeping in the arms of the cellist, who had shown up for the occasion in his elegant concert outfit, the rest of the family disappeared discreetly, exceedingly embarrassed, when we sang an off-key 'Internationale' in a chorus. At the next meeting of the Secretariat we unanimously approved that the space set aside for press conferences, a decrepit cubicle crumbling into dust, with empty

beer bottles in a cupboard without a door, be named the Alfredo da Conceição Pires Room, and we unveiled a picture of the old man on the tiny wall
between two windows where the valiant comrade smiled in his lacquer frame
the unfocused grimace of an instant shot in a picture booth."

"Twenty-seven months," the second lieutenant answered. "Twenty-seven
and something months, the same as in the war."

"Any day now, when least expected," the lieutenant colonel muttered with
a pensive little sigh, "the one who's going to kick off with a stroke will be me.
One of these days I've got to go to the doctor to have my blood pressure
checked."

During the early days, mother- and father-in-law, brothers- and sisters-in-
law, Inês, Mariana, three maids, and he were all crammed into a tiny
apartment in São Paulo, where they kept bumping into each other and the
endless array of heavy trunks, whose metal catches would suddenly open like
chrome grasshoppers, vomiting out socks and shorts, they slept on mattresses in the hall, in the living room, in the kitchen, where a broken pipe
perfidiously dripped the whole night through, the city looked disagreeable
and gray to him, stifled with traffic, Portuguese friends of Inês's parents
would appear and disappear continuously like the settings on a barometer,
complaining and bitter, cursing the Army, the rabble, the communists, the
lady with purple hair swore that the Vatican was a den of Russian cardinals
around the pope plotting heretical conspiracies against the Virgin of Fátima.
The mother-in-law, her hair undone, always in a bathrobe and slippers,
presided over the confusion between shouts and tranquilizers, dresses and
jackets hung on hangers hooked onto cords, dozens of children would come
out from under the furniture, filling drawers, from the depths of the trunks,
and they never stopped crying, they would eat standing up with plastic
spoons and paper plates tasteless lunches that smelled of drainpipes, dried
shit, and automobile exhaust, and Do you see what freedom has given us,
Jorge?, Do you see what democracy has given us, Jorge? and, every once in a
while, Inês's mother put the key into a small case, rummaged secretly inside,
got dressed, disappeared with a funereal air for a morning or an afternoon,
and would return younger, her hair set with presents for everyone and a
handful of bank notes in her wallet: At first, Captain, we lived off her pawned
rings until I got a job in an office and we moved to another apartment in
Santos, almost on the waterfront, next door to a middle-aged Neapolitan
couple who would occasionally spend entire nights arguing, shouting, and
drinking Chianti, and playing operas during the intervals.

"And underneath the picture," the communications officer explained, "we
hung a plaque that said Dedicated to Alfredo da Conceição Pires, Martyr for
Freedom. When Marxism-Leninism-Maoism finally defeated the bourgeoisie, we'd give his name to an avenue, a garden, a factory, a whole
neighborhood, a municipal swimming pool, a fish hatchery, we wrote to the

widow on the letterhead of the Organization, congratulating her on the soon-to-be future immortality of her husband, after a week or two we got back a letter addressed to Olavo and there inside, covering the middle of the page in capital letters, GO TO HELL."

"A stroke," the lieutenant colonel was talking to himself with rounded eyes fluttering over a forest of bottles, "why in hell didn't that idea ever enter my head?"

"Cholesterol fine, X-rays fine, EKGs fine," the doctor barked, pushing away the reports with a disappointed face. (The cupolas of the Basílica da Estrela were gleaming in the sun behind the nurse's square hairdo.) "Would you like to swap your state of health for mine, maybe?"

"Say, Jaime," the mother-in-law asked her subdued husband, pipe between his teeth, facing the eternal voiceless television set, "have you read the news from Lisbon yet? They had a revolution to put an end to the communists and when it was all over they knocked us down again. The poor people who stayed behind there, I don't even want to think about them."

You could see the wharves, the docks, dirty moorings sticking up, the brownish sea, lots of smoke, foreign ships at anchor. I'd leave early in the morning, work the whole day through, come home late on the bus, squashed in by women, bundles, and mulattoes, I'd leave Inês sleeping, grazing on the pillowcase with her open mouth, and I'd find her all sleepy, lying on the sofa in the small living room with a magazine with a colored cover on her knees, and Mariana trotting around her, waving a cloth giraffe, demanding and restless. The ships gave off the round mooing of oxen, black stevedores, insignificant in the distance, disappeared under the crooks of the cranes or into the wooden warehouse buildings, the laundry was piling up in a wicker basket, the dirty dishes were piling up in the kitchen, a smoky, melancholy, foul-smelling night was floating about in the bedroom, and while I was lighting the stove for dinner, listening to the unending epic arguments of the neighbors as they bubbled over and twisted through the aluminum gratings, the demanding ring of the telephone, and while I was putting the pot of water on the burner to cook the spaghetti, Did you read how the communists are still in power in Portugal, Jorge? Did you read how those atheists are still the masters of everything?

"There are people," the communications officer was resigned, "who no matter how much they've been knocked down, no matter how scientifically they've been shown the truth, will never get to understand the revolution: look, you don't have to search too far, Pires's widow was one. She'd got it into her head that Marxism had killed her husband, and from then on, what can I say, Captain?"

"An aneurism," the lieutenant colonel went on in an airy way as if he were dreaming, "a guy suddenly kicks the bucket, he's perfectly fine and chatting and, boom, his body fills up with blood and that's that."

"I've got to talk to Inês urgently," the lady with purple hair said on the landing, "and you won't even invite me in."

"Did they still carry on, even in Brazil, Lieutenant?" the soldier was indignant. "Even in Brazil the shameless bitch kept it up?"

You sweated all the time, just like in Africa, Captain, the same disgusting humidity, the same smell of dead meat, the same rash around your neck, your armpits, your groin, it was hard to breathe, the atmosphere was always heavy, always crushing, the ships' boilers fed on it and warmed up, there were too many people, there was too much traffic, too much noise, there were too many Portuguese shut up in groups in crowded little apartments, the office manager didn't pay him much and the check was always late (He treats you that way because he thinks you're a pauper, his wife argued, tell him where to go and to get lost), at lunchtime he would lean on the counter of the first stand he ran into, chewing a dirty sandwich and thinking One of these days the ships are going to come right into the city, knocking down houses, sailing with an unbearable noise of engines on the cracked pavement of the streets, thinking I want to go back to Lisbon, I want to see my parents, I want the yellow paper lampshade on Mãe d'Água, I've had it up to here with the old woman's phone calls, the sugary smell of marijuana and the pupils of my brothers-in-law dilated by cocaine and horse, thinking At this moment she and the other one are rolling around on the bed, rubbing each other, licking each other like sheep, laughing, saying bad things about me, swapping stories about my physical defects, my tics, my manners, thinking, Captain, What am I doing here? thinking I love you, thinking I don't love you, thinking I detest you, thinking, idiotically, In Brazil, in India, in China, in any old shit place, wherever it is, I'd really like to be happy with you.

"Just a little urea, not too much, Colonel," the doctor told him (and the cupolas on the Basílica da Estrela quivered and vibrated, set against the unalterably blue sky, and a medieval bell was tolling in the distance), "but if you stay away from meat and eggs you'll be as good as new overnight."

"Didn't I tell you, Artur?" the cloud of perfume exclaimed, triumphant, crawling over him like a kitten, with hanging breasts and pleats of fat that quivered in a complex of bracelets and necklaces, "didn't I tell you that the second dose of capsules would fix it?"

"Inês isn't home," the second lieutenant assured her with his hand on the door, barring the vestibule, looking at the lady with purple hair with an icy rage that was growing. "She went to São Paulo with her sisters, to my in-laws' place, and she won't be back till the beginning of the week as far as I know. Do you want me to give her any message?"

"Ilka?" Inês's sharpened voice asked from inside, startled. "Is that Ilka, Jorge?"

"I tell you it was absolutely beautiful, sweet," the cloud of perfume, stretched out on her back on the sheets like a beached codfish, assured him, caressing his damp, dead tool with her hand. "My word, I've never had so much pleasure with anyone, so, you see."

"So much misunderstanding hurts," the communications officer lamented. "Refusing to give her husband's name to a street, to a nursery, to a kindergarten, to a hospital, to a simple bandstand, just imagine. It was things like that that led me to doubt that it would ever be possible to set up Marxism-Leninism-Maoism in this country, it was things like that, Captain, that took my spirit away completely. Because no revolutionary, no matter how hardened, no matter how accustomed to our national conservatism, to the people's atavistic fear, their innocence exploited by priests, to the resistance of the petty bourgeoisie, and to the shadowy plotting of international capitalism, because no revolutionary is made of wood, gentlemen."

"Yes, darling," the lady with purple hair replied with an angry little sob, passing quickly under his arm and going to the living room. "I only got here just now because of this awful traffic and I was chatting with your husband."

"You five come with us, without any protests or noise," the soldier announced with complete assurance, pointing to the women at the table. "We'll pay the bill and beat it out of this dump as fast as we can."

"I give you my word, it was marvelous, my little dear," the cloud of perfume went on, kissing the back of his neck, "I give you my word, you were heroic."

Inês, in pajamas, unkempt and happy, cross-legged on the sofa was playing with her painted toes, the lady with purple hair, her back turned, was serving herself some whiskey with ice and club soda from the cabinet (The way she knows every corner of the place, the second lieutenant thought, the way she went straight to the bar), the street door was open and the Neapolitan, very fat, in his undershirt, was shooing the cat down the stairs, a tanker flying the Turkish flag was going slowly off in the gray day, pursued by a flock of birds: I'm getting out of here, I'm not getting out of here, I'll sit down in a chair in front of you two, I'll leave you alone, a waiter dropped a piece of paper onto the table in passing, the way seagulls shit in the middle of their flight, alone for your honeyed caresses, your imbecilic nibbling, your swinish carrying on, the communications officer flicked on his lighter in order to decipher the feces, his features fell into worried seriousness, Almost three contos, shit, shall we call over the manager and complain, Commander?, Does anyone know what three contos divided by five comes to?, A wild lay, Artur, the cloud of perfume classified things, her breasts spilling out over her ribs, I never make mistakes, you know what I mean? as soon as I saw you on the Terreiro do Paço I said right off Here's the man I've been waiting for all these years, the pair of them were talking in low voices, with their mouths almost together, Captain, as if I didn't really exist, as if nobody else were there, Six hundred clams and a little something for the tip, the communications officer calculated, no more books or movies until the end of the month, A couple of whacks for each one, the second lieutenant was thinking, motionless on the rug looking at them, a couple of whacks for each one and to the dame with purple hair Get the hell out of here, you whore, and a swift kick outside, the Turkish tanker was disappearing, wrapped in sad and pestilential smoke, a few lights were going on here and there, the noise of the cranes had ceased, the city seemed to be puffing up behind him, Who's got change of a conto? the lieutenant colonel asked, wallet in hand, leafing through bills, pictures, cards, papers, She must have a rotten body, Inês, withered breasts, varicose veins, disgusting folds in her belly, what charm can you find in that crocodile, why does her gray-haired pubes attract you? the ship smaller and smaller, insignificant, nonexistent, the docks and barges deserted, the sound of traffic changing in color, in intensity, in tone, I never felt so foreign and so all alone as in that apartment, Captain, I never felt so perplexed, the purple-haired lady's ice cubes tinkled around me like a lot of wild laughter at an orgy, mouths opening and closing, and I couldn't make out a single sound, the soldier picked up the leftover bills and coins, Whoever's got change coming, speak up, stealing away from the mulatto woman's slow appetite, Prepare yourself, Artur, because you're never going to get away from me again, the cloud of perfume warned, prepare yourself because I'm not going to rest until I get you to the altar, And are you telling me that she brought it off, Colonel? the communications officer asked, are you telling me that the madame hooked you in the blink of an eye? the Italian was shrieking at his wife on the other side of the wall, the orchestra attacked a tango, an older character with a camellia in his lapel got up in back, buttoning his jacket, shepherding a skinny adolescent, the vocalist detached the microphone from its stand, got untangled from the wire, and came forward on tiptoes, smiling, over to the dull-colored bulbs of the platform, With those and other bits of nonsense, you gentlemen understand, the concierge said, threatening her son with a wooden spoon, that bitch got him all tangled up, Inês laid her hand familiarly on her friend's knee to whisper a secret in her ear, Go fix your faces, the soldier ordered the women, and in five minutes we'll meet you at the door, the camellia passed by them with ridiculous little leaps, out of time with the music, Tomorrow I'm telling your parents what kind of a woman you are, the second lieutenant thought, I'll closet myself with your mother in her room, warn her, Prepare yourself, and let her in on everything, in addition to the tireless guy with the flower, there were only two or three motionless couples left, entrenched behind walls of bottles, half-hidden in the shadows, their location guessed by the tips of their cigarettes which grew larger and smaller, the manager said good night, obsequiously rubbing his pale hands, but his tiny evaluating eyes were not smiling, the whores, whose jackets made them fatter, were waiting for us in a fierce cloud of cologne, chatting with the doorman, who was blinking his owl eyes leaning against the posters with photographs of beauties in bathing suits, like those in Miss Universe contests, it still wasn't daytime and yet the night was imperceptibly whitening along the edges of the houses and the unequal angles of the roofs, the municipal street-cleaning truck, with an amber light blinking on top, was slowly dragging along, washing the streets, a man was rummaging through garbage cans with a stick, dogs lying beside the leafless trees watched us with trepidation, Two taxis, hurry up, the lieutenant colonel demanded of the doorman, beginning to look for his socks amid mother-of-pearl knickknacks, Say, Jorge, the lady with purple hair, exhibiting her lighter, asked, I've run out of cigarettes, just think, would it be too much to ask you to go down for a minute and get me a pack of Marlboros, the docks, the ships, the city were swarming with lights, the motor of a last derrick was thumping its irregular valves on a barge, Ma'am, sir, your daughter is a lesbian, and the wide eyes of his mother-in-law, and her open mouth, and the hands that fumbled blindly, suddenly trembling, for a chair on which to sit, Don't speak so loudly, her husband was alarmed, my sons out there might hear you, the lieutenant colonel squatted down on the rug, lighted by the pink halo of a porcelain lamp with a pair of doves at the base, Did you see where my shorts went? what a mess, We're going straight to heaven, my jewels, the soldier suggested, shooing the mulatto woman and her friends into the cars like geese, Inês? the mother-in-law asked, as she adjusted her bathrobe with her scaly hands, looking as if she'd taken on fifty years in one minute, Inês is the last one in whom I would have expected that, Jorge, and by the way where's the bottle of tranquilizers that was here? he finally found them under the bed, alongside a high-heeled slipper, a pompon over the arch, fallen on its side by the rug, the cloud of perfume, her makeup undone, her eye shadow running down her cheeks, was smiling at him carnivorously from the pillow, and the lieutenant colonel remembered, as in a dream, touching the plastic plate of the woman's false teeth several times with his tongue, sticky with a greenish film of saliva, Inês and Ilka, impossible, the father-in-law stated energetically, even before we fled here we went to Fátima together to the candlelight procession, The shop on the corner, Inês said, doesn't have American cigarettes most of the time, only those Brazilian rat-killers, but there's a dealer three or four blocks farther who sells everything, even marijuana, his shorts, damp in front, his trousers, his shoes, he went to the mirror to fix his tie and found in the glass the plump body, chubby with folds like a baby's, of the cloud of perfume, whose clenched fingertips were sending him hazy kisses, inside the cars the women's smell grew thick and spread out like the dew of corpses, it still wasn't daylight, but any indefinite and vague thing was dissolving the night like an acid, gnawing away at the shadows, reducing the shrubbery and trees to gesticulating, fleshless bones, discoloring building façades and conferring upon faces the restless masks of the dead, the magician's assistant was searching in her purse for her cigarette holder, the communications officer was dozing with his chin on his chest, the lieutenant colonel's hair was sparse between the bottom and top of the back of his neck, Look how old these bastards have become, I thought, the way these mother-fuckers have become middle-aged and vulnerable and soft and resigned and sad, Inês? the mother-in-law snorted, aggressive, sucking on a capsule, Inês, do you swear? it wasn't day yet and still a phosphorescent acid was burning the gums of their smiles, immeasurably increasing the incisors and the bones of the faces bringing the yellowing hands over breasts and immobilizing features in an anguished serenity, the father-in-law was knocking his extin-guished pipe against the hollow of his palm, One little goodbye kiss at least, you rascal, the cloud of perfume asked, at least a squib of tenderness, sweet, he went down in the elevator premeditating Get your own fucking cigarettes, you cow, balls' will be done, you bitch, and while the taxi went on, rubbing against deserted corners, he realized in panic (It's going to be dawn, it's going to be dawn, it's going to be dawn, it's going to be dawn) that the whores were leaving the low-down cabarets on Conde de Redondo, he perceived the threatening calmness of the city and the terrible silence of the statues and the squares, the damp afflicted color of the musty sky reflected on the glass of store windows and the pleated skin of pools, the mother-in-law recovered her composure little by little, became rejuvenated again, took on vigor, recov-ered complete control of herself and her husband, Now, Jorge, she advised, don't come to me with these foolish bits of rumor because I've got a lot to do, the lieutenant colonel finally finished attacking his shoes, buttoning his jacket, went into the bathroom and combed his hair and finally leaned over the cloud of perfume and smelled the flat, agreeable odor of the woman's arms that hung over him, heavy, around his neck, we crossed the Avenida, went through the Praça da Alegria where the shrubbery spread thickly in a whispering disorder of leaves, the second lieutenant started walking, aimlessly, hands in his pockets, in the direction of the broad nothingness of the port, the woman's mouth sucked on his, her tongue came into his like a wet sigh between his teeth, and at that moment one of the lieutenant colonel's legs slipped out from under him, he lost his balance, and he fell unprotected onto a soft pile of lace, flounces, bows, ribbons, satins, pleasant, padded masses of sweaty flesh that closed around his body like the last wave over the drowning head of a castaway.

"Please don't pay any attention to the mess, gentlemen," the second lieutenant asked on the landing, looking for his keys in his pockets, "but the cleaning woman didn't come by once this week."

The microscopic vestibule, with the little windows of the gas, electricity, and water meters set into the wall, the living room–bedroom divided in the middle by a bookcase, banners, porcelain dolls, pictures, the tranquil animal rumble of the refrigerator, the rusted, petalless corollas of the gas jets, and on the left a narrow corridor with cabinets painted white, Mariana's former bedroom smelling of dust and mustiness, the bathroom with the plastic shower curtain drawn, the shaving brush and safety razor on the glass shelf supported by chrome brackets mounted on the tiles and by the window the stairs down to the tall trees of Príncipe Real, the illuminated stone of the fountain, with its dark recesses and its round and porous wrinkles, and from the other side of the street, Look, Captain, the soldier said, grabbing me by the elbow, the painter's apartment almost within reach of my fingertips, if I took a good leap off the balcony, look, I could even touch it, if I could leap over the parapet, over the clump of parked cars, I'd land in the middle of the old man's canvases again and the black man's fetishes, the necklaces of *missanga* beads, the bottles of turpentine, the cans of paint, the canvases, the cloth from the Congo, the newspapers on the floor, it's impossible that our second lieutenant never saw me, it's impossible that our second lieutenant hasn't been covering up, the mulatto woman was looking at a porcelain hunchback playing the mandolin, Melissa the striptease goddess was looking for where the glasses were kept in the drawers beside the washing machine, the skinny girls with dyed hair shut themselves up, lipstick in fist, in the toilet, Five soldiers and five drunken whores, shit, the second lieutenant thought, with regret, I hope they don't wake up the neighbors at least, all we need is for the concierge to come pounding on the door, Isn't there any music to put some life into these corpses, the magician's assistant asked, I've never been to such a draggy wake, I've never been with such dumb people in all my life, the communications officer discovered a battery radio behind a curtain and tried to get it to work, sitting on the couch with the instrument in his lap, rocking it tenderly as he would a child, Pay no attention to the mess, pay no attention to the trash, the second lieutenant requested, pushing a bucket and a plastic mop away with his knee, quickly rinsing out the glass ashtrays in the sink, filling the ice bucket, opening bottles of soda water and tonic, the mulatto woman lay down on the bed, crossing her thumbs over her throat, closed her eyes and a minute later was snoring, her chin drooping, exhibiting the fillings in her teeth, I can't believe that you didn't catch me naked, Lieutenant, the soldier was alarmed, jumping around like a grasshopper, on top of the black man, on top of the painter, the bronchitic flush of the toilet could be heard with a sobbing of pipes and almost immediately the two skinny girls, dressed like twins, came into the room with smiles of relief, If what you want is to break up with Inês, you swine (Don't say anything, Jaime, I'll settle this matter quite well), at least have the honesty not to come to me with such imbecilic accusations.

"That's funny," Melissa the striptease goddess commented, pointing to the lamp with the yellow paper shade which the breeze from outside was making swing like a pendulum, "in what store did you find that spinning ball?"

"The bastard got married and went to live in her place," the concierge grumbled, furious. "Do you think if he stayed here I'd have given them a moment's rest?"

"He not only didn't bring me the cigarettes," the lady with purple hair was indignant, "but he went off and spread awful stories about me. I haven't even told a thing to Greg, poor dear, I was afraid it would give him some kind of attack. There are people capable of anything, Captain."

"What if I take you to court for defaming my daughter, eh?" the mother-in-law roared. "What if I drag you through the bitter streets, how'd you like that?"

It smelled of rotting wood and hawsers, decomposing fish, stagnant water, and mingled breezes, and the oval rings of the streetlights revealed rain puddles, mud, scum, tramps lying facedown on bags and bales: I've got to arrange for another cleaning woman to clean up the port for me, sweep away the drunks, the warehouses, the docks, the cranes, another cleaning woman who would sew up night properly for me, stopping the morning light from penetrating through a rift in the shadows, preventing me from seeing myself in the mirrors with the cruel impiety of the sun coming through the windows, stopping my movements from becoming white, out of synch, and ordinary like those plaster angels in provincial cemeteries, chatting uselessly with an inaccessible, distracted sky, preventing it from digging wrinkles in my face of resignation and fatigue, the deep folds of forty years marked on my neck, the melancholy wrinkles at the corners of my mouth, a black man naked from the waist up was smoking, lying over the hatch of a Dutch, or Belgian, or Uruguayan freighter, Leave it, the twins said at the same time to the communications officer, who had picked up a waltz on the radio between squawks and squeaks, And in any case, Captain, the communications officer observed, inexpressively examining the equal, spiritless, graceless windows of the building across the way, the iron vases and arabesques on balconies, the scratched blinds and railings, the gutters like sad hanging intestines, the unexpected death of Pires destroyed, without our realizing it at first, an incentive, an urge, an impulse of some kind, the Maoist drive that raised our spirits and drove us on, the coffeepot at headquarters didn't work for days on end, the banners were growing musty, the flags were drooping on their wooden staffs, unexpected shells of dust and toadstools were blooming on the bald heads of Lenin's busts, the cellist signed up to go fight in Cambodia and left with his instrument case full of plastic machine guns and pistols, the meetings of the Central Committee turned toothless with no impetuous and energetic comrades, the dissipating haze of smoke let one see the sick, damp walls, the defaced, torn posters, the stains of soot, the sprouts on the ceiling, the thousand scratches and streaks and abrasions and defects and water bulges in the stucco, The dues don't even cover the rent, the treasurer was bleating desperately, one of these days you're going to see the landlord hitting us with an eviction notice and, boom, we've tried raffles and no go, we've gone with lotteries and candy sales, we've organized a dance, but the neighbors wouldn't let us go through with it, we've asked for the support of an enlightened proletariat and the peasantry who know best and we haven't received a single cent, until just before Christmas when a gentleman with a small mustache and vest, escorted by a gentleman with a briefcase who was waving a typed piece of paper for all to see, a policeman with his hands behind his back spread majestically, the spies from the neighborhood, and a half hour later, in spite of the protests of Olavo, who was howling his Marxist wails, dragging his overcoat along the ground, behind a couple of moving men with shoulders like cabinets, we found ourselves disconsolately on the sidewalk, watching over a pyramid of chairs missing a leg, one-legged tables, piles of manifestoes, flyers, cans of red and black spray paint for writing on walls, clumsy typewriters, a broken-down photocopier, helmets, camouflage suits, binoculars that didn't focus, Carnival masks, scratched dominoes, Roman gladiator boots, gaudy tinplate bazookas that shot tomatoes and melons, and the broken plaster beards of countless Engels, sternly dreaming, of the most diverse dimensions, looking at the river, sitting on the last warped sofa, whose springs stuck through the cloth of the cushions blackened by the burns of matches and cigarette butts, while boys, Gypsies, drug smugglers, blindmen, fruit peddlers were stealing our furniture, emblems, and badges, the moving men, armed with sledgehammers, knocked off forever the immortal name of the Organization from the front of the building and the gentleman with the little mustache and vest went off accompanied by the gentleman with the briefcase in a gilt Opel, with striped seat covers, which left moaning, lowing through vegetable stands and vagrants leaning against tavern doors, until it evaporated, with one last belch, around the knife-edged corner of an alley where an old woman, sitting on a three-cornered stool, was foisting newspapers and rubber flowers onto the indifference of beggars.

"It had been a long time, I don't know how long, since someone treated me that way," the lieutenant colonel justified himself. "It had been years since I'd known what a woman's washed body was like."

"If you don't retract what you said at once," the mother-in-law warned (Shut up, Jaime, all you can do is cough up jackass notions), "I'm going to talk to my lawyer the first thing tomorrow."

"So you got married just like that, Commander," the soldier said in disgust. "So you buried yourself with the first one who came along."

"We waited an hour or two after for someone to help us," the communications officer explained: "Olavo telephoned a friend who had a van and no dice, Dália asked some cousins to help but they never came, and we ended up going off and leaving the mess right there, in the middle of the street, as if none of it belonged to us, understand, while the Gypsies and the blindmen had a tug-of-war over manuals and portraits of Ho Chi Minh. In the Bairro

Alto there must be a lot of busts of Mao Zedong on doilies on tops of refrigerators."

If I close my eyes quickly, the second lieutenant thought, leaning against the window frame, the darkness will go on and on and save me from seeing dawn on the lengthened faces of these dames, because there's nothing worse in the world, Captain, than the mug of a whore in the light of day, after hours and hours of smoking and fake champagne, nothing worse than those dull bat eyes, those tawdry fur stoles without any fur, those torn jackets, those shoes with crooked heels, those spangled purses, those tragic clowns with long red hair, or frosted, or blond, or the color of black shoe polish, that mortuary smell of sweat and cheap perfume, that endless tinkling of bracelets, that swish of clothing, that rubbing of necklaces, those tarantula women with net stockings and very short skirts, with lifted eyebrows and great scarlet laughs on their painted cheeks, who lift me up off the ground, grab me around the neck, undress me with the skilled swiftness of nannies, double me over on the bed, straighten out the pillow for me, open up the sheets and lay me out on the bed.

(I'm not going back to the apartment, goddamn it, I'm not going back up there)

so that if I close my eyes quickly the darkness will go on eternally and I won't see the soldier embrace the sleeping mulatto woman, I won't see his fingers feeling her up, hastily, along the broad dune of her stomach covered by a dark, sparse and harsh and repulsive meadow, I won't see the striptease goddess Melissa who is frantically pushing her body up against the lieutenant colonel's on the dirty rug, squealing and wiggling and wriggling like a beast being born

(Tomorrow I'm going to send for my things, the bundle in the study, clothes, letters, books, tomorrow I'm going to leave your daughter on her own)

I don't see the communications officer pushing, grunting, against one of the sisters, up against the bookshelf that moans and sways, I don't hear her shouted comments, her little squeals, her feigned protests, her faked orgasm, amid the thrashing, knocking down framed pictures, antique coins, little ivory objects, I'm not present in the stony, unpleasant silence afterward, nor do I see the mulatto woman moving off her huge thighs nor the soldier, ass in the air, on all fours, buzzing like a restless insect around her puddinglike breasts and belly, I won't see you, Captain, bury your chin in the neck or shoulders of the other skeletal twin, grab her around the waist, scoff at the protests, at her monkeyish anger, at her genuine enjoyment, I close my eyes quickly and I don't see the legs pedaling in space, or the wet bellies, or the hoarse, urgent voiceless voices

(All right, ma'am, I take back everything I said, nobody said anything, your daughter and your family can fix things up any way you want) or the epidermis that quivers, rubs against, scrapes, suppurates, close your eyes fast

(In five months, maybe not that many, the lieutenant colonel said in a murmur, through the embarrassed tips of his lips, we'll have been married seven years come May)

make a devilish effort and don't think about you, your agitated trunk, almost without any breasts, like a lizard with tetanus, in your incurable perpetual disorder, in the cluster of purses hanging from doorknobs, your horrible scorched dinners scraped out by a fork from the bottom of the pots, the lumps of starch that you always left on my shirts, the mulatto woman was whistling fibrous snores in her sleep

(Don't worry, I'm going away, ma'am, don't worry, I'm going away right now)

and the fountain, the trees, the steps up to Príncipe Real, my loneliness growing old on the third floor on the Rua da Mãe d'Água amid dust and disorder, the soldier lifting his weary bones to vomit in the toilet, more whiskey, more gin, more martinis, more beer, more of that leftover vodka from the army in the pantry, I open the bottles and hold back the morning, I have them close the metal blinds and night goes on, nobody, no face from the past appears in the dead mirrors, no deformed face is reflected on the polished surfaces, my parents are sighing in the next rooms, the clock in the small living room drips metallic and equal minutes, it's always five o'clock, Inês, it will always be five o'clock in this place, the paper lampshade will sway eternally, the magician's assistant touches me on the shoulder, the lights on the garbage trucks go on and off like great green hearts through the ribs of the drawn blinds

(Seven years married, add them up, being bored to death, getting hopelessly screwed up, seven years married with a sinister mother-of-pearl peacock in front of my nose)

somebody drops a glass or china object on the floor, when it breaks it hurts me like a wound, the magician's assistant pulls on my tie, my jacket, unbuttons my shirt, more whiskey, the pulp of her mouth advances and retreats, forming words, whole phrases that dissolve without being heard, a little froth of gin is bubbling on her chin just like peroxide on a boil

(I never saw Inês again, Captain, I never heard anything about her again)

we float in a density of water, down the hallway, to Mariana's defunct room, painted white, facing the extinguished spotlights, the fountain in the dark, the endless whispering of the trees, my shorts get stuck at my knees and my socks get stuck on my feet

(But what revolution, goddamn it, there'll never be a revolution in Portugal)

## The Revolution

I trip over the lieutenant colonel, who's on all fours like a child, looking for a swallow of gin, and I end up sinking down, with one sleeve of my jacket hanging from my wrist, in the midst of the paste dolls, Bakelite ducks, and felt bears, who examine me, sitting on the shelves, with their dense, inexpressive, stupid plastic eyes.

*Part Three*

# AFTER THE REVOLUTION

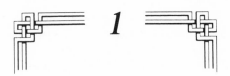

*1*

"WHEN Odete left," the soldier said, "the old man and I were all alone in the place, Captain, chewing in silence the horrible little army rations that the nurse brought, she would run an almost nonexistent cloth over the furniture from time to time and would change the location of our clothes and rearrange the tableware in the cupboard drawers. I even thought Now's the time he's going to hitch up with the bookkeeper, now's the time I'm going to have to put up with that dame's puss at the table, but, who in hell can say why, he never let anyone take Dona Isaura's place, never invited anyone at all, ugly or pretty, into the enormous black wooden bed. So at night we'd sit on the same sofa, like a couple with nothing to say, in front of the lighted television set, while he scratched his belly beneath his undershirt or squeezed his asthma spray into his open jaws, getting redder and redder, shorter and shorter of breath, more and more afflicted, at the end of the program, he would drag himself along, scuffing his slippers and wheezing, toward the distant shadows of his bedroom, I could hear him blowing his nose and coughing at the other end, turning faucets off and on, checking the gas heater, barring the door, I could hear the creak of the springs and the boards as he got into bed and when I turned out the light in my cubicle, there it was, in the garden, the dark, shimmering glow of the kale, lightly waving against the dilapidated café au lait–colored garden fence. But what impressed me most, Captain, was the deathly silence of the deserted rooms, the sudden, inexplicable sadness of the cupboard and the chairs, the suddenly befogged, suddenly distant photographs, objects suddenly laden with an unexpected meaning, the complete absence of voices, altercations, whispering, and domestic sounds, the nothingness of a fishbowl, the absolute, irremediable, thick nothingness of the fishbowl that we were living in. Because when Odete left, you see, we began to go slowly into our death throes, great insects or black caravels ran or floated idly across mirrors, the broken pipes dripped hourglass minutes into plastic pails, burned-out bulbs lighted up the darkness of the bitter, distant faces of the past, the sounds from the street imperceptibly took on the texture of the mold or mildew that spreads across the tables and the clothing of the dead. Uncle Ilídio, in pajamas and muffler, would sneeze throughout whole Sundays, playing solitaire on the lumpy little couch in the living room, the hens would appear and disappear, severe and stupid, on the windowsill, the sky over the rooftops, the stone arches, the rusty little chimney covers, was a melancholy water that coagulated, solidified, and dissolved again, a vertical sea, with its tiny ships and enormous castaways, the old man's dirty fingernails would shuffle and deal the cards, but even his former carnivorous, permanent rage was losing strength and direction, the workers didn't obey him quickly as before, deliveries were behind, the vans took a hundred years to come back, stopping at every bar in successive celebrations, we were losing customers every day, every day there were the irate complaining barks on the telephone, They damaged my piano, Two armchairs are missing, What happened, please tell me, to my cabinet with little drawers, only the flower in the vase seemed to prosper in the glassed-in office, with files lined up and bills in order, growing in color and size, only the flower, which would burst out through the windows, creep across the warehouse, and inevitably devour all of us, vans, workers, rats, furniture, dust, huge, scarlet, tentacular, carnivorous, the flower which would climb into the street, digesting us, on its way to the hospital beyond and to Conde de Redondo, with its mangy whores and pastry shops with no one in them, Odete came back with some boxes, helped by a skinny, insignificant guy with an overcoat down to the ground, to carry off books, papers, photographs, the posters with bearded guys and unpleasant-looking workers hanging on the walls, she said Hello to me from the door and shut herself up in her room, going through drawers, the skinny guy, standing very straight beside her in order to look taller, was advising This has some interest, This hasn't got any, This is indispensable, This you can leave, This would be better burned, because with the bourgeoisie rearing its head anything can happen, comrade, and me standing there stupidly, with my mouth open, looking at the body that had filled out, the breasts that had grown larger, the round hips under her dress, the eye shadow, the brown hair loose down her back, me thinking Do you still peel pears over your fish bones? the old man crossed paths with her, snorting with indignation, tossing a murderous glance at the overcoat, as if he, Captain, had been the one cuckolded, as if it had been his head that was heavy, Odete (or should I call her Dália, Lieutenant?), was emptying whole shelves, dumping out drawers, leafing through notebooks, respectfully wrapped the bust of a bald-headed man with a frown in a piece of paper, Do you still peel pears over your fish bones, Odete? and then the little one came to mind and, of course, I got emotional, and then I picked up her smell and, of course, I was moved, a different smell from the mulatto woman's, gentlemen, an aroma without perfume, only of washed skin and flesh and soap (Do communists take baths too? the second lieutenant asked, do revolutionaries deodorize their armpits too?), the skinny friend, staggering under the weight, carried the boxes down to the street for her, while she, kneeling, back toward me, was closing up the suitcase that held her clothing with straps and cords, and my voice came out without my wanting it to, just like that, out of my throat, Do you still peel pears over your fish bones? just like that, I swear, exactly that way, Do you still peel pears over your fish bones? no anger, no recrimination, no grumbling, just Do you still peel pears over your fish bones?, Odete stopped what she was doing, stunned, staring at me, her eyebrows coming together over her nose like the circumflex accents of the roofs of houses, What? she asked, what's this business about bones and pears?, Uncle Ilídio was coughing recriminatively far off, making his asthma spray whistle, purposely rattling pots and pans in the kitchen, Why doesn't the dame leave, why is that dame hanging around here, The pears for dessert at the end of dinner, I explained, you used to push aside the remains of the fish to the edge of the plate with your knife, you never looked at us, you never said anything, you would smile, and the years would roll back loose in my memory and I would get the times mixed up, confused in my mind, getting back from Mozambique, Dona Isaura, the Republican Night School, my father's building in Buraca, your sarcasm, your amused indifference toward me, the mulatto with dark glasses and Hawaiian shirt examining me silently from the threshold, the pitiless and rapid passage of months, but what a hell of a life, what a complicated life, don't you think so, Captain? the way everything was figured to be so simple and clear when we got back from the war, Any more boxes, Dália, the skinny guy asked behind me in a kid's voice, Pears? fish? Odete was repeating, her forehead wrinkled, searching, the fellow clutched the bust of the bald man against his chest like a priest with his host and stood, gazing at it again and again, with the ecstatic look of a holy man, Pears? fish? my mother?, Odete was frowning, not understanding anything, Throw that bitch out into the street, Abílio, the invisible old man ordered from the end of the hallway, skating on his muddy tone of spittle, I don't want that loudmouth woman here for a single minute, the one who called her Dália hesitated, frightened, backed into the vestibule with the scowling bust by his face, Why not take the trunk along now too? I suggested, didn't you come here to pick up more things?, Are you strong enough, Olavo? Odete asked, can you carry all that or do you want some help? and outside the window the hens, and outside the window the kale, and outside the window the little gardens, separated from each other by board fences, watercress, tomatoes, parsley, potatoes, dwarf lemon trees here and there, burlap scarecrows, wash hanging on the line, cats, Olavo sank the Most Holy with the bald head into his pocket (the ceramic eyes peered sternly at me from under the cloth) and he tugged the trunk with both hands, as with a corkscrew, the room, without books or notebooks or pencils seemed as naked to me as the face of a blindman, Odete got up and her body had really grown bigger, and her hips fanned out underneath the firm ring of her waist, the asthma spray was going continuously, a dog was howling in the alley," I kept a picture of Ezequiel, he confessed to Odete, in spite of everything he looked like you, and the soldier thought This is it now, damn it, now's the time I won't be able to stand one hellish bit of it anymore, now's when I'm going to collapse like any old faggot, and yet he didn't, and yet I didn't collapse, Captain, and I still stood up under it, a few pieces of adhesive were left, some thumbtacks, the corners of posters stuck to the plaster, half a dozen books, a notebook here and there containing the pus of her handwriting, I dug my nails into my hands as hard as I could and shoved my hands into my pockets to control myself better, I tried to smile, wrinkling my face, getting rid of lines on my cheeks, pulling up the corners of my mouth, You don't even remember what he was like anymore, Odete, you don't even remember what it was like here at home, Are you going to give her a kick in the ass or do I have to come out there?, Uncle Ilídio roared in the distance, in the midst of television commercials and his muddy cough, Olavo must have been waiting for her outside, purple from the effort, putting the junk into a rented tricycle and settling himself in the driver's seat, Shifting into first, gunning the motor impatiently, Ezequiel died, Odete, I answered with difficulty, I'm more interested in the living, and the picture came back, obliquely, of the little white coffin with chiseled rings, the priest, the curiosity of the neighbor women, the slow line of taxis following the hearse to the cemetery, sweaty palms, sweaty kisses, sweaty flowers, the strange empty relief afterward Why didn't you throw her out right away? the second lieutenant asked, Ezequiel's dead, I'm much more interested in you, why didn't you come right to the point, why weren't you sincere, you old dummy? the howling of the dog went away down the street, the hens looked at him with their usual sour indifference, Odete (or should I call her Dália, Lieutenant?) twisted her mouth in a grimace of rejection or sarcasm or pity that I didn't understand, She was probably explaining to you that nothing you had to offer her was of any interest, the lieutenant colonel said, she was probably trying to explain to you that a whole string of years had gone by and a whole bunch of things and that you were refusing to admit it, that you were refusing to admit that neither of you was the same as before, I'll give you five minutes,

Abílio, the old man roared from the parlor, five minutes, second by second, People don't change that much, Commander, the soldier protested, people don't change that way, me, for example, I felt capable, just imagine, of swallowing boring movies, starting to study, starting to read, Dália, the overcoat called, worried, you're taking too long, Dália?, Your trouble is that you won't accept the fact that we're not always the same, and that's that, the second lieutenant argued, your trouble is that you want to be like a broken-down machine, that's it, there's no clock, you see, that can toll out the time that's already gone by, And in spite of it all, hell, you had the same face as before, the same eyes as before, the same shoulders, the same teeth, the same stringbean-shaped mouth as before, what would have happened if I'd grabbed you, if I'd hugged you, if I'd kicked the door closed, if I'd stopped you from leaving, if I'd proposed Let me see you peel a pear after dinner over your fish bones, Four minutes, Uncle Ilídio bellowed threateningly, furious, any minute now I'm coming in there and there'll be one hell of a mess, Dália, the runt was peeping, look, it's getting late, Dália, a bantam rooster leaped up to the windowsill and hung in the air, the tiny cartilaginous hand of an old woman or a corpse, Odete clutched my arm, smiling in a kind of complicity of tenderness and I thought What she really feels is pity for me, the only thing she really feels is pity for poor old me, I haven't eaten any pears lately, Abílio, she whispered, one of these days you invite me to lunch and I'll peel one in front of you, a truck blew its horn in the alley, brushing up against the wall, and the rooster disappeared into the garden with a hop, Fifteen seconds more, the uncle shouted with weary energy, I'm on my feet now, Abílio, Dália, the skinny guy implored her, invisible in the vestibule, for God's sake, Dália, Odete released his arm, stopped smiling, passed close by me on her way to the door, When I peel a pear again I promise I'll let you know, Abílio, she went down the two worn steps behind the overcoat onto the street, the truck blew its horn again and a crust of stucco broke off the ceiling and fell to pieces on the floor beside the tangled fringes of the rug, right underneath Dona Isaura's gaudy Sacred Heart of Jesus, some older neighbor women were watching the scene from their windows and their unaffectionate eyes looked like the rooster's, bulging and hard between rinds of skin, Odete and the midget hurriedly got into the backseat of a taxi along with the bundles, the truck driver was gesticulating with indignation from his cab, Uncle Ilídio, in pajama bottoms and gripping the rubber spray, stationed himself beside me on the threshold snorting with hatred, the exhaust pipe of the taxi was trembling and vibrating to the rhythm of the motor like the lower lip of a child close to tears, The twenty-sixth of February, Captain, I'll never forget, the same month that Ezequiel got sick, Odete's silhouette began to go slowly down the alley in an irregular puff of smoke, the neighbor women, leaning on their windowsills, made signs to each other or whispered secretly, as in church, If you never telephoned me at work it's because you never peeled a

pear over your fish bones again, Uncle Ilídio closed the door with unexpected delicacy, made me sit down in his place on the couch where there was
a yellowing little plastic rectangle on the back, handed me a glass of Spanish
anisette from the bottle with a monkey on the label that the bookkeeper had
given him at Christmas, Drink some of this shit, boy, don't turn fairy on me
because of this, they were advertising a detergent on television and I downed
such a swallow that I gagged and broke into coughing, my eyes full of stinging
tears from the belching.

"Time passes, damn it, time passes," the lieutenant colonel's father muttered jovially from his invalid's chair, waving at us with the varnished tip of
his cane.

"Situations like that, even though they don't look it, are hellishly hard,"
the second lieutenant murmured to nobody in particular, contemplating his
empty glass with excessive fondness. "If Inês appeared before me now I'm
damned if I know what I'd do."

"Olavo?" the communications officer said, surprised. "Living with Olavo?
Jesus, what did she see in a camel like that?"

"Why don't we get married?" the cloud of perfume asked ethereally, in bra
and panties (there were abundant rolls of reddish flesh hanging out over the
elastic bands), while she fixed her makeup with a tiny brush. "An intimate
ceremony, Artur, just the best man and maid of honor, no one else: I haven't
got the slightest inclination for these secret meetings, I haven't got the
slightest inclination to go on being your mistress."

"Maybe the old man liked me, Captain," the soldier explained, "but he
wouldn't let me like him. For example, if he got sick and I brought him some
broth in bed, he'd insult me."

"And later on, if you were stationed outside Lisbon, I could still go with
you," she explained, putting on her false eyelashes with the skill of a min-
iaturist, prolonging the angles of her eyelids with a stroke of her pencil. "You
weren't meant to live all alone and I was born to take care of you, love."

"What are you snooping around here for, you swine?" the uncle shouted in
a rage, covered with blankets and sheets, from the deep well of his pillow.
"Get out of here and go throw that poisoned soup away: if you think you're
going to inherit what I have, get that idea out of your head, your sister's the
one who's in line to get the moving business, you swindler."

"Make up your mind, I won't take no for an answer, you'll move in here
next week," the cloud of perfume concluded in an authoritative way, pushing
the dog away with the heel of her slipper, "and don't worry, I can close the
boutique for an afternoon and take care of the papers. Come here, give me a
hug the way it should be done, but without messing up my hair, silly."

"Someday, without thinking about it, you're going to die, boy," his father
warned, extremely satisfied, gesturing with his cane. "And I'll be there on the
other side pushing up the daisies and laughing, waiting for you."

"In the Beato conservatory, at five o'clock, the last Friday in April," she revealed. "I've already taken care of the rings, I sent your suit out to be cleaned: now confess that you're happy, sweet."

And later on, with time, with soccer, with work, it's like taking a suppository, a pill, an aspirin, Captain, the toothache continues but farther away, in the distance, spread out, bearable, I stopped gagging, the bottle of Spanish anisette went back in the cupboard, the glasses were arranged two by two on the shelf, Mr. Ilídio locked up Odete's room, where the hens pecked freely among the remains of notebooks and loose sheets of paper, roosted on the chairs and shat and scratched the strewn straw from the mattress with their feet, I kept on going out with the quiet man and the old man, we would get the job done as fast as we could and hang around for the rest of the afternoon until quitting time, wandering around bars with no one noticing or bawling us out, They've got some wild grape liquor in Chelas, the old man would announce, and we would drive the van there, bouncing along, I discovered some cherry brandy that's out of this world in Moscavide, the quiet man would reveal, and let the customers wait, tapping their feet with impatience, while we hunkered down in miserable little dark and pestilential dives talking to drunks, Gypsies, loafers, gas meter readers with greasy briefcases under their arms, over nauseating codfish cakes and tasteless squid salad, which left the soft taste of the wet cartilage of a child on your tongue. In those days, Captain, after a few fingers of strawberry brandy, or three or four shots of eau-de-vie, the toothache disappeared completely, an immense, cosmic, fraternal joy made me belligerently embrace the surprised stranger who was drinking his martini lunch in a corner, I would vomit up my mouthful on the nearest shoulder, the remains of lunch, purple membranes, almost whole potatoes, mashed pieces of meat, the floor was beginning to spin and sway, slanting, in whirls that grew faster and faster, an inner storm made me hang onto the bar, the chairs, the slippery, runaway corners of the tables, an atrocious agony persistently floated in my stomach, the voices of the quiet man and the old man echoed too near or much too far away, shouting phrases or commands or reprimands that I didn't understand too well, somebody lifted him up by the armpits and the hands that held him up on his feet hurt like metal hooks, in the cold, objects took on a bit of shape, cars, building façades, faces, dogs, cellophane trees that swayed, Hold me up I'm going to vomit again, he said, and it was just the dry heaves, dizziness, a string of spittle hanging from his chin, nauseating tastes on his palate, just his pants being wet without his knowing why, he climbed up into the moving van pushed by an energetic foot, and the steering wheel and the gearshift and the pedals grew tremendously, coming up to meet him, I'm going to split my head on the door handle, I'm going to smash my nose on the rubber floor mat, but the body of the old man and the body of the quiet man held him propped up, stopped him from tumbling down, from falling, the engine made the seat shake and my guts swirled around in my belly in sharp successive twirls, he was startled by the feeling that he was going to fall apart at every intersection, every corner, every gigantic building façade, and later on, little by little, with the breeze in his face and the minutes on the clock slipping by like snails, the world, with difficulty, got back onto its usual tracks, things gradually diminished in size, his stomach, pacified, was quieting down, he pushed his hair back from his ears with an unsteady hand, the vomiting was over, the nauseating taste was over, the anguish was over, the agony was over, the wheels squealed as they always did at the entrance to the warehouse, the hood rose up in the air like the nose of an airplane before sinking, pitching down the ramp, going by the birdcage office with Uncle Ilídio inside, sitting at his desk, the bookkeeper gesticulating in front of him with the flower in the vase in between, I'm better now, goddamn it, I'm steady on my feet now, piles of furniture jumbled together in the shadows, a bulb without a shade hanging on a twisted cord from the half-rotten roof beams, and up above the dirty strips of broken glass on the roof and the beginning of the vaguely blue geometry of the crates: at first, Captain, that was how I cured the toothache of memory, that was the way I managed to tolerate the steps of the hens in Odete's room, scratching with their nails against the notebooks and paper, I managed to watch it dawn without panic over the sea of kale in the garden, black and silvery against the broken boards of the fence, the outskirts glimmering metallically with the first slanting, difficult light of day, breaking like sebum out of the painful swelling of the clouds.

"The bookkeeper quit," the quiet man suddenly revealed during lunch on the second floor of the warehouse, spearing his fork vertically into his metal can like a hook for catching octopuses in a break between rocks. "She was trying to force your uncle to hook up with her, the guy said no, and right then and there the dame got mad and left."

"One less person to order people around," the old man consoled, throwing a chair in the direction of the swift fleeting shadow of a rat: the herds of the creatures seemed to have grown in boldness and quantity, the little animals squeaked in unison behind broken plush linings like sick babies. "Believe me, if bosses caught swine fever it would be great."

"Do you prefer round or flat wedding rings, sweet?" the cloud of perfume asked, with the stinking dog in her lap, during the television serial.

"Since the business is going under," Dona Emília barked like a woman possessed, fists on her waist, "what blessed interest would I have, just tell me, in marrying an ignorant animal like you?"

"Olavo," the communications officer said, shaking his head, "I swear I could have imagined anybody but that character."

"The death of your wife and the Revolution have finished you for good," the bookkeeper whined, forcefully putting her glasses and the ball-points into her purse, "you're no good even for singing a blindman's song anymore, you're good for nothing, you boob."

And really, just as the quiet man had announced, the woman didn't come to work in the warehouse office the next day, or the one after, or the one after that, Uncle Ilídio was indifferent to the telephone, to the flower, to a cross-eyed character in a pearl gray necktie who was complaining with insults about a delay in service, he would stare at the empty vase with the asthma spray in his hand, the workers lazed around on the ramp, went up outside with a lighted cigarette cupped in the palms of their hands to flirt with the women coming and going from the drugstore across the way, they played cards behind the trucks on tables that they cleaned with their sleeves, they dozed in the vans, leaning against the backs of the seats, their mouths open, like the corpses of drowned men.

"And you didn't take charge of the business?" the second lieutenant asked, "didn't you have the balls to help the old man out at a time like that?"

All I did was drink, Captain, he excused himself, all I did was try to forget Odete, the little guy in the long overcoat, and the pears peeled over her fish bones, all I wanted was to be called into the office, be told Household furnishings from Cruz Quebrada to Marvila, get the job over as fast as possible and then sink into a lukewarm atmosphere of flies, alcohol vapors and breaths, leaning my elbows on a zinc bar tattooed with the wet marks of glasses, order a vermouth, watch the lemon peel drift around the brown liquid, order a second vermouth in order to soften the pecking of the hens in my head, order a third vermouth in order to forget the sharp accusing eyes of the creatures, a fourth so the toothache of nostalgia would be transformed into a distant, diffuse, bearable anguish, the quiet man would stick his fingers into the glass (he was missing a joint on his index or middle finger, I can't remember which) and suck the little pieces of lemon, the old man, in a very good mood after his sixth grape liquor, was smiling amiably at every-body, there were always Cape Verdeans with switchblades in their pockets, and hoodlums, unshaven and with slow, globular eyes, one or two fat, ugly women, poorly dressed, in slippers, swilling their brandy in the shadows, the quiet man would go over to them, flirt, joke with them, belch, scratch his crotch, laugh, Tomorrow without fail I'm going to enroll in the Republican Night School, the soldier planned, indifferent to the flies that were crawling over his ears and forehead, tomorrow without fail I'm going to start studying to be a doctor, he would get a job in a hospital and the doormen would call him sir and bow to him when he came in, he'd wear a medical gown, give orders, admit patients, sign prescriptions, operate, beautiful nurses would hover noiselessly around him, with the slight, almost imperceptible swish of their starched uniforms, Mr. Ilídio had completely lost interest in television, he would turn his head away, not look at it, if they were showing a soap opera he would mutter softly Turn that off, stay gasping and squeezing his spray the whole night through, Why don't you make an appointment at the Health Service clinic? the soldier suggested to him one night, Uncle, you're probably going around sick and don't know it, you probably need to visit a shrink, but the old man told him to go straight to hell with his former sneering vigor and he stormed off, scurrying down the hallway like a cockroach before he slammed the bedroom door, he still took time to bark If you mention doctor to me again I'll kick your ass into the middle of the street and you can go fuck yourself, and the next morning, Captain, he began to give sharp orders at the warehouse again, answer the telephone, argue with customers, rail at the workers, tidy up the glass cage, forget consignments, scribble telephone numbers on the wall with the tiny pencil stub, the vans came and went with their former industry, with the boss waiting for us at the door, watch in hand, frowning, he sent out for three boxes of rat poison and ordered that the warehouse be cleaned up the way it should be, we looked at each other surreptitiously, astounded, there were no longer any flowers on the desk, no longer that strange little vase covered with facets and reliefs, every time he passed me he would grab me by the shirt and roar So I need a doctor, do I, you bastard, so you got it into your head that my nerves are shot, did you, you son of a bitch? at dinnertime he would look at me with a diabolical little smile and ask between his teeth Do you think I'm better now, dummy?, Will you give me a clean bill of health, you dirty dog? and yet there was something tender, something thankful, I can't explain it, in the middle of all that, maybe, Captain, he liked me just a little, maybe, Captain, he had some interest in me.

"I saw a beautiful engagement ring in a jewelry store in Areeiro, Artur," the cloud of perfume whispered ecstatically at lunch, spreading the gravy from the meat over an imposing silver center in imitation of a giant sunflower. "Platinum, with a pearl and two little diamonds, all for eight contos, just imagine: don't you think that's quite cheap, sweet?"

"Olavo," the communications officer repeated in disbelief, scratching his cheek with his fingernails, crossing and uncrossing his legs, serving himself some of the yellowish liquid from the unlabeled bottle with extreme care, lighting his cigarette at the filter end. "Dália and Olavo, God give me patience, you can say what you want, but I don't believe it."

"There's a bigger one, Artur, a real delight," the cloud of perfume explained, as her open gestures wrapped around him like vines around Amazonian trees, "but even if they promoted you to brigadier, I wouldn't dare confess the price of that one."

"That dame caught you with your guard down, Colonel," the second lieutenant laughed, "that dame hooked you good."

Odete was finally disappearing little by little from his mind, one night, mechanically, without thinking, he opened the door to her room, turned on the light, and he found, without any feeling of anxiety, a devastated room, naked, terribly filthy, with fragments of straw and paper everywhere, dry shit stuck to the floorboards, translucent feathers floating softly in the light, two spotted hens, who when they saw him disappeared in terror out the window, tacks and rusty nails buried in the walls like warts, the abandoned photograph of a fat Chinese looking at him with the false benevolence of a judo wrestler, and outside, the rectangular outcroppings of balconies, a sound of choking, sobbing, murmurs, scurrying in the chicken coop, the lemon tree and the medlar in the garden, twisted with unmoving cramps, and no longer any discomfort, any affliction, any pain, Captain, I was cured: a kind of lightness, a gassy relief in his head, he closed the window, went to the kitchen in search of a broom and dustpan to clean the room, scratched the hardened chicken excrement off with a knife, tore the Chinaman's round head into a thousand pieces and threw it in the garbage, Nobody ever lived here, he said to himself, I've never been there, how strange, it's the first time I've come in here, he slowly withdrew to the doorway, locked the door tightly with the key, dropped it into the broken china jar with a dragon at the bottom, halfway down the hall, he heard Mr. Ilídio rolling around in bed, wheezing and coughing, and when he passed by the bathroom he heard the old man's alert sarcastic voice, piercing the resistance of his phlegm and his sheets, So you finally got free of her, you dimwit.

"The larger one is sixteen contos, sweet," the cloud of perfume revealed, spectacular with lace and frills, picking up the plates with precious gestures: from the wall the apostles at the Last Supper, disguised as marijuana smokers, were following the movements of her buttocks with mystical lewdness. "I didn't want to, Artur, I swear I didn't want to, you were the one who made me tell."

"Soda, huh? You want a drink of soda?" the quiet man was startled. (The hunchbacked bartender was cleaning the stone counter with a rag.) "You haven't turned fairy, have you?"

"If it hadn't been Olavo you can bet it would have been somebody else," the second lieutenant said to the communications officer: "They've got it in their blood, dames can't make it alone for very long. If you only could have seen the miscarriage Inês took up with, a guy my father's age, like a skeleton, poorly dressed, who spits when he talks, you'd drop your balls right out of your chair."

"Just yesterday (Give me the dessert spoons from the drawer there, these are for coffee, silly) I spent over an hour at the jeweler's looking at it," the cloud of perfume whispered, serving a baroque, complicated dessert in which icebergs of egg whites were swimming in a dark, indescribable syrup. "The clerk was ever so pleasant, he took it out of the case, cleaned it with a special cloth, let me try it on, and with a little conversation I got him down to thirteen or fourteen contos at the most. Fourteen contos for a ring like that is a steal."

"His liver's probably acting up," the hunchback joked. "He's probably got a weak bladder and the doctor's put him on a diet."

I wasn't going to tell them about Odete, Captain, I wasn't going to tell them about the empty room and the hens and the trash and the kale at night, I wasn't going to tell them about the strange toothache of nostalgia, Your uncle wants you up in the office, the old man told him while he was unloading a stove from a van, and much less that I'd been cured and didn't need grape liquor or brandy or wine to drive the dark clouds out of my head. My uncle? the soldier thought, what does that bozo want now? a few weeks back they'd hauled some furniture from a flat in Graça, from an old building next to the firehouse (Aha, the communications officer said, aha, Colonel, this has to do with you), above a square with trees and the fat red trucks with hoses, the owner had left the key at the warehouse, but no sooner had they entered the vestibule than the concierge came out of her hole dragging a kid in glasses, one eye covered by a patch, by the arm, and she went up in the elevator with them, looking mistrustfully at those huge guys in coveralls, with ropes and hooks sticking out of their pockets. A woman still young, Captain, thirty-five, forty years old, who can say, sometimes life uses people up so much that you can't tell their age, good enough legs, big tits, she was walking behind us not saying anything, from room to room, with a furious look on her face, but after half an hour she loosened her tongue and began to talk, she called the owner of the furniture every name in the book, and when she saw the picture of a fat lady, all covered with jewelry, she spat on the carpet in disgust, Come in here, boy, and shut the door, his uncle growled angrily at him, rummaging around his desk, there wasn't really much stuff and with all our practice we had the junk all downstairs in a jiffy, and every minute or so the siren at the firehouse kept breaking out into a horrible song and even the pavement of the street shook with the noise, the kid with the patch over his eye, indifferent, on all fours, was playing with a toy car on the balcony, the old man and the quiet man took advantage of the quick job to slip into a bar almost directly opposite, a legless invalid sitting on a blanket on the sidewalk begging at the entrance, the concierge stopped spitting and grumbling and was gradually calming down, she took a hairpin out of her apron, fixed a lock of hair over her ear, and smiled at me, she was missing a front tooth and an eyetooth, her hands were red and thick and her feet were big but her behind quivered like liquid and her hips stood out, wide, underneath her skirt, Sit down in that chair there, Mr. Ilídio ordered, as his curved shoulders now hid the calendar with a naked chick, grabbing the asthma spray and sticking the little glass tube into his throat, sit down there because it's long past the time for you to learn how to run this old firetrap, the old man and the quiet man weren't about to come back and she and I took advantage of it to have a little chat, her husband had been in France for seven years and for the last three she hadn't had a letter or a single cent, she wrote

to Paris and no dice, she tried a cousin of his and nothing doing, she
telephoned the consulate and nothing, Maybe he's in Germany, they
answered her, maybe he's in Belgium, in Luxembourg, in Austria, in
Sweden, In any case, as far as I'm concerned, he's dead, she declared to the
soldier, I've lost interest, you can't rely on men, there isn't a single one who
isn't an absolute liar, I'd rather bring my son up all by myself, *Vrrum, vrrum,*
snorted the brat on the balcony pushing his car, You're not exactly right, I
disagree, let me tell you there are still some decent men around, our voices
echoed like loudspeakers in a political campaign within the empty walls in a
funny way, the concierge made a gesture of disbelief with her arm and I
caught the strong, bitter smell of her armpit, a dame with muscles, Captain,
a dame like me, a dame as strong as an ox, he looked at his Uncle Ilídio,
startled, and he, then, with disdain, If you don't want to you can get out, you
good-for-nothing, I could see right away that you'd rather go on with your
carousing, I could see right away that you'd rather go on with your boozing,
the quiet man and the old man finally blew the horn down below and their
brandy breath was like a fatal blast of pesticide, Did you get to do something
with the chippy? the old man asked and I answered no, but on the following
Sunday I was going to meet her by the corner of the building and we'd take
the trolley to Belém, the little one, whose name was Eliseu, sat on the seat in
front of us and from time to time his mother would give him an educational
pat on the behind for this or that reason, esplanades, cafés, the river, the
tower surrounded by tame little waves that were like curly hair, Keep your
mouth shut, answer the telephone, and don't talk nonsense, Uncle Ilídio
ordered me without my having stuttered anything, there's the chart with the
moves and then you can see about the dates available, the naked girl on the
calendar, kneeling, was smiling, holding up her breasts, the concierge was
smiling, eating chestnuts with me, facing the Tagus, boats were coming and
going, slowly plowing the murky water, the traffic was making the big iron
beams of the bridge buzz like seashells, whole families were eating soft
turnovers and chicken wings on the yellow grass, she invited me to come
watch television the following Wednesday in the cubicle where she lived, a
kitchen with a cot for the child, a bedroom, a bathroom, and a tiny living
room with a lot of crucifixes and illustrated postcards and lumps from the
dampness on the walls, there were two canvas beach chairs beside the
television set which had a round doily on top and a trinket which was some
kind of ceramic candlestick, the woman opened a cupboard, took out a goblet
and a bottle, and poured me some sharp vinho verde which burned my
tongue and bubbled down my chest on its way to my stomach like a painful
magnesium fuse, the program was a boring dance affair with music like the
kind at funerals that never ends, guys and girls, tireless, leaping, moving
their wrists to one side and the other, I was sipping the poison out of
politeness, all stiff, not knowing what to do, vaguely thinking about Odete,

the kale, the midget in the overcoat, the siren would whistle and shut down, I left at ten past eleven, returned home half-dazed, making confused plans during the bus trip, I went back on Saturday, I went back on Tuesday, I went back on Thursday, I finished the bottle, I started a new one, the alcohol didn't burn my stomach as much anymore, Odete didn't appear when I was with her anymore, on the sixth or seventh visit I didn't find the television set in the parlor but in the bedroom, on a wicker table at the foot of the bed, a Spanish doll in a full skirt and hands in the air by the headboard, I ceremoniously placed the tip of my behind at an angle to the bedclothes and the springs creaked much more than I had supposed, on the screen they were showing comedy films full of chases, running, pratfalls, tumbles, guffaws, an orange-colored, cardiac light endlessly licked the window frame, the concierge took off her shoes, stretched out on the sheets, was getting undressed quite naturally, item by item, as if she'd known me for a hundred years, the glass of wine was dancing in my hands, I ended up putting it on the rug beside me, and while I was curling up, huddling out of timidity and embarrassment, the enormous face of a clown (or a woman? or the lieutenant colonel? or the magician's assistant? or all of you all at the same time?) completely filled the screen (more gin), grinding and twisting (more whiskey) with sharp, endless, pathetic (more vodka) masks of derision.

# 2

"LET me be the first to congratulate you on your promotion to general, General sir," Major Fontes told the lieutenant colonel with an enormous lackluster smile on his gums. (Where in hell could he have hidden his teeth, the lieutenant colonel thought, so that all that can be seen is that spongy, repulsive orange peel of flesh?) "No need to explain to you how proud the officers here in the Ministry are with your appointment as director of the Military Academy: if our Brigadier Ricardo were alive I can only imagine how pleased he would have been now, he expected so much of you."

"Look, it was the boy from the cleaners with your blue suit," the cloud of perfume called to him, pushing away the little dog with her leg, shaking in front of him, like a bullfighter, a cellophane package hanging on its plastic hanger, inside of which entrails with sleeve buttons were softly swaying. "I'd better put it in the clothes closet so you won't sit on it with your usual absentmindedness."

"And you didn't make her, dope?" the second lieutenant asked, "you didn't hump her right off?"

"Of course we had relations," the soldier answered, "of course I laid her; do you think I'm some kind of hick or something?"

Even after Brigadier Ricardo's death he continued to occupy the tiny office in back, with the same filthy cobwebs in the corners of the ceiling, the same rotting furniture, the same excessive mounds of paper, the only difference was that now he had been instructed to work in reverse, to undo what he had done, to bring back the people cleaned out and to clean out the ones who had done the cleaning, urgent orders were constantly arriving from the top, Hurry up, Carry this out, Get this moving for me, Cases number 128 to number 156 have to be ready by the end of this week without fail, Colonel So-and-so and Colonel So-and-so and Colonel So-and-so are immediately and for obvious reasons put into reserve status, leaning over his desk like a calendula, bifocals on the tip of his nose, he took notes, scratched out, underlined, made crosses in the margins, wrote, a sergeant typed up his reports, Lieutenant Cardoso, who was interested in literature and always carried his little novel under his arm, corrected the Portuguese, chewing on the rubber eraser of his pencil, traffic on the Sodré docks growled and jingled ceaselessly, the trains on the Cascais line came and went at the station in the distance, the December dampness was increasing the number of lilac mushrooms on the walls, another brigadier, fatter, older, even shorter, who kept repeating We've got to keep the Army calm, we've got to calm down our superiors, now occupied the large room with heavy church hangings facing the broad rusty rectangle of the square and the statue that was trotting toward the river, They raised me in rank but didn't give me a better cubbyhole, they raised me again and the aide-de-camp to the chief of the General Staff announced to me on the telephone My friend, starting in March you're going to run things at the Military Academy, and hung up, Now they want me to be a scoutmaster, the lieutenant colonel thought, furious, roasting Major Fontes with his eyes, Now they want me to spank those who don't memorize their multiplication tables, the lieutenant colonel thought, looking exasperatedly at the cloud of perfume, the fifteen-conto ring on her finger, who was having tea with a green, silent, and snuffed-out friend, as fragile as a stalk, who was leaning over to offer pieces of toast to the lapdog, making sparkling waves with her bracelets, after so many months as a clerk they want me to be a nursemaid, he thought, rolling and unrolling behind his back the marching orders that Major Fontes had handed him with the pomp accorded a parchment diploma, Brigadier Ricardo's replacement, suddenly subordinate, accompanied him to the hallway, hopping with respectful, amiable, little leaps, The Ministry is going to feel your absence like an irremediable loss, General, The courageous and competent work that you accomplished here, General, The lucidity, the critical spirit, the benevolence, the care and admirable impartiality that from the beginning set the standard, down to the tiniest details, of your conduct here, General, How greatly our poor youth, unhappily adrift today, will benefit certainly from your guidance and example, General, and me, to myself, your aunt's snatch, and me, to myself, Fuck your whore of a mother, you oily little shit, the orderlies came to attention in the attic rooms, the personnel in the Secretariat snapped to attention, In spite of everything you managed to make general, his mother said, with a rabbit stole around her neck, lazily installed in an armchair decorated with gold studs, powdering the wrinkles on her cheeks with a pink puff, mind you don't mess it all up with one of your silly stunts, and Uncle Mendes, Uncle Pinto, Uncle Conceição smiled paternally, glass of port in hand and well-starched handkerchief in jacket pocket, It will be difficult, the brigadier was reciting, for us to fill the breach in the composition of the officer assignment unit left by the absence of your wisdom and zeal, and the lieutenant colonel, hastily, Are you listening, Mother?, I doubt that anyone with your high intelligence, General, will appear soon to work with us in the arduous task of presiding over the destiny of our glorious national armed forces, and the lieutenant colonel, in short pants, How are you, Uncle Pinto? he went down the steps to the street still accompanied by the chubby brigadier's flexuous and excessive discourse, sprinkled with gestures, and by the approving smiles of Major Fontes, Lieutenant Cardoso, other vague characters, other dim individuals whose names I can't remember, I had to take my boxer to the vet in an emergency, the green friend lamented with a vegetable sigh, there wasn't any pill that would stop its diarrhea, they took leave of me under the arcade in the middle of that usual total confusion of beggars and soldiers and Gypsies, And the doctor told me right off, as soon as he felt its belly, another day or two, Dona Clarisse, and your dog would have died in your arms, they went back into the building amid salutes and bows, the Black Mercedeses and Volkswagens of the Army were lined up along the sidewalk, the drivers with corporal's and sergeant's insignias on their shoulders were chatting, leaning on the hoods, Naturally, when he told me that, I was close to fainting, I sincerely don't see the use in giving awful news to people, the Barreiro ferry was filling with people, an insignificant drizzle was hanging in the air like saliva, the lieutenant colonel folded the marching orders four times, stuck them in his pant pocket, and started walking, hunched over, along the columns to the subway station on the Praça da Figueira, I'm sick and tired of telling you to straighten up, Artur, his mother said indignantly, bent over like that you'll be quick to turn into a hunchback, Lord always goes to him, the cloud of perfume answered, and so far he's been right about all of his illnesses, I'm fifty-one years old, Mother, the lieutenant colonel argued, peeking into a store window and finding himself terribly old, at my age what difference does it make if I'm hunchbacked or not?, Fifty-one already? the second lieutenant was surprised, I wouldn't have taken you for more than forty or forty-five, Being right is fine, the green friend asserted, what I'm angry about is the brutal way he talks to us, the subway to Anjos, the bus to Sapadores, the filth, the sweat, the disrepair, the torn advertising posters (women in bathing suits, faces with dark glasses, deeply bronzed muscular Apollos, a blond guy, pleasant look-

ing, with a mustache, in the uniform of a municipal street cleaner KEEP
YOUR CITY CLEAN), the vigorous or timid political slogans written in
capital letters on building façades, exhausted, faded, ugly, sad people, There
wasn't any revolution, Lieutenant, convince yourself of that, the soldier
insisted, apart from less money and more disorder, what difference can we
see between 1974 and now? and on Sapadores your place five floors above
the boutique, filled with vases, Chinese knickknacks, horrible paintings of
waterfalls and nymphs, easy chairs too large for the dimensions of the living
room's unequal cheap baroque luxury, and pictures of you when you were
young, Edite, everywhere, you in a bathing suit at the beach making daring
faces like movie actresses, He forgets that we have feeling for the little
creatures, the stalk said, refusing with her hand more tea, besides that, it
could be that animals understand what people are saying, the *Reader's Digest*
has an article this month about that by an American, Knocking everything
down to rebuild it just the way it was, the soldier persisted, one of his legs
over the mulatto woman's, is that change, Lieutenant?, General, eh? his
mother warned, if I happen to catch you in some mess I swear on my life that
you'll go for a whole month without any dessert, the young sales clerk with
firm skin and blue eyes who greeted him as if he were a grandfather, always
reading photo-novels behind the counter of the boutique (I wonder what she
does Saturday nights? the lieutenant colonel thought, does she go to the
movies, does she have a boyfriend, is she a virgin?), she put the magazine
away in the drawer for orders as soon as she saw him, he went up in the
smelly, extremely slow elevator with a door grating that quivered and trembled like a cable car with the flu, feeling, inside that narrow box, with a pale
nose and hands crossed over my fly, tight and stiff, like a corpse in a coffin,
Who do you want to see, the surly soldier at the main entrance to the Military
Academy asked mistrustfully, and farther on inside he could make out boys
running, sports fields, trees, barracks, he wiped one foot after the other on
the mat, Artur? the cloud of perfume shouted from the kitchen, is that you,
sweet?, What do you want? the sergeant of the guard barked, lighting a
cigarette, pistol on his belt, never mind the conversation, I haven't got time
for sweet talk, It was my impression at the time that the Revolution was so
people could live better, the soldier was worked up, I didn't know that the
important thing was for everything to stay the same, Lieutenant, It's obvious
that they can understand, Clarisse, the cloud of perfume explained, scratching the lapdog's ears, any child can tell you that animals are much sharper
than we are, the sergeant deciphered the marching orders, sniffed, read
them again, suddenly turned scarlet, saluted with the cigarette in his hand,
the surly soldier, beret on the back of his head, opened and closed his mouth,
not understanding what was going on, Please excuse me, General sir, the
sergeant stammered in panic, but in civilian clothes like that I couldn't guess,
he sat down in the living room, took off his jacket, turned on the floor lamp,

took the newspaper out of his briefcase, looked for the sports pages, Artur, sweet, is that the way it is now, you don't pay any attention to me? the overworked voice from the kitchen whimpered, do you come home now without even a kiss?, Go to the movies with you? the girl in the boutique asked with a nervous smile, no, I haven't got a boyfriend, but if Dona Edite ever dreamed, I'd lose my job like that, General, This way, General, please, the breathless officer candidate with a red armband whispered, leaning over and talking with the unctuousness of a clerk, we didn't figure that you'd be coming today, much less in civilian clothes, Director sir, and out of the corner of his eye the lieutenant colonel saw the surly soldier straightening his beret, his tunic, his sleeves, his buttons, giving his boots a difficult shine with his pants legs, he saw the sergeant of the guard anxiously assembling his shift, the bugler galloping over, a corporal quickly distributing white gloves to the men, he sensed a confused agitation (people, faces peeking out, tripping, gestures) behind the windows of the first floor of the main corps building, If Dona Edite doesn't know anything about it, maybe, the girl agreed, and her eyes mocking me, and the corners of her mouth pulled up, mocking me, and her breasts swelling under her blouse, shouting at me You can't you can't you can't, Colonel Ramos, General, at your orders, a guy in glasses with a boil on his cheek, followed by a silent legion of majors and captains, introduced himself, a bell was ringing for class (or calling the students?), quartermasters scurrying like cockroaches were lining up platoons, orders and shouts could be heard in the distance, youngsters in uniform were walking toward a cement courtyard with a basketball net above it, a customer entered the boutique, the girl got up and the lieutenant colonel immediately fell in love with the display case of rings and necklaces, No sooner were you promoted than you start doing foolish things? his mother reprimanded him, calling on Uncle Pires as a witness, can't you see that I'm completely right in taking his dessert away from him, Afonso?, Wouldn't you like to meet the officers of the Academy in the main hall before making contact with the students? the colonel in glasses proposed, ill at ease, wiping his sweaty palms on his behind, please excuse the improvisation, General, but it hasn't been the custom of directors to arrive like that in a taxi, in civilian clothes, through the main gate, Call me Artur, that's my name, do I seem so old to you, kid? he got up out of his chair, crossed the parlor, a nauseating smell of roast meat that was agonizing and growing, pots and pans hanging from hooks, an ironing board, blue plastic bowls, clothes drying on the back balcony, Edite in an apron and hairnet with a package of flour in her hand, Good evening, dear, Hello, sweet, A real woman, his mother considered, one who's lived, has experience, money in the bank, upbringing, seriously, I've never seen anything stupider than a man, On weekdays it's difficult because of my parents, the girl said, her fingernails chewed and her hair less shampooed than it had seemed at first, only if I lie to them, General, only if I tell them I'm sleeping

at the home of a girl friend, At your service, General, the one in glasses
agreed with a kind of genuflection (the branches of the trees were waving like
feathers around the back of his neck), leave the ceremonies of protocol till
tomorrow and I'll show you your office and your quarters, But what can he
see in an insipid girl who isn't even eighteen, is she? his mother was irritated,
twisting her gnawed stole with the skeletal fingers of a bird, what does a child
hardly out of the cradle know about satisfying a male? more trees, a parade
ground, sports fields, a pack of children kicking a ball, the officers dispersing
slowly, hesitantly, dragging their feet, Edite held out a cheek soft as a pillow,
where the makeup, liquefied, was running down, damp from the heat and
the steam, you could write your name with your thumb on the glass fogged
up with steam, We're leaving here next week, the lieutenant colonel
announced, looking without emotion at the plastic and clay bowls, the tank
on the balcony, the tiles in poor taste, a wicker basket piled high with
clothespins, I've been promoted to general, he muttered, and I've been
offered a kind of living quarters at the Military Academy, so you can say
goodbye to this place for a while, And you insisting on the Revolution,
Lieutenant, the soldier wondered, sharing his last cigarette with the mulatto
woman, listen, the ones who are running things in the country, aren't they
maybe the same ones who were running things before?, Hello, Mother? the
girl in the boutique said (The good thing is that they live in Alcochete and my
girl friend hasn't got a phone, she whispered, covering the mouthpiece, the
good thing is that they won't let me travel on the ferry alone at night), I
wanted to let you know that I'm working late here at the store, so I'm going to
sleep at Suzete's, an office with the portraits of the former directors on the
wall and the usual standards between two bookcases, the usual baroque
desk, the big high-backed chairs as always, and going on to the residence
under the whispering of the dry leaves of the plane trees, Colonel Ramos
rushing to open and close doors, to turn on the lights, to demonstrate the
heating system, the refrigerator, the water heater, the appliances, calling a
corporal to fix a window frame, calling another corporal to oil a latch, there
was trash, pieces of paper on the floor, It needs a good cleaning, General, it
needs a proper waxing, we have to spray the rooms with insect repellent, for
example, but I guarantee you that tomorrow morning, when you arrive here
to take possession, not a speck of dust, not an ant will be seen, and, indeed,
the next day they were waiting for me with martial bugle calls, starched,
combed, shaven, polished, Colonel Ramos gave a speech, consulting note
cards, before the battalion of cadets on the cement yard, The historic deeds
of the Portuguese armed forces, The crusades, The navigators, Vasco da
Gama, Ferdinand Magellan, Bartolomeu Dias, the great Afonso de Albuquerque, Dom João de Castro and the siege of Diu, The unmatched courage
with which we freed ourselves, gentlemen, from Spanish domination,
French domination, Dutch domination, not to mention the unforgettable

saga of Africa, Mouzinho de Albuquerque, Paiva Couceiro, Caldas Xavier, The way in which we fought the unjust colonial war that the Salazarista dictatorship (Give it to them, give it to them, the communications officer commented) so cruelly imposed on us, Edite, abounding in pins and lace, was triumphant on the platform, exchanging intimate smiles with the insignificant wife of the colonel, who, in the meantime, had turned to me, proud, solemn, majestic, all in one person like a figure in a procession, And for you, Excellency, I can only wish the greatest success in the exercise of your thorny duties, A distinguished officer molded by a thousand diverse experiences, A man of war and the halls of government, To watch over the education of the future military and civilian leaders of the Nation, This school and its ancient traditions, Dozens and dozens of its illustrious sons well attest to the incomparable level of instruction practiced here over the decades, and then my timid, roundabout, confused thanks, Edite fanning herself, my mother repeating in my ear You're acting like a fool, Artur, tonight, as punishment, you're going to bed without any supper, chests covered with medals, visored caps, drums, cornets, the parade of countless little organ-grinder monkeys with rifles on their shoulders, Where in hell is the bottle of gin I left in the bathroom?

"And did you go to the movies with her, Colonel?" the second lieutenant was interested, "and weren't you afraid of your wife, Colonel?"

"The living quarters are a delight," the cloud of perfume, resting the enormous fifteen-contos ring on Colonel Ramos's restless sleeve cackled. "With a little feminine touch here and there, flowers, some doilies, some knickknacks, some pictures, you'll see how marvelous it will look overnight."

"I didn't touch it, Commander sir," the soldier swore, "you don't have to give me that suspicious look, ever since three o'clock in the morning all I've done is drink grape liquor."

"If the dog gets sick on me again," the substanceless voice of the green friend at the other end of the parlor lamented, "word of honor, I won't know what to do. That vet is going to give me a heart attack one of these days."

"At eleven o'clock, midnight at the latest, I'll be in bed, Mother, I promise," the girl shouted into the telephone.

Not a first-run movie house, naturally, the ones where you find yourself in a compromising position by running into familiar faces during intermission, friends of Edite, people who have visited you at home, my brother-in-law, stupefied, bulging eyes, trying to cover up in vain, but a hidden one, a neighborhood house on the Praça do Chile, full of unemployed people and metal cuspidors, to see a very old, scratchy film, a musical comedy with startling cuts, a good-looking character would appear, in a bow tie, singing, and, boom, it would switch without any transition to a dance scene, the cone of light from the projector leaped as if it were bouncing about the booth like a wagon on a narrow, rocky trail, the seats had a disagreeable plastic smell, the spectators stomped their feet on the floor in indignation, a pair of little old ladies, heads together, were reading the subtitles to each other in the monotone of a dictation text, her elbow touched mine and withdrew, I felt her shoulder against my shoulder for an instant, the smooth smell of legs, stomach, body, I moved my knee closer by feeling, trembling with anxiety and upset, eighteen years old my eye, nineteen or twenty at least, the girl wriggled, annoyed, in her seat, She's had enough of this, the lieutenant colonel thought in panic, she's terribly sorry she came out with me, a fireman, standing, kept blowing his nose in the corridor and his axe was gleaming like a gold tooth, What excuse am I going to give at home? he asked himself, bringing his knee a little closer, where did I spend the night? a meeting, an emergency, orders from the minister, the threat of a coup? the elbow touched her again, this time more forcefully, and she withdrew just a tiny bit, the character in the bow tie was on a terrace excitedly kissing a lady in a silvery dress and fur jacket, his knee finally found the resistance of a thigh and stopped, the girl's shoe stepped on his lightly and her head leaned over toward his neck and the intensity of the smell increased, eighteen years old, my eye, Uncle Pinto, twenty-three or twenty-four and that's a low estimate and with a lot more experience at this than I, I can almost bet that the telephone call to her mother was a fake, I can almost bet that it was a signal set up with some pimp, he groped her hand and squeezed a damp, limp, slippery bundle of fingers, he turned his chin around to kiss her and brushed the oily dandruff of her head with his mouth, I wonder what her breasts are like, the lieutenant colonel thought, I wonder what she's like naked, how many lovers she's had already, how many abortions she's had, and at that point the movie stopped, the lights came on, an advertising sign moved slowly down from the ceiling and covered the screen, garages, oculists, funeral parlors, restaurants, The Avenidas Furniture Store, tailors, musical instruments, used cars, intermission, the salesgirl sat up in her seat, she carried a tiny blue plastic purse in the shape of a parallelopiped, wore a knit jacket over her shoulders, and a ring with her initials on her little finger, maybe she really does live in Alcochete, maybe her mother does exist, maybe she's not lying to me, they went out single file, with slow, oxen steps, to look at the shop windows, children's clothing, watches, household utensils, photographic supplies, small, critical myopic eyes behind glasses pointed at us, a cluster of movie buffs in muddy shoes drinking coffee and buying chocolates at the counter, a flow of serious scarabs was going up and down the steps to the toilet with no apparent surcease, the girl took a cigarette out of a braided-straw case while the lieutenant colonel searched, without finding them (I have to say something, we have to talk about something), for the redeeming phrases of an impossible conversation, Shall we bring our mother-of-pearl peacock, sweet?, Edite proposed, shall we bring the Indian collection of ivory elephants?, The hardest are the opening words, the lieutenant colonel thought, the hardest is to find a subject that's worth something, they walked silently around the lobby, side by side, heads down, like a pair of condemned criminals or strangers, a big-bellied policeman was standing guard over a cuspidor, the fireman with a cold was studying the posters for coming attractions, all very old, frightful films, with actors with hair parted in the middle and little mustaches, See, Alice? Colonel Ramos said in an accusing tone to the insignificant little woman, do you see how our general's wife has managed to give it the feeling of a home in the twinkling of an eye?, The bottle of gin, Colonel, is the one you've got in your hand, the second lieutenant defended himself, you haven't stopped drinking from it for a single minute, the usher with gold buttons was contemplating the sad street outside, I'm going to ask the girl what her name is, the lieutenant colonel decided, let's give this a beginning, middle, and end, he cleared his throat, opened his mouth, but a small, irritating, endless bell, coming as if from beneath the floor, making ankles and soles of feet itch, was summoning the audience for the continuation of the film, the bar emptied, the spectators filled the seats as if their heads were teeth emerging from the plastic gums of the chairs, the advertising panel with its musical instruments, oculists, garages, rose, crooked, with a squeal of pulleys, on its way to the ceiling, the lights slowly dimmed, scattered coughing went on and off, the beam from the projection booth quivered again, the well-built fellow was arguing on the screen with a bearded gentleman who was gesticulating and becoming furious, I courageously put my arm around the salesgirl, her moist fingers stroked my chin, my pants suddenly felt too tight in the fly, where a pinched piece of me was trying to grow and expand, Twenty-five years old, my eye, Mother, the lieutenant colonel thought, if I went for her ID card I'd find thirty, There are those who are just the opposite too, the communications officer said, taking off his socks, there are those who look sixty and are thirty too, Dames trick you, boy, dames trick you, the grandfather roared from his invalid's chair, trust anything in the world except a circle of skirts, he pushed on his dick with his free hand to help it get free of the prison of his shorts, and a wet roll of flesh, thick and hard, climbed up him instantly, almost to his navel, her legs grasped mine, her tongue rose out of the darkness, quickly brushed around the shape of my ear, disappeared, the old women reading the subtitles fell quiet, scandalized, the old gentleman with a white beard was carrying on vehemently in what looked like a theater dressing-room with the lady in the fur jacket, who was answering him with disdainful grimaces, the communications officer carefully put his socks inside his shoes and dove, like a swimming student in a municipal pool (the little organ-grinder monkeys disappeared around a curve in the parade grounds), between the hairy, open thighs of a woman.

"General, sweet? (The cloud of perfume was pondering him, absolutely motionless, marveling amid the smoke, the steam, and the smell of meat beginning to scorch, clutching the package of flour tightly against her enormous, imposing breasts: and me thinking, bitterly, All this happiness isn't for me, damn it, because underneath it all she doesn't give a damn for me, but for herself, only for herself, for living with a prestigious guy, for having managed to marry an important fellow.) You a general, Artur? I'm going to phone Clarisse to tell her (Didn't I say so, Mother?), poor dear, her husband never went beyond second lieutenant."

"Revolution, Lieutenant?" the soldier insisted, tireless, repeating his martinis and pushing the skinny girl by the arm, "in order to make a real revolution in Portugal you'd have to kill all the priests, all the soldiers, all the doctors, all the rich people, half the country at least."

"Right this afternoon, ma'am," Colonel Ramos announced amiably, "they'll be putting up the curtains and laying down the rugs that are missing (they're two very fine ones, from Arraiolos, and are supposed to be delivered at five o'clock) and I can guarantee you that by tonight this place will be perfectly livable."

More arguments, more conversations, more singing, more endless dancing, the machine shaking and breaking down, the screen zebra-striped with scratches, the screeching waves of sound, the stomping and shouts of protest from the audience, the older gentleman's beard that would leap out of focus from time to time, the girl's tongue appeared out of the shadows, licked my throat, disappeared, the lieutenant colonel lowered his chin and her mouth tasted like chewing gum, dentist's cement, and stew, the lady in the fur jacket, with a very strange baroque hairdo now, leaned her enchanted cheek against that of the man in the bow tie, the music swelled, nasally, THE END in blue letters stamped on the faces of both, and underneath, in Portuguese, in smaller letters that went off and on, FIM, the lights in the theater all went on, suddenly revealing awakened and concave faces, drapes opened with a tinkling of rings, the street outside looked more tawdry to me, more insignificant, poorer, the night over the buildings looked like a lumpy piece of canvas full of cracks and holes, Some revolution, some stinking revolution, the soldier snorted with hate, they went on for a few years fooling us all with that, A boardinghouse, a flophouse, a room? the lieutenant colonel hesitated going up the marble steps, arm in arm with the salesgirl, to the Praça do Chile, shall I just go with her into any old boardinghouse?, Hello, Clarisse, is that you?, Edite bellowed euphorically into the telephone, I'll give you a piece of candy if you can guess what's happened to Artur, the magician's assistant, taking pins out of her hair, was dancing on top of the table striking precarious poses, rubbing her belly against the paper lampshade, Get down from there before you hurt yourself, the second lieutenant begged, get down from there, you'll ruin the top of my table, A heart attack?, A heart attack? the cloud of perfume howled, outraged, oh, Clarisse, do you think I'm living with an old man perhaps? they went down two or three blocks on the

Avenida Almirante Reis, through the window of a beer hall a swarm of men could be seen drinking and smoking, little plates of lupine seeds, pool tables in back, old men in berets leaning over chessboards, closed shops with grillwork shutters (haberdasher's, goldsmiths, home appliance establishments, cubic and white in the shadows), an ambulance whining, traffic lights, military police jeeps, the dull, dream-walking traffic of midnight, Can the little run-down hotel in the Bairro das Colónias still be in existence, with its vertical sign and mangy front, with the same disheveled young boy still on guard by the panel of keys and the guest register, the same threadbare carpet, fastened to stairs with metal staples? Some women were slowly patrolling the corners, majestic, excessive, and funereal, Hotel Lemos, Hotel Dias, Hotel Maracujá, Hotel Colonial, Hotel Chicago, tiny rooms, burned-out bulbs, dirty sheets, windows opening onto hazy inner courtyards from which, mixed in with the meowing of cats, a dew of garbage evaporated, shouts and slaps and the jerking of springs, stiff as nails, drilling the wall continuously, how many dawns like that, how many venereal diseases (seven, eight?), how many glass dishes overflowing with cigarette butts, how many bitter, bilious, repentant, difficult, ash gray awakenings?

"He's been promoted to general, Clarisse, he's been named director of the Military Academy, just imagine," the cloud of perfume challenged, adjusting a terrible earring the size of a chandelier, which scattered light in a thousand different directions, with her free fat hand. "By the way, I was chatting with Artur just now and the thought came to me that your husband never went beyond second lieutenant in the Auxiliaries, isn't that so?"

"Shall we look for a bar where we can have a drink?" the salesgirl asked, her arm becoming lighter on mine, her trunk, impassively, growing harder, smaller, withdrawing.

"I know very well that he started low, I know very well that he began as a sergeant," Edite went on, unperturbed, grinding her friend into uncountable, tiny little pieces of meat, mistreated and humiliated. "In any case, his getting to be an officer was devilishly good luck, the messes for quartermasters and corporals and the rest of them (I can't tell one from the other, what do you expect of me) are so awful, good Lord, their food is so common, don't you think? And their uniforms, horrible heavy material, making them dress up like traffic policemen without helmets."

"There's a crazy place with music on Martim Moniz," the girl suggested. "I go there with my friends sometimes."

I not only went to them when I was an adolescent, with a group of school chums, the lieutenant colonel thought, not just in his youth, solitary as a fox, with his mustache beginning to sprout, but during marriage too, and especially after your death in the cancer hospital, so as not to stay home all alone, you see, trembling with fear, awake in the dark, rolling his blind eyes around in search of the brighter lard color of the window, listening to the sounds of

349

underbrush and footsteps from a distant Africa, which the ticking of his wristwatch on the night table and the spraying of the water trucks washing the street below gradually dissolved. Especially after your death in the cancer hospital, you have to know, when there wasn't any wine in the pantry or stumbling over chairs, he couldn't find a bottle of whiskey or grape liquor in the cabinet, tormented by the gaseous claws that pinched and pulled him, by shapes in white smocks and rubber gloves, equipped with bloody scalpels, dissecting pale corpses laid out on stone tables, by fingers that pointed fiercely in his direction, You killed her. An unlighted sign on a corner, Hotel Angola, Rooms, Second Floor, an iron lamp swinging above, surrounded by large black moths, What's this? the boutique clerk was indignant as they went in, what's this? a character in shirt-sleeves dozing behind a broken-down piece of counter just like the fragment of a wharf, the lieutenant colonel showed the tip of a card to the other man's indifference, he wrote the date and signed his name on a slip, received a key, Third door on the right, shooed her down a kind of tunnel that smelled of urine and stale preserves, turned a knob, felt around for the light switch on the molding of the door, What's this? what's this? she repeated in a low voice with a metallic tone that bent over and gave in, a ceiling light with a metal shade went on unexpectedly, as if someone had pulled an adhesive bandage from the hairs on my thigh, a bed, a stool, a decrepit cabinet with a mirror, with one of its legs replaced by two loose tiles, a glazed pitcher and a small basin with dusty swirls where tiny cobwebs slanted downward, a small window on the street with dotted little curtains, holes and cracks in the plaster, small raffia mats, the cloudy, immemorial, thick, ancient silence of an attic, and at that point, without my expecting it, without warning, without a sound, the girl threw her purse onto the bed, sat on the stool, bent forward, buried her nose in her elbow, and began to cry.

"They'll bring breakfast to your place at whatever time you tell us, ma'am," Colonel Ramos explained, "and the same goes for lunch and dinner if you don't feel like doing any cooking."

"Say, Artur," the cloud of perfume said, running her little finger over the back of a piece of furniture to check its cleanliness. "You must remind me to invite Clarisse, poor thing, over this week."

Her father was probably a railroad worker, or a metal worker, or a chauffeur, her mother a seamstress, or a cleaning woman, or cashier in a department store, and the lieutenant colonel, unnerved, not knowing what to do, imagined a cold cave of a place in a sad building in Alcochete: photographs of the girl as a baby all over the place, a nail keg, unmatched chairs, innumerable crying children, shouting neighbor women, clotheslines, gulls dozing on the river mud, the trombones of the Philharmonic rehearsing in the distance, her face staring at him, resentful, afflicted, repentant, fat with tears, almost bellowing, You think I'm a prostitute, General, but you're mistaken, you think I'm a loose woman, General, No, I make no judgments, word of honor, calm down, the lieutenant colonel was getting restless, I'm not judging anything, seriously, be quiet, look you're scaring the other people, a dump below a hospital, or by a soccer field, or on the way to Lisbon, or by the bullring, opaque china dolls, a huge radio, the picture of a customs inspector with a mustache on a shelf, If Edite finds out about this she'll fire her, if Edite finds out about this she'll kill her, he imagined the cloud of perfume, extracting herself from an Army Mercedes, falling apart in roars, gigantic, alarming, pitiless, the kid, dismayed, took a few lost steps across the room, he cracked his knuckles, peeked out through the curtains and nobody was on the street, hazy haloes surrounded the neon signs, an invisible airplane droned in the solid interior of the sky a few timid little pats on the salesgirl's back (Now now now) as she noisily blew her nose, pushing her hair back over her ears, making a great effort to smile, You can invite anyone you please, ma'am, Colonel Ramos enlightened her, flexuous, the house is completely independent, there's an entrance for cars at the back gate, the magician's assistant, off balance, stuck a fingernail into the paper ball that was torn into yellow shreds, twisted wires, its transparent plastic rods breaking with the small noise of a cracked knuckle, Completely independent, ma'am, if the general wants a sentry there, we'll put one there, Come here, the lieutenant colonel said, thinking about the cave in Alcochete and her metal-worker father, rest a little on the bed and as soon as you feel like it we'll leave, he helped her to lie down, took her shoes off, put pillows under her head, the garbage collectors, almost all Cape Verdeans, with wide orange suspenders, were furiously slamming the containers onto the avenue, amid scurrying, orders, the sobbing and swallowing of machines, I spent the night at the Ministry, dear, putting up with the secretary of state, an emergency meeting because of some idiots with a mania for revolution again, I'm dead beat, fix me some good, strong coffee, if it's not too much trouble, and the cloud of perfume, in a dressing gown, fatigued in turn, and her hands pulling the sheets softly over him, and the lapdog scratching with its claws by the glass door to the kitchen, invite Clarisse, invite my brother-in-law, invite Ramos and his wife, aperitifs, drinks, dinner, me chewing, looking at the Last Supper on the wall, listening to the terribly remote, mixed conversations without interest as they came closer and went away, her seamstress or cleaning-woman or department store–cashier or sausage factory–worker mother, the childhood photographs, the straw chairs, all different, around an oval table, That's how people live, the lieutenant colonel thought, taking off his jacket and placing it carefully on a wooden hanger, it's in the midst of this absurd idiocy that the days succeed each other in a vegetable way, without surprises or hope, one after the other, necktie, shirt, undershirt, the girl was looking at him without weeping, but with the tears of a while back still motionless on her round cheeks and the poor-quality eye shadow getting lost along her temples in the roots of her hair, her legs were close together like those of a dead person, one of her hands like a visor over her forehead and her eyes astute, slightly curious, slightly frightened, his shoes, his pants, his socks, his shorts, It's in the midst of this absurd idiocy, the lieutenant colonel thought, this bitter, unquestioning tranquility that the flabby jelly of the days slowly evaporates, he turned out the light and the square of the window grew larger, suddenly neat in the dark, the color of the sounds became sharp and lucid, a dull, acrid wind moved his insides, Keep your trap shut, he said aloud in the silence, look, you're bothering other people, and he was hit by the certainty that he was really talking to the seagulls and marine birds of Alcochete, dozing among the grasses in the river mud.

# 3

I DON'T know this night. I don't know this place. I don't know these smells, these tastes, these voices, I don't know these women or these men. I don't know these early-morning dogs in the street outside, the sounds, the pasty dawn that butters the window frames, the dead body prone beside me on the carpet, why dead, by whom dead, how dead? Esmeralda, my god-mother, Dália, you? I go to your apartment twice a week, on Tuesdays and Fridays, right after dinner, I drink, I talk, I listen to music, I clean my glasses with my handkerchief or with that little piece of cloth the doctor gave me and which I'm always losing, I get undressed, I slip between the sheets, I kiss you, I get inside you or you get inside me, or we both get inside each other at the same time, like lobsters, full of claws, antennae, legs, hair, hard red cartilage that turns red, we murder each other with our nails, our fingers, and our teeth, at eight o'clock you wake me up with the breakfast café au lait, I take a bath, comb my hair, put on my shoes, you say goodbye to me in a dressing gown, dragging your broad, hesitant crustacean feet on the rug, in the swaying of the bus on the way to the Ministry I can feel last night's scratches on my back and the marks of canine teeth on my neck, I get back at night, the giraffes and the hippopotami of the carousel looking at me through the window the way this dead woman I don't know looks at me, the way the prisoners looked at me in jail, the way the inspector looked at me, compassionate and avid, before beating me, the way these dames and these guys are looking at me, dully, as if underwater, moving out through the hallway, half-naked, with the difficult, twisted movements of crabs, to vomit in corners the whitened-meat contents of their guts. But I don't know them nor do I know you, sitting there, listening to me, my aunt died, Dália disappeared, Esmeralda is in a home staring at the wall in front of her without responding to what I say to her, and if I stroke her hand she grabs me around the wrist with the endless vegetable stubbornness of a tendril, it's not Tuesday or Friday today and therefore it's not you I'm touching, it's not you I'm talking to, I got up a little while ago to urinate and outside I saw, even without my glasses on, an enormous fountain, trees, buildings, I belched and a taste of champagne came into my mouth, I tried to go out and I couldn't find the door, I tried to escape through the frame of a picture and I didn't fit inside, to hide inside a jug and my heel got stuck in the opening, so I understood then that I was back in Peniche, in Caxias again, on the fourth day of standing like a statue, that behind the fountain and the trees and the buildings the afflicted, repetitious calf moans of the sea were hiding, I understood that I'm probably at political police headquarters, with the cells and interrogation rooms disguised by clumsy constructions of cardboard and cellophane and a set of mirrors into an ordinary apartment in an ordinary neighborhood, in order for them to make me confess more easily and I don't know what to I don't know to whom, the Organization, Olavo, Emílio, Baldy, Lopes, Pires's death in the hospital, I understood that these women and these men are agents of the secret police who are disguised as friends, who kiss me, who pat me on the back, who chat with me about this and that and Mozambique and themselves, that they pretend to be drunk, bareass in front of me, with their pistols hidden in their wallets or their pants pockets, with microphones and recorders in the drawers of the furniture, I hit upon the idea, you see, that this night is an invented night, a night with glossy paper hung over the windowpanes, that it's really eleven-thirty, or noontime, or three o'clock outside, that if I pierce those black sheets with my nose or my elbows I'll come upon the sun I suspect is there, with the light they're stealing from me, with the August that I guess at, so you can go to hell, Captain, or rather: go to hell, my dear inspector, tell your people to withdraw, to stop this stupid charade for me, get me free of this dead woman, with the smell of a dead woman and the breath of a dead woman and slippery skin, get her far away from me, I abandoned politics a long time ago, word of honor, what do I know about Olavo, what do I know about Lopes, what do I know about the Central Committee, I shat on the Revolution some months ago after Pires's heart attack, at a stormy meeting in Estefânia, I resigned, understand, I resigned, by the bones of my godmother, I resigned, I swear that I resigned once and for all, the guy with the pipe, coveralls, and wild hair who was chairing the session looked around, embarrassed, cleaning the bowl of his pipe with a matchstick to give himself time, he looked around again in search of some kind of support from the featureless faces, smooth and absent like apples, that the smoke was putting out of focus, he ended up pushing the piece of paper along the threadbare arm of the easy chair in the direction of the communications officer, and asked, feeling him out, cautiously, stumbling over his words like a drunk doing his best to walk straight, What's this?

"Your aunt has broken the collum of her femur," the doctor, still a young man, still sufficiently insecure to be concerned. "She needs an operation, it's no use saying more at the moment. Yes, she'll stay here, of course, we'll see what the specialist decides. In any case, at her age it's serious."

It wasn't an out-patient clinic, inspector (when are your gorillas going to start beating me, tell me? especially that one lying on the bed there next to the mulatto woman), I loved that old woman too much to subject her to hours on end in a filthy corridor full of moaning litters, sick people sitting on the floor holding their bellies, with the hazy eyes of patients in their death throes, guys with bandages, pregnant women, already dead many years ago, whom the stretcher-bearers forget all day, nurses leaping with difficulty, like lobsters, over the sobs that crawl along, just like worms, among the sheets and dirty pillows, so that when she fell downstairs on her way to mass, the beads of her rosary scattering everywhere, and my godmother lying prone on the landing like a toad, we took her, Esmeralda and I, to a hospital on the Rua Conde de Valmor (which is always confused with Visconde de Valbom and no one ever knows for certain where it is), a creature in a blue smock asked me for my name and address and a deposit of five hundred escudos (We've been cheated so many times that now we have to take precautions, you understand), she gave us a cardboard disk with a number and told us to wait in a room filled to the brim with sties and boils, whose walls were decorated with scratched posters of red crosses and the imperious command NO SMOKING underneath, An ill-humored lady in a cap stuck her unpleasant head between the doorjamb and the door and called people with sharp barks, Seven, Eight, Nine, Twelve, my aunt was softly whimpering, wrapped in a thick quilt, and the doctor, as soon as he lifted up her skirt, immediately picked up the telephone, Do we have an empty room?, Esmeralda was digging for her handkerchief in her purse, But the one with breast cancer died yesterday, the doctor was arguing, she left the bed empty a long time ago, and to us Come back at two o'clock sharp, the specialist usually comes in at that time.

"It's my resignation request," the communications officer, half-lost, without looking at anyone, sitting in one of the wicker chairs in Olavo's apartment, said, "I'm sick of politics, damn it, so what?"

Lopes raised his hand, I want the floor, we had a quick lunch in the kitchen, Esmeralda turned her back to me from time to time to dry her eyes

(I bet she's going to drop tears on the fried egg, he thought, tears on the watercress, the fried potatoes, the meat), at ten minutes to two they rang the inaudible bell at the hospital again, the attendant in the blue smock demanded one conto six hundred more in advance and gave me a receipt that I put in my wallet without reading (Because she's staying here as an in-patient, the woman explained, because it's more than just an out-patient consultation), she told us to go up to the second floor by some stairs that cried out with pain from our steps, we passed a nurse almost as old as my aunt and a chambermaid in rubber boots and a checkered apron, who was carrying a basin of urine or menstrual flow down the hall, the communications officer advanced a step, consulted with her in a low voice, she told us to wait in a kind of cubbyhole impregnated with an unbearable smell of disinfectant and medicine, a very drawn-in girl, in bathrobe and slippers, fluttered across the floor like an apparition, and in a while, the same doctor from the morning appeared, his gown open and a stethoscope around his neck, looking more adult and responsible now, he gruffly ordered the girl back to bed and to them The specialist is waiting for you, come this way.

"Anyone else signing up?" Olavo asked, taking notes with his ball-point on a pad. "First Lopes, then Dália, followed by myself, and you, the last of all, hoping you'll reconsider: you don't give up ten years of militancy like some-one drinking a glass of water, and even a battle-hardened Communist has his little right to sporadic discouragement and disbelief."

Lopes stood up, put out his cigarette darkened by spit, raised his didactic hand, and we found the specialist examining X-rays of bones against the light of the window in a cancerous office, his rear end against a corner of the desk, a ringed calendar on it, a pile of clinical forms, a glass covered by a plastic saucer, packages of medicines, a bunch of disposable syringes in their cello-phane wrappers held together by several turns of worn rubber band. The relatives of the patient in eighteen, the morning doctor announced, and the specialist, in his forties, threw us a bored look out of the corner of his eye, softly stroking his bald spot with slow fingers:

"She's recovered consciousness now, we're going to operate this afternoon, put a steel pin in her hip, she can't have any visitors": an exhausted, neutral voice, dull little eyes, a mouth that looked like a string bean, with the corners turned down where the teeth quivered as he spoke, like little rotting pieces of fruit that were poorly attached. He looked for cigarettes in his pocket, took an age to find his lighter: "Around about nine or ten I'll be able to give you more concrete news."

And I shouldn't have allowed you to murder my godmother, Inspector, I shouldn't have left her like that, in that squad room posing as a hospital, waiting with Esmeralda the whole afternoon, made a fool of, in the cub-byhole off the hall, while the guards handled her, anesthetized her, laid her down, with masks on their faces and cloth boots on their feet, in a brightly lighted room glimmering with tubes and metal, a Martian in a white helmet covered her face with a kind of suffocating muzzle, another searched for her vein with a needle, injected a police serum into her blood, a very thin knife approached her hip, he went down to the receiving room to telephone the Ministry in spite of the ill will of the receptionist in a smock, and there came the grunt from the Terreiro do Paço, Hunh, Connect me with the officer placement unit please, the clatter of typewriters, mixed conversations, exclamations, murmurs, a familiar bell, Yes? and me, without any preliminaries, without any idle talk, without any questions, Say, Ananias, tell Major Marques that I'm not coming to work this afternoon because my godmother had a fall, without remembering that you people were listening to me, without remembering that you were recording me, without remembering that at headquarters guys in shirt-sleeves were typing up my words, appending them to my case, sending them to Caxias, to Peniche, to the Englishmen and the Belgians and the Italians of Interpol, without remembering that you were most certainly examining me in that very hospital, spying on me, following me, Let the comrade take time to reflect if he wants, Lopes orated, but in no case can he leave the Organization, we've all worked enough time for socialism to be more than sufficiently aware of doubts and fatigue, we're human, damn it, and yet, comrades, the bourgeoisie is melting away, capitalism is devouring itself as the result of its irreconcilable internal contradictions and the complete absence of a coherent plan capable of bringing the masses together, clouds of smoke, the bust of Cesário Verde rusting in the little square below, the cars clustered one against the other, like potatoes, on the sidewalks, it's certain that we're few right now but it's no less certain that in the factories, in the shops, in the schools, workers and ardent youths, thirsty for justice, are impatiently awaiting our direction and example, he paid the receptionist in a blue smock for the call, and wearing earphones she was plugging and unplugging colored jacks on an ancient switchboard directly linked to FBI headquarters, he went up the stairs, found Esmeralda installed on the edge of the easy chair, clutching the metal clasp of her purse with her icy fingers, Did you find out anything about the lady, child?, Esmeralda liked us, you know, she spent her life worrying about me, and now, when I go to visit her in the home, she doesn't hear me, doesn't know me, doesn't talk to me, she belches up indistinct grunts wrapped in saliva out of the corner of her mouth, I can hear the feces coming out of her body under the sheets, when it began to grow dark a nurse who was pushing a chrome cart filled with plates of soup turned on a tired bulb in the alcove and its yellow light made us as dead as the dead people here tonight, that mulatto woman entwined with the dead redhead, that naked woman, that middle-aged guy clutching the empty bottle, on his back on the carpet, the other drifters whom you put here to make me confess I don't know what, maybe my nausea, my urge to vomit, my heavy head, Lopes stopped speaking, Dália started speaking on a signal from Olavo and yet, you see, I'd stopped listening to them completely, I wanted to get up, leave, open a window because it was suffocating inside there and beat it out of that place as fast as possible, go to a movie, close my eyes in the darkness and stay motionless hours on end, as quiet as you, as quiet as your pals, waiting for you to wake me up for breakfast, the sound of the bath being drawn, and an enormous, friendly lobster smile, full of claws, antennae, legs, hair, hard red cartilage that turns red, while tenderly, methodically, efficiently, you murder me. No, don't move in your chair, don't say anything, it's not worth it: I know that she belongs to the police too, she's part of the plot too, she works for you too, she poisons my café au lait and toast with some kind of powder, she asks all kinds of questions while she hands me the towel, helps me dry myself, changes the blade in my razor for me so that I can cut my throat, puts the toothpaste on my brush for me, pushes me toward the elevator with my sweater on backward, Dália fell silent, Olavo was smiling at the communications officer moving his mouth with inaudible phrases, and, finally, Inspector, Do you have anything to say? and me I do, I need some air urgently, this smoke has made my eyes sting, I went out the door and I never saw them again, I could still hear them calling me from the landing when I got to the vestibule, but the Revolution, understand, was all over for me, Marxism-Leninism-Maoism suddenly had stopped arousing my passions, I almost never left the apartment (Don't make that face, it's true, you certainly must have complete reports, Inspector, photographs, maps, diagrams, sketches about how I spend my time, my daily life, the isolation of my existence since then), I would listen to music, read science fiction novels, the earth invaded by beetles, are you familiar with the genre? or ants or octopuses or extremely intelligent amoebas manning spaceships, I aimlessly watched the dust collect on furniture, the faucets drip, the washbasin fill with hairs, I would get up at seven-thirty, wait ten, fifteen minutes at the bus stop, get to the Ministry punctually, settle down at my desk and go over current business with the sergeant, a thousand pounds more of potatoes for the Chaves post, twenty more bags of rice for Tavira, The people in Beja are still complaining about the quality of the goods, Lieutenant, they've got the idea now that they want champagne and caviar, a cough way off in the distance, then closer, someone shaking me on the shoulder, Wake up, child, you fell asleep, child, Esmeralda apologizing for him, ashamed, to an imprecise far-off person, He works hard, Doctor, he's very tired, I'm worn out from telling him that five hours sleep aren't worth anything, he opened his eyes as if he were pushing away a huge weight from his face, he covered them with his sleepwalking fingers, all tangled because of the bitter light of the alcove, sniffed like an animal at the smell of medicine, he got a whiff, running his tongue over his lips, of pharmacy, the specialist, cream-colored cap, green smock, and cloth boots, aiming his dull little neutral eyes at him from above, the peas of his teeth trembling for a second in the string bean. Her heart couldn't take it, she passed away without any suffering on the operating table, my condolences, Lieutenant.

"Just like that, brutally, nothing else?" the second lieutenant asked. "They killed your old lady and you Fine, all right, thank you very much, good night, you pay the butcher's bill where you come in, right?"

I didn't pay right off, I waited for them to send it to me at home through the mail, but what I had to dig up the next day, or two days later, was money for the undertaker who took charge of the burial, and a donation for the priest which the sexton came for right there in the cemetery, pulling a greasy little receipt book from under his cassock and wetting a tiny pencil stub with his spit, If you'd care to leave a little something extra for our church's social work, a funeral with Esmeralda and me bouncing along on uncomfortable seats inside the hearse, dying from the smell of stearin and the waxy perfume of the flowers, the driver chatted the whole time with his helper about the fearful atrocities committed on his mother-in-law by a dentist in Anjos, molars extracted without anesthesia, drills out of control perforating gums, prostheses unwittingly swallowed when she drank water, from time to time one of the funeral attendants would turn around, straighten the cloth that covered the coffin, and give it a loving pat, Esmeralda was saying her rosary without cease to the rhythm of the missing motor, but you people certainly must have filmed all that, I'll bet the gravediggers, with caps, spades, and a photographic device hidden in their pockets, belonged to the police squad and were taking notes on my reactions, movements, and words, I'll even bet that the tombs and crosses, artificially sculpted, were part of the ingenious machinations of the secret police, Esmeralda lamenting and keening in her room, her ankles in a basin of salt water to alleviate the swelling in her feet, I drank a glass of cherry brandy and ate a codfish cake at a little place on São Domingos called The Wayfarer's Pearl, with a low counter and walls lined with showcases of moldy candy and biscuit tins, a lot of cars parked on the streets, a lot of new buildings, identical vestibules that monotonously followed one after the other, with the same tasteless tiles, the same plants, the same hammered-glass elevator doors, Building 1, Building 2, Building 3, Building 4, Building 5, he rang the bell for eight three times, waited, rang twice more and almost immediately the lock leaped with a click, I'll bet you were waiting for me on the balcony, I'll bet you were watching the street with binoculars from the enclosed balcony, the scarlet elevator button that throbbed, the arrow pointing up dark, the arrow pointing down lighted, the metal box climbing through the jaundiced light of the landings in oily haste, and on the doormat, smiling, in slacks, playing with the shell necklace, you.

"And who's that lady, Lieutenant?" the soldier asked. "What lover is it you're hiding from us?"

"I've seen those seashell necklaces, they're terrific," the magician's assistant said, sitting on the floor, struggling against the cap on a beer bottle with her teeth. "They go beautifully with a beach outfit I have."

"If you'd care to leave a little something extra for our church's social work, please," the sexton requested with an odious, sullen, cadaverous, toothless smile.

They continued calling him (or he thought they continued calling him) almost to the wall of the Estefânia Hospital, its anemic silence, its ravenous trees, the voices thinned out and dispersed, They must have gradually abandoned politics, he imagined, forgotten about Lenin and Marx and the Chinese, found a job at an insurance company or in a factory office, or a bank, who's still worrying about the Revolution, Inspector, who persists in this country in wanting to change the world when in Portugal, isn't it so? the world is what changes us, people change, they get old, they abandon, desist, but institutions never, there they are the way they always end up sooner or later, getting back to keeping afloat, eternal, intact, stubborn, inviolate, always the same skeletal hungry dogs, the same rich people, the same poor people, the same unalterable, melancholy, narrow landscape you can barely squeeze into standing, and suddenly, one fine night, unexpectedly, a night I don't recognize, like this one, people I don't know, like these, bring me to an apartment I don't know, like this one, stretch a dead woman out beside me on the rug, scatter other corpses, other dying people about the rooms, install a naked woman drowning in her own fat between the bedsheets, hide perverse little microphones in the hollows of the chandeliers and under the tabletops, and in a short time the inspector from Caxias will come in here, the inspector from Peniche, You again, you bastard? you again, you cocksucker? and punches and kicks and slaps and curses and squeezing balls, who, how many, where, hurry up, and right away the dizziness, and right away the illness, the nausea, the strange taste in your mouth, the urge to vomit that I have now, What did you people put in the dinner?, What did you put in the drinks? this feeling of death, this lack of strength, this irrepressible surrender, the toothless sexton brandishing the greasy pages in his face, If you'd care to give a little something extra for our church's social work, please, the specialist pointing me out to Olavo, Dália, Lopes, the rare, puzzled survivors of the Central Committee who were looking at him, very serious, in black ties, contrite and confused, Her heart couldn't take it, she passed away on the operating table, my condolences, ladies and gentlemen, I'm going to fix you a cup of strong coffee, the second lieutenant said, before you go completely out of your head, the communications officer, his jaw tied with a handkerchief, was looking for his godmother with his desperate myopic eyes, I wasn't the one who died, it was she, but no cry, no sound, no whisper, The old lady is the one who broke her leg, the old lady is the one who fell downstairs, the old lady is the one whose life was hanging by a thread,

Esmeralda approached the lieutenant, drying her runny eyes with her handkerchief, and she placed her green hands on his chest, she put a crucifix in his
hands, combed what hair he had left, One of those effervescent tablets, the
soldier suggested, they perk a person up in a minute, if the man goes on
delirious like that and hanging on the curtains, he's going to wreck your
place, he said to the second lieutenant, can't you see how he's torn a drape
and knocked down a whole shelf? the bald inspector from the Caxias interrogations, followed by two huge agents, genuflected in front of me and
crossed himself unctuously, It was a question of a good prisoner in spite of all,
he behaved reasonably, he didn't upset anybody, he didn't shit in his cell, I
made an enormous effort to open my mouth, I tried desperately to move my
arms and nothing doing, if I rolled my head over far enough I'd find the old
woman's coffin beside me, and my godmother in her Sunday dress inside, as
yellow and as delicate as the corpse of a sparrow, Explain to them who died,
Aunty, show them the wound in your thigh, your halted pulse, your death
certificate if necessary, with the name of the doctor, and the signature, and
the stamp, and the inevitable bureaucratic bullshit as always, If you'd care to
give a little something extra for our church's social work, please, the sexton
asked Olavo in his insistent gelatinous voice, We'll wait for nightfall, it's
always more discreet, Lopes said, addressing Esmeralda, and we'll bury him
over there, next to that building under construction, in a plastic bag or a
shoebox, Discretion, discretion, one of the sergeants from the Ministry
approved, placing a spray of hyacinths and camellias at his feet, It was four
contos five hundred for flowers alone, paid for by the State, Captain Ananias
elucidated, Major Marques didn't economize on expenses this time, he told
me that he was coming later in the afternoon in person to present his
condolences by giving the family a posthumous eulogy, Me, for my part,
pearl necklaces or nothing, Melissa the striptease goddess stated, with a
silver paper star on each nipple and a vine leaf over her pubes, those seashell
trinkets give me a hellish allergy on the throat, A double cup of coffee at least
and an aspirin, because we won't get anywhere this way, lads, the lieutenant
colonel, turning handles at random and bringing a match vaguely toward the
gas jets of the stove, if you don't cut off his drinking he'll start leaping around
like a lizard with epilepsy, His glasses? the second lieutenant asked, pushing
away pillows, did any of you step on his glasses?, Esmeralda, bustling, was in
the kitchen preparing tea for the wake, my aunt rose up suddenly, gigantic,
cruel, stern, raging, in front of me, Why don't you put him in the same slope
where he put the dog, why not in the same pile of dirt and weeds and sand
and garbage, why not with the same construction shovel, why not at the same
time? and she smelled bad and was rotting and was dead and yet she was
talking and gesticulating and scolding as before, and her bun was loose, gray,
over her shoulders, the police inspector agreed, the secret police agents
agreed, Dália and Olavo agreed, Grab him, the bum wants to jump out the

window, one of the skinny blond twins shouted, hurry up and grab him before he does something foolish, and a short way from here the carousels, a short way from here the Pit of Death, a short way from here the Great Ferris Wheel, a short way from here the nauseating, sweet vapor of the crullers, a short way from here the rheumatic mechanism of the Electronic Flying Saucers, a short way from here the aluminum of the loudspeakers, Today's Friday, I thought, it must be five o'clock, it must be almost seven o'clock, you're waiting for me on São Domingos, spying from the balcony, spying from the ledge and they won't let me go, I rub my feet on the doormat and I'm not me, I'm amazed as always at the tiny little clay and cloth objects on the furniture in the vestibule, monkeys, elephants, cats, little pitchers, microscopic flowers, plastic babies, miniatures of the Eiffel Tower and the Monastery of Alcobaça, a Belgian boy with his dick out, a paperweight with snow inside, If you'd care to give a little something extra for our church's social work, please, Major Marques, with a row of medals on his chest and his cap under his arm, gave a silent greeting to my aunt, Esmeralda, the inspector, Olavo, leaned over me as over the mirror of a lake with a puzzled wrinkle on his brow, took one or two steps back to the rear of the room, disappeared. Maybe taking him out and walking him up and down on the street, the soldier advised, there's nobody who won't come to with a little wind in his puss, phantasmagoric drunks staggering, holding each other up on Mãe d'Água near the illuminated and twisted cardboard of the fountain and the sad trees of Lisbon, the whores were peeping down from the window above at a cluster of disheveled heads, I never thought you were so bad at holding your liquor, the second lieutenant reprimanded him, that you'd go down on the canvas like this from cheap champagne, a night watchman was checking doors, the shrubs on Príncipe Real were branching out in the shadows, How are you doing, boy, the lieutenant colonel asked, did you or didn't you vomit up your whole stinking dinner? the communications officer was snuffling and spitting, suffocated, heaving, hugging a tree trunk, When was the last time this happened to me? how many years has it been since I felt like this? the ground was swaying, the building façades wavered, the shoes and legs of his companions were suddenly coming closer

I'm going to fall

and went back again, not to Mozambique, damn it, not when the orders sending us off arrived, guys drunk on beer shooting in the compound, singing, shouts, howling, elbowing, cursing, silhouettes zigzagging, effusive and enthusiastic, not when they surrounded the Largo do Carmo and put an end to the secret police and fascism, Lopes, a bottle of red wine between his knees, vociferating against American capitalism and Soviet revisionism with his clenched fist raised, I can't drink champagne, that's obvious, only sangria and white wine, a glass of grape liquor from time to time and that's it, help me the way you should, damn it, hold me, lift me up, my bones have given out on me.

"We'd better go back inside before we wake up the whole neighborhood," the second lieutenant was nervous. "And stop kicking the garbage cans, fuck it, the one who's got to put up with the other tenants tomorrow is me."

"A good worker and a good soldier," Major Marques praised him. "His leftist bit in time gone by, but a serious person."

"He had a good reputation, no lovers, parties, music, noise," the concierge reported, "I never noticed anything out of line up there."

"And why is it you got to dislike politics, Lieutenant?" the soldier asked, "and while we're at it, why did you break with your friends?"

"And who's that chick you keep so well hidden," the second lieutenant was interested, "are you hooked up with a cabinet minister's wife or what?"

"I'll bet it's mine," the lieutenant colonel said merrily, holding the communications officer up with both hands on his waist. "Don't be afraid, boy, you'd be doing old baldy a favor."

"Burying him like the dog is a splendid idea," the sharp, authoritarian voice of his aunt approved. "Go down there, Inspector, and borrow a shovel from the watchman at the construction site."

Because they were still building across the way, on the other side of the street, Captain, skeletons of depressing buildings, horrible, all just alike, dull colors, where people's skin must have got wrinkled and yellow like old newspapers in a storeroom smelling of rat urine and feces, where old commodes and chairs wobbled on uneven legs, where photographs in round frames slowly dissolved, leaving heavy-lashed orphaned eyes floating on vague, iodine-colored faces, in a small shed between two fences an old man in a dark uniform was holding his hands over a handful of burning pieces of wood, and right behind him, tiny and varied, piles of rubbish were accumulating, cones of remnants, twisted pieces of metal, hillocks of weeds and stubble, disemboweled bidets, stray dogs, a provincial silence that the noise of the bumper cars and the small wagons of the Ghost Castle startled with a tremulous diarrhea of lights. Not counting the nurses' quarters that grew in number on a dead-ended side street with its clotheslines, its frantic phonographs, its loud laughter, its gabble, its agitated gatherings of silhouettes behind the windowpanes, he lived in the same immemorial, silent peace as always, with the same smell of chicken, sardines, and burned sugar at night, Can we go back upstairs again, Lieutenant? the soldier was concerned, are you sure you're all right, Lieutenant? shots in my head, mortar shells exploding like watermelons into kernels of light, breeches that opened and closed like latches, fleeting flashes lighting up the tents, a truck, its headlights on, melting away piece by piece like a chocolate bar in the sun, Go in there to the closet in my room, the aunt commanded one of the police agents, and fetch me a shoebox from the stocking drawer, I have hopes that the secretary of state, in spite of not sympathizing with him, Major Marques whispered, will at least award him the bronze medal third class for ten years of service with no punishment, So you finally got back, Melissa the striptease goddess was angry, we've been here parched and we couldn't even find a beer, We'd like to take part in the funeral, the magician's assistant requested, we'd form a lively procession all the way to the other side of the street, don't you think? the communications officer tried to shout at them It wasn't me who died, wanted to explain to them The only problem I've got is that I can't move or talk, but he felt them lifting him up bodily, laying him down on a hard surface, Dália and Lopes enclosing his head in tissue paper that had a strong smell of shoe leather and polish, and that the sounds (the voices, the music from the amusement park, the carts, the carousels, the barker for Little Gypsy Dora, the crackling of oil for fried potatoes) were coming, muffled, from the outside, to die on the rims of his ears, more shots, more bullets, more sparkling watermelons of lead exploding, one more tree knocked down and rolling on the sand, You people, the ones who didn't go into the jungle, the lieutenant colonel said disdainfully, were always weaker than us, Who's the dame, you old devil, the second lieutenant was intrigued, confess to me here in secret, I won't tell anyone anything, Let him go, the drunk belongs to me, the skinny blonde shouted, clean the vomit off him and give him to me, the yellow ball from the lampshade was shriveling up, crumpled in a corner, I don't know this night, the communications officer thought, glancing around myopically like a stranger, I don't know this place, I don't know these smells, these tastes, these whispers, I don't know these women or these men, it's Tuesday, it's Friday, I'm certain that you'll be waiting for me at the entrance, that you'll kiss me, that you'll smile at me, that you'll pull me inside by the timid, afflicted sleeve of my jacket, very far away he could hear the inspector talking to the old man at the construction site, Dália, who joined in the conversation, loaded with unanswerable, seductive arguments, Olavo, who was giving his opinion, pompous, some phrase or other, the clash of metal, a pause, a shovel digging, he could make out the heads of his aunt and Esmeralda side by side behind the curtains of the apartment, It was you who kicked the bucket, you whore, you're all mistaken, you swine, he was vaguely aware of their lifting him, throwing him, limbs loose, into a hole in the ground, and while the first stones, the first weeds, the first clods of earth were falling onto his chest, his legs, his shoulders, his belly, through the tissue wrapping paper he made out the soldier's modeling-clay mouth from an infinite distance, relieved, It's good to see you OK again, damn it, happy again, drinking again, but what a big scare you gave us, Lieutenant.

A FEW weeks later he got a second job in the business office of a newspaper whose noisy rooms, perpetually lighted by dull globes, abolished daytime in a melancholy way, followed by a third in a publicity agency drowning in debt, run by a Portuguese with a small mustache and the gloomy face and manners of a professional dancer waltzing to his ruin, who was married to a Chilean midget who had worked some time previously in a circus and cheated on him with the fairy photographer, and lastly a position as head of sales in a pesticide factory, where the workers, poisoned by the gases, turned yellow and feeble by three in the afternoon, like gnats in their death throes. In the room at the boardinghouse where he lived, the boat whistles and lights of the ships kept him from sleeping, his sheets getting all wet with insomnia's sticky lard. The mulatto woman on the other side of the wall would come in at five or six in the morning, all painted up, reeking with whiskey, the heels of her shoes echoing unsteadily down the hall, the water from the shower, at the opposite end of the place, hit me square on the head, a tenacious mosquito kept approaching my ear in sadistic ellipses, the sharp, stabbing motors of trawlers gnawed at my brain and my insides with their propellers, beginning at seven o'clock the voices on the street wounded like fishhooks, in desperation I bought a bottle of pills at the drugstore, which instead of pushing me into a coma entangled me in confused dreams, scary and disconnected, and kept me all day in the stupefied prostration of a mangy lion encaged in his clothing, while the pesticides turned my bladder and skin gray, and one by one the stenographers fell, kicking, tongues hanging out, over their typewriters, murdered by cockroach powder. He almost always found guys in the toilet lying on their backs on the tile floor, their hairy legs drawn up on the chitin of their bellies, staring at him with foggy, empty eyes. The flowers withered in their vases like a flaccid penis, dead salesgirls were drooped in strange positions over their counters, here and there an executive would flutter for a few seconds, dying, in his office, trying to reach the lock on the window with his fingers, pounding his head against some print on the wall, collapsing into contortions on the floor, flapping the alpaca wings of his jacket, which disgorged a pollen of credit cards and traveler's checks, finally coming to rest with the expression of a fly on the glass lens of his spectacles. In the cellar laboratory, bristling with alembics, sterilizers, retorts, thermometers, and Bunsen burners, chemists in green lab coats, enveloped in dark lethal fumes, were rolling around in the corners like dessicated beetles. People came out of neighboring restaurants holding their hands to their heads, vomiting, the ships docked along that stretch of waterfront were consumed with a granulous acid of rust, opening suppurating wounds on their hulls, sinking with the sulfuric clatter of useless tin cans, and with the tips of their smokestacks sticking out of the water like carbon corollas. Every morning energetic workers wearing gas masks would sweep into the street dozens of empty, weightless, and porous corpses that fluttered before the brooms like plane-tree leaves, which a rheumatic truck would carry off moaning to some dunghill on the edge of the city, where children amused themselves by playing with dead executives and chemists whose false teeth poured from their jaws in a diarrhea of molars. For three or four months the second lieutenant had no news of Inês, Mariana, the brothers-in-law whose eyes and smiles were dilated by cocaine, the Portuguese who were selling their silver and rings for a trifle to delighted pawnbrokers, characters who considered democracy a personal insult thought up by a perverse communistic evil, who imagined Russia as the shadowy incarnation of hell and were waiting for Our Lady of Fátima to dissolve hammers and sickles in a serene, pious, magical puff of a canon's censer. He'd made friends in the meantime with a Lebanese biologist, the author of a six-volume treatise written in cramped script on the sexual aberrations of geese and the tenant in the room at the boardinghouse next to the toilet, eternally impregnated with a smell of ancient turds, and after work he would accompany that tiny and lucid connoisseur of the carnal appetites and intimate ailments of birds, listening to the night gasping in my throat, the wounded-ox cries of the ships, the altercations of workers and whores, a piano in the shadows, shirt cuffs over the keys, fingers that withdrew and advanced, American, English, and

Spanish tunes that circled our necks like tendrils, I never felt so good in spite of the heartburn and the uncomfortable feeling in my throat, in spite of the tenacious, whimpering tale about the abracadabra of feathered coitus, I never missed you, my daughter. The Lebanese was preparing a small supplement, in three compact volumes, to the previous six, he would write on his knees, sitting on the bed, surrounded by illustrated atlases (peacocks, turkeys, swans, cockatoos, ostriches), flasks of liquor, notebooks, crumbs, lumps, little pieces of tobacco, the picture of an old woman on the night table, innumerable books scattered around the floor, the only window opened onto an inner courtyard or a labyrinthine succession of yards that were lost among houses with herpes all the way to the docks, the waves doubled over themselves on the sidewalk below, the small mirror on the wall reflected buildings, balconies, rolling clouds, the dirty sky, smoke, the Lebanese, forefinger in the air, would discourse excitedly about the diverse, unthinkable, and voluptuous kinds of coitus among Bantam hens, illustrated by pencil sketches on envelopes printed Brazilian Academy of Ornithology, I would listen to him, flabbergasted, on the edge of the bed, testing, in order to pass the time, the various bottles of ancient liquor spread about on the sheets, until one day, without realizing it, I asked the landlady for the use of the phone, she was a nervous, skinny woman who patrolled the hallway constantly, armed with a terrible broom, chasing rats and spiders, I dialed the number of the apartment, hearing the irregular pulsing of my blood in my ears, one ring, two rings, three rings, four rings, five rings, I got the numbers mixed up, he thought, She went back to São Paulo to her parents' place, he thought, She's living with the lady with purple hair in Rio de Janeiro and they stroll braless and holding hands along the beach, he thought, a click, a metallic sound, his muscles all halted, in suspense, waiting, the skinny woman passed by at a trot, chasing some unhappy vermin with the huge piassava broom, and finally, after an eternity in an abyss where his body was sinking, lost, rolling around in successive twirls of anguish, the familiar voice of Inês right here, clinging to me, alive, in the flesh, questioning, bewildered (I love you), furious (I interrupted your sleep, oh shit), Hello.

"Me, when I'm waked up in the middle of the night, I'm worse than ruined," the magician's assistant stated, lying on her side on the sofa, scratching one cheek of her behind with the scarlet nail of her forefinger. "I spent a few months with an old man who at four o'clock in the morning, boom, he'd turn on the light and start shaking me because he couldn't get to sleep."

"Mariana's not with me," Inês growled, "she went to London with my mother to see the eye doctor. And listen here, by the way, do you think this is any hour to call a person up?"

"Célia," the guy with insomnia would call out in the dark, "have you seen my bottle of tranquilizers by any chance, Célia?"

"I went around with a real hangdog look," the magician's assistant complained. "I was nodding my head like an old woman in a corner, with the dark rings I had under my eyes I had on double makeup for the show. The day I got rid of him I slept almost a whole week straight through."

"No, she's fine, she's never been better," Inês yawned triumphantly. "But Mother had to go there to change the lenses of her glasses and got it into her head to take her along. Ilka says you can never go wrong getting examined by a foreign specialist."

"On your night table, Célia," the man squeaked, "look in the drawer, be patient. I just wanted you to know about the horrible nightmares I've had."

"He was a salesman in a car lot," the magician's assistant supplied the detail, massaging her navel. "I never saw a guy who could talk so good, so sure of himself, so much on target. And later on, at night, as soon as he got his pajamas on, he'd start getting pale, shaking, looking for pills in cupboards, grabbing me, stuttering, Oh, I feel so strange. Oh, I'm sweating all over. Oh, something's happening to me. Oh, if you leave me now my heart will stop for sure."

"They might be back in March," Inês cut him off, "Mother wants to go to Switzerland, a family meeting because of the bank. What I can't understand is your interest in Mariana now, because for ages you haven't given a damn about her, you haven't come to see her once."

"I don't feel well, Célia," the old man wept, pushing the bedclothes away. "I'm not at all well, I need air, I've got a tightness here, hurry and get me a glass of water so I can swallow the capsule."

"And your little ass bathed in perfume, and a butler at your command, and a chauffeur at the door?" the magician's assistant, furious, rolling up under the covers, covering her head with her pillow, pushing his trembling hands away with the crook of her elbow. "Go to hell, leave me alone, don't bother me."

"Try calling in April or May," Inês proposed generously. "In spite of the nonsense you hit my parents with, I'm not against your visiting her every two weeks. But you'd better not want anything more than that, don't even dream about it, you'll be getting a letter from my lawyer soon with the conditions for a divorce."

But not in April and not in May, I phoned from time to time and there was no answer, the skinny girl, in a blaze of glory, was showing me a dead rat from a distance, holding it by its tail, done in by the sinister broom, the biologist was going on fervently about the psychological factors in premature ejaculation in turtledoves, the lawyer proposed, in florid juridical gibberish, the alimony of a millionaire, the possibility of spending two hours with Mariana every three weeks, the authorization to see her only after the agreement, in June, no sooner had I said Hello? than they hung up in my face, the next day I leaned on the bell to the apartment, the intercom bellowed a distorted Yes? and I from the street, like a man possessed, I want my daughter, you bitch, I want my daughter, you slut, people turned around to look, startled, after a couple of hours of that, coming at a trot from a corner, three huge blacks appeared, an older one with a greasy necktie and two dressed like dockworkers, they made sure that I was the one in question, pushed me against the wall, their thick breath blew into my nose, they threw me to the ground, punching and kicking me, my cut lip hurt, my ribs ached, one of my shoes was lost in the gutter, the skinny woman with the rats took care of my bones, carefully binding them up, the biologist abandoned the private difficulties of turtledoves for a moment to supply me with the address of a lawyer cousin, very reasonable, an expert, according to him, in matrimonial troubles, and I found a very dark character, barefoot, cooling himself with a straw fan at the entrance to a filthy little house, inside of which a monkey, held on a leash tied to the handle of a cupboard, was merrily destroying, tearing up into a thousand pieces that floated about the office, trial briefs, petitions, and codes. The expert got behind his desk, stroking his stomach, pushed the animal away with a pat, took a bottle out of a drawer to stimulate his understanding and his innards, listlessly straightened up two or three ruined books, and asked me, with the stumbling pomposity of an alcoholic, So what's new, Engineer? so of course I ended up accepting her conditions, Captain, so I ended up signing all the papers they sent me, Captain, child awarded mother, yes sir, father's rights nil, yes sir, obligation of monthly payments at fifty percent of my salary, yes sir, the barefoot lawyer scolded the monkey and sighed We're on a bad track, Engineer, we're giving up too much, Engineer, but the huge blacks hauled him inside the cabin one afternoon, dislocated a shoulder, broke all the dishes that were still undamaged, and the man immediately began to cooperate with a zeal that was touching, You can see the little one every four weeks, you can see her every two months, a shorter interval would get her too used to it, Engineer, children like to be dealt with from a distance, Engineer, if you turn over ninety percent of what you make you'll still have a little something left at the end of the month, isn't it so, also, what the devil do you need so much money for, hell, getting out of this without any further trouble is the miracle of your life, friend, the monkey was mimicking on a shelf, dumping out files, chewing on pencils, inspecting his testicles, catching fleas on his groin, the attorney solemnly tied a necktie the thickness of a hawser around his neck, laboriously put on a pair of gigantic muddy boots that he first cleaned with the sleeve of his shirt, took down from a hook a jacket that once had been white, decorated with a mapa mundi of wrinkles, spat on the dirt floor, the saliva bubbling then shrinking away between his feet, and accompanied me, reciting Lebanese prayers and juridical formulas in Latin, to the tumbledown courthouse, squat under the sun amid palm trees and puddles of stagnant water, on a square of unequal buildings, from whose tiled crests enormous scrawny birds were observing us with limestone indifference.

"Célia," the guy with insomnia was imploring, "have pity on me and call an ambulance, Célia."

Walls with holes, crumbling corridors, drowsy secretaries, portraits of fat military men evaporating in their frames, foul-smelling policemen, characters going about with reams of paper or trays of coffee, and then a larger chamber, Captain, that looked like a schoolroom, with desks and benches for the pupils or the public, where a mist of urine fluttered about in slow ellipses, a kind of throne with a little old man wearing dark glasses and coughing perched on top of it, Inês, with the face of a deserving orphan, sitting near a well-dressed gentleman with graying hair who was tranquilly thumbing through the contents of a briefcase, neither of them looked at us when we came in, neither of them seemed to hear the enormous, worn boots that were crashing down like a rhinoceros's feet onto the loose boards of the floor, the Lebanese bent over like a jackknife with successive bows to the little old man in dark glasses who responded with a mask of impassive displeasure, a man came suddenly from behind a curtain and ordered them harshly to sit down, the court clerk, the lawyer informed me in a low voice, and that hundred-year-old mummy is the judge, Silence, the one giving orders bellowed severely, at the first sign of the slightest disrespect for the court the chamber will be cleared immediately, What an ugly word, I thought, what a horrible verb, *to clear*, and you hadn't changed at all during those three months, Inês, the same profile, the same trim little breasts, the same twin buttocks tight against each other like two kernels of a fleshy nut, the same way of resting your chin in your hand, throwing your hair back with a quick toss of your head, of emptying the light from your eyes when people were talking to you, What right have you got to talk about other people? the communications officer protested, if the minute you laid eyes on that dyke you collapsed with passion.

"The same thing every night, just imagine," the magician's assistant went on, "just tell me if that isn't enough to drive a person batty in a minute."

The well-dressed gentleman made mincemeat of the Lebanese (who in the meantime had spotted with terror the three blacks smoking on one of the school benches in the rear) with a shower of baroque arguments taken down in shorthand by the court clerk, who would throw at me, I don't know why, bloody sidelong glances of disapproval, one of the blacks, with a very bad cold, kept on sniffling behind me, the palm trees brushed against the windows, the little old man was nodding in his pulpit, my lawyer leaped to his feet, Every three weeks, certainly, Two hours maximum, obviously, more than two hours would be an exaggeration, Sixty percent of income, what a coincidence, that's precisely what he was going to propose, No objection to any point, my illustrious colleague (and the blacks were heaping tons of threats on his shoulders), to your learned and fundamental observations, abandonment of the home, insults, moral annoyances, the structurally neurotic personality of my client, the court clerk interrupted his writing, stood, and rapped with his fingers on the edge of the papal throne of the judge, who awoke with a start the way babies do, wildly waving their spasmodic tiny, little limbs, Who told me to trust that nut with his turtledove ejaculations, the second lieutenant thought, who told me to be that big a fool, the well-dressed gentleman was smiling abstractly, contemplating his fingernails, Inês was smiling slightly, like a martyr on a scapular, the Lebanese was ceaselessly sweating orgasms of affliction, the judge composed himself like a stork on his wooden chimney, tremulously fluttering the opaque gleam of his glasses about, he bleated the belch of a goat Divorce granted, the threatening sniffles of the black man disappeared completely, a guy in uniform shooed us out into the street with the irritated gestures of someone chasing chicks out of a garden, a difficult sun was lighting up the puddles outside, a lukewarm breeze was disarranging the trees, it must have been close to dusk because the shadow of houses was lining up and moving in a slow rotation of petals like a sunflower of shadows searching for night, with the sea moaning on our flank, we returned in silence to the lawyer's office where the monkey, sitting on the floor, was banqueting on the tattered remains of a dictionary, the man of law took off his boots and insulted them (They don't know how to make shoes in this country, Engineer), hung the inconceivable planisphere of his jacket and his dirty tie on their hook, dropped into a wicker rocking chair that seemed to break into splinters with every movement of his body, threw his black nails around a flask of liquor, and affirmed with satisfaction, snatching his fly in the semidarkness, We took real good care of them, Engineer, my speech had its full effect in spite of the judge's antagonism, I destroyed them, I wiped them out, I pulverized them completely, we got a lot more than I expected at the beginning, sixty percent of your earnings is a real pittance that anybody can afford.

"Calling to me the whole damned night, driving me off my nut the whole damned night," the magician's assistant said, shaking her head. "I spent more than a month taking vitamins to get back in shape, you see."

The lawyer spat on the floor several times, he studied the crusty spaces between his toes, concentrated in scowling, interminable meditations, lighted a small branching lamp over the monkey who was dozing on a chest, he pulled a pen out of a pyramid of trash, wiped the tip on his hair, and began to add difficult columns on the back of an invoice, itemizing aloud official paper, so much, tips to office boys to speed up hearing, so much, court costs, so much, bus rides to courthouse to find out how things were going, so much, private conferences with my colleague on the other side, so much, he drew a line underneath, made a mistake several times, finally reached some conclusion because he tossed the pen disdainfully into the shadows of a corner, smoothed the piece of paper with his fingers, showed it to me from a distance, tipped the flask into his gullet for a minute, and announced with esteem, with friendship, with the whisper of an accomplice, You owe me one hundred thousand cruzeiros, and let's not talk about this anymore, Engineer.

"Célia," the car salesman whined, clutching at his chest with sweaty hands, "if you don't hurry up and call the male nurse in the building next door I'll kick the bucket right here and now, Célia."

"A hundred thousand cruzeiros?" the second lieutenant asked, startled. "Are you crazy or what?"

"An injection in the vein, Célia," the man was sobbing, "a tank of oxygen, a bottle of serum, any kind of miracle that will save me."

"To say a hundred is to mean fifty," the lawyer quickly compromised. "Money's not going to destroy this friendship, Engineer."

Dozens of black cellophane moths were fluttering around the bulb, handcars or cranes or lifts were rolling about in the shadows with metallic jerks, the monkey was merrily shuffling through a drawer, with his black knuckles turning over pads, staplers, letter openers, erasers, typewriter ribbons, spools of thread, calendars, the lawyer, buried in his chair, was sailing from flask to flask with the indefinable expression of a happy castaway, from fifty we went to thirty, from thirty to twenty, and from twenty to ten, we closed the deal for five thousand cruzeiros in twelve monthly payments (Money's not going to ruin this friendship, Engineer), to seal the pact I tried the attorney's brandy, which turned my stomach into a sulfuric burr, bristling with a thousand heartburn thorns, his eyes floated out of control from wrinkle to wrinkle on the surface of his skin, he ended up snoring with his mouth open while his behind sank through the broken straw seat, and his knees came up to his chin in the position of a decrepit fetus reeking with alcohol, the water whirled, curling around under the wharf, as if it were softly biting into the foundation of the house, the burr grew smaller with the second swallow, became inoffensive with the third, and disappeared completely with the fourth, the second lieutenant stumbled out over the stones, cardboard boxes, and empty cans that bounced in the dark, dogs sleeping in cabin doors came over to sniff him, emphysematous, with stupid, sharp yellow eyes, the following Sunday, huddling under a tenacious drizzle, I went to the Santos apartment (and this time no enormous blacks, this time no kicks, no insults, no punches, this time an exclamation amplified by the intercom, Oh, is it you? and the lock immediately sprang open) to visit Mariana who cried in terror as soon as I tried to approach the playpen, they'd rearranged the furniture, there were prints I wasn't familiar with, fat sofas, a picture of the lady with purple hair on a small table between the lamp and the telephone, Inês, arms folded, kept an eye on me the whole time, leaning against the door with tense disdain, I said Hello to her from a distance and she answered with an evasive expression, she looked fatter to me, with better coloring, better dressed, prettier, Mariana was peering at me with fear, brandishing a nerve-racking plastic rock, new curtains too, the records lined up in a special rack, an exhaust fan in the kitchen, a dubious sweet smell in the room, after an hour I got up, limping from a leg that had gone to sleep, from the uncomfortable pillow I'd sat down on, with the useless bait of a cloth doll in my lap, I tried one last caress for Mariana, who immediately drew back from me, stepping on toys, to the opposite side of the playpen, from the hallway to the vestibule I noticed a new bed in the bedroom, lower, stronger, wider, a second picture of the lady with purple hair, in a bathrobe and hair curlers, with a dog like a powder puff in her arms, it hurt me to breathe, my limbs were swaying, I said So long, Inês, and it was a different voice, Captain, an unexpected voice, disenchanted, sharp, that was having a hard time putting the words together, I extended my mouth to kiss her cheek and her body stiffened, and her face, frowning, drew back, she looked at me as if I were some kind of strange beast, gelatinous and odd, as if she'd never been married to me, as if I'd never seen her naked, as if she'd never felt my dick inside her, as if I made her sick, Captain, she closed the door in my face before the elevator arrived, I went down with a Japanese gentleman and a little hunchbacked old lady, each of us in his corner of the metal box that whistled and shook, thinking I'm going back up there and kick your ass, thinking I'm going back up there and break all the furniture and give you a good beating until you squat down and beg my forgiveness, the port outside, jammed with ships, smelled even worse than usual, and the ebb tide was leaving behind a scum of vomit on the piers that the reflection of the lights on sterns was drowning, stringy algae, bones of planks, wicker baskets, mingled trash, a Turkish flag danced on a mast, a fellow in a seaman's cap was raising the Polish flag on a freighter, I want to go to Portugal, the second lieutenant thought by the entrance to the building, what am I doing here all mixed up with this dirty water, these ships, these panicky daughters who don't recognize me and reject me, this foreign house, closed up to my absence like an indifferent conch, Célia, the car salesman bleated, don't be inhuman, don't let me die like this, Célia, and that night, Captain, the biologist and I, you see, all by ourselves, drained the city's entire beer supply.

"And in spite of everything that wasn't the worst of it," the magician's assistant, trying to put together the wire and plastic rods of the yellow paper lampshade, said, "I could still make it with the guy who used to die early in the morning. But right after that I got involved with a nut who made me put on his mother's wedding dress before he'd get into bed with me. He'd go over to a trunk, pull things out of it, careful, like a dentist, pieces of cloth with holes and rips, a stinking veil, a wreath of wax orange blossoms, he would hold that rotten shit out to me like a treasure, order me Lock yourself up in the bedroom and put this on, quick, when you finish take the roses out of the vase, hold them in your hand, and address me as my son when you call me, and he would appear before me in blue velvet knickers, his hair in bangs, wearing a ruffled shirt, repeating Mama Mama Mama Mama Mama Mama in the little whine of a child."

To tell the truth, it wasn't just that night, Captain, we kept on drinking, just like today, for three or four days on end, I got time and memories all mixed up, liquid, floating in my head like jellyfish, the Lebanese would talk endlessly of the exquisite, infinite voluptuousness of hens, I vaguely remember fat mulatto women in sordid little rooms with toothless black men, graying kinky hair, opening their enormous gums in silent guffaws, that my wallet was stolen, papers, keys, money, of walking along the beach, arms over each other's shoulder, belching, wheezing, and insulting each other, pouring bottles of cane liquor over each other's head, maudlin and happy, until we dropped anchor at the boardinghouse again, amid the atlas, dictionaries, notes, the monkey, excited by the smell of alcohol, was leaping from bench to bench with anguished sobs, a stuffed albatross which confronted us furiously from atop a pile of books, and when I returned, stupefied, with an acid taste on my tongue, to the pesticide factory, I found the management office full of dead administrators, one last stenographer tossing about on the floor in her death throes, the absolute, solid, mineral silence that comes after railroad wrecks was filling the offices with an unusual polar atmosphere where the slightest object (a date pad, an eraser, a stamp, a china cup with pens) suddenly took on a meaning that was mysterious and obvious at the same time, I paid myself in the deserted payroll office, where the open drawers looked like mandibles that had lost their strength, with office-boy cockroaches drying up under the tables, in the whole neighborhood creatures with dark circles under their eyes were staggering along the streets in front of me, until they collapsed on the corner with a small, stagnant sigh, trees just like withered, plucked kale plants were bending limply to the ground, the biologist, commiserating, employed me in the laboratory where he was now studying the postmasturbatory melancholy of owls in a room lined with cages of dozens of birds with thick, frowning, far-sighted, worried eyebrows, made all bristly by strong light bulbs and whistles from complicated instruments, full of buttons, indicators, gauges, thermometers, needles, the Lebanese and a cross-eyed girl assistant who smelled intensely of mathematical equations and a lack of water, both in lab coats and glasses, bustling all over the place, they peeked through the bars, dictating mind-boggling notes to each other, it fell to the second lieutenant to feed the creatures generous lunches of lizards, rats, and slugs, brush their feathers, and scrape their feces out of the bottom of the cages with a kind of knife or trowel, an older, freckle-faced gentleman with a Polish accent, whom all respectfully addressed as Professor Rdwkvsmky, a famous specialist in owl sperm, would come from time to time to examine the creatures' wombs with a critical magnifying glass, he advised them to flood the walls with photographs of oil lamps and church bells (There's nothing like religion to excite owls, he maintained forcefully, there's nothing like Catholicism to stimulate the most libidinous and perverse instincts of birds), we went about for a whole week, noses in the air, taking pictures of sacristies and chapels, stealing bells from entranceways, hanging crucifixes on gas jets, in the center of the room we triumphantly placed a huge ceramic Saint Anthony with a Christ Child who looked like Mickey Rooney hanging about his neck, and the owls, Captain, grew sadder and sadder, colder and colder, more and more silent, more motionless, more nervous, hiding, trembling, in the corners of their cages, Professor Rdwkvsmky tried without success to stimulate them with a long hook, the end of a broom, a piece of wood, a jet of water, the Lebanese and the cross-eyed woman uselessly waved posters at them, the Vatican, the Sistine Chapel, the cathedral of Chartres, they replaced the monstrous Saint Anthony with a life-sized Christ, with oakum hair, cheeks concave from a lack of beefsteak, varnish drops of blood on his forehead and neck, and a terrible cross on his shoulder, staring at us all the time in accusation as if we were the Pilates of birds, we would stumble over his huge ankles and vacationing-German sandals and hasten to say an Our Father of apology, the owls, far removed from any sexual activity whatsoever, were cheeping pitifully in their cages or they would take to dropping dead without warning, piling up in grayish clumps of feathers, and their feet, Captain, looked like the repulsive, hard, wrinkled, cartilaginous fingers of the lady with purple hair who opened the door to the apartment in Santos on my next visit to Mariana, vapid, pleasant, relaxed, carnivorously crafty, with limbs spotted in the rare places uncovered by bracelets and rings by the pale freckles of menopause, who asked me to excuse the disorder (I didn't see any disorder), went from room to room with proprietary familiarity, offered me something to drink (orange juice? whiskey? gin?), offered me a chair, offered me ashtrays, praised my looks (You look much better like that, a little thinner, Jorge), picked up Mariana, smiled at her, dandled her (Inês ought to be back soon, she went down to the supermarket for a minute and promised me she wouldn't be long), she got indignant over the communists (All that's missing is for them to turn Fátima into Red Square, Jorge), she got sick over the Portuguese newspapers (Paid for by Moscow, believe me, run by their embassy, I haven't any doubts about it), she informed me of the death of her husband with a resigned raise of her eyebrows (Lung cancer, just imagine, horrible suffering, poor thing), Mariana kept her eyes on me, nervous, in panic that I would come over to her and touch her, the woman settled down opposite me, crossed the repulsive tangle of bones and tendons that were her legs, and the second lieutenant thought, surprised, What fucking interest can you have in this fossil, Inês? he thought The way her joints must creak, all buckled, in bed, he thought In a wheelchair one of these days, pissing in her panties, soiling herself, drooling, and you, all passionate, cleaning up her doodoo, giving her spoonfuls of medicine, taking her to the doctor, reading the newspaper to her, chatting with her, he thought about the house on Mãe d'Água and the fountain in the trees and the imperious acid phone calls from his mother-in-law, he thought about the place in Carcavelos and the enormous dogs leaping through the shrubbery, Don't you think that Mariana is the image of her mother? the old woman asked, devouring the little one's cheeks with her long anthropophagous yellow teeth, and at that instant in the vestibule, a noise was heard, the sound of a latch being released, your voice singing I'm going to put the groceries in the kitchen, dear, the lady with purple hair stopped chewing on my daughter for a moment and smiled at me, And what if I smashed that porcelain lamp over her noggin? the second lieutenant imagined, what if I stuck that little letter knife in her belly?, Did Mariana behave herself, love?, Inês asked from up on the dizzy heights of her high heels, coming into the living room, What if I killed the two of them with a bread knife? the second lieutenant thought, realizing suddenly that he smelled of owl shit and cane liquor breath, Good afternoon, he said in an audible murmur without looking at anyone, he went down the steps, diminished, stumbling, trying to calm the uneven beating of his heart and to put some order to the ideas that were evaporating, riding each other, melting into each other, Apply electric shock to his penis three times a day, Professor Rdwkvsmky ordered, pointing him out to the Lebanese and the cross-eyed woman, we've got to get him to masturbate effectively like the other owls, solitary pleasure distends the nerves and stops ulcers, wave posters of naked women, singers, dancers, actresses, old sweethearts, prostitutes in front of his cage, bring in a tape recorder with abundant sounds of coitus, talk to him about the blond teacher, very proper, who taught him French at school, the catechism teacher with a mustache, the inaccessible mothers of his schoolmates, the restless summers in Ericeira, the girls who made him quiver at night with dark desires, he entered the laboratory skating like a bird, dazzled by the lights reflected on the tiles, intrigued by the pointers and the viewfinders of the apparatus, possessed by a damnable hunger for lizards and rats and slugs, I stroked my breast feathers with my beak, I defecated quick yellow spittle on the floor tiles, I settled, perplexed, in a corner of the cage, the cross-eyed woman turned a knob and a storm of tolling for the dead solemnly filled the compartment, Professor Rdwkvsmky poked him on the shoulder, on the testicles, on the chest, with a sharp stick, Masturbate, he shouted, hurry up and give us some decent drops of sperm, show him a picture of his daughter to get his reproductive glands worked up the way they should, Five thousand cruzeiros in liquor and dictionaries for the monkey's lunches, the lawyer was explaining, putting on and taking off the huge muddy boots, five thousand cruzeiros for my speech is a trifle, Engineer, If he really got divorced, why the devil doesn't he come back here? his father asked, coughing amid the lead dust of the print shop, in the big abandoned house in Carcavelos, where the shrubbery was growing in a hirsute fury, the German shepherds were growling and eating the carpets, the designs on the Persian rugs, the damask drapes, knocking over my father-in-law's broken television set, the eighteenth-century consoles, the glass cabinets filled with

Chinese plates and the plaster busts of the grandfather, Two cubic centimeters of sperm, the biologist begged of me, at least two tiny little cubic centimeters of sperm, And besides treating him as a son, the magician's assistant said, I had to tie a napkin with Donald Duck printed on it around his neck and slip the soup into his mouth with a plastic spoon, the second lieutenant began walking toward the waterfront, toward the sea, melancholy buildings monotonously followed one upon the other, the garbage was piling up on the street in a nauseating stew, the uninterrupted traffic was deafening, traffic lights now amber, now red, now green, they were changing color constantly in a painful mechanical hurry, And how long after did you come back to Portugal? the communications officer asked, how much longer did you still put up with that pit trap?, Bring his wife if necessary, Professor Rdwkvsmky advised, fix up a divan, a mirror on the ceiling, black garters, lace panties, nail polish, lipstick, undress her, lay her down under him, on top of him, but get it, remember that the State, contributors, foundations are collaborating with us, the whole country, they're paying you to study scientifically the sexuality of birds in order to reveal to the world the unusual eroticism of owls, Five thousand cruzeiros, Engineer, the barefoot lawyer growled between two swigs, what are five thousand cruzeiros in times like these, The separation has been good for all of you, the lady with purple hair approved maternally, wrapping one of her necklaces about her forefinger, you've got better, Inês has got better, even Mariana has got better, a few months from now, going on like this, I'll bet that you'll get along marvelously, like God and his angels, I bypassed a rotting dock, dark, almost deserted, with just one boat moored and dancing on the black water and coils of rope and cork floats left on the wooden planks, a second barge nudged by rusty tugs like cows in a manger, the creamy thick smell of the waves didn't come from the water but from the warehouses heaped in the shadows where large red letters stood out, trade marks, numbers, emblems, I've got the sea behind me, the second lieutenant thought, I've got the sea, how strange, leaning over my shoulder like a frightened head, he went close to the reflections cast by the lights of the ships that glimmered and moved like worms on a kind of silent and stationary dark surface, an acid breeze mussed his hair, mussed his feathers, Masturbate, Professor Rdwkvsmky shouted, and he huddled trembling in his roost on a jetty, the Lebanese and the cross-eyed woman came down the gangway of a Swedish liner and adjusted thermostats and voltmeters around him, the magician's assistant rose from the floor with submarine sluggishness and threw the yellow ball of paper from the lampshade out the window, in the direction of the hesitant morning in the street, After all that did you stay in Brazil for a very long time, Lieutenant? the soldier asked, poking his belly too with a stick of wood, or a catch, or a fishhook, or a wire, the music of the bells in the laboratory grew progressively more intense until it became an unbearable, confused slew of sounds, huge posters of church belfries came and went by his blind eyes, Have another whiskey and leave off that business of rubbing your fly, the lieutenant colonel advised, if you take another whiskey I guarantee you that you'll lose your erection completely, I won't manage anything, the second lieutenant thought, grasping the soft little rag of his dick, I won't even get a visible erection, and at that point, Captain, my intestines vibrated, my stomach became distended, a stream of stuttering little farts came out of my ass, a driving turbulent, unknown, salty swelling arose in successive swirls from my belly, I leaned as best I could against the bookcase, spread my legs, opened my mouth, stuck my neck out, and turned myself loose, vomiting up the sea.

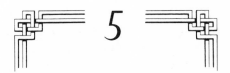

"IF you take a good look at things, I never did anything right in my life,
Captain," the soldier said. "Even at work, Jesus: my late uncle put me in
charge of the moving business and today if we get one job a week we're
lucky."

"On the first plane I could catch, a week or two later," the second lieutenant answered. "My wife's lover was so happy to see me leave that she loaned
me the money for the ticket right on the spot."

"Today, to Lisbon, Jorge?" the lady with purple hair asked. "Of course I
can lend you the money, I always carry my checkbook in my purse. Yes, I'll
tell Inês, yes, I'll give Mariana a kiss, rest assured, I won't forget."

"All I've got left now are a van that's rotting away and a sick tricycle rusting
in the warehouse," the soldier said. "And, as for workers, the only ones left
are me and the quiet man, growing old and playing checkers all afternoon in
the office."

"Sometimes at night I still wake up with the bedspread covered by the
trawler lights, hearing the ships on the waterfront and the toilet in the
boardinghouse," the second lieutenant related. "Sometimes at night I still
wake up shooing off owls with my arms and if I sit up in bed I discover
feathers and yellow excrement under my behind on the sheet."

"Tired of thinking about getting rid of all that shit for a song," the soldier said. "But when the dough runs out, what am I going to do about eating, Captain?"

"Hardened bits of excrement, like the scabs on wounds, like what pigeons leave on roofs," the second lieutenant explained. "You crumble it with your finger and there's no smell, no weight, no taste: a funny thing, crystallized sputum, a kind of dust, understand? Sometimes at night I think I'm still a bird, Captain."

"Are you like the other one too?" the concierge asked, mistrustful. "Are you going to leave me too, just like that?"

He would visit her once or twice a week, on Wednesdays and Saturdays, bring a cake or a package of hard candy or a tin car for the child, dine with her, almost without speaking, eyes on his plate, leave before dawn, penetrated by cold, vaguely repentant, vaguely guilty, while the morning light was brutally pulling out of the shadows the trees and houses and garbage cans that had been emptied and scattered the night before. His steps produced enormous explosions in the silence, as if he were walking through the echoing nave of a deserted church, he would open the glass office at the warehouse, sit down behind the desk, stupidly staring at the telephone that never rang and the street up above that was slowly taking on a density without mystery: the owner of the drugstore was taking down the shutters, the mechanics at the garage were coming down the sidewalk in small groups, smoking, the early timid sun was licking the worn cement ramp. No hunger, no sleepiness, no thirst, just a fleeting, hopeless sad feeling that floated liquidly inside him: he would set the checkers up on the board, clean the crud from his eyes with his open hand, the sound of engines, conversations, shouts, the squeaking carts of fruit and vegetable vendors: what now?

"A bird," the second lieutenant went on. "Quiet, afflicted, worried, flapping its wings on its perch, waiting. An unusual bird that shaves and gets dressed and puts its shoes on, and who talks, in the midst of tolling bells, posters, hooks that scratch my belly, orders from the biologist, the Pole, the cross-eyed woman. And on top of all that the ships in the port, now closer, now farther away, anchored in the diffuse haze of my sleep, that never stop, you see, calling me."

"An Army man, an old guy, a pervert who couldn't get a hard on," the concierge said, "one of those people who if they can't make it come up with excuses and carry on: I'm damned if I didn't learn a lesson from it. So with me, my fine fellow, either you get the papers in order or you hit the street."

The quiet man would get in at nine o'clock, a quarter after, his fingers unsteady already, smelling impetuously of wine already, his bilious eyes floating in his face like specimens in a jar of alcohol, his bones sticking out, sharp, just like a chicken's cartilage, his shirt threadbare. Uncle Ilídio would put in a yearly appearance, look the warehouse over with a dull, uninterested glance, withdraw panting and continuously sucking his asthma spray with the urgency of a baby sucking its bottle, only a suitcase with clothing and no one to see me off at the airport, passengers with the funereal faces of an air disaster sitting amid sacks, waiting for the flight, if that little woman gets on the same plane I do something will certainly happen, if that fat guy ends up next to me I'll bet anything that a reactor will go on the blink and they'll tell us to fasten our seat belts, and the stewardesses will get nervous, and some voice will start hollering, there goes my bag sliding along a rubber runner and disappearing, I felt tiny, insignificant, useless, defeated, the quiet man moved a piece forward and leaned back, searching for a pack of matches in his pockets, even today, Captain, the second lieutenant went on, after all those years, all those troubles, all those uncertain moments, all those morbid sad spells, if, for example, I'm with a woman, if I touch her arms, if I stroke her breast, if I lean over her mouth as if over my own face in a mirror, what comes to mind, I don't know, is like I've got a toothache, like I've got thrush on my tongue, I lost five pounds that last week, like twenty minutes from now, rubbing the sweat of my side against the sweat of her side, I'll light the cigarette of disillusionment and boredom, the rats trot across the broken furniture in the warehouse, the broken windows on the roof scratch the puffy, musty, mourning skin of clouds, of the sky, the telephone remains obstinately silent with the severe, halted face of a corpse, the old man, lying in bed at home, spends his days desperately trying to breathe, the quiet man's match zigzags and misses the extinguished tip of his butt and trembles, and if I don't hold my stomach as hard as I can, Captain, the soldier explained, if I don't tighten my stomach muscles, if I don't close my mouth fast, if I don't get to imagine that I'm all alone, a sharp, salty sob catches me in the throat, my bladder moans like a boat run aground, an ebb-tide cloud turns my eyes gray, I have to steady the quiet man's hand with mine until his cheeks contract like a bellows, the tobacco becomes luminous and red and two puffs of smoke spiral out of his nose, the hardware man, plump, gelatinous, in a striped duster, is hanging brushes and brooms and wooden broomsticks on display hooks, maybe I'll put another vase and flower here, maybe a calendar with a nude dame, maybe a china clown with great big shoes, a tilted little hat, and a microscopic umbrella to make the office more cheery, maybe that way the customers will come back, maybe that way the orders will increase, we'll clean up the warehouse, we'll sell the tricycle for scrap, we'll dust the furniture, we'll put the files in order, we'll repaint the green lettering on the front of the building, I've got to make a naked run to the toilet, the second lieutenant said, squashing slippers, shoes, clothing, magazines, which twisted and protested under his feet, lean over the effervescent toilet bowl, and, like on the dock in Santos, vomit up the sea.

"If you were obliged to live with a wife like mine," the lieutenant colonel sighed, "I guarantee that you'd vomit up the sea every night."

"The old man never, never asked me a thing about the business," the soldier said. "From the minute he handed Ilídio Movers over to me, the only thing that worried him was to still be alive the next day."

Earth-colored wrinkles, the olive oil–colored panic in his eyes, his white nails clutching the rubber asthma spray, his graying hair that looked just like sheep's wool peeping out of the not-too-clean openings in his shirt: such fear of death, such stubbornness in hanging on, and any day now there you are emptied of blood, memory, saliva, fear, urine, there you are in a necktie, vest, and shoes shined as bright as a teapot, in a casket with brass handles made to look like silver, and the quiet man and I sitting up with him in the parlor, playing checkers on the dining-room table with a bottle of brandy and an extinguished religious candle on the coffin. Weeks later my sister will put in her inevitable appearance, when the smell of the corpse reaches her nostrils or some solicitous neighbor tells her that you kicked off, she'll show up sloppier, more unkempt, more beaten down, uglier, with the usual cluster of children hanging on her and the inevitable mulatto in dark glasses behind, demanding, in a squalid pudding voice that dissolves into misery, melancholy, and fatigue, half of the business, once again I'll think, perplexed, How you've changed, God, the way you've become so horrible, repulsive, and once again I'll remember grandmother, on guard over her army of whores, barking in a rage, stirring a pot of soup with her enormous spoon, You and your sister and your mother and your uncle are all made out of the same shit, fuck it, nothing but garbage came out of my cunt.

"I want to be an owl too," the communications officer demanded, crawling over the carpet with the lethargy of an octopus.

"And what's your problem about getting a divorce?" the concierge was annoyed. "What kind of a game is that, did the dame cheat on you or didn't she?"

And in fact, Captain, the old man kicked off and three days after the funeral she showed up at the office with hundreds of dark-skinned kids, all filthy as the devil, with flat noses, clutching at the varicose veins in her legs (probably the same kids as the last time, a few years ago, that too many flies and too little food had stopped from growing), followed by a skinny, very short black man in a green jacket, blue pants, a red and yellow polka-dot bow tie around his neck, sandals and the scar of a knife wound in his exuberant kinky hair, Shameful, a mob of black great-grandchildren, the grandmother roared, indignant, stirring up the coals in the stove, Let me be an owl, you faggots, the communications officer asked, drooling on the rug, let me be an owl for just a little while, the quiet man's arm made a hesitant ellipse over the checkerboard, the black man's mustache was sweating like shower tiles after a hot bath, his convex temples were gleaming, they took the tricycle, half of the worm-eaten furniture in the warehouse, along with the chinaware, silverware, and the wobbly junk furniture in the uncle's room, Melissa the striptease goddess, rolled up on the couch like a dying snake, was sharing the rubbing alcohol with the lieutenant colonel, It's going to dawn, it won't be long at all, the soldier thought, it won't be long before it'll be day. The black man made a phone call in the office in incomprehensible vehement squawks and a couple of hours later an uncountable crowd of locals in gaudy rags poured bubbling out of a truck even more decrepit than ours, laughing, elbowing each other, talking in howls in a colorful language, disappearing voraciously into the shadows of the warehouse like so many worker ants in the grass, adding to the usual rustle of the rats a rustle of whispering, shuffling, and whistling, the worm-eaten commodes moaned and moved like underbrush in the jungle, the steamy warmth of Mozambique closed its damp fingers around our throats, the breeze from a thunderstorm was blowing from the rusty hill of the truck down there, They're going to fire on us, I thought, trembling, crouching under the protection of the office desk, they're going to kill us both, partner: the flash of mortars, bazookas, shouts, shots, protests. The quiet man, engrossed, was moving pieces on the checkerboard and his chest, wounded by a primrose of grenades, opened like a cabbagy flower of bone and blood, the helicopter with the doctor (or just a jet landing at the municipal airport?) brushed the tops of the trees through the skylight on the ceiling, the sun of the light bulb grows immeasurably and spins and twirls and oscillates like a record, the ants pile cupboard upon cupboard into the ancient truck, take the tricycle apart with crowbars, monkey wrenches, and hammers, I grabbed the pistol of a pencil and kneeled behind the shelf with invoices, where, mounting up, empty, were the quiet man's red-wine bottles, gray nephews were playing on the chipped floor with ropes, pieces of wood, metal hooks, trash, All made out of the same shit, fuck it, the grandmother was growling, you, your sister, your mother, your uncle, nothing but mangy garbage came out of my cunt, Otília and the skinny black man finally climbed up into the cab of the truck, the ants piled up on top of a pyramid of drawers, unfolding endless accordions of teeth, one of the kids was holding a rat by the tail, the engine crackled, vibrated, fell silent, crackled again, and no shot, no wounded, no wall knocked down by the thunder of an explosion, no mine rising up like a geyser from the floor, no medic trotting over to us with bags of serum, tourniquets, bandages, shots of morphine, You don't know if the dame lives in Lisbon? the concierge asked, you just take it easy, I'll tell you by next week, the wheels of the truck began to leap rheumatically over the pavement as if they were square, or pentagonal, or hexagonal, Your hair's so dirty, your skirt's so wrinkled, the soldier thought, looking from the door at the sister's dull profile, the rats, puzzled by the absence of the furniture, were anxiously feeling their way through the empty shadows, and a few months later I read in the paper that the skinny black man had stuck you in the navel with a knife twelve times and the police found you in the kitchen of the Buraca building (your picture, out of focus, left a pollen of lead on our fingers), arms and legs open, biting the tiles with your broken teeth.

"As though she could have ended up any other way," the grandmother grunted, spelling it out over his shoulder. "A person who doesn't know how to be a whore, boy, should keep her legs together and go straight."

"Your wife is living in Cova da Piedade with a stunted little midget," the concierge announced, putting the piece of paper with the address in his pocket. "Go over there, tell her that you want to get married, ask her for a divorce, and that's that."

I didn't go to the funeral. I didn't go to the police. I didn't go to the place in Buraca, and if I happen to pass by there with the quiet man, Captain, I go around the neighborhood by going behind the railroad stop, so that over the reeds growing on both sides I only see stagnant water from the sewer, television antennae, and chimney tops, a roof or two, and the trees in the woods, mingled, blue and tall in the distance: I presume that the ants on the truck took my dark nephews and nieces to some shack made of loose boards and corrugated metal in Benfica or Damaia, you know what it's like, narrow streets, an unbearable stink, cats with their guts hanging out in mud puddles, ragged shirts in plastic washbowls, hysterical radios, I bet there isn't a single piece of silverware left, a single sock, a single picture, not even one of those magazine pages used to line dresser drawers, I bet that the faucets, the doorknobs, even the showers were detached and taken away, probably even the smells and memories and the ancient tastes of childhood, my father still young, with a mustache, in his undershirt, combing his hair in the small framed round mirror on the wall, my mother leaning over the sink and scaling fish, nights of undefined fears and troubled insomnia, terrifying faces threatening my sleep, they certainly must have carried off my first sperm on the sheets, the specter of the old aunt who would cough ceaselessly in a wheelchair, they sold the toilet valve to Gypsies, my sister's adolescent behind and the thump of the gas in the heater, and they bought more loud shirts, more big dark glasses, more transistor batteries, more belts with great big gold buckles, they drank up the glass chandelier and my father's heart attack in neighborhood dives, so, Captain, I was suddenly left without a past, without a family, without a birthday, without a date of birth, without a childhood, without school chums, without distant winters, suspended, transparent, deprived of the consistency of flesh, of weight, with my white hair and my present age, a sad little wrinkled, worn-out baby moving disenchanted checkers in a devastated office.

"Take the ferry at the end of the afternoon," the concierge told him, "ring the bell, go right in without so much as a howdy, give her a couple of whacks, since they never hurt anyone, if necessary give the scarecrow a couple of kicks in the balls, and after the introductions are over, very calmly sit down in the best chair in the house and give that bitch a week to turn in the papers to the court."

## After the Revolution

"The guy going Mama Mama Mama Mama Mama, with a lollipop in his fist, licking my ears, my neck, biting me on the shoulder, feeling my tits, snapping the elastic on my panties, slobbering all over me, grunting and chewing on the flowers scattered in my lap," the magician's assistant complained, "and me, to myself, out of my mind, Christ almighty, what a mess, Christ almighty, what have I got myself into, when is this son of a bitch of a wise guy going to finish his charade."

"If you people won't let me be an owl," the communications officer warned cancerously, sipping the beer froth out of the empty glasses, "I'll never come to another battalion dinner."

He closed the warehouse earlier than usual (almost a month had gone by without any customers, almost a month without a move, so he had to sell some broken-down cupboards cheap in order to pay the quiet man's salary), and he walked down Martim Moniz toward the Terreiro do Paço, pushed along by the irrevocable and thick swirl of people coming from work, from offices, firms, stores, bakeshops, taverns, people, trolley cars, automobiles, lights, peddlers, policemen, beggars, the same old landscape, gentlemen, the same old city, gentlemen, the same old faces, gentlemen, I'll bet that no earthquake, not even twenty earthquakes coming someday could change this shit, there was Martim Moniz, ambiguous, unbalanced, slanting, with the first whores and the first pimps being born, still uncertain on the orangish, reddish, greenish, yellowish, blue sidewalks, the pale blotch of the Mouraria, the Praça da Figueira, and now, just like the legs and long antennae of a lobster, coming out of the square's crustacean body, the geometric streets leading to the river, sad window boxes on windows inhabited by women who take in knitting or interpret French, the sky already dark, streaked with delicate black coils, clinging and separating like a breathing gill, a turn to the right, to the left, straight ahead again, a hundred earthquakes, a hundred revolutions, a hundred civil wars, the soldier thought, and this shit always the same shit, goddamn it, the mannequins in store windows staring at their own reflections with oval eyes, bald women, men with elbows bent in delicate static gestures, amputated legs wearing black stockings with little flowers, neckties, cuff links, eels of belts, shoes and slippers on plastic columns or chrome brackets, not an invasion of Martians, not a hail of meteorites, not two hundred atom bombs, fuck it all, darkened balconies, nameplates of expediting agents and chiropodists, the Rossio station in back, swallowing and vomiting crowds of people, banks and credit agencies closing zealously, like fists, over harvest baskets of twenty-escudo notes, buses that sway like fat gentlemen running, a trolley perpendicular to me giving off silvery sparks, the archway of the Rua Augusta and the sudden square breadth of the Terreiro do Paço, melancholy ministries like lay cloisters, where guards and office boys are dozing, the pestilential smell of the water (Take the ferry at the end of the afternoon), the propeller stirring up the dull jelly of the Tagus, the night wind on the river and its smell of a decomposing corpse, a cemetery, intestines, What will I say when I get there? find words, make up sentences, conversations, huffs, refusals, arguments, hemmed in by a gentleman with his newspaper open and a small poorly dressed woman who nods from fatigue or sleepiness, in the seat opposite two girls are whispering without looking at him, mingling their smiles and their hair, the boat leans from one side to the other with a deep sound of intestines, I ring the bell, Odete or the guy opens the door for me, and what then? He feels stiff with embarrassment, the back of his neck is burning, he has an urge to urinate, he holds back an afflicted fart with his buttocks, the little ship describes a slow curve, slows down, the noise of the engine changes in intensity, pitch, a lot of small waves lap the hull like tongues, a movement of shaking back and forth, a thump, crewmen outside rolling hawsers that somebody has thrown from above around thick iron pegs, the passengers get up, go down a narrow gangplank onto the dock, night has come on completely and the gentleman with the newspaper and the poorly dressed little woman and the girls with mingled hair disappear into the current of shapes hurrying toward the bus stops, he thinks Even if the planet exploded I swear this dump of a country would stay the same, he hesitates about having a shot of grape liquor in a nearby café to get his courage up, a single customer with a beard and a knapsack on the chair next to him is chewing on a gloomy piece of beef, rubbing his jaws horizontally against each other like a dray horse, but the drivers are blowing their horns, people are getting on board the lighted fishbowls of metal and glass hurriedly, No spitting on the floor, a dirty rectangle next to the roof warns, low little houses, anemic vacant lots that melt into the shadows, packs of worried, skeletal dogs, workers on motorcycles whose enormous helmets and jeans make them look like pauper astronauts, A whack or two never did anyone any harm, there's nothing like a kick in the balls to help clear up any difference of opinion, what do you want that body for anyway, you ninny? he leans his ear against his own ear on the glass and the quivering and vibrations of the vehicle shake up his brains and his bones, they go through insignificant settlements submerged in the almost solid density of the night, tumbledown walls, a factory, another factory, trees, brick buildings, more walls, the bus gags, sneezes, belches, shakes the feathers of its mudguards like an indignant duck, stops, goes forward, stops, goes forward again, its headlights pull a sign out of the shadows, Cova da Piedade, This is it. He gets out of the vehicle with his legs weak and loose and his stomach throbbing like an oyster, night, little mangy buildings along a long street, cross streets that disappear in a dim haze of streetlights, lighted signs floating like dead fish, a gasoline pump where an old man in a beret is wiping his incredibly tiny hands on the cloth of his pants, the soldier goes ahead listlessly, I don't feel like it, I don't want to, I'm afraid, he shows the piece of paper from the concierge and the old man solicitously puts his broken glasses on his nose, leans, just like the flame of a candle, in the direction of a milky neon tube, sinks into the slow deliberations of a hound dog, his cheeks and his forehead are creased with wrinkles, a hundred, a hundred and fifty, two hundred years old, what can the age of this bastard be? the old man folds the glasses wrapped over and over with pieces of adhesive tape, straightens up, points with his finger in the gesture of a prophet, into vague, infinite distances, Keep going straight, friend, when you get to a drugstore turn left, Let me kiss your peepee place, Mama, let me lick your peepee place, Mama, the one with the lollipop was asking, kneeling on the bed, breathing like a seal, trying to put his nose between the tight thighs, a six-wheel truck stopped by the pumps and the driver, in shirt-sleeves, leaps out of the cockpit with the aerial spiral of a trapeze artist. It doesn't smell of river here, the soldier thought as he walked, it smells of smoke, insomnia, numb mornings, poverty, men playing rummy in filthy dives, a kind of chapel or church or hospital emerging from the shadows, lighted windows and rooms with no one in them, oleographs, modest cupboards, tables set, the skinny guy opening the door Yes? and me embarrassed, nervous, speechless, feeling like running away, on the landing, Odete opening the door for him and me, as if I didn't know her, Sorry to bother you, it's nothing, excuse me, I got the wrong floor. Faded buildings, ocher, pink, lilac, closed garages, tobacco shops, thread stores, Odete grabbing him by the sleeve, Wait a minute, don't go away, come in: two or three children just like the skinny guy were trotting softly around the living room, a lot of books, a lot of posters, a lot of pictures of the angry man with a goatee, peasants brandishing sickles and rakes demanding I don't know what from I don't know who, the scare-crow (Olavo, isn't it?) who looks at him with a welcoming and timid half-smile, a school, the drugstore, advertisements for sunglasses and toothpaste in the window, a scale, shelves full of packages, bottles, syrups, pillboxes, plastic spoons, baby bottles, shampoos, lotions, creams, baby food, tubes of lacquer, vaporizers, combs, a clerk in a lab coat with the face of a Siamese cat behind the counter waiting on customers, I want to suck your belly button, Mama, I want to suck your titties, Mama, Turn left, the old man had told him, a narrow and muddy alley, weeds on the edges, streetlights from time to time, lanterns where during the day they must have been putting in pipes, sewers, telephone lines: it was getting hard to make out the numbers on the doors in the dark, which side the odd ones are on, which side the even ones, he went up to the front of one of the buildings, peered at the top of the doorframe and over the bells, a metal plate, Dr. João Simões, General Practice, Hours 2 to 7 PM, and he imagined a sour individual listening with his stethoscope to bronchitis and prescribing pills and shots, the buildings gradually became sparser and unforeseen hummocks sprouted in the spaces between, sand, bags of cement, iron rods, rolls of wire, the outlines of houses, the pointed crests of cypress trees, the greasy odors of a cemetery: he unbuttoned his fly, drew out his dick through the difficult opening in his shorts (who was the son of a bitch of a garment worker who invented those cheap clothes?) and he urinated against a shiny mound of tar, feeling he was slowly emptying out a part of himself, Looking at things clearly, none of us has done anything right in our lives, boy, the lieutenant colonel said, wake up the mulatto woman, stick your tool up her ass and ten minutes from now you'll be on top of the world, by God, number sixteen, number eighteen, number twenty, the entrance to a workshop, number twenty A, and afterward an empty space where his shoes stumbled on stones, on unexpected holes, on soft humps, on the uneven ground, a three-story cube with a half-dozen lighted balconies, Unfortunately, the soldier thought, the old man at the pump wasn't fooling, I've arrived.

"*Hoo hoo hoo,*" the communications officer howled, twisting on the carpet. "If anyone in this room is more of an owl than I am, raise your hand."

"When I first came back here," the second lieutenant said, "none of the appliances were working, the shithead neighbors upstairs had flooded the toilet, and it stank of mustiness. I had to sleep for more than a month with all the windows open to air it out, I used up gallons of air freshener, if you could have seen the bill for repairing the machines you'd have died. And without Inês and Mariana I got hellishly sad, I'd wake up crying in the middle of the night, I'd dream about the dame with purple hair all the time. So, Captain, I spent a few weeks with my folks to get myself together again."

"It was about time," his father muttered in the print shop, without looking at him, without showing any joy, without returning his kiss. (The rotary presses were gobbling up paper, the floor was shaking, the outlines of the workers were distorted in the fog of smoke, coal dust, dirt, mingled silhouettes were moving about angularly in a jaundiced light.) "Maybe you should think about calling your mother, she ought to be happy knowing you're here."

"More than an hour there by her door, not moving, with a stomachache, my hands sweating, my feet sweating, getting up courage," the soldier murmured. "What am I saying, an hour: two, three hundred years before I dared lift my finger and ring the bell."

"The old lady and my sister treated me like a king," the second lieutenant said. "The meals I liked, the desserts I liked, money, tickets to the movies, neckties, records, seats at soccer matches on Sundays. They straightened up my place, hired a cleaning woman, bought new sheets, changed the curtains on the windows, called in a guy they knew to restuff the couches. They sneaked out the pictures of Inês, the telephone began to ring again, my sister introduced me to a number of her girl friends, she was always inviting me to nightclubs, get-togethers, picnics, parties."

"A hundred years there not knowing what to do, waiting a long time in the dark, leaning against the doorjamb," the soldier whispered. "And the voice in my head ordering me You get there, you give her a couple of whacks, him a kick in the balls, you give her a week to turn in the divorce papers to the court, one or two more slaps so they won't forget what you want, you turn your back, you come away."

"*Hoo hoo hoo,*" peeped the communications officer, swimming on the rug. "Watch me fly, you dummies."

"You can always work here until something better turns up," his father conceded, pointing to the shapes and the leaden haze with his chin. "For someone used to delicate jobs this must look like a punishment, a sentence, going from a horse to a stinking donkey."

He rang the bell, waited, rang again, and at that moment realized, surprised, that the street door was open. A light was on above, a mangy vestibule, worn-out mailboxes on the wall, pots with puffy plants on the stairs, strips of matting: his ankles had a hard time lifting, as if they were dragging along tons of shackles, his heart was turning over inside his liver, his intestines were rising up tumultuously into his throat, his lungs were a pair of bellows weighing down his sides, What am I going to say, what am I going to do, how can I get out of this? Who is it? Odete asked, invisible up there, sucking in air, expelling air, sucking in air, expelling air, sucking in air, expelling air, What kind of a game is this getting to be, did the dame cheat on you or didn't she? another curve in the railing, a new set of stairs, Who is it? a whining little male voice repeated, a man's shoes beside a woman's shoes, legs without stockings, uncreased pants, a jacket, a dress, hands, elbows, shoulders, the surprised face of the skinny guy and, a little bit above, Odete's intrigued look: It doesn't smell of river, he thought, it smells of fresh paint, sewers, the absence of comfort, fried oil, ohitsyoudontstandonceremonycomein, such a neutral pitch, such a natural tone, Captain, as if we'd only seen each other the night before, you see, as if we'd only just separated, you see, I love you, a couple of whacks, a valiant kick in the balls, the concierge's son crawling on the floor, yellow, silent, pointy faced, pushing a tin car with his finger, and, in the end, no posters, no pictures of the stern man with a goatee, not many books, no peasants, no rakes, no sickles, no children: a tiny living room, wooden chairs, a picture of Dona Isaura on the radio, another one of Odete, arm in arm with Olavo, on a low table, one or two cheap lamps, the newspaper opened on the couch, the smell of a still warm meal, ashtrays, mats, the bedroom with an unmade bed, the kitchen in disarray, stacks of dirty dishes in the sink, pots, bowls, pans, did she cheat on you or didn't she? Can it be that I love you, the soldier thought, or is it just timidity, just bashfulness, just the usual anguished hesitation? Comeincomein, the skinny guy consented with an obsequious little invitation, folding up the newspaper, opening up his wine-colored gums in a disagreeable and humble smile, and he, to himself, I bet they're living just as short of dough as me, I bet they're counting pennies like me, I bet that during the last days of the month they buy on credit at the clothing store, the grocery store, the butcher's, eating on credit in stinking little restaurants, Give me some olive oil to drink, the communications officer asked, crawling toward us, the only nourishment a proper owl can stand is olive oil. You haven't changed a bit, Odete commented, smiling too, an impersonal smile, dull, distant, without disdain or affection, the years have gone by without touching you, Abílio, and me like a bear, Captain, like an elephant, like an enormous animal, with no place for my hands, my body, my legs, sucking in air, expelling air, sucking in air, expelling air, sucking in air, expelling air, the concierge telling me to beat them up, ordering me to go in there shouting and kicking balls and me looking at the place and looking at the two of them, understand, with as much pity for them as for myself, I tried to put some rational order into the business, the second lieutenant explained, but with my father it was an impossible chaos, there was no accounting system, there was no order, there wasn't the slightest administrative plan, for every measure I proposed, the old man would answer by running an annoyed pen across a pad, frowning, sulky, on one occasion we broke into shouts, eyes flashing at each other, and never again after that scene did we look straight at each other, You're completely out of your mind, the father barked, do you think this is a goddamned bank or something? until I ended up getting a position with an insurance company and it was a relief for the both of us, He tried to force the lemon lollipop between my legs, the magician's assistant said, he wanted to play the bass fiddle on my clitoris with that sticky piece of shit.

"I ended up sitting down on the living-room couch, Captain, right on top of the scarecrow's newspaper, which crackled under my ass every time I moved," the soldier sighed, "as if I was carrying the whole of autumn in my behind. So I listened to them and talked to them all quiet like, very bashful, terrified at the idea of filling the conversation with paper farts."

"What kind of a trick is this getting to be, what were you up to stuttering over there?" the concierge was indignant. "I don't understand, I swear, I don't understand, did the dame cheat on you or didn't she?"

"After a quarter of an hour there was nothing to talk about," the soldier complained. "The periods of silence got horribly longer, if they shut up, my heart would fall into painful empty pits, my mouth was dry, I didn't have any saliva in my mouth, my muscles went soft, I tried to get up and the newspaper *trrrrr trrrrrr trrrrrr* giving me away like a watchdog."

"What?" the concierge exclaimed, dumbfounded. "You came away empty-handed, you jackass, you came away without demanding the divorce?"

"*Trrrrr trrrrrr trrrrrr,*" the newspaper threatened.

"No, nothing special, seriously," the soldier whispered. "It just happened that I had to come by here on a job and I remembered Let me go see how Odete is, let me see how her husband is."

"*Trrrrrr trrrrrr trrrrrr,*" the pages said.

"But what a fine fellow of a dunce you are," the concierge howled, "what a beast you turned out to be."

"*Trrrrr trrrrrr,*" the pages warned.

"Good night, don't bother coming to the door," the soldier protested. "If another moving job in these parts turns up in the next month or two I'll come by and look in on you."

"*Trrrrrr trrrrrr trr,*" the pages vibrated.

"You felt sorry for them, you were moved by their pleasantness, the way they received you, treated you?" the concierge was appalled. "And who's sorry for me, fuck it all, who's moved by me, you bastard?"

"*Trr,*" the newspaper sobbed.

"Yes, I got fat, I weigh almost two hundred pounds," the soldier informed them. "I can barely fit into chairs, you can see it."

"*Trrrrrrr trrrrr trrrr,*" the newspaper guffawed.

"I'll holler as much as I like, damn it, am I in my own home or am I not? fuck the neighbors, fuck the kid," the concierge howled, pounding on the television set. "And if you raise your voice to me again I'll hit you over the head with this bowl, you faggot."

"*Trrrrrrr,*" the newspaper lamented.

"So I was messed up for two nights with one stroke, Captain, the little night at Cova da Piedade and the great big night in Lisbon, I got to two vestibules, I closed two doors, I got away from two buildings simultaneously," the soldier said, on his back on the bed with his open palm on the sprawled, chocolate-colored back of the mulatto woman. "And still today, after so many years have passed, I still don't know, did you ever see such a piece of foolishness? which of the two scared me the most."

"*Trrrrrrrrrrrrrrrrrrrrrrrrrrrrrrrrrrrrrrrrrrrrrrrrrrrrrrrrrrrrrrrr rr-rrrrrrrrrrrrrrrrrrrrrrrrrrrrrrrrrrrrrrrrrrrrrrrrrrrrrrrrrrrrrrrrrrrrrrr rrrrrr-rrrrrrrrrrrrrrrrrrrrrrrrrrrrrrrrrrrrrrrrrrrr,*" the newspaper concluded.

6

"WOULDN'T the concierge take you back after that?" the second lieutenant asked. "After she got over her rage?"

"We'd go out to dinner every so often or to the movies, or to a bar," the
lieutenant colonel said, "on one occasion she dragged me by the hair to dance
at a discotheque. She'd phone her mother and make excuses that involved
girl friends, I'm going out, I'm staying over at this one's place, I'm staying
over at that one's place, I'd invent meetings at the Ministry, summonses from
the secretary of state, school dinners, and I'd get undressed without turning
on the light, dopey from gin, while Edite and the dog were snoring horizontally in the darkness of the bedroom, threatening and just as big as my fear of
them, my uneasiness, my fatigue."

"I won't be through before one o'clock in the morning, Mother," the
boutique clerk explained, leaning against the counter of sweaters on
sale, twirling a lock of hair with her finger and winking over the mouthpiece.
"Get that idea out of your head, I'm going to Amadora and I'll stay with
Graciete, her godfather will come by to pick us up in his car when we're
through."

"She telephoned the warehouse three or four times," the soldier
answered, "are you all right, how are things going, I'm sorry about the other

392

day, Abílio, I lost my head, I misjudged you, and me, I've got my pride, not a peep. But a dame like that when she gets a bee in her bonnet won't give up."

"It's the third time this week you're going out at night," the cloud of perfume complained. "Is that all your military colleagues know how to do?"

"And in a discotheque, figure that one out," the lieutenant colonel laughed, stroking his uncertain foot along the behind of the striptease goddess, who moaned on the couch wrapped in her soft, twitching brandy sleep. "Can you people imagine me bouncing around in a discotheque?"

"I was afraid you were going to be like that other bastard, Abílio," the concierge argued. "Come on, don't be foolish, come on over tonight, hell."

"I'm spending the night with Suzete, with Bernardete, with Lizete, with Mariete," the boutique clerk said, sitting on the aluminum counter in the shop, blowing clandestine kisses with her pursed lips. "Their husbands drive us home, Mother, I shudder when I think about getting on the ferry at eleven o'clock."

"We went on like that for more than six months, Lieutenant," the soldier replied, "her repeating to me, Come, come, come, come, come, come, come, and me acting like a prince, saying no. But the Lisbon night is so deep, Captain, that a guy all alone, without any help, is bound to break down: so one Wednesday I took her up on her invitation, OK, don't bug me anymore, cook me some onion stew as bait, see you later."

"Every so often it occurred to me what if I told them they've got another grandchild, what if I suddenly spoke up at dinner about Ilda's pregnancy?" the second lieutenant said. "But then I'd think No, it can't be that way, me opening my mouth and the old folks falling over backward, pale, twisting and frothing at the mouth."

"Artur," the cloud of perfume warned, bathing the little dog, "watch your step, because if I smell a trick I'll wring your neck."

Hotel Cabinda, Hotel Pérola, Hotel Baptista, Hotel Açoriana, Hotel O Meu Ninho, the Dallas Residence: the same filthy stairs, the same sleepwalking clerks, the same uninterested sidelong glances, the same beat-up registers, dull voices that requested Write your little old ID here, friend, furtive couples slipping down the hall, women all painted, glowing adolescents, elderly gentlemen hiding their faces behind a hand, and always the same room, you see, no matter where it is, in Picheleira, in Arco do Cego, in Baixa, in Graça, in Alvalade, in Lumiar, identical beds, lumpy sheets, bidets on iron legs, bulbs that exhaled, like breath, the sick light of a hospital, half-closed windows blowing an icy, treacherous breeze on our backs, and then the usual difficulty, the usual affliction, the usual sweating, the hurried, solicitous fingers that squeezed, insisted, the quick little surge, the instantaneous tightening of muscles, it's done, just a little while till morning (Did I fall asleep?), the sock lost God knows where, the two of us, sticky, irritated, puffy, batting our heads against the headboard, crawling on the floor, the victorious sigh, yours or mine, I found it, the brown trim on the uniform collar, the undershirt, suddenly unpleasant, which gave me goose pimples, your perfume on the palms of my hands, on the back of my neck, on my nose, it seemed impossible to me that anyone would notice, that anyone would be surprised, that anyone would catch on, Colonel Ramos came into the office quite serious, the majors and the captains came into the office quite serious, Edite, in a tunic, was removing the fish bones for me with imperial gestures and her false rings glistened like a chandelier, Tomorrow I'm going to be nineteen, the boutique clerk announced, naked in front of me, fastening her bra over her shoulder blades, I still want to see the present you're going to give me.

"Give her a bracelet or a necklace, Commander," the communications officer suggested, belching up the third glass of Alka-Seltzer in a row (and the effervescent tablet rose and fell and rolled around and grew smaller in his esophagus, giving off a trail of bubbles). "Dames go crazy over intimate, personal little presents."

"The long nights I went through for six months, Captain," the soldier murmured, "listening to the sounds from the window, wide awake, the kale rustling, the chicks, the metal shrubbery of antennae shaking and swaying. I'd come in the next day with the teeth in my gums ringing with scurvy as though I'd taken an endless nightmare voyage on my sheets."

"So I kept my trap shut so as not to upset the old folks, Captain," the second lieutenant said. "When you came right down to it, I didn't even know anything about the child, and, besides, an awful lot of babies die, isn't that so?"

"Another meeting with the minister today?" the cloud of perfume's voice was surprised in the midst of the dog's sharp barking. "But there aren't any more revolutions in sight, are there, isn't everything quiet down there, didn't Colonel Ramos assure me that all the shooting, all the plotting, all the coups were finished?"

"And were you in love with the girl, Commander?" the second lieutenant asked.

I don't know about being in love, a guy forty-seven years old is way past the age of foolishness, he can't chase after the first idiotic notion that puts in an appearance, and yet he'd telephone her at the shop three or four times in the morning, and yet he'd interrupt meetings and work sessions to listen anxiously to her breathing and her laughter on the other end of the line, and yet he'd accompany her, ever so bashful, to nightclubs booming with music and colored spotlights, in order to caress her and stroke her at a discreet table, immediately invaded by groups of rowdy, lively young men without neckties who would smoke his cigarettes, drink his whiskey, and treat him familiarly in a kind of ceremony that paralyzed him. Huddled in a corner, annoyed at sharing his seat and the small dish of fried potatoes or peanuts or popcorn with a boy with a mustache, the boy with a mustache's girl friend with mountainous breasts, the boy with a mustache's fat sister, and a mulatto who smelled and every so often would release a Niagara of guffaws, the lieutenant colonel, who felt as out of place as a clown at a wake, would become painfully aware of his baldness, his white hair, his wrinkles, his lumbago, he bitterly remembered the doctor's advice (Small meals with not too much salt and watch your heart), he'd put his necktie in his pocket and unbutton his shirt in the futile hope of rejuvenating himself by a few months, he'd let the boutique clerk bite him earnestly on the ear, let himself be pulled by the arm into the middle of the dance floor where, cornered by the music, by the strobe lights, by the shouts, the laughter, the faces that ceaselessly approached and withdrew, he'd initiate a clumsy pantomime made up of contortions and hops, he'd use his handkerchief to wipe the sweat off his cheeks, his clavicle, his neck, he'd feel the girl's tongue snake over the wire and plastic plate at the roof of his mouth, he'd ask the attendant for his topcoat, help her put on her jacket, the foul-smelling mulatto would squeeze his ribs effusively, the one with the mustache would give him some knowing pats on the behind, he'd put a twenty-escudo note into the delighted hand of the doorman, sneeze from the cold outside (I'm going to catch cold, I'm going to catch cold for sure with this weather), the car's windows and headlights were covered with dripping mist, more kisses, more hugs, more tired squeezing as the engine, dull, tremulous, sobbing, warmed up, the windshield was clear outside and cloudy inside like the bottles where seven-month fetuses are kept in yellow liquid, and afterward the Hotel Jasmim, Hotel Moçâmedes, Hotel Paris, Hotel Alabama, Hotel Antunes, Marvila Rooms Hot Water and Shower, a vaguely curious sidelong glance at the boutique clerk, an indifferent sidelong glance at him, a dirty nail or thumb pointing to the printed line. Sign your little name here, friend, that's three hundred escudos in advance, please, the same wallpaper with its medallions, the same damp pillowcases, the cirrhotic light, taking off his topcoat, his shirt, his pants, his shoes, his socks, burying his nose in the sheet, his bones rattling from discomfort and cold, and suddenly a slithery flank slipping over his back, a breeze under the covers, a cold little hand squeezing his testicles, Cuckoo.

"I know an engineer," one of the little blond twins said, "who'd pay me to screw with him and with a clothes dummy called Alfredo. He was very refined, thin, a managing director for eighteen years, his wife had died on him of a stroke and one day when he was going along the Rua dos Fanqueiros, he saw the dummy in a store in full dress and he fell in love. So that before the two of us would roll around on the mattress, the guy would undress Alfredo very carefully, comb and brush his oakum hair, deodorize him, perfume him, run a razor over his pasteboard cheeks, lay him down beside us, all nice, with his head on a little lace pillow, and tell me Give him a kiss too or else he'll be peeved, you can't imagine how jealous Alfredo can get."

"Why don't you separate from your wife and come live with me?" the boutique clerk suggested, putting on her glossy boots. "It'll save all that trouble of lying to my mother, Artur."

"Just look at him, poor thing," the engineer nudged her, "just look at how angry with us he is. Are you so inhuman that you can't fondle him a little maybe?"

"Cuckoo," the lieutenant colonel answered in a thin little voice, feeling imbecilic, ridiculous, lethargically searching under the sheet for her nipples, the curve of her navel, the sparse little hairs of her pubes.

"A chick of nineteen, Commander," the communications officer opined, stirring the eighth effervescent tablet with his finger as it winked out its gas like a soluble deep-sea diver, "is a pack of trouble."

"I had to rub up against Alfredo," the twin sobbed, "I had to pretend I was coming on top of him."

"We could rent part of a house," the boutique clerk enticed him, "and we could go dancing at the Tubarão every night. In Linda-a-Pastora, for example, there are flats that aren't too expensive."

"See how happy he is?" The engineer was merry. "See how he's smiling to say thank you?"

"Well, finally," the concierge exclaimed, opening the door for him, poking him in the belly. "I never knew anybody so proud, God almighty."

"I've got to look for that child," the second lieutenant said, "I'll be damned if I won't find him this very day."

"So how did you shake her off, Commander?" the soldier asked, "how did you get out of that mess?"

"One afternoon," the lieutenant colonel said, "I went into the boutique and came face to face with her mother. I never saw two people who looked so much alike."

They'd spent the night before in a little bar in Alcântara, smoky and dark, where a thread-thin character with a goatee was torturing an upright piano, and which, after two o'clock, after the shows finished, filled up with actors, journalists, poets, drunken moviemakers nodding against the French posters that covered the walls of the tiny place, with bulbs enclosed in red cellophane and little benches and dwarf tables around the bar. The bald man in shirt-sleeves who was impassively pouring fierce drinks into cocktail glasses, with a maraschino cherry and a lemon twist perched on the ice, served them brandy glasses full of a greenish liquid and an additional toothpick so that they could give a light stir (Careful, the bald man advised, drawing back) to that strange liquefied dynamite, capable of reducing a person's intestines to crackling sulfuric briquettes with the very first swallow. The lieutenant colonel vaguely remembered very ugly women, hair loose, in Indian tunics and sandals, hanging over the artists with proprietary airs, painters vigorously spewing pork rinds and hake over each other, gray-haired novelists accompanied by adolescent girls in blue jeans, imbecilic and ecstatic, immersed in schoolgirl meditations, photographers with dirty fingernails pushing back their inspired mops of hair with knuckles yellow from acid. He remembered that his temples had a hard time holding in his gassy brains, that out of the clay mug that was his heart, through his belly and limbs, a bush of wire arteries was emerging, buried in his flesh, whose harp sound hurt him, that his feet insisted on flying, loose, in the atmosphere saturated with smells, belches, laughter that unfolded like a coil, grunts and sighs, he remembered wanting to punch, for hazy reasons, a blond saxophonist, and of having hugged, weeping, the knees of a comatose editor in chief, he remembered the street rolling up and unrolling, elastic, slippery, wet with rain, under his feet, the sarcastic dancing of the lampposts, the building façades that kept tumbling down onto his shoulders, and then the taxi (Hadn't you better take your father to the hospital, kid?) and the sound of the engine that scraped across his perineum, the Hotel O Meu Lar, next to the Mint, whose blue lamp wavered, microscopically on the other side of the world, of having crouched on the sidewalk, insulting the windows with nobody in them, calling them bitches, your helping me up the stairs, paying for the room, pushing me with all your might onto the bed, nauseous, dizzy, without any energy or will, putting out the light, pulling your shoes off, and I watched you get undressed, item by item, in the foggy morning that was just beginning, with gestures that evaporated fluidly from my eyes like the casual smile of a baby.

"Her mother, just like that, in the store?" the soldier whistled. "What a hell of a mess, Colonel."

"Good afternoon," the lieutenant colonel said in a pale voice (If I could drop dead right here I could get out of this), going over to the boutique clerk with the painful slowness of a condemned criminal. "Do you carry babies' bonnets by any chance?"

He awoke all alone at noon, lying across the bed, startled by a dream in which his grandfather was scolding him from his invalid's chair, threatening him with the silver head of his cane (Silver?). Long threads of rain were falling monotonously outside, boils of pus were suppurating down the windowpanes, mushrooms were sprouting and blistering the medallioned wallpaper, a cockroach who was scurrying along the baseboard disappeared into a crack in the floor. There were ashes and hardened mud and cracker crumbs on the design in the rug, a dead moth, feet in the air, was in its death throes on the night table between the bottle of water and a dusty glass. His muscles were burning, his tendons were burning, his joints were burning, his bones filled him with piercing knives and nails at the slightest movement, his eyelids, dilated like hemorrhoids, defecated his eyes. He got dressed without washing (not even a glimmer of water in the china pitcher), one or two girls wrapped in towels stumbled like moles along the hallway. Where did we go yesterday? Where did I leave the car? the desk clerk, who was shaving in a little mirror beside the key rack, demanded a hundred escudos extra (It's half past twelve already, pal, you know the rules, pal), while his ears palpitated, emitting froth like those of a dead horse. One afternoon when he was little, the lieutenant colonel had gone to the beach with his mother just when the lifeguards were using ropes to drag out a dead mare, devoured by crabs and bloated with gas, limpets and moss clinging to its enormous jaws, and every so often, without warning, if he closed his eyes, in Africa, at mess, at the dentist's, at dinner with friends, the image of the drowned horse, its mane hanging down like the fringe of a rug and its great vacant eyes covered with clusters of flies and red insects all jumbled and seething, would appear washed up on the beach, dragged toward the little wooden bathhouses, followed by the desperate hunger of the gulls.

"A baby's bonnet with ribbons," the lieutenant colonel repeated, panic-stricken, anxiously feeling the ridiculousness of his question, the beating of his heart diminishing and slowly extinguishing in his chest like a candle. "A grandson of mine is being baptized on Saturday, miss."

He paid the hundred escudos, left twenty more as a tip to calm the desk clerk, who was blocking his way, razor in hand: the man pocketed the money, annoyed (They're trying to have some fun for nothing, they're trying to take me for a fool), muttering confused threats, spitting mentholated froth at the top of the stairs, the rain was bouncing angrily off the pavement, dozens of castaway mares were piling up, shapeless, in the gutters, a thunderclap rattled over the rooftops preceded by a quick jab of light, and the lieutenant colonel, his jacket collar turned up, shivering under the eaves, was trying to reconstruct the puzzle of the night before, tying together novelists and painters, explosive drinks, tragic adolescents, and muses in Indian tunics who didn't fit together: Did we come in a taxi from the Flamingo, the Blitz, the Bunker, the Lontra, the Lareira, the After Eight? He got names mixed up, smells, atmospheres, alleys, confused routes, shuffled faces, was mistaken about the dinner menu, the drinks, the portions, the topics of conversation, until far off in the distant reaches of his mind there was a labored clearing, some motor began working in his brain, his mother, the bathhouses, and the dead horses evaporated from the gutters and a cloud of perfume rose to warn him with a finger, Clarisse was knitting with downcast eyes, the dog barked in the kitchen, scratching on the doormat with its long claws, Alcântara.

"I'm sorry, Commander," the second lieutenant said, "but babies' bonnets don't go with a dirty old man."

He found the car crucified on the corner of an alley, with a parking ticket, ink running in the rain, under a rubber windshield wiper, small houses, little suburban shops, and there in the background, as always, encased between two walls, gray or the color of dirty milk, speckled with boats, out of focus in the rain, the river. And not just the river, the bridge, and not just the bridge, the statue of Christ the King on his hill, the dull earthen outline, squat settlements in the cheek folds of the hills, the distant sea beyond the mouth of the sewers, with thousands of dead mules drifting along, from wave to wave, obliquely, in the direction of the beach. But the Volkswagen wouldn't start, he pushed on the pedals and a cluster of tin cans shivered and fell silent, the battery gave off a few weak groans of protest, the horn moaned the tenuous laments of a puppy, a group of youths came out from under the awning of a café, bent over the rear mudguards and pushed, the car picked up speed on the stone-paved surface, dancing on the gleaming trolley tracks, the lieutenant colonel put it into second, let out the clutch (Is there the smell of cheap perfume inside here or am I the one who smells of cheap perfume?), the car leaped, halted suddenly, leaped again, they shouted at him Steponit steponit steponit steponit with the squawk of an albatross in a storm, he stepped on the pedal, heard, confused, some confused sobs of connecting rods, STEPONIT, the birds roared farther and farther away, the hood broadened like the chest of a diver on a board, the cylinders flowed together and joined in an uninterrupted hum, the needle on the speedometer began to move, his shirt, his pants, his jacket were drenched, his tie was swinging back and forth from his neck like a rag, an itchiness was growing in his nose (Am I going to sneeze?), third, fourth, he reached a square, a wider street, big faded buildings, an avenue, a traffic circle where trucks and cranes could be glimpsed, round traffic lights, the green side of a boat, he took his cigarettes out of his pocket, but the pack, nauseating and sticky, had been turned into a kind of muddy mush, What will Edite say, what kind of a face is she going to put on for me, what lie can I give her, the boutique clerk's mother, forehead wrinkled, took a step toward him, clutching her purse in both hands over her stomach, as if to protect herself or to attack, the daughter, chewing gum with a cheap beaded ring on her little finger (Her poor taste is so obvious to me, the lieutenant colonel thought, surprised, her defects are so clear to me now), was huddled behind the counter like a sick badger, Go take a walk around the block, Lucília, this gentleman and I have some urgent business to transact.

"A devil of a problem," the lieutenant colonel said, getting out of his wet clothes, "the Chaves Cavalry regiment was getting ready to come down here on a war footing. I don't know how many hours it took us to convince the second lieutenants, the captains."

He turned the shower on, hurriedly hid his drawers in the bottom of the wicker basket, took a quick shower, brushed his teeth, shaved with a dull blade that wounded his chin without cutting the hairs, he rubbed his face, neck, shoulders with cologne that made the scratches smart, the pale lapdog came over to inspect him, sniffing at his heels, he pushed it away with a kick of hatred, Get over there, I don't even want to look at you, What?

Artur? the cloud of perfume asked, spraying her hair in the bedroom, Nothing, he answered, I was just cursing those dunces in Chaves without realizing it.

"The little one was a virgin, General." The clerk's mother blinked her concerned eyes: "What now?"

She wasn't thinking about raising a rumpus, none of that, she didn't want any mess, she didn't want any disputes: almost up against the lieutenant colonel, without any shrieking, without any rancor, without any fury, she was chatting in a flowing, relaxed, abracadabralike diplomatic tone, because in a certain way, General, in spite of my legitimate feelings as a mother, in spite of the call of my blood, in spite of the undeniable affection that links me to Lucília, it was a kind of, let us say, business deal, a commercial transaction that she had come to propose to him: she smelled of cheap soap, two rings of sweat were spreading under her arms, her frazzled dress was hiked up around her belly, the wrinkles around her eyes were just like the ones by her mouth, as if three stones had fallen into the yellow puddle of her face at the same time, her great toe pierced the tip of her shoe like the flattened head of a snail peeping out of its shell, her dull hairs quivered like antennae, a business deal, General, some ridiculously small material and moral compensation, the least that could be demanded since he was the first man Lucília had had, so either you marry her, sir, or you set her up in an apartment and take on the expense, or if you don't do any of that I'll find myself obliged, with great regret, believe me, to inform your wife of the truth in this matter, and all the while she was smiling, imagine (he told me), talking with her lips close to mine, tugging on my tie in a familiar way, pouring into my nose a pestilential, fetid breath where old lunches were decomposing, wedding buffets, sautés, rotten eggs, the tart breath of an ebb tide.

"The engineer wasn't any big deal, what's another lunatic more or less, I've gotten used to everything with time," the twin said, "the dummy stretched out there now, smiling like a dead person, smelling of hair tonic and perfume, gave me an awful impression. And then you'd touch him and there'd be nothing between his legs, only the smooth pasteboard of his skin and the plastic joints of his hips, nothing that vibrated, that grew, that got hard, that got wet, that filled your hand. I kissed him and couldn't find any tongue, hugged him up against me and the guy didn't react, I licked his ear and there was no answering quiver."

"And you dropped like a wounded duck, Colonel," the second lieutenant cackled. "You had your pants scared off you by the dame's blackmail."

"Just one more kiss, just one more kiss," the managing director peeped, pushing her head down. "Alfredo is such an affectionate person."

"The mannequin would look at me with a little smile and right away I'd feel sick," the skinny girl said, "glass eyes make me nervous."

"In my opinion," the boutique clerk's mother advised, "there's nothing like an apartment on the Avenida de Roma, below the Alvalade movie house. With all the stores around there the little one won't get tired shopping."

"The woman wrapped you up nicely, she had you in the palm of her hand, Colonel, and you could only watch," the second lieutenant laughed, "I'll bet you had the girl all set up the following week."

Not the following week, but the following month, not next to the Alvalade, but two blocks from the Vox, over a Chinese restaurant with a display case full of fans, porcelain spoons, horror-movie waiters, and chandeliers with scarlet fringes: a bedroom, a living room, a kitchen, a shower stall, a rear balcony, electric appliances, rugs, a brass bed with arabesques, so well polished that it hurt your eyes to look at it, a television set, a record player roaring out music, little iron tables here and there, and any number of knickknacks: little bears, gnomes, birds, glasses with printed decorations, a ceramic fairy with a silver star on her crown. The rear balcony, like dozens of others, overlooked a rectangular square with trees and gravel beds and eternally deserted benches, empty establishments with windows painted white, and there must have been a school or an academy in the neighborhood because right after twelve noon bands of children aged ten or eleven crossed the square diagonally to disappear into a kind of tunnel, in the direction of the Júlio de Matos Hospital, where the lunatics clamored among the bushes, greenish and convulsed. He had to borrow money for the apartment, behind the back of the cloud of perfume, and every time he put his key in the door he'd find her brothers and sisters, or her cousins, or her uncles and aunts, or her friends, or her parents installed in the living room, sipping Maintenance whiskey, nibbling Maintenance hors d'oeuvres, devouring Maintenance meat, chatting, nudging each other, laughing, Excuse me, Commander, the soldier grew sad, but it was a stroke of luck for them, Lucília quit her job at the boutique, dyed her hair red, painted her toenails, hired a maid, bought a horrible Pekingese, topped it off by acquiring menopause buttocks and breasts, flooded the closet with black dresses with very low-cut necklines, and she'd suck on licorice candy from morning till night, imperially spread out, creamy, almost liquid, on a plush couch, leafing through photo-novels with an ill-humored little look. In time the lieutenant colonel ended up making friends with her father, a retired railroad engineer who was missing almost all of the fingers on his left hand, whose favorite topics of conversation were locomotives and derailment and who invariably ended up asking him, after several circular flights of a famished buzzard, if he might not have two or three extra conto bills in his wallet, because I'll pay you back tomorrow night without fail, debts to friends are sacred to me, you know, and in spite of all, of course he never paid him back, doubtless because he'd forgotten and the lieutenant colonel was ashamed to remind him, Lucília lost interest in bars and nightclubs, determinedly dedicating her time to buying outfits and putting on weight, she would complain every week, standing naked on the scale, her fat quivering, I've gained more than six pounds, Artur, and one fine morning Colonel Ramos, after his report, asked, respectfully, May I make a small observation, General? the lieutenant colonel in his haze answered yes, and the other one, very serious, The officers think you're neglecting the administration of the Academy, General, just the day before yesterday the secretary of state paid a surprise visit and found no one to receive him, unfavorable things, intrigues, stories about skirts are being whispered about in the halls of the Ministry. He thought about asking What things? but desisted, he thought about telling them all to go to hell and he forgot to, he wanted the fellow to disappear so he could tell the orderly If anybody calls me on the phone I've gone out and close his eyes for five minutes in the leather easy chair, How long has it been since I've had a proper night's sleep? the sound of the chocolates won't let me rest, your incessant jaws keep me awake for a long time, the sound of the foil paper being opened gives me a start, Say, General, Lucília's mother shouted, pointing with a circular move-ment of her arm to the overloaded closets, this girl hasn't got a thing to wear, look at her, Say, General, some cousin would announce, inspecting the pantry, all I can find in the place are empty bottles, Making love to a managing director and a pasteboard dummy is a hell of a job, the skinny girl explained, I was beside myself trying to get an orgasm out of Alfredo, two or three mechanical little shakes and that's that, two or three little nothing leaps and all set, Another business dinner? the cloud of perfume was angry, maybe it would be better if you moved your bed to the Terreiro do Paço, the secretary of state insists on talking to you, Commander, the telephone operator warned him, pulling him out of his sleepwalking mist, Do you want me to put the call through, sir?, I can't get along on twenty contos a month, Lucília said, clutching a pencil, doing some difficult sums on the wrinkled back of an envelope, either I get more money or starting on the fifteenth there'll be nothing to eat, fortunately the cloud of perfume opened a second boutique in Areeiro and almost immediately thereafter one in Campo de Ourique, one in Estoril, and one in the Baixa, Colonel Ramos's wife went into partnership with her in the business, Clarisse ran the one in Estoril, located between a travel agency and a branch bank, with bitchy, avaricious detail, Excuse me, Commander, the soldier put in, but I'd almost bet that the dame was going to bed with someone else, Hello, hello? the secretary of state asked irritably, a small, insignificant, and short-tempered man, very close to the president of the Republic, damn it, man, I didn't recognize your voice, are you drunk or something? The lieutenant colonel straightened up in his chair, wiped the crust from his eyes, coughed, quickly buttoned his uniform jacket, hurriedly shuffled through some papers on the desk, For the love of God, Brigadier, not by a long shot, I was even looking over a plan for remodeling the mess halls. Your face looks awful, Artur, the cloud of perfume noted, why don't you get a chest X-ray, Your face looks awful, Artur, why don't you get a blood test? and me running desperately back and forth between one and the other, without really being with either one, without any erection, without any pleasure, without any patience for either one, nodding over the newspaper like an eighty-year-old in the first chair I can grab, catching sight of their expressions of annoyance and fury before I doze off, A chest X-ray, an opaque enema, a blood test, a urinalysis, a search for eggs in the feces, What? the secretary of state roared, enemas, analyses, urine, eggs, what the hell kind of foolishness are you braying about?, Fifty contos at least, Lucília concluded, definitively, with anything less than fifty contos I'll certainly starve to death, and she owed the butcher, and she owed the grocer, and she owed the dressmaker, and she owed a fortune to Maintenance, not to mention that she'd got it into her head to take a bus trip to Egypt, It certainly seems to me that either you're drunk or you're off your rocker, the secretary of state said with amiability that augured no good, be in my office at five o'clock. I wonder where Ilda is living? the second lieutenant whispered, an ugly dame like that couldn't have gone too far. Another man? the lieutenant colonel answered, finishing the medicinal alcohol, at first I didn't have any suspicions at all, damn it, they were all cousins, you understand, all family members, all childhood friends. He put on his best uniform, headed the Volkswagen toward the Terreiro do Paço, corporals, sergeants, second lieutenants coming to attention, corridors, the baroque jewel-box smell of the enormous salons, Lieutenant Cardoso, with a folder of papers under his arm, greeted him fleetingly from the distance with a bothered and bashful smile, some extremely busy officers who pretended not to know him and me to myself right off These bastards must be cooking up something against me, what's the secretary of state got up his sleeve? Please be good enough to wait a few moments, General, a quartermaster asked him, reading the sports pages in an armchair next to a damask drape, I'll announce you right now, and me indifferent, bored, out of it all, dizzy from lack of sleep and fatigue, the steps beat on the marble floor and echoed, distorted, inside my skull, I'll announce you right now, I'LL ANNOUNCE YOU RIGHT NOW, I'LL ANNOUNCE YOU RIGHT NOW. I confess that another guy never entered my mind, who'd be so stupid to lose the free ride I represented, her parents treated me like a son-in-law, her brothers considered me their brother-in-law, Lucília's family seemed to find all of that quite natural, as there was never any lack of drinks, cheese, croquettes, music, laughter, shouting, when you came right down to it, I spent more time in Alvalade than at home and I might just as well have divorced Edite, and I might just as well have shat on the cloud of perfume, and I might just as well have married the little one, twenty-seven years difference in age is nothing these days, I met a guy who would masturbate in front of his daughter's dolls, the communications officer said, but living with a dummy, now, that's too much, The brigadier is waiting for you, the quartermaster declared with a glance at the soccer results, please follow me, General, balconies opening on the tranquil, olive-colored Tagus, row-boats, the sky fat with clouds, people leaving and entering moored fer-ryboats, the secretary of state, in civilian clothes, eyes lowered, consulting files, the second lieutenant found a bottle of beer rolling loose under the stove and shared it, taking great swigs, with the soldier's bottomless thirst. As long as I had money, the lieutenant colonel said, I was welcome, and when the dough ran out they would raise holy hell, insulting me, calling me names, sending anonymous letters to Edite and leave for good, the quartermaster coughed lightly as he left, the secretary of state raised his eyebrows, stared at them (As if you didn't know that we'd been here a long time, you son of a bitch), Oh, it's you, General, sit down, sit down, an uncomfortable easy chair lost in the oceanic office, rugs, prints of battles, a photograph of a boy in uniform in a coral frame, the president watching us, martially, from the wall, the quartermaster retired backward, Using his daughter's toys to mastur-bate, the communications officer was appalled, a horrible character, kneeling in the middle of the clowns and dolls, drooling and beating on his fly. I saw a very pretty blouse, natural silk, only nine contos, Artur, the boutique clerk sighed, don't you think it's a steal, tell me? The secretary of state examined him slowly, his fingers interlaced on the polished top of his desk, and his little whitish eyes dissected him acrimoniously: the lieutenant colonel crossed his legs, uncrossed them, crossed them again, he felt unprotected and tense, like an acrobat on a high wire, the focus of light from the window, dusty and pale, lighted him up obliquely as in a circus, I'm going to fall off, he thought, my muscles won't obey me, my body won't obey me, and I'll be flat on the ground any minute now, Another lunch, another dinner, another night away from home, Artur? the cloud of perfume was puzzled, when am I going to spend an evening with you like before? and he glimpsed her heavy naked limbs slowly caressing his trunk, her mouth smoothing what was left of his hair, his throat, his belly, his knees, his pubes, with slow skill, the platinum hair hiding his face, spreading on the pillow, shaking with spasms: There have been complaints, there's been gossip, the secretary of state asserted in a disagreeable, fragile tone, with reference not only to your duties at the Academy but also to your private life, letters from students' parents, verbal complaints, reports, If Edite separates from me, the lieutenant colonel thought, apprehensively, how am I going to support Lucília and her family on my salary, how in hell am I going to manage with the expenses I've got? Her railroading father would explain at length with the help of three tooth-pick holders and four water glasses the famous Ovar derailment of 1945, The price of food has gone sky high this month, the mother informed him in a friendly way, poor Lucília is going to have to scrape along to feed all those mouths, be quiet, Hermínio, I'm talking to our son-in-law just between us two here, with no one hearing us, if you don't raise the ante, General, I can see things getting very dark. The secretary of state in the distance, at the far end of the room, waved a corroborating and threatening file, I wanted to let you know that under the circumstances I've suggested to them upstairs your immediate transfer to reserve status, you're tired, General, please believe me that all of us here at the Ministry not only understand perfectly, but also feel that it's getting to be time for you to have a little well-deserved rest, the chief of the General Staff has proposed the silver medal for distinguished service and even though these matters should remain confidential, I can add that I absolutely agree with him, Steady on the wire, Artur, for the love of God don't lose your balance now, Of course you'll lose some prerogatives, the secretary of state put in, shooing away the insects of objection with the back of his hand, but you'll continue to receive full pay and you can dedicate your time completely to your favorite pastimes, because according to what I've heard (a smile of understanding) you've arranged for a nice little young bit of amusement in the Avenida de Roma neighborhood, which I find excellent as long as it doesn't prejudice the service. Another man? the lieutenant colonel asked, I only became aware of it months later, in April or May, I was going into the living room and a fellow with a mustache suddenly moved away from the boutique clerk, I stayed very quiet, I pretended that I didn't notice a thing, the next day I got there two hours earlier and wham, coming from the bedroom were the expected yells and sighs, her mother was standing guard in the vestibule, crocheting in a little low chair, she looked at me, looked at the closed door behind her, looked back at me again and her blood froze, she was afraid I had a gun and would riddle her daughter with bullets, that I'd pull a knife and slice her up, Have pity, General, they're only a couple of kids, and me swaggering on the outside and singing on the inside Tomorrow I want the place vacated, madame, And if that one should ever come to end, the secretary of state said with a perverse little laugh, there are plenty of salesgirls working in fashion establishments, at our age we always need some kind of recreation, General, It was me and the quiet man, Commander, the soldier informed him, who took your junk from Alvalade in the van to be auctioned off by weight, as proof, we accidentally broke a pane of glass in the cupboard, I'm sorry about that, Starting in January, which is the month for tomcatting, the secretary of state wrinkled his eyes, you'll have twenty-four hours every day for all the fun you want, get a place in the country, take up gardening, buy a boxer dog, fornicate, and I laughed too, amid the drapery, without feeling like it at all, to make him feel good, but the worst was yet to come when I discovered that Edite was also carrying on, I never found out who with, She would come to my place, Colonel, the communications officer confessed, like someone vomiting up too big a meal, I've got a weakness for women fat and forty, we'd stay there together, hugging, smoking, watching the carousel horses on the ceiling, we'd spend hours looking for your wife's earrings in the sheets, the beads from her broken necklace, her panties, a garter, I never saw Lucília again, the lieutenant colonel sighed, not listening,

# FADO ALEXANDRINO

I never saw the fellow with the mustache, I began to spend afternoons in bed, not looking at anything, not thinking about anyone, until I began to put down roots of flesh in the mattress, like a fetus, my blood swirling about in the placenta of the floor, transformed into a kind of mineral or like a chrysalis fastened there, waiting in vain for the feathers of wings to grow on my back, you understand, to be able to fly.

## 7

"So, finally, was she the mystery woman?" the second lieutenant asked the communications officer severely. "So, finally, was she the dame you didn't want to talk to us about?"

"With all these holes in the boards we're going to land on the neighbor downstairs someday," the cloud of perfume nightingaled, hair loose, on all fours on the rug, eye makeup running down her neck like war paint and onto the great cheeses of her breasts. "Help me find my purse, sweet."

"I'm sorry, Lieutenant," the soldier scolded, "but cheating on the commander is really dirty."

They would meet at first, in spite of the mute, disapproving sidelong glances of Esmeralda, who would bless herself from image to image, in the apartment behind the amusement park, looking out the open window at the microscopic little seats of the Great Ferris Wheel and the red and yellow lights on the Electronic Flying Saucers (Word of honor, all I knew was that her husband was in the Army, I had no idea who he was), but the cloud of perfume's rheumatism had trouble adjusting to the narrow bed, my restless sleep shaking and pushing her, the small, drafty bathroom with a single towel at the end of the hall beyond the seven or eight horrible crucifixes and dozens of plaster saints glowing their accusing virtue in the dark, she had a hard time adjusting to the cockroaches, the giraffes, and the dust, and he ended up renting an apartment in São Domingos, right next to the woods, near the railroad tracks that thundered at night with hoarse, melancholy mooing and the stuffy sniffles of brakes.

"I lived in an apartment by the woods," Melissa the striptease goddess said, "and I had to move two weeks later because of the racket the crows made."

If you got up, Captain, to get a drink of water, wash in the bidet, or urinate, if you got close to the balcony, leaned your nose against the doorframe and peeked outside, what you could make out was a dark green mobile mass of pointed heads of trees, elbows of branches, hair of leaves, and later on when a pale halo began to separate tree trunks and windows gradually began to appear as squares on the featureless faces of the buildings, blackbird fruit fell one by one out of the trees and the crows began to fly in a circle around the still damp, undivided shadows of the city, floating over the restlessness of dogs and the cardiac alarm clocks of sleeping notaries, shouting out the afflicted calls of a child. Crows with yellow eyes and beaks curved like old people's nails, opening the broken umbrellas of their wings in a growing morning, crows that appeared, disappeared, reappeared grazing the chipped walls and iron grillwork of balconies, touched walls, went away, rolled over, came back, swift and funereal, coloring people's insomnia with the broad, musty hangings of death. In Africa, the communications officer thought, the crows were bigger, crueler, heavier, stranger, more laden with threats and omens, and they would rise, not out of the dawn, but at the beginning of night, in the sudden, solid night of the tropics, heavy with salamanders, snakes, insects, thousands of fierce or neutral vegetable eyes, listening, spying, throbbing, hating, dissecting, and the old black women hidden in their thatch huts on their knees would repeat Ah, the crows, shaking their fragile and sinewy frightened heads. So that whenever he slept on São Domingos, in the apartment next to the woods, the communications officer would get the time and place mixed up, the Mozambican jungle and the rotting city that floated down the river like flotsam toward the sea, and he would open the fly of his pajamas facing the toilet bowl as he would that of his camouflage pants facing an invisible eucalyptus tree, erect in the darkness like an enormous wooden penis. The present gurgling of the plumbing and the past squeaking of bats mingled sharply in his mind, his own shape, faded in the mirror, reduced to a vague, painful, and motionless silhouette, looking like a wounded guerrilla fighter, his dick hanging out, bleeding piss, in a dawn of misfortune, the quiver of the tiles shaking and glistening, like submerged marijuana plants waving their flat, ribbed leaves, and he would go back to bed as though he were coming back, dragging his feet full of blisters, from a three-day patrol, gaunt, tired, bone weary, unshaven, leaving a furrow in the ground behind him from the leg gone to sleep that was like a rifle (Don't have anything more to drink), and a reflection of animal terror in his dull eyes.

"Doctor, doctor," Melissa the striptease goddess complained, "fix me up with some kind of medicine because my nerves are frazzled from the noise the crows make."

"With those trains and all those birds," the communications officer said, "what else could I do but spend the whole night drinking."

He would put the pack of cigarettes, the bottle of whiskey, and an empty ashtray on the night table, and right after dinner, after the nine o'clock express, while the cloud of perfume was clearing away the dishes and the pictures shook on the wall, I would swallow two or three fingers of alcohol in order to get through the night, two or three fingers for the mail train at twelve past ten, two or three fingers for the freight train at eleven-twenty, two or three fingers for the limited at one-thirty-three, the cloud of perfume would stroke my hair and I wouldn't even feel her nails, she would put her nipple in my mouth and I wouldn't even recognize the taste, she would call me sweet and I wouldn't even hear her purring, she would squash up against me and I wouldn't even catch her smell, fleeting serpents of windows lighted up the ceiling, china objects rattled in the cupboard, the toilet flushed all by itself with a squeal of brakes, Don't you feel sorry, Lieutenant, aren't you going to ask the commander to forgive you for screwing his lady? the soldier asked, the platinum locks rolled and twirled underneath, with sighs, between my legs, I didn't have the slightest idea who she was, the communications officer defended himself, how could I have guessed the name of the dame's husband?, I came almost without noticing around the tenth train, I came again with the forty-ninth, the old girl would dress me, undress me, rock me, kiss me, lick my navel, nibble my skin, stick her long nose under my arms, the whiskey light dimly illuminated my insides, my bladder was going on and off like the diesel fuel in boats, with the fiftieth train she was breathing heavily, exhausted, Until tomorrow, sweet, and my feet were glowing, skeletal and symmetrical, at the foot of the bed, pointing the scaly relief of their calluses at the ceiling. The crows, I thought, I wonder what's happened to the crows? but there weren't any crows, Captain, there wasn't any woman, there wasn't any apartment, only the trains passing incessantly through my body and my penis inflated and thick with veins lying sideways on my groin, only a confused space where my voice was slowly sinking, farther and farther away, Until tomorrow, sweet, disappearing in a vestibule dissolved in the sound of the high heels, the throbbing of the blood in my head, and the almost inaudible swish of clothes, Crows, ma'am, the doctor inquired delicately, crows that you imagine or crows in cages you have at home? and no sooner did I go off to sleep than the alarm clock jabbed an unbearable, tenacious, painful fishhook in my ear, and right after shaving, showering, brushing teeth, the urge to vomit when I got to the street, the bus to the

Ministry, the bumping that brought on palpitations in my heart, nausea, sleepiness, a wish to die, my green face in mirrors, my hiccups of cheap liquor and cholorphyll, my uncombed hair, the sickening salutes from sergeants and soldiers, steps, corridors, steps, more corridors, the desk full of papers waiting for me, the doctor was young, ingenuous, inexperienced, blondish, he was looking, frowning, his pen suspended over the card, at Melissa the striptease goddess, and she was thinking, furious, This idiot thinks I'm crazy, this idiot doesn't believe anything I say: she'd put on her best clothes, was clutching her best purse on her knees, she'd pulled back her hair over her neck with a chaste bow, she wore practically no makeup, just an insignificant touch of carmine on her lips, and she was trying doggedly to smile: I live next to the woods, Doctor, the crows, you know what it's like, they holler at me the whole night through under my window, there must be something in the drugstore, a pill, a shot, a powder, anything against birds, cotton in the ears is no good, Really, the second lieutenant agreed, going to bed with our commander's wife is something quite serious: at eleven in the morning, when my brain began to clear up, as sure as anything the telephone would ring and it would be her, the challenging little voice, the warm breath of the syllables, Hi, sweet, Artur just left for the Academy, I can't live without you, tell me you love me, come on, and me sharpening a pencil trying to orient myself in that loving tempest, and me arranging rubber stamps, groggy, like someone looking carefully for the trembling needle of a compass, the complicated name of the cities and rivers on my day's map, but her words were pushing me again, brutally, into the confused agitation of the night before, a train was passing pell-mell through the room, crushing the typists' machines which fell apart in a rain of screws and keys, Our lieutenant, the soldier stated energetically, should be punished immediately, Captain. Woods?, Crows? the doctor asked, interrupting, hesitant, is this the first time you've been to see a doctor because of nerves?, You could request a transfer to the provinces and we could run away together, sweet, the cloud of perfume proposed, can't you imagine how happy we'd be in Viseu, for example? Bring me a cup of strong coffee, because everything's swimming, the communications officer, covering the mouthpiece with his hand, asked Captain Ananias, while a second train was noisily crushing chairs and cabinets, scattering metal locks, hinges, files, fragments, a cup of good strong coffee before I leave this world for a better life, friend, A kick in the balls never did anyone any harm, the concierge explained, serving the soup, there's nothing like a couple of swift kicks to straighten a man out: the young doctor got up, put out his cigarette, said One moment please, went out, through the office window a branch bank could be seen, plane trees, roofs, a few people, the watery sun, clouds. Melissa the striptease goddess was listening, unable to understand, to the buzz of conversations of the people in the waiting room outside, crowded into a tiny little compartment, Maybe a glass of anisette would do me more good than coffee, the communications officer thought, on the verge of fainting or vomiting, there's nothing like a cordial to bring a guy around, Punishing him is a good idea, the second lieutenant agreed, does the colonel want us to lock him in the toilet? It wasn't just the locomotives, Captain, the communications officer lamented, I could still take the locomotives, it was the whistles, the tooting, and the urine incense of the grade crossings, the villages, the buildings, and the poles going very quickly backward, Saying Viseu is the same as saying Peniche, sweet, the cloud of perfume whispered on the telephone, wouldn't it excite you to live with me by the edge of the sea? Captain Ananias finally appeared with the coffee, a thimbleful of black liquid quivering in the demitasse, the saucer trembling, the pack of sugar trembling, the tinfoil spoon trembling, the man's hand trembling too, Take it, quick, damn it, before I spill all this, Captain Ananias asked, all this rattling bothers me, the young doctor came back accompanied by another one quite a bit older, tall and bald with the wrinkles of a man in charge on his forehead and a huge dark mole on the side of his nose, who sat down behind the desk, took measure of Melissa the striptease goddess, and benevolently ordered Now let's unravel this story about pigeons the way it should be, the sun, more and more watery, touched a tile roof that immediately caught fire, They're not pigeons, Doctor, the blond fellow corrected respectfully, pointing to the index card with his thumb, it's written here that they're blackbirds, Blackbirds or pigeons, it's all the same, the bald man cut him off, ultimately, it's a case of bird delirium and that's enough: It wasn't just that roof that was burning, Melissa the striptease goddess observed, red flames were also rising from two or three more nearby, television antennae hung like the bones of dead people, and a few chimneys were melting and twisting like candles under the action of the heat: These animal schizophrenias, the older doctor explained, putting the tips of his fingers together and leaning back in his chair with satisfaction, are the commonest thing in the world, I can't understand how you were taken in by sparrows. The buildings were being consumed outside, one by one, reduced to little cones of ashes, in the bloody light of afternoon, the embers of plane trees were collapsing noiselessly into the wilted yellowing grass, tall and split like long underarm hairs, a dog with his muzzle and neck in flames disappeared into a barrel-like dark alley. You want some pills to chase away the little birds, right? the bald man asked amiably, well, you're absolutely right, ma'am, they really do bother people a lot, and to his disciple, didactically, With three hundred milligrams and not contradicting the patient, my dear friend, there isn't an ostrich who can resist. What if I don't have a home anymore, Melissa the striptease goddess wondered, terrified, seeing the city silently crumbling around her, what if when I get there the neighborhood is a pile of smoking ruins: the communications officer reached out his arm for the cup and spilled the coffee, dropped the saucer, dropped the little spoon, dropped the sugar, Captain Ananias (Damn, damn, damn) was shaking his soaked trousers complaining, When you say home, Melissa the striptease goddess thought, you mean the antique dresser that cost me twelve contos on the Rua de São Bento, you mean the Empire bed, you mean the big flowerpot by the entrance, you mean the tea service, Sir, the soldier asked the second lieutenant, furious, do you think locking the lieutenant up in the toilet is punishment enough? The noise of the crows in the woods? the old doctor was startled, crumpling up the prescription, how could I guess there were crows in the woods. In Peniche, at the edge of the sea, the cloud of perfume's sinuous little voice insisted, with waves and seagulls and ship- wrecks and the two of us, could you get any more romantic? You fucked up my new uniform, damn you, Captain Ananias was angry, drying the wet splotches with his handkerchief, the laundry won't even be able to get this shit off. There are dozens of crows making a racket in the woods, Doctor, the young doctor elucidated, submissively leaning over the bald-headed man at a right angle, one of my aunts moved to Xabregas because of them, an albino nurse, in a cap, opened the door to whisper There are still twelve patients waiting, chief, they've already come into the records section twice to com- plain, very rude, Let them wait, the bald man roared, scarlet, a vein pound- ing strongly on his temples, I'm dealing with goldfinches here: He ended up advising me, Melissa the striptease goddess said, to take some blue capsules that dried up my mouth, started my heart leaping, made me urinate all the time, and stopped me from getting a wink of sleep the whole blessed night, What kind of a disorder is this, you bums? the bald man roared in the corridor, I don't allow any ill-mannered communists in this place, Swimming together at the beach, the cloud of perfume whispered, lying down side by side on towels, putting lotion on each other, reading the newspaper in canvas chairs, and the communications officer imagined that nauseating fat old woman with a ridiculous straw hat on her head, dark glasses with Mickey Mouse on the frames, successive rolls of pink flesh overflowing her bikini: naked children stopped to stare, grave people carrying their shoes were flabbergasted, openmouthed, and I felt like hanging up the phone, and I felt like changing residences, and I felt like running away. And to top it off, he still dares to say bad things about the wife of our commander, to top it off he puts her down, to top it off he detests her, Lucília died of typhus last year, the lieutenant colonel reported, groggy on the couch, distractedly stroking a man's shoe with his fingertips, Edite told me at dinner: Can you see me getting her all greased up, Captain? the communications officer wailed like a condemned prisoner, can you see me spreading that brown cream all over her back, Captain? The crows won't bother you anymore, the young doctor promised, the crows will never annoy you again, night had fallen completely now and when Melissa the striptease goddess went outside the streetlights of the city were going on, great shapeless shadows, still clear, still daytime, still neat, wavered on the building façades, sounds were taking on a sharp glassy tone, the first bats were rising and falling rapidly in the silence, the sky was shriveling up over the rooftops, and in the end, the buildings remained intact, except more mysterious and threatening and dense, and in the end, the trees survived the fire, and in the end, the crows survived the capsules, and she sighed, relieved, stopped, anxiously crushing the leather of her purse with her fingers, because everything was continuing as before in the usual tranquil and serene and habitual almost geometric order.

"What I felt deep down was loneliness," the communications officer murmured to no one in particular, as softly as if he were praying, contemplating the empty glass with hollow eyes. "And besides that, with Esmeralda's illness, dust was piling up, garbage was piling up, unopened mail was piling up, the apartment, you can see, was gradually becoming uninhabitable."

"I gave the mother five hundred escudos to help with the funeral, I sent a wreath of flowers with a note," the lieutenant colonel said: "I don't know how many years it had been that I didn't see her. It seemed that she weighed two hundred pounds, that she got tired because of anything and because of nothing at all, that she was being kept by a contractor."

"I was the one who did the cleaning, the vacuuming, the cooking," the communications officer psalmed, lifting his glass with a tremulous, pontifical gesture. "And I would make Esmeralda's bed, poor thing, and change her clothes, and put the bedpan under her legs. In time the poor thing had stopped being able to hold back her feces and urine."

"Have you people got any idea," the lieutenant colonel asked, "how much a funeral procession from here to Alcochete costs?"

"She spent her days in a high-backed chair," the communications officer detailed, "looking at the street with the eyes of a statue. I would chat with her, Good evening, Hi, How do you feel, and the old woman, not a word, it was just like there was nothing there."

"And a stone angel, eh, to decorate the plot?" the lieutenant colonel went on, pushing away the shoe. "An angel about a yard high, that's all, weeping, with an open book in its hand and Rest in Peace on the base?"

"She didn't know me, she didn't answer me, she didn't talk, it seemed as though she didn't hear a peep," the communications officer said, blessing the glass. "I sold the whole bunch of saints and all the little shrines in order to put her into a home."

"Since the war ended dying has become hellishly complicated, Commander," the soldier put in. "In Africa, at least, it was duck soup: a shot, a coffin wrapped in the flag, the company cook putting fewer potatoes on the table, no ceremony, no fuss, no tears, a telegram to the family KILLED IN ACTION IN THE PROVINCE OF MOZAMBIQUE, and then the hold of a ship to Lisbon and that was that. You came to envy how easy it all was, remember?"

"Retire me?" the bald man howled sarcastically in the hallway, "retire me? Another peep and I'll be the one who retires you, my fine son of a bitch, and I'll cut off your consultations once and for all. It's been several shitty months since there's been an end to revolutions."

"A little bitty contribution, General, no matter how small," the mother humiliated herself (A different person, the lieutenant colonel thought, a completely different person): "my daughter thought so much of you."

"We've got rooms for three, five, and eight contos," the director of the home listed, her hair in a bun and wearing a checkered smock like governesses twenty years ago, the same severe eyebrows, the same slippers, the same hairs in the nose, the same disagreeable tight mouth. "There's no vacancy in the three- and five-conto ones, in the eight-conto ones someone happened to die the day before yesterday, the widow of a cabinet minister, and if you'd like to inspect the facilities, please come this way."

"I scoured the newspapers, I bothered friends, I went all over Lisbon looking for a decent place," the communications officer justified himself, majestically multiplying the blessings, "but an old folks' home is harder to find than a virgin in a whorehouse. Until I finally discovered that one on the Calçada do Combro."

A grocery store on the corner, smelling of barley and dried fish, a poolroom on the right (cues crossed over a red ball), and an ancient and skinny building, two stories high, with a metal plaque by the bell, PIUS XII HOME FOR THE AGED, A CHRISTIAN SHELTER, closed windows, vague motionless faces behind the glass, indistinct features by the folds of the curtains: he rang the bell and a sharp jet suddenly broke the silence inside, ripping blankets and startling footsteps, the door opened noiselessly, a vestibule with tiles, a hat rack, a table against the wall with a china plate on it, a wind guard with green and yellow granular glass, a maid on all fours, ass in the air, waxing steps: the eight-conto room was located on the upper floor and the communications officer made out, in passing, on the ground floor, a large parlor, with a turned-off television set and a dozen old people sitting quietly, the color of gray paper, hands on their knees, around the room, steps, a handrail, a landing. It's number fourteen, the director explained, shuffling along, rapidly and stiffly, in front of him: she took a bunch of keys out of her pocket, a lock resisted, squeaked, turned, finally leaped with a click: Here you are, the woman said, it has to be straightened up, of course, the final cleaning: a bed in poor condition, an irregular mattress that had waves in it, a dresser with chipped drawers, little saints hanging from nails that dug rhomboid holes in the plaster, Pope Pius XII, in glasses, thrusting forth his mystic bird's nose, a vague smell of stale urine, lavender, medicine, musty clothes. The communications officer pulled back the curtain that almost evaporated in his fingers and there was the Calçada do Combro, faded in the October morning, a man with hands in his pockets on the threshold of a modest shoe store crammed with baby booties, small restaurants with checkered tablecloths, workshops, barbershops, the dim display case of an antiques store, a fellow with a tape measure around his neck running across the street. The fish eyes of the governess weighed a ton on my back, a cockroach with millimetric antennae was strolling across the baseboard: The minister's widow, the communications officer thought, must have died from looking at that dismal, hopeless landscape every day, those cheap dives, those tailor shops, that lack of sunlight, roof after roof after roof after roof and after them even more roofs, the autumn rain that makes things sad and doesn't wet, the cold that doesn't ever get to be cold and yet freezes, the flinty coughs I hear from down below, chimneys, depressed dogs, Cape Verdean municipal workers in torn shirts destroying the pavement with pickaxes, led by a fellow countryman who points to the gutters to be fixed with the dirty tip of his boot, tomorrow I'll bring you here in a taxi, Esmeralda, sitting beside me in silence, and I'll come to visit you three or four times a year with a package of cookies and an enormous urge to get away as quickly as possible, until they call me at work or at home, regretful, pausing against a background of electrical explosions, She died, I'll arrive, this dame who shrivels me from the back with her eyes, will be waiting for me, very grave, by the door, and you'll be laid out on the bed in black, your chin bound up with a handkerchief and a crucifix in the dry vine-roots of your hands, as distant as ever, as deaf as ever, as silent as ever, as indifferent as ever, The window has no latch, the governess advises, in order to avoid temptation, more than once we've caught our patients at the last moment trying to leap over the sill, a pawnbroker, too, almost on the corner, displaying gold watches and worn-out radios, tomorrow I'll sell the shrines in the hallway with the shame of someone smuggling out the precious bones of his grandmother, I'll pay a few months in advance and I'll be able to rest easy: a column of ants was marching assiduously toward a zigzagging crack in the wall, a bulb without a shade in the ceiling, a cigarette butt squashed on the floor, I'll pack up your things and empty out the drawers, the slips, the nightgowns, the stockings, the panties, the hairpins, that big mother-of-pearl comb, the ceramic Our Lady of Fátima, and goodbye and until always and accept your fate and me too, the guy with the tape measure crossed the street again with his coattails flapping in the wind and his head bent down against the rain, he turned to the director thinking Now my childhood has really kicked the bucket, and said aloud, in a tone of one, bothered, handing down a sentence without appeal, Save the room for me, the two of us will be here tomorrow at three in the afternoon.

"Everything's so expensive, General," Lucília's mother wept, drying the nonexistent tears with her balled-up handkerchief. "And her friend, as soon as she got sick, abandoned her like a dog. If my husband or my sons had anything down there where they're supposed to they would have given the bastard a going-over for sure."

"Or Évora," the cloud of perfume moaned, running the tip of her tongue over his ear. "I bought a small plot there some time back and, besides, the Alentejano accent is so charming, sweet."

"I still think what our lieutenant did is shameful," the soldier declared. "But since nobody here seems to be bothered by it, let's drop the matter."

"Hey, daddy," the fat mulatto woman muttered in her sleep, "get your fine self over there, you're taking up the whole bed, Jesus."

"We can always kill him," the second lieutenant suggested, laughing. "Everybody in favor of capital punishment raise your hand."

"Nurse, nurse," the bald man howled like someone possessed, "call the orderly if you have to, but I want this stinking communist out of here immediately."

"The doctors didn't understand her illness," Lucília's mother said, her hair in disorder, soft purple bags puffing out under her thick eyelids, "and they kept sending her home with vitamins and suppositories. What happened was that the fever never stopped going up and when they gave her a blood test it was too late."

"In the state he's in," the magician's assistant put in, "all you have to do is blow on him and he'll go out like a match."

"If you officers and gentlemen vote in favor," the soldier hastened to say, rolling up his sleeves, "I'll bust a beer bottle over his noggin."

"I changed her, I washed her, I cut her nails, I explained to her that we were going away, that she was going off to the PIUS XII HOME FOR THE AGED, A CHRISTIAN SHELTER," the communications officer droned on, I kissed her on the forehead because the old lady had raised me, you might say, in spite of everything, even with Esmeralda in that state, blind maybe, and mute maybe, and deaf maybe, or maybe only indifferent to me, distant from me, shitting on me from her perch and on the apartment, and the cleaning and the little bit of cooking, all we had was each other, isn't that so? and she impassive, not moving a muscle of her face at all, not smiling at me, not looking at me, we went down the steps with my grasping the railing with all my strength, holding her around the skinny fish bones of her waist, leading her all the way on the legs that were going soft on her, chatting with her in a low voice and with the useless nonsense that we drool on occasions like that, I put her cardboard suitcase, an imitation of a Wild West trunk, beside the taxi driver, I settled her and myself in the backseat, and said Take us to the Calçada do Combro, chief, number thirty-five, chief, And if you won't be quiet, the bald doctor advised the young woman who was protesting, your visits will be over too, What can she be thinking? the communications officer tried to imagine during the trip, what ideas are taking shape in her noodle? It was still raining, the same dusty light rain, the sky looked like the contractile belly of a salamander and the pigeons in the Chiado were taking shelter, necks hidden in their unfolded wings, in the niches of the churches. The tires skidded for a moment on the trolley tracks, the shoe store, the little restaurants with checkered tablecloths, the workshops, the inlaid dressers at the antique shop, the narrow little building, the poolroom with its crossed cues over a ball, Whoa, back, chief, this is it. And once more the bell tearing the bedspreads like a knife along with the fragile, chitinous throats of the old people, the maid with her ass in the air, ugly, unpleasant, and sad, polishing metal and knobs with a bottle of yellow liquid, the governess examining Esmeralda in silence, examining the trunk, leading us to a room that announced OFFICE in cardboard letters on the door panel, shelves with cardboard files, bills, receipts, stamps, a jar full of pens and pencils, a typewriter wrapped in a plastic shroud on a folding table. They must have opened the bar by now, the second lieutenant announced in the death rattle of a pelican, I'm going down there for a minute to buy some wine, the Rua da Mãe d'Água, pale, was growing and shrinking like a gill, If I fall off the bed, the mulatto woman muttered, turning stomach down with great confusion, I'm never going to sleep in this place again. The communications officer took the money out of his pocket, the director looked mistrustfully at the bills on the table, filled out a receipt in a primitive, cramped hand, inscribed Esmeralda in a thick, square register, Two quarts at least, the lieutenant colonel requested, deeply interested now in his own fingernails, this early morning without wine has become an unbearable wake, Príncipe Real and the Calçada do Combro came together beyond the rather dirty windowpanes, with the same miserable muddy water, with the same feeble little wind of an asthmatic having a seizure, with the same tepid cold that froze things, with the same faded roofs, identical in all sections of the city, with the same establishments and little shops and stores without customers, with the same scruffy, abandoned leftovers, with the same ragged ambulant vendors, Three quarts, boys, the magician's assistant said, because I can put away a quart and a half in a minute, the director and the communications officer carried Esmeralda bodily up to the next floor, aided by the doorknob maid, who carried the suitcase, an old man in slippers was dragging himself painfully along the corridor toward a balcony with plants, Into your room, now, Mr. Martins, the governess barked in an authoritarian way, what shitty kind of disobedience is this?, They'd straightened out the sheets, run a rag over the furniture, hung a few more accessory martyrs in sandals and with great chaste eyes on the walls, expurgated the cockroaches and ants, placed some dead flowers in a vase, You'll live like a queen here, Dona Esmeralda, the governess promised, and, just think, today we're having meatballs with mashed potatoes for dinner, we seated her by the window facing the roofs and the commercial establishments and the grayness of the afternoon and she didn't move a twitch, no frown, no comment, no snort, no smile, I pushed back her hair, brushed my lips quickly across her forehead, and it's possible that she saw me in the street, bent over in the rain, getting away as fast as I could toward the bus stop, it's possible that she recognized me by my movements, or by my curved shoulders, or by the way I walk, it's possible that she wondered where I was going, it's possible that she felt sorry for me, thought about the empty years, the amusement park, my godmother, the dog dying on the kitchen tiles, the noise of the carousel and the fantastic animals passing by in circles on the ceiling, and when I got home, Captain, there was an enormous silence in the rooms with no one else in them, lighter rectangular areas where the furniture I had sold was missing, the lack of cleaning and the usual filth, and in the kitchen, when I leaned my nose against the window frame, I perceived outside, down below, roofs upon roofs upon roofs upon roofs, the chimneys and little shops of the Calçada do Combro in the October dusk, and a guy running across the pavement with a tape measure around his neck, opening his arms to the hazardous cars of the roller coaster.

"Are five quarts enough?" the second lieutenant asked, dragging across the floor behind him a jug encased in wicker that was salivating and drooling the purple froth of bronchitis. "It must be eight o'clock, they should be opening the bar right now."

"Eight o'clock? Shit," the lieutenant colonel was surprised, interested in an anonymous sleeping knee. "If I don't get the hell out of here right away my wife will bawl the hell out of me."

"So where do we stand, officers and gentlemen?" the soldier was growing impatient. "Shall our lieutenant be killed or not be killed?"

"It wouldn't take too much, sweetie pies," one of the little blond twins put in. "All you have to do is put a plastic bag over his head and hold it tight."

"Borges," the bald-headed man ordered a fellow with no forehead and an obedient look. "These four louts out of here, right now."

"How amusing," the magician's assistant said, draining a big glass. "Up till now I've only witnessed executions in the movies."

"Or Manteigas, sweet, have you considered Manteigas?" the cloud of perfume suggested with the sinuous intonations of a siren. "The Estrela Mountains are beautiful in winter."

"It's funny the way how, with time, Captain, things little by little turn off in your head," the communications officer was ashamed, sorrowful. "This year, for example, I forgot all about her birthday."

The trees on Príncipe Real, he thought, in the daylight now, had lost the mystery and thickness of night, the depth of the buildings, of faces, of things has lessened, the barks of dogs were no longer like mirrors dissolving and breaking interminably, the voices, and the heels of shoes had stopped hurting me, the huge shadow of the sleeping mulatto woman, legs wrapped around the sheet, was reduced to the simple and human proportions of a body, workmen were hammering and erecting scaffolding in a neighboring building, the ocher or uniform-colored sky weighed down, swollen, above the rooftops, it's going to rain again today the same thin, idiotic rain as always, suspended drops that don't fall, without consistency or substance, only the discomfort of the damp air, and clothing sticking to your back, socks soggy without your understanding how, If it's eight o'clock, the communications officer thought, the greenish flora and fauna of the bars must be vomiting up the last whiskey now and the last piss against the tiles of the toilet, they must be lying on their beds with their clothes on, listening to the afflicted sound of their blood limping through their limbs, the water in puddles between boxwood trees retreats with wrinkles that come and go, wrinkles on the forehead, concentric lines, transparent bladders, Esmeralda has certainly awakened by now, is catching now, tense, in silence, the minimal sounds of the home, the coughs, the cutlery, the steps, a distant vacuum cleaner, she doesn't recognize or she pretends not to recognize my voice (It's me, hello, good afternoon, I came to pay you a visit, here I am), but she listens to the plants growing in their pots and the knots of wood that throb, retract and expand like wooden hearts, the bushes in the Botanical Garden have thrown off their cocoons of shadows and are climbing slowly toward the light, every day waiting, just think, at the job or at home, for the phone call that doesn't come, for the whisper of regret that isn't spoken, for the ceremonious pauses that don't come, who knows, maybe you'll outlive me, Esmeralda, who knows, maybe you'll go on eternally, with your nose by the window frame above the melancholy stores and the tangle of chimneys on the Calçada do Combro, the second lieutenant was distributing the wine, the liquid was spilling into oval stains on the pile of the rug, the fat mulatto woman sat up in the bed, opening her gigantic hippopotamus jaws, teeth of yellow metal inserted at random, like screws, in her gums, Everybody in favor of capital punishment raise your hand, the soldier repeated with the rubbery insistence of drunks, Manteigas is it, then, the cloud of perfume concluded triumphantly, a fireplace, stone jugs, coarse gray blankets, and us inside there, Edite must be charging around already, mad as hell waiting for me, the lieutenant colonel was frightened, she must have already gone to get the shears from her sewing box, Captain Ananias, in the bathroom, was rubbing his pants with soap, muttering insults in a low voice, the governess, with a frown on her face, was organizing the old people's breakfast, One of these days I'm going to write you a letter, Esmeralda, telling you how the apartment has got bigger, how the worms are eating up my closets and my veins, how even at three in the afternoon the sideboards run aground like ships in a motionless sunset, how hard it is to breathe in that silence, how when they open the amusement park and the rasping music of the loudspeakers shakes the curtains and the giraffes roll in a spiral on the ceiling, none of them will find me in the parlor, because I'll be living in Manteigas or in Peniche or in Évora or in Viseu with an unbearable madame with dyed hair and a horrible tiny dog, Everybody's agreed, the soldier said in a calm fury, except for the captain, who didn't lift a finger, I'll take a suitcase of clothing, the communications officer thought, a few pictures, a few books, the conch shell I picked up on the beach at Areia Branca when I was small and which brings a slight breath of the sea to my ear, the electric razor and Dália's letters and post-cards, the magician's assistant staggered back from the kitchen with the bread knife, Stick him, stick him, the mulatto woman encouraged the twin with the mannequin story, clapped her hands with delight while her sister, hugging the lieutenant colonel, was smiling into space with the inexpressive, stupid smile of a sheep, Stick him, the second lieutenant shouted with the wine running down in two frothy threads over the starched front of his shirt, I promise I won't miss next Christmas, the communications officer thought, that I'll go in person to pay the monthly bill instead of sending the usual money order, that I'll go up to the second floor, that I'll see you, I promise that I'll take an interest, I'll telephone, I'll ask about you, I'll visit you even if I'm living in Manteigas, even if I'm living in Peniche, even if I'm living in Viseu, even if I'm living in Évora, Stick him, Melissa the striptease goddess reacted, fierce, squeezing the jug between her knees, traffic on Príncipe Real was getting heavier, trolley cars were tinkling up above, blue sparks lighted up the walls, the concierge's fat little dog, Stick him, her tethered morning hate croaked, On Sunday right after lunch, the communications officer thought, mixing an Alka-Seltzer in his wine, I'm going to take a bus to the Calçada do Combro, between the shoe store and the poolroom, and on the way to the PIUS XII HOME FOR THE AGED, A CHRISTIAN SHELTER, there will surely be, gentlemen, so many doves on Loreto, so many doves on Camões, and he leaned over to serve them a handful of aspirin tablets for the dizziness and vomit, and he peeled them, one by one, like peas, from their green wrappers, so he didn't see the soldier get up, grab the long knife with both hands by the rough wooden handle, and bury it with all his strength into my back, like a calf being butchered. And not even Esmeralda, even though she had her nose up against the window frame, noticed the body lying face down on the sidewalk of the square, fifty yards away from her, amid the indifference or the fright or the hunger of the birds, among the chimneys, the trees, the garrets, and roof after roof after roof after roof that hid the river.

"W HAT'LL we do with the corpse?" the magician's assistant asked, worried, touching the communications officer's body with the tip of her toe to see if he would move. "In three or four hours, boys, there'll be a stink in here that no one will be able to stand."

The blonde imagined police photographers running back and forth through the disorder of the apartment, taking a raft of pictures, characters on their knees looking for fingerprints on doorknobs and bottles, inspectors clutching ball-points interrogating neighbor women, cars with lights on their roofs blocking off the Rua da Mãe d'Água, while patrolmen in uniform used sweeping gestures to drive people's curiosity away, and guys in medical jackets put a long form bound with straps and wrapped in a coarse blanket into an ambulance.

"What about the bloodstains?" Melissa the striptease goddess asked. "There are bloodstains all over the rug: where the devil do they keep the detergent here?"

BODY ON PRÍNCIPE REAL: CRIME OF DEBAUCHERY OR POLITI-CAL CRIME?

"The solution," the lieutenant colonel proposed, "is to wait until it's night again and leave the guy in a small park or on some bench, like a beggar.

Maybe the dogs will eat him, maybe the garbage trucks will take him away, and there's plenty of time, we needn't worry."

"I was the one who discovered him," the cleaning woman announced victoriously to a crowd of newspaper people who were filling her mouth with microphone molars. "As soon as I put the key in the lock I right away got a whiff of a dead person coming from the pantry."

"It was only to scare him, Captain," the soldier justified himself. "Word of honor, I just brushed his shirt with the knife, word of honor, I never thought he was going to play that trick of dropping dead on us."

DECEASED MEMBER OF NOTORIOUS EXTREMIST LEFT-WING TERRORIST ORGANIZATION FOR MANY YEARS: A SETTLING OF ACCOUNTS? NEO-FASCIST REVENGE? DON'T MISS STATEMENTS TOMORROW BY MAJOR PARTIES ON REVOLUTIONARY VIOLENCE AND DEMOCRACY.

"In the pantry," the concierge gave details, "sitting on a crate covered with old newspapers, with a package of dishwashing powder upside down."

"At first," the toilet attendant said, "lying on his back on the grass with his nose in the daisies, all proper, I thought he was asleep. Only when the mutts began to growl around him and pull at his pants did I get suspicious and take a look."

More photographs, more fingerprints, more autopsies, more questions in the building, the outline of the communications officer drawn in chalk on the carpet, pictures with big headlines on the front page of newspapers, and the five of us in handcuffs in a room full of indifferent men and women typing, before a fat fellow answering telephones, opening the mail with a wooden letter opener, sucking on angina pills, and severely questioning us at intervals, lifting his authoritarian little nose. Who killed him?

"Look, Captain," the soldier was indignant, "I spent twenty-six months in Mozambique with the lieutenant, was I going to sink six inches of knife blade into him now?"

The PMC, Party of Monarchist Christians, painfully aware of the wave of criminality that we are going through at the present time, alerts all Portuguese men and women to the current dangers of so-called Modern Civilization and celebrated Democracy, corrupters of nostalgic national customs, and appeals to the armed forces, the bishops, the industrialists of the North, married couples, wholesale merchants, and Catholics in general, with an aim to join forces, in order to put an end firmly and unhesitatingly to the socialist tendencies that a Muscovite atheist minority is trying to impose on us, and which carry along with them rape, robbery, disrespect for established institutions and our age-old national history, mongoloidism, goiter, pornography, a drop in priestly vocations, therapeutic abortion, birth-control methods, uterine contraceptives, Swedish movies, lace brassieres, single mothers, parricide, divorce, bikinis, and other equally deleterious forms, equally cruel, of the destruction of Home, Family, East India Company tureens, and the traditionally conservative and agrarian values upon which our well-being, economy, and Future are based.

"What a shitty mess," Melissa the striptease goddess complained, scrubbing the rug, gripping a brush, up to her neck in a cloud of brownish foam. "This crap is spreading all over, damn it, it won't be long before it starts dripping into the apartment below."

"The rug wasn't anything great, Captain," the second lieutenant said, "but since Inês had bought it, I liked it."

And still, even with the place changed and rearranged by his mother and sister, even with all possible vestiges of the past disguised or banished, it would happen sometimes that he would open a closet and come across a forgotten jacket, find an old photograph album behind the books on the shelves (smiling groups at the beach, family lunches, a woman with a baby hanging on her neck), a broken necklace in a drawer, sanitary napkins in the bathroom, the mark of another head on the bolster, and those fragments of the past, joined together with splinters and little pieces of lost episodes in his memory, would bring back, coming together and blending, years and more years that pained him softly now like a back tooth, and would make him wander, eyes ensnared, from room to room, sniffing like a dog through the new smells of furniture and drapes and paint, the irremediably evaporated urine of Inês's presence, Inês's laugh, Inês's body on the sheets, the silent, huddled, shaken fright of her pleasure.

"That's the least of it, throw the man out the window," the magician's assistant proposed, "and everybody will think the poor guy committed suicide."

THE MUTILATED CORPSE ON PRÍNCIPE REAL: MORE DETAILS OF CRIME INTRIGUING LISBON.

"We were playing, of course, Captain," the soldier said. "I know regulations, I'd never lay a finger on an officer."

COULD DECEASED BE HOMOSEXUAL OR DRUG DEALER? COMPLETELY EXCLUSIVE INTERVIEW WITH HEAD OF DRUG SQUAD.

"Just like that," the concierge explained to the reporters, "sitting on that wine case, his jacket on his knees, half-rotten already, looking at me. Naturally, I couldn't sleep for a week after that."

PRISONERS SENTENCED TO FIFTEEN YEARS SOLITARY CONFINEMENT. UNABLE TO BEAR WEIGHT OF HIS GUILT, MILITARY RESERVIST HANGS SELF IN JAIL.

"Inês came back from Brazil five or six years ago with Mariana and a new woman lover," the second lieutenant said. "She settled down in her parents' house with her daughter and her friend, in the middle of the dogs, the cocaine, the brothers, and either she or the little one, I can't remember which, phoned me after a few weeks."

"He started off in a not-too-important position as assistant director of the Personnel Section," a very well-dressed, well-combed gentleman with white hair, a decoration in his buttonhole, sitting behind a huge desk said, "and in time, slowly and with difficulty he went up a few notches. Insurance is an unpleasant business, my friend, and, besides, it was a question of an employee who was sad, apathetic, introverted, without any initiative, anonymous, invisible: on one occasion, for example, he was out sick for three weeks and nobody noticed his absence."

FORMER SECOND LIEUTENANT IN MOZAMBIQUE EXPEDITIONARY FORCE INVOLVED IN TRAGIC MURDER?

"Hello is that you I didn't recognize your voice are you all right?" Inês recited all in one gush, "if you want to visit Mariana in Carcavelos tomorrow we'll be home after three."

The same rusty gate, far from the Marginal, up there where the sea could be seen, the same gravel drive that the tires were crushing, scattering, chewing, the same trees and shrubs in disorder, the same dogs with red eyes, except older and less turbulent, barking, biting each other, putting their enormous paws on the windows, the empty swimming pool, with tiles and broken statues, full of branches and dead leaves, the house, with drapes drawn, rotting in the sun. He approached the veranda by the front door (How long has it been since you were here, damn it), he went up two or three trimmed steps, at the base a pair of stone lions, lacking noses now, he rang the bell and the rhomboid sound of other times echoed, like the sound of the flight of a partridge, through the rooms and empty parlors, getting lost in the infinite distance of the kitchen, the pantry, the laundry room, low-ceilinged, narrow, windowless, where a funereal maid, her hair in a bun, was ironing a Himalayan pile of sheets.

POLICE INVESTIGATING POSSIBILITY OF A SETTLING OF ACCOUNTS BETWEEN RIVAL GANGS.

He rang the bell again, surrounded by the curiosity of the dogs, who were watching him with raised ears and tongues hanging out, their broad dirty chests rising and falling, another partridge echoed through the halls (Eleven years already in April, fuck it all), rapid shoes, closer and closer, the horrible groans of hinges, a strange, instantaneous smile, lacking in affection, from a woman: You're Mariana's father, aren't you? The same furniture in the vestibule, the same smells, the same vague outlines of brothers-in-law sliding along in the background, almost without touching the rugs, consumed by the flames of heroin: everything was just the same, Captain, except we'd grown a little older, a web of wrinkles growing around eyes and lips, backs aching with changes in the weather, three sets of stairs would bring my phlegm-filled lungs into my mouth. Age can break us at any moment, gentlemen, stones appear in our kidneys and bladder, our hair gets scarcer, our muscles get soft, our sex is a useless rag for pissing, insignificant and dark. Until finally I'm a corpse in some church, a handkerchief around my chin, double-breasted jacket and tie, whispering, tiptoes, people in black, old women sitting around in chairs, a jaundiced, dying light in faces and gestures, transforming relatives into contrite, mute, mourning fish.

"Cut out that morbid philosophizing," Inês ordered, "the kid's coming."

WAS LIEUTENANT PIRES RAPED BEFORE THE MURDER? IMPORTANT REVELATIONS BY CORONER ON INSIDE PAGES.

"Put the dead man in the bathroom," the other twin suggested, "and I'll bet everybody will think he died from straining, that in squeezing out the shit his guts came out his backside."

"Oh, sweet," the cloud of perfume said, spraying lacquer on her hair, in a bathrobe, sitting on a stool, "just imagine, they told me your daughter is living with another woman in Carcavelos."

There were other automobiles in the gravel yard, almost all big and new, with dignified chauffeurs reading the newspaper behind the wheel. From the second floor came loud laughter, exclamations, the confused sounds of conversation, steps, Inês and the other girl, forgetting about him, seemed to be mutually preening each other's breasts with their beaks. A tall and sandy-haired cousin nudged me without looking at me, whiskey glass trembling in his freckled hand, in a smoky oil painting like the ones in churches a gloomy Christ was scratching himself on the cross with the long movements of a worm, and just then, coming from a cabbage-shaped shadow of drapes and curtains, a clump of blond hair in disorder, vague breasts being born, my father's nose, a pair of chubby, disjointed legs, a bashful smile, Hi.

"Or in the kitchen with a slice of bread in his hand," the magician's assistant counterposed, frowning as she searched for ideas that would save them. "He was cutting away on the bread and the knife slipped out of his hand and boom."

MODEL WORKER, SOLE SUPPORT OF AGED SERVANT IN A HOME: FELLOW WORKERS DEMAND EXEMPLARY PUNISHMENT FOR MURDERER OR MURDERERS.

"A very wealthy woman, the granddaughter of bankers or something like that," the cloud of perfume informed, eyes glued to the mirror, sketching with a pencil, with infinite care, the evasive, millimetric arcs of her eyebrows. "They met in Brazil and are living in a palace full of carpets, crystal, statues. It's funny that your daughter never said anything to you, Artur."

Where can a person take a child of fourteen for an outing, a child he doesn't know too well on top of it all, Captain? I tried the Zoo (a disinterested look at zebras and camels), a traveling circus (we left before the clowns came on), a museum with more cuspidors than paintings where Mariana spent the whole time chewing bubble gum, contemplating an empty wall like a cow, São Jorge Castle, with peacocks among the vines that cover the ruined battlements and busloads of tourists, standing stupefied before a pond with three famished ducks, the beach (a disagreeable little breeze penetrated the marrow of your bones and after a time the sky suddenly clouded over and it began to rain), and we ended up returning, dispirited, at the end of the afternoon to Carcavelos, watching the sea leaping over the wall and biliously sweeping the Marginal, the pale streetlights were on, reflected upside down on the wet pavement, patches of buildings, trees that leaned from one side to the other with disordered bows, and then the turn to the right, the muddy drive bordered by shrubbery and the pretentious chalets of emigrants, where the tires of the car skidded and slid, a rabbit who appeared and disappeared in the tremulous beams of the headlights, the rusty gate, the gravel driveway, the German shepherds weaving in the darkness, the blind rectangle of the swimming pool where the imprecise reflections of reflections moved, my tender, timid hand on your knee, already fleshy, already round, already that of a woman, which withdrew, embarrassed, under my fingertips, the body hardening on the seat, I can only say that I had a great time, Father.

ALUMNI ASSOCIATION OF GIL VICENTE SCHOOL ORGANIZES HEARTFELT PILGRIMAGE TO GRAVE OF SORELY MISSED MEMBER ON OCCASION OF THIRTIETH DAY AFTER HIS DEATH.

"People searching for a sincere relationship with children, at least," the second lieutenant complained, "and always lies, always subterfuges, always evasions, always nonsense, always bored yawns, always condescending friendliness, always distracted sidelong glances. So how can you make me believe that we're not always alone, Captain?"

"In Carcavelos, yes," the cloud of perfume affirmed, riffling impatiently through the plastic hangers in search of a dress with a floral pattern. "If you don't believe me go see for yourself, damn it."

"Back already?" Inês asked, surprised. "Don't tell me there wasn't anything interesting to see in Lisbon."

"Are you sure about the garbage container?" the magician's assistant doubted. "Will a whole person fit with his knees doubled up?"

"In Carcavelos, in a huge house, a palace," the cloud of perfume barked at him, pulling up her back zipper. "I've got the number here, dummy, take it, give her a call."

"How strange, my father was in Africa more or less at the same time," the other girl said, very much at ease, massaging the shoulder with an energetic, masculine palm. "Nineteen seventy, seventy-one, wasn't it? I was still married to that boob then."

"The lady with purple hair stayed behind in São Paulo, shacking up with an ex-nun who would parade in the Rio carnival dressed as a man," the second lieutenant related. "Those bitches never lose any time, Captain."

"What a silly idea, Mother," Mariana countered with surprising adult naturalness. "We went to lots of places, we were on the go all the time, this place, that place, you can't imagine what a good time we had. Father, when he wants to, can be quite funny."

And me there, among the three of them, Captain, smiling stupidly, mouth open like a mongoloid, looking at one then the other, feeling the pack of cigarettes with my fingers and too bashful to smoke, having the urge for a beer and too ashamed to ask, ceremonious and stiff, suffering through the periods of silence and keeping calm throughout the secrets, the gestures, the conversations, perceiving against the light, between two doors, the carnivorous profile of Hilária showing me her long, unpleasant, fierce teeth, listening through breathing periods to the sound of the television set in the small parlor, where the old man must have been nodding, whiskey in hand, in his usual armchair.

"The pair of them there, understand," the second lieutenant said, "leaning against the antique chests and furniture under the saints, the landscapes, the still lifes, hips rubbing, knees rubbing, knuckles rubbing, as if the little one didn't exist, as if I didn't exist, as if nobody existed, damned impudent and bold. I swear, all that was left was for them to get undressed and devour each other's tits, right in front of me, like hungry insects."

"So where are you living now?" the lieutenant colonel asked in a casual way, trying in vain to make a cigarette lighter work as it sputtered and slipped out of his fingers. "You never look me up, you never phone, you never want to know what I'm doing, it even looks as if my life has completely lost interest for you."

"So which of you gentlemen killed him?" the fat policeman suddenly became concerned, a telephone receiver at each ear. "Which one of those present stuck the pretty little knife into the deceased?"

"In Carcavelos?" the lieutenant colonel was surprised. "So far away? And in whose house, if I may ask?"

"Say, maybe it was you, eh?" the fat man asked severely, pointing to the magician's assistant with his pencil.

"And then the funniest thing, Captain," the second lieutenant went on, "is that I was there watching them, holding Mariana by the hand, annoyed, upset, furious, and right then, bang, without thinking, I pictured them naked, stroking each other, kissing each other, licking each other, biting each other, I began to picture the tangle of legs and arms and behinds, and when I came to, you can imagine, I had a hard on."

EMINENT NOVELIST PREPARING NOVEL ON LIFE OF UNFORTUNATE LIEUTENANT.

"Inês?" the lieutenant colonel commented, startled. "No, I don't recognize the name, is she a new friend?"

"After that one," Melissa the striptease goddess asked the second lieutenant, pulling the jug toward her, "how many dykes did you get mixed up with?"

"He can stay here stretched out attending the party," one of the twins, with a Cesarean scar on her belly, conceded generously. "Even though he's dead, he's got the same rights as the rest of us, right?"

"Your daughter is a tennis teacher, Colonel, she smells of rubber, good health, and muscular sweat, she wears a little white skirt and her oily hair is tied back with a green ribbon, she taught my ex-wife how to hold a racket": she would stand behind her to explain to her better, push her breast against her shoulder blades, her stomach against her back, her knees at the curve of her legs, she would grip her by the shoulders, the elbows, the wrists, demonstrate to her how to volley, approach the net, position herself on the court, and after the lesson, in the slatted bathhouse heavy with sun, a shower together, the pleasure of warm water on the head, on tired tendons, on the skin, small breasts glassy with drops of water, trunks dried with Turkish towels, and after the third, or fourth, or fifth day, the second or third week, the seventh, eighth, ninth, or tenth hour, when their looks lingered longer, appraising, attentive, impassioned, loving, the curve of the hips, the waist, the nape of the neck, the buttocks, the throat, the proposal Do you want me to massage your back? Do you want me to put some oil on your tendons? the body lying facedown on the leather-covered settee with tufts of straw peeping out of the holes, soft slaps, the coolness of pomades, liniments, kneading that became caresses, movements of a soft, persistent, infinite slowness, noses that came together, mouths, foreheads, wet hair mingling, We went on the roller coaster twice, Mother, once on the merry-go-round, once on the bumper cars, the kind that have a big pole attached to them and give off electrical sparks, you put a plastic token in a slot, step on the pedal, and they start up, vulvas rubbing against each other now, clitoris or anus being offered to a tongue, a taste of something damp and soft that contracts, hips that wrap around and move and tighten and go away, the sky with small round clouds almost on fire in the window, a kind of wave or rumble becoming precise and growing in the distance, the liniment running down from the navel like oil, And we even went to the beach but it rained, and to the Zoo but there was a crowd of people, all of them throwing peanuts and pieces of bread and paper and trash at the monkeys, their tiny goldsmith fingers, their tiny little eyes, surrounded by bristles and long hair, always moving about, their puffy naked asses, movements that grow faster, mouths that open, breathing that quickens, the rumbling spreads out, spherically, turgid, enormous, about to explode, Next Saturday I'll come back again, the second lieutenant promised, retreating toward the door like a ceremonious flunky, stronger laughter upstairs, exclamations, protests, Getting away in a hurry before Inês's mother puts in an appearance at the top of the stairs with playing cards in her hand, before I have to greet this uncle or that uncle or the other uncle, solemn old men, serious and hunched over, well dressed, clean-shaven, fine smelling, and me with these flannel pants, this jacket, this chin stubble, this wrinkled shirt and no tie, Inês smiles, her friend smiles, and the eyes of both of them are vacant, inexpressive, and polished, like those of dolls, pushing the dogs away with my elbows, closing the car door, turning the key next to the steering wheel, leaving, Mariana comes to the veranda to say goodbye, well mannered, adult, my friend? her arm lifts and waves, and I'm startled by the idea of that daughter-woman I don't know, who doesn't know me, who suddenly went from pacifier to marijuana, the fat inspector came out of a window space, telephone to his ear, and pointed the compass needle of a pencil at me: Was it you?

"Listen," the lieutenant colonel asked, "do you intend to settle down there permanently?"

LADY OF HIGHEST RESPECTABILITY WHO INSISTS ON ANO-NYMITY CONFESSES TO OUR REPORTER SHE WAS MADLY IN LOVE WITH VICTIM.

"Clean this matter up completely for my sake," the cloud of perfume whispered, hovering over her husband's shoulder like a vulture. "Something like this in the family is a real scandal, what will our friends think?"

"I'm not too bothered by it," the fat mulatto woman said, rubbing her armpit, "but it's nine o'clock and the body is already beginning to stink."

WELL-KNOWN MOVIEMAKER PLANS FILM ON RUA DA MÃE D'ÁGUA CASE. ITALIAN DIRECTOR, FRENCH BACKER, LEADING ACTORS CONTACTED.

"Dykes—as far as I know she was the only one," the second lieutenant answered Melissa the striptease goddess, who was rummaging through drawers with a dreamy curiosity, strewing pieces of paper and envelopes over the floor. "The only woman who came after, besides, I don't think I would be attractive to any lesbian."

The wave, the rumble, the turgid, spherical balloon full of snorts and kisses finally burst in a scattering of shouts and froth, a heel that was pedaling frantically on the settee, knocking over the bottle of liniment, which spattered on the floor with a dull sound, a long thread of saliva hung from a lip, joints and veins and bones creaked, bath towels became entangled, monograms of legs quivering and stretching, Can Mariana have ever witnessed that? the second lieutenant thought, can Mariana have ever participated in that? it's impossible for her not to have heard, it's impossible for her not to be aware, not to know, and me, made a fool of at the amusement park with her, and me, made a fool of at the Zoo with her, whisperings at school My mother's a lesbian, she sleeps in the same bed with her tennis instructor, I put my ear to the door every night to listen to them saying how much they love each other, the tumbling, the moans, the whispering, the giggling, The knife went in all by itself, Captain, the soldier swore, word of honor, the knife went in all by itself, Your parents probably haven't noticed anything, Inês, busy as they are with television, and card games, your brothers prefer pills, cocaine, heroin, the old folks' friends and relatives drink whiskey and smoke American cigarettes sprawled out on sofas, Mariana methodically flunking her courses, goes out at night, gets high on pot, and I play the fool planning to buy her a doll, a child's table setting, a rubber bear, some childish foolishness for Christmas, and me refusing to believe that you've grown up, Do you want to go on the merry-go-round, in the Ghost Castle, the idiotic little jungle carts, a gorilla with a man inside threatening us in the dark how funny, and you pretending to be frightened so as not to displease me, startle me, disillusion me, All by itself, Captain, I swear it went in all by itself, I went down the gravel walk pursued by the disorderly gallop of the dogs, through the dark, squat shrubbery into the dark night, past the ghosts of the trees and the house back there like a cube of shadows, broken here and there by the yellow rectangles of the lighted windows, DIRECTOR OF HOME WHERE SERVANT OF UNFORTUNATE LIEUTENANT LIVES STATES: MURDERED MAN WAS ANGEL OF DEDICATION AND KINDNESS, You didn't kill him for making it with my wife, you bumpkin, who do you think you're fooling, the lieutenant colonel said to the soldier, shaking him angrily by the shirt, you knocked him off more because you thought he was cheating on you with Dália, the mulatto woman, disgusted, pushed the body with her foot toward the kitchen mats, murmurs and a rustle of clothing were coming insistently from some place in the apartment that was hard to pinpoint, Mariana was spying through the keyhole now and through the oval opening a buttock appeared and disappeared, the hourglass shape of the small of a back, backs with freckles, hairs, a flared nostril that was violently emitting and taking in air, I take you for a boat ride at Campo Grande, the second lieutenant thought, I take you bicycling, I take you to see the swans, while in his daughter's eyes, demoniacal, insistent, convex, twisted, the two female forms grew denser, evaporated, blended, sobs, spasms, rabbit squeals, the gargling of a suffocated throat, Don't look, he went through the rusty gate, skidded several times on the downgrade, the headlights bounced from one side of the road to the other, revealing stones, pebbles, bumps, enormous holes, a disemboweled cat, dirty pleats of mud, and suddenly, unexpectedly, the streetlights on the Marginal wrapped in a bluish cellophane of mosquitoes and mist, cars slipping along the wet pavement like beetles, the lights of ships, large rectangular shapes in the black pit of the river, vague little microscopic dots twinkling on the opposite shore, You killed him out of revenge, you bastard, the lieutenant colonel said to the soldier, pouring himself some more wine, you killed him out of revenge for Dália or for Odete or for who the hell knows, the car became stable on the asphalt, seemed to grow, get longer, speeded up, a huge truck loomed in front of him with its load tied to the cab with ropes, Don't look, Put him under the couch, the magician's assistant suggested, pointing to the deceased, hide him there once and for all, HUNDREDS OF PEOPLE JOIN SPONTANEOUSLY IN FUNERAL PROCESSION THAT WAS CONSPICUOUS, HEARTFELT, UNMISTAKABLE, IMPRESSIVE SHOW OF MOURNING, Get to the Rua da Mãe d'Água, open a bottle of gin, drink until little blue flames come out of my teeth and tongue, until my stomach twists in my belly like a worm, until my face smiles back at me in the mirrors, a bunion on the communication officer's foot sticking through a torn argyle sock was pointing mockingly at the ceiling, the police searched the room for clues, opened closets, moved pots, spread a kind of chalk dust over smooth surfaces, leaping like grasshoppers over our outstretched bodies, one of them, on all fours over the mulatto woman, was examining her breasts in great detail with a magnifying glass, Inês and her friend were pinching each other brazenly in the vestibule, under the copy of *Guernica* cut out of a magazine and glued onto a piece of wood or cardboard, a car from the roller coaster came in through the window, with a horrible sound of brakes, and it gently laid Mariana on the sofa, Don't look at me naked like this, Don't go to the entrance, Don't look, HIS EXCELLENCY THE PRESIDENT OF THE REPUBLIC REPRESENTED AT FUNERAL FOR MEMBER OF HIS MILITARY STAFF, the red wine scratched and hurt the throat, the glass mouth, surrounded by straw, spat out the last gulps of purple froth, a heavy, disagreeable nausea, bounced off the walls, Inês lay down on her back on the chest, stretched out her arms, pulled on the zipper of the slacks and leaned over the body of her friend, Don't look, he leaned over her slowly, avidly, the pitiless light of nine o'clock was inventing repugnant lumps of vomit on the carpet, separating the sticky nocturnal jelly from objects, revealing legs and arms and breasts and mouths and eyes and noses spread at random, clothing on the floor, bracelets, necklaces, overturned ashtrays, twisted beer-bottle caps, and creases and wrinkles and bald spots and flab, the workers in the building across the way, their shirts and pants crusted with plaster, were climbing up the scaffolding like squirrels, with deliberate ease, Mariana and the fat man were searching for my shorts and pants among the shorts and pants on the floor, Don't look, My father, Inspector, could never be capable of a terrible thing like that, my father is a dope, he'd never kill anyone, I aimed the pistol, fired, Don't look, and Inês and her friend jumped like frogs at the impact of the shots and finally lay still, eyes bulging, as in a huge squeeze, the second lieutenant raised himself with difficulty on a soft elbow that kept slipping (this wetness here on my legs, damn it, is it sperm or piss or shit?), held back a belch, reached out his free hand and grabbed a perfumed leg, or a gelatinous thigh, or a piece of buttock, How many dykes after that one? Melissa the striptease goddess asked, miles away from him, in a thin glass voice, there are guys who can only make it in bed with lesbians, Now can you see that he was the one? the fat man said to Mariana, he's knocked off two more, no less, I was careful to fix myself up with a midget woman, the second lieutenant stammered in embarrassment, in phrases, in words, his head spinning dizzily, who here is nuts enough to get involved with a chick four feet tall.

"A midget?" the lieutenant colonel became interested, hair uncombed, studying the wicker wing of the jug like an entomologist. "Explain to me how you make love to a midget."

"That fat cow Dália, Commander," the soldier asserted, pounding his chest pompously, "as sure as I'm alive I don't even remember her."

"Clean up the blood, wash it away with soap and water," the mulatto woman advised, pointing to a constellation of black or wine-colored or very dark purple splotches that emphasized the symmetrical designs on the rug. "If the cleaning woman finds it here there'll be hell to pay."

"A midget?" one of the twins, in bra and panties, laughed, clapping her hands in amusement. "Where did you ever find a midget woman, you devil?"

I didn't find her, the second lieutenant thought, cleaning a toenail with a fingernail, she found me, in a suburban pastry shop across from the insurance company, where I was drinking my usual coffee and eating my usual custard pastry after work, idly observing from the counter speckled with fly shit shelves of cakes, sandwiches, baskets of egg sweets, cartons of chocolate milk in a kind of metal box and sweating. The Largo de Santa Bárbara, he thinks, at the end of the endless, narrow, melancholy Rua de Arroios, ancient buildings, a sloping and irregular oval, exhausted trolley cars arriving from Conde de Redondo, Estefânia, Gomes Freire, squealing on their tracks, other employees of the company eating, standing up like sheep, with empty eyes and elbows on the barrelhead, napkins in plastic glasses, bald-headed old men reading the newspaper at solitary tables over empty beer steins ringed with foam, women who came in to buy cold cuts, to buy cheese, to buy ham, little dogs pulling on the dames' leashes, wrapping them repugnantly around their ankles, the floor filthy with pieces of paper, cigarette butts, rinds, crumbs, and getting change from the cashier, and then I saw microscopic arms and legs, a huge head sitting on an almost nonexistent body, tiny, ugly, disagreeable, misshapen, poorly dressed, you.

"A midget woman?" the fat inspector asked Mariana. "Besides being a murderer does your father suffer from some mental defect, kid?"

CRIMINAL LIVING IN GREATEST LUXURY WITH UNFORTU-NATE, PHYSICALLY HANDICAPPED WOMAN.

"A midget?" his mother commented, shaking her head, looking at her knitting in a basket. "My Carla introducing him to so many nice girl friends and look at what the boob sets his eyes on in the end."

DON'T MISS NEXT ISSUE WITH EVERYTHING ABOUT THE MONSTER OF THE LARGO DE SANTA BÁRBARA.

"A dwarf, just between you and me, is too much, Jorge," the lieutenant colonel took exception, stroking the dead man's knee. "If she was a cripple or a hunchback, maybe."

IMMORALITY IN PORTUGAL REACHES UNHEARD-OF PROPORTIONS AT THIS MOMENT, TRIAL JUDGE TELLS OUR EDITOR.

"Can I buy you a cup of coffee, ma'am?" the second lieutenant offered, bending at an angle like a carpenter's rule.

"Underneath it all, Jorge didn't know what he was doing, poor thing," Inês lamented. "I always thought there was a lot of mental instability in him."

LAWYER FOR MIDGET IMPLICATED IN CRIME ACCUSES RA-

DIO, TELEVISION, PRESS OF DEFAMATION AND HANDS OUT STRONGLY WORDED PRESS RELEASE AT CONFERENCE.

"Her name was Adelaide and she was a gynecologist at a maternity hospital, Captain," the second lieutenant supplied details. "She specialized in sterility of the tubes, it seems that she would unplug them with a very thin needle."

FAMED INSPECTOR BORGES MAKES OPTIMISTIC DECLARATION TO US THAT POLICE ARE TIRELESSLY PURSUING NEW LEADS THAT WILL HELP REVEAL MURDERER.

"Coffee? What's that about coffee?" the midget asked with a startled frown. "Talk louder, I'm deaf."

Her skin was shriveled ocher, her hair dull and brittle, fingers tobacco stained, her clothes drooped randomly from her narrow shoulders, one of her shoes looked taller than the other to the second lieutenant, with more buckles and laces (Can she be crippled?), her face twisted upward in a grimace of mistrust, puzzlement, surprise (Coffee? you want to buy me coffee?), with the saliva crystallized like a third lip at the corners of her mouth. She smelled of disinfectant and sweat and maybe she didn't even measure four feet, but three feet, three and a half at most, a real midget, Captain, a tiny little thing, a strange little miniature, And do they make love like regular people? the mulatto woman was interested, Her voice was what got me most, her voice was what made the biggest impression on me, hoarse, broken, with sudden rises in the middle of a sentence, Of course, he answered, their vaginas are just the same, it's just that they wiggle more, get worked up more, are more like caterpillars, more insatiable, have more pleasure, A cup of coffee, yes, if you'll do me the honor, the second lieutenant bellowed, I'd have the greatest pleasure if you'd have a cup of coffee with me, she lived in an apartment just like ours behind the Bureau of Identification, with everything just like regular people's, dishes, pots and pans, electrical appliances, tables, and pictures and books and clothes closets and a settee and a normal bed, just like mine or yours, *Guernica,* the Last Supper, the Sacred Heart, Our Lady of Fátima, the midget twisted around to him again, Maybe it would be better if you and I sat down, sir, she bellowed with imperious amiability, the ladies with the cold cuts and the ham turned to observe them, Adelaide's spherical ankles swayed in the air, like those of children, without touching the floor, He announced to me last week that he wants to get married, his mother grew sad, leaned over to lower the volume on the radio, tell me, sincerely, can you picture me as grandmother to a whole tribe of monsters? a waiter cleaned off the table with a cloth the color of crap, dirtier than the top, and put two cups on it, a table setting with napkins, and a saucer with wrinkled croquettes, She served me some tonic liquor, climbing with difficulty, like a duck, up onto chairs in order to reach the glasses and the bottle, And did you make her the first time? and jump on top of her hollering Adelaide as soon as you got inside the door?, HAVE POLICE INVESTIGATIONS FINALLY FOUND REAL CRIMINALS, OR HAS NEW FALSE LEAD CONFUSED OUR DETECTIVES' SEARCHLIGHT?, The fact is, I think you're pretty, the second lieutenant justified himself with shouts in the pastry shop, your green eyes caught my attention, I don't care if she's a gynecologist or a pediatrician or an engineer or any other fucking thing, his father roared, brushing the lead dust off with his open hand, that bastard always did have a sick attraction for freaks, What first caught my eye in her apartment, the second lieutenant recounted, was the unbelievable number of conchs and seashells everywhere, in cupboards, on shelves, on dressers, on tables, large, medium, small, white, dark, brown, black, speckled, shells the size of a fingernail, the size of leaves, the size of a hand, THIS NEWSPAPER PRESENTS EXHAUSTIVE INQUIRY INTO PUBLIC OPINION, Not the first night, no, he replied, the fifth or sixth one after, in a room piled high with medical books and chrome equipment that opened and closed, Thirty, forty, fifty years old? the second lieutenant thought, looking at the greasy wrinkles on the midget's neck, elbows, and face, how old can this dame be?, You're marrying that watch fob? his sister laughed, you really must be crazy, And when she's naked, he said, she's not as ugly as you people imagine, she's got well-shaped breasts and thighs, for example, I hate croquettes, the midget roared at the waiter in an unexpectedly full voice, bring me some chicken tarts or shrimp cakes instead, we talked about this and that, and I was hoarse from talking to her, I was bending over to reach her ear and after half an hour my backbone was throbbing and aching, the next week and the next and the next I waited for her by the entrance to the maternity hospital, leaning against an iron grill alongside some shrubbery and trees, and I saw her, tiny, coming out of a leprous side building with some other doctors or nurses and limping toward him, with a twisted smile on the ashen parchment of her cheeks, he had an urge to turn and flee, disappear, escape from that strange being who was approaching, from her short moans, her sharp panting, her doll dresses, I didn't even mean to wound him with the knife, Colonel, the soldier insisted, how can I prove to you that I didn't even want to wound him? he curled up in a ball to kiss her, like a bedspring, and some kids playing ball sneaked looks at us and laughed, At least with this one, the second lieutenant thought, at least with this one there's no danger, who's going to love her? he shouted Hello darling, stuck his hand possessively, reassuringly under her arm and, with Adelaide, went down to the pastry shop on the Largo de Santa Bárbara, on the way to their conjugal snack.

$F_{ROM}$ two nights a week at the concierge's little apartment the soldier went on to three, then four, then five: he would have dinner, nod sleepily in the canvas chair in front of the television set, vaguely listening to the sound of dishes, coughs, and pots and pans, Eliseu's cot in the next room that creaked as it received him, the late-night footsteps of tenants in the lobby outside, the woman's slippers coming and going, glasses being put away, sounds that mingled in a stew of noises and gradually dissolved into deep waters that had no memory, until someone or something shook his shoulder and made him return hurriedly to the surface like a deep-sea diver, with a rain of the bubbles of unfinished nightmares in which blacks with rifles had risen out of the grassland of the past and were advancing toward him in a confusion of shouts. After a few weeks he began bringing his dirty laundry and shirts that needed buttons in a suitcase or a bundle, after a few months, without giving it any notice, he had a drawer in the bedroom dresser filled with his socks, undershirts, and shorts, and a suit or two hung on wire hangers in the closet amid the concierge's dresses, well starched, with empty sleeves swaying like those of one-armed lottery vendors. Little by little he was growing used to the various smells of the apartment, each with its own density and space, the volume of its shadows when he awoke suddenly had lost its threats and mystery, he knew the rhythm of the breathing and cracking of the furniture, the jaws of the rats who were minutely devouring the fringes of the rugs and the darkness, the dogs and roosters of dawn leaping over each other in neighboring gardens, your body next to me with your open mouth squashing down on the pillow, I learned to distinguish your legs from mine and your urge to pee from my full bladder pinching me, and when we separated in the darkness, sweating and breathing heavily like suckling pigs in their death throes, your arching was separated from mine, like a blindman moving rapidly through the labyrinth of a square or a garden memorized too well.

"Sometimes, damn it, I think that's what marriage is all about," the lieutenant colonel growled, his legs open on the floor (a tangle of dark hair grew out of the twin chestnuts of his testicles), struggling in vain with a sock that was turned inside out, doubled over, resisting: "People taking a long time to find out just which one of us they are when they wake up."

"It's up to you people, it's up to you people," the mulatto woman put in, stretching on the bed, "but you can't help but notice that the guy is smelling so bad he's starting to stink."

"Until I finished shaving I was the midget," the second lieutenant explained, "so small and huddled down that I couldn't even see myself in mirrors. Only when I brushed my teeth did I start to grow, take on size and shape, the cough of a man, a thick voice, phlegm, crusty eyes. I'd tie my tie, shine my shoes, and right away, when I got back to the bedroom, I'd come face-to-face with a yellowish, myopic caterpillar, hair mussed, on the sheets, struggling with the tray of coffee and cookies and roaring Good morning at me with the painful squeaks of a doll."

"Seriously, can't you people smell the stench?" the mulatto woman was puzzled. "If you don't get him away from me soon, any second now, I'll throw up."

From time to time the soldier would sleep over at the place in Campo de Santana to take care of the chickens, the nits on the medlar trees in the yard, and the snails on the kale: the city seemed to be growing hairy everywhere, in buildings, blocks, alleys, cross streets, shantytowns, just like a seedbed of boils, seeming inexplicably stagnant alongside the mental hospital, where characters in pajamas chatted with the walls, looking at cracks, fences, and fissures with the luminous eyes of the prophets of some absurd religion: the same gardens, the same yards, the same old women on the same crumbling windowsills, the same rotten hours on the same wall clocks, the silk of the same cats on the roofs, where the mold from the gutters covered the television antennae with the same death-throes green. Even the termites and the bugs echoed in the rooms without furniture, he thought he could hear the electricity slipping through the wires, the water from the faucets running, muddy and rusty, like sobs in the stone kitchen sink, whose drain was frightened and round like the throat of a dead man. The soldier would shut

himself up in his old room in the back with a slanting ceiling like the grimace
of a stroke victim, would arm himself with a musty pile of magazines, cover
himself carelessly, half-dressed, half-undressed, with a blanket that burned
his skin, and if it wasn't raining and the tiny drops didn't carry him off with
the leaves from the trees and the lighter trash in the direction of the sewers,
he would turn off the light of the metal lamp after an adventure with the
Cisco Kid, Zorro, Mandrake and out there beyond the small window per-
ceive the restless sea of kale rustling in the night, the gleam of aluminum
froth where an abandoned washtub was floating, the quiet of the chicken
coop, handkerchiefs of wings waving on the roosts, the memory of the quiet
man snoring in Pontinha, surrounded by children, his mother-in-law grumbling in a hammock, his wife pushing away his body thick with alcohol, her
arms open, the concierge in the big bed without me, laying her breasts, her
cheeks, her stomach on the acid smell of skin with which I had fertilized the
sheets. He stayed at the place in Campo de Santana, the bedspread hurt him,
the dreams made shifting hard, like a cold motor, and the feathers of the
chickens fluttered, white, on the other side of the glass panes, Uncle Ilídio's
asthma and Dona Isaura's snoring startled him, a dog growled the whole
night and he had the urge to get up and go down the hall because maybe
you're still studying, Odete, because maybe you haven't gone to bed yet, but
the red posters with the outlines of factories and peasants with clenched fists
repelled him, all those books, all those notebooks, all those dictionaries, all
those pens and pencils in ceramic mugs frightened him, Come in come in,
Olavo invited formally, smiling, Come in come in, the communications
officer invited in a friendly way, cleaning a speck off his glasses with a
fingernail, and if this were Mozambique, damn it, he'd pick up the nearest
machine gun, wipe them all out with one burst, and disappear into the jungle
at a trot.

"Too bad the others aren't here," he said aloud without realizing it,
wrapping himself in the blanket or the mulatto woman's body like an animal.

"It's going on ten o'clock," the fat woman was surprised, installed on the
queenly throne of the bed. "If you people don't make up your minds right
now about what you're going to do with the dead man, I'm going to beat it out
of here like a bat out of hell."

Ten o'clock, the soldier thought, how many checker games has the quiet
man played by himself in the glassed-in office of the warehouse since nine
o'clock, indifferent to the bleating of the telephone, to the clear or rainy day
outside, to the rats galloping over the dusty furniture or nursing their
squeaking litters, lying on their side, baring their canine teeth in the seat
stuffing of the van? Ten o'clock, our lieutenant is rotting, ankles sticking out
from under the thick cover of the couch, the leafy trees on Príncipe Real are
the scrawny trees in Omar, the sparrows the speckled, long-legged river
birds, this chill at carpet level is the grass dampened by the drizzle, and, you

437

know, Captain, the way knives can stick into flesh without you noticing, it reminds me of how weapons go off in Africa without anybody touching them, the way prisoners are beaten without us even noticing, the way they make babies in black women without seeing how, lying facedown, with their clothes on, fly open, on the dirty mats in thatched huts, dripping sweat and saliva and wax-colored drops all over, wherever they can secrete or exude, you peek out through the little windows carved in the adobe and in the sudden, instantaneous morning you make out a pale clearing, black men squatting, the barbed wire of the post, the crazy people who make faces in the huge wards in the Campo de Santana, flattening their hands against the walls, the whitish kale that is now puffing up like the breast of a turkey, Odete's smile that comes and goes, Are you sure you don't want to come in, Abílio? the Tagus softly shaking off the reflected lights of the boats, I had a lot to drink, he thinks, stretches his body out, and pours himself some more wine, the thick purple foam tints the edge of the glass, so that a few hours from now, when the police cars finally get here, they'll grab me sleeping, I bet, wrapped in the blanket like a cocoon amid a confusion of trembling, afflicted, destroyed bodies.

"Sitting on one of the toilets, with the door wide open," the attendant explained to reporters, "leaning forward, with his eyes open, like a guy taking a shit. Only some time later I began to wonder about him and I went back to see and I came across that knife hole in his back."

"If you'd open the window," Melissa the striptease goddess said, wallowing on the rug like a mare, fixing herself a kind of mattress with the soft pillows, "we wouldn't smell the guy's stink so much."

"And did you always know when you woke up," the lieutenant colonel wondered, "which one of the two you were? I'd go to bed with an Omega on my wrist, thinking that way, I would know the next day that the one with the man's watch would be me."

"Also, would it be too much trouble to raise the shade a little?" the twin with the Cesarean scar was annoyed, on all fours, looking for the towel. "If there's no more respect for people's feelings you can go fuck yourselves."

"Listen here, why didn't the two of you get married?" the second lieutenant asked the soldier.

He would wake up with the exhausted impression of having fought all night, of having not slept, of having been pushed and pulled and beaten and bruised by guerrillas in uniform, of having his veins and his bones crushed, his muscles felt dissolved like those of corpses in alcohol and with the heavy weight of a boot on his belly, he opened the kitchen door that led to the garden, in shorts and socks, in order to wash at the spigot, the sky was piling up with the superimposed boulders of clouds and my piss crystallized in the damp winter air and foamed on the ground, the chickens were looking at me, tilting their heads, mistrustful, at your place there was a heater, hot water, slippers, deodorants, bathtub, cockroaches that hid behind the trimmed piassava palm, ants that climbed and walked obstinately over the broken tiles, a big yellow sponge, a nail brush, rust spots around the faucet, me motionless in the water, with only my head showing, and the fire sirens blowing in the street, ambulances, hook and ladders, a whirring of motors that squeaked, choked, leaped, hesitated. Until one afternoon, coming back from a moving job, he found an unknown, halfbreed-looking man, middle-aged and with a serious expression, waiting for him in the warehouse with a thin portfolio under his arm.

"Naturally, I called the police right away," the toilet attendant answered. "I've worked for the City for twenty years, I don't want any trouble in my toilets."

"They started to carry the body down to the street and stopped," the concierge explained, pushing the cat away with her foot, "there are still half-scrubbed bloodstains on the landing, in the vestibule. It was only after that that they must have got the idea of the pantry as a way out."

"Are you Mr. Ilídio da Conceição Gaspar's heir?" the little man with the briefcase asked sternly, opening and closing his beardless jaws, where the corner of an unbelievable set of false teeth gleamed.

He took some printed papers out of his case, waved them threateningly at the soldier like an aggressive fan, cited decrees, codes, and numbers.

"We have proof that no one is living in his house, that none of his descendants are using it in accordance with the law, that only rarely does someone sleep there to take care of the animals, the garden. I'm here to inform you that starting with the first of the month we will consider it completely unoccupied."

"You should make a little effort," the second lieutenant advised, "get on a ferry, a truck, a taxi, anything, hell, go back to Cova da Piedade, have a nice talk with Odete and Olavo, convince them. On my daughter's life, I'll bet they'd be delighted with a divorce."

"Isn't there some of that stuff to get rid of smells?" the mulatto woman was getting impatient, desperate, trying to get up to reach her bra while the vast rolls of fat around her kidneys went up and down like saddlebags. "To be perfectly frank, I can't take it anymore."

"As soon as I touched him with a finger he collapsed onto the floor," the toilet attendant reported as the cameras alternately lighted him up and left him in darkness. "Headfirst onto the trash and piss and wetness, with a trolley ticket or a cigarette butt or a piece of toilet paper on his cheek."

"The landlord had been around to grease the neighbor women's palms, Captain," the soldier said, "and as soon as he had enough proof, he sent the guy with the briefcase to bug me."

Still, he went to an office to complain, then to another, from the second one they sent him back to the first and from the first to a third, where people were standing in line out to the street, and where a bilious-looking secretary made him fill out dozens of forms, told him to get a certificate from the Neighborhood Council, authenticated by eight competent merchants, a certificate from the Criminal Registry, six passport-sized photographs, his military booklet, and a declaration with the stamped seal of the Anti-Tuberculosis League guaranteeing that he didn't suffer from lung disease, and that he must present everything the following day, not to forget his fourth-grade diploma and his driver's license for light and heavy vehicles, at eleven o'clock in the morning at a window in Chelas, in order to have his request eventually considered by the director general of Housing and Rents. He arrived at seven o'clock and the line stretched for over two hundred yards, turning at least five corners and losing itself in the confusion of the market, a lot of old people, a lot of women with faces of hunger, poorly dressed types, snot-nosed children crying, sometimes there were protests, shouts, arguments, heated blows, a policeman with his hands behind his back, who was guarding a bank, got angry with a mammoth Gypsy selling belts and neckties, around nine o'clock the sky grew dark, lowered, and it began to rain, one of the old men buried the rib of his umbrella in the eye of another down to the cloth, the snot-nosed children leaped and ran, the policeman grabbed the Gypsy by the jacket and in no time at all a car with three guys in uniform appeared and they took him away with shoves in a confusion of insults and kicks, the rain tripled in ferocity, the soldier, dripping water, kept looking at the requirements, the photographs, the certificates, If I lose any of these papers I'll be fucked, until by ten o'clock he'd reached the entrance to the building, a nauseating squat little structure, filled with people crammed together who smelled of dog doodoo and cold tobacco, a creature in mourning, right in front of him, was telling a sympathetic cross-eyed woman friend about the sudden death of her husband, dragged back and forth in the emergency room of the hospital, on a litter, among broken legs, guts hanging out, and moaning, until he died, for obscure reasons, exactly halfway between the oxygen tanks and the dusty plaster-cast room, the soldier went up a step or two every quarter hour, stumbling attendants went up and down the stairs shouting Excuse me, carrying tons of yellow papers in their open arms, he hated the landlord, he hated the little man with the briefcase, he hated the neighbors who must have reported him, whispering over their windowsills to officials on fearsome errands, at ten-twenty he began to make out above the curve of a counter, a wall of frosted glass, a sign NO SMOKING, another NO SPITTING ON THE FLOOR, people obsequiously bent over the rectangular openings of windows, voices lowered, respectful coughs, he had trouble breathing through his nose, he felt a tingling in his nostrils, shivers, and a strange feeling, like a fever, in his body, I've caught a cold, the wet shirt was sticking to his skin like a leech, his damp legs were like uncomfortable fish scales, his feet sloshed in his shoes, wrapped in the rotting rags of his socks, ten-twenty-five, ten-thirty, ten-thirty-three, ten-thirty-seven, ten-forty, through a window missing a pane he saw the buildings opposite, out of focus, through the water, blind rows of windows, rolls of clouds, the difficult, swollen, melancholy, oily light of winter mornings, more attendants, a clerk in shirt-sleeves with a big book in his hand and an expression of disdain, elbowing people, hazy silhouettes, like amoebas, on the other side of the windows, the creature in mourning sighed and her enamel medallion with the picture of her husband (a character with a mustache and the fateful look of those promised a macabre death right from the cradle) bounced impetuously between her breasts like a bottle cap, the dull sound of rubber stamps could be heard, the squeak of drawers, registers being leafed through, the clearing of throats, the snot-nosed children, smothered by the crowd squeezing up the stairs, were whining in a way that got fainter and fainter, If I wanted to go back now, I couldn't, the soldier thought, looking at the beehive of heads and eyes and mouths buzzing on the landings below, the old people took ages at the counters, perplexed, asking questions, making mistakes, hesitating, Six still in front of me, the soldier counted, five, four, three, bored clerks held their cigarettes between thumb and forefinger, going through dossiers, examining cases, endlessly slow, picking their nails with little metal instruments, making crosses in pencil on the margins of stamped paper, a sneeze climbed up my throat and disappeared, noiselessly, into my nose: A whole week of tea with lemon, he calculated, a whole week rubbing my ribs with mentholated ointment, the widow in front of him reached the window, sighed again, the effigy of her husband leaped, and from her purse she took an incredible number of wrinkled documents of various sizes and colors, which she smoothed out with her fingers before a clerk wearing glasses and a complicated brooch at the low-cut neck of her dress, who limited herself to brushing them off with the back of her hand, whistling through her pursed lips, Without a deed nothing can be done. The cross-eyed friend, who seemed literate, immediately broke into overlapping explanations, the deed must have been in Lagos, ma'am, except that there was a fire in Lagos and all the files burned up last August, and the municipal government couldn't, you understand, ma'am, give out photocopies of something that didn't exist anymore, no one took the responsibility of putting the white stamp on empty certificates, you see, starting next year, maybe with four witnesses with more than thirty years and eight months of residence there you could get it, but the old folks are almost all rotting away in the home in Tavira, and the ones left had been bought out by land speculators who were building apartments and houses everywhere close to the ocean, the widow was nodding agreement and the one in glasses listened to them without hearing, fingering the monstrous brooch, the rain had stopped and a lozenge of pale blue sky, still framed by clouds, appeared unexpectedly in a corner of the window, Without the deed nothing can be done, next, the clerk ordered, letting go of the brooch, as if she had awakened from a strange lethargy, the ones waiting behind me seemed to form a single, repugnant, soft, spread-out body that throbbed, the smell of tobacco and the smell of dampness, clotted and thick, rolled around in his stomach and guts, the widow began to weep, the cross-eyed woman angrily started her discourse from the beginning (The deed must have been in Lagos, ma'am, except that in Lagos there was this big fire last August), the soft body gave off a breath of grunts of impatience and discontent, Next, the woman in glasses spoke, unmoved, the cross-eyed woman grudgingly withdrew, consoling the widow and protesting, at five to eleven the soldier finally rested his chest against the window, while on the left a frightened Indian woman, with her son around her neck, watched a sheet of stamped paper being covered with rectangular and oval marks, from my pockets I took the pictures, the documents, the forms, the identity card, the sputum analysis, a little green envelope which contained the microfilm of the X-ray from the Anti-Tuberculosis League, which was a piece of film with clearer marks asymmetrically printed on the heavy dark background, Why are you showing me all this stuff? the clerk in glasses asked, surprised, and now the clouds had completely disappeared and the sky was becoming thick with colors, several layers of transparent paper, an airplane slipped between two chimneys, a flock of pigeons in disorder described a broad, rising semi-circle, They want to throw me out of my house, the soldier said with an anxious little pound on the counter, they want to get rid of me just like that, the woman in glasses examined the papers with a broad frown, schematically initialing the corners with a red pencil, the phone rang behind her from a desk where a bald-headed individual, biting the top of his pen, was solving a crossword puzzle in the newspaper, a redheaded clerk answered and kept grunting interminably, hip against the desk, playing with a paper clip, running his lips along the little ridges, Does anyone know a batrachian with seven letters? the bald man inquired, jaw hanging, waiting, Your uncle's wife's death certificate is missing here, the woman in glasses advised, irritated, it's unbelievable how people in this land of irresponsible people never bring the necessary documentation with them, the wet clothing was drying on my skin like the water of a river on its bed of grasses and stones, the redheaded man hung up the phone and stood staring at a cardboard calendar with an idiotic expression, A city in northern China with four letters? the bald man asked, frowning, caught up in geographical meditations, the sky was becoming clouded with a thin mist that was dragging toward the west, They accuse me of abandoning the place, ma'am, the soldier explained, did you ever hear of anything so unfair, a gentleman with a briefcase looked me up at the warehouse yesterday morning with an order from the judge, the clerk in glasses thought for a couple of seconds, indecisive, squeezing her brooch, and then she ruffled through a huge pile of bulletins, official releases, telegrams, codes, volumes of decree-laws, the redheaded clerk, requested by the bald-headed man, was searching in vain, counting on his fingers, for the name of a lake in Finland with eighteen letters, NO LITTER-ING, a sign ordered, and pigeons and buildings in the window and a bit of the river, It's almost eleven o'clock and I've had it, the soldier thought, they're going to throw me out on the first of the month, now what? a man better dressed than the others, who, from his serious look, his vest, and his proprietary movements must have been in charge of the section, appeared amid the desks, coming in by a discreet little side door, pointed to the round wall clock with his arm, shouted Close the windows immediately and tell the taxpayers that haven't been taken care of that we'll reopen at two o'clock, Did you bring the baptism certificate, a bladder stone, and a urinalysis of the deceased's wife? the woman in glasses asked, the soldier searched his pockets, the contents of his wallet, on the floor (It was still possible that he had them, that they'd fallen, that someone had stepped on them without noticing), the head man evaporated through the small door that slammed shut, driven by a spring, the bald man, who had hidden the newspaper, asked around, pointing to the crossword puzzle with his pen, What's the word for bread in Croatian? the window to his right came down along its wooden strips with the sound of an execution, a second one, farther off, also closed, a sound of slow, annoyed footsteps dragged slowly down the stairs, the soft body gradually grew smaller in volume, And has the deceased woman's voter's card also disappeared by chance? the woman in glasses asked wearily, when are you people going to learn, please tell me, how to live in society?, Maybe the concierge will take me back, the soldier thought, I can still keep the furniture that's left at the warehouse, but what am I going to do about the chickens and the kale? and all of a sudden a deep sadness came over him as he thought about the dark hallway in Campo de Santana, the walls rotting away, the splotches of mold on the baseboards, the cracks in the paint in the corners of the ceiling, the little yard, the garden, Dona Isaura, his uncle, Show me the electrocardiogram of your maternal grandfather at least, the clerk hinted, her hands on the supports of the grill now, with the sad, impatient tone of an examiner facing an ignorant student, since you know or ought to know that the lack of your maternal grandfather's electrocardiogram is subject to judicial procedure, Mississippi, the redhead suggested timidly, the feverish feeling was crawling up his legs, branching out into his fingers, accelerating his pulse, filling his blood, the pigeons were coming and going in afflicted flights, I knock on the door to Odete's room,

Who is it?

I go in and she was smiling at me in the middle of notebooks, books, shelves of diction-aries, encyclopedias, class notes, political essays, novels, As far as the house is concerned there's nothing we can do, the landlord's blood test shows a quantity of white globules that can't be overcome, the one in glasses advised now, lowering the guillotine of her window, but if you don't present the electrocardiogram within forty-eight hours you'll receive the notice of a fine at the warehouse, Mississippi shit, the bald man refused, a cleaning woman, in an apron, with brush and bucket, began to scrub the floor energetically, and when I went down the steps of the General Office, Captain, there was no longer anybody on the landings or on the stairs, except for one or two snot-nosed children crying on the steps all alone, only bulbs with no shades and signs and service notices fastened to windows, outside a flag was wrapping around its staff on the second-floor balcony, a thin rain was slipping lightly across the tile roofs, a miserable little pastry shop was jam-packed with customers drinking coffee, the pigeons had disappeared, the old people had disappeared, the piece of blue sky had disappeared, something was tickling him in the nose, it suddenly squeezed his chest and he sneezed, he felt like lying down, not moving, dozing off, his muscles softened, lost strength, his eyelids, red, were tingling, an infinite indifference was added to a kind of nausea, what do I care about the house, what do I care about the chickens, what do I care about the kale, what do I care about my uncle, just stretching out on the sheets, just closing my eyes, just being left alone, he took a bus to the concierge's street and his teeth were chattering with the sound of chinaware, a strange coldness was squeezing his bones, the rain kept stopping and starting again, he went into the dismal place seeing objects as if they were sunken in a painful, uncomfortable mist, the furniture was leaping over itself, Odete put her textbooks aside and began to get undressed silently in front of him, he made out the shape of a back, a thigh, flesh-colored lace panties, he reached out his hand to her, lost his balance, the concierge supported him, took off his shoes and wet socks, went to the closet in her son's room to get a blanket that smelled horribly of mothballs and covered him the way the guys in ambulances cover people killed in accidents, after centuries had gone by he felt them putting a thermometer under his arm, calling him, asking him questions, listening to him with a stethoscope, holding his head to give him a bitter pill, the voice of the concierge repeating Yes Doctor, yes Doctor, yes Doctor, diffracted like images in a fishbowl, steps, the cough of a man who seemed to be giving advice or warnings, one of the hens in the garden who was watching him, perched on a bureau, with its inexpressive or accusing glass eye, and then the voices and figures dissolved in a whitewashed silence of the dead, where from time to time a gurgle of murmurs broke out with the rush of my blood, and then the soldier was going down, this way and that, with a swaying motion, the malaise in his legs disappeared, the tightening in his chest went away, one of Odete's arms, separated from her body, waved a long maritime farewell to him from very far off, the waves entered through his ears, nose, eyes, navel, the thousand pores of his skin, his hair waltzed, his chest shuddered with a final sigh, and he went under:

"And you didn't make your mind up after that?" the second lieutenant asked, indignant. "And even after that you didn't go live with the dame?"

On the third day, the doctor, a pleasant, wire-thin fellow, unkempt hair, poorly dressed, with the dirty tips of his collar pointing upward and prescription pads sticking out of all his pockets, tears and holes in his jacket and pants, informed me in a friendly way, while he was taking my temperature, looking at the thermometer, head to one side, leaning like the stalk of a plant toward the light from the window, beyond which the firemen's sirens never ceased blowing and hooting, With a case of pneumonia like this you were close to kicking the bucket, friend, if your wife hadn't called me right away you'd be fertilizing the cypresses in the Prazeres cemetery right now, Eliseu, crawling on the floor, with stupid insistence was pushing a little wooden car against the legs of the resident, my ribs had almost stopped hurting, just a little jab in the shoulder if I breathed deeply, I felt like eating some rabbit and rice, or a tuna-fish salad, Brussels sprouts in oil, the world had become neat and clear again, no more shadows, the concierge, still mistrustful of the miracle, was looking at me out of the corner of her eye as if I were a cataleptic Lazarus, Keep on giving him the syrup and the little capsules every six hours, the doctor advised, giving me exploratory taps along the ribs with his fingers, and maybe by the end of the week, if the cough disappears, he can get up, the soldier swallowed, without any pleasure, soups, broths, roast chicken, a microscopic slice of fish that the concierge brought him on a wicker tray, that afternoon he got up to piss, had a dizzy spell, and came back to bed practically on all fours, leaning on the furniture, urinating in his pajamas, his legs shook, his arms shook, the tendons of his neck shook, he was sweating, exhausted, as if he'd been running for hours on end, he thought, I'm going to go under again, I'm going to sink again, the concierge, who was chatting with a tenant in the vestibule, ran back inside, railed at him, hoisted him up by the waist onto the bed, Not even out of gratitude, damn it, the second lieutenant was horrified, not even to pay her back for the hard work she put in for you? the capsules resisted going down his throat, the drinkable liquid in ampules tasted bitter, the apartment was dark, long and sad like a coffin of the dead, the bedpan next to him stank, he stayed all day with his hands resting on the sheet, silently studying the ceiling, on one occasion he asked Eliseu for a small mirror, and imprisoned in plastic he saw a skinny, lightless face, full of teeth, endowed with a beard, They're fooling me, I'm going to die, he felt he was like Dona Isaura after her stroke, like his uncle, dressed up now, with a handkerchief tied around his jaw, in his coffin, Odete would smile at him from time to time and disappear, the dogs in Cova da Piedade brushed up against the night tables and barked, through the only window in the room a dull and graceless light crept in, the pleasant, rumpled doctor rang the bell right after the television program (a boring dance, commercials, boring politicians arguing in a boring way, commercials, boring news, com-

mercials, a preview of tomorrow's boring programs), he took his temperature, listened to his heart, joked, reduced the dosage of the capsules,
prescribed big vitamin pills and some drops to raise his blood pressure,
Sometimes at night he goes off his head a little, the concierge reported,
sometimes at night he starts talking about his uncle, the doctor took out some
pills to prevent dreams and recommended a cooked pear and small glass of
port wine after dinner, You smell terrible, Odete commented, making a face,
you're never going to be anything but a halfwit, you bumpkin, Come in,
come in, Olavo invited, waving the newspaper, Word of honor, I really and
truly can't stand it anymore the mulatto woman said, either you shut him up
in the pantry or I'm leaving, You killed him for yourself, the lieutenant
colonel accused, cut out the excuses, you boob, Don't even think about going
out before the end of the month, the doctor forbade him, laughing, wasn't
the shower the other day enough for him? the concierge took good care of
me, poor woman, she was concerned, she was interested, she fed me, gave
me my medicine on time, so he swore to her without conviction As soon as
I'm well I'm going to ask for a divorce, I'll go to Cova da Piedade, I'll talk to
them and that will be that, but, of course, I didn't do anything of the kind,
Captain, I rented an apartment on Santa Marta and invented a whole string
of excuses, the quiet man visited him on Friday, at lunch time, while the
soldier was munching disconsolately, surrounded by bottles and boxes of
medicines, in the mortuary shadows of the room, on a tiny little cutlet, he sat
on the edge of the bed, very ceremoniously, reeking from alcohol, A third-
floor room on Santa Marta, the soldier said, in the building below the
hospital, the idea of living with a woman after my experience with Odete
terrified me, he started thinking right away What if she gives me a hard
time?, What if it turns out bad? and What if she falls in love with some guy
and leaves me? so that till today, at the age of forty, Captain, I haven't been
able to make up my mind, the concierge has adjusted by now, she doesn't
holler anymore, doesn't complain, the quiet man, who sat motionless in the
room like a mannequin, left a long time later, exhaling his wine breath,
without having opened his mouth, on the twenty-ninth day the doctor
announced that I could get up and sit in the living room, I sat there melancholically looking at a row of pigeons perched on the peaks of roofs and the
cream-colored February sky, I listened to the concierge singing as she
scrubbed the steps, every so often one of the birds would shake its neck, its
head, its wings, and disappear, I no longer felt flashes of light-headedness or
that strange weakness in the arms and legs, But you promised her you'd get a
divorce and you didn't, the second lieutenant said, I would say you were
lower than a cockroach, Put him on top of the crate, the magician's assistant
advised, just like that, if it wasn't for the smell, I bet they'll think he fell
asleep, we folded his jacket over his lap, one of the blond twins emptied the
box of detergent on him from the head down and the white powder spilled

over his tie, shirt, pants, pointed shoes, What sad pusses dead people have, the soldier thought, what soft rubbery mouths, like a sick clown's, and their hands, Captain, so quiet like that, hanging down, pale, whether it was from the vitamin pills or the ampules, I was soon able to stand on my pins and shuffle along from room to room without any help, the day after tomorrow the little man with the briefcase will dump the furniture into the street and take over the house, the day after tomorrow, the soldier thought, they're going to kill my uncle for good, Odete stopped visiting me, waving, smiling, I'm fine, he remembered Olavo in the apartment in Cova da Piedade, newspaper open on his knees, staring at him a little unwillingly with furtive eyes that tried unsuccessfully to congratulate themselves, to be happy, the ferry shaking and leaping on the waves, the trip of the truck to the town, the following day, in the afternoon, he got dressed and sneaked out of the building while the concierge went to pay the electric bill, he walked two or three blocks feeling the elastic sidewalk under his shoes, and it was as if he'd had a good beating and his muscles and shoulders had been pounded, if, for example, he had tried to move faster or run he certainly wouldn't have been able to, he caught a trolley down by the little square, it was hard to breathe, the air entered and left his lungs with difficulty, he got off at the Rua Gomes Freire and had some hot dogs, boiled eggs, and a platter of chicken giblets in a bar called the Prego de Ouro (The Gold Nail), frequented by pawnbrokers, factory workers, sleepy whores who worked in the neighboring blocks, drifters, guys from the Courthouse, and little pimps with loud ties and checkered jackets with shoulder pads selling smuggled American cigarettes and shelling dishes of lupine seeds in a macho way. Bent over the zinc counter he recognized an apprentice from the garage near the Ilídio Movers warehouse, a fellow with acne-scarred cheeks, a defect in his fingers as though he had double nails on his stubby thumb, and some old men who were accustomed to occupy the slat benches on the Campo de Santana, the shadows and the swans slipped along the surface of the pond, under the tall dark trees the color of eternally nocturnal eyebrows, the guy drawing draft beer was downing tarts and croquettes behind the boss's back, he ordered a glass of applejack to give him strength and courage (something, a spring, a screw, an engine, seemed to be on the point of breaking inside him), the second lieutenant locked the door to the pantry with the corpse of the communications officer inside and they returned in a procession to the living room, half-naked, half-dressed, bumping into doorframes and walls like butterflies, he paid, left a tip of a few dark little coins, got off the stool, which suddenly seemed of a Himalayan height, with difficulty, dizzy, as if he were on a scaffold, a layer of boxes and trash cushioned his fall, the afternoon was growing dark around the fringes of the outlined tiles and the roof drain funnels, an appliance store, where washing machines were lined up in dazzling parallel rows, lighting up the depths of its display, the zigzag filaments of the bulbs were a touch red, he went along toward the house almost hugging the wall of the hospital, and his legs, gentlemen, were bearing up, his muscles were bearing up, his head was bearing up, just a little dizziness, just a little lethargy, just his brain bubbling, as if gasified, there was the alley, winding and steep, in the accumulated sunset shadows, the small bordered yards of the low, little houses, the whitish mongrel dogs barking from the stoops, the noise of cutlery, lace curtains quivering, religious prints framed in plywood on the walls, he touched the key in his pocket, amid change, loose cigarettes, and a box of matches, here we are, the yellow façade of Mr. Assírio, who dealt in smuggled radios, the pale blue of Mr. Alfredo from the drugstore who was scolding the parrot on the metal perch, its neck feathers raised, the little man with the briefcase pointed his fragile, definitive little chin at him Starting with the end of the month, we will consider the house unoccupied, What about the garden? he thought, and the chickens, and the furniture, and the feet of the dead on the floorboards? no one saw me and if anyone did, who would have recognized me with a week-old beard? the latch opened easily, the vestibule, the hallway, Odete's room right there on the left, the little footsteps of rats in the attic, light, cautious, instantaneous, the confused mixed smells of the past still floating in the kitchen and the living room, the odor of cooking, sweat, dampness, medicine, hen turds, mildew, I reached the backyard, I cut the clothesline with my jackknife, chased the chickens over the fence as they cackled in panic, scattering feathers, into the neighboring yards, I tore up the wire from the rotten-wood chicken house, I trampled the kale, the potatoes, the tomatoes, which squashed under my heels like the cartilaginous skulls of babies, my ankles were heavy with mud, my kidneys really ached now, my brain was getting gassier and gassier, I turned over the washtub, broke the water faucet with a hammer and a silvery spurt arched out into the shadows, vanishing and making the cultivated earth gleam here and there, I split the rotting window frames and a splinter of glass cut my hand, the ball-shaped tiles in the bathroom, the marble of the bowl, ancient turds spread over the tile floor, the water sobbed its way along the floorboards, I knocked over chairs and furniture, dumped out drawers, threw a stone at the electric meter which broke with fireworks of thunder and lightning, I turned my uncle's bed upside down and tore open the straw mattress with my fingernails, voices outside were coming closer, the afflicted exclamations of a woman, shouts, calls, interjections, dogs barking, a man asking Who's there? a flashlight was glowing dimly at the end of the hall, feeling along the wall I still had time to tear a shelf down, another, I heard someone shout in the street Call the police, someone's wrecking Mr. Ilídio's house, I wanted to explain that it wasn't so, I wanted to tell them it was me, I still had time to turn over a low table, break a pot, but my feet were slipping out from under me, my body was going back on me, a wire was wrapping itself around my ankles, I fell, unsupported, onto my back on the floor, amid the mud and the water and the crap and the nails and the loose boards from the furniture, a dog grabbed my shirt, the flashlight lighted up my face, several tall figures surrounded me, but I stayed down there, stretched out on the floor, bleeding from the wrist and face and knees, looking at them, Captain, my eyes suddenly without hate, calm and peaceful, the kind animals have when they die.

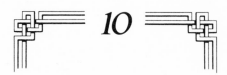

# 10

"BEING in the reserves," the lieutenant colonel said, pushing away the empty jug with the palm of his hand, "is the same as being dead."

He would wake at five or six in the morning, instantly, without feeling sleepy, without feeling fatigued, as if it were two or three in the afternoon and he'd never lain down, in an imprecise way he could make out the contours of the bedroom, the cloud of perfume's bulk snoring beside him, the tables by the head of the bed, the dresser, the silence of nighttime sweat, the parallel lines of the blinds were dim with a creamy light, tiny ships of insomnia sailed on the large oval mirror with pictures stuck along the molding, shipwrecked dreams wavered on the walls, he would feel for his cigarettes, matches, the concave crystal of cold glass that was the ashtray, he would lean on the pillow up against the wood of the bed, sitting on the mattress in his pajamas, smoking, drilling the shadows with his wide-awake eyes, and then, to himself, What shall I do today? and then, to himself, How shall I spend the day? empty, endless hours, interminable, getting a shave at the barber's, reading the newspaper, lunching somewhere on a plate of sad fish, looking at the store windows on the Avenida de Roma or in the Baixa, going to the movies, returning home, Edite all fired up, behind schedule, hair uncombed, concerned, hurriedly fixing a pin, an earring, a brooch, a button, dining across from her in a silence of glasses and silverware that was heavy with contained recrimination, lack of interest, fatigue, mutual accusations, and later on, at eleven o'clock or midnight, getting undressed by the foot of the bed, folding my clothes on their creases over the arm of a chair, watching her take off her makeup, transform herself into a different woman, much older, much uglier, into a repugnant, almost decrepit old lady who was anointing herself with creams, pomades, pastes, tying up her hair with a schoolgirl's purple ribbon, or a lapdog's, with a ridiculous little bow at the top of her head, she would put on an absurd short nightgown frothy with lace, slip in between the sheets without looking at him, a scandal sheet between her long nails, DID DALAI LAMA RENT LUXURY APARTMENT IN BIARRITZ FOR FORMER CLEANING WOMAN IN MOVIES; WILL FAMOUS GREEK SHIP-OWNER DEMETRIOS PHOPHOPOULOS DIVORCE HEADSTRONG MODEL JANE BUBBLE TO LIVE WITH IRANIAN PRINCESS?, I would sit there without reading, eyes on the ceiling, scratching my testicles, chang-ing position, thinking about the naked girl in the film at the Odeon, detesting you, you would fold over the corner of a page without finding out if the last king of Egypt really did lash his concubines with a metal-studded whip, you would sigh, turn your back full of pimples and freckles to me, Good night, you'd pull on the light-switch cord and the room would suddenly become dark, as if all of a sudden it had turned inside out with us inside, Good night, the lieutenant colonel would answer in a low voice, with the tone of someone grumbling Shit, the rustle of clothes, silence, the rustle of clothes, more silence, a pair of buttocks touching and moving away from me, the sole of a foot touching and moving away from me, What is it about me that makes her sick? the lieutenant colonel thought, surprised, what is it that she hates in me? what would she do if I tried to hug her? the hands on the electric clock were glowing in the dark, forming frowns, smiles, grimaces, signals, my body broke away from the bedclothes, floated a little, came back, stood erect in the air, hesitated, swayed, left, and my head, concerned, went after it, my thoughts, my anger, my vague desire for you, my inertia, all more and more mingled and mixed inside him, all more and more imprecise, more diffuse, the clock was microscopically sailing along, miles away, the darkness was giving way to a kind of white peace, a kind of absence, he still thought And what about tomorrow? and nothing pained him anymore, offended him, made him uncomfortable, worried him, they'd left the house at the Military Academy and were living in Edite's apartment once more, amid the innumer-able knickknacks (small china objects, fans, Indian arrows, small items of ivory and bamboo) and her imposing poor taste, the dog would scratch its nails on the kitchen tiles, various moments of silence would pile up and follow one another, drifting, and right then, immediately, smack, five or six in the morning, the parallel ribs of the blinds, the ships of insomnia in the large oval mirror on the wall, I shave, read the newspaper, have a fish as disconsolate as I for lunch on the first terrace at hand, I look at the store windows on the Avenida de Roma or in the Baixa, I go to the movies, and why in hell don't I have a heart attack, a stroke, some kind of crap like that at the first intermission, and why in hell doesn't this shit end now, tell me that, once and for all.

"You shouldn't have had so much to drink, Commander," the soldier remarked respectfully, applying a second pat to the empty jug. "When the wine turns sad it takes a lot of strength to resist its pull."

"If he got a job," the green friend said to Edite, giving her a second lump of sugar, "he wouldn't be such a burden to you, he wouldn't be hanging around the house so much. I know a garrison corporal who does the accounting for a business."

"So how long did you live with the midget?" Melissa the striptease goddess asked.

"When I say accounting I also mean working behind a counter, as a warehouseman, a doorman, a traveling salesman for a boutique," the green friend had her vengeance, triumphantly stirring her tea. "A job that would distract him, you know how it is, keep him busy, keep his spirits up."

"I'm still living with her," the second lieutenant answered. "With a normal dame it's the easiest thing in the world to break up, but just show me, please, how a guy can get free of a midget."

The barbershop smelled of monotony, sublimity, and cheap lotions, two or three guys were sitting in the chairs, towels around their necks, ever so solemn, and snippets of hair kept falling around them, like the feathers of a chicken being plucked, swept out onto the sidewalk by a diligent little old man in a smock who also emptied spittoons and ashtrays, changed cloths, arranged newspapers, and went out at intervals, hands in his pockets, to contemplate the street, buildings, automobiles, people, the monotonous grayness of March. The facing mirrors multiplied ten, twenty, a hundred times the razors, the faces, the shaving cream, the scissors, and the combs, the people waiting, leaning against the wall on backless little benches, the fluttering movements of the barbers, washed hair dripping the drops of a castaway, the sleepy eyes of the lieutenant colonel from time to time would meet others also drifting along, also vague, on the glass surfaces and the chrome frames, I wish this would never end, I wish haircutting could be eternal, the hairs falling onto the towel like dirty snow or, itching and uncomfortable, getting onto your neck, the scissors were opening and closing their chrome bird beaks, flashing against the back of a neck, or around an ear, on excessively long hair by the temples, soft fingers raised his chin, lowered his chin, smoothed his cheeks, a phantom in a mustache next to him, with his hand out holding a cigarette, was moving about under a kind of sheet, thumbing through a magazine, Do I know him? a calendar, the framed rectangle of the price list, the advertisement of a brand of hair cream with a very well-combed boy surrounded by enthusiastic adolescents, Shall I trim it? the barber asked the phantom, leaning over in a friendly way and pointing to the mustache with his shears, the guy raised his eyebrows, outraged, Do I know him? but memory kept betraying him, names and places got mixed up in his head, just a little while from now a small grilled trout, just a little while from now the movies, buying an aisle seat, giving the usher a tip, sitting in the dark, not to follow the film but to think about life, thinking immediately about nighttime and dinner, thinking about tomorrow, It must be this, this empty anxiety, this hollow despair, that the guys I used to put into the reserves felt Good morning, General, the phantom greeted him, smiling in the mirror, while the barber applied alum with a wooden stick, the aging manicurist with incredible breasts was waddling in the space between chairs, his memory opened up inside him like a watermelon, that face, that mustache, that slim body, those spider fingers, that's it, the Encarnação Artillery Regiment, the early morning of the military coup, the priest's communist plot paranoia, Colonel Ricardo roaring into the phone, the uniformed officers in the commander's office, Captain Mendes, in camouflage dress, peremptory, inviting, advising, threatening, giving orders, advancing or withdrawing on his long, thin legs, but couldn't he be mistaken, damn it, couldn't his memory be playing tricks on him as always?

"Mendes, in the reserves?" the second lieutenant asked, surprised. "I remember hearing about that, reading about it in the papers during the November twenty-fifth business, but I thought they'd reconsidered their decision and reinstated him."

"Most of them, yes, but not him," the lieutenant colonel answered, crawling toward a floral-patterned couch. "They always considered Mendes to be a very dangerous communist, the perfect communist, understand, as dangerous as a snake, capable of killing his whole family with a hammer and sickle. Colonel Ricardo, for example, was scared to death of him."

"How have you been, General?" Captain Mendes inquired obsequiously, smiling amid the rain of hair.

"I hate those bastards so much I don't even want to see a picture of them," the soldier stated. "If I ever catch one in the street at the right time I'll fuck him up good right there."

"We left the barbershop together," the lieutenant colonel said, snuggling into the pillows, "and we went to have some codfish and beans for lunch at a restaurant on Loreto to rehash old times. Incidentally, they've got a red wine there that you've got to take your hat off to."

"As far as I'm concerned, I'd like to shoot the lot of them," the soldier was indignant. "I'd line them up against a wall and bang bang bang bang bang bang bang bang from the first one right down to the last without stopping. You people can laugh if you like, but if it wasn't for socialism there'd be no poverty in Portugal."

"At first I didn't remember anything," the lieutenant colonel explained, "but later on, little by little, things came back. Even the smells, even the sounds, even what was going through my head at the time, so many years before."

Captain Mendes finished first and stayed waiting for him by the door, looking at the buildings on the Avenida da Igreja, chatting with the old man in the smock who was emptying the spittoons and ashtrays, while the manicurist, leaning over, emery board at the ready for the fingers of a man of position, was lovingly perfecting his nails, smoothing his skin, wiggling her shoulders, emitting a string of seductive warbles, exclamations, quivers, laughs. The barber brushed the back of my neck, making me shiver, a drip passed through the obstacle of the towel and descended along my back, Six, seven, eight, how many years for certain? the razor singing over his skin, the Army trucks squealing on the gravel of the parade ground, platoons shaping up, officers running back and forth, the manicurist sank the important man's hands into a little glass of soapy water, and there were Colonel Ricardo's squeals of panic on the telephone, there were the frightened eyes of majors, my indifference, my boredom, my sleepiness, clumps of hair were going up and down, weightless, in the dim, tarnished shrubbery of the barbershop mirrors, alighting on the scissors in the washbasins, on the gestures, the newspapers, the glass shelves, the price list, the extraordinary breasts of the manicurist, attendants brushed off the customers' shoulders, the little old man brought out a broom from behind a curtain where in a small space piles of towels could be seen, bottles, dozens of razors in their cardboard cases, and out into the street he pushed hair, cigarette butts, almost transparent little pieces of paper, I slept through the whole uprising in spite of the chaplain, in spite of the majors, and when I awoke, cabinet ministers arrested, armored cars, a strange exaltation in the city, soldiers with machine guns on the corners, radios blaring, Captain Mendes leaning toward him over the salt and pepper, The custard here is excellent, would you like to try it, General?

"Why don't you people hide the dead man in the public toilet outside?" the magician's assistant asked. "Dress him up nice and fine, carry him out on your shoulders, sit him down on a toilet, leave, and that will be that."

"That Captain Mendes," the soldier declared, lying alongside the mulatto woman with his face covered by her arm, "must be a royal son of a bitch. Send him to me and I'll take care of him."

"Starting tomorrow you will stay away from the regiment," a guy with thin gray hair and huge shoulder boards said. "We don't want any more adventurism, any more mad ideas in the Army, friend."

"Literally, overnight, General," Captain Mendes lamented, spitting out his olive pits onto the edge of his plate. "As soon as I came on the post they called me to the office, and right there, in front of the sergeants, the colonel started shouting at me, provoking me, insulting me, there'll be no more of this shameful business, no more anarchy, report to the Military-District headquarters, because you've had it."

"Don't worry about it," Melissa the striptease goddess argued, "if you do it carefully, nobody will catch on, just another bunch of drunks walking through the park."

"And in São Sebastião da Pedreira," Captain Mendes said, "I was received at the entrance by a chubby, effeminate little lieutenant who gave me a typewritten piece of paper, Your transfer to reserve status, and he disappeared immediately down the hall, swinging his behind without even giving me time to answer him. I stood there with the piece of paper in my hand like a fool, all alone in the midst of orderlies and stucco cornucopias."

The restaurant extended out onto a kind of glassed-in terrace, with more tables and chairs, potted plants, large clay figures, an image in a niche, pots, hanging clumps of onions, a truck unloading barrels onto the sidewalk across the way, men in shirt-sleeves, the stone-crushing sun of two o'clock: Captain Mendes had unexpected wrinkles around his eyes now, dark creases on his neck, he'd got fatter, a small cylindrical belly was growing just below his ribs, So I'm a civilian, General, I work in my father-in-law's hardware business, I sell locks, keys, hinges, burglar alarms for houses and cars, are you interested in a security system against burglars by any chance?

"It's funny how everything went so fast back to what it was before the coup, Captain," the second lieutenant said. "That's how it was, except for a few walls covered with graffiti and a few dummies who fucked themselves up for nothing."

"You again?" the dumpy little lieutenant was surprised, nervous. "The order from above, as far as your case is concerned, is irrevocable, Mr. Mendes."

"There are only foolish old men on Príncipe Real, half-blind, sunning themselves on benches," the magician's assistant explained, scratching her right hip with her silvery fingernails. "Do you really think anybody's going to take the trouble to look at you?"

"The funniest thing, General, is that at the time they cashiered me I was more innocent than a nun," Captain Mendes said, pushing away the fish bones with his fork. "I got married right after April twenty-fifth, I started getting interested in the hardware business, and I took it easy: revolutions, you see, conspiracies, Leninism, the working class, all that bother, didn't rouse me one fucking bit."

Not just fatter, the lieutenant colonel thought with the second carafe of red wine, but less energetic, less sure of himself, with less hot air, softer, with the smile of an altered tomcat, the voice of an altered tomcat, the eyes of an altered tomcat, a signet ring on his finger, a silver cigarette lighter, gray hairs, tailor-made clothes, the oily, friendly manner of a merchant, a sudden, unexpected tolerance, no sharp corners, no edges, no uncomfortable, discourteous, bothersome remarks: The fact is, he got old too, the second lieutenant suggested, he got tired of this shitty country too, he left the rebellion up to schoolboys too.

"Nowadays, if a person rebels," the soldier stated, "it's by writing son of a bitch on the walls of the subway and that's all. But if anybody has any doubts, I'd give that guy a good whack on the noggin."

"Business is good," Captain Mendes was pleased, "because car alarms are selling like hotcakes. We're agents for a whole bunch of foreign businesses, in five or six months we're going into computers. When you come right down to it, General, my getting kicked out of the Army was a damned-good piece of luck."

"Let me fix his tie," one of the little blond girls demanded, taking hold of the dead man's neck. "I was a clerk in a department store, there's nobody here who can tie a tie like me."

The sound of the conversations in the restaurant rose and fell and wavered like the sea, numerous, multiple, small, the truck that was unloading barrels onto the street across the way left, through the windows of the terrace a florist's shop could be seen, a pawnbroker's, a clinic, a boardinghouse, the graceless buildings of Lisbon, the faded grass dried out by dog urine, the implacably blue sky, the entrance to a laboratory with a doorman stretching by the entrance, the waiter alongside them, expectant, Do you want some coffee, General?, Captain Mendes offered with an urbane gesture, they put the communications officer's shoes and socks on, the wound in his back had stopped bleeding, the tear that the knife had made in his shirt was barely noticeable, the mulatto woman combed his hair, holding her nose with her free hand, His glasses, damn it, the second lieutenant remembered, put his glasses in his pocket, One coffee and one Nescafé, Captain Mendes ordered, lifting his nose toward the waiter, they have an excellent liqueur here, how about it? the fellow in the pawnshop was struggling to open his shutters, a window full of watches, another with toasters, gold chains, necklaces, and radios, We're thinking about an optical section for next year, Captain Mendes announced with pride, in case the government, of course, extends some convenient protection for private enterprise, what have they done for business so far? and the lieutenant colonel, aloud, Yes, a liqueur, and to himself, appalled, The way people change, Jesus, What would you expect, General? Captain Mendes said energetically, if we want to be part of Europe we've got to take some initiatives, we've got to keep up with the foreigners, and inside the shop a confused, tumultuous, abandoned shadow of objects, Where could his glasses have gone? the twin with the Cesarean wondered, has anyone seen the guy's glasses?, It's funny how the dead become serious with time, the lieutenant colonel thought, surprised, looking at the deceased, this fellow's face has turned to stone in just a few hours, The nationalization of banks, for example, Captain Mendes discoursed, annoyed, besides being stupid, is an economically catastrophic recourse, numbed soldiers getting into the Mercedes trucks, into the personnel carriers, into the jeeps, machine guns, bazookas, recoilless cannons covered with oilskin sheaths, Captain Mendes barking orders on the parade grounds, the heroic morning full of the echo of boots on the gravel, the chaplain moaning They're going to outlaw pilgrimages to Fátima, they're going to outlaw mass on Sundays, they seated the communications officer on a chair to fix him up better, And the labor laws we have, just let any businessman dare, tell me if I'm wrong, invest, make his business grow, create job opportunities, But wasn't this guy there? the lieutenant colonel thought, confused, hadn't this guy demanded all that? really, the only thing that's worth anything now is writing son of a bitch in the subway, the liqueur slid down his throat with a pleasant burning sensation, smoothly, If I were on active service, he reflected, the one who'd pull off a military coup now would be me, I'd storm into Edite's apartment, tear up her dresses with a bayonet, break her ivory peacocks into a thousand pieces, tomorrow the barber again, the newspaper again, the communications officer's head kept bouncing listlessly on his chest, the movies again, the silent dinners again, tense with indifference, threats, hatred, I just so happen to be looking for a man with experience in personnel relations for the optical project, Captain Mendes said with a conspiratorial smile, there would be a basic salary and a percentage of sales, after so many years of command, why don't you give the matter some thought, General? the cloud of perfume was spreading boutiques all over Lisbon, organizing fashion shows, paying for ads on television, setting up a factory in Barcelos, he had two more glasses of the liqueur that no longer burned his throat, only a delicate dullness in his body, his fingers groping on the glass, and a heavy satisfaction in his blood, he patted Captain Mendes on the back, laughed, That's good, at several off-color jokes, stammered, hesitated, accepted the position, There you are, Melissa the striptease goddess said, with one last tug on the dead man's tie, now you can get rid of him in the toilet whenever you want, Come around to the company tomorrow, General, Captain Mendes gave him a hug, so we can get this matter all set up, so I can introduce you to my father-in-law, I'll get home, the lieutenant colonel decided, tripping over his shoelaces, and I'll bark into her puss, I've got a job, and I'll tell her to go to hell Stick your money up your ass, you shitty old bag, Captain Mendes got into a huge, luxuriously chromed car, replete with antennae and accessories, you pushed one button and the windows opened, you pushed a second button and the windows closed, you pushed a third button and auxiliary headlights came out of the hood, you pushed a fourth and a little mahogany bar rose up trembling out of the plush upholstery, the automobile went off with a dull hum of reactors, took flight, turned down the Avenida da Igreja, disappeared around the corner of a movie theater, the lieutenant colonel returned to the apartment on foot, spirits high, but the effects of the liqueur were rapidly dwindling in his head, the insults to his wife disappeared one by one in his mouth, his steps stopped weaving, the satisfaction of moments before evaporated, his frothy bones hardened again, he reached the neighborhood along the green painted wall of a stadium, and the one-handed man at the newsstand greeted him, shops, garages, a tiny bookstore in whose belly uncertain shapes were moving, the bakery, closed at that time, kids playing in a kind of park, building entrances, the drugstore, a digestive rest in the empty taverns, bark into your puss I've got a job, tell her to go to hell Stick the money up your ass, you shitty old bag, Lord barking, Clarisse dropping her teacup, Edite looking at him with eyes round with surprise, veneration, fear, sudden respect, he put the key in the door, went up on the elevator with a well-dressed couple who were arguing in low voices, fierce and stiff, showing their sharp canine teeth, capable of devouring each other, growling, in front of me, The way people who live together hate each other, the lieutenant colonel thought, the way people who live together at best put up with each other, the man's quivering nostrils were steaming, one of the woman's knees was trembling with rage, the hairs of his overcoat and her stole were standing on end like the angry backs of two cats, the guy was twisting a brown glove in his hand, whispering indistinct phrases, while his enemy, with a dazzling hairdo, was delving into her purse in search of a dagger or a mirror, I'll get off up there and tell her right to her puss I'm going to work in optics, you whore, separate my things because I'm going back to Sapadores tomorrow, and the cloud of perfume, weeping, clutching him, really hanging onto him, stroking his hair, Don't do that, sweet, don't abandon me, don't leave me, Dames are like that, the soldier philosophized, the more you whack them the more they love you, the alcohol was evaporating, the exaltation of a few hours ago had given way to a sullen and cloudy melancholy, in the vestibule, while he was hanging his jacket on the rack, the lieutenant colonel heard the voices of Edite and Clarisse, who were whispering in the living room, the poodle came to sniff his ankles silently, its dark nails scratching his shoes, Beat it, don't bother me, scram, and the animal ended up sitting down on its hindquarters, pensively rubbing its ear with its paw, the washing machine was shaking in the kitchen, swishing sheets, the clothes on the line on the inner balcony were fluttering, there was dirty china on the stone-topped table and a mixer had fallen to the floor beside a cupboard, the smell of hot bread and rolls, sideboards with pigeonholes in the hallway, dishes in lighted niches, I got a job, damn it, you can stick the boutiques up your fart-hole, and there were the two of them, sitting on the living-room sofa without even looking at him, heads together, conspiring, surrounded by huge, sickening sprigs of gladioli in ceramic vases, Clarisse paler and thinner every time, talking about illnesses, Edite, with platinum ringlets down her back, her front wide open with a low neckline and lace, the lieutenant colonel took the timid, oblique step of a crab forward on the rug, leaned over to pick up a cigarette and lighter from a silver box, thought, Don't they even see me or are they ignoring me on purpose? they'd placed the tray of tea on a table in front of them, cookies, crumpets, toast, rolls, Just imagine, I met a former captain of mine, very close to me, who's set up a complicated business, he reported, and his voice was growing weaker, hesitating and starting up again on the edge of extinction, like the flame of a stearin candle in a draft, he's asked me to manage a branch of his business (Not like that, damn it!), and I start work with him tomorrow (he lighted the cigarette with difficulty), don't you people think that's a great piece of news?, Clarisse swallowed a sip and was lost on the opposite wall, most interested in a painting of an old woman squatting on a stool and fanning the pale embers in a clay fireplace, Edite stared at him for an instant, frowning, as if he were some kind of insect, raised her eyebrows to the sky, turned her eyes away, shrugged her shoulders, turned to her friend, And when is it they're going to operate on your myoma, she asked.

"The best thing would be to hold him up under each arm," Melissa the striptease goddess said, "and the third one can go in back just in case: pulling here, pushing there, taking the place of one of the others if he has to. And as soon as you've finished, bring me a little bottle of eau-de-vie on the way back, I've got a thirst the likes of which you've never seen."

"A corpse in a pantry isn't an everyday affair," the fat inspector informed the reporters on the landing as they took notes, took pictures, held up the microphone wires. "Generally, as you gentlemen are quite aware, murderers will take the precaution of dragging them far away from the scene of the crime. And, then, the tenant of the apartment has disappeared."

"Since you're such an expert, damn you," the second lieutenant was excited, "just explain to me how you give the gate to a dwarf."

"According to the concierge, a person of the greatest responsibility," the fat man said, "a real gentleman. No, we're not discounting the theory that he was killed too."

"Goodbye, I've had enough, thank you very much, it was great, so long?" the second lieutenant roared, scarlet, shaking the soldier by the sleeves. "You're sick in the head, Abílio, you can't even dream what a leech she is."

"Or an accomplice, of course," the fat man admitted, puffing up his jowls like a turkey. "As we begin, gentlemen, no possibility is being overlooked."

"A little eau-de-vie to cleanse the stomach," the magician's assistant repeated, "really more refreshing than anything else. A drink that lifts up your heart, helps your liver, something that will send us away in a good mood."

"She clings to me like a tick," the second lieutenant lamented, "she shows up at my job at all hours, making me have lunch and dinner with her, she's suspicious of any woman, she's jealous of everything, she threatens, whines, cries, makes scenes, gets the whole building stirred up, I've already changed secretaries twenty times, even my getting together with you guys was a tragedy. And now, since she's got it into her head to have a child, all that's left is for her to lock me up on the back balcony like an animal."

"So far we don't know very much," the fat man said. "He works for an insurance company, he hasn't got a police record, he got divorced from one of the biggest names in the country. Until a few months ago his mother or his sister would come by here to take care of his laundry, do the cleaning."

"If you don't hold him around the waist the guy will only keep falling down," one of the twins advised, tucking in the dead man's shirt, smoothing his hair, picking up his glasses from the floor. "Pretend he's a girl friend, get worked up, hug him."

"A bottle or two," the inert mulatto woman added, spread liquidly on the bed like a dish of pudding. "Maybe it will help me get rid of the guy's smell."

"A job as manager, tomorrow," the lieutenant colonel grew faintly animated, the cigarette forgotten between his fingers, "fifty contos base pay, working expenses, a percentage of sales, trips abroad in first-class hotels, a car, what do you people think of that, by God?"

"The doctor still hasn't decided," Clarisse answered, "he wants to repeat the tests, he wants to see me again. Two weeks at the most, I think."

Captain Mendes's business was in Cabo Ruivo, beyond the oil tanks, next to the abandoned seaplane, halfway between the docks and the train tracks sunk in weeds and stones, where, rotting on the slopes, broken-down freight cars stood. There were no seagulls or rats or river birds because the water, pasty and motionless, had died and it stank, hugging the wooden warehouses and the keels of trawlers, the breath of corpses spread through the air, a shantytown in back was spread out irregularly along a strip of land, its twisted shacks like sick molars, rising and falling in garbage gums, broken crates, pieces of cardboard, cracked bidets, baby carriages without wheels, an ancient car sunk in the mud without doors or windows, its hood up, like the mouth of a hippopotamus, over tonsils of cylinders and wires. He got out of the taxi, with the driver protesting, angry, stuck crosswise in a puddle, without looking at his tip, he splashed away through pools of dark mud where dark clouds rolled, reflecting the dark sky, huge, fat rats scurried through the bushes, a myopic dying dog was pointing the jelly of its eye toward no one in particular, he passed an abandoned house, a wall in ruins, a tractor reduced to a skeleton of rusty iron, he pushed open a gate, stumbled up a slippery ramp, and came out onto a dirty terrace, with three or four trucks around a decrepit little building, looking empty, with a sign proudly proclaiming Assis & Mendes, Ltd. under the crumbling eaves, and there inside, sitting motionless behind dusty desks that faced each other in a leprous room, an old man with shaggy eyebrows, vest and watch chain, squashing piles of invoices with his fat hands, and Captain Mendes, squeezing a blackhead on his nose, holding a little round mirror with the photograph of a naked woman on the other side in his free hand.

"Look natural, damn it," the magician's assistant roared from above, leaning over the windowsill. "You all look like you've swallowed a broomstick."

"Well, well, please come in," Captain Mendes greeted him, effusive, putting down the little mirror, "you haven't met my father-in-law, have you?"

The seaplane, in the distance, looked like a toy, a distant carbon flame was burning on the metal top of the chimney at the oil refinery, the river was like a cream pudding, without any definite color, thick with sugar, the old man's eyebrows, Pleased to meet you, General, came together with the look of an accomplice, the collar and cuffs, not too clean, were twisted on his body, Optical Division? the lieutenant colonel thought, what the hell am I doing here? the communications officer's body was dancing between them, held by the tendons and joints of his limbs, they had to stop on almost every step of the stairs to Príncipe Real in order to get a better grip on him, to catch their breath, to rest, the leaves on the trees were brushing their heads now, This guy smells like shit at low tide, the soldier said, the mulatto woman's right, damn it, this guy smells like all the sewers in the city put together, in the adjoining room a muffled typewriter was beating along with worn-out keys and the lieutenant colonel pictured a woman with no breasts, all yellow and sad, installed in a cranny of a room copying an endless memorandum with a single stiff finger, he pictured Clarisse's mocking smile, Edite's superior smile, the portholes of the seaplane were little round eyes making fun of me, In six months we'll be bringing out microscopes and sunglasses, Captain Mendes's father-in-law announced proudly, trying in vain to open a warped drawer, bear with me for just a minute while I show you some catalogues, seen from above the fountain the buildings were joined to each other like fingers, a microscopic lady was walking a dog that could barely be seen, tiny little cars were going slowly down the street, We're not going to be able to cross the park with him on our backs, the second lieutenant was alarmed, pretty soon he's going to slip out of our hands into a flower bed, everybody knows that dead people's skin, Captain, is more slippery than an eel's, everybody knows that dead people's skin gives off a little green sweat like a caterpillar's, Here it is, in Japanese and in English, the not-too-clean old man said, triumphantly exhibiting an illustrated pamphlet, do you happen to know any foreign languages, General?, That over there on the other side of the river, those little buildings wrapped in a fog of smoke, the lieutenant colonel thought, isn't Barreiro, it's Seixal, it doesn't look like factories, shipyards, docks, a guy on a bicycle was pedaling down there, on the highway, appearing and disappearing behind mounds of rubbish, pursued by an irate pack of dogs, Are you going to sell dark glasses from door to door like a Gypsy? Edite inquired sardonically, are you going to force microscopes on neighborhood haberdashers?, These quarters are temporary, Captain Mendes assured him, next week we're opening a new office in the Chiado, That is, the lieutenant colonel explained to me resting openmouthed on a bench with the communications officer's body almost hanging over him, a fifth-floor walk-up on the Rua Garrett, above a store that sold accordions, guitars, violins, electric organs, xylophones, and drums, which whined all the time in a flow of thunderous music, just as run-down, rotten, and ancient as the building beside the river, large rooms with high, musty ceilings, splotches of mold defacing the paint, floorboards that groaned and broke underfoot, and, as for the rest, you see, there were the same two dusty desks, Captain Mendes picking blackheads off his nose, the father-in-law triumphantly showing me his worm-eaten catalogues, and the infernal typewriter slowly leaping from key to key with anguishing pauses, during which you held your breath, your heart stopped, your muscles became suspended in the middle of a movement, waiting for the relief of the next letter, which would appear at last, with a dull little thud, just like the contraction of a dying gill.

"We found him in the pantry on the Rua da Mãe d'Água, gentlemen, we found him in a toilet," the fat inspector explained to the reporters. "A single corpse in two different places is more common than you think."

"It isn't just the smell, it's the weight," the soldier lamented, wiping his sleeve. "I've never seen a guy as heavy as stone like our lieutenant, Captain."

And there was the smell of the shrubbery and the plants in the garden, the squat red pear of a sun drifting between two branches, a gasoline pump, the awnings of antique shops, alleys that descended unexpectedly, almost straight down toward the river, an enormous cedar tree, characters on benches with canes, nobody paid any attention to them, nobody noticed the body, Being in reserve status is exactly the same as being dead, the lieutenant colonel thought, they'd fixed up a third desk for him and the three of them stayed there the whole day, not looking at each other, watching the pigeons on the balcony and the buildings across the way, the tonalities that would change, move, light up, grow dark in the sky, until a small Oriental arrived, with a necktie and an artificial smile, expressing himself in the oxygenated language of a deep-sea diver, who took more catalogues out of a briefcase, more pamphlets, more single pages with charts and illustrations, more incomprehensible advertising, they picked up the corpse again, headed like hoboes in the direction of the toilet, Our agent in Tokyo, Captain Mendes announced pompously, our representative in Japan, Better selling glasses from door to door, Clarisse conceded generously, cookie in hand, than sitting there doing nothing, as far as I'm concerned, a husband shut up at home all day would make a nervous wreck out of me, and after the Chinaman came crates and crates of microscopes, pens, magnifying glasses, radio sets, recorders, toys, calculators, pocket computers, cheap useless objects from a bazaar, assorted baubles, the floor was covered with straw and tissue paper, the man in the tie would exhibit the objects with the gestures of a magician before lining them up carefully on a blanket, the typewriter went on along its stumbling way from syllable to syllable, *Glu glu glu glu glu glu,* the man from Tokyo oxygenated, I thought about everything except his getting involved in smuggling, the cloud of perfume said, upset, in spite of socialism there are still some honest jobs around, What if some person, some dog gets suspicious, the second lieutenant thought, frightened, they'll call the police and we'll have had it: the communications officer lost a shoe and they had to load him onto another bench in order to put it on, the beard was growing on his sucked-in cheeks, purplish lumps ran across his wrists, his nails looked like a parrot's claws, The way dead people are resigned, the soldier said to himself, surprised, the way dead people are obedient and calm, and yet it's impossible not to notice the smell, not to tell from his paleness that he's dead, You'll be in charge of the distribution and control of the merchandise, General, Captain Mendes ordered, we're going to hide all this in the warehouse by the river, the office here will be left for two or three little unimportant legal agencies, Democracy is good for people getting disentangled, the father-in-law added, winking, the Treasury police today aren't what they used to be, and, besides, the sergeant (another wink) is from my part of the country and a buddy of mine, understand?

"One fine morning," the cloud of perfume related, serving herself from a sparklingly clean silver-rimmed teapot, "we hadn't even had breakfast yet, both asleep in bed, it must have been six or six-thirty, judging by the light in the window, twenty to seven at most, and bang, bang, bang, horrible pounding on the door, you can imagine the fright it gave the neighbors, you can imagine my fright, Lord barking like crazy, the lock bursting with a loud noise, broken, I sat up in bed, reached for my robe, and right then, into the room, elbowing each other, slipping on the rug, knocking my things over, came eight or nine hoodlums in uniform carrying rifles, led by a tall man with his shirttail out and a holster on his belt, who was aiming a horrible big pistol at Artur, So it's Japanese tape recorders, is it, so we finally caught up with you, eh boy?"

"In spite of everything," the fat inspector declared, blowing his nose, "the pantry version, as far as you can decide anything in matters like this, seems to have more credibility than the other."

"Is the toilet that enclosure over there in the middle of the geraniums, Lieutenant?" the soldier asked. "That rusty little balcony just beyond the trees?"

"Good heavens," the green lady moaned in fright, forgetting her sugar, terribly shocked.

"Hurry up and get dressed, my dears," the man with the pistol ordered, "we've got the patrol wagon waiting downstairs."

"*Glu glu glu,*" the little yellow fellow smiled, pointing to a crate of transistors.

"Here are your subordinates, General," Captain Mendes said, introducing him to a pair of obtuse rhinoceroses, enormous and browless, who, with the help of crowbars, were making the nails squeal on the two crates.

"We couldn't get another pair like these," the father-in-law amplified, "they've both done twenty years in the penitentiary."

"Do you want us to bring you breakfast in bed with flowers?" the man with the pistol was impatient. "Get a move on out of that fart-sack, I've got other things to do."

"The toilet is still a good hundred yards from the building," the inspector explained. "Dragging a corpse there, going up the fountain steps, crossing a street and a park, and even then avoiding the eyes of the guard takes a lot of doing."

The following day the lieutenant colonel went back to the warehouse by the river, escorted by the former penitentiary guests in a truck where, when they hit a bump, microscopes and glasses would rattle: it had rained and the tires skidded and spun in vain on the mud and wet grass, a family of Gypsies was having lunch beside a skinny donkey, successive copper-colored clouds were rolling across the slanted sky, just like the ceiling of an attic, the seaplane was rocking as if it were going to break away from the dock like a great swollen and rotten piece of fruit, the flame from the refinery was fumigating things with thick swirls of carbon, No, I didn't wonder about anything, no, I didn't have any doubts, I wanted to be able to throw the salary in Edite's puss, I wanted to shout at her Go fuck yourself, I don't need you, a week later we began the distribution, I would record what came in and what went out, the poor victims of the penitentiary carried the items here and there, Loures, Mafra, Torres Novas, Alcácer, so many computers, so many watches, so many calculators, we would check the money when they got back, the three of us sitting at a wobbly table, on Mondays and Thursdays Captain Mendes, still complaining about freedom, communists, democracy, elections, trade unions, would come to Cabo Ruivo to oversee the remittances and the escudos, the dogs in the shantytown barked, indignant at the sunset, the rhinoceroses, suddenly timid, huddling in a corner, would drink, sharing a jug of white wine, stray cats made noise in the garbage on the other side of the tumbledown walls, The little list for next week, Captain Mendes said, almost everything to Ericeira and Sintra, the bulb in the ceiling multiplied the shadows and put them out of focus, faint lights trembled in Seixal, we reached the edge of the toilets and went down the worn, slippery steps, sliding on litter, it smelled like a zoo, an artificial anus, abandonment, and a stable, the watchman, cap on the back of his head, was nodding on a plank bench, a row of porcelain basins aligned at fly level, separated by vertical marble slabs, white tile, insults written in pencil or scratched with penknives on the doors, a beggar buttoning up, lighting a cigarette, leaving, his jacket and pants flapping around his body like filthy cotton fins, at times the mist that rose from the river would smother the warehouse, diffuse shapes swam in a colorless phosphorescence, Please get in, my dears, please get in, the one with the pistol invited with a broad, clownish gesture, pointing to a van with barred windows that was blocking traffic on the street, At seven in the morning, blear-eyed, hair undone, no makeup on, her jacket thrown over her shoulders, Edite looked like a stumbling, dying sixty-year-old woman to me, like a snakeskin hanging on the shrubbery of her bones, we left the communications officer in the first available toilet, went back to the park, and from above (Now, will you just tell us where all that Japanese shit came from, my dear fellow?), a view of the mist from the Tagus covering the benches, the flower beds, the retirees, the trees, the buildings on Príncipe Real, the fountain, the Rua da Mãe d'Água, the body of the mulatto woman leaning out, so that barely distinguishable, in the room or on the river, was the outline of the seaplane, lightly swaying by the dark stone of the dock, just like an anchored albatross.

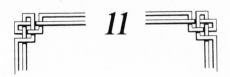

# 11

I KNEW that he'd died even before they told me anything, because neither they nor I, as long as I've been alive, said or say anything, just as I know that sometimes he slept with a woman at the other end of the city, far away from the river, in a place beside some woods or some bushes (and the leaves of the trees tremble in my blood), surrounded by crows and trains. When they brought me my breakfast coffee and roll at ten o'clock he was already dead and the face of the usual maid was only the face of the usual maid, a face as indifferent as my father's when I was small, in Beira, with all those pine trees and those granite walls squeezing my chest, I was sitting on the lowest step of the vegetable garden with a piece of mica in my hand and my father, enormous, was in the shed, uncoupling the donkey from the cart full of straw, hitching the animal to a ring in the wall, giving it a pat on its rump, coming out, and the flies, and the heat, and the smell of trampled figs and urine. I thought He's going to stroke my head, but the gigantic shoes and pants passed by me without stopping, and there was the slanting shadow of the chestnut and another vineyard after our vineyard, separated by a barrier of loose stones, more barriers, springtime, scattered donkey dung here and there, the outline of the mountain range very far away and my hatred for them all throughout the afternoon, growing, spreading like the brook in January.

I also knew of my father's death before a neighbor woman called me to my grandmother's house on the dark alley behind the station or what would come to be the station, with a clock, scale, ticket office in one corner, in a cubicle with a little iron grill and a man in a cap, a flag and a cornet in his hand, and I remember, because it wasn't lunchtime yet and it was hot, a nest of wasps was buzzing in a hole beside us, my blind sister and me, squatting on the ground, each with her piece of mica in her hand, dividing the light into dozens of little colored beams, and then I suddenly sensed his death in my blood and had a heavy urge to urinate in my bladder, and when the neighbor woman appeared in her apron at the top of the alley, I already knew the exact words she was going to say, the exact expression, the surprising, oily tenderness with which people speak to orphans, the smell of not-much-water and sweat and earth of the poor. My blind sister began to weep for no reason, as happened with her on so many occasions, because of a change in smells, or the tonality of the wind, or because of an unexpected coolness on her skin, a low sobbing, almost noiseless, almost without tears in her empty eyes. There were old women staring at us without emotion from the doorways, only out of curiosity or indifference, She sensed it already, poor thing, the neighbor woman explained, and I can report that old women's homes are just as old inside, dark as the inside of a barrel, with portraits and furniture scattered about according to the secret order of the years. The neighbor woman picked up my sister without understanding that she was crying because the horizontal cello sound of the wasps coming and going and climbing over each other in the hole had disappeared, and I noticed the restlessness of the sheep and the goats and the cows, looking at everybody with their big round frightened eyes. In my grandmother's house, below the market square, where shreds of tissue paper were always floating, running up against the posts of the tumbledown stalls and the columns of the church, I saw men with their hats in their hands, outside, rolling cigarettes, I saw figures that appeared and disappeared in the windows, I saw an enormous silence inside the silence of the people and trees, I saw trousers and skirts that drew aside to let us pass, lighted tallow candles in saucers on the tables and the sideboards, swinging their hips through the nighttime of the house as they wouldn't have dared on the square in the March morning, and on the big bed, with a yellow crocheted bedspread, under the hazy picture of a man with a mustache, gravely seated on a kind of throne, I saw my father, wearing a jacket and tie, a rosary entwined in his fingers, a handkerchief tied around his jaw, and a coin on each eyelid, calmer and more peaceful than I had ever seen him, with his Sunday boots at the bottom of the sheet, and maybe even capable at last of touching me on the head, taking an interest in me, resting his hand on my shoulder, if my mother and my aunts and my grandmother let him, because they all held him prisoner with their wails and the gestures of their displeasure, hair uncombed and dressed in black, leaping around him in the filthy theatrics of misfortune. My blind sister, stretched out on the floor, stopped crying and came along feeling her way, smiling, her blank eyes vibrating with joy, toward the bed, her hands in front of her, testing the air like antennae, until she stood stock still, inches from my dead father, from having sniffed a different odor in the air no doubt, that rotten-chestnut and mud and chicken-house smell of dead people, and somebody then lifted her up under the arms and carried her quickly out to the square, like a chicken being carried into the backyard to have its head chopped off, my father's setter broke into howls amid the paper and trash that March had mingled, and my mother fell down at the foot of the bed, held up by the compassion of the neighbor women, her face tightened in a grimace of aversion or sorrow.

That he'd died from a shot I only learned later, after the burial, when we were returning home in a column through the village, in the middle of the afternoon, with the priest in front of us sprinkling holy water left and right with a holm-oak branch, and right then I heard the explosion of the shot in my ears and the quail of my sweat rose in panic, and the fields of my body echoed their surprise from pigsty to pigsty, and the rabbits of my teeth grew round with fear, I heard the shot coming from the eucalyptus grove on the edge of the mountains and I saw my father fall off the seat of the cart onto the load of firewood, I saw the donkey continue his trot along the trail and the tree trunks calmed down again, the crickets which had been singing in the earth emerged again from the roots of the raspberry bushes, the branches in the woods calmed down, I saw the other man leap, with the gun under his arm, over a gate, another gate, another gate, and disappear at a run among the brown leaves of the cornfield, I saw his pale narrow nose and open mouth, his dirty beret, just like the fuzzy lining of a purse, and I recognized him among those who, in their Sunday best on that sunny Wednesday, accompanied my mother, my grandmother, my aunts home, avoiding the hens pecking at the sand and the tails of the animals rhythmically swarming with flies in the wine-covered shadows of the corrals.

And two or three years later, during the month of my first menstruation, when the man in the beret married my mother, I knew without having heard their conversation that they would send my blind sister away to an asylum in Viseu, that the bed in the room next to mine would begin to sigh and sway for nights on end once more, that the walls would vibrate like beehives from the mute anxiety of their combat, and I hated them just as minutely, just as carnivorously as I hated his huge shoes and pants that passed by without touching me, just as I hated the November cold and the rain outside pounding on the roof with the force of a catastrophe. I hated the gun hanging on a hook behind the door along with the cartridge belt and the knapsack and the beret, and in April or May, weeks after my sister had left and the gun was settled in our house, with the smell of my father's blood circulating in the veins of the barrels and the thunder that killed him still echoing in the trigger and the butt and the complicated iron fittings, with carvings and designs, of the weapon, I was sitting in the reeds by the bank, looking at the water, and the frogs the color of the water, and the mud the color of the frogs kneading the pebbles, and I heard the sound of earth being trod behind me and stones and clumps of mud rolling down the embankment, and I turned and looked, and my stepfather was taking off his vest, his shirt, his pants, unlacing his boots and coming toward me, without a word, blowing strongly through the fife of his lips, with his quail-hunting bitch trotting at his heels, and he was so skinny and fragile and ridiculous that no one would ever have said he was capable of killing a man of such absolute indifference as my father, and he sat down beside me and grabbed me by the shoulders and made me lie down, and he smelled of gunpowder, of dog fleas, and the sheets in my home, my hair mixed with the weeds, my behind mixed with the shale, a toad slipped by my ear with the heavy, sick walk of the village druggist, and I received his weight on my body, I embraced his lower back and closed my eyes in order to hate him even more, with a hatred as great as the cries of owls during the insomnia of August, roosting on street corners and in deserted garrets, announcing the afflictions of the dead to those dwelling in the houses.

And after he got dressed and went away, with the dog nosing his feet and his testicles, damp from me, hidden in the folds of his long underwear, while I was washing his medlar juice and the violet, almost black stains off my thighs, I perceived that that week, or the next, or the next, or the next my mother and he would send me away on the train, much farther away than the farther away I could conceive of at that time, much farther away than Viseu, or Santar, or Tondela, or Mangualde, or Mortágua, or the villages from which the silversmiths came on market days, carrying suitcases of earrings, gold chains, rings, pins, and silver rowboats behind their saddles. They said goodbye to me at the station without touching me, as if my mute hatred for them was a skin disease, they gave me a cardboard suitcase with clothes and a basket of food to last me through the trip, and after hours and hours of tumbling over hills and passing between houses, pastures, flag stops, clusters of buildings, ruins of castles, and the astonished silence of the fields, I got off in Lisbon, in the steam of the brakes and the horrible metallic squeals of protest, in a place like an enormous church, full of railroad cars, newspapers, baggage, noise, and the Lady, with an umbrella, tall, serious, grave, dressed in a way that was so strange to me, like that of images in processions, was waiting for me with the Husband, watching people getting off with the sharp, quick eyes of a bird, until she spotted me, touched my arm with her glove, called the Husband, who was mopping the sweat off his neck with an enormous handkerchief, and they took me to their home behind what much later would become the amusement park and was at that time a vacant lot surrounded by dizzying buildings of three or four stories, full of windows and strange balconies, and there they gave me an apron, gray uniforms, and a starched cap for my head, the likes of which I never could have imagined, and they told me You're going to be a maid, and they taught me how to serve at the table, dust, polish metal, put a thousand and one objects into a thousand and one drawers, iron and fold clothing, and they fixed me up a closet with a mirror next to Cook's closet and a bed next to hers in the room behind the pantry, and I spent the whole night, and several nights after that night, awake in the dark, listening to the tiny, almost inaudible footsteps of the rats, who trotted among the packages of pasta, salt, barley, smelling the new, unknown odor of the pillowcase, startled by the creaking of the furniture and the sleeping and the coughing, and the strange and frightening vibrations from the street, and thinking about my blind sister in the asylum in Viseu, without any mica, or wasps, or dark alleys, or familiar voices scolding or inviting her, walking hand in hand with other blind children in a graveled playground, she, too, hiding her rage and her hatred inside the eggshells of her empty eyes.

I never again had a man inside me because my body closed, and I felt it close many years ago, fifty or sixty, like fat flowers at night, because the lips between my legs closed with the soft and insistent selfishness of corollas after my stepfather pierced me and perforated me and brushed my chest and stomach with his fingers stained with my father's fright and my mother's intimate liquor, that waxy serum that I secrete sometimes if I touch myself, feeling in the fork of my thighs a damp worm that hardens and quivers, stuck to the pelvic bone, until a kind of sob grows inside of me, a quick little spasm contracts my muscles and my skin, my teeth gnash in my mouth like a fork against another fork, and my insides quiet again, pacified, in an enormous weariness, without hatred finally, devoid of rancor, only the stickiness of sweat under my arms, in my groin and the joints of my limbs, and my heart running very fast from out of my trunk like a dog, chasing its own tail of blood. I never again possessed any man because their urgency, their hands and their hair, the heavy bones of the mushrooms and lichens of their own death inside, because their small, sterile paps, dry as raisins, all sicken me, and those pendulous dark sacks hanging down below, swinging when they walk, almost coming out of their bellies like the navels of newborn babies. I'm not just talking about the morning, or afternoon, or evening when my stepfather lay on top of me and broke the watery membranes of my belly with the sharp edge of his plow, because it wasn't just that time on the bank that I gave in, but also a lot of other times, in order to hate him more, in the donkey's wine-colored stable, with the animal's shit falling on my knees from time to time, on the man's back, on his shoulders, the back of his head, my throat, on the brick threshing floor of the mill up there, from where you can see the village and the mountains and the fields turn blue and mysterious like the blue and mysterious cheeks of sick people who can see beyond objects and through them and subvert the relative distance of things, and up to the last coitus, on my parents' bed that sighs, swollen with straw, as if the sunset wind were slowly blowing inside the cover, and while my stepfather moved and arched, sinking my body, and I gripped his legs with my legs and his trunk with my elbows and nails, hearing once again the explosion, seeing my father falling from the seat of the cart onto the load of firewood, I would bury my eyes in the ceiling and hate them silently, fiercely, all of them, the people in the village, my relatives, my blind sister, and myself, I hated myself so much that I couldn't even face myself in the shard of a mirror in the living room, out of rage at the face and the mouth and the hair that rose, out of focus, in the glass, implacably returning my fury to me with unbearable intensity. And then I discovered, with a strange feeling, that there were two, the one who was observing herself and the one who was observing me, the one I lived in and the other one nobody lived in, so different from what I supposed that I peered at her, and turned, and came back, and tried to surprise her the way you surprise people who think they're alone and in whom we discover expressions and movements different from the usual ones, unpoliced movements, abandoned and free, and yet, even in Lisbon, many years later, in the building by the amusement park, I would find a tense and alert shape in a starched collar and dark uniform, growing old with the same desperate slowness with which I myself was growing old, gray hair, wrinkles, cords of veins around the neck, the body more and more bent, these droplike lumps on the fingers and hands, and the age spots that reproduce and flow together in a kind of milky way of splotches. And I came to Lisbon and never heard from them again, because nobody wrote to me and I didn't write to anybody, I didn't answer the telephone when a telephone was installed, and I put the images of the village and its people out of my head, and if I felt any death in my blood I would expel the dead ones from my thought the way you put out a hunting dog that's come into the house without permission, even my mother, even my stepfather, even my blind sister in the asylum in Viseu, accompanied by hundreds of blind women, motionless in their chairs with dull, panic-stricken eyes, waiting for dinner, but in Beira there is always a blind person, male or female, feeling around with a cane, with infantile wisdom, for some road to take, blind people who sleep in nests in the wall like wasps, huddle in the churchyard in summer like old pigeons on cornices, blind people with rusty tin cans on their knees, not talking, not chatting, not shouting, not playing the guitar or the accordion or the violin, and every time one of them died, a kind of little jump would take place in my body, a vibration in my stomach, a shiver in a finger, menstruation dripping on my clothes before the time for my period, so that almost every day the death agony of blind people would upset me, the silverware and china in the kitchen would slip out of my hands, I would upset a gravy boat on the tablecloth, and the Lady, startled, frowning, What's got into you? and I answering, without words, It's the blind people in the churchyard, ma'am, it's the village between two mountain ranges that's turning loose inside of me, the maze of alleys, sad with flies and shadows and silence and sharp smells without water, It's the winter wind spreading through a row of tree-tops, among the pines, and the snow, and the cold, and my grandmother lovingly lining the walls with little paper saints, it's my father fallen on his back, arms open, on top of the load of firewood, it's all the years of my childhood stored here in pain, and since I could never explain that to the Lady because city people only understand what is understood or what can't be understood, I would then clean the gravy off the tablecloth with a rag soaked in warm water, as if I were attending a woman in the pangs of childbirth, the Husband would twirl his wedding ring around his finger, watching the spot that was disappearing, and once everything was done and the world again spinning like the balance wheel of a watch with majestic slowness, the Lady and the Husband would pick up their spoons again, relieved, swallowing the soup just like mechanical dolls, the chandelier in the ceiling spread a sunlike light, filtered by a thousand glass droplets, and I would go back to the doorway, hands crossed over my navel, hugging against me with all the strength I had the hairy, thin, hateful buttocks of a man.

And twelve or thirteen years later, about the time of the Husband's accident, at a time when the place was beginning to fill up with crucifixes and little shrines, I was washing clothes on the balcony, across from the balconies and windows of other buildings, where women like me, leaning over basins like mine, were washing clothes with the same movements as mine, and I saw a square with a statue, a steep sidewalk, and the trolley car skidding and jumping its tracks, leaping onto the sidewalk amid shouts and yellow sparks, crushing one man, a second man, I saw people running away and hollering, and the car finally coming to a stop, glass breaking, pieces of wood exploding, metal twisting, running into the display window of a bookstore, whose volumes and magazines and newspapers scattered all over the street, and even before the ambulance crew got there with their useless apparatus and their druggist's smocks, I saw him lying prone on the ground, his face as unrecognizable as those in childhood photographs, looking at nothing as if he were still sitting at the table, all proper, watching me clean the lumps of gravy from the tablecloth with a wet rag, his spoon held suspended between the plate and his mouth, and his watch ticking more slowly than the pendulum on the wall clock between a pair of Chinese buffets or consoles or sideboards, a yellow disk that came and went

came and went

came and went

tolling every so often the medieval time in its vertical lignum vitae case.

I hated that one not because he'd done me any harm, not because he would appear in my room if he found me alone, opening and closing his mouth and breathing like a fish, not because of the fingers that felt under my skirt and the soft moans of a puppy dog, but simply because he was a man, because he smelled like my father and my stepfather in spite of the perfume that smelled like perfume, like wine, like shoe leather, like tobacco, like haste. I hated his body slinking into my insides, and the enormous hernia of a testicle that made him try to penetrate sideways, unsuccessfully, the closed corolla of my womb, the lips of my legs that tightened and fused into the soft and stubborn selfishness of a corolla, and in spite of that, or for that very reason, when the corpse arrived from the Morgue, I helped the Lady wash and dress him with a secret joy, a hidden satisfaction, in their bedroom where the springs hadn't squeaked or groaned for many years, under the huge crucifix the size of my whole arm, with the Christ twisting under the nails like a worm, other smaller crucifixes, a gigantic painting showing the Passion, cobwebs of rosaries here and there, and a woman standing on a cloud, her naked heel stepping on a serpent, surrounded by a colored group of tiny angels, just like late-night moths around an oil lamp.

Consequently, I helped the Lady fix him up the way they'd fixed my father up in the village all those years before, and how, in spite of everything, I hope they will fix me up here, in spite of the indifference of the maids and the dislike of the oldest one, the one with the ring of keys on her belt, never smiling, never raising her voice, never softening her eyes. I hope they will tie my wrists with a broad ribbon and fasten my jaw shut with a handkerchief, and lay two large, ancient and almost green copper coins on my eyelids, and I helped the Lady shine his pointed shoes, put on his socks, tighten his tie, light candles with artificial plastic tears at each of the four corners of the bed, avoiding my face in the mirrors and my shape, which pursued me on the polished surfaces, deformed by the convex varnish of the wood, avoiding the other one, the one that's not me and that repeats my movements, and copies my clothes, who is just as afraid of me as I am of her, and then, on the table in the dining room, on top of it, next to the stack of dishes and the dozens of glasses, I set the cold chicken and cakes and wine and cheese and butter for the dead man's friends, for the ones who'd come to pay their respects to the Lady and smoke in the corners, for the women who pray aloud around the corpse, for the young boys who laugh and whisper in low voices and laugh again in the little sitting room in back, and it's strange how the place changed, I thought, how the oil paintings and the furniture and the portraits took on a stiff and artificial unexpected solemnity, the way the blue of the sky is a different blue, more ceremonious and distant, the way the vibration of the sounds hurts me inside my arms, in the cluster of little tubes where the blood flows, I close my eyes and I can see the desperate efforts of the dead man to penetrate my thighs without an opening, the sealing wax of my vagina, the spiral lips of my womb, I close my eyes and my father falls backward off the seat of the cart, onto the load of firewood, while the donkey continues trotting along the trail to the house, pursued from far away by the echo of the shot and the barking of the dogs.

Days after the funeral, when everything had slowly gone back to what it had been before, Cook had an argument with the Lady, she was fired, she received her notice and I stayed on, not because I liked her, but because I really had no place to go except the village whose streets were now mixed up in my head and whose smells and hiding places and shadows I'd slowly forgotten, the village at the end of a railroad line that I didn't know, with flag stops, scoop-wheels, farms, open spaces that I didn't know, the village that certainly wouldn't recognize me and which I certainly wouldn't recognize, since things change in our absence and rot away, the same as people's wants and feelings and will. They certainly must have built buildings like this one here and there, and avenues and parks, and set up horrible motionless statues, and done away with the marketplace, and the cedars in the cemetery, and the brooks, and the trees, so there wouldn't be anything more to hate unless it was ourselves, so that hate doubles back on us, trembling, into our own bodies, like the stinger of an insect, and with no other way out we hang ourselves by a rope from the eucalyptus tree by the well, the one that lifts up the flagstones of the house with the hellish energy of its roots, and brushing the soles of our feet against the surprised faces of the living, of those who still haven't realized how much they hate themselves because there's nothing else to hate, a father, a mother, a handful of aunts, a blind sister attentive to beetles and wasps, smiling or weeping according to the angle of the shadows and the tonality of the smells, not even a distant relative to hate, or a dog, or a trousseau trunk and its smell of starch, or a gun behind the door, or a thin man in long underwear coming toward us through the mud of the bank, nothing to hate, nothing of nothing, absolutely nothing, not the emptiness that swells up in us, piling up hollow clouds like rain over the mountains, preceded by the short, instantaneous, phosphorescent traces of lightning flashes.

So that after the funeral and Cook's leaving at six in the morning so as not to miss the bus to her village or what had once been her village and today was part of the city's suburbs, bristling with buildings and statues and melancholy squares of colorless grass, just the Lady and I and the pictures of the unknown people on shelves and bureaus, nicely resting on their lace doilies, were left in the apartment, she giving me orders from the sofa and I obeying her orders without complaining, cleaning, washing, dusting, receiving the deliveries by the baker and the milkman, buying things at the greengrocer's below or the drugstore on the next block, lighting the stove that spat and vomited scarlet sparks through its sooty pores, and one day, after talking for hours on the telephone in the tone of somebody arguing or convincing, or getting mad, the Lady went out and when she came back she had the Boy with her, a child four or five years old like my blind sister when our father died, but with eyes that saw and caught things, serious and hard and dry like those of lizards in cracks in walls, and we fixed up a room for him in the Husband's study, and we left him sleeping, hugging a rag doll, among chairs and desks and rows of thick books filled with a compact, incomprehensible, tiny little hand, and from time to time, through the night, one of us would get out of bed, slipping unwillingly along the hallway with photographs and clocks, and turn on the light to look at his small, vulnerable body, lying on his side, his fists clenched, the shadow of his lashes on his cheeks, the ribs that went up and down like gills, his features of a man in the incomplete likeness of a child, and the second or third time I observed him I knew, terrified, about his death thirty or thirty-five years later, I knew that it was going to be violent and unexpected and quick and without any suffering, none at all, in a building at the base of a fountain with tall trees crossing branches and shading the top of the roof, I knew that he would die early in the morning among drunken men and women with their bodies sprawled about and that I wouldn't be able to do anything more for him except to know that and be silent, that I wouldn't be able to do anything more for him except witness in silence, tense with fear, the approach of that moment, feeling my blood boiling like nitric acid through the flute holes of my bones, seeing him fall back, unsupported, not onto a load of firewood but onto the dirty pile of a rug, with a blade stuck in his back and all the horror in the world in a soundless moan. So I never hated him, not even on the long rainy afternoons when the surface of everything suddenly takes on the terrible cruelty of mirrors, reproducing me from room to room with an obstinate and sadistic irony, and in which the air wavered around us, strewn with threats, with echoes, and with specters, instead I felt, from the first moment, as if the corolla of my vagina had expelled him from me in one painful, single, slow vegetable contraction of muscles, a kind of son now that I was beginning to be too old to carry something both familiar and foreign in my belly, a microscopic man with a beard and a mustache and an urge to defecate and mute anxieties and fierce joys being constructed piece by piece in the oils of my uterus, a son now that my breasts were sagging and my own blood disobeyed the cycles of the moon and failed, a son in this city that surrounds me on all sides, imprisons me, constrains me, and I finally lay down when the silhouettes of the buildings were illuminated by an ashen light and the municipal workers were crashing garbage cans onto the street, thinking that my father was going to die again in the death of the Boy in fewer months from now than one judges months can last, and when I fell asleep the pines of the village fanned my nerves and the cold of winter dampened the sheets of the mosses and fetuses of an October promise.

And in order to postpone his death and the roar of the gun in my childhood ears, in order to postpone the fear of seeing another body fall inside my body, looking above the sky of my skin with the infinite innocence of the dead, I made him grow carefully, with compotes, and confused prayers, and cookery, and tender warnings, like a crocheted border, and I brought him milk in bed at night and in the morning, and warmed his bath, and hid the piece of chinaware he'd broken, and defended him from the Lady's heavy love with my love for him, as if those poor maneuvers could conjure away the future, as if the course of things could be altered by my useless gestures, as if I could manage to be stronger than the force of inevitability that was written without having been written in the head of my head and in the guts of my guts, and that's why I decided, after a certain time, not to hear anyone or talk to anyone, with the intuition of keeping the blood in me silent, I decided not to ask, not to answer, not to move an arm or leg, not even to look, I decided to become like my blind sister in the asylum in Viseu, shouting mutely all the time until ceasing completely and forever to recognize my own voice.

Therefore, ever since the arrival of the Boy there were three of us at home, not counting the oratories and saints with which the Lady kept surrounding herself more and more, dozens of oratories and hundreds of saints, of wood, plaster, ivory, glass, paper, material I don't know or don't know how to describe, and then they moved the amusement park from the amusement park to here, to the other side of the street, separated from us by a fence and ten or twenty yards of asphalt, and during the whole summer the night was inhabited by a deafening swarm of noises just like those of the loudspeakers of faith healers, and the microphones of those who peddled God and out of a sack drew snakes, white rats, monkeys, and strange little animals, the smoke from the food stands grew sugar sweet around bulbs, rosaries of lights drew near and went away with the wind, swaying like a ship, the ceiling was inhabited by spinning shadows, the Lady took effervescent aspirin at dinner-time, stirring the liquid with a small spoon, complaining about the noise, and at that moment I became aware, surprised, that we were both old, the same age as all old people, that it had become impossible to tell, even after observing us for a long time, which was younger and which was older, I became aware that it was hard for us to walk, that it was hard for us to bend, that our eyes and ears had trouble perceiving images and sounds, and at that time the Boy was already a man, a thin lad with glasses who would always come in and go out without speaking, who wouldn't answer questions, who shut himself up in his room, who avoided the Lady's company, inventing pretexts or without any pretext whatever, the only man in my life that I didn't want to or didn't get to hate, even if he behaved toward me the same as all the others, with the same lack of interest, the same muteness, the same quick steps grinding on the floor, and the same vague, directionless eyes, rather, I loved him because he was like the son I didn't have and therefore he wasn't like anybody, once I had understood very early that all men are like each other in their depression and their weakness, that they all try to delve into our insides with the keys hanging from their bellies, to deposit in us the drop of snot that they're made of, and they all get dressed without looking at us, getting tangled up in the dozens of buttons on their clothes, leaving right away, furtively, like thieves of our bodies, thieves of the dull pleasure they'd had, with boots on, slipping through the primroses, up the bank, in the ill-smelling mud by the stream.

I would iron the Boy's clothes, tidy up his dresser drawers, sweep the nighttime giraffes and horses from the amusement park out of his room, serve him his meals when he ate at home, and watch, terrified, closer and closer and clear and detailed and certain, his death, seeing a kitchen knife, a dawn of insomnia, men and women sitting in chairs or stretched out drunk on the floor, chatting with pale, soft, death-rattle, wine voices, seeing the one who was approaching behind his back, leaning over him and drawing back again, and the wound, just like the separated lips of my body when my stepfather had me, drooling some purple drops, some sticky dark stains, and I wondered if my blind sister would also see the same thing, would also know the same thing, whether at the asylum in Viseu, among the other women, all in striped robes and slippers, her mute shout would splinter the white tiles of the wall, her breathing, all by itself, would fog up the windowpanes, whether since the days of the wasps and the vineyards and the shadows in the village she knew the same thing and was hiding it like me, because if she told anyone they would send her to a hospital in Coimbra, with an iron grill fence, and nurses, and bowls of food, the same as pigs, and a priest on Sundays, a hospital full of skinny weeping figures, of guys with heavy eyelids squatting on the ground, drawing parallel lines on the earth with a stick, my sister most likely knew, my mother most likely knew, all other women most likely knew, because women's heads work on a slant and through the future while men's go straight ahead and are as useless and stuck in the present as a dried-up olive tree, only capable of adding and subtracting and calculating harvests and the price of furniture and the urge to fornicate and despair, and maybe all women know the same thing I know and are afraid to confess it to other women because they don't know if they know and they're afraid of disbelief and mockery, or because men make us that way out of relief and defense, and they turn us against each other like goats in different corrals, scratching the shale of the ground with the hornlike persistence of their hooves.

And one morning, in January, the Lady and I said goodbye to the Boy, who was leaving with hundreds of other men in uniform, with faces just like empty coffins, on a troopship for Africa, a fat, white ship with three stacks that whistled and smoked through the still oily winter water. There were a lot of people on the dock, and rain and cold and military marches, people who were crying, handkerchiefs, cigarette butts, paper, crumbs, scraps, circles of spit on the concrete pavement, the sound of drums, creatures who must have come from very far away to witness the horizon thick with clouds and seagulls into which the ship was slowly going. The Lady took her handkerchief out of her purse and called me under her little red and black umbrella, more black than red, the people went to the edge of the pier shouting, shouts mingling with the gulls and the music and the clouds, and the Lady said to no one in particular in a low voice, God grant nothing should happen to him and I understood then that she at least didn't know what I knew, that is, that nothing would happen to him of course, that he would come back two years later as healthy as my father coming back every day from the pine grove, until the knife finds him in Lisbon, without a care and having forgotten all that, so drunk and dirty and confused and stained with vomit and saliva and rheum, as if he'd been traveling all afternoon in a cart on a slope in the vineyard, waiting for his sudden encounter with a bullet so as to fall back onto the load of firewood, without a word, like a plaster saint shattered on the floor.

He came back from the war only a little balder and a little thinner, and when the Lady called me and I came out of the laundry room with an iron in my hand and saw him, I felt once more the strange absence of the usual hatred for men that always, ever since the beginning, he awoke in me, that kind of affection or tenderness that softened my bones and my voice, and when I went close to him I knew about his painful and difficult and approaching death, much more painful and difficult than the Lady's death or the dog's, so I thought I've got to die before he does, I've got to invent some way of escaping the suffering of knowing he's in a coffin, sewn up by doctors on their stone-topped tables, smelling of manure, and olives, and the rotting entrails of sheep. And it was the time of the dog's slow dying in the kitchen, staring at us, one by one, as if she wanted to carry us with her to the slimy purgatory of animals, and the Boy laid her in a shoe box and buried her with a construction shovel, at night, in the vacant lot across from our building, and the Lady died after the dog did and I watched them both with the same mineral indifference of days gone by, of sixty years ago, the time of my father in the dark house, full of holy images, at the entrance to the village, knowing that the Boy would follow them and tormenting myself every day with the idea of him dead, not having managed to hate him since he was the son I never had, because it had been too late to have one for so many years, and which my closed-up body hadn't expelled, I've got to die before him, I thought, I've got to find a way to escape from here, but the village no longer existed, the wasps and the accomplice shadows of other days didn't exist, the familiar faces of childhood didn't exist, so I lay down on my bed, in my own urine and my own feces, and I stopped talking and listening and answering and seeing until the Boy took me to this building down by the river, with its indifferent maids and its mutely scolding and severe director, where the sound of his death won't reach me, nor the hateful eyes of other days, spying on me from the reeds bordering the bank, waiting for me to get undressed so they can get undressed too and come toward me in the long underwear, frightening the frogs and grasshoppers and lizards and minnows, transparent, on the shore, lying down beside me without a word, turning me over on my back like a stone and penetrating me so quickly, with a single thrust, like a knife in the back, making my blood howl amid the protesting toads.

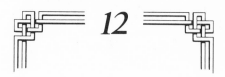

# 12

"You bastard," the midget growled in the vestibule, furious, waving her twisted little limbs at the level of the second lieutenant's knees. "Is this any hour to be coming home, you bum?"

He'd come on foot, counting his nausea attacks all the way from the Rua da Mãe d'Água, going down the Praça da Alegria, where the cabarets, closed and unlighted, had their entrances covered, wrinkled like appendicitis scars, crossing the Avenida, deafened by its traffic, by the sparrows, by the leaves on the trees, by a truck that went by roaring out the address of a raffle, exhibiting the first prize dashing automobile on its cab. He'd climbed up Conde de Redondo, hugging the walls, without looking at the ground that was dizzyingly far away, because of the effects of the wine, a Gypsy was spreading blouses and slacks on the sidewalk and I must have stepped on some items because he cursed me, I bumped into the cart of a woman selling fish who loomed over me, enormous, smelling of chitterlings, I stumbled over a child who whimpered like a little dog, two middle-aged ladies got out of my way like people carefully avoiding a mud puddle, rolling eyes looked me over with reproof, I passed the photomat on Gomes Freire, the gardens by the Bureau of Identification, swarming with people, and three buildings ahead, my own place, the woman who was scrubbing the lobby steps with a bucket and a brush, the mailboxes, the ever-present dying flowers in their vases (Maybe I'll make it without vomiting, maybe I'll be able to act normal), the finger that I stuck into the elevator button like the one I stuck into my nose as a child, rrrring, and now the torture of the key (Which one is it, damn it?), my disobedient fingers slipping, the effect of the grappa, the effect of the champagne, the effect of the whiskey, the effect of the gin, and immediately thereafter the face of the midget at my navel, the purse that bounced around my ankles, the noonday light filling the living room with dust, aging the furniture, Tell me, you swine, who were you with all night long?

"What a great bender," the quiet man praised, setting up the checkerboard in the warehouse office. "So you've finally joined the club, old buddy."

"Nobody, dear," the second lieutenant justified with a belch, losing his balance, taking a step backward, grabbing the saving support of the umbrella stand with both hands. "People I hadn't seen in a long time, you know how it is, talking about this and that, remembering Mozambique, friends from the Army."

"A genuine amateur crime," the fat inspector answered disdainfully. "Thousands of clues, fingerprints all over the place, an ideal case for a beginner in police work. In two or three days I'll have the entire little story for you."

Just to sit in any old chair, the second lieutenant thought with anguish, supporting his stomach muscles with his hands, just to sit quickly before he heaved the whole mess up out of his mouth: he went around the record player (I'm going to fall), a swirling sofa approached and withdrew like a post seen from a moving train, he touched the arm of an easy chair like a blindman, dug his afflicted nails into the fabric, slid with relief, with the feeling of a cascade, onto the floral cushion, loosened his collar, lowered his burning eyelids, listened from very far away to the midget whining around him, his heart was slowing down, his bladder seemed to have started functioning again, just a headache, just the shattered bones in the back of his neck, just a weariness of centuries in his legs, but I'm not falling down anymore, I'm not vomiting anymore, my body was floating in the morning light, if this dame would only shut up for five minutes I could certainly fall asleep.

"Are you going to play or not?" the quiet man was indignant. "If you move the pieces like a bumpkin it's no fun beating you."

"No pictures, they'll prejudice the ongoing investigation," the fat man refused in a friendly way, lifting his chubby hands to the ceiling. "Later on I'll give you some shots of the murderer, the scene, the victim. But if, in the meantime, you want to take pictures of the building, the Príncipe Real park, the concierge, the neighbors, the toilet attendant, be my guest: the readers always like that sort of thing."

I'll doze off for an hour or two, the second lieutenant thought, I'll take a shower, swallow an aspirin, change my clothes, explain at work that my father got in from France, that I had to make a hurried visit to the doctor, that I had a hell of a toothache last night. The midget's indignation was moving farther away, her tiny trunk was twisting in the haze, the easy chair rose in the light, Melissa the striptease goddess, lying on the bed, was lazily rolling on a stocking, the magician's assistant was fixing her makeup, the mulatto woman was putting her gigantic breasts into the Breton caps of her brassiere, five minutes, damn it, sleeping five minutes until the nausea passes, until my blood beats its usual rhythm, until my insides calm down, until the twin with the Cesarean scar finishes getting dressed. You dirty bastard, the midget hollered, what did you do yesterday, you dirty bastard? the thighs of Melissa the striptease goddess were rubbing against mine, a strong perfume was enveloping and exciting me, Five minutes, the second lieutenant begged mentally, five little nothing minutes, her vagina was exuding a thick liquid, hairy and pink membranes were moving away, the flesh of her navel looked edible to him, tender, soft, his pubis moved forward on the floral sofa, he smiled, roughly searched for his fly, What's this, what's this? the midget's voice bleated, appalled, the magician's assistant's tits, with dark black nipples, were swelling and shaking, Just five minutes, he begged, just touching them just coming and I'll get right up, the mulatto woman was pulling up the zipper on her skirt, the other twin was quickly brushing her hair, a tiny film of dandruff was spreading over her shoulders, falling weightlessly in the room like a kind of snow, But what kind of indecency is this, what kind of disgusting behavior is this? the midget was indignant, If I open my eyes, the second lieutenant thought, I'll see the lacquer clown hanging on the wall, I'll see the bouquet of artificial flowers on top of the cupboard, the headache wasn't bothering him anymore, the bones in the back of his neck, fitting together well, stopped vibrating, Melissa the striptease goddess was slowly stroking his testicles with a patient back-and-forth motion, his groin, his penis, the easy chair was exploding, faster and faster, faster and faster, the lieutenant colonel put the key in his pocket, took a quick look in the vestibule mirror, straightened his tie, walked down the hall with the step of a recruit, went into the bedroom smoothing his jacket (the mother-of-pearl peacock was growing larger on the dresser, cackling, a Barcelos cock was mocking me), and he found the cloud of perfume filling a suitcase, emptying the marble top of the dressing table of brushes and flasks, putting high-heeled shoes into little plastic bags.

"So early?" she asked, surprised, or irritated, or afflicted, or indifferent. "I didn't expect you until one o'clock, one-thirty as best as I could figure. Ever since you've been in charge of your friend's computers you're never on time for anything."

"Let the boys from the Morgue through, let the corpse through," the fat inspector ordered the reporters, pointing to a stretcher with a long shape covered by a sheet, and two guys in caps clumsily stumbling down the steps with it. One reporter, squatting in front of them, leaping like a grasshopper, was taking pictures of them from step to step: CORPSE OF UNFORTU-NATE LIEUTENANT MOVED TO MORGUE: HORRIBLE DETAILS AND STATEMENTS BY MAIN WITNESSES ON PAGE TWELVE.

"Abílio," the quiet man asked, replacing a missing checker with a button from his uniform, "did something happen to you?"

The rats, the color and size of small rabbits, were galloping through the enclosures in the warehouse, the dirty panes in the skylight were breaking one by one, revealing fragments of sky just like pieces of naked skin, a huge truck, with the driver way up high, moving from one side of the steering wheel to the other, hid the sidewalk for a moment, the puny little garden on Luciano Cordeiro, the old buildings with twisted, broken blinds: How many days without a moving order, how many weeks, fuck it all? The concierge had loaned him money for the rent, every so often she would leave a hundred or two escudos in his pants pockets for cigarettes, for meals, for the bus home: The way things are going, the soldier thought, I'm going to have to go back to catching fairies before too long, leaning up against a tree at night by the Sodré docks, listening to the boats and smoking, waiting for the faggots' cars.

"Clarisse invited me to spend a few days in a house she's rented in Malveira," the cloud of perfume said, her hair more silvery than ever, gathering together necklaces and earrings in a small heart-shaped leather box, and the lieutenant colonel to himself immediately, You don't even know how to lie, you boob, what kind of a face will you be coming home with later on in the afternoon? "We decided all of a sudden, sweet, I didn't have time to tell you yesterday. But I guarantee I'll be back on Monday without fail, missing you all the time, I promise. I was going to leave you a note in the living room, right next to the telephone, explaining everything."

The eternal perfumed pink cards with doves, or baskets of flowers, or kittens, or a little girl crying in the corner, with your name in gold letters, underneath the grammatical errors in your purple ink, the gooey tenderness of menopause, the repulsive diminutives, the lipstick encircling the compli-cated signature, and, in contrast, the sharp instructions to the cleaning woman, on graph paper torn out of a looseleaf notebook, Miss Ilda prepare roast kid for dinner and try to get the hall and bedroom like they ought to be the last time they were positively filthy, thank you very much Edite, the midget was tugging at his sleeve in a rage, her voice was coming closer again, impossible to locate in an orangy fog, You smell like a stinking whore, you asshole, you spent the whole night fooling around, you bastard, the second lieutenant cautiously opened one eyelid, his head instantly began to ache again, and there was Adelaide, Captain, microscopic, waving her arms, her features twisted with rage, her angry little gnome fists advancing toward my nose.

"In two or three days, boys," the fat man promised, "it's a matter of probing the case more deeply and there'll be a lot more stories. And you over there, get away, don't you lift that sheet, we don't want any problems with lawyers during the trial."

"Some wild party last night, Abílio?" the quiet man was impatient. "That's the second time now that you've moved a man backward."

The lieutenant colonel turned on the faucet in the bathroom, filled the tub to the top, and sat down on the bidet, elbows on his knees, underneath the cosmetic shelf, looking at the tiles and the mirror slowly growing dim, the faucets, the shower head, and the chrome pipes were beginning to sweat, fumes of lye rose from the inlaid rectangle on his left, while Edite was telephoning for a taxi, making her voice double up and roll around itself like a seductive caterpillar. Pieces of cotton were floating in the toilet bowl, almost transparent fragments of toilet paper, a cigarette filter, candy wrappers, and Edite, excited, passionate, transported, all nervous, with a room reserved at an inn in Azeitão or Palmela, thinking about the communications officer, vibrating over the communications officer, dreaming about the communications officer, writing him long letters in purple ink on her horrible pink paper, hanging from his thin neck with little sighs of consent, submission, surrender, wiggling the cellulite of her hips in the double bed, calling him sweet and begging him Don't tickle me, telling him Stop it, Celestino, laughing. He got undressed, dropping his clothes at random on the floor tiles, testing the temperature of the tub with the tip of his toe, stretching out motionless in the water, as in a boiling pot, I'm going to lose a shipment of stuff this afternoon, he was a little worried, scratching a buttock, and Captain Mendes will fire me, the Japanese must certainly have been waiting for him for hours in the warehouse by the river, surrounded by crates and sacks and the obtuse hesitation of the rhinoceroses from the penitentiary, the seaplane at Cabo Ruivo looked like a stuffed seagull, two beeps of a horn on the street, I'm leaving, sweet, see you Monday, the cloud of perfume shouted in the hallway, and at that instant an ambulance gave off its howl in a crescendo beneath the window, the Japanese was complaining to the puzzled father-in-law in his deep-sea-diver bubbles, Inês, naked, anointed with oil, rolled languidly on the massage table, her armpits were little ovals with black spots that were growing, her eyes were two little black spots too, but sticking out, taking things in, and ironic, her muscular legs were moving away, her buttocks, very white, were growing tense and spherical, a ball was bouncing on the floor in the compartment next door, deformed voices were chatting and laughing, the outside door slammed, the lieutenant colonel listened from the tub to the metal elevator cables squeaking, I'll get there at five, I'll get there at six, I'll get there when I get there, what do I care about the job, the transistors can go fuck themselves as far as I'm concerned, and a softness in his body, an endless fatigue, absolute alienation, he imagined, as if he were dreaming, a bed with curled legs empty at the inn in Palmela, the screech of the ambulance made his ears reverberate like echoes in a seashell, a second woman leaned over Inês's extended body, licked her longingly on the shoulder, on the other shoulder, on the curve over her kidneys, You're going to spend hours on end waiting like a fool, suitcase beside you, in the place where the two of you planned to meet, the lieutenant colonel thought, amused, looking all around, crossing and uncrossing your arms, tapping your foot on the floor, more and more impatient, more and more furious, trying a phone call or two without success, stopping, not understanding, getting frightened, I'll bet something's happened to him, I'll bet he's sorry, I'll bet another woman, a girl came in and went out humming with a pair of tennis rackets under her arm, the blinds were softly turning the light green, the oils in the bathhouse had a strong mothball smell and word of honor I saw the dame lying down, the younger one, the one who wasn't my daughter, stroking Maria João's chin and asking her Kiss me on the behind, and asking her Stick your finger up my ass, and it was at that moment that the soap slipped out of my hand and I fell asleep.

"Some business with your lady friend, Abílio?" the quiet man asked, all worried, while the soldier's pieces were disappearing, evaporating from the board.

"Anybody who pisses out of turn and out of the pot," the inspector warned, pointing to the photographers, "isn't going to get one single detail of the crime when the time comes."

"If you think you can get away from me you're very much mistaken," the midget barked like a person possessed, leaping around the second lieutenant like a little dog. "I want your sweetheart's name right now and right here."

The stretcher with the corpse disappeared through the rear door of a blue van, which mingled immediately with the thick, jostling afternoon traffic: Faster, faster, harder, Inês was begging with an urgent tone, the headache was a kind of wire that was tightening and slackening, the nausea, reduced, had withdrawn into the depths of his stomach like a frightened little animal. The second lieutenant got up from the sofa, went into the bedroom, changed his clothes, and his movements seemed light and directionless, like algae, his feet floated on the carpet, his shirt and shorts wouldn't obey him. The mulatto woman, the magician's assistant, the little blond twins, and Melissa the striptease goddess, sleepy, diurnal, charmless, abandoned their provocative poses, rolled on their stockings, put on rabbit-fur jackets, stained and worn all of a sudden, perched on their crooked heels, made their way to the street: a half hour from now the company again, the secretaries' typewriters, the desk covered with a pile of forms, rubber stamps, ball-points, papers, his jacket hanging on the chair, the vague smell of perfume floating through the rooms, and when the lights went on, when the newsboys were hawking papers in the street and people were piling up at the bus stop, it would be taking the elevator, going down, greeting this or that person at the clock by the reception desk, heading home, alone, on foot, hands in his pockets, empty of ideas, plans, stimuli, glancing indifferently into shop windows, illuminated ground floors, the girls passing by without looking at him, and tomorrow the same thing, goddamn it, and the day after tomorrow, and all week long, all month long, all year long: It's been some time since I've felt well, the lieutenant colonel thought with satisfaction, lazily rubbing his sides, I haven't felt so great in a hundred years.

One of the twins was gripping the straw-covered jug by the handle, the soldier remembered, looking at the checkerboard in the infinite perplexity of his insomnia: the mulatto woman's stockings looked like a drooping spider web, the silver-plated buckle of the magician's assistant's belt was missing: Two, three days at most, the fat man emphasized energetically, we'll have the nightingale here peeping in our hand and us whistling, arms around each other, stumbling on the landings, doormats slipping underfoot, a wondering crack opened and closed, revealing an eye, a long nightgown, the tip of a slipper, and outside the trees were trembling in the sunlight, the leaves quivering and flashing like mirrors, our blind-owl beaks blinked, and the one with the Cesarean was making wild signals with her arm for nonexistent taxis, Príncipe Real, gigantic, perched above the fountain, was leaning over as if it were going to lose its balance and fall, the soldier moved any old piece forward and tried to remember if they'd left the dead man in the toilet or in the pantry, whether buried under boxes of detergent and rice or amid the fetid urine that gurgles in the drains: the taxi blonde was shouting at automobiles, limping along, brandishing the jug, on one of her broken heels, stupefied noses peeked out of windows at the dizzily low-cut necklines, the uncombed hair, the exaggerated and unfinished makeup, the very tall heels, Melissa the striptease goddess vomiting in the gutter, There's a policeman back there, the soldier thought, and what if he sees us? whores at eleven o'clock in the morning are something suspicious, Captain: the second lieutenant finished buttoning his clean shirt, tying his tie, noticed a mud stain on his shoes, a private car stopped on the corner, the door opened, a man's hand could be vaguely seen, the twin with the jug parleyed for a few seconds and disappeared inside in a whirlwind of skirts, the tires squealed on the pavement, went on their way, the lieutenant colonel, softened up in the tub, was rubbing shampoo onto his temples, the back of his neck, the crown of his head, She went off because she was afraid, the soldier said, I'll bet that later on in the afternoon the dame will be strutting about in a cathouse in the country, If you have any idea of getting away from me, the midget whined at the second lieutenant, hanging on his belt, you're very much mistaken, my fine fool, I recognize him perfectly, Inspector, the manager of the Bar Club Madrid nodded, impeccably shaven and smelling of lotion, elegantly leaning against the orchestra's piano, looking at a shiny photograph, he was here last night in the company of some friends, I always cooperate with the police, ask Chief Castro, who drops by every so often to have a drink with me, the dance floor empty, the tables empty, the chairs with their legs in the air, a small, irregularly built man clumsily sweeping the floor, a thin stream of light creeping hesitantly through the keyhole in the entrance door: the second lieutenant got his wallet and his change out of the other jacket, dug through the pockets, got free of the midget with a quick movement and she skidded in her slippers and fell, sitting, startled, against the washbasin, Inês, on her back, was offering her neck now, her chin, her ears, to the avidity of her friend, who was chewing and swallowing her with the cannibalistic, angular motions of a locust, It seems they took along a bunch of the girls who work here, the manager added urbanely, I've got their addresses on file in the office if you want them, are you sure you won't have one little beer, Inspector? Do you want to kill me, Jorge?, Inês bleated, with one flat breast outside her bathrobe, do you want to kill me, you bum? the lieutenant colonel soaped his left knee, his right knee, his ankles, put his head under the cold spray of the shower, reached out for the Turkish towel, the sweat on the tiles was slowly disappearing, the mist in the bathroom was dissolving, the frosted glass in the window was a gleaming golden plaque, But what a devil of a day, he thought, the weather must be wild along the river.

"Five girls, eh?" the fat inspector was surprised, going through files in the office, muttering names, taking notes on a pad. There was a desk, a metal cabinet full of narrow drawers with chrome handles, a small bar with glasses and bottles of whiskey and vermouth in a corner, a door onto a yard with garbage cans and crates of tonic water where a mangy German shepherd was limping about. "We know three of them well, the other two, the ones who look like sisters, must be new in the business, right?"

"Abílio," the quiet man said, shaking the soldier's wrist, "the phone's been ringing for ten minutes and you don't even hear it."

"Not exactly," the manager answered smoothly, delicately picking up ice cubes with some pink plastic tongs. "They came here three months ago from a branch of ours in Oporto."

"Don't stop don't stop don't stop don't stop don't stop," Inês begged in a dying voice, curling up like a civet on the table.

"And how many fellows were there, do you remember?" the fat man inquired, cleaning his ear with his ball-point: "Three, four, five, six? I need an exact number, damn it."

"Hello, Abílio?" the concierge hesitated on the telephone, as always, walking from syllable to syllable like a timid lobster (and the fire sirens could be heard rising and falling continuously behind her). "I wanted to see if later on you could bring me a package of candied fruit for the kid's cake."

"They're good, professional women, Inspector," the manager informed him, raising the glass to eye level and examining the yellow liquid with a critical eye, "they'll cooperate with you in whatever's necessary. The number-one thing in our business, our golden rule, is not to give the police any trouble." And his polished fingernails had the opaline consistency of the sclerotic nails of dead people.

On the corner of the Praça da Alegria the other twin and the mulatto woman said goodbye, mingling their lipstick with the lipstick of the others, holding their suddenly ceremonious and distant hands out to us, timid fingertips, they both disappeared, staggering along a landing on the steps, wiggling scarlet behinds that evaporated into the vestibule, that grew smaller and diminished and disappeared into the shadows, reduced to little red undulating dots. You're a criminal, Jorge, the midget was howling, on all fours on the rubber mat, you're the worst kind of trash, They must have candied fruit down there, the concierge was sure, steadier now, walking more securely on the words, and hard candy, and cream puffs, and candles, the second lieutenant brushed his dirty shoe, straightened up again, examined himself in the mirror, Tomorrow just the same as tomorrow and tomorrow and tomorrow and tomorrow, he thought, depressed, the lieutenant colonel folded the bath towel and hung it up, whistling, on a metal rack, I'd better hurry up and get dressed if I want to catch the bus to Cabo Ruivo.

"If there were five chippies," the fat man muttered to the manager, cleaning his little fingernail with a matchstick, "the men, at the price lays are, must be around the same number. We'll start with the nearest address, and if I get any feeling that you're obstructing justice, I'll screw you."

"Abílio," the quiet man was alarmed, "don't you think you should see a doctor maybe?"

"Oh, Inspector sir," the white-haired man said indignantly, "if you don't trust me, just ask Chief Castro what he thinks."

"Get up and quit playing the fool," the second lieutenant ordered the midget, "I've got to get my ass to work."

"The clinic, the hospital, the São José emergency room?" the quiet man insisted. "Or would you rather I called a doctor on the phone?"

"On second thought, I'll accept a cold beer," the fat man relented, collapsing into an armchair.

They finally caught a taxi, but Melissa the striptease goddess lived on Penha de França, the magician's assistant in Campo de Ourique, and they argued, clinging to the door, kicking and shoving each other, while the driver, a young fellow with a mustache, laughed at them with his elbow over the back of the seat, alternately rooting for each of them and egging them on, Give it to her, rusty, don't let her get one-up on you, chubby. A crowd of people looked on from the corner, the policemen in their booth in back looked at us two or three times: But what kind of shitty mix-up is this, the second lieutenant thought, alarmed, this is all we needed: even the trees on the Rua da Mãe d'Água are pointing at us with their leaves, even the buildings are leaning over accusing us. The remaining twin disappeared hurriedly down a side street, the driver was starting to get impatient now, he insulted them, patted the wrist of one, hit the arm of the other, unglued their hands from the door handle, started up, the magician's assistant was pulling out whole clumps of hair, Melissa the striptease goddess was digging her long nails into her rival's throat, the crowd on the corner was growing, reinforced by truck drivers and neighborhood merchants, windows were filling with spectators in bathrobes. The best thing is for us to beat it the hell out of here, the soldier suggested, the best thing is to get away before anybody gets a good look at our faces, don't forget that there's a dead body up there. Not up there, in the toilet, the lieutenant colonel corrected, he's just another guy taking a shit, who's going to notice anything in that, hell: each went off in his own direction, wobbly, elbowing indignant creatures who protested, Under arrest at the station house for disorderly conduct, you say? the fat man was amazed, bring those royal highnesses to my office right away. Murderer, coward, male chauvinist pig, pervert, the midget was squealing, holding her head, if you're not back here by five o'clock I'm going to raise holy hell like you've never seen, Cool, nice and cool, the inspector approved, holding up his stein, with thick lips of froth around his mouth, Me, the lieutenant colonel thought, looking for a pair of blue socks in the sock drawer, I came onto a sloping alley that had no end, my legs seemed to be burying themselves in the limestone pavement, my heart was huffing, all exhausted, behind its muscles, and all of a sudden, in the space between two buildings, the circular complex of the city, derricks, a strip of river, tiny boats, So, a fight, the fat man commented, amiably rubbing his belly, now please have a seat, your highnesses, and give me a blow-by-blow description of the boxing match: the lieutenant colonel supported himself, collapsing with fatigue, on an iron railing, the sun glimmered here and there, white or copper-colored statues were waving their arms in disorder and dozens of pigeons took flight from a small clump of trees just below. A uniformed policeman stationed himself to the right of the inspector and without looking at anyone, put sheets of paper and a wine-colored chemical into an archaic typewriter, Five-thirty, Jorge, not one minute more, the midget warned, or I'm going to go into the manager's office and get you fired right there, the lieutenant colonel finished getting dressed, sprayed some cologne on his handkerchief and his hands, went down to the bus stop, he looked at the clock, two-twenty, Most likely the Japanese has already got his ass hot by this time, furious, gargling strange curses in his little sparrow voice, most likely Captain Mendes has appeared, like a man possessed, cursing the rhinoceroses while kicking the crates, the second lieutenant went agonizing down toward the Praça da Alegria, the soldier set out for the Bairro Alto, leaping across alleys with his enormous legs. You don't know anything, your highnesses, you don't know anything about anything? the fat man asked jovially, chewing on a pork sausage sandwich, the crumbs of which were raining down onto his belly, didn't it ever occur to you to maybe take a few little tablets, some little pills to jog your memory? the portrait of the president on the wall was staring at everybody with military severity, the soldier took a trolley to the warehouse below the Misericórdia church, on a square full of sparrows with a kiosk in one corner, he squeezed between a fireman and a student with acne and continued on with a tightened heart all the way from the Rua da Escola Politécnica, beginning to breathe freely only after the Largo do Rato, going down Alexandre Herculano, where a sea of anonymous legs and bodies and arms and heads was trotting along the sidewalk, obstinate and blind, like cockroaches without antennae, going in and out of registration offices, pastry shops, haberdashers, clothing stores, Get up, you naughty girl, a character with a cigarette in his mouth and accordion-pleated pants ordered the twin with the Cesarean, not concerned with the middle-aged customer lying next to her, who was looking at him with terror, just think, a colleague of mine down at headquarters, just imagine, is very interested in you.

"Even if it's only to take your blood pressure, Abílio," the quiet man insisted. "You've got the look of someone risen from the dead and it's a sorrowful sight."

The double-decker bus to the warehouse bounced along the irregular pavement of 24 de Julho, skidding on successive trolley tracks, disappearing into pitch black tunnels, reappearing, like a seal, on hillsides, snuffling sparks and steam through the hairy nostrils of its motor, there were a lot of people with suitcases at the entrance to the railroad station, and beyond that individual railway cars abandoned on the tracks, submerged in trash and weeds, the large warehouses in ruins on the riverbank, the city, which was beginning to thin out beyond the walls like the hair on the crown of the head of a man of forty, a few threads of graying houses and the skin of the earth appearing underneath, useless boats, belly up, on the spongy stones of the docks, iron rings, a brown trawler falling apart among the railway cars, far from the water, its keel in the mud, like Noah's Ark anchored on its mountain, swift circles of turtledoves, slow circles of gulls, buildings with caries, a few limping dogs, nobody, Captain Mendes's automobile parked on the slope bordered by skeletal little bushes, the wooden shack behind some wild fig trees, one of the rhinoceroses urinating, trunk-heavy, against a pole.

"I was only supposing that maybe you people could help us here with a minor little murder, a little old corpse of no importance," the fat man said good-humoredly, blowing the crumbs off his tie, "but you've lost your memory, right, so what are we going to do? Look, here comes the missing one: squeeze over a little on the bench, have a seat, your highness, with your arrival the team is complete."

"Don't you forget what I told you, Jorge," the midget whined on the landing, perched on the railing like a deformed bird. "Five-thirty without fail and this is the last time this is going to happen."

When he put the key in the door the second lieutenant was already feeling normal, only a slight heavy feeling in the belly, nothing else, a little insignificant discomfort in the esophagus or stomach, but the smell of cold tobacco from the ashtray made his guts swirl, caused a nauseous urge to vomit, and the bones in his head began to throb and ache again: What excuse am I going to give at work, he thought, a toothache, an uncle's illness, a funeral? and he glimpsed the boss's tight face, the mute censure of his fellow workers, the icy reception from the clerks, the typists, he glimpsed his own timid smile, his shyness, his indisposition: something boiled up inside him with a lurch, his throat was turning sour, if only he'd bought at least some capsules for the liver, if he only had a tranquilizer in his pocket.

"Well, let's start this mess right from the beginning, your highnesses," the fat man asked patiently, tapping his pencil on the desk like a maestro calling his orchestra to order. "There are some dissonances here that don't please me."

"So, finally, General," Captain Mendes growled, perched on the corner of a crate with his hands in his pockets. "Had you forgotten that there were goods to be delivered today?"

"Abílio," the quiet man whispered, perplexed, his open hand resting on the board, "don't you hear the telephone ringing again, Abílio?"

The seaplane was still rotting by the wharf, with its little peephole eyes looking melancholically at the mud of low tide, the stone outcroppings covered with rubbish, algae, moss: a dead man's mist rose from the absence of reflections on the water, the little white commas of seagulls could be glimpsed, the clumps of buildings on the opposite shore, dirty clouds crossing the green sky diagonally, Inês, twisted into a grimace, was biting her own lips in the bathhouse, more sounds of tennis balls, more spraying of showers, more loud laughter from the girl on the other side of the partition, the second lieutenant opened the car door at a red light and dumped the contents of the ashtray into the street, but the discomfort was still there, he rolled up all the windows, turned on the air conditioning, breathing: The glee club is sounding better, the fat man applauded softly, let's try a different tune now, your highnesses, the samba entitled Whose Idea Was the Knife, for example, how about that? The soldier picked up the receiver and nobody was there, just a vibrant silence, concave, on the line, Crossed wires, he snorted. I'm late, the lieutenant colonel answered with a smile, imagining the cloud of perfume becoming annoyed, getting restless, going back home, putting her clothes back into the closets, I had dinner last night with some of the boys and it went on late and I overslept: the rhinoceroses, frightened, huddled in a corner, looking at each other with infantile terror, the strident laughter of the girls in the bathhouse was shaking the wooden slats on the platforms. Go down and bring up the truck, we've got a moving job at four o'clock, the soldier ordered, and he imagined that he saw the sporadic start of the motor frighten the rats, shaking the balcony on the upper floor, the indifferent face of the communications officer crucified on the carpet: Overslept?, Captain Mendes repeated, stupefied, we've got a big job and you're telling me that you overslept?, They were in Africa together, the fat man barked, stroking his double chin, at the fellow with the cigarette in his mouth and the pleated pants, it shouldn't be too hard to find them, go over to Military-District headquarters and see if you can find me anything useful: The seaplane is still there after all, the lieutenant colonel thought, lighting a match casually, it hasn't taken off like an albatross in my absence after all: and more clouds, and more stray dogs, and a great silence all around, no wind rustling the bushes, disarranging the weeds, the air from the engine, disagreeable and lukewarm, paralyzing his lungs, and the second lieutenant, agonizing, finally pushed the button and shut it off, he switched on the radio to distract himself and he turned it off at the second song, a terribly sad Spanish number accompanied by funereal violins, If I get home before five maybe Adelaide will leave me alone, maybe Adelaide won't get on my back too much, I'll punch in, I'll sign the correspondence, and I'll come back, he didn't remember the communications officer, only the drinking bout of the night before and the hairy thighs of the magician's assistant slowly opening like a marine polyp in front of him, only the bulging belly and tits and flattened face in the background, far away, impossible to reach within the simple range of an arm, Well, you should know that because of you we're losing thousands of contos in transistors, Captain Mendes shouted, extremely angered, you should know that your sloppiness has cost us a solid customer, the Japanese man came to the office to inform us that he isn't going to supply us with even a single battery, and the lieutenant colonel not giving a damn, not hearing him, watching the river, the broad darker spots on the water, the struggling little ships and their wakes of foam, a Gypsy boy with blond hair pulling a mule by a rope toward the shantytown: What a wild day, he thought, it's too bad I learned to enjoy life so late.

"I'm beginning to catch the tune, your highnesses," the fat man approved condescendingly, scribbling quick phrases on a sheet of paper. "The one who stuck the knife in, your ladyships swear, was a big beetle-browed tough with a crew cut?"

"The result of this," Captain Mendes growled, his eyes sharp with hate, calling the rhinoceroses as witnesses, "was getting my deal and this pair's jobs fucked up. And anyone who fucks up a deal of mine gets himself fucked up immediately thereafter."

The second lieutenant had to leave his car three or four blocks from work and go on foot along the Rua de Arroios, carrying the inconvenience of his indisposition to the company's modern building, with the air-conditioners sticking out of the windows, and an office boy beside the time clock, spelling out the difficult cuneiform characters of the newspaper in a low voice, as if he were praying. In the tile-floored lobby, beyond a monstrous abstract sculpture, there were elevators with colored arrows and numbers that went on and off, and a semicircular counter with a pair of receptionists, whose hairdos he vaguely perceived, putting plugs into a switchboard full of the buttons and little bulbs of a spaceship, and taking care of people in front of a battery of telephones, with the gelatinous ultraviolet eyes of inhabitants of Mercury: If I planted a bomb in the lobby, he thought, what would become of all this shit?

"Let's see if we can get to some kind of understanding about the place where they left the corpse, your highnesses," the fat man advised, drawing thoughtful spirals on the paper. "This tale of the toilet and the pantry has frankly got me at my wit's end."

"Yes, Mozambique, 1970," the sergeant at the Military District answered the fellow with the cigarette in his mouth and the pleated pants. "Do you want the names of all the personnel in the battalion?"

The second lieutenant pushed the button for the sixth floor and the aluminum box mutely went into motion without any jerks, with an astral whistling, as if it were slipping in an oily, dizzying way into the atmosphere of the stars, to drop him off with surgical delicacy onto a red carpet, fire extinguishers hanging on the walls, plywood doors under which coughs, noises, the dull sound of bells were escaping, exhausted voices asking questions or answering them or employees in neckties dictating to ageless secretaries: You two are let go, Captain Mendes said to the rhinoceroses, you can thank the general here for this unexpected little holiday. The second lieutenant's office was located right next door to a kind of storeroom, across from a narrow fire stair and a glass case containing the snake of a hose and an axe. Now you're singing a song that's nice to hear, the fat man applauded, let's go through it all again for the last time, Sampaio will accompany you as best he can on his typewriter piano, and when we're finished your highnesses can very wisely put your signatures underneath. The second lieutenant, standing, without sitting down at his desk, still watching the clock, ran his eyes over the circulars and interoffice memos, canceled one appointment by telephone and set up another, told a secretary to bring him some coffee, jotted down the next day's business on his calendar, took a file out of a locked drawer and quickly thumbed through it, a carefully combed colleague stuck his head in the door, said Hi Borges and disappeared: And it isn't just you people, Captain Mendes added, kicking the crates, the general, for example, can go straight to hell where he came from. The second lieutenant put the file away, pushed aside the calendar pad, threw half the correspondence into the wastebasket, piled the other half into a kind of jointed plastic receptacle, the hands of the clock were spinning at a frantic speed, four-ten, four-twelve, four-fifteen, four-twenty, How long, he asked himself with anguish, will it take me to get from here to home, and he fearfully saw the midget's flashing eyes, her mask of rage, pitiless, hateful: You've got six hundred and thirty-six names there, friend, the sergeant at the Military

District offered, enough to entertain you for at least a year. Get there early, the second lieutenant thought, go in, kiss her, sit down in the usual armchair and open the newspaper, the laughter of the tennis girls was echoing stronger and stronger inside his head, the soldier climbed up into the broken-down truck, settled beside the quiet man in the cab decorated with illustrated postcards, images of saints, stocking caps, horns, and miniatures of naked women swaying from the rearview mirror, the trees on Luciano Cordeiro, the ancient houses, the Capuchin Hospital, the engine buzzed and clattered, dozens of loose tin cans hitting each other, the smoke rising in fiery rolls through the holes in the red rubber flooring by the pedals, the loud noise hindered conversation, If you pass a candy store pull up, the soldier asked, shouting, cupping his hands to his mouth, I've got to buy a package of candied fruit and seven or eight birthday candles for the little bastard.

"This just isn't any good," the fat man said to the fellow with the cigarette in his mouth and the pleated pants. "Fix me up with some photographs of these guys from the files so their highnesses can take a look, and in the meantime have Mamede and Soares contact them one by one."

"Get out of my sight, you shit general," Captain Mendes barked, threatening him, desperate, his fist clenched. "Get out of here and go hide in some nice little hiding place, because if my father-in-law catches you, he'll break every bone in your body."

"What?" the quiet man asked, his profile all in a kind of January fog from the gases from the engine.

The soldier turned on the windshield wipers in order to make out something of the street ahead of him, but his eyes felt red and burning and the smoke in the cab hurt his throat, making him salivate, spit, cough: it was a long haul from there to Vila Franca and they were sure to die of poison like cockroaches somewhere along the concrete strip of the highway, legs in the air on the torn plastic seat cover, two light little corpses, crumpled, chitinous, hairy with the long stems of their antennae. The window handles were broken, a nauseating, unbearable heat was wrapping his feet in slippers of hot blasts, the quiet man was driving too fast, making the city spin, bristling with buildings, in a carousel of windows, traffic lights, people in terror jumping out of the way of the rusty hood, a traffic officer stood looking at them, petrified, in the middle of a signal, the second lieutenant locked the drawer again, went down a corridor in the opposite direction (one, two, three, four, five red fire extinguishers with the instructions printed on the casing), he pushed the elevator button, which flashed a green arrow pointing down, a skinny woman clerk drew back timidly into the car, and once more the sidereal whistle of the mechanism, the interstellar passage to the lobby, compressed like an astronaut in the aluminum capsule. The time clock clanked like a piggy bank when he put the perforated card into the slot, the office boy looked at him with the submissive tranquility of a sheep, chewing a

matchstick, the girls with curled hair at the switchboard, foreheads at counter level, were taking care of a short little character with a cigarette in his
mouth and pleated pants, accompanied by a uniformed policeman, who
seemed to be discreetly showing them some kind of document.

"You'll be staying here a few more days, your highnesses, we've got more
than enough rooms," the fat man answered, digging into his ear with his
pencil. "I've gotten used to you now and my heart would break if we were
separated."

Leaving Lisbon, passing by the airport, where the airplanes were lined up
by a long, glassed-in building, the highway went over a viaduct by the Army
post where they had been discharged ten years before, with the dampness of
Mozambique still in their guts, and had moved toward the grillwork of the
gates where a noisy, confused human octopus had come together: the soldier
could vaguely make out the barracks buildings, military vehicles lined up on
the parade ground, the flag on the command post, antlike troops here and
there: the light suddenly turned green, the quiet man stepped on the gas, a
jet of smoke invaded the cab, and even so he saw it, I saw it: a small
automobile, dark blue or black, crossing in front of them, a woman's head,
other heads, the little car hesitating, stalling, starting up, stalling again,
someone blowing a horn desperately on our left, Stop, he shouted, the quiet
man stepped on a pedal, spun the wheel, the tires squealed, slipped, blew
out, gave way, an axle, a spring, some vital part broke like a branch under our
feet, the truck rolled over, It was down there that the war came to an end, the
soldier stupidly thought, there that the ambushes stopped, the mines, the
dead and wounded, the quiet man let go of the wheel and protected his face
with his arms, the little car disappeared, unhurt, behind us, Candied fruit,
hard candy, candles for the little bastard's birthday cake, his anemic little
breathing, his pointed sparrow face, the decrepit truck crashed into the wall
of the viaduct with a rain of glass and bricks, We're going to fall down there,
he thought, we're going to land right onto the gravel of the post, one, two
turns in the air, bodies thrown against each other, a bureau broken apart, a
scraping of sand and the smell of rubber and a taste of blood or crushed flesh
in the mouth, an interminable suspension, the certainty of floating eternally
over a second road against the wall of the post, the octopus of people
undulating and calling them, the duffle bag with clothing and African baubles
was heavy on my shoulder, the asphalt nearer and nearer, the howl of the
quiet man echoing as in a drained swimming pool, taking a taxi to Buraca,
coming upon my sister's hostile frown, my waist or kidneys being crushed,
without any pain, without any suffering, without any sound, ear wet with a
dark, sticky paste, legs imprisoned in metal joints, the speedometer loose,
floating in the cab, a fleeting wooded landscape and me running with my
weapon in my hand toward the village, and right afterward, and before the
boom and the explosion and the tall yellow flames, nothing.

"Hey, Nunes," the fat man called jovially, examining the point of his pencil with great interest, "take their highnesses here to the bridal suite."

"If I were you, my dear general," Captain Mendes advised, hands in his pockets, circulating through the warehouse dust, "I'd rent a little room off in the country where nobody could find me, where they couldn't even smell me: somebody who's made us lose thousands of contos is going to end up paying for them one way or another."

Five after five, the second lieutenant thought, consulting his watch with alarm, I should have been on my way home already by this time, I should have been leaning over to kiss the midget, I should have been running my fingers lovingly through her hair, folding over the pages of the newspaper with my fingernail, sighing with marital satisfaction, looking around at the furniture, the doilies, the portraits in their silver frames, feeling myself obligatorily happy, saying I love you, but he couldn't find the blasted car, as usual he'd forgotten the block, the sidewalk, the exact location, the license number, so he was wandering about anxiously looking at the parked cars, tiny sweat drops of fear were wetting the hair of his temples, his insides were growling and a heavy urge to urinate was stiffening his legs, making it hard for him to bend his knees, Inês, dripping oil, was now slowly caressing her friend's triangle of hair with her nose and chin, moaning as she nibbled at her groin, her navel, her hip bones, a crippled lottery vendor pursued the second lieutenant for a few yards with the sticky insistence of a fly, he took note of a grill, a headlight, a green mudguard, It's this one and it wasn't that one or the other after it, or the other, or the other, five-twenty, five-twenty-one, five-twenty-three, five-twenty-seven, the midget, a bandage on the back of her neck, was probably watching the kitchen alarm clock, counting the minutes in the same way, trembling, getting angry, getting furious, rolling down the hallway with a heavy object in her hand, Still here? Captain Mendes roared with surprise, you still haven't got the good sense to beat it?, It'll be night in just a little while, the lieutenant colonel thought, a cool breeze was trotting along at weed level, the tide was coming in like a sighing breast, the outline of the seaplane, much clearer, extended out against the dull mud color of the water, in the shacks in the shantytown lights, campfires could already be seen, a roundup of hens and dogs was coming home, Five-thirty, the second lieutenant said to himself, the midget was waiting for him behind the door like a bulldog, clutching a bottle, the lottery vendor again and his miserable clothes, his constant sniffling, his slips of paper, his interminable drunkard's sentimentality, the lieutenant colonel started down the slippery incline toward the road, tripping over stones, an invisible dog was howling, the rolls of clouds that had been crossing the sky diagonally were disappearing, Five-forty and not just my bladder, my asshole too, if I don't come across my car I'm going to sit down on the curb and let myself go, Adelaide will kill me, Captain, she'll bring a bronze statuette down onto my skull, dozens, hundreds, thousands, of parked cars all around him, hemming him in, encircling him, squeezing him, cars with empty seats, unoccupied, mocking him, sarcastic, waiting, a damp substance escaped from his dick or his anus, he leaned a hand against a tree, I'm going to vomit, a fellow with a cigarette in his mouth and pleated pants, accompanied by a uniformed policeman, helped his heaving with a few pats on the back, a van with a light on top was waiting for them placidly with its wheels up against the sidewalk, the lieutenant colonel (The way night comes on so fast, damn it) took a ridiculous little leap to the side in order to avoid a mud puddle, and the older rhinoceros's punch caught him full in the face (Get in, get in, the one with the cigarette invited pleasantly) and as he fell he saw that the seaplane at Cabo Ruivo was taking flight like an exhausted archangel, rising up with difficulty through the empty degrees of evening on its way to the sea.

# About the Author

António Lobo Antunes is the author of seven novels. He currently resides in Lisbon.